WHEN DOCTOR MANKY
STROLLED IN

Also by Tim Thompson:

When Frank Offcut Went Missing – *Book Two of the Silver Button Saga*

WHEN DOCTOR MANKY STROLLED IN

BOOK ONE
of the
Silver Button Saga

TIM THOMPSON

 A catalogue record for this work is available from the National Library of Australia

Title: When Doctor Manky Strolled In / Tim Thompson, author.

ISBN 978-0-6451994-0-6

Graphic design and typesetting: Lead Based Ink
Map drawings: Tim Thompson

Typeset in 11.5/15pt Adobe Garamond Pro

For happy wanderers, wherever they may be.

CONTENTS

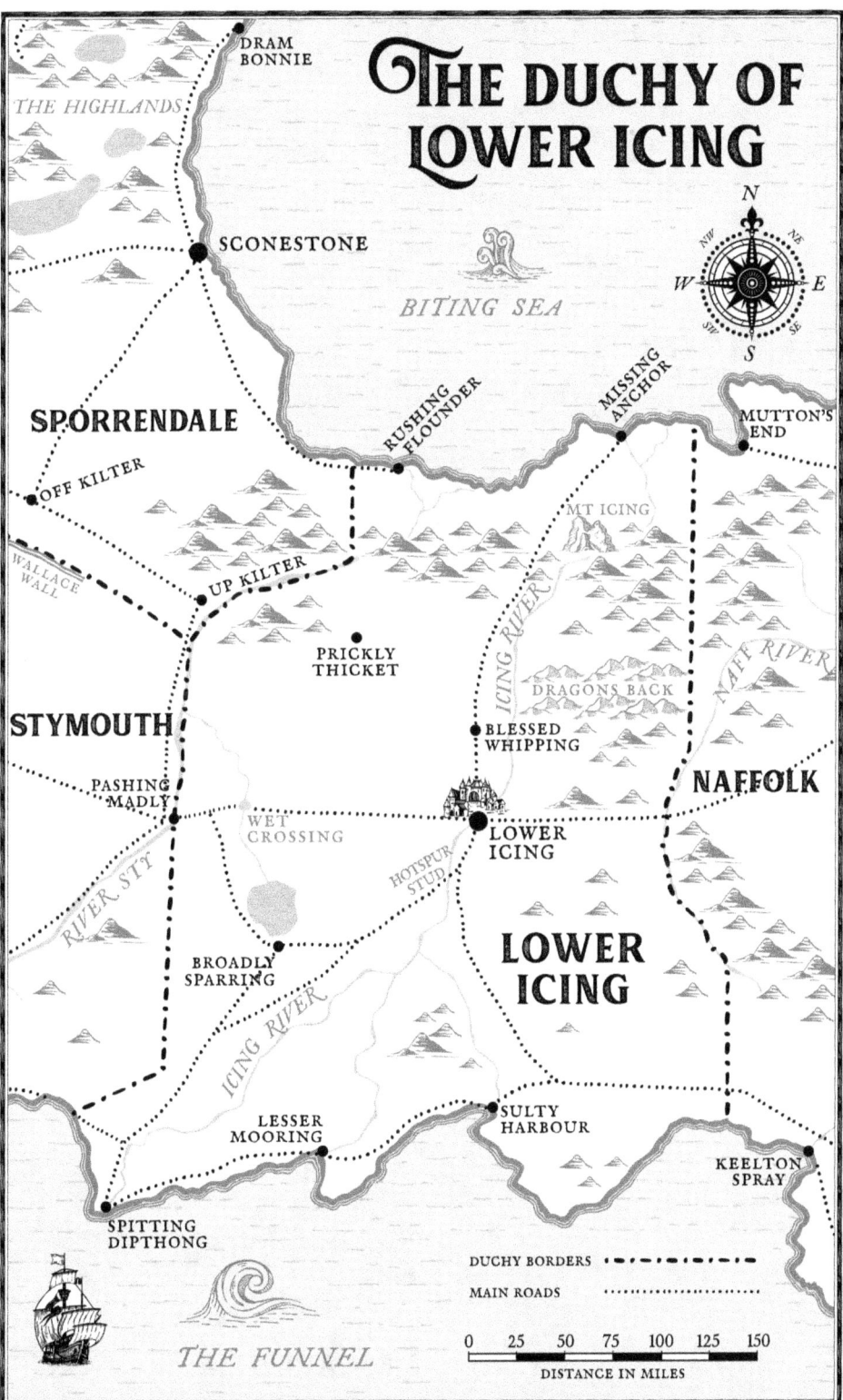

THE DUCHY OF LOWER ICING

DRAM BONNIE

THE HIGHLANDS

SCONESTONE

BITING SEA

N
NW · NE
W · E
SW · SE
S

SPORRENDALE

RUSHING FLOUNDER

MISSING ANCHOR

MUTTON'S END

OFF KILTER

WALLACE WALL

UP KILTER

MT ICING

PRICKLY THICKET

ICING RIVER

DRAGONS BACK

NAFF RIVER

STYMOUTH

BLESSED WHIPPING

NAFFOLK

PASHING MADLY

WET CROSSING

LOWER ICING

HOTSPUR STUD

RIVER STY

BROADLY SPARRING

LOWER ICING

ICING RIVER

LESSER MOORING

SULTY HARBOUR

KEELTON SPRAY

SPITTING DIPTHONG

DUCHY BORDERS ·—··—··—·
MAIN ROADS ················

THE FUNNEL

0   25   50   75   100   125   150
DISTANCE IN MILES

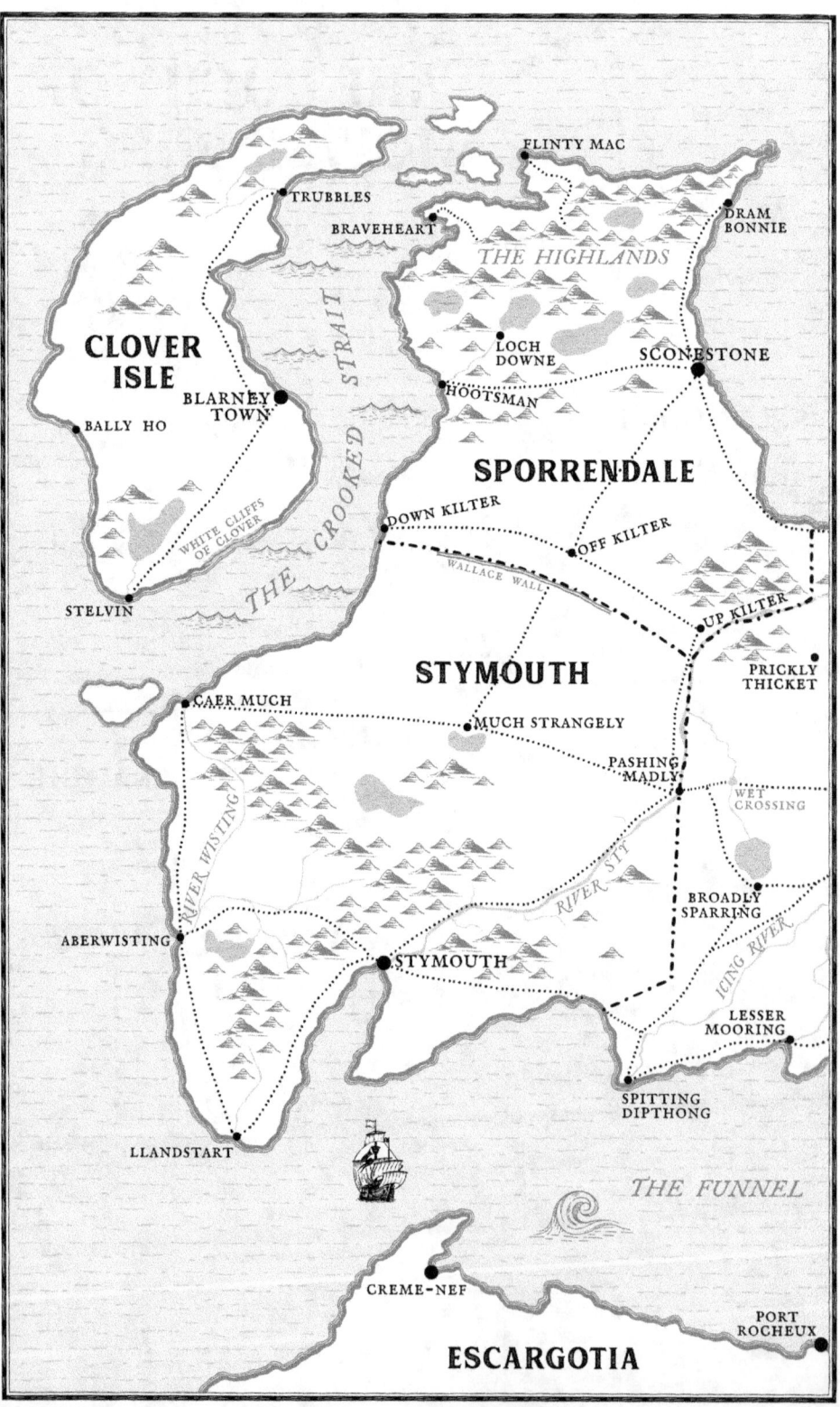

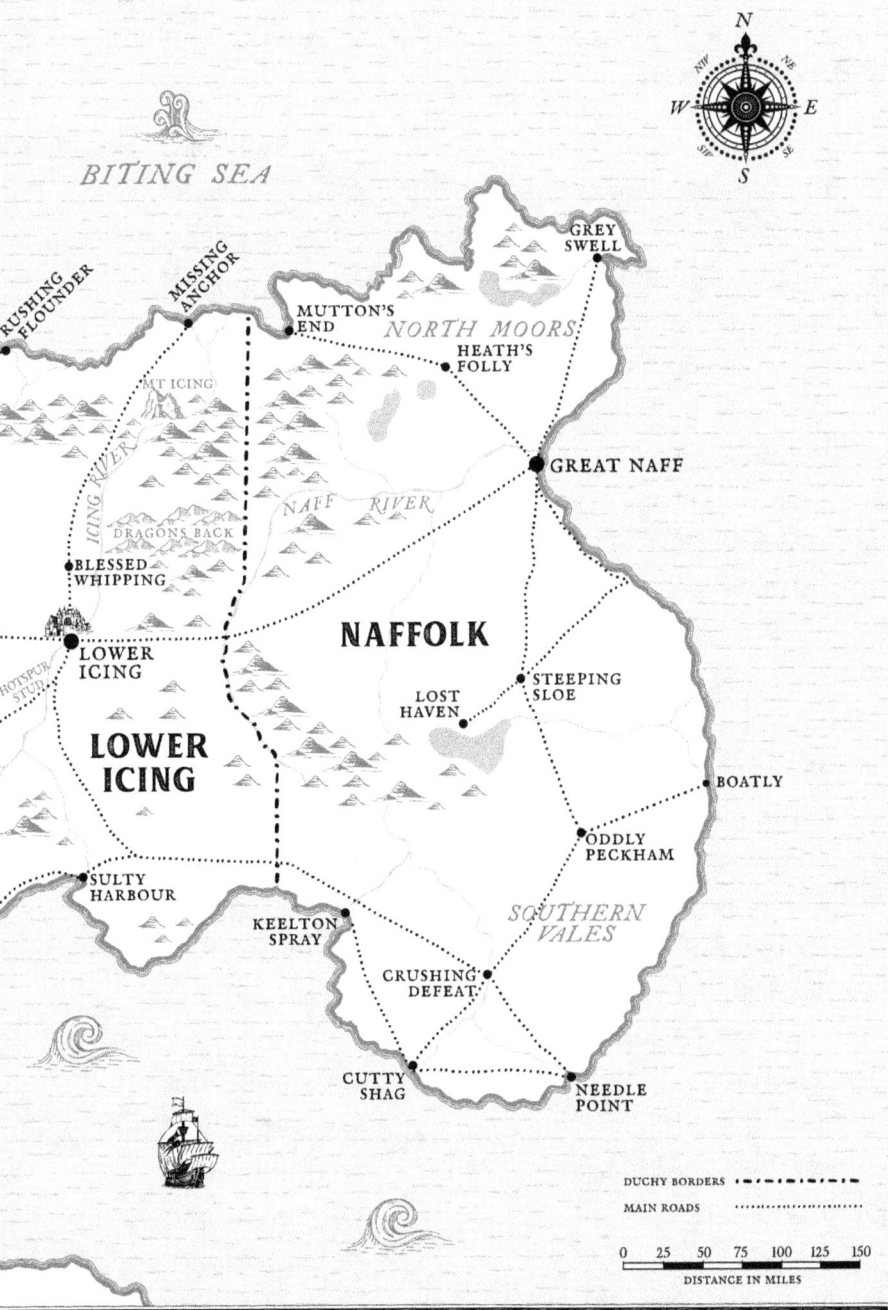

THE FIVE DUCHIES

BITING SEA

GREY SWELL

RUSHING FLOUNDER

MISSING ANCHOR

MUTTON'S END

NORTH MOORS

HEATH'S FOLLY

MT ICING

ICING RIVER

NAFF RIVER

GREAT NAFF

DRAGON'S BACK

BLESSED WHIPPING

NAFFOLK

STEEPING SLOE

LOWER ICING

LOST HAVEN

HOTSPUR STUD

LOWER ICING

BOATLY

ODDLY PECKHAM

SULTY HARBOUR

SOUTHERN VALES

KEELTON SPRAY

CRUSHING DEFEAT

CUTTY SHAG

NEEDLE POINT

DUCHY BORDERS ▪–▪–▪–▪–▪
MAIN ROADS ·············

0   25   50   75   100   125   150
DISTANCE IN MILES

Places of Interest

THE TOWNSHIP OF
LOWER ICING

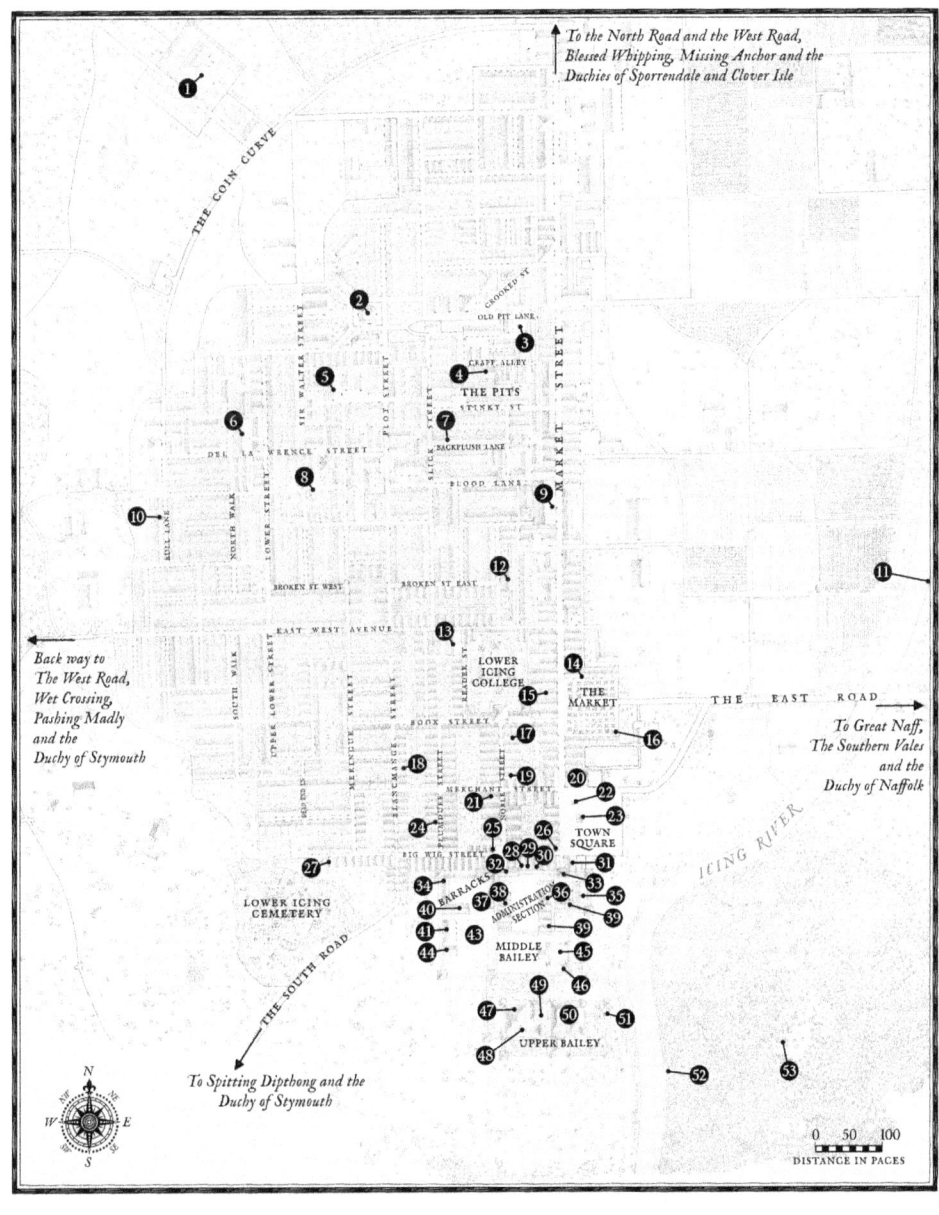

PART 1

SID

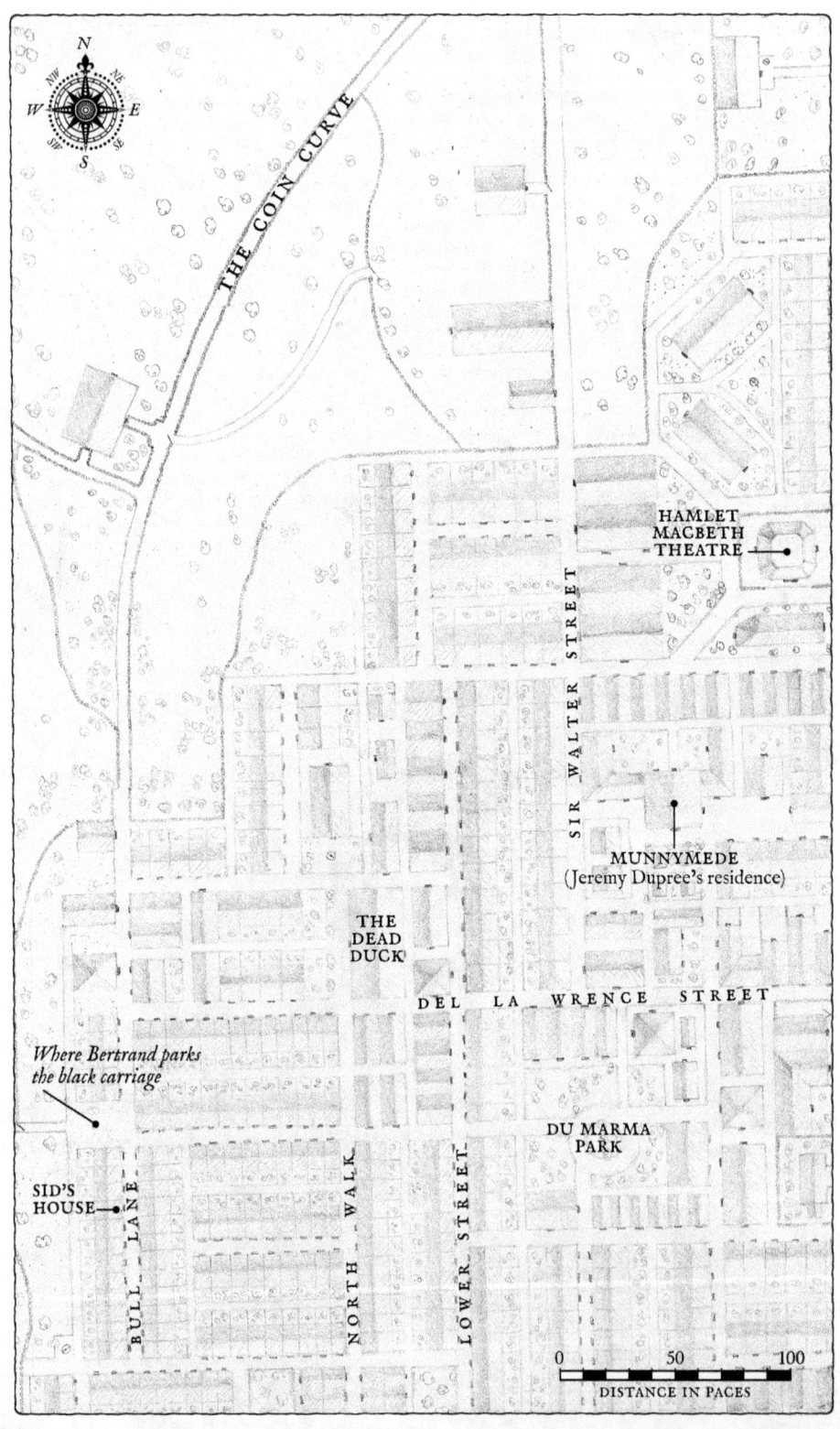

Introduction

The consummate burglar

SID EVILY COULD be described as ruggedly handsome — his hair was dark, like his eyes, and his face was often covered in stubble, but he radiated an easy-going, boyish manner that left a positive impression on most people he met. At twenty-eight, Sid had reached a stage in his life where he felt confident in his abilities, content in his surroundings, relaxed with his crowd and generally happy with his life. Sid had definitely found his niche. Well, actually, if he was honest, it was more of a comfortable rut.

He lived on the western edge of Lower Icing, the largest town in the Duchy of Lower Icing (which was one of five duchies on two islands known as the Five Duchies). Lower Icing had a massive castle rising on a hill to the south, but, more importantly to Sid, there was an inn just down the street from where he lived. He could be found at The Dead Duck most days and nights. Such was his patronage that he had his own booth.

Sid was a Venturer — a term *he* used to describe his trade. Basically, any venture he could profit from, he'd happily be involved in. Most of them were, if you were going by the letter of the law, illegal. However, the letter of the law had never bothered Sid, and his current ventures were child's play compared to what he used to do, back in the days when he described himself as an *Ad*venturer.

In those days (over six years ago now) he was the consummate burglar — a master lock-picker with a keen eye for the valuable and a cat-like ability for coming and going. Sid was also very intelligent. He could read and write, and he spoke with a refinement and articulation that was highly unusual in the world he lived in. He had his sister, Olivia (or 'Liv' as he called her), to thank for that.

Liv had virtually raised Sid. Their father had run off when he was five, and their mother had drunk herself to death by the time he was nine (and Liv fourteen). Liv was also blessed with intelligence, but intelligence wasn't an appreciated trait in a Lower Icing woman, so she had concentrated her efforts on educating Sid in the hope that, one day, both of them would benefit from it.

Throughout Sid's childhood, adolescence and into adulthood, Liv intoned the importance of becoming a gentleman of means and social standing. She made him study books on etiquette and fashion, as well as more practical topics like economics and politics. None of it had interested Sid. However, he did acquire a certain appreciation for the finer things in life. The trappings of wealth displayed by the 'castle set' (as Liv called them) were a constant distraction, particularly since she often took Sid on excursions to Big Wig Street, where the richest merchants had their shops.

It had been on one of these excursions that Sid discovered his talent for thieving. It was the week before Liv's eighteenth birthday. They were browsing in 'Charles Bling – Jeweller to the Duke' when Sid spied a pair of silver earrings in an open display cabinet. They were just lying there, asking to be stolen, and Sid had deftly obliged. It had seemed such a natural thing to do, and the rush of excitement it gave him was a wonderful new experience.

Liv had been delighted when he'd presented them to her on her birthday, but she'd queried how he'd afforded such an extravagant gift. At that time, Sid worked in the castle kitchen, mainly helping the Head of Pastry (a man called Reg Puffy) balance his books. At thirteen, Sid already had a better head for figures than most adults. He explained to Liv that he'd simply been putting aside coppers, and the odd silver piece, for the past year. This had delighted Liv even more than the earrings.

Over the next few years, unbeknown to his sister, Sid's shoplifting became more sophisticated and targeted. However, not once did he resort to thuggish robbery — there was no art or challenge in that. The sophistication and targeting was due to Paul Peabody, a self-professed entrepreneur, who had approached Sid shortly after he'd pilfered a pair of boots. Initially, Sid had been wary (and shocked that Paul had noticed his thievery), but he'd also been intrigued by what Paul had to say: that if they combined their skills, they'd both profit greatly.

Paul lived in The Pits — a cramped area of squashed housing and dark alleyways not even the men-at-arms were willing to patrol. Through Paul's guidance, Sid graduated from a shoplifter to a master burglar. Paul knew a lot about the castle set: where they lived, and, most importantly, what they owned. He even had floor plans for some of the homes. This amazed Sid, but Paul refused to reveal how he'd obtained them. Each burglary took weeks (and sometimes months) to plan, and Sid only ever stole one specific item at a time (as identified by Paul). Each burglary went off without a hitch, and Paul paid him an agreed fee in gold. By the time Sid was sixteen, he was quite well off, yet he still worked in the kitchen and still spent time studying social etiquette. Paul had impressed upon him the need to retain an outward appearance of normality, and that included not being flashy with his coin.

In the end, it was this normality that became Sid's undoing. Shortly before his twenty-second birthday (by which time he was working in the Administration Section of the castle) Liv found his stash of coins under the floorboards of his bedroom. It was only because he'd accumulated so many (and spent so little) that the floorboard had dislodged as she swept.

The discovery had left Sid with no choice but to own up to his nocturnal profession, but he revealed nothing of Paul's part in his Adventuring. To say Liv was shocked was an understatement. But it was more the fact that he'd been able to live a double life for so long that she had found hard to come to terms with.

It took her days to calm down. When she was finally able to speak civilly to Sid it was to tell him the only way he could redeem himself was to return the money. His initial reaction had been one of outrage — he'd be arrested and probably hanged! But she'd formulated a plan. They would put the coin in the tin chest Liv used to store her sewing accoutrements and hide it amongst the discarded junk that littered the laneway behind their house. She would simply say that she had found it. Liv had become quite friendly with the Captain of the Guard, and assured Sid he wouldn't ask too many questions.

Sid hadn't been happy about the plan at all. It was over two thousand gold pieces she wanted him to surrender: enough for them to leave Lower Icing and set up somewhere new. Liv, however, was adamant. He either agreed to let her return the gold or she would turn him in. It was for his own good, she'd said, and he'd thank her one day. (Over six years later, that day still hadn't arrived.)

Still, back then, he'd felt like he had no choice, and, amazingly, Liv's plan had worked: there was no investigation and no recriminations. It was as if nothing had happened at all. However, there was also no money, and Sid was not happy about that. And, as a further blow, Paul terminated their partnership, citing that Sid was now too much of a risk, that his sister had drawn attention to herself, and, by extension, to Sid. In fact, Paul was disappointed and angry at him for allowing Liv to act in the way she had. It was a most unpleasant parting in which Paul revealed an unnerving side of his personality: one that bordered on the madly obsessive.

Over the next few months, Sid and Liv's relationship gradually restored itself somewhere near to what it once was. It was as if Liv had decided to sweep the whole incident under the floorboards. Sid, however, had found it hard to adjust to a mundane world of administration; he missed the thrill of Adventuring.

During this time, he became more and more pre-occupied with organising another foray into the realm of the castle set, even though he'd promised Liv he would never steal again. Trouble was, he no longer had the benefit of Paul Peabody's meticulous planning. Which home? Which floor? Which room? Which item? How many locked doors? How many people in the house? Any noisy pets? These were just some of the details Paul had provided. Sid's only option was to visit a place he'd burgled recently, but Paul had made it clear he should never 'revisit' a home within a year — the inhabitants were still wary and more security conscious.

To break out of his dull routine, Sid began frequenting The Dead Duck. If he couldn't satisfy his needs climbing up walls and breaking into the homes of the castle set, he could certainly gain some satisfaction climbing up the skirts and breaking into the corsetry of the inn's enthusiastic barmaids. Sid's inn-life soon became habit, and the desire to Adventure diminished. So did his willingness to be a quill-scratcher at the castle, and six months after Liv had found his cache, he resigned from his position.

Sid had thought Liv would be furious, but she hardly batted an eyelid. Nor had she really admonished him about his descent into drinking and debauchery. At the time, Sid was nothing more than pleasantly surprised by his sister's acceptance of his changing lifestyle.

A month later, it was Sid's turn to be shocked and outraged when Liv casually announced she'd sold their house — because it was *hers* to sell — and that she was soon to marry the Town Crier. Sid didn't know which declaration was more astounding, but Liv offered no explanation. She simply said she would give him half the coin from the sale of the house (which would proceed within the week).

True to her word, Sid found himself homeless (with a pouch full of gold) a week later. He was smart enough to know he couldn't fritter away the coin on ale and women, and he made a concerted effort to find a new abode. The effort paid dividends. Within the month, Sid had bought a home — the one he lived in still — and came out of the exchange with a third of his gold remaining.

Two weeks later, Liv had married Gerald Hiepants, the Town Crier. Sid had been amazed and hurt to find out *after* the event. She'd fobbed off his disbelief by saying it was just a small, private ceremony.

As the years past, Liv became more aloof and snobby. When he visited, it was always Gerald playing the host, while Liv became increasingly resentful towards him. Sid had tried talking to her, but she refused to engage in any conversation on the matter. Eventually, he became just as offhand and resentful towards her, and happily fell into his Venturing life, which was centred on the merry world of The Dead Duck.

Yes, Sid was content enough, even if it was a far cry from the exciting life he'd once led. The Dead Duck was a joyous establishment, filled with good-natured people who enjoyed their fair share of drinking, singing and cavorting. Sid was partaking in two of the three — he wasn't one for singing — when Doctor Manky strolled in and literally stopped the show.

Chapter 1
Some sort of benign ghoul

Friday, June 27

IT WAS A boisterous Friday evening at The Dead Duck and Maddy (one of the barmaids) was singing 'The Ballad of Saucy Sarah' to a bunch of appreciative regulars. Everyone was in a good mood.

Suddenly her voice quavered and she looked like she'd seen a ghost. And to most people there, she had.

The man was dressed completely in white, from top hat to shoes. But what was even more striking (and disturbing) was the person inside the clothing. His skin looked as if there wasn't a drop of blood flowing through it, his hair was as white as freshly fallen snow, but his most frightening feature was his eyes; they were pink, like bacon. The Dead Duck had become deathly quiet. He removed his hat and smiled.

"Good evening, ladies and gentlemen." His voice was clipped and precise, like it was used to getting exactly what it wanted with minimum fuss. "Please forgive the intrusion. My name is Doctor Horatio Manky. I'm looking for a Master Sid Evily."

Sid couldn't believe it; this freak wanted to see *him*? What the frig! No-one said anything, but just about everyone was looking at him. The man nodded his appreciation, tucked his hat under his arm and walked towards the corner booth where Sid was sitting… where he *always* sat. As the white man approached, his pink gaze shifted from Sid to Elsie. Sid had done a pretty good job of chatting her up and would definitely be taking her upstairs tonight.

Elsie smiled nervously. Sid felt wary and self-conscious; he could sense the silent stares upon him as the white man stopped at his table.

"Do you work here, my dear?" the white man enquired politely.

Elsie's mouth twitched as she jerked her head up and down.

"Very good. Would you be so kind as to fetch a bottle of your finest wine?"

Elsie scampered towards the bar.

His pink eyes followed her. "Thank you." Then he noticed the still-stunned patrons. "And open a keg of your finest ale for all these good people. Please, enjoy yourselves."

The silence broke into a muttering of thanks; a far cry from the rowdy cheering that would normally occasion such generosity. Then the music returned and Maddy was soon chiming out the ever-popular 'Keep Your Pants On, Mister Winkle'.

As the atmosphere returned to normal, the white man's attention turned to Sid, pink eyes piercing out from his bloodless face.

"Well… what do you want?" Sid snarled; his erotic dreams of seducing Elsie had been interrupted by this bizarre nightmare.

"May I sit down?"

It didn't sound like a question. Sid indicated the bench opposite him.

Manky smirked. "Thank you, Sid — may I call you Sid?"

Sid was in no mood for pleasantries, at least not from a man who looked like he'd spent his life bathing in milk. "Just spit it out, Manky — may I call you Manky? What are you after?"

"Ahh… a man who comes straight to the point," Manky said as he sat down. "I think we shall get along very well."

Sid wanted to tell him to go sling his hook; he was pissed off by the white man's passion-killing appearance. However, there was something oddly compelling about his freakish looks and calm demeanour. Manky regarded him from across the table, pink eyes appraising, while the rest of The Dead Duck returned to their drinking, cavorting and singing. He felt oddly removed, like the booth was no longer part of the inn but a separate world inhabited by people with white skin and pink eyes. Mind you, he'd had a few ales.

"Information."

The word took Sid by surprise. "What?"

"I wish to be kept informed. And I'm told you're the best man to provide the information I require."

"What information? And told by whom?" Was this a jest?

Manky was about to continue when Elsie arrived with a bottle of wine and two wooden cups. "Thank you, my dear," Manky said.

Elsie smiled at him… coquettishly?

Sid experienced a quick pang of jealousy. "We're still on for later tonight, right, Elsie?"

Elsie looked confused. She placed the wine and cups on the table. "Will says this is our best... somefin' from Naffolk. A red, anyways."

"Sounds perfect, my dear," purred Manky.

What the frig was happening here? Elsie had been all over him five minutes ago. "*You* know…" Sid persisted, indicating upstairs with his eyebrows, "…later?"

"I dunno wha' you're on about, Sid Evily." She seemed genuinely perplexed. "And that'll be twenty silvers, fanks… for the keg an' all."

"Of course," said Manky, reaching into the pocket of his white pants. Sid half expected him to pull out twenty *white* coins. Instead, he handed her two gold ones (worth the same as twenty silver, but more valued). Then he produced a silver coin. "That's for you, my dear," he said, smirking at her.

A *silver* for frig sake?

Elsie took the coins, pocketing the silver. "Mos' gen'rous, fank you kindly."

"Not at all, my dear."

What the frig! "Elsie—"

"Now, if that's all, I got uvver fings to get on wiv." With that, she turned around and merged into the crowd of revellers.

"That's women for you, Sid: unpredictable."

Manky's smirk was beginning to irritate Sid. "There was nothing unpredictable about it," he snapped. "You've obviously put the wind up her. This better be good, Manky, otherwise I'll give you a good reason for looking so bloody pale."

The threat seemed not to bother Manky in the slightest. "Very well, Sid. I believe your sister is married to Lower Icing's Town Crier."

"So?"

"And you are on good terms with him?"

"Yes. So?"

"And he tells you things?"

What was he on about? "He's the Town bloody Crier! He tells things to *every* bloody body!"

A few nearby heads swung in the direction of the booth. Manky paid them no heed; he seemed totally unflappable.

"Very true, Sid, but I think you'll agree there are things and then there are *things*."

What did he mean by *that*?

"The tidings your brother-in-law voluminously announces to the people of Lower Icing are sanctioned by the Duke, are they not?"

Sid didn't respond, because he knew it wasn't a question.

"Therefore, not all news is shared with the people, and *that's* what I would like you to remedy, Sid. I would very much appreciate being kept informed of the stories people are *not* hearing from 'Gerald the Herald'."

Sid regarded Manky's bizarre visage; the man seemed immune to emotion. He could deal with people who were angry, abusive, annoying and even threatening — it went with the territory. However, he wasn't used to someone with Manky's demeanour.

"What makes you think I'll do anything for you? In fact, what makes you think I *can* do anything for you? Who are you, anyway?"

The annoying smirk persisted. "Which question would you like me to answer first, Sid?"

"You choose, but make the answers good, because your face is starting to irritate me, and I don't put up with irritations for long."

Once again, Sid's brusque manner had no effect on Manky.

"Right at this moment, Sid, I doubt you *would* do anything for me. And, as yet, I'm not certain you *can* do anything for me. As for who I am… let's just say that I'm a potential benefactor… one who rewards well."

Sid felt a strong urge to punch Manky in his over-confident smirk, but the thought of being well rewarded stayed his hand. Sid was always on the lookout for ways of making money, and, truth to tell, he could do with a new challenge. His main venture had become rather routine: Sid acted as kind of middle man between Reg Puffy (who was now Head of Kitchen at the castle) and The Dead Duck. Basically, he ran a non-sanctioned pastry service, supplying the inn on a weekly basis with 'hot' pies, pasties and buns (and Reg Puffy with coin). Occasionally, the Duke's Gamekeeper took him hunting and allowed him to keep his quarry. Again, it wasn't exactly law-abiding, but who was going to worry about the odd pheasant. And there were other 'one-off' ventures that cropped up from time to time and supplemented his income.

"How well rewarded are we talking, Manky?"

Manky offered a self-satisfied smile, "Well, that depends on your information, Sid. I shall, however, offer you a retainer of, let's say… five gold pieces a week. How does that sound?"

Sid thought it sounded unbelievable. His combined ventures made him three gold pieces on a good week, and that was hard work. Now he was guaranteed almost double that for buying Gerald a few ales and asking about his week at the castle. But Sid wasn't counting his coins just yet.

"So, when do you want the information, and, more importantly, when and how do I get paid. You don't expect me to trust you, do you?"

Manky reached inside his coat and pulled out a small leather pouch. He tossed it on the table. It clanked. As Sid reached for the pouch, Doctor Manky started pouring the red wine. Inside the pouch were ten gold pieces.

"Look at it as a gesture of good faith, Sid — something to encourage you in your pursuits," Manky said as he finished filling both cups. "Next Friday at midday, we will meet, as we are now, to discuss the political climate, and you will leave at least five gold pieces heavier. How does that sound?"

Sid fingered the pouch of money. If nothing else, he'd just made ten gold pieces, and there was probably a lot more to be had if he played his cards right. Sid smiled at Manky — two could play the confidence game — and raised his cup. Manky followed his lead. "It sounds…" Sid paused for effect "… acceptable."

"Excellent, Sid." Manky smiled, and the cups touched like swords before a duel.

A warm breeze wafted through the open window next to his booth, and, in the fading evening light, Sid watched as Manky climbed aboard a dark carriage drawn by a single black horse. A man, dressed in a pale blue robe and who looked very much like he'd been raised by vultures, opened the carriage door.

"I trutht your meeting wath thuccthethful, Doctor Manky," lisped the man in a monotonous voice. Sid wondered if Manky was actually a doctor. He couldn't imagine he'd have many patients.

"I believe it was, Bertrand. Thank you for asking. We shall know soon enough."

With that, he turned his head towards the window, smiled and tipped his hat at Sid like some sort of benign ghoul.

CHAPTER 2

A bad influence on Gerald

THE FOLLOWING MORNING Sid woke in a bad mood. All his attempts at coaxing Elsie upstairs at The Dead Duck had failed. It was Manky's fault. He'd done something to turn her off; she'd been all over Sid until Manky's icy appearance. In desperation, he'd offered her one of his gold pieces (five times the going rate), but it might as well have been a dead rat for all the enthusiasm she'd showed. So, Sid had walked home much less drunk and much more frustrated than he was accustomed to on a Friday night. He had a bad feeling about Manky.

Sid was thinking about this again as he strolled, depressingly clear-headed in the mid-morning sunlight, along the cobbled streets of Lower Icing to his brother-in-law's house (although Gerald always referred to it as *Olivia's* house).

Now, on the verge of turning thirty-three, Liv was a bitter, humourless woman. It was as if the life had been sucked out of her, leaving only a heightened sense of propriety. Position and appearance were Liv's two guiding lights. Added to this, she was a particularly particular person and Sid certainly didn't cut the mustard in the ham sandwich of Olivia's world, and hadn't done since he'd 'forgotten which side his bread was buttered'. She also thought he was a bad influence on Gerald — the man she'd unexpectedly married six years ago because he was going places. No doubt she'd been thinking of more important places than the Town Square at two o'clock twice a week, and, no doubt, she still was.

Liv and Gerald lived on Plumduff Street, a wide thoroughfare of terraced housing that was typical of the dozen or so grander streets in 'Upper' Lower Icing. Elegant façades stared snobbishly from both sides, looking down on the smattering of well-dressed people strolling up the incline towards the castle or, perhaps, to Big Wig Street, where they might browse the upmarket shops. These were the type of people who would never visit the actual market, a mere five-minute stroll in the opposite direction. Sid garnered some wary looks, but he paid them no heed; they went with the territory.

The door to Liv and Gerald's house was easily recognisable, not because of the white door (they all had white doors) or the small iron '8' which was hammered into it, but rather due to something far more distinctive. Just to the right of the front door, the morning sunlight highlighting it brilliantly, was a polished brass plaque. It was his sister's most prized possession. They were the only ones in the street to have a brass plaque. In Liv's mind, it was a status symbol that gave them 'position in society', and she kept it spotless. It read:

ABODE OF GERALD HIEPANTS
TOWN CRIER OF LOWER ICING

Sid knocked. Moments later, the door opened, revealing a smartly dressed man with an open, smiling face and cheeks as red as his three-quarter-length coat.

"Oyez! Oyez! Oyez!" Gerald bellowed from the doorway. "Sid Evily has come to see his brother-in-law!"

Sid grimaced at the pronouncement. After seven years of being Town Crier, his brother-in-law found it hard to leave his work at the office. "Yes. Thank you, Gerald. But I'm not sure my arrival is *that* news-worthy."

Gerald looked slightly embarrassed. "No, no, of course not. Ridiculous behaviour… Not that it's not good to see you, of course… I mean, it's always good…" He shook his head. "Your pardon, Sid. Please come in."

"No need to apologise, Gerald." Sid gave him a good-natured pat on the shoulder and entered the house, where he was ushered down the hallway into the kitchen at the rear of the home.

"I think Olivia is in her dressing room. I'll just go and tell her you're here."

"I have a feeling she already knows," Sid mumbled to himself as Gerald disappeared back down the hallway.

He returned alone a few minutes later. During his absence, Sid had overheard muffled snatches of his loving sister's voice coming from the floor above: "What's he want now?" and "He's trouble, Gerald. Get rid of him." and "I don't care if you like him; he's a common criminal." (She managed to make 'common' sound more undesirable than 'criminal'.)

Gerald approached the kitchen table at which Sid was now sitting. He grimaced. "Olivia's a bit… busy. Would you like some cider?"

Sid hated cider. It was the only alcoholic drink he was ever offered in the Hiepants' house and he had a sneaking suspicion that was because Olivia knew he hated it. "I'll be fine. Thanks anyway."

"Perhaps some—"

"Look, Gerald. I need to speak to you."

"Of course, my good fellow, speak away. I'm almost as good a listener as I am a speaker, and I am quite the speaker, as you know."

"Yes. Yes," Sid muttered. "Gerald, I need to speak to you in private." He pointed to the kitchen ceiling, indicating Liv's approximate location.

Gerald looked uncertain, before understanding dawned. "Oh, I see... anything in particular?"

"I can't talk about it here. What do you say I meet you at The Harey Rabbit after you've finished at the Town Square, and I'll tell you over a few pints?"

"Sounds positively intriguing, Sid," Gerald replied.

"Just don't tell..." Once again Sid indicated the floor above.

Gerald nodded as he tapped the side of his nose.

CHAPTER 3

A useful conversation piece

IT WAS ALMOST two o'clock, and the Town Square was busy with the usual assortment of townsfolk waiting to hear what news Gerald had for them. Sid couldn't remember the last time he'd actually listened to one of his brother-in-law's inane oratories. The snippets he'd happened to hear over the years were ridiculously overblown and pompous. As Doctor Manky had alluded to, they all consisted of castle-sanctioned drivel: references to a few prominent citizens and their minor achievements, the great job the men-at-arms were doing in making Lower Icing a safe place to live, and mildly amusing anecdotes to remind the population how fortunate they were to have decision-makers with a sense of humour. In Lower Icing's case, the decision-makers consisted of the Duke, one Lord Marmaduke DuMarma, and the Duke's closest advisers — the closest and most influential of whom was Sir Richard Upson, the Seneschal of Lower Icing.

Sid usually had better things to do on a Saturday afternoon than listen to a man in a red coat with a loud bell bellow forth proclamations that had little or no effect on his life. Today, however, he'd decided to see his brother-in-law in action. If nothing else, his proclamation could prove a useful conversation piece.

The traditional 'Oyezs' had stopped and the last peal of Gerald's bell dissipated in the afternoon breeze. The crowd waited in silence as Gerald unrolled the proclamation.

"Hear ye all," his voice boomed out. "The Duke wishes it to be known that last night a brazen act of trespass occurred at Lower Icing castle. A hooded figure was discovered in the Duke's private chambers."

The crowd murmured their disbelief, Sid included.

"It is believed the brigand was attempting to steal from the Duke's private coffers."

The murmurs turned into cries of outrage. Sid was more intrigued than outraged. There'd been a time when he'd considered using his talents to break into the Upper Bailey. He had no doubt he would have succeeded, but there didn't seem any point. He didn't want to steal from the Duke, and he didn't feel like risking the hangman's noose on a pointless challenge. His thoughts immediately turned to Doctor Manky. *He* obviously suspected something was amiss at the castle, something *major* enough to invest ten gold pieces.

"The Duke grappled bravely with the intruder, but, unfortunately, he made good his escape. The Duke was unharmed and the villain left empty handed."

This brought about a half-hearted cheer. The crowd seemed unsure what to make of the news. Sid was beginning to feel uneasy. If Manky was somehow connected to the attack, then, by association, so might he be.

"However, he left behind a clue to his identity."

At this point, the officer in charge of the six men-at-arms who always guarded Gerald stepped forward. Sid recognised him: Jethro Fowler. Fowler was a bloody 'Cake Eater' — one of the lieutenants who wore a *purple* and gold uniform, to set them apart from the run-of-the-mill men-at-arms who wore blue and gold. He and Fowler had had a few run-ins in the past, so Sid kept himself well immersed in the crowd.

Fowler pulled out something small and shiny from a black leather pouch and held it aloft between his thumb and forefinger. The crowd let out a collective "Oooh".

"This silver button," Gerald bellowed, "tore off the villain's clothing as he fought against the Duke. It has a distinctive design etched into it: a feather above a broken sword, a likeness of which will be posted on the news stand. It is the duty of all citizens to help bring this malefactor to justice, and the Duke is prepared to offer a reward of a hundred gold pieces for information leading to his capture."

A hundred gold pieces! This news was met very positively by the surprised crowd; *that* kind of reward was unheard of. Gerald looked rather pleased as he signalled for Fowler to put the button away and return to his place. However, it did nothing to quell Sid's bad feeling — quite the reverse.

Gerald raised the parchment again. "It is the Duke's pleasure that I now relate the story of the man with a wooden eye and the girl with an axe-scarred face."

The crowd cheered, and laughed uproariously when Gerald delivered the bawdy punch-line, even though most of them would have heard it a dozen times or more.

Beaming with pleasure, Gerald finished with an enthusiastic reminder about the Duke of Stymouth's royal visit two weeks hence, something each

Lower Icinger should recognise as a great occasion.

"It is an opportunity for all of us to show pride in our town and our Duchy," he yelled, triumphantly.

The crowd response was half-hearted to say the least. Stymouth was the Duchy that bordered Lower Icing to the west, and that was all most of the townsfolk knew or cared about it. Gerald tried not to look deflated, but failed. Sid tried not to feel worried, but failed.

Chapter 4

It's just a name

TWO INNS BOOKENDED the north and south sides of the Town Square. The Harey Rabbit was situated on the southern, elevated side, adjacent to the castle's East Gate (which led to the castle kitchen). It was where all the well-to-do folk congregated with restraint and decorum. Directly opposite, on the market side, stood The Bloody Bell (so named because it was closer to where the Town Crier and his 'bloody bell' addressed the crowd). Here, the not-so-well-to-do folk rolled up with boisterous enthusiasm to get totally smashed.

It was with laboured steps that Sid walked up the slight incline towards The Harey Rabbit. It had nothing to do with walking uphill and everything to do with where he'd rather be drinking. The Harey Rabbit wasn't Sid's idea of an inn. He'd only experienced its 'tasteful' interior twice before, many years ago, as a part of his 'education' in social etiquette. It had no atmosphere, and that, Sid knew, was because most of the patrons were vacuous toffs. Still, Gerald was an amiable chap and a generous drinking partner, and Sid now had a few pertinent questions to ask him.

Saturdays were traditionally the 'big news' days which attracted a larger crowd to the Town Square, and, consequently, more people to the inns. Today was no exception; as Sid walked through the entrance of The Harey Rabbit, the quiet drinkers were in full voice.

Sid knew Gerald wouldn't arrive for another half an hour at least; he was an integral part of the 'Posting Ceremony' — a farcical official act that took place at the purpose-built news stand erected between the Town Square well and The Bloody Bell. It involved a superfluous collection of orders barked out by an officer, the resultant foot stamping and sword waving by his men, and the slow, deliberate movements of Gerald as he replaced the old proclamation with the new one. Only a smattering of children thought the ceremony was worth hanging around for. They pulled faces and made funny noises in the hope of breaking through the apparent seriousness of the occasion. They always failed. Gerald then had to return to the castle to complete the administration side of the ceremony, whatever *that* entailed. Putting the bloody bell back on his desk, Sid supposed.

Sid ensconced himself at a table next to the bar and bought a tankard of ale. As he drank from it, he observed the inn's patrons. He didn't much like what he saw or heard; there were too many people with influence and position — rich merchants discussing greater protection measures with high-ranking officers, a young man, presumably studying medicine, explaining to his companions how Chicken Pox was actually carried by pigeons, and, right next to him, four lawyers joking about applying the death penalty to anyone who wore a yellow waistcoat. At a corner table, a group of well-dressed women daintily sipped wine and occasionally smiled at each other without actually breaking into conversation. It was all very stuffy and uncomfortable, and, like the ale, was leaving a bad taste in Sid's mouth.

Surprisingly, not many seemed to be discussing the events at the castle. He doubted any of them had actually heard Gerald's proclamation; they were too wrapped up in their own self-importance. When the Duke *was* mentioned, it was in relation to the Duke of Stymouth's impending visit — seating positions at the Ducal Banquet seemed to be foremost in the minds of the nobs at The Harey Rabbit. He did, however, overhear someone with a loud 'ra-ra' voice mention that if the button was indeed silver, then it must have been a "rather wealthy intruder, what".

Sid wondered if there was any connection between Stymouth's visit and the intruder. He had no idea where Manky had come from. He hadn't thought to ask the unflappable apparition… or *why* he wanted to know what was happening in the castle. A potential benefactor was how Manky had described himself. He could well be in the employ of the Duke of Stymouth; he'd arrived and left in a coach, and he had an 'attendant', so he had money and position.

Then again, Sid thought, no-one in their right mind would use Manky if they wanted to gain information secretly. However, his sudden appearance *had* to be linked to the intruder at the castle. One thing was for sure, it was going to be interesting to hear what Gerald had to say about it all. And now that he was thinking about his brother-in-law, why hadn't he mentioned anything about this intruder this morning? It was very unlike Gerald the Herald to keep news like *that* to himself, even if it did mean 'breaking the seal' on an official castle missive.

Sid groaned inwardly. In truth, he really couldn't give a toss about the Duke or the tossers at The Harey Rabbit, and he was no longer sure he should be part of whatever scheme Doctor Manky was involved in. Maybe it was best to just walk away.

He was on the verge of getting up and seeking out the normality of The Bloody Bell when a huge noise exploded into his right ear. "Oyez! Oyez! Oyez!"

Sid's first impulse was to punch Gerald in the face — a fat lip was definitely what he was asking for. But, as he looked up, he saw Gerald had a big smile on his face and two large tankards of ale in his hands. "Admiring the lovely ladies in the corner, eh, Sid?" Gerald winked and sat down.

Sid grimaced. "Bit proper for my way of thinking."

Gerald smiled, sliding one of the tankards towards Sid, "Don't worry, my good fellow. A few more of these and I guarantee you'll be having *improper* thoughts about them."

His good cheer was infectious. Sid grabbed the tankard as Gerald sat down. "Cheers, Gerald."

They clanked tankards. Sid guzzled down a few mouthfuls of the tepid liquid and decided he would, after all, go to work for Doctor Manky. He was curious what his brother-in-law might actually know, and the extra coin definitely wouldn't go astray. He placed the tankard down and wiped his lips. "Nice bit of Town Criering today."

"Thank you, Sid. Most kind. It's not often I have such sensational news. Terrible for the Duke, of course, but... well, there was no real harm done, and someone *may* recognise the button... teach the blighter a lesson, what."

Sid watched his brother-in-law gulp down more ale. It was a hot day, and very close inside The Harey Rabbit, and Gerald's face was a brighter shade of red than his Town Crier coat, which, unbelievably, he was still wearing. Beads of sweat ran down the side of his face and merged with the rivulets of ale that trickled from the side of his mouth. Eventually, he came up for air and stated loudly, "I'd say by this time next week we'll be toasting the capture of the Silver Button Thief."

Gerald's confident declaration had been overheard by some of the nearby nobs. "Here! Here! Well said, Town Crier!" responded one of the anti-yellow-waistcoat lawyers.

Gerald smiled and raised his tankard in acknowledgement of the sentiment. This was not good. The last thing Sid wanted was an all-in discussion, especially with someone who'd like to hang everything (except the expenses).

"Olivia!" Sid blurted out.

The mention of his sister's name had an immediate effect. In the blink of an eye, Gerald's expression transformed from cheerful to fearful. His eyes darted back to Sid, then he twisted around in his chair, twitching his head nervously. "Where is she?"

"Relax, Gerald." Sid could almost see Olivia's thumb print smudged onto his brother-in-law's sweating forehead. "I just wanted to know if you'd told her about our meeting."

Gerald's relief was palpable. "I say, old chap, don't do that to me. My life wouldn't be worth living if she thought I was drinking with you. No offence — you're a top fellow and all — it's just that Olivia... well... she lets me have these Saturday sessions to socialise with people of influence, as she puts it."

Gerald looked apologetic, but Sid smiled. "Well, that's alright then; Liv's always talking to you about *my* influence."

They both laughed.

Satisfied he had regained Gerald's attention, Sid continued. "So, what else has been happening in the castle?"

"Not much, old chap. The preparations for the Duke of Stymouth's visit are well underway in The Keep — Master Scaffold is a most ingenious man. This infernal heat is playing havoc with the Upper Baily gardens — some of the more temperate blooms are beginning to shrivel. The kitchen is running low on marzipan, or so I'm told, and... that's about it, really. The Silver Button Thief has taken precedence over everything else."

This was going to be a waste of time. Gerald had completely missed the intent of the question; he just wasn't the intrigue type. And, in any case, who would trust him with sensitive matters of state? No, he was far too honest and open to be included in any inner circle of knowledge. Sid was about to dismiss the subject when it suddenly occurred to him: Gerald had referred to the castle intruder as the Silver Button *Thief*.

"The intruder... how did he get his name?" Sid's tone must have sounded serious, because Gerald's expression became wary.

"I would have thought that was obvious, dear boy. We found a silver—"

"Yes. Yes. I understand the silver button bit," Sid interrupted, "but, in the Town Square, you said nothing was stolen."

Gerald looked slightly perplexed. "Well... that's correct. Nothing was."

"So why do you refer to him as the Silver Button *Thief*?"

Sid waited a few moments for Gerald to reply. He obviously hadn't realised the epithet's connotation. "I have no idea, Sid." He looked bewildered. "It's just the name Sir Richard calls him."

"The Seneschal?" Sid thought out loud, intrigued.

"The very same."

"Hmm… interesting."

"What do you think it means, Sid?"

"Who knows." He was still thinking out loud. "But don't you think it's odd to refer to someone who hasn't stolen anything as a thief?"

"Well… yes… that is… I suppose so." Gerald seemed uncertain.

Sid's next question was cut off before it had begun by the voice of a woman. It had a rather nice sing-song tone to it. "Looks like you and your gentleman friend could do with another drink, Gerald."

Gerald looked relieved by the interruption. "Oh hello, Mary," he said, smiling up at a rather pretty brunette. She was obviously some sort of barmaid, but she had a sense of authority about her that Sid found immediately attractive. "Your timing's perfect as usual. What do you say, Sid — same again?"

"Good of you to offer, Gerald, but it's my round. How about we sample a bottle of The Harey Rabbit's fine wine?"

Gerald looked pleased at the prospect. "Delightful idea, old chap."

Sid shifted his gaze to Mary. She smiled back at him, blue eyes twinkling between shining rivulets of ebony hair. Her skin had a healthy, golden tone that suggested an active life outside The Harey Rabbit. It wasn't until Mary spoke that Sid realised he'd been staring at her.

"I'm not sure what establishment you usually frequent, sir, but the custom here is to pay for your drinks," she said in good humour, which eased Sid's embarrassment somewhat. He quickly fumbled through his money pouch and handed Mary a coin. As it turned out, it was one of Manky's gold coins, and probably enough to buy a whole cask of fine wine.

"Why, thank you, sir. Most generous of you, since it's also the custom here to allow the serving girls to keep the change."

Sid was now awake to Mary's good-natured teasing and his natural flirtatious manner came to the fore. "As long as *you* were the serving girl, Mary, I would consider every gold coin well spent."

With that, she laughed and walked off. Sid watched her as she made her way across the crowded room.

Gerald smiled knowingly as Sid's gaze returned to the table. "She's a beautiful woman."

"You won't get any arguments there. Is she spoken for?"

Gerald chuckled at that. "I think you'll find she's quite capable of speaking for herself."

"I'm delighted to hear it." He drained the last of his watery brew and said, "So, getting back to this thief business, Gerald. What do you make of it?"

In response, Gerald's smile became a wince. "Do we have to discuss this, old chap? I mean, it's all very interesting but… well… this is my afternoon to get merrily drunk, and I don't want to spoil it by talking shop, what. And, in any case, now that I think about it, I'm not entirely sure who came up with the Silver Button Thief name, and I don't see what difference it makes — it's just a name."

Gerald appeared somewhat flustered, so Sid decided not to pursue the subject. He was fairly sure Gerald knew very little about events at the castle, and any further discussion on the subject would only frustrate both of them. Gerald was right: it was time to get merrily drunk.

"You're a wise man, Gerald. Let us drink and speak of more enjoyable things — like getting to know Mary better. I'd wager you could tell me a few of her secrets."

Gerald nodded happily, but what he said took Sid by surprise. "Speaking of secrets, didn't you have something you wanted to tell me in secret?"

Sid had forgotten about his little ruse. "Ah… yes…" Sid scanned the room, pretending to make sure no-one was listening as he tried to think of a response. Ironically, it was his sister who provided it for him. "Well, to tell the truth, I probably exaggerated a bit… It's just that it's Liv's birthday soon and I thought this year I'd make an effort to do something special for her. I wondered if you might have a few ideas?"

After a short brainstorming session, in which Gerald suggested Sid might like to buy Olivia some personalised stationery, or maybe even a silver locket, the brothers-in-law spent the afternoon and evening talking, laughing and drinking.

The last thing Sid remembered as he stumbled out into the warm night to relieve himself in The Harey Rabbit's stables was how surprisingly nice the inn was, and how lovely that lovely, lovely Mary was. Her lovely face — wild and intelligent — was etched into his mind, her lovely, lovely midnight hair surrounded by a haze of candlelit revelry. He was unaware of anyone lurking in the shadows, had no idea what opportunity his presence presented, and had absolutely no warning of the heavy blow that rendered him unconscious.

Chapter 5

An ethereal beauty

THE HUMMING DRONE was familiar to Sid, but he couldn't quite place it. He concentrated, and gradually the drone became distant voices. Now he could hear random spurts of laughter and the occasional name being yelled. Sid jerked awake and tried to sit up, but was defeated by a stabbing head pain. He heard himself groan as he sank back into the comfort of a... bed... but not *his* bed. How? He hadn't drunk *that* much had he? Just a few quiet ales and a bottle of wine with Gerald. What had happened to Gerald? His brother-in-law had left The Harey Rabbit well before him, hadn't he? Sid had stayed because of Mary... Mary with the blue eyes, the dancing voice. He felt so tired. Lucky he was in bed.

"You right, sir?" asked the voice of a young man.

Sid opened his eyes, but only one obeyed. For some reason, his left eye remained shut. Through his right eye, Sid saw an anxious face, but his mind couldn't comprehend what was going on.

"What's happened to me?" he croaked. The left side of his face hurt with every movement.

"You been attacked, sir; hit in the 'ead, like," the face informed him. "I'll just go an' fetch Mistress Mary. She wanted to know when y'woke; straightaway, like."

By the time the lad had finished speaking, he'd almost retreated out of the room. Attacked? What the frig was going on? He reached for his money pouch, but realised he was dressed only in his undergarments. How long had he been here? And where was *here*, exactly?

He was propped up on a pillow — from his position he was able to take stock of his surroundings, and that made him feel even stranger. It appeared he was in a woman's bedroom. The walls were painted light blue, the ceiling white; to his right was a small bedside table, with lavender and wildflowers arranged in an earthenware vase; the wall to his left contained a large window from which shaded light filtered through sheer cotton curtains that wafted in a warm, gentle breeze, carrying with it the faint redolence of stables; next to the window, in the far corner, was a dressing table, complete with mirror and side drawers; on the table was a neatly arranged collection of hairbrushes and small, colourful glass bottles; directly opposite him was an empty fireplace, with an ornately carved, polished timber mantlepiece above it; placed at each end of the mantle-piece were more flowers, guarding three intricately worked glass figurines of an owl, a squirrel and an otter; to the right of the fireplace was a timber wardrobe, with a number of hat boxes sitting neatly on top; directly opposite the window, in the wall to his right, was a doorway. Standing within its frame was an ethereal beauty. Sid wondered if he was dreaming. Everything seemed hazy and dislocated, except for the pain in his head.

"Mary?"

"How are you feeling?" Mary said, quietly, as she entered the room.

Sid felt like someone had removed the insides of his head and put them back the wrong way; everything from the bottom of his chin to the top of head ached, the area around his left eye throbbed, his mouth felt like it was stuffed with nails, and his jaw creaked painfully.

"I've had better ends to a night of drinking," he said as she floated closer and sat down on the edge of the bed.

"Doctor Whysman says you'll recover. Nothing is broken."

Sid didn't remember seeing any doctor. The last thing he recalled was relieving himself in the stables of The Harey Rabbit. She leant towards him, appraising his condition. Her tanned complexion was flushed and her forehead shone with perspiration, yet she smelled wonderful, like wildflowers, and her blue eyes were as bright as a summer sky. If this was a dream, it was the most vivid one he'd ever had.

"And it looks like the swelling's gone down slightly."

His thoughts turned to his condition. What damage had been done? He gazed over to the dressing table mirror. From his position on the bed, he couldn't see his reflection, but he could see a hand mirror lying on top of the table. "May I use your hand mirror?" he asked softly — he really was finding it painful to speak.

Mary's right eyebrow arched, and she looked at him appraisingly before retrieving the mirror.

The head that stared back at Sid looked like something out of Lurchalot's Travelling Freak Show. His one good eye focused on the area where his head had, literally, been split open. A two-inch long gash above his left eye was trying to congeal through neat stitches as it sat atop a swollen lump about the size and colour of a large plum. The eye itself had been forced shut by the swelling. The angry bruising extended down the side of Sid's face, turning from a lighter purple to a sickly yellow at his jaw. In stark contrast, the right side of his face appeared completely normal. Yes, he looked freakish.

"Glad you think the swelling's gone down," Sid commented, placing the hand mirror on the bed.

Mary looked at him intently from the edge of the bed. She seemed almost annoyed. His mind was swirling and his memory was muddled — had he done something wrong... offended someone?

"Why did this happen to you?" she asked.

What did she expect him to say to that? "I have no idea. The last—"

"Don't lie to me! I'm not a fool."

Mary suddenly produced his leather money pouch and slapped it into his right hand. It felt warm and light. "You've been robbed," she said. It sounded like an accusation.

"Then I suppose the *robber* is why this happened to me!" His angry response produced a throbbing pain across the left side of his head.

The look on Mary's face was also pained: a mixture of sympathy and disappointment. "Look inside the pouch."

Sid sighed. "I can see it's empty; robbers don't often leave change."

"Robbers don't often leave pouches," Mary countered.

This was all becoming too much; what did Mary want from him? He'd been beaten and robbed, but she was acting as if *he* was somehow to blame. She had a point about the money pouch though. Why hadn't the cutpurse simply cut his purse, instead of risking capture by emptying its contents?

Clenching his hand around the leather, he could feel something round and hard inside. He loosened the leather ties and tipped the object into his left hand. It was small, round and silver. It looked like a button. There was a design etched into it. Sid brought it closer to his good eye; he was having trouble focusing. Slowly the design became crisp and clear. It was a feather over a broken sword.

What was going on? Why would someone leave a silver button in his pouch? Suddenly, the fog cleared. Gerald's proclamation! The Duke's intruder! The Silver Button Thief! (Even though nothing had been stolen.)

Mary's stern voice broke through his thoughts. "Well?"

Realisation hit him like another blow to the head. Mary thought *he* was the intruder. "I have no idea how this got here," he said, his mind beginning to focus.

Mary looked unconvinced. She plucked the button from Sid's hand. "It's a warning, isn't it? You know what happened at the castle, don't you?"

Was she serious? Mary was holding the button as if it was irrefutable proof of his complicity. His head hurt, his bad eye throbbed painfully under the swelling, and his good eye was watery and raw; he wanted to close it and let sleep take him away from this madness… but *her* eyes compelled him.

"I swear to you, I know nothing of what happened at the castle, or why I was attacked."

She regarded him, blues eyes searching; he could see that she wanted to believe him. Then there was a knock at the door. Breaking eye contact, Mary stood and opened it. A young lad entered holding a tray. Sid recognised him as the person who'd been in the room when he regained consciousness. The lad placed the tray on the bedside table; it held a bowl of broth and a small loaf of crusty bread. He gave Sid a nervous glance and a twitchy smile before turning his attention to Mary.

"C'n I do anythin' else, Mistress?"

Mary shook her head and smiled. "You've done enough, John. Thank you."

Sid heaved himself into a sitting position as Mary shut the bedroom door behind John. His head swam and throbbed — for a moment he thought he was going to black out. Then he felt Mary's arms around his back, propping him up while she rearranged the pillows. The dizzy spell passed as Mary reached for the tray and placed it on the bed cover over his lap. The aroma of the broth was mouth-watering — literally — and Sid realised he was famished. He picked up the spoon and submerged it in the vegetable-filled broth. Mary studied him as he brought the spoon to his mouth. He suddenly felt self-conscious. The situation became even more embarrassing when he was forced to slurp the contents into the right side of his mouth. The left side was in painful bruise territory, and he couldn't open it enough to fit the spoon, let alone the pieces of potato, carrot and turnip.

After successfully inhaling most of the spoonful, he glanced up at Mary. For the first time since coming into the room, she conveyed sympathy, and when she spoke it was with tenderness. "Please tell me the truth. If you're in some kind of trouble…?"

Painful as it was, he obliged by telling her about the strange meeting with Doctor Manky. During Sid's account of events, Mary's attitude towards him mellowed considerably — Manky was too bizarre to fabricate — her doubt replaced by disbelieving acceptance. He explained that Manky had approached him because of his relationship to the Town Crier, that he'd wanted information about any unusual goings-on in the castle, things that weren't public knowledge, that he was prepared to give Sid ten gold pieces just for picking Gerald's brain. So he'd taken up the offer — that's what had brought him to The Harey Rabbit. Gerald's brain, however, contained very little information, unusual or otherwise, and had proven to be totally devoid of any intrigue.

"Manky must have either known about or been involved with the intruder," Sid surmised. "It's too much of a coincidence."

"This is madness. What have you got yourself into?"

He looked at her sun-kissed face and wished he was the sun. His mind really was all over the place, and he was finding it hard to retain focus, so he said the first thing that popped into it. "Well, by the looks of things, your bed, so it can't be all bad." His attempt at humour caused him to grimace in pain.

"Sid, this is serious." Mary was fighting back a smile. "What are you going to do?"

"I haven't decided yet. I'll see what Manky has to say for himself," he said, slurping down another mouthful of the surprisingly tasty broth.

"And what if *he's* responsible for your beating? This Manky could have set you up."

Sid placed the spoon in the bowl. He could see her point, and yet, for some reason, it didn't ring true. Manky didn't strike him as dim-witted, and that's what he'd have to be to incriminate himself so obviously. "No, it doesn't make sense. I think it's more likely I was marked out by someone in The Harey Rabbit. I'm not exactly one of the regulars."

"How do you know it wasn't me?" She smiled, but there was a challenge in it.

"I don't, but I'm not about to accuse the angel who's given me her bed and nursed me back to health."

The evening was surrendering to the dark, but even in the reddening light, he saw Mary blush. "Well, it was cheaper than calling the undertaker." She gazed at the window and then stood. "It's getting dark. I'll just light—"

"Mary…" Sid reached for her arm as she moved off the bed. She turned to face him. He took her hand in his. She gently squeezed it and smiled… with genuine warmth. It lit up the evening gloom. "Thank you."

CHAPTER 6

Best go tell Mistress Mary

MARY HAD LEFT Sid to rest, and it wasn't long before he'd succumbed to an overwhelming desire to sleep, which he did well into Monday evening.

When he finally rejoined the world of consciousness, his head still ached, but the fuzziness had dissipated somewhat. However, the memory of the last two days was still rather vague. He knew where he was and what had happened to him, and he was pretty sure he'd had a conversation with Mary about the silver button and Doctor Manky. There was also half a memory of someone talking to Mary about his condition and how she should treat it, but that all seemed too hard to think about.

Sid thoughts turned to more immediate matters. It was time to leave. He felt as if he'd been confined to Mary's bed for weeks. Pulling off the sheet, he levered himself into a sitting position on the edge of the bed. Apart from a throbbing pain over his swollen left eye, the manoeuvre hadn't caused him any duress. He noticed a hand mirror resting on the bedside table and it jogged another memory: one of a gruesome visage. He wondered whether he should reacquaint himself with the reality of his injury. He wasn't sure it was good idea, but in the end, curiosity won out.

His memory, unfortunately, had been accurate. He still looked like a nightmare — the contrast between his injured left and unscathed right was morbidly fascinating. Placing the mirror back on the table, he scanned the room for his clothes. He was naked except for his hose undergarment. However, there was nothing sartorial in view, so he carefully slid off the side of the bed and stood up, almost knocking over an empty piss bucket. Had he pissed in the last two days?

He waited for a wave of dizziness or nausea, but only the aching throb persisted, and he could deal with that. Sid headed for the wardrobe in the corner by the window. The light outside was fading, the courtyard and stables shrouded in shadow except for a tinge of copper glow on the stable roof. Not a breath of air flowed through the window. Sid opened the wardrobe, and there, amongst a collection of dresses and various feminine accoutrements, were his black trousers. Below them were his boots, but he couldn't see his white shirt. Oh well, at least his trousers and boots offered him enough comfort and decency to make his way home. Grabbing his items, he sat back down on the edge of the bed. A small wave of dizziness flowed across his head, but nothing like he'd previously experienced. He put on his trousers without any problem. He then slipped into his calf-length leather boots easily enough. He was about to do up the buckles when a young lad of about fourteen appeared at the bedroom doorway. He looked shocked.

"Something the matter?" Sid asked.

"No, sir… That is, yes, sir… Sorry, sir, it's jus' tha'… you're outta bed, like."

"Apparently so." Sid winced; talking made his head hurt.

"But… you ain't been—"

"Well, I am now," Sid interjected, even though he had no idea what the lad was about to say. "And I'm leaving."

The lad looked worried. "Best go tell Mistress Mary."

"You do that."

Sid was still fumbling with the buckles of the first boot when Mary appeared in the doorway. Her blue eyes radiated surprised and concern. Sid couldn't help but smile at her — she was just so beautiful. "Hello, Mary."

"What are you doing, Sid?"

"Something I mastered around the age of five," he replied, returning his attention to the leather straps on his boots in an attempt to hide the pain of speaking.

"Very funny," she replied.

He could hear the sarcasm in her voice, but he didn't know what to say. He was overwhelmed by her, by what she'd done for him, but he was also embarrassed that he'd been such a burden. He wanted to reach out to her, tell her how he felt, but instead the words "I seem to be missing a shirt" came out of his mouth.

"I'd say you were missing more than *that*," she retorted, moving into the room. "Sid, you're badly injured; you've barely been conscious for the last two days. You can't suddenly wake up and…"

He'd turned his attention back to the straps. He didn't feel worthy of her concern.

"Sid, are you listening to me?"

He pulled the strap through the buckle, his mind searching the depths for the right words. "Mary," he said, standing. "I feel fine, fully rec—"

Suddenly, the world lurched and bright lights sparked in his vision. He lost his footing and stumbled forwards. Then, somehow, Mary was supporting him; his left arm wrapped around her neck, but he was still falling. He felt his knees touch the floor. He reached out with his right hand for balance, his body falling in slow motion until his hand found the floor. Then his head began to clear; he could hear himself breathing. It was strange… it sounded so heavy, like he'd been running. "Sorry," he panted.

CHAPTER 7

Leavin' the right impression

SID WAS MUCH more alert and mentally restored when he awoke early the next morning. Mary arranged a bath and provided him with a new shirt. Apparently, his old one had suffered just as much damage from the attack as *he* had and was too badly blood stained. Not even repeated scrubbings by Mary's washer woman could clean away the evidence of Sid's cracked head. "If Juanita can't remove the blood from your shirt, then no-one can," Mary had said.

As he soaked in the cool water, Sid considered his next move. He could leave Manky to find another monkey and live the straightforward, comfortable life of supply and demand. Trouble was, he wasn't in the mood to be comfortable. He'd been made to feel decidedly *uncomfortable* by his attacker; he wanted answers *and* he wanted the satisfaction of returning the favour. He had to remain cool-headed though. He'd seen enough bluster and bravado end badly to know that thinking was best done before acting.

By the time Sid was washed and dressed, he felt like a new man. Although still very tender, his head no longer ached. The swelling had gone down somewhat and the gash looked to be on its way to healing, but the bruising still looked angry and his left eye remained sore and useless. However, it was with renewed vigour and purpose that Sid Evily finally left the feminine confines of Mary's room that Tuesday morning.

The bar room of The Harey Rabbit was empty, except for a table occupied by a well-dressed couple in their fifties. Mary was serving them breakfast. As Sid approached, Mary turned and smiled at him.

"You've scrubbed up alright."

"I know," Sid agreed, happily. "I should get bashed more often."

Mary gave him a withering look, and moved to the side of the table, giving Sid a clearer view of the couple. The man seemed to be appraising Sid, as if he was considering the purchase of an old horse. The woman was smiling at him, as if she knew her companion would make the purchase. It made Sid feel very self-conscious.

"Sid, this is Doctor Albert Whysman and his wife, Petronella," Mary said formally. "Doctor Whysman is the person who's been treating you."

Sid bowed formally. "Delighted to make your acquaintance, Doctor," he said in a voice he saved for people of position. "Thank you for all your kind and timely ministrations."

"Don't mention it, m'boy. Young Mary, here, did all the work." Doctor Whysman seemed a jolly sort.

Sid then turned to Petronella, smiled amiably and bowed again. "A pleasure to meet you, madam."

"Why thank you, Master...?"

"Sid will do nicely, thank you, Mistress Whysman."

Petronella floundered slightly at the breach of protocol. "Well... Sid, I am glad my husband was able to help you. You've obviously been hurt quite badly. It's dreadful to think one cannot walk the streets safely at night."

Sid wondered what fantasy part of Lower Icing Petronella lived in. He couldn't imagine *any* night-time street — outside the castle grounds — being safe from cutpurses, muggers, or anyone else desperate or stupid enough to risk public flogging (or worse) for financial gain.

"Well, quite," Sid said politely. "And now, alas, I must take my leave. Thank you again for your assistance, Doctor Whysman. I will, of course, recompense you for your time as soon as—"

"No need, m'boy," Doctor Whysman stated.

Sid was slightly taken aback by this. He was naturally suspicious of people who did — or offered to do — things for nothing.

"I insist, Doc—"

"Mary, here, has already been most generous on your behalf," he remarked, indicating the breakfast spread.

Sid looked at Mary. Her eyebrows were arched, as if daring him to argue. "Well," he said, "it seems I am indebted to you in more ways than one, Mistress Brewer."

"Do not mention it, *Master* Evily," Mary said, mimicking Sid's formality, though it sounded forced. "Allow me to escort you to the door."

Sid smiled — partly because his play-acting was making Mary uncomfortable, but mainly because it felt so good to have his mind back.

Mary turned and smiled warmly at her guests. "I shall return directly,

Doctor, Petronella. In the meantime, please enjoy your breakfast."

"Thank you, m'dear," the doctor replied cheerfully, and then said to Sid, "And you rest up, m'boy. Your body is still repairing itself. Take care not to overdo things."

"No need to concern yourself, Doctor." Sid smiled. "I intend to take very good care of… things."

"What was *that* all about?" Mary enquired once they were outside. The morning street noise was a sharp contrast to the quiet confines of the inn.

"What do you mean?" Sid grinned.

"The way you were speaking in there, all formal, like a *regular*."

"Well y'see, me lovely," Sid said, affecting a common accent, "there ain't no 'arm done in leavin' the right impression."

Mary grimaced at the change in his voice, then countered with, "I didn't think you were the type to worry about what people thought of you."

"You're right, Mary," he replied, once more in his normal voice, "I'm usually quite comfortable being Sid Evily, but I don't know this doctor, and I don't know the world he lives in." Then he added dryly, "It's a wise man who is wary of a Whysman."

"Oh *very* droll." A reluctant smile broke across Mary's face. Then she realised what he was implying. "Surely you don't think *Doctor Whysman* was involved?"

"Who knows? I have no idea why this has happened," Sid said, pointing at his face. "But until I find out, you're the only one I'm willing to trust."

CHAPTER 8

Let Sid go about his business

THE SUN WAS beaming down, turning the warm morning into another hot summer's day. As Sid walked along the cobblestone streets, his head began to pound in time to his steps. He also felt light-headed, and it came as quite a surprise when he bumped, literally, into Gerald and Olivia just outside their terraced home.

"Mind where you're walking, there's a good fellow," Gerald muttered amiably.

As Sid turned to apologise, he was treated to two quite different expressions: shock and concern from his brother-in-law and a mild, contemptuous glare from his sister. They were the last people he'd expected or wanted to see right at this moment.

"Good heavens, Sid! What's happened to you? Are you alright?" Gerald's voice boomed painfully.

Sid forced a smile. "Oh, you know me, Gerald," he said as casually as possible, "always fall for a pretty face."

Olivia's cool voice cut through Sid's attempted levity. "I'd like to say I'm surprised, Gerald," she said, still gazing at Sid, "but Sid looks for trouble as much as he looks for the ale jug, and both tend to leave him with a sore head."

"Come now, Olivia. Poor Sid's obviously been hurt quite badly. The least we can do—"

"The *least* we can do," Olivia cut in evenly, whilst maintaining her veil of decorum, "is let Sid go about his business."

In an odd way, Sid felt grateful for his sister's dismissive attitude. "Right you are, Liv," he agreed. "I *do* have business to attend to." Looking at Gerald, he added, "Many thanks for your concern, Gerald. I'm much better than I look. Good day to you."

Sid walked off, leaving an awkward-looking Gerald arm-in-arm with Lower Icing's frostiest woman.

The front door of Sid's humble abode had never looked so welcoming. It was a place where he knew he could rest and take stock of his situation. After retrieving a small barrel of ale, cheese and bread from the cool confines of his cellar, Sid sat down with quill and parchment and began to write. He needed to get his thoughts down on paper, because his mind was whirring with possibilities of who might have attacked him.

The castle intruder? Found out his mistake after Gerald's proclamation.

Someone at The Horey Rabbit?

Yellow waist-coated tosser lawyers? No, they wouldn't have the balls!

Just the wrong place at the wrong time... probably.

No frigging idea... exactly!!!

Sid was frustrated. There was no use trying to work out the whos and whys. Doctor Manky was the only person who could help him. He put down the quill, reached into his trouser pocket and retrieved the button, which he placed on the table. Then he picked up his tankard and took a long, slow draught of ale, all the while staring with his good eye at the engraving on the silver button.

The realisation was such that Sid almost sprayed the contents of his mouth over the table. He'd placed the button next to the quill. It wasn't a feather on the button; it was a quill. He picked up the button and examined it: a quill above a broken sword. It symbolised a well-known saying: The written word is more powerful than physical force.

So, was this just a button? Or did it have a more sinister implication? Sid's head was pulsing with wild possibilities; the whole thing seemed too fantastic. He'd drained a couple tankards, and now felt drained himself. He clambered upstairs and spent the day resting in his bedroom. As he drifted in and out of sleep, he tried to sort through what he'd learnt and what it could mean.

CHAPTER 9

Something to tell you

SID TRIED TO block out the sound, but it persisted. It was a loud thumping noise, but it didn't seem to be causing him any pain, which was a relief in itself. Now his name was being shouted, adding to the din, when all he wanted was peace and quiet.

With a start, Sid woke. Someone was knocking at his door. His bedroom window was open and he stumbled towards it. The afternoon heat was oppressive; Sid could feel the trickles of sweat running down the sides of his face. The bright sunlight made him feel even groggier. As he gazed down into the street, he could see a woman thumping at his timber door, her dark hair shimmering. It was Mary.

"Would you like an axe?" Sid croaked loudly.

She stopped immediately, looked up and smiled. "Well, would you believe it, I've finally made enough noise to wake the dead."

"Can't get enough of me, eh?" Sid said, still trying to adjust to consciousness. "I'll be down shortly."

Sid unbolted the door and revealed a vision more radiant than the summer sun. Mary was wearing a simple white dress that accentuated her tanned face and made her blue eyes almost glow. Her smile was magic, and, once again, Sid was spellbound. It took a second or two before he realised Mary was speaking to him.

"…such a hot day, I thought I'd see if you'd made it home in one piece."

"Sorry, Mary… I… er…" His brain was still asleep and his head was spinning from the trip down his stairs. "I suppose I'm still a bit dazed. Please… please come in."

Mary gave him a wry smile. "Why, thank you."

Sid ushered Mary into the main room of his house. In the centre of the room stood the table, with Sid's half-eaten cheese and bread still lying next to the empty tankard. His parchment and quill were also part of the arrangement.

Next to the parchment, shining in the small amount of afternoon light provided by the room's single window, was the silver button.

"Welcome to the abode of Sid Evily," pronounced Sid, offering Mary one of the two chairs at the table.

Mary smiled as she sat. "Has a woman ever set foot in this place before?"

"Plenty of women, but never a lady."

She smiled knowingly. "So, how are you feeling? You look a bit better, particularly for a man who died six years ago."

Died six years ago? Had he missed something? "Was that a jest, Mary? My head is still rather foggy."

"Not according to Petronella Whysman. She's under the impression you fell from a roof."

Sid groaned in realisation. "Let me guess… my sister?"

Mary nodded.

As far as Liv was concerned, she had no brother. It still bothered Sid — he had no idea what had triggered her deep-set resentment of him. "And here I was thinking you'd come to cheer me up."

"I'm sorry, Sid; it's just that Petronella Whysman seemed quite shocked when I told her who you were."

Sid sighed. "Liv decided long ago that a dead brother was more socially acceptable than the live version."

"Well, you can hardly blame her for *that*." Mary wore a playful smile.

Sid barked out a laugh, then instantly regretted it as the left side of his face erupted in pain.

Mary shook her head (as if he should know better than to laugh in his condition), then reached over and grabbed the parchment. "What's this?"

Sid made no attempt to retrieve it; he'd written nothing he hadn't already discussed with Mary. He watched her face as she read. A smile played upon her lips. Maybe it was due to the point about the dick-pulling lawyers.

"Hmm… some interesting thoughts."

"Amusing ones, by the look."

Mary paused, blue eyes aglow; she seemed to be savouring the moment. "In a naïve sort of way."

"*Naïve?*" His outrage caused his face muscles to move in directions his swollen eye wasn't ready for. The pain was severe, and, with a curse, Sid snatched back the parchment. Tears blurred his vision as he gazed down at what he'd written, but what happened next was totally unexpected.

Mary had moved to Sid's side of the table without him realising; he could feel the warmth of her arms around his neck as she gently embraced him, the softness of her lips on his cheek, and he could smell the scent of wild summer flowers.

Then she kissed him softly on the mouth. To Sid, it was a moment of sheer joy — pain turning into unexpected pleasure — and for that moment there was nothing else in the world. As the parchment fell silently from his hand, he reluctantly allowed Mary to withdraw from the kiss.

"Does the abode of Sid Evily have a bed?"

Their coupling had been passionately gentle, or, possibly, gently passionate. Both of them were acutely aware of Sid's injury, and while it had no effect on his performance, it did inhibit his ability to express himself more… creatively. In any case, this wasn't just another quick 'get your rocks off shag' with Elsie; *this* was Mary… and it was magical.

Sid gazed at the beautiful woman lying beside him. Was she a dream? Had she really woken him, banged on his door, and called out his name?

Then the dream spoke. "I have something to tell you."

Sid smiled. Her husky voice sounded real enough. "That sounds ominous," he croaked. "Should I have heard this *before* you had your way with me?"

She softly stroked his face. That felt real too. "I don't know what to make of you, Sid Evily, but I am not ashamed to admit you have made my heart fly."

"And you mine."

He reached out to embrace her, but she stopped him.

"Wait. You need to know something about me."

The relaxing, dreamlike feeling suddenly disappeared, Mary's voice suddenly sounding *too* real.

"If we are going to be open with each other, this must be said."

"Very well, Mary. I'm all ears."

Mary looked as if she was about to open a door she knew was probably best left shut. She took a deep breath, and then informed him that Sir Richard Upson was her half-brother.

CHAPTER 10

Woman of means

SID STARED AT her anxious features, trying to equate the woman of his desire with the half-sister of Sir Richard Upson. It didn't add up at all.

"Say something, Sid," Mary said softly.

He should be angry, but, actually, he felt quite calm. "Does that mean you know what happened at the castle?"

"No," Mary whispered urgently. "I know nothing about any of it. I am not my brother's confidante. We rarely see each other, and when we do, we talk of the weather or other such inane things. We live in two different worlds and have nothing in common."

Sid didn't know what to say. A dozen things were running through his head — is this why Mary kowtowed to the nobs and put up with their crap?

Mary looked worried by his reaction and began answering his yet-to-be-asked questions. "Richard and I have the same father — the late Sir Walter Upson," she explained, taking his hand in hers. "My mother was one of Sir Walter's servants. She died giving birth to me. Of course, Sir Walter could not raise me as he would a daughter born in wedlock, but he did look after my wellbeing and made sure I was cared for. He sent me to live with John and Kate Brewer, the owners of The Harey Rabbit. They had no children of their own, so I was a blessing to them. They raised me as their daughter and treated me with love and kindness, and I always regarded them as my parents. At my coming of age, they turned the running of The Harey Rabbit over to me. I was so pleased and proud."

Sid noticed tears forming in the corners of Mary's eyes.

"The next two years saw both of them dead from influenza. And then a year later, Sir Walter succumbed to old age — if you call sixty-one old. After he died, I found out that he'd bought the deed to The Harey Rabbit and put it in my name. So, at the age of twenty-four, I was suddenly a woman of means. That was just over two years ago."

Two rivulets of tears made their way across Mary's cheeks, one heading for her nose, the other heading for the pillow she was resting her head on. She took a deep breath and sighed. Sid caressed her right cheek with his thumb, wiping the tear before it reached her nose. He remembered the news about Sir Walter being sympathetically bellowed out by Gerald, though at the time it had meant very little to him — just another nob dying in luxury.

"I swear, Sid, I know nothing of this silver button business," she whispered.

"I believe you, Mary," he said quietly, and he meant it. Mary could have kept her relationship to Sir Richard a secret and he would have been none the wiser. In any case, Sid understood the vagaries of family — you couldn't help who you were related to; Liv had made that point loud and clear on numerous occasions.

"Thank you," she said drawing him close.

Suddenly, Mary was leaving. She had to get back to The Harey Rabbit before her staff began throwing pots at one another. Sid tried to coax her into staying, but she was adamant that the inn required her presence. She promised she would stay with him tomorrow night, after closing. Reluctantly, Sid acquiesced.

He was escorting her through his living room when he remembered the silver button. He stopped and looked back at the table. It was still there, lying next to his half-eaten cheese and bread. How could he have forgotten? The answer to *that* question was standing in front of him, looking slightly impatient.

"Look, Sid," Mary said. "I'd love to stay, truly, but I have to get back to the inn."

"I've discovered something about the silver button," he said, retrieving it and taking it to the window, so she could see it in daylight. "Come and have another look at it."

She gave him a dubious glance before following him. He placed the button in her hand, and, as she studied it, her expression turned from curious to puzzled.

"Look at the etching," he prompted. "The feather…"

Mary studied the shiny object closely and murmured, "I still can't see what…"

"It's a quill," said Sid, unable to maintain the suspense.

Mary seemed unimpressed by the revelation.

"Don't you realise what this means?" He was bewildered by her calmness.

Mary shrugged her shoulders. "The person who drew the likeness has poor eyesight?"

Was that a jest? She was smiling, so it must have been. She kissed him on his cheek, then whispered playfully in his ear, "I suppose it could be a secret message."

Sid was finding it hard to see the funny side in this. "My thoughts exactly," he replied as she drew back.

Mary's playful smile vanished.

CHAPTER 11
A sign of bad news

SID SPENT THE rest of the afternoon pondering the circumstances surrounding the silver button. During the process, he drank his way through another jug of ale. By the end, his thoughts were swimming in a morass of alcohol and stuffy heat. 'No friggin' idea' was still the best he could do. He'd even lost enthusiasm for his 'secret message' theory. Why would he be the recipient of such a message? He knew nothing and no-one of importance, apart from Tom Skinner (the Duchy's Gamekeeper) and *that* was more of a passing acquaintance. No, it was ridiculous to think the button was meant for him, but *why* had it ended up in his money pouch? If it was a set up, it hadn't been thought out very well; none of his clothes had that button. In any case, it was obvious he'd been attacked and the button planted on him. Mary would certainly attest to that. Perhaps he should turn himself in and plead his case. He laughed out loud at that, and then collapsed into a drunken slumber.

Sid didn't wake until late morning, but felt much better for the extended sleep. He decided not to waste any more time on the silver button. Instead, he would attend to the business he knew and understood.

Wednesdays, Sid went to see Reginald Puffy, the Duke's Head of Kitchen, to negotiate the week's savoury pastry order. This Wednesday wasn't going to be any different, regardless of the events on Saturday night. In fact, he was in a very content mood as he strolled through the sun-filled streets of Lower Icing towards the castle.

The route to the castle kitchen actually took him past The Harey Rabbit, but he resisted the urge to pop in and see Mary. As usual, there were a couple of guards milling around at the East Gate, keeping an eye on the comings and goings. They mostly let people go about their business; after all, they recognised just about all of the traders and barrow-boys by sight. Occasionally, they'd check the contents of a person's cart, but it was just a token effort at security.

Sid, of course, was well known to the guards — he usually slipped them a coin or two, because it made getting the pork pies and other culinary delights out of the castle a lot easier.

"Ah well, look what we 'ave 'ere, Ronnie," said one of the guards in a jovial tone as Sid approached the gate. "Looks like young Sid Evily's been on the wrong side of an argument. Who was she, Sid?"

Ronnie laughed, and Sid acknowledged the jest with a winced smile. As he passed through the gate, the guard followed up with, "Better watch out Sid, the kitchen's full o' tarts this mornin'."

What the kitchen *was* full of was people going about their duties: peeling vegetables, kneading dough, plucking pheasants, gutting fish, sweeping floors, cleaning benches and what seemed like a hundred other jobs all happening in fast motion. But everyone had one thing in common: they looked bloody hot. The hues of faces ranged from mild pink to vein-bursting plum. Sid was searching for the latter.

It didn't take long to spot the rotund shape and almost completely bald head of Reg Puffy. Dressed in a white smock and brown trousers, he reminded Sid of a large Christmas pudding with a cherry on top.

As Sid approached, Reg was overseeing the rolling of pastry and the filling of pies. "No, no, no. Not like that, girl. You need to flour the roller first. How many times must I tell you?"

"Sorry, Mista Puffy," the girl mumbled.

Sid took the opportunity to make his presence known. "You know, Reg, I've always thought of you as a bit of a high-roller," he said.

Reg kept his gaze on the girl and the application of flour, and it was obvious he didn't find Sid's remark the least bit amusing. "What do you want, Sid?"

Sid was a bit taken aback; Reg would often bluster at his kitchen workers, but he'd always been quite jovial with Sid. Perhaps the heat was getting to him; his head did look like it could erupt any second.

"Well, apart from your delightful company, Reg, it is Wednesday," he responded breezily. Too breezily, as it happened, as the left side of his face gave him a sharp reminder of his injury.

"I am well aware what day it is," Reg said without looking up, and then addressed another girl in the pastry-rolling section. "It's still too thick to cut." He prodded the pastry, and the girl began re-rolling. He seemed unusually flustered, and his attention remained fixed on the pastry rolling. "Look, Sid, you can see I'm busy. I can't take your order today."

Sid was gobsmacked; Reg had never said that to him before. "What are you talking about, Reg?"

Finally, Reg met his gaze. His eyes widened as he stared dumbly at Sid's face. With what seemed to be a great effort, Reg extended his hand and pointed directly at Sid's left eye. "*That's* what I'm talking about."

A few minutes later, Sid watched as Reg produced a parchment from a drawer in his office desk.

"This arrived this morning," he said, shakily handing the parchment to Sid.

The first thing Sid noticed about the document was the perfect penmanship; it looked to have been written by someone trained in the art of calligraphy. The second thing he noticed was the absence of a signature. In Sid's experience, anything unsigned was always a sign of bad news. This was no exception.

Reginald Puffy
Head of Kitchen
Lower Icing Castle

Dear Sir,

I am aware of your arrangement with one Sid Evily. I fear I cannot, in all conscience, allow it to continue, and insist you cease all dealings with him forthwith. It is my opinion that Sid Evily has used his greed and guile to lead you astray, but now it is time for you to return to the fold. I believe you to be a loyal subject of the Duke and do not wish you to be the subject of any *harmful* investigation. I am confident you will make the morally correct decision and avoid the unpleasant alternative.

"I'm sorry, Sid," Reg said after Sid had finished reading, "but you can see I have no choice."

Sid could hardly believe it. Reg had been supplying him with pork pies and other pastry delights for almost two years.

"Who gave this to you, Reg?"

"No-one; it was just lying there on my desk."

"When did you notice it?"

The letter had clearly upset him. "Um… 'round eight this morning — it's when I do the inventory."

"And before this arrived," said Sid, shaking the document, "when were you in here last?"

Reg sighed as he massaged his forehead. "I don't know. About midnight, I suppose." Then his tone became more resolved and he looked straight at Sid. "Look, Sid. I have to take it seriously. I'm sorry, but there's too much at stake. As far as I'm concerned, our little venture is over."

CHAPTER 12

Odd sort of foreboding

SID'S MIND WAS racing as he paced the cobblestones of Big Wig Street. What was going on? If he'd known meeting Manky was going to give him this much grief, he would have told the bloodless creep to find some other bloody idiot to do his dirty work.

Big Wig Street ran east-west, parallel to the castle's northern wall. It was where all the high-class merchants sold their wares, including Charles Bling: Jeweller to the Duke, the scene of Sid's first foray into professional thievery. Today, however, there was no feeling of nostalgia as he strode past the glittering shop front. Continuing down Big Wig Street, he crossed Noble Street (which led to the West Gate of the castle) and, for the second time in two days, he literally bumped into his brother-in-law.

"Sid, my good fellow!" exclaimed Gerald in a somewhat strained voice. "You need to keep a good eye out where you're going." Then, realising his poor choice of words, his voice softened, "Your pardon, Sid. My mind is elsewhere, I'm afraid. Things are a bit unsettled at the castle, what." Then, more buoyantly, he added, "So, how are you feeling, old chap?"

"I'm fine, Gerald," Sid replied dismissively; he was far more interested in what Gerald had just said. "In what way unsettled?"

Gerald sighed. "All this silver button business. It's set the cat amongst the pigeons, what. I had to cry yesterday's proclamation without Lord Marmaduke's endorsement, and that's never happened before, not without advance notice."

Sid decided to take a sympathetic tack with Gerald. "Yes, I can see how that would be very frustrating for you, but I suppose the Duke has a lot on his mind."

"I think it's Sir Richard who has more…" Gerald looked self-conscious and somewhat abashed.

"More what?" Sid prompted.

"I'm sorry, Sid. I'm not at liberty to say."

"How can that be, Gerald? You are our Town Crier. If anyone is at liberty to say anything, surely it's you."

"That's where you're wrong, Sid!" He sounded angry, which was totally out of character. As if realising this, he added in a more restrained tone, "Now, if you'll excuse me, I must be about my duties." Before Sid could say another word, Gerald was striding purposefully towards the castle.

Sid was left shaking his head; it felt like his world had been turned upside down while he lay unconscious in Mary's bed.

Sid's next stop was one he usually looked forward to, but as he approached the familiar sign depicting a lifeless duck being held by its feet, he felt an odd sort of foreboding.

Frivolous sounds of laughter and animated conversations drifted out from the open windows of The Dead Duck. The Duck was always busy; Will Plucker ran the place with a perfect mixture of friendliness, bawdiness and drunkenness, and, like Sid, people enjoyed its unpretentious atmosphere. What's more, the food was bloody good. Joan Plucker made a wicked rabbit and parsnip broth (amongst other things) and it was the only inn in Lower Icing to sell food prepared in the castle kitchen. But, thanks to whoever was behind this silver button business, there'd be no more culinary wonders from Reg Puffy's kitchen to serve the punters.

Sid entered the front door of the inn and was immediately set upon by Elsie.

"Aw my gawd, Sid! What 'appened to ya face?" She looked genuinely distressed. "Who done this to you? What you bin up to, Sid?"

"I'm fine, Elsie," Sid replied, calmly.

"Fine? Jus' look at the state of ya!" She was looking at him as if he had two heads.

"Really, Elsie, I'm fine." He gave her a peck on the cheek. "But thanks for your concern."

Elsie looked unconvinced. "S'pose you 'ere to see Will. I'll send him over wiv a jug. You sure you're—"

"Elsie. Really…" he gently squeezed her arm in the hope of reassuring her, "it was just some ruffians who caught me by surprise and got away with a few coins. I'm much better than I look. I promise."

Elsie gave him another dubious glance before turning away and heading towards the bar. Sid made his way through the early lunchtime crowd to his corner table, repeating assurances of wellbeing to all who made eye contact.

Ironically, the effort needed to convince people he was fine was making his head ache.

He plonked himself on the wooden bench at his booth and waited for Will to join him. He would not be happy when Sid told him his news. Will was not a man you wanted unhappy — he could smash an empty wine barrel with his bare hands. Fortunately, Sid and he got on well together, and Sid was relying on that friendship to see him through this awkward situation.

Sid was staring out the window, watching the people go about their business, when he was disturbed by the thud of something heavy hitting the table top. He looked around and saw a large jug, ale sloshing from its open top and splattering around its base. Sitting across the table was Will Plucker.

"That looks nasty," Will said as he placed two tankards next to the jug. "Don't s'pose you got a look at the bastards?"

"No."

"No... 'course not; bloody cowards," Will muttered as he began pouring ale into the tankards. He had the kind of face that accentuated every expression; deep laughter lines down his face were in direct competition to his furrowed brow, each highlighting opposite emotions. At the moment, the furrows were winning. Adding to his disgruntled appearance were his bushy, frowning eyebrows and unkempt mop of black hair. Sid was quite impressed with Will's hair, because there wasn't a speck of grey even though Will was well into his forties.

He finished pouring the ales, handed one to Sid, and grabbed the other. "Your health, Sid," he said, before taking a large gulp of the frothy fluid.

Sid attempted a smile. "Cheers, Will." He sipped at the large tankard; his face was still too sore to drink normally.

Will downed a few more gulps before getting down to business. "So, Sid, what's on order this week? I wouldn't mind some more of them pasties; they sold like 'ot cakes. Speakin' of which, can you get any more—"

"I won't be getting anything this week," Sid interrupted calmly.

Will flicked his eyes at the purple side of Sid's face. "Got somethin' t'do with that, 'as it?"

"I'm not sure. But probably." Sid felt quite removed from the situation, as if he was watching himself talk to Will.

Will stared at him for a moment before topping up both tankards from the ale jug. "Goin' to tell me what 'appened, then?"

"All I know is that someone attacked me after I'd been drinking at The Harey

Rabbit on Saturday night, and today Reg tells me he can't supply me with any more food."

Will stared at Sid over the rim of his tankard as he drank from it. Then he placed it gently on the table. He shook his head. "Got t'be more to it than that, Sid."

Will was no fool, and he'd certainly earned Sid's trust. He nodded. "You're right. There is more to be told, but most of it is just guesswork, and I don't want to cause you any trouble."

"Trouble? What you got yourself into, Sid Evily?"

"I don't know." Sid sighed, feeling very tired all of a sudden. He picked up his tankard and drank as deeply as he could. Will's eyes were still boring into him, the furrows on his forehead protruding like a freshly hoed field.

"Tell me what y'know. I'll risk the trouble."

It was already getting dark by the time Sid left The Dead Duck; the lights from windows shone in the thickly clouded remnants of the day. The dark sky was a welcome sight as he ambled along the cobblestone streets to his home — it might rain, finally.

Chapter 13

The delightful company of Sid Evily

AS SID APPROACHED his house in the fading light, he could see a dark shape of someone slumped next to the front door. Sid was alert enough to meld quickly into the shadows of the street, even though he'd been drinking most of the afternoon. His heart beat fast, blood pounding through his ears, as he slowly moved towards the still outline. It wasn't until he was within pouncing distance that he realised the person was asleep (or, at least, appeared to be asleep).

Sid wasn't taking any chances. He grabbed the body by the shirt-front and, with both hands, jerked it up against the wall of his house. Then he pressed his right forearm into the figure's neck, pinning him to the wall. And it *was* a 'him' — he could see that now — a lad about fourteen years old, lanky, with scruffy, light-coloured hair. It was hard to distinguish his features in the gloom, but one thing was radiantly clear: the absolute terror in the boy's wide-eyed expression.

"Spread your arms out where I can see them," hissed Sid.

The boy obeyed immediately. He was breathing quickly; Sid could feel the warm puffs of breath on his face.

"Who are you?" Sid asked, releasing the pressure on his neck. The boy was far too frightened to make any moves, and there was something familiar about him.

"John, sir," he gasped out.

"What brings you here tonight, John?"

"Mistress Mary, sir. She wanted me to wait for you, like; t'make sure you'd come to no 'arm."

Sid stood back from the quaking figure. He recognised him now — he was Mary's odd-job boy who had, according to Mary, spent some time watching over him as he lay unconscious. John's arms were still spread out against the wall, and Sid felt a pang of guilt as he realised the shock he'd caused the young man.

"Take your ease, lad. I'm sorry I frightened you, but I'm a bit… wary these days."

John let his arms slide slowly towards his sides, like he expected Sid was playing a trick on him.

"How long have you been here, John?"

"Mistress Mary sent me 'bout six o'clock, sir. She was worried 'bout you on account you weren't home, like… when she visited."

"That's odd. She said she would visit after closing," Sid pondered out loud.

"She can't, sir. Tha's what she came t'tell you."

Sid was suddenly aware that their conversation, quiet though it seemed, was actually echoing down the street.

"Better come in, John," said Sid. "You look like you could do with a drink."

"Yes, sir," John murmured obediently, and then followed Sid as he unlocked his front door and went inside.

They sat in Sid's candle-lit room. John scoffed down one of Reg Puffy's pork pies like he hadn't eaten for a month (not realising he was ingesting something fit for a Duke) and washed it down with a tankard of ale.

Sid was eager to know why Mary was no longer free to see him, but the young man had waited at his front door for almost three hours in the cloying summer heat, loyally carrying out his mistress's instructions; the least he deserved was some sustenance.

"Feeling better, lad?" Sid asked as John finished off his last mouthful with a swig of ale.

"Yes, sir. Thank you, sir," he responded dutifully.

"Well then, perhaps you'd like to tell me what's preventing your mistress from spending tonight in the delightful company of Sid Evily?"

Sid was being flippant, but John flushed with embarrassment. "Oh! Your pardon, sir! 'Ere you are waitin' t'know what Mistress… I was just so 'ungry an' all, an'—"

"It's fine, John. Just tell me the message."

"Yes, sir."

"And stop calling me 'sir'. I'm not one of those toffs who demand respect because they blow their snot into a silk handkerchief. Sid's my name."

John smiled awkwardly. "Right you are then… Sid."

Sid nodded his approval and refilled their tankards. "So, John, you were saying?"

"Sorry, sir-id… the mistress said she 'as t'see t'some importan' guests tonigh'… in the private dinin' room, like. She's sorry, but there ain't no way she can't be there."

"I see," replied Sid, but he *didn't* see at all. Mary hadn't told him about any important dinner yesterday. If it was *that* important, surely she'd have mentioned it. "Who's it for, do you know?"

The lad's eyes dropped under Sid's scrutiny.

"John?" Sid pressed.

John kept his gaze lowered. "I ain't meant t'say nothin'," he mumbled. "The mistress said…"

"What did the mistress say?"

John looked up. He had a strange expression on his face, and Sid realised the ale was already beginning to have an effect on him. Talk about a one tankard wonder.

"Promise you won' tell the mistress?"

"You have my word, John."

A slightly dazed, conspiratorial smile formed on his lips. "It's for Sir Richard Upson. Patricia says 'e's 'er 'alf brother, but I think she's jus' 'avin a lend."

Sir Richard? Mary had said she rarely saw her brother, that they lived in two different worlds. Yet, here she was, a day later, organising a *dinner* for him! What was she playing at?

"Sid… you alrigh'?" John was looking at him with unfocused concern.

"I'm fine," Sid said tersely. "When was this arranged?"

"Yesterday, jus' after the mistress come back from visitin' you." John started giggling. "She was 'avin' a bath. An' she 'ad to get out quick, like… Put 'er in a real tizz, it did."

Sid failed to see the humour. "So, she wasn't expecting Sir Richard then?"

"No. 'E def'nitely caugh' 'er by surprise."

If what John said was true — and Sid believed it was — then Mary *hadn't* known she'd be hosting a dinner for her brother tonight. She *hadn't* hidden anything from him. *That* was a relief.

Still, it was a strange coincidence. In fact, it couldn't be coincidence; it had to have something to do with the silver button. What if Mary had decided to tell her brother about him after all? But, no, she couldn't have; he'd have been arrested by now. He really wasn't thinking clearly; he'd had too much to drink this afternoon. He *did* trust Mary; she wouldn't betray him.

"And who else—" Sid began, but the lad was looking down into his tankard, his head lolling and jerking, fighting against sleep. Bloody hell! Had the lad never drunk ale before?

Sid banged his hand on the table. "John!"

He burst awake. "Comin' Patricia," he said obediently, and stood. Then, realising where he was, he stumbled out an apology and said, "Think I bes' be goin'. I ain't feelin' righ'."

John *was* already looking a bit under the weather, and Sid doubted he knew anything of significance anyway, especially where Sir Richard Upson was concerned. In any case, he didn't want him decorating the floorboards with ale and pork pie.

Sid led John to the front door. It was well and truly dark now, the cloud cover blocking out any light from the moon and stars. "Will you be alright, lad?"

John nodded. "You won't say nothin' t'the mistress 'bout Sir Richard, like?"

"Rest easy, John. I'll say nothing. Not even to Patricia, whoever *she* may be."

"She's the cook," he mumbled.

Sid smiled; the poor lad must get barked at regularly by Patricia. The thought of being down-trodden suddenly evoked concern for Mary. "Will you do me a favour?"

The dark outline of John's head nodded.

"Keep your eyes and ears open tonight. If there's any trouble, I want you to come and get me. Do you understand?"

"Trouble? Like wha'?"

Sid wasn't sure what he meant either, but he didn't like the sound of this dinner. "I don't know exactly. Just... keep an eye out."

"Right you are, Sid."

"Good lad." He patted John on the back as the lad stepped onto the street.

"Night, Sid," he said, and then disappeared into the darkness. Sid lingered in the doorway as the sound of John's footsteps faded. He wondered if John *would* be able to keep an eye out. He obviously wasn't the sharpest sword in the armoury. And if he did bring news, what would Sid be able to do about it?

Sid was brought out of his reverie by a drop of water hitting his head. Then another one. It was raining. Seconds later, it was pouring. He stepped onto the street, looked up, and let the heavy drops drench him. Windows and doors along the street flew open, and people ran out to enjoy the downpour. The rain belted down noisily, splattering on the rooftops and cobblestones, almost enough to muffle the cheers and squeals of delight. It was beautifully refreshing. Hopefully it would revive John and keep him focused.

By the time Sid went to bed an hour later, the rain had abated to a steady drizzle. However, its gentle pattering was not enough to lull Sid to sleep. Instead, he spent half the night in worried wakefulness, expecting to hear the sound of footsteps running towards his door. He heard none.

CHAPTER 14

Now who is keeping secrets?

SID WOKE UP to the sound of heavy rain. He bolted upright and leapt out of bed; grogginess and injury compounded to make him feel dizzy and disorientated. He stumbled to the window and leant out into the rain. Heavy drops splashed onto his head and he quickly withdrew — the rain didn't feel as refreshing as it had last night. Then again, last night he hadn't had a hangover.

He clambered into some clothes and made his way downstairs. There, he breakfasted on bread, cheese and cured beef. It was a slow process, because he was feeling decidedly slow. However, with each forced mouthful, his mind, as well as his body, crawled back towards normality.

An hour later, he'd recovered sufficiently to attempt the journey to The Harey Rabbit. The memory of last night's conversation with John, though slightly muddied, was clear enough for Sid to be concerned about Mary. Why, exactly, had Sir Richard suddenly decided to impose himself on Mary's hospitality? And what ramifications did it have for Sid? Well, he'd find out soon enough.

The rain had stopped. The lane outside his door was cluttered with chatting women and children running around playing, intoxicated by the fresh air. As he passed by, Sid acknowledged his neighbours with a 'good morning' and a smile. Some smiled back, but most looked warily at his beaten face. Some of the children screamed when they saw him — just what his aching head needed.

Sid took a zigzag route through the lanes and streets of Lower Icing — The Harey Rabbit was situated on the opposite side of town. As he made his way south and east, Sid's thoughts turned to the letter received by Reg Puffy, and the fact that he no longer had a pork pie venture. The largest slice of his livelihood had been sabotaged. What was he going to do about *that*? And who wrote the bloody thing? Whoever it was had an educated hand. But it still begged the question 'why'. And why had he been attacked? And why had incriminating evidence been planted on him? Why?

In the end, it all came down to Doctor Manky. Sid was due to see him tomorrow, and he was now looking forward to the encounter. This time *Sid* would be asking the questions, and *he'd* be making Manky an offer *he* couldn't refuse! In the meantime, he needed to make sure all was right with Mary.

As Sid turned right into Plumduff Street, the sun found a hole in the clouds. The western façade of stately homes was suddenly bathed in sunlight and the rain-washed red bricks gleamed magnificently. Casting his gaze ahead, Sid saw the bright red shape of Gerald emerging from his doorway. He smiled to himself at the unlikelihood of it all. In general, he was lucky if he saw Gerald once a month. Now his brother-in-law seemed to be popping up everywhere he went (or maybe it was the other way around).

Gerald started pacing purposefully up Plumduff Street towards the castle, and Sid broke into a half jog to catch him up.

"Gerald!" Sid called as he closed.

The big man turned. "Ah, Sid. How are you feeling, old chap?" Gerald asked kindly, although he looked agitated.

"I'm well, thanks, Gerald," Sid said, trying to ignore the *un*-wellness of his hangover. "And you?"

"Rather busy, I must say. In fact, I'm late for a rather important meeting." Gerald started walking again, setting a fast pace.

Sid followed. "Is something amiss?"

"It is as I told you yesterday, Sid: I'm not at liberty to say."

Sid's frustration suddenly overflowed into anger. He darted in front of Gerald and pushed him in the chest.

The Town Crier stumbled backwards, wearing a look of surprise and anger. "What is the meaning of this?"

"Exactly," Sid hissed. "What *is* the meaning of this?" He was pointing at his bruised face.

Gerald looked perplexed. "I don't understand what you—"

"The coward or cowards who did this to me have got something to do with that silver button thief. And, more than that, they've threatened people I know and are trying to ruin me. Funnily enough, Gerald, I'd like to find out who they are. So, if you have any idea who's behind this, I'd like to know."

Gerald stared at Sid, confusion turned to suspicion. "How do you know?"

"How do I know what?" Sid snapped.

"How do you know your attackers have a connection to the silver button thief?"

Sid felt blood rush to his head and silently cursed himself for being so loose-tongued. "Let's just say it's an educated guess."

Gerald smiled mirthlessly. "*Now* who is keeping secrets, Sid?"

Sid was momentarily taken aback by his brother-in-law's astuteness. "Gerald. This is me, your friend. All I'm asking is your help in finding the people who bashed me."

Gerald breathed in deeply and then sighed. "You ask much, Sid, for I am not privy to the thoughts of the Duke and his advisors. And, as a friend, believe me when I say I know little about the silver button thief — perhaps even less than you — and I *certainly* know nothing about your attacker." Gerald looked up the street, suddenly aware their altercation was attracting a few quizzical gazes. "Now, please," he said self-consciously, "will you allow me to go about my business?"

Reluctantly, Sid stepped out of the way. Gerald smiled awkwardly. "Well, good day to you, Sid," he said, tipping the point of his black, triangular hat, before continuing his journey towards the castle.

"Let me know if you do find out anything, won't you, Gerald?" Sid called after him.

Gerald showed no sign that he'd heard.

CHAPTER 15

Allow me to introduce myself

IN ORDER TO avoid the disapproving glares of the haughty nobs, Sid entered The Harey Rabbit through a gate set into a high stone wall that bordered the Town Square. It was the same gate he'd used last Saturday night, the same gate someone had followed him through to bash, rob and frame him. It opened onto a courtyard, which was used for hanging bed linen as well as providing much-needed space between the kitchen and the stables.

Sid turned his attention to the kitchen. The sounds of food preparation could be heard coming from the open doorway. Through it he could see two women, dressed in uniform, sitting at a table — one with her back to him, the other a side profile. Sid was about to make his presence known when John's gangly figure appeared in the doorway. However, he didn't notice Sid, because his attention was focused on someone inside the room.

"Right you are, Mistress," he said, shifting his feet, eager to be on his way. "I'll be sure to tell 'im." Then he darted out of the doorway and nearly jumped out of his skin when he saw Sid.

"Bloody 'ell, Sid," gasped John. "Y'scared me 'alf t'death!"

"Be sure to tell me what?" Sid smiled at the boy while he recovered his composure.

"Well, Mistress 'as to…" His reply wilted as confusion blossomed on his face. "'Owja know I was comin' to see you, Sid?"

"Educated guesses are becoming my specialty," he replied cryptically. This seemed to confuse the lad even more. "Don't concern yourself about it, John."

John looked quite deflated. He'd obviously been excited about the prospect of escaping from his kitchen duties and the bellowing Patricia.

"Why don't you pretend I never saw you and take off for a while," Sid added brightly. "Go on," he encouraged, nodding towards the open gate. "No-one's looking. Mary can give me her message in person."

John eyed the gate as if considering Sid's suggestion, then flicked his gaze back to Sid as he began to move towards the kitchen. "Y'can't go in there, Sid," John said, blocking Sid's approach. "Mistress said she weren't t'be disturbed."

Sid stopped. "Why?" he asked. What was Mary playing at? She'd left him high and dry last night; he wasn't about to be fobbed off again.

"Well… um. She's busy, like, with a guest," John said, obviously floundering between the truth and his instructions from Mary.

A thought suddenly occurred to Sid: what if one of Sir Richard's nob dinner guests had charmed Mary into… His heart sank at the thought of her in the arms of another man. "I see," he said quietly.

He brushed past John, determined to find out exactly where he stood with the innkeeper of The Harey Rabbit.

"No. Wait! Please, Sid!" John yelled from behind.

Four faces turned in his direction as he burst into the kitchen. He vaguely remembered the girl to his right (the one who hadn't been able to wash the blood from his shirt); her eyes were tearing from her proximity to a pile of chopped onions. The two girls he'd seen sitting at the table looked up at him in surprise; one of them began giggling. The squat, rotund woman standing at the bench on the other side of the table, cutting up chickens, wasn't so accepting of his sudden appearance. If he had to make another educated guess, he'd say the scowling expression belonged to John's task-mistress, Patricia.

"Now listen 'ere!"

That was the last thing Sid was going to do. Ignoring the outraged cook, he called out Mary's name.

He heard John behind him, turned around and fronted the boy, who looked terrified.

"Where's Mary, John?" Desperation made him sound angry.

"You leave that boy alone!" demanded the cook.

The washer girl piped in with a heartfelt, "Oh, eet ees *so* romanteek," in her foreign accent — it sounded Icarumban.

Sid's attention remained fixed on a clearly upset John. "Sid… it ain't what you think," he said frantically. "The mistress said to tell you that she'd—"

"Visit you this afternoon," Mary's musical voice chimed in from behind him, and it had an ominously sharp note to it. Sid spun to face her. She stood with folded arms, framed in the doorway that opened into the washroom. "At three o'clock to be precise," she added meaningfully. Sid was momentarily taken aback; she seemed so… matter-of-fact.

"What?" He was confused.

She stepped into the kitchen as he moved towards her.

"You have to leave," Mary said, her voice low. She looked worried.

"What's going on?" His voice betrayed his hurt.

"Not now, Sid," she whispered, and began ushering him back towards the courtyard doorway.

"Please, Mary," he said, stopping her and holding her by the arms. "I need to know what's going on."

"You 'eard the mistress," announced the cook from the corner of the kitchen.

Mary glared at her. She shrugged her shoulders and went back to cutting up chickens. Looking back at Sid, Mary's expression was apologetic. "I *will* tell you, Sid," she said softly, "but not now. There are… things I have to take care of first."

"Things?" He released her arms and took a step back from her. More bloody secrets? One of the seated girls giggled. What was going on here? Were they playing him for a fool? Blood began pounding behind his damaged eye.

Again Mary's attention was diverted. "Mandy, I don't employ you to chop vegetables. You and Lillian get back to the bar."

Both women stared at her.

Mary snapped. "Now!"

Discarded knives rattled on the table as they jumped up and made their way to the door next to where Patricia was cutting into chicken carcasses. Then Mary addressed the Icarumban girl. "Be quick about those onions, Juanita; that linen won't wash itself."

The girl nodded and sniffed, but still managed a knowing smile.

Mary shook her head in frustration. Then she took a deep breath, closed her eyes and slowly breathed out. When her beautiful blue eyes reopened, they were directed at Sid. Her features softened as she reached out and gently wiped away a tear that had escaped from his swollen eye. "I'm sorry," she whispered. "I know how this must seem, but you have to trust me."

Sid gently took her hand; he could feel the moisture of his tear. "I could ask the same of you."

She squeezed his hand. "I *do* trust you."

"Um… Mistress," John murmured from behind Sid.

Mary's expression suddenly turned from tender to tense, and she threw Sid's hand away from her like she'd been caught playing with something she'd been told not to touch. Standing in the doorway adjacent the washroom entrance was a tall, clean-shaven man with a sardonic smile.

Clearly flustered, Mary turned to face him. "What do you want?"

Was *this* her idea of trust?

The man reproached her calmly. "Come now, Mary. I heard an aggressive male voice and was concerned for your wellbeing. However, this gentleman — though *clearly* not gentle — seems to have your… confidence."

The figure stepped into the kitchen. He was dressed entirely in black except for a finely engraved silver belt buckle. His clothes appeared plain, but he wore them like they were made for him, and his bearing and manner suggested he was used to parading around in something more… splendid.

"Allow me to introduce myself." His dark brown eyes bored into Sid's as he moved to stand the other side of Mary. "I am Sir Richard Upson."

In one way, Sid was completely taken aback: the man looked nothing like Sir Richard. This man had no close-cut, sculptured beard or free-flowing shoulder-length hair; he was clean-shaven and his hair was short… No, actually, it was tied back. It certainly gave him a more youthful appearance; younger even than he'd appeared years ago when Sid had worked in the Administration Section of the castle. But in another way, his introduction came as no surprise. Sid always recognised Sir Richard's type, no matter *what* they looked like. And now that he was looking, there *was* a slight resemblance between the half-siblings — they'd obviously inherited the same mouth and cheek structure. Still, regardless of his appearance, Sid's overriding feeling was one of relief. Mary wouldn't have slept with her half-brother; this wasn't the highlands of Sporrendale!

There was no way he was going to show any weakness or deference to *this* puffed up ponce. Holding Sir Richard's scrutinising gaze, he introduced himself with forthrightness. "Sid Evily."

"Sid was just leaving, Richard," Mary said pointedly.

Sir Richard appeared not to hear her. "Evily? Curious name." His voice and manner was smooth and refined, like his shaven face.

"You could ask my father about it, but it's been a long time since I've seen *him*."

"Ah." Sir Richard smiled knowingly. "That would explain the…" He casually twirled a finger near his left eye. "… lack of discipline."

He felt Mary gently squeeze his left arm. "Sid, you said you were in a hurry."

It was clear she wanted him to leave, but Sid wasn't one to be led away from a challenge. "More like the lack of discipline in your so-called men-at-arms."

Sir Richard just smiled. He was like the black version of Doctor Manky. "Speaking of which," he said amiably, "you could save me the mundane task of ordering a couple of them to—"

"Richard! Please!" Mary implored. "Do you really think *this* is the appropriate place to be discussing your affairs?"

The Seneschal's gaze darted from Mary to Sid, then back to Mary. "You are quite right, Mary," he acknowledged with a half-smile. "I should know when to… *button* my lip."

The sod! He was either fishing for information or Mary had told him what had happened. Well, he wasn't going to get any reaction from Sid. He wouldn't give the tosser the satisfaction.

Mary, on the other hand, looked as if her composure was about to desert her. Turning back to him, she said, "I think you should leave, Sid." Her tone was insistent, but her expression apologetic.

Reluctantly, he obliged. "You're right. I *do* have important things to attend to."

She looked grateful, and gently squeezed his hand. Wrenching his eyes away from her sunshine face, Sid regarded the black cloud behind her. "Alas, Sir Richard, it seems we are not to become better acquainted, for the moment at least."

As hoped, Sir Richard raised an appraising eyebrow at Sid's sudden formality. "So it seems," he acknowledged, "but no doubt you'll be invited to another family gathering." Then he added mockingly, "Perhaps when you're looking a touch more… presentable."

It was all Sid could do to stop himself from smacking the smugness out of the smarmy git. He felt his hand being squeezed again; Mary's expression had become pleading.

"I will see you later." He'd meant the words to sound earnest, but they came out like a summons.

"Yes, you will," she assured him.

Regardless of Sir Richard's looming presence, or more likely *because* of it, Sid kissed Mary on the cheek.

"Oh! El amor es bello!" Juanita said dreamily while sniffing back tears (possibly from the onions).

"That's enough of that kind o' language, my girl," admonished Patricia.

"No. You no understand. Ees—"

"Enough!" Mary snapped, closing her eyes and shaking her head in frustration. Then, unexpectedly, she returned his kiss. "I will see you at three."

Sid nodded. He wasn't happy, but his intuition told him to trust Mary. Whatever game her half-brother was playing, she was on *his* side. With one last squeeze of her hand and a dismissive gaze at a bemused Sir Richard, Sid took his leave.

As he headed for the door, Mary's voice sang out. "John. You go with Sid. I won't be requiring you for the rest of the morning."

Sid was about to tell Mary that he didn't need looking after — if that's what she intended — but the lad's face brightened so much he didn't have the heart to contradict her.

John fell into step next to Sid as he walked across the courtyard.

"Right, lad. Since your mistress wants you to keep me company, I'll tell you what I have in mind."

"Right y'are, Sid," John replied dutifully.

"Well, my young friend," he said almost jovially, because he'd suddenly thought of someone who might be able to enlighten him as to what was going on at the castle, "we're off to see another friend of mine."

As they stepped through the gateway and into the Town Square, Sid clapped a hand on John's bony shoulder. "And, along the way, you're going to tell me all you know about Mary's dinner last night and what Sir Richard Up-His-Arse is up to."

John winced.

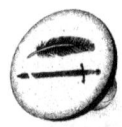

CHAPTER 16

Tom Skinner's cabin

JOHN WAS NOT exactly a fountain of information, more like a wet blanket. Sid had to wring out every detail, and, in this particular case, the blanket had only been mildly damp to start with.

John had missed the arrival of the dinner guests because he was waiting for Sid to return from The Dead Duck. Upon entering the kitchen of The Harey Rabbit, he was jumped on by a worried Mary wanting to know where he'd been and if Sid was alright. John told her all was well with Sid, but that Sid was worried about *her*. She wasn't best pleased with John, because she could tell he'd been drinking. She'd made him change out of his wet clothes, and then he'd helped out in the kitchen.

Mary had spent most of the night in the kitchen, overseeing the food preparation for her secret guests. She was the only person allowed to enter the dining room, and she only did so to deliver food. During one such delivery, John had asked his fellow kitchen hands if any of the guests had revealed themselves. Juanita said she thought she'd heard the voice of one of "dee bad rat lawyers" but no-one had any real idea. To maintain secrecy, Patricia, Juanita and the rest of the staff had been ushered upstairs while the party made their clandestine entrance via the kitchen. No-one saw them leave either — the meeting was still in session when Mary dismissed them for the night. John and Juanita, who resided at The Harey Rabbit, retired to their respective quarters. John had fallen asleep immediately.

By the time John had finished his account, they'd crossed the Town Square and were heading east along the East Road (which led to the Duchy of Naffolk and, ultimately, the bustling port city of Great Naff).

Sid's destination, however, was a lot closer. Just across the Icing River from the castle, hidden within the Duke's Forest, was Tom Skinner's cabin. The Gamekeeper preferred a more natural existence and was very content in his woodland world. Not that he and Tom had that much to do with each other, but the occasional times their paths had crossed (usually at The Dead Duck), he and Tom always shared a few laughs; enough, at least, for Tom to invite him on the odd hunting trip *and* allow him to keep some of the quarry. He'd once told Sid that he and Sir Smarmy Friggin' Upson had a long-standing friendship and that they shared a passion for big game hunting. Well, hopefully their friendship had been standing long enough for Tom to have been informed about the happenings on Friday night. Friendship aside, Tom was also a nobleman (his family owned an estate to the west, along the border of the Duchy of Stymouth), which added to the likelihood that he might well be in the know, and why Sid was willing to take the chance that he was home.

The sun was trying to reassert itself through the cloud cover; the day was turning out to be unpleasantly humid. They'd travelled about two hundred paces down the East Road, through the steamy, cultivated fields and pasture land that bordered the Icing River. Sid was already sweating profusely. Adding to his discomfort, the left side of his face had begun to throb. He cast his gaze at the workers tending their patches; they appeared to be moving in slow motion, their energy sapped by the oppressive conditions. The ones toiling close to the road looked upon him with wary weariness (or was it weary wariness).

Just ahead of them, spanning the Icing River, was a flat wooden bridge some forty paces in length and wide enough for two large carts to pass side by side. As they crossed, there was a noticeable cooling of the air and a wafting breeze from the north. Sid looked upriver, in the direction of the breeze, and inhaled deeply. The patchwork of fields and orchards grew wider as the river angled away slightly from the town. The reed-filled banks were dotted with people fishing. He wondered how many of them were licensed — anyone caught fishing without a license would have to pay a hefty fine or be locked up.

As they left the Icing behind, the stickiness returned. Fifty paces on and all remnants of the breeze had been simmered away by the baking East Road. Neither he nor John had said a word since the account of Mary's dinner. Apart from the goings on at The Harey Rabbit, he had nothing in common with the lad — John was greener than the pea & sprout soup Joan Plucker served at The Dead Duck.

Ultimately, it was their route that provided Sid with an opportunity to say something. "This is where we leave the road, lad."

"Right y'are, Sid," John replied amiably, following as Sid turned right onto a verge of parched grass. Wasn't he curious about where they were going?

Judging by his smiling acceptance, Sid supposed not. The lad was far too trusting for his own good.

The grass stretched a hundred paces south before the Duke's Forest began to assert itself. They were grateful for the oak, elm and elder trees that provided most of the shade, but with the shade came the insects, buzzing and hovering around them, looking for some form of moisture (blood, sweat and, in the case of Sid's swollen eye, tears). Still, if Tom could come through with the goods, it would be worth the discomfort.

Five minutes later, the outline of Tom's cottage suddenly appeared between the trees. They were almost upon it before the wooden structure revealed itself, standing in the middle of a small clearing.

"Here we are, John," Sid announced. "The majestic abode of Lower Icing's Gamekeeper."

John just nodded.

"Don't you want to know why we're here?"

"To see the Gamekeeper?" John ventured.

Was he joking?

John looked at him expectantly. No, he wasn't bloody joking.

Sid nodded. "Come on. Let's see if he's in."

Even before Sid reached the front door, he knew he was out of luck. There was no sign of life and the windows were shuttered. Next to the cottage was a stable. By the time he reached the front door, he could see it was empty. If Tom was within five hundred paces, his horse would be there. Hanging from a nail in the door was a sign. It looked official.

RESIDENCE OF THE GAMEKEEPER OF LOWER ICING
UNLAWFUL ENTRY IS PROHIBITED
AND SUBJECT TO PROSECUTION
BY ORDER OF MARMADUKE DU MARMA,
DUKE OF LOWER ICING

At the base of the lettering was the Ducal Seal of Lower Icing: five crowns under a unicorn's head.

That nailed it; Tom definitely wasn't here. Sid was wondering what constituted 'unlawful entry' when John piped up with, "Ain't y'goin' to knock, Sid? See if 'e's 'ome, like?"

Sid just shook his head. It made it throb… again.

They were hot, sticky, thirsty and insect-crazed well before they emerged from the forest. In the distance, to his left, the buildings of Lower Icing shimmered into view, the castle a steaming grey beast, come down from the clouds to engulf the town.

Sid's attention turned to the Icing River some fifty paces away. He couldn't remember the last time he'd immersed himself in its frigid water, but now seemed the perfect time to refresh his body *and* his memory. He swung towards the river and picked up his pace. John followed dutifully in his wake.

The brown-baked grass suddenly became green as the land banked down to the deep, cold water. There was very little sand on this part of the river, just a merging of grass to reeds. They were about a hundred paces south of the bridge, where a farmer was leading a horse with a cart load of hay towards Lower Icing. *Better him than me*, thought Sid.

Villagers tended not to use the river south of the bridge, particularly on the eastern side where Sid and John were. It was where the Icing angled west towards the castle, and the bend increased the flow of water significantly. It made fishing, washing, and any other river pursuit more perilous. Still, Sid wasn't thinking peril as he carefully edged his way down to the reeds; he was thinking cool relief.

In the end, the process turned out to be quite straightforward; the reeds were so thick they helped support Sid as he squatted down and splashed his face with the clear water. It was a shock — the river was still icy cold even after the unusual bout of hot weather — but its effect was immediate. Not only did the water refresh him, it numbed the pain in his face. Then, cupping his hands, he scooped the soothing fluid into his mouth and drank deeply.

It was only after he'd slaked his thirst that he realised John hadn't joined him. The lad was sitting on the grass just behind him. "What's the matter?" he asked. "Not thirsty?"

John looked the epitome of thirsty: red-faced, sweating forehead, matted hair, clinging shirt. "Can't swim," he mumbled self-consciously.

"Nor can I," replied Sid. "Fortunately, swimming is not a skill you need for drinking." Sid knew what John was angling at — he was afraid of falling in— but the lad really needed to start manning-up. Sid had been Adventuring for over *two years* by John's age!

John looked at Sid dubiously. Sid reacted by scooping another mouthful of water. "See, it's perfectly safe."

John nodded unconvincingly, and then began edging his way down the slope on his arse. After half a dozen reluctant shuffles, he made it to the reeds. Slowly, he leaned forward and dipped a single hand into the reed-filled river, the other he used to anchor himself to the bank. It was painful to watch. Eventually, however, he managed to slurp half a mouthful.

"There," Sid said, trying not to sound too condescending, "not so hard after all."

John smiled back, and, by the fourth safe scoop, he'd started using both hands. Then he propped himself on his haunches and splashed himself. Then he began laughing and splashing Sid. Then he fell forward into the water and reeds.

Fortunately, he'd been squatting upriver from Sid, and as he scrambled and thrashed in the water, Sid was able to haul him back onto the bank with little effort — the lad was reed thin.

As soon as his head was out of the water, the relative peacefulness of their surroundings ended with an explosively wet coughing fit. Sid flung John onto his back, then grabbed the front of his shirt and pulled him, spluttering, into a sitting position. He gave John a healthy slap on the back. John expelled a huge cough of water and then inhaled deeply, gasping for air. Sid let him go, and the lad collapsed back onto the bank, panting with his eyes closed.

Sid shook his head in despair. "Your pardon, John. I forgot you couldn't hold your drink."

CHAPTER 17

A mug of The Bell's finest

TEN MINUTES LATER, John had recovered enough to continue the walk back to Lower Icing. In between recovering from the shock, he'd spent the time apologising. Sid had been sorely tempted to throw him back in.

As they both squelched their way to the bridge (Sid was almost as wet as John) the lad was suddenly a lot more talkative.

"I ain't never been in the Icin' before. Come to think on it, I ain't never *drunk* from the Icin'... not d'rectly, like. Only from the well, but I s'pose that *is* from the Icin', ain't it, so I s'pose I *'ave* drunk from the Icin'."

John managed to spout on about what water he'd drunk, washed in and washed *with* the whole way to the bridge. Still, it didn't require much input from Sid, and his mind began to wander back to Manky and the silver button.

The common thread between him and Manky was this intruder. Manky must know who he is and suspected he would attempt to rob the Duke. Sid was the intruder's opportunistic victim. Manky was before the fact; Sid was after the fact. It was as simple as that — too clumsy and risky for anything else, and Manky certainly didn't strike him as either a klutz or a risk-taker. He wouldn't orchestrate something so obvious, would he? It *had* to be coincidence, didn't it...?

It was midday by the time they reached the Town Square. It was hot and steamy and full of people to-ing and fro-ing or lining up at the well with empty buckets. Sid was no longer sure if his clothes were damp from the river or from sweat. The refreshing effect of the Icing had well and truly evaporated in the heat.

"Well, lad, thanks for your company and your entertaining thoughts on our water, but, alas, this is where we must part company."

"Oh," John said, taken by surprise at Sid's sudden dismissal. "'Course. Right y'are, Sid."

"Tell Mary I will be expecting her at my place this afternoon. And tell her to bring plenty of answers with her, because I have plenty of questions for her."

"Yes, Sid." He seemed to be struggling with the notion that their little excursion had come to end.

"Good day to you, John."

Without another word or glance, Sid headed home. He'd made it as far as the north-western corner the Town Square when, on a whim, he decided to have a drink at The Bloody Bell. His head was beginning to ache again; he needed refreshment and something to numb the pain, and a mug of The Bell's finest would do both.

Unbelievably, it was even more humid inside The Bell. Sid forced his way through the crowded stuffiness to the bar. As he waited to be served, he scanned the bustling room to see if he could see anyone he recognised. His gaze fell upon a couple chatting in a gloomy corner under the set of stairs that led to the first-floor accommodation. They were standing in front of a half-open door that led to who-knew-where, but it looked as if blue was the predominant colour scheme.

What intrigued Sid about the couple was their demeanour — they were stiff and formal and, now that he was looking, the woman seemed too well dressed to be in The Bell. Although she had her back to Sid, he could tell the woman was agitated. The man (who appeared to be in his twenties) looked wary, as if he were being asked to do something underhand. Sid's curiosity was piqued as he watched the pair in close conversation. Even though they were little more than five paces away, it was far too noisy to hear a word of what they were saying, but some agreement seemed to have been reached. Then the woman produced something wrapped in black cloth from her small handbag. The man looked very serious as he gently took possession of the bundle. The woman's body language suggested she was apologising or imploring. The man reached out and tenderly squeezed the top of her arm, reassuring her. Sid's good eye was gradually adjusting to the dim light and he could see that the man's expression had become empathetic. Then the woman kissed him tenderly on the cheek. This embarrassed the young man.

Sid's attention was snapped away from the intriguing scene by the chirpy voice of a barmaid. "What'll it be, love?"

"A tankard of your finest, darling," replied Sid, giving the young woman a flirtatious wink with his good eye. He realised it probably looked like some demented twitch when paired with the disfigurement of his left eye. He watched her as she picked up a metal tankard and filled it to the brim with the brown, foaming liquid. Sid could hardly wait to down the lot, and he would empty it a lot quicker than she was filling it.

"There y'go, love," said the barmaid, placing the tankard carelessly on the bar, spilling some of its contents. "That'll be four of y'finest coppa pieces, ta very much."

Sid gave the girl a five-copper piece and told her to keep the change. Then he attacked the tankard with gusto. For about fifteen seconds all Sid could see was the inside of the tankard as he drained its contents without taking a breath. After the last drop had made its way down his throat, Sid, once again, had a view of the tavern. His first glimpse caused him to drop the tankard in disbelief.

The woman who had been chatting with the grave young man (who must have disappeared back into the blue room) was now making her way through the crowd. Her hat was pulled down, obscuring her features to most onlookers, but Sid was in no doubt; the stern set of the jaw, that expression of barely concealed contempt could only belong to one person — his sister, Olivia.

Sid could hardly believe it. Had Doctor Manky put some sort of curse on him? One that made all the people he knew — or *thought* he knew — act totally out of character? For starters, Elsie had refused to spend the night with him, Gerald had been unusually cagey about the goings-on in the castle and then, of course, there was Reg Puffy, who was no longer willing to supply him with pork pies and other assorted pastries after receiving that mysteriously threatening letter. And *now* his sister was engaged in some furtive activity in, of all places, an inn! And not just any bloody inn: The bloody Bloody Bell!

Sid snapped back into reality and watched Liv exit through the open double doors in the corner of the building. Sid was through them moments later, and he quietly followed her as she walked stiffly down Merchant Street, towards her house.

It was about a five-minute stroll from The Bloody Bell to 8 Plumduff Street, just a couple of blocks then turn left towards the castle. Liv stuck to her course without deviation; it was like she couldn't wait to get off the street. Sid followed at a discreet distance. He'd already decided against the direct approach because, where his sister was concerned, observation was far more productive than confrontation.

Liv arrived home. However, before going inside, she used her sleeve to rub the brass plaque next to the front door. (It could never be too clean.) Sid decided to wait for a while, to make sure Liv was staying put. After half an hour, it was obvious she'd had her fix of furtiveness for one day. He decided to head off home and wait for Mary. He'd had enough of the sun, and the effects of downing that tankard had taken hold.

On the way home, Sid felt somewhat detached from the world. People and faces floated past him in a broth of grey humidity. His thoughts swam at the unreality of it all. Had the world gone mad? Was he sick and delusional? Had he really met Doctor Manky? He laughed out loud to himself. A completely white doctor — it was a hilarious notion. And Mary, surely she was just a dream? His mind was playing tricks, trying to make real something that could never be.

Sid managed to drift home, and then collapsed on his living room floor.

CHAPTER 18

Doctor Whysman's most important patient

SID OPENED HIS eyes, his left one taking painfully longer to focus on the concerned face of Doctor Whysman.

"Welcome back, young man."

It took a few seconds for Sid to realise he was lying on his bed. He instantly tried to get up, but was gently restrained by the doctor.

"Be at ease, Sid."

"How is he, Doctor Whysman?" It was Mary's voice, quiet and hollow sounding.

"Mary?" Sid tried to sit up again, and was once more held down by the doctor's firm hand.

Eyes fixed on Sid, Doctor Whysman said, "He'll be fine if he rests and gives his body a chance to heal."

Mary suddenly appeared behind Doctor Whysman; she looked concerned in an angry sort of way. He'd seen that look before, shortly before she'd produced the silver button.

Sid was immediately suspicious. "What's happened?"

"Now, Sid," Doctor Whysman's quiet tone demanded attention. "Listen to me; you've been over-exerting your mind and body. To fully recuperate you need rest and proper nourishment."

Mary shook her head and folded her arms across her chest. *That* was not a good sign.

"And that means no more gallivanting around the countryside or drinking gallons of ale."

Sid's eyes flicked between the doctor's earnest expression and Mary's challenging one, before settling on the former with what he hoped was an earnest expression of his own. "Doctor Whysman, I have been foolish in the extreme. I will, of course, heed your wise council."

Doctor Whysman nodded in satisfaction.

Mary's reaction was quite the opposite and, scarily for Sid, far more insightful. Throwing her arms up in frustration, she yelled, "You're impossible, Sid Evily! Don't waste your time on him, Doctor Whysman." Then she stormed out of his room, slamming the door behind her.

Doctor Whysman turned back to face Sid. His kindly features were a mixture of confusion and suspicion. "Just mark my words, Sid." Then he, too, left the room.

What the frig was happening, Sid wondered. He kept waking up to concerned faces. Couldn't he be allowed to pass out in peace? He forced himself into a sitting position. With a shock, he realised there was still someone in the room.

"'Ow yer feelin, Sid?" asked John.

"Never felt better," Sid said sarcastically. "Especially after my lovely nap which, by the look of things, lasted half the afternoon." A few moments of uncomfortable silence followed before he added, "So, John, do you know how I came to be tucked up like an infant? Last thing I remember was waiting outside Liv's for her to—"

Sid's mouth came to a halt as his memory clicked into gear. Liv... the man at The Bloody Bell... the black bundle... the kiss.

"For her to what, Sid?"

"Oh, never mind, just my mind wandering."

"Who is she?"

"Liv is my so-called sister. It's her birthday tomorrow and... Look, it's of no consequence to my current state... You were about to tell me how I came to be Doctor Whysman's most important patient."

"Oh... right y'are."

John stumbled through his explanation, telling Sid how Mary had come to visit him at three o'clock as arranged and found him unconscious on the floor. After failing to revive Sid, she had run back to The Harey Rabbit and sent John to fetch Doctor Whysman. They'd arrived to see Mary resting Sid's head in her lap, wiping his face with a damp cloth. They'd carried Sid upstairs to his bedroom, so Doctor Whysman could examine him properly. After the examination, he'd mixed up an elixir and waved it under Sid's nose. Apparently, the effect had been almost immediate, and Sid had woken up.

"... And then the Doc said you needed to rest, like, and you said—"

"Yes, yes," Sid interrupted, "I was here for that bit. Remember?"

John bowed his head. The boy really was quite pathetic, but he was also well-meaning.

Sid sighed. "I'm sorry, lad. As you can tell, I'm not right in the head at the moment. I appreciate your help."

John looked up and nodded. "You'll be right, Sid."

Sid said nothing.

John stood. "Best leave you t'get some rest, like."

Sid grimaced. "You know what they say — no rest for the wicked."

John smiled awkwardly, as if wondering if Sid was joking, and then left the room.

Sid's gaze turned to the window. The clouds seemed gloomier, like his thoughts.

A few moments later, Sid heard his front door open and Doctor Whysman's voice wishing Mary a good afternoon. He clambered out of bed and stumbled dizzily towards the bedroom window. As he looked down on the overcast street, Doctor Whysman and John were making their way towards the castle. Standing there, Sid felt the faintest touch of a cool breeze blowing through the humidity. He breathed deeply in an attempt to clear his head. It made it spin instead, and he had to brace himself against the window sill.

As the sound of their footsteps faded into the grey afternoon, he heard another set coming up the stairs. Sid stumbled back into bed — he didn't want to push his luck with Mary.

CHAPTER 19

Bad things are happening

MARY LOOKED WORRIED and defiant at the same time, and Sid knew this was not the time for his usual flippancy. As she approached his bed, she gave him a half-smile. Encouraged by this, Sid returned the smile and coupled it with an apology. Her smile became broader as she sat on the edge of the bed and gently stroked his hair away from his slowly healing eye. Then she kissed his forehead.

"I'm sorry too," she said softly. "I shouldn't have yelled at you. But I'm worried about you and… other things."

Then she leaned over to the small bedside table and lit the candle. Her eyes shone in the muted light, and, for the first time, Sid saw the hidden depths in those blue pools, eddying with unseen emotions. He suddenly realised they were shining because she'd been crying, and wished he could take back his disingenuous words to Doctor Whysman.

"Mary, I'm—"

She softly shushed him, and then took his hand. "Please just listen, Sid. Richard has…" Taking a deep breath, she continued. "There are things I want to tell you, but I need to be able to trust you."

Trust; it was such an easy word to say, yet it was so hard won and so easily lost. "Didn't we have this discussion earlier today in your kitchen?" he said, edging himself into more of a sitting position, back resting against the wall. His head was aching.

"It's just that… Richard would not be best pleased at my being here."

That was hardly a revelation, but Sid's senses weren't so clouded he couldn't see the conflict in her expression, searching for reassurance from him. He squeezed her hand. "You can trust me, Mary."

She smiled and nodded. "Very well, Sid. What I'm about to say must go no further than these four cracked walls."

Sid flicked his gaze to the wall on his right; there were so many cracks he'd stopped noticing them. "I promise… So, are you going to tell me what occurred last night, or would you like me to plaster the walls first?"

Mary smiled. "Well, it wouldn't hurt." Then her expression became earnest and she began her tale. "So… after our afternoon of wanton pleasure on Tuesday—"

"Ah… *that* would explain all the cracks."

She treated him to a withering look. "Richard came to see me at The Harey Rabbit. I couldn't believe it, particularly after what I'd told you."

Yes, that she hardly ever saw him. It still seemed unreal that she was the half-sister of that tosser.

"I knew there was something wrong. He's usually so…"

"Smarmy?"

Mary's eyes narrowed. "Unreadable."

Cagey more like, Sid thought.

"I asked him what was wrong and he told me that…" Again she paused, her eyes searching his. "Remember, I'm trusting you to keep this to yourself."

"*Really?* You should have said."

"*Sid!* This is important. What Richard told me is *why* I agreed to host his dinner, which, by the way, you can't tell anyone about, and *why* I didn't want you coming to The Harey Rabbit."

Sid was suddenly filled with a sense of foreboding, and his eye began to throb.

"He said that Gerald's proclamation on Saturday was only partly true. A silver button *was* found in the Duke's chamber, but the Duke wasn't the victim of an attempted robbery, he was attacked with a poisoned blade, and—"

"What?" Of all the things he'd expected Mary to say…

"He remains in an unconscious delirium. Doctor Whysman's been treating him, but he's worried the poison has taken hold."

Sid felt the pit of his stomach lurch, and the throbbing in his head became more intense. What had he got himself into? *Not all news is shared with the people*, Doctor Manky had said. Had he suspected the attack? *Inform me of the stories people are not hearing from Gerald the Herald.*

"I can hardly credit this, Mary," Sid said, heart pumping, head throbbing, body moving to get out of bed — this was not news he could take lying down.

"Yes, it is hard to take in," Mary agreed, moving so he could get up. However, as soon as he swung his legs over the edge of the bed, a wave of dizziness forced him back onto the mattress.

"Sid!" Mary was immediately solicitous. "Are you alright?"

"I'm not sure," he said honestly. His head was spinning with a thousand thoughts, spinning like a button. Suddenly, he remembered Sir Richard's snide comment from this morning about buttoning his lip. "The silver button — you told him!"

Mary's upset face was swimming in front of him. "Yes, but only because—"

"You talk about trust."

She pressed her hands against his shoulders, looking him directly in the eye, making him listen. "The silver button is Richard's. He told me so himself. It was found clasped in the Duke's hand, and, because of it, he is no longer Seneschal."

It took a while for the words to sink in, but they still made no sense.

"Richard is as much in the dark as you are. That's why he held the meeting at The Harey Rabbit. I think he suspects someone at the castle, but I know nothing more than that."

This was incredible. "So, why doesn't he suspect *me*? Surely I'm the obvious candidate, or at least the easy mark?"

Mary stopped pressing against his shoulders. "That's why you're *not* a suspect. Richard isn't stupid; he realises you've been set up. The perplexing thing is the button; Richard can't understand how…"

Mary appeared momentarily lost in thought.

"How what?"

She blinked and shook her head. "Oh, it matters not. If Richard knows anything, he certainly hasn't shared it with *me*."

Sid regarded the face hovering above his. It was full of concern and compassion, softening as she stroked the right side of his face. Still, he had the feeling she was holding something back, as if she wasn't entirely convinced of her half-brother's intentions where Sid was concerned. The Seneschal, or *former* Seneschal, could still point the finger at him.

"How do you know your half-brother *didn't* attack the Duke?"

Her dark eyebrows furrowed.

"Why not?" he said, levering himself into a sitting position. "He could have easily carried out the deed. Then, realising he'd left incriminating evidence behind, created a fabricated version of events for Gerald to proclaim, then arranged for one of his silver buttons to be planted on some unsuspecting bastard like me."

Mary was shaking her head. "Doctor Whysman is right; the knock to your head *has* addled your senses. If what you are suggesting were true, Richard would have already arrested you. Yet, here you are, being confided in by his sister as well as being tended to by the Duke's doctor."

She raised her eyebrows, daring him to gainsay her logic. He couldn't.

"In fact, Sid, he asked me to get the silver button from you. He wants it back. Hardly the act of a man trying to deflect blame in your direction."

"I think I lost it…" He suddenly remembered he'd felt for the button while watching Doctor Whysman and John leave, but found his pocket empty. "…plucking John from the Icing."

Mary gave him a dubious look.

Then again, he said to himself, he may *not* have; he seemed to remember playing with it as he entered The Bloody Bell. Truth was, no matter how illogical his thoughts, he didn't trust Sir Richard bloody Upson and wouldn't put *anything* past him.

"Richard won't be pleased."

He shrugged, and waited for Mary to press him on the issue. Instead, she changed the subject completely.

"Why did you go looking for Tom Skinner?"

"I know him."

"Is *that* the extent of your explanation?"

"I thought he might know what had happened at the castle."

Mary smiled ruefully. "If only I'd known, I could have saved *you* the walk and *John* the drenching, *and* you'd still have Richard's button."

Her expression changed, becoming… resigned? Sid had a bad feeling about what was coming next.

"Tom also stayed at The Harey Rabbit last night. He's helping Richard, and he's just as tight-lipped."

How cosy. "Yes, well, you weren't exactly in the mood for a conversation this morning, and I wasn't about to announce my intentions in front of your high-and-mighty half-brother."

Mary didn't look pleased by his response. She pushed herself off the bed and walked over to the window.

What did she expect from him? A game was being played, and Sid felt like the sacrificial pawn. He watched as Mary stared out into the grey afternoon, breathing deeply. His frustration soon turned to sympathy. None of his plight was her doing.

"I'm sorry, Mary."

"It's just that bad things are happening," she said, her gaze fixed outside.

Sid edged off the bed.

Mary regarded him as he walked groggily towards her. "I need someone I can turn to, Sid, not someone who will turn on me."

Sid stood next to her, using his left arm to brace against the window sill, while wrapping his right arm around her waist and drawing her close. Mary rested her head against his shoulder, and for a while they stood together in silence, looking out at the gloomy afternoon sky. Apart from a wafting cool breeze, nothing stirred, not even the ubiquitous feral cats that usually lurked on the rooftops and hunted the streets for any scrap of food. Sid definitely wasn't a cat person, but he did feel a certain kinship with them; they were expert survivors and seemed to enjoy the freedom their lifestyle brought. It was an odd thing to think about, but at least it was something he could relate to.

"Will you stay with me tonight?" Her voice was soft, like the breeze.

Sid knew he should say something simple and heartfelt like *There's nothing I'd like more.* Instead, what popped out was a flippant, "Are you sure it's safe for me to be surrounded by all that ale and wine? You know what Doctor Whysman said."

Fortunately, Mary took it with good grace. "That's just it, Sid; *I* will be in control of everything that passes your lips."

With that, she pulled him towards her and kissed him passionately. It was a pleasure and pain moment. When she released him, she gave him a determined look and said, "See?"

For the first time since waking up with a silver button in his pouch, Sid burst into laughter, and then gasped in pain.

CHAPTER 20

Sid is rotten to the core

AN INSISTENT VOICE was calling his name. There was a pressure on his left shoulder, shaking him. It was a woman's voice.

"Mary?" he said urgently, jerking himself into a sitting position. His head immediately throbbed and spun.

"We have to go," Mary said from somewhere to his left.

"What's happened?" He grimaced as he turned to face the sound.

"We've slept through the afternoon. It's past six o'clock. I have to get back to The Harey Rabbit."

Back to The Harey Rabbit? Where *was* he? Suddenly the room came into focus, and so did Mary. She was standing over him, untangling her hair with her fingers. "How are you feeling?" she asked, squatting down next to him.

"I'm fine," he replied, trying to remember how they'd ended up in bed.

"Are you sure?" She looked concerned, her blue eyes searching.

They'd been talking at the window. Then Mary had kissed him… "Never felt better."

Her reaction was dubious. "Sid. Perhaps it's best—"

"I'm fine, Mary." She'd asked him to stay with her. It was all flooding back now — Sir Richard's dinner, the Silver Button was *his* and… bloody hell, the Duke had been poisoned!

She still didn't look convinced.

"Truly," he said, getting out of bed. Surprisingly, he managed the manoeuvre without pain or dizziness. He kissed her hand and said, "Lead on, my lady."

Mary shook her head, but she was smiling.

The humidity had gone entirely, replaced by a cool breeze that meandered its way down the streets of Lower Icing. Window shutters were flung open to allow every swirl of freshness into people's abodes, and many of those people were standing at their windows, quietly embracing the change. Some people called out to Sid as he and Mary walked up his street (which had no official name, but was referred to by the locals as Bull Lane), commenting on the beautiful evening or making lewd suggestions about his new lady friend. Oddly enough, there were very few people actually on the streets, just the occasional couple in conversation and smatterings of scurrying children (and slinking cats).

However, as they strolled closer to the castle, things became a bit livelier: men-at-arms patrolled in groups of three, and the more affluent people who inhabited this part of Lower Icing were out and about in their fine clothes. The cooling northern breeze carried their voices and filled the early evening streets with laughter and conversation.

Sid, walking arm-in-arm with Mary, had fallen into a reverie. He was imagining his meeting with Doctor Manky tomorrow. He would stride to the bar, order a jug of ale, and tell Will Plucker that he needn't join him for the meeting because he was going to take care of everything. Then he would casually walk up to Manky and give him a look that would turn his skin a few shades whiter. Manky, smugness replaced by fear, would say, "Goodness gracious, Sid. We *do* seem to be running into each other rather a lot lately."

It took a few seconds for Sid to mentally re-join the here-and-now and realise the words had been spoken by his brother-in-law. Gerald was dressed in a bright combination of green trousers tucked into black boots, white cotton shirt with yellow waistcoat and black cavalier's hat with a green plume. It was strange to see him out of his Town Crier garb, and he looked rather chuffed with himself. The woman linked to his arm, however, was a severe contrast, both in her dress and expression.

"So, how are you, old chap?"

Sid was still taking in the scene before him, and before he could respond to Gerald's enquiry, the jolly man had responded for him. "Not too bad, I'd say, having a pretty lass like Mary on your arm, what." Then, giving Mary what he supposed was an endearing smile, he enquired, "How are you, m'dear?"

"We're both well, Gerald," Sid interjected pleasantly, finally finding his voice. "You're looking rather dashing. In fact, there seems to be a few people out in their finery tonight."

"Yes, and we must be joining them, Gerald," said his sister, evenly.

"Is there some occasion then, Mistress Hiepants?"

Olivia treated Mary to an expression of imperious indulgence. "We have been invited, along with other distinguished guests, to dine with the Duke at the castle."

Mary couldn't hide her disbelief. "Surely the Duke is not—"

Sid stopped her words by squeezing her arm. Either Doctor Whysman had found a miraculous remedy, or, incredibly, Gerald and Olivia knew nothing of the attack and this dinner was some sort of… What? Announcement? Perhaps the Duke was dead.

In any case, he didn't want either of them knowing that *they* knew. Fortunately, his sister's snobbery saved Mary from any embarrassment. "I hardly think *you're* in a position to query anything to do with the Duke. You should attend to matters more appropriate to your station. And if you'd take some good advice, I suggest you choose your associations more wisely." She glanced disdainfully in Sid's direction.

Sid could feel Mary's arm tense, but her expression remained calm and assured. "Thank you for the advice, Mistress Hiepants," Mary replied, politely. "However, I know a bad apple when I see one."

Sid almost burst out laughing. Bravo, he wanted to yell. Gerald grimaced and Olivia simmered.

"Then you should see that Sid is rotten to the core," she retorted.

"Really, my dear, I rather think—"

"Be quiet, Gerald!"

Then, with undisguised contempt, her baleful gaze returned to Sid. "And as for *you*, why don't you crawl back to your world of dirty whores and pathetic drunks."

Sid smiled ruefully, shaking his head; he'd heard this all before. He wasn't angered by her words, just *weary* of them. "I think you'd be surprised by *my* world, Liv. You see *all* types at the places I drink… particularly The Bloody Bell."

There was a moment, *just* a moment, when Olivia's icy demeanour looked like it was about to crack, but she held firm. "Come, Gerald," she said coldly. "It's time we were on our way."

Sid couldn't help but admire her composure.

"Right you are, m'dear," Gerald murmured, cowed by Liv's tone. He doffed his hat and wished them both a good evening, before they rejoined the rest of the castle nobs.

"This is Richard's doing," Mary said as they continued walking east down Big Wig Street.

"Yes," Sid agreed. It certainly seemed the most likely explanation.

"But I don't understand. The Duke can't possibly be hosting a dinner."

"No," Sid agreed again. "Unless, of course, honest Richard and good Doctor Whysman have been lying about the poisoning."

Mary lowered her voice to a whisper. "Do you seriously think they would fabricate such a thing?"

Sid shrugged.

"To what end?"

"I have no idea." In truth, his thoughts were already shifting away from the castle; away from a place where he couldn't gain entry to a place where he could. "However, it's given me a rare opportunity."

"What rare opportunity?"

He increased his pace.

"Sid?" she asked, stumbling to keep up with him.

"I'll tell you when we get back to The Harey Rabbit."

CHAPTER 21

Public drinking is beneath her

THE SHORT WALK down Big Wig Street flashed by in a haze of fashion and shop-front glitter. As they entered The Harey Rabbit, Mary looked bemused by the lack of clientele and the muted atmosphere, the inn starved of its usual Thursday-night custom by a dinner at the castle. A few groups of people (obviously not important enough to be invited) sat and talked in murmured voices.

Two serving girls (the ones who'd been chopping vegetables in the kitchen) and Mary's barman were chatting behind the bar. They welcomed Mary and Sid as they approached.

"It seems we have competition from the castle tonight, Dave," said Mary, addressing the burly, bearded man of middle years.

Dave nodded, eyes glinting with mirth. "Aye. Given me a chance to work me charms on these two beauties 'ere."

One of the girls hit him playfully across the arm; the other shook her head and laughed before they resumed their serving duties to the crowd of leftovers.

Sid gave Dave a knowing smile, and the barman responded with a knowing wink. "'Ow y'feelin', Sid?"

"Much more clear-headed, thanks, Dave," Sid replied cheerfully. In fact, *focused* was probably a better word — he was about to go Adventuring for the first time in over six years!

Mary's thoughts, however, were centred on the goings-on at the castle. "So, when did you find out about this dinner?"

"Jus' after y'sent John to fetch Doctor Whysman; a few hours ago, s'pose. Same as the guests, I reckon."

"What do you mean?" asked Mary, leaning across the bar and lowering her voice.

Sid hunched closer to Mary as Dave explained quietly, "Well, two castle servants, dressed all formal like, come in 'ere an' start 'anding out sealed parchments to the more importan' folk. It caused a big to-do, I can tell ya. Just about ev'ryone went rushin' for the door; it was like somebody 'ad fired a cannon or somethin'. Turns out the parchments were invitations from the Duke to dine with 'im at the castle tonigh'." Then his jovial manner returned. "Blimey, you shoulda seen them ladies when they realised they only 'ad a few hours to get ready."

A few minutes later, Sid and Mary were sitting in The Harey Rabbit's private dining room. The same room in which Sir Nob-Up-His-Arse had held his secret meeting last night. And now, tonight, all the nobs were swanning off to some fanciful dinner with the Duke — the Duke who was *supposed* to be in a state of delirium after being poisoned. The invitation had to be a ruse; either that or the Duke hadn't been poisoned at all. Sid didn't like the sound of either alternative.

"What do you think is going on at the castle?" Mary asked as she poured red wine into two glasses. It wasn't often Sid drank out of a glass; he was more of a tankard man.

"I have no idea," he said, almost to himself, "but as I said, it's given me an opportunity to delve into something else."

"You mean your sister's appearance at The Bloody Bell?" Mary asked, placing a filled glass in front of him.

Sid was momentarily taken aback. "Have I told you?"

She took a sip of wine. "Only vaguely; I don't remember anything significant. It was just before we fell asleep."

A vague recollection was better than none; he couldn't recall mentioning *anything* to Mary about Liv. He took a couple of gulps of wine, and then began relaying the moments leading up to his sister's bizarre presence at The Bloody Bell. "After my jolly jaunt with John, I'd built up a bit of a thirst and was feeling a little worse for wear. My head was a bit... foggy." He wanted Mary to understand that he hadn't gone into The Bell because of what had happened at The Harey Rabbit. "In any case, I needed to get out of the heat and recover my senses."

Mary nodded her understanding as he swigged the rest of his wine. "It obviously had *marvellous* recuperative affects."

Sid acknowledged the dig with a smile. "I was at the bar, waiting to be served, when I noticed a man and woman standing in the doorway underneath the staircase in deep discussion. I couldn't see the woman's face, but the man's expression was intriguingly intense. It was a strange thing to see in a place like The Bell. Then the woman took a small cloth bundle out of her bag. I couldn't really see it in the gloom, but it appeared fairly small and thin. The woman seemed to be apologising or reassuring the man in some way; it was too noisy to hear what they were saying. The man accepted the bundle gravely. Then she kissed him on the cheek. He looked a bit taken aback by that. I didn't see what happened next, because the barmaid had handed me a tankard of ale. By the time I'd finished downing it, the man had disappeared and the woman was making her way back through the bar. I thought my mind was playing tricks on me, but... even *with* her hat pulled low, I recognised Liv's sour-cow expression. I couldn't believe it, Mary."

"Yes, it *does* seem an odd place for you to see your sister, even though I've only just met her. Are you *sure* you weren't mistaken?"

"As you say, you've just met her — would you now mistake her for anyone else?"

Mary shook her head, seemingly lost in thought.

"The point is, Mary, my sister was in a public house."

Mary looked blankly at him. "Is that... unusual?"

"Unusual?" Sid blurted incredulously, sending a stab of pain through his eye. Then, in more subdued tones, he added, "It's bloody unbelievable."

Mary's eyes narrowed. Obviously she hadn't grasped the meaning behind his words. He put his empty glass down and reached for the bottle of wine. "Let me put it this way: Gerald drinks here every Saturday afternoon, brown-nosing with all the nobs of Lower Icing, but I'd wager he's never been accompanied by Liv." He topped up her glass and refilled his.

"You're right. I've only ever seen her *outside*, walking with Gerald. This evening was the first time I've spoken to your sister."

"That's because she believes public drinking is beneath her." He placed the bottle back on the table. "And if that includes the salubrious confines of The Harey Rabbit, what the bloody hell was she doing in The Bloody Bell talking to some strange man? And what the frig was she giving him?"

"She *did* flinch slightly when you mentioned The Bell."

"Ha! Yes! I wanted to see her reaction."

"So, what do you have in mind?"

He took a few more mouthfuls of the wine; it was quite easy to drink for a red. After a few gulps, the glass was empty. That was the trouble with glasses: they emptied far too quickly.

Mary's blue eyes gazed at him disapprovingly in the soft candlelight. "Remember what Doctor Whysman said about resting and… drinking?"

What did she expect? *She'd* supplied the wine. "I remember," he said, dismissively, "but this is a chance to *put* my mind at rest."

Mary looked dubious.

"I'm serious, Mary. This castle dinner is the perfect opportunity for me to look around my beloved sibling's home and possibly find out what she's been up to."

"Do you think she's involved with what's happened at the castle?"

"Your guess is as good as mine, but I wouldn't put it past her. Gerald's been tied to that Town Crier's bell for over six years now, and I reckon Liv's more than ready for him to have a position that has a better ring to it."

"Yes, I can imagine that." Mary looked distracted. Like Sid, she seemed to be trying to process all the facts. Then, focusing back on him, she added, "But going to such lengths as poisoning the Duke?"

Sid agreed; it seemed bizarre to even suggest such a thing, but after this past week, the bizarre was becoming commonplace. First Manky, then the attack on the Duke, Gerald's misleading 'Silver Button Thief' proclamation, being bashed, waking up in Mary's bed, finding the silver button in his pouch, being treated by the Doctor-to-the-Toffs, Mary revealing her relationship to the Seneschal of Lower Icing, the threatening letter to Reg Puffy (*Bloody hell!* He'd almost forgotten about it! The threatening friggin' letter to Reg Puffy! What the frig was *that* all about?) the secret meeting at The Harey Rabbit, the altercation with Sir Up-His-Arse, and, to cap it all off, the behaviour of his prim and proper sister in the seediest establishment south of the Pits… and all this going on while he battled a massive, dizzy headache.

"I have no answers, Mary," he said, quietly, the candlelight reflecting in his empty glass as he tilted it, "but I may find some at 8 Plumduff Street."

Mary regarded him for a moment. "Just be careful, Sid."

CHAPTER 22

Enough light to come home to

FIFTEEN MINUTES LATER, Sid had left The Harey Rabbit and was heading back down Big Wig Street towards Plumduff Street. He'd been quite surprised by Mary's acceptance of the situation. He put it down to curiosity coupled with his sister's unfailing ability to rub people the wrong way. Still, he had to be back within the hour or she and John would come looking for him.

Big Wig Street was now eerily deserted. The evening light, dull and gloomy under the canopy of clearing grey sky, added to the sense of desertion. Even the light glowing behind the windows seemed dull; it was almost as if the shops and homes were falling asleep. Then it occurred to Sid that many of the people living here were likely at the castle and had only left one or two candles burning, giving themselves just enough light to come home to.

The freshening breeze wafted in Sid's wake as he stepped hurriedly past the West Gate. The guardsmen were talking and laughing amongst themselves and only cast cursory glances in his direction. Not that he was worried about being accosted by any of them, but it was interesting to note their demeanour — whatever was happening at the castle tonight, the guardsmen didn't appear to be any more guarded. They were bloody hopeless, the lot of them.

As he approached Plumduff Street, his heart began beating faster and he felt slightly woozy; the thrill of Adventuring was still there after all these years. However, this was unlike any Adventuring he'd done with Paul Peabody; he was not stealing a piece of jewellery or a precious ornament from a stranger's safe box, he was after something far less tangible, something that may or may not exist, something that explained his sister's presence in The Bloody Bell. What the frig had she been doing there? Was *this* the information Manky had been expecting, hoping Gerald would let something slip about his *wife*? Assuming, of course, *Gerald* knew what she was up to! It just seemed too incredible to even imagine.

Sid slowed his pace as he made his way towards the door next to the brass plaque of 8 Plumduff Street. It was as quiet as midnight, even though the sun was still an hour from setting. There was not a soul to be seen or heard; no glimpses of people inside their homes, no sounds of domesticity permeating through walls. The elegant street was deserted.

Sid's objective was to gain quick and silent entry into the abode of Gerald Hiepants; the anticipation of the task was an intoxicating mix of fear and excitement, a feeling that he'd all but forgotten.

He undid his belt and removed a small leather wallet from a virtually unnoticeable pocket next to the buckle. It was cunningly worked into the leather with elaborate stitching to give the appearance of design. Inside the wallet was what Sid liked to refer to as his 'Adventure Kit'. In reality, it was his lock-picking kit, and, for the last six years, it had been nothing more than a sentimental reminder of more intriguing and profitable days.

The wallet and belt had been a gift from Paul Peabody; an investment in their future was how he'd phrased it. Memories of their successes brought a smile to Sid's face. Then his smile faded; his sister had loved and cared for him in those days.

The wallet contained numerous metal picks, individually secured in pockets. They ranged in length from two to four inches. They also had varying diameters ranging from a delicate 1/32 of an inch to a more robust 1/8 of an inch. They were all finely crafted with kinks and niches, cleverly designed to open the most intricate of locks. Even so, they were useless in unskilled hands. They required a deft touch; so much of lock-picking was about feel. Sid had been adept at it. He wondered if he still was.

After choosing the third largest pick, he squatted down and inserted it into the keyhole. It was amazing how familiar it all seemed, and the mechanism proved no match for his skill: within a matter of seconds, the unmistakable click of an opening lock briefly disturbed the silent street.

Sid gently pushed the door and slipped inside, quietly shutting it behind him. He was standing in the small reception hall. Sitting upon a small, ornate table was a pewter candlestick. A single wax candle, hardly used, was proudly providing an even-glowing flame, revealing the immediate surroundings. To his left, six steps led up to a small landing before turning ninety degrees right to follow the wall up to the first floor.

Straight ahead, the reception area became a hallway that ran parallel to the staircase. At the end of it was the laundry and the kitchen, where Sid had spoken to Gerald about meeting him at The Harey Rabbit last Saturday. However, the light from the candle was not strong enough to reveal that particular detail; it barely reached the six feet required to illuminate the first door on the right: the one that opened into the formal lounge where the Hiepants entertained those Liv deemed worthy. Sid, of course, had never set foot in that room. However, he wasn't the slightest bit curious about its interior, and he very much doubted he would find anything of interest there. No, Liv would keep her private life *private*.

Sid ascended the stairs, more with anticipation than excitement. It was a strange feeling; not quite the rush of a complete stranger's house, and yet with every step that took him closer to his sister's inner sanctum, he felt enlivened. Liv had lit another candle at the top of the stairs, making it easy for Sid to move with confidence. He did note, however, that this candle was well used and placed in a simple wooden bowl on the floor. To Sid, it highlighted perfectly the difference between what was for show and what was real. He shook his head; to live a life where *everything* was appearance must be very depressing. Then, out loud, he murmured, "No wonder you're such a bitter cow."

Sid knew the upstairs layout mirrored downstairs: one large room at the front — the bedroom — and three smaller ones at the back. He picked up the bowl containing the candle and moved down the hallway to the back rooms. A few paces along, the candlelight revealed a door to the right. It opened into a small room that contained a leather-top desk and a large wardrobe. On the desk lay a quill and a sheet of parchment. Sid walked over to the desk. Written in scratchy handwriting on the parchment were three words: Oyez! Oyez! Oyez!

"Bloody hell, Gerald," Sid muttered in disbelief. What sort of Town Crier actually writes down his Oyezs?

There were three drawers on either side of the desk, but they contained nothing of interest. Sid turned his attention to the large wardrobe on the opposite side of the room. It was taller than Sid and both of its full-length doors had brass locks with keys in place. Sid turned the key of the right-hand door and it creaked open. The flash of red gave him a bit of a start. Hanging in the wardrobe was Gerald's official, three-quarter length Town Crier cloak, its gold braiding catching the candlelight. Opening the other door revealed a selection of trousers, shirts and a pair of well-polished black boots. Sid relocked the wardrobe and left the room.

Down the corridor, towards the back of the house, the next door opened to a room on his left. Upon walking in, the first thing Sid noticed were three large chests running neatly along the entire length of the opposite wall. He went over to the first chest and opened it. It was full of Liv's dresses. most of them serviceable colours like grey, brown, and mauve. The second chest contained mainly hats of the same mundane hues. The final chest was divided into three compartments; the smallest one contained needles and thread, spare buttons and other dressmaking equipment, the middle-sized compartment contained gloves and undergarments, and the largest was full of shoes and boots. Sid took care to leave everything in the chests just as he found it.

As he surveyed the rest of the room, he caught sight of his gruesome visage, eerily lit by candlelight, in a window that, during daylight hours, looked down onto the back yard. He snarled at the image, "I'm every child's nightmare." (On a brighter note, his facial movements were becoming less painful, the swelling had receded significantly, and the stitched gash was now flat across his forehead; it was more the ugliness of the purple-grey bruising that marred his face.)

Next to the window stood a dressmaker's model consisting of a head and torso. It was modelling a finely laced white corset and bustier. Sid regarded the piece with a mixture of intrigue and bemusement. "Perhaps I've misjudged you in more ways than one, dear sister," Sid whispered to its featureless face.

Adjacent to the mannequin was a dressing table, backed by a large mirror. Once again, Sid looked upon himself, morbidly fascinated by his appearance. He stepped towards the table for a closer inspection. There was a collection of hair brushes and a wooden box of hairpins neatly arranged on the table top. A larger, more ornate wooden box, delicately carved with swirls and inlaid with gold-leaf, contained Liv's jewellery. Under the table top was a wide, shallow drawer containing Liv's collection of rouge, powders and other beautifying lotions. He let out a deep breath: apart from Liv's surprising taste in underwear, there was nothing revealing in this room.

Sid turned his attention to the door that led to the other room across the hallway. It was locked. "Well, well. What've we got in here?" he enquired of his flickering shadow.

Placing the candle on the floor, he fiddled through his set of lock-picks. Choosing the one that had opened the front door, he began manoeuvring the intricate item. Again, it didn't take long before he heard the satisfying click of the lock opening. Retrieving the candle, he entered the room.

He was immediately confronted by lines of shelving that ran the entire length of the opposite wall. There were five levels, the lowest some two feet from the ground, the topmost around seven feet in height. The top shelf and half the one below held a series of leather volumes packed tightly together. In contrast, the bottom three shelves held a haphazard array of objects ranging from rolls of dress material and sewing equipment to a collection of comical mugs and a marble statuette of a town crier.

But Sid's attention was quickly drawn to the desk situated in front of the window. Lying next to a book (oddly entitled *Do Well-to-Do Well* by Lady Violet La Fleur) was an unfinished letter. It was addressed to Doctor Whysman's wife, Petronella, and read:

Dear Petronella,
It is with great pleasure that I accept your kind
invitation to morning tea next Wednesday at 10 o'clock.
I am looking forward to seeing the new drapery that you

Sid shook his head in disbelief as he sneered distastefully at the flowery handwriting; the same hand had penned the warning letter to Reg Puffy. What was the point of it all? It had been so long since he and his sister had been estranged, she was telling people he was *dead* for frig sake! So why would she suddenly care what he was doing? It just didn't make any sense — *another* thing that didn't make any sense. Bewilderment soon turned to anger as he thought about what she'd done. "So, dear sister, you think you can put your fingers in *my* pies without getting them burnt?"

He scanned the desktop. There was nothing else of interest. There were, however, four drawers to explore, two on either side of a tucked-in chair.

He opened the top left drawer. It contained Liv's personalised stationery and some spare quills. He glanced back at the letter again, just to make sure the handwriting was the same, but there was no mistaking the precise lettering. He was surprised he hadn't recognised it when he'd read the letter to Reg. How frigging bitter could you get! He took a deep breath and tried to clear his head. He needed to concentrate on the task at hand and not be distracted by thoughts of his sister (in the pillory being pelted with a barrelful of pig shit).

The drawer below stored sticks of red wax and the Hiepants seal. On the other side of the chair, the top drawer was empty except for some folded, ink-stained cloths. The one below it was locked. Again, Sid delved into to his Adventuring Kit, this time choosing one of the smaller picks. The drawer was fiddly compared to the two doors and he had to change to an even smaller-sized pick before the lock was conquered. (He wouldn't have made that mistake six years ago.) Still, it had only taken him minutes rather than seconds.

The drawer contained a flint and another book: *Poetry in Potion* by Doctor Horatio Manky.

CHAPTER 23

Too much orange-spotted mushroom

SID FELT SURPRISINGLY calm as he shut and relocked the front door of 8 Plumduff Street. He was satisfied he'd left everything exactly the way he'd found it, including Manky's book locked away in its desk drawer.

As he walked along the still and darkening streets, he thought about his sister. He'd discovered two things about her this evening: she'd written the warning to Reg Puffy and she knew Doctor Manky. Well, she had his frigging book, at least, so there must be *some* connection. Sid wondered if his sense of calm was actually shock, because if finding the book hadn't been shocking enough, what he'd found inside certainly had been.

Poetry in Potion had seemed harmless enough when Sid first leafed through its pages. It consisted of recipes for various potions, mostly treatments for common ailments like influenza and body aches, but there were also some more complex mixtures for things like the pox and even the Black Death. Sid had laughed when he'd seen those; the main ingredient in each of these potions had to be Manky's deranged ego. However, the scoffing had stopped when Sid reached a small section at the back of the book entitled Special Potions. One of the potions in this section had been underlined in black ink. It was called Paloma Coma. The list of ingredients included odd things like fermented potato skin and orange-spotted mushroom, and it seemed vitally important to stir the mixture with a dove's feather. The end result was a potion that would supposedly put the imbiber into a deep sleep. This was particularly beneficial, according to Manky's explanatory notes, for patients who needed painful procedures like limb amputation. However, what had grabbed Sid's attention was the small heading printed at the bottom of the page. It consisted of a single word: Warning. Underneath, the potion-maker was alerted to the danger of using too much orange-spotted mushroom. It could cause the imbiber to become delirious and feverish, and, if untreated, death was a likely outcome. The whole warning had been incriminatingly circled in ink…

possibly the same ink that had been used to write Reg Puffy's poisonous letter.

Sid could hardly credit what it meant: his sister must have played a significant part in the attack on the Duke. It was… unbelievable. And what did that make Manky? Her accomplice? Or perhaps she had stolen the book, and Manky therefore suspected she was planning an attack on the Duke. And what of Gerald? Was *he* involved? *That* was even *more* unbelievable! And, if so, why would Manky target *Gerald* for information? But, then again, there *was* the fabricated proclamation. Perhaps it was *Liv* who'd made him write it. Then there was the encounter at The Bloody Bell. Now that he thought about it, the young man she'd met had looked resigned, accepting of his fate as he took charge of the object wrapped in black cloth… an object that could well have been a knife or small dagger.

"What have you done, Liv?" He breathed out loud. And, more to the point, what had *he* done, getting himself involved with Manky? Perhaps Liv had found out about his meeting with Manky and then organised the beating. It was too much to take in; a whirlwind of possibilities blew through his mind, and, as if on cue, his head started spinning. He had to prop himself against a nearby wall until the dizziness passed.

As Sid approached the corner of Big Wig and Noble streets, three patrolmen suddenly appeared from the West Gate and began walking in his direction. Instinct took over, and Sid pressed himself against the façade of a nearby shop, melding into the shadows created by its ostentatious entranceway.

"Reckon the shift'll finish early t'nigh, Jack?" said one of them as they ambled towards Sid. "Ain't nothin' much 'appenin'."

"Don' bet on it, Fred," replied Jack. "There's a banquet full of people what need seein' 'ome safely."

"Aye," agreed the third, as they passed Sid.

Fred wasn't happy. "Bloody hell. Wha's the Duke playin' at? Ain't no-one seen 'ide nor 'air of 'im since tha' intruder got in. Now, 'e's suddenly decided to throw a big nosh-up for anyone who lives this side of bleedin' Merchant Street. I mean, wha's *tha'* all about?"

"Yeah, well I wouldn' go sayin' things too loud," said the nameless soldier.

"Why?" said the other two in unison.

"Well, somethin' ain't right."

"What ya sayin?" asked Jack.

By this time Sid was straining to hear the soldiers' voices as they strolled farther away from him. The nameless soldier was now speaking very softly, and

Sid could only pick up hints of his reply.

The response from Jack, however, couldn't have been clearer: "Dead?"

The word echoed down the empty street, quickly followed by the sound of a helmet being slapped.

Sid made it back to The Harey Rabbit with almost twenty minutes of his allocated hour remaining. Nothing had changed much in the cosy confines of the inn; the smattering of patrons talked amongst themselves, no doubt wondering why they hadn't been invited to the castle while casting aspersions on those who had.

Mary was at the bar as Sid entered. She came straight over to him, looking both relieved and worried.

"I'm fine, Mary," he said, anticipating her question. "We need to talk in private; you won't believe what I've discovered."

They had just sat down at a small dining table in one of The Harey Rabbit's eight well-appointed guestrooms. Mary told him some of her guests preferred to dine in privacy. How nobbish could you get, Sid thought; there were much better things to do in privacy. The dim glow from the single candle played across Mary's sun-browned face. Her blue eyes shone with concern, full lips pressed in anticipation. Sid was suddenly distracted by thoughts of 'much better things to do'. Then a waft of air caused the flame to flicker and his mind to re-focus.

"Liv has something to do with the attack on the Duke," he said. Mary sat in stunned silence as he revealed what he had discovered at 8 Plumduff Street. "And, to top it all off," he finished, "she also wrote the threatening letter to Reg friggin' Puffy!"

She stared at him, confusion playing across her dancing eyes. "What threatening letter?"

Was she serious; surely she couldn't have been *that* distracted. Then it occurred to him that he may not have actually mentioned it. "Didn't I tell you?"

Mary shook her head; she seemed genuinely unaware of the matter. "When did this happen?"

"Yesterday morning… I thought I told you."

"No," she assured him. "Understandable, given the circumstances."

Yes, like being cracked over the head by a bloody coward possibly hired by his bitter, scheming sister. Sid told Mary about the letter, and how Reg Puffy was no longer willing to supply him with pork pies or any other pastries.

It sounded quite comical in the grand scheme of things.

"What the frig, Sid!" Mary breathed, shaking her head; she was just as bewildered as he.

"Exactly." Sid sighed; he suddenly felt tired.

"What are we going to do?" she whispered.

We. He liked the sound of it, but this was something *he* had to do. If his sister and Doctor Manky were conspirators in the attack on the Duke, he didn't want Mary getting involved and putting herself in danger. "I'm seeing Manky tomorrow… Well, supposed to be, at least. The bloodless creep might not come back if he's heard what's happened."

The look she gave him was unreadable, but that was probably because he was struggling to keep his eyes open. He yawned. "Sorry, Mary… I just feel so…"

Next thing he knew, she was standing over him, massaging his shoulders. "I'll fill you a warm bath and then put you to bed."

He was already half asleep when he replied, "That's the best plan I've heard all week."

Chapter 24

Ill-considered thoughts

SID WASN'T SURE whether it was the bright sunlight or the erratic street noise that woke him. He momentarily felt disorientated before realising he was in the guest room he and Mary had talked in last night. Then, like the morning sun, the memories of what had happened yesterday evening came streaming in. Bloody hell! His sister! It was unbelievable; more like a bizarre dream than reality.

He jumped out of bed and dressed. Oddly enough, he felt invigorated; the bath and the sleep had obviously done wonders, and he was driven by the thought that he would be meeting Doctor Manky today. Yes, he could hardly wait to see his bleached face again, assuming, of course, he hadn't done a runner.

Sid looked at himself in the mirror and was surprised to see a cleanly shaven visage. Mary must have done it last night while he was in the bath. It was all a bit hazy; he'd never felt so tired. He must have been functioning on pure adrenalin while he was at Liv and Gerald's. Still, his face was gradually getting back to normal. He gently ran a finger across the neat stitches; his left eye was only slightly swollen, and, in the bright morning light, the bruising appeared more yellow and greenish-grey than purple, certainly more benign than the image he'd seen in Liv's window last night. Regardless of his appearance, he was beginning to feel like his old self.

After unsuccessfully calling for Mary upstairs, Sid headed down to the bar. The Harey Rabbit was an amazing place, Sid thought, as he was greeted by the hum of muted conversations. It wasn't so much that the place was patronised (albeit sparsely) at this time of the day; it was more the fact that its patrons hadn't been there all night (as was the case with most morning activity at The Dead Duck).

Mary was standing by a table, dressed in a black uniform, talking to a group of four gentlemen, one of whom was the lawyer Sid recalled as having a distinct dislike for yellow waistcoats. (Gerald was clearly of the opposite opinion, judging from his castle attire.)

Mary was one of those people with the rare ability to make those she spoke to feel special — even pompous, arrogant nobs. He tried not to grimace as he surveyed the morning gathering of well-to-dos. The smattering of people who made eye contact with Sid gave him varying looks, from disdain and suspicion to pity and revulsion. (He wondered if it was the bruise on his face or the cut of his clothes.) Oddly, their reactions made him think about Doctor Manky: he must feel this way every time he came into contact with people, confronted by the wariness in their eyes. It had to be depressing. But, then again, Doctor Manky hadn't seemed depressed. On the contrary, he'd seemed to be in a natural state of self-satisfaction, one where he believed himself superior to those around him. He dismissed thoughts of Manky and concentrated on his immediate surroundings.

Mary was now walking towards him with a strange expression: a mixture of concern and joviality (if that was possible). Sid wasn't sure what to make of it; perhaps it was her morning 'hostess to the nobs' face. It actually put Sid in mind of Elsie and a successful night at The Dead Duck. If he *had* shared a similar experience with Mary last night, he had no recollection of it, and that would be a real shame. But had anything happened, he would surely remember it. After all, the images of their first time together were still burned in his brain.

"Good morning, Master Evily," she said pleasantly. "I trust your stay at The Harey Rabbit was to your satisfaction?"

What was she playing at? Was this an act he should be joining in on? "I'm not sure, Mistress Brewer," he said with a suggestive smile. "I seem to have fallen asleep prematurely." Judging by her uncomfortable expression, Sid hadn't played his part very well. "Please excuse my foolish jest," he added formally, and then, in a louder voice, "Your hospitality is unsurpassed. Thank you for a most satisfactory stay." He bowed politely.

She smiled gratefully. "Why, thank you."

Something was wrong, and Sid had a fairly good idea where the wrongness was sitting.

"No doubt you're hungry. May I suggest you be seated at one of the booths overlooking the Town Square?"

The booths were well away from the four gentlemen; by the look of their tailored garb, they were *all* lawyers.

"I'll have a hearty breakfast sent to you shortly," she added meaningfully.

"Sound's delightful," Sid replied with mock formality. However, he was rapidly losing his appetite. "I'm sure it will be most… fulfilling."

"We aim to please," she smiled. "Depends how—"

"Gel!" Nearby, a prissy-looking spinster-type was clicking her fingers at Mary.

Mary gave Sid a despairing look. "If you wouldn't mind seeing yourself to your table, Master Evily. I'll be with you soon."

Sid nodded and forced a smile. "Not at all, Mistress Brewer." He watched as Mary walked over to the uptight-looking woman, whose expression was pinched and disapproving, as if she'd just drunk sour milk. Her snobby voice carried across the room. "This tea is too weak and co-eld."

Mary began apologising while Sid headed towards the booths Mary had indicated. He could have chosen a more direct route and steered clear of the four sombrely-dressed lawyers, but their superior demeanour irked him. He wanted to let them know he wasn't intimidated by their presence. Mistress Brewer might have to massage their egos, but Master Evily certainly didn't.

The yellow-waistcoat lawyer clocked Sid first, his jowly visage regarded him through heavy-lidded eyes. A mocking smile appeared on his lips as they made eye contact. Sid held the lawyer's contemptuous gaze. His eyes were grey and watery, like the slurry from a laundry bucket. His nose was bulbous and pock-marked, and his neat, shoulder-length hair was a similar hue to the charcoal-grey clothes he was wearing. As Sid approached, the man slowly turned his gaze back to his three companions.

Sid smiled in satisfaction. He knew the type: weak individuals who got what they wanted because they held a position, who never got their hands dirty because they paid (or coerced) people to get *their* hands dirty. Yes, Sid had come across their kind quite a few times before.

As Sid walked past, he heard a refined, drawling voice say, "Yes. She's obviously slumming it at the moment. But haven't we all, what?" This was followed by knowing chuckles.

Sid turned around and saw the mirthful expressions on the faces of the other three. The man in question now had his back to Sid. One of his companions noticed Sid's reaction and indicated the situation with a slight, bemused nod and flick of his eyebrows. The yellow-waistcoat hater twisted casually in his chair and smiled challengingly at Sid. "Something I can help you with?"

Sid wanted to pound his smarmy expression right up his cavernous nostrils. There was a period in time, after his life of Adventuring had ended and his life of drinking had begun, when he wouldn't have hesitated, but he'd learnt a few things since then, and one of them was keeping his emotions under control.

A cold anger welled inside him, but he used it to keep his voice even and eyes fixed on the smirking, toad-faced lawyer. "No. Absolutely nothing, but there *is* something I can help *you* with."

The lawyer regarded Sid with barely hidden contempt. "Oh? Do tell."

Sid forced himself to smile as he softly said, "If you're unable to keep a civil tongue in your head, I can help you find a more appropriate place to put it."

This seemed to amuse the lawyer. "Did you hear that, gentlemen," he asked rhetorically, without taking his gaze from Sid, "this good-for-nothing just threatened me. He obviously has no idea who I am. Hardly surprising, I suppose." He gave Sid's face a fleeting appraisal. "By the look of him, he makes a habit of choosing the wrong people in whom to convey his ill-considered thoughts."

"Well said, Jeremy," chimed in one of his companions.

Looking directly at Sid, Jeremy continued. "I suggest you be about your business before I decide to take offence. And, believe me, I *know* how to handle an offence."

"Oh, very droll, Jeremy," added the same companion, while the other two guffawed their amusement.

Jeremy kept his eyes fixed on Sid, daring him to say another word. Sid knew he was in dangerous territory; this man could, and no doubt would, have him arrested if he pushed the matter. Swallowing back vitriol, he forced himself to turn and walk towards his table. This was done to the accompaniment of superior chuckling.

Sid was seething as he sat down, but he knew there was nothing he could do about it. Whether he liked it or not, some people wielded too much power to be met head on. You just had to deflect the blows until you found the opening for a knockout punch.

The altercation seemed to have gone almost unnoticed by the rest of the patrons. Mary was no longer in the bar room, and nobody else seemed to be paying him or the puffed-up bunch of tosser lawyers any undue attention. Sid turned his gaze from the interior of The Harey Rabbit and stared out the window towards the Town Square. It was actually later than he'd realised; the carts that haphazardly littered The Square on Fridays — when the real market was closed — were well ensconced in their positions and set up with food, clothes, trinkets, cure-alls, and anything else people without an official market license thought they could sell. The once-a-week vendors were in full voice trying to attract custom.

The loudest voice, however, was the one ranting inside Sid's head. Damn it all, it said. He was better off working out this mess alone. Mary was complicating matters; she was too connected to the nobs (like those tosser lawyers) and too involved with her smarmy half-brother and his bloody silver button.

Sid had spied the button against the wall, on the floor under the table, as he and Mary left his house yesterday evening. He had no memory of how it got there, but it had probably dropped when he collapsed. In any case, as far as *he* was concerned, it was *his* silver button until he found out what the frig was going on. And he could do that without Mary's help. It would be better that way; she was too worried about him, and their relationship was already being noticed by people whom he considered enemies… his sister included. It could be used against him, and the last thing he wanted was any harm to befall Mary. No, she was better off without him. She was too good for him anyway.

His thoughts turned to Doctor Manky. For the most part, Sid could hardly wait to hear what the ghoul had to say for himself, particularly the connection he had to Sid's vengeful sister. (Assuming, of course, there was still going to *be* a meeting.) And then there was Gerald. Had he known about Liv's misdeeds? Had he played a part himself? Sid very much doubted it: he didn't have the wherewithal, and Liv wouldn't trust him to keep his mouth shut, especially when being Town Crier was not only his job but his passion. He thought about the leather-bound volumes, shelved in chronological order. From the brief time Sid had spent leafing through them, they appeared to contain copies of every proclamation Gerald had made: over six years' worth, all written in his scratchy handwriting and each beginning with Oyez! Oyez! Oyez! It would be funny if it wasn't so sad.

"Mornin', Sid."

The chirpy words wrenched him away from his thoughts and he looked up to see John smiling down at him, using both hands to hold a large wooden tray of sausages, eggs, mushrooms and bacon.

"Oh. Hello, lad," Sid said, trying to focus back on the here and now. John held the tray in front of him, piled with enough food to feed a brigade of men. "I know Mary thinks I can't feed myself, but that's a tad excessive, don't you think?"

John's initial reaction was confusion, and then realisation arrived. "Oh, righ'. Nah, this ain't f'you." Then his naturally bright disposition reasserted itself. "Bes' keep goin' 'for I drop it. Be back to take your order in a tick, Sid."

Sid's gaze followed John to the table of lawyers, watched him smile as he placed the tray on their table, saw the pompous arse-wipe, Jeremy, slip John a coin, and John play the grateful serving boy.

The sense of wellbeing Sid had felt before entering the bar room had now well and truly disappeared. And disappear was exactly what Sid had just decided to do. He'd had enough of *this* side of the Town Square, where people clicked their fingers and flicked their coins as if they were born to it. They frigging deserved each other!

Mary still hadn't reappeared from wherever she'd disappeared to; probably personally seeing to the correct tea temperature for Mistress Plum-In-Her-Bum. He was no longer interested in what Mary had to say. It was an opportunity to leave. Sid took it.

CHAPTER 25

We're all family 'ere

SID MARCHED ACROSS the Town Square towards The Bloody Bell, vaguely aware of the morning bustle around him. The inn not only marked the north-west corner of the Town Square, it was also at the intersection of Merchant Street and Market Street, Lower Icing's busiest thoroughfare. Merchant Street formed part of Sid's usual route (to and from Reg Puffy's) but it intersected Plumduff Street, and Sid had no intention of tempting fate by accidentally (or otherwise) running into either Hiepants. His sister could wait; she'd get what was coming to her in good time. Right now, there was another calculating individual who was about to experience the wrath of Sid Evily — the supposed meeting with Doctor Manky at The Harey Rabbit was less than two hours away.

The first thing Sid needed to do was speak to Will Plucker. Sid could handle Manky alone. There was too much at stake; he didn't want to drag Will, or Joan for that matter, into the same mad conspiracy in which *he'd* been ensnared. Those puffed-up lawyers had actually done him a favour by acting so full of themselves. They'd helped him focus on the task at hand. Namely, draining every last drop of information out of the bloodless doctor.

Sid pushed his way through the clogged intersection outside The Bloody Bell, and headed down Market Street, away from the castle, The Harey Rabbit and 8 Plumduff Street, and directly towards The Dead Duck.

Sid entered the relatively serene environment of The Dead Duck to the yearning sound of Maddy singing "She Lost Her Leg For Love" (a poignant ballad about a woman who saves her lover from being run down by a horse). She and a couple of other barmaids were engaged in their morning routine of making the inn presentable. This mainly consisted of chucking out all the semi-conscious revellers from the night before and scrubbing away anything they'd left behind. They'd done a good job, because The Duck was pleasantly free from the odour of vomit and piss. In fact, there was an enticing redolence of baking; perhaps

Joan Plucker had made a batch of her famous pigeon and onion pies.

The girls all smiled when they saw Sid, Maddy doing so while singing. Sid gave them a brief nod and headed straight for Will's private quarters. He knocked on the door before entering. Will was sitting at a table talking to Joan. They both looked at him with a mixture of annoyance and concern.

"Pardon the interruption," Sid said without preamble, "but I need to talk to you, Will."

"Wha's happened now?" asked Joan "You gettin' y'self into more trouble at the castle, Sid Evily?" She sounded cross, but Joan was a compassionate woman who had always looked out for Sid. Her gruffness was all show.

Sid was thinking how to answer her, when Will did it for him. "It's alright, love, Sid and I have a small matter to discuss."

Joan cast both of them a dubious glance. "Wha', like the small matter that got 'im beat up, an' me 'avin t'go back to bakin' pies?" She didn't give Sid or Will the chance to respond. "If this 'as anything to do with The Duck, then it's *not* alright, Will Plucker." Crossing her arms, she directed her challenge at her husband. "Well?"

"It has nothing to do with Will or The Duck, Joan," said Sid, moving towards the table. "It's my problem, and that's what I've come to tell you."

"Wha' you on about, Sid?" Joan asked irritably, realising she'd been kept in the dark about something important.

Sid looked to Will, not wanting to say the wrong thing. Will closed his eyes and sighed. Then he faced his wife. "That white bloke what came in las' Friday… Sid reckons 'e was the start of 'is troubles, and 'e's comin' back 'ere to meet with Sid today, so I thought I might join in… see if we couldn't sort a few things out… together, like."

Joan eyed both men; it was like waiting for a cannon to fire.

"Too right, Will Plucker!" Joan exploded, smiling proudly at her husband.

Sid felt awkward; this was not what he wanted. Manky was *his* problem. Other people and their good intentions were only complicating matters. Sid looked at them both, trying to work out what to say without revealing what he knew about the Duke and the silver button.

His reluctance must have been obvious, because Joan Plucker broke the silence with a compassionate, "We're all family 'ere, Sid."

Will Plucker reinforced the sentiment with a determined nod.

Sid sighed. What could he say?

He settled for something appropriate. "Thank you."

CHAPTER 26

Like he'd never stopped wearing them

THERE WAS A sense of déjà vu as Sid approached his house. Leaning next to his doorway, head bowed, was the scraggly form of an adolescent boy. And just like last time, Sid was able to walk up to him without being noticed.

"I wonder how this wall has stood all these years without *you* propping it up, John."

John jerked in surprise. "Sid... sorry... I, er... that is, the Mistress wanted me t'say—"

"She was worried about me?"

"Well, yeah, but—"

Sid wasn't in the mood for the boy's spluttering explanation; it was obvious why he was here. "Look, lad. Tell Mary I'm fine and everything is in hand. I will see her when I can."

"But, Sid—"

"Listen to me, John. This is for the best. If you care about your mistress, you'll want to keep her safe. And that's what I'm trying to do. Do you understand?"

John looked Sid in the eye and nodded. Sid could tell he wanted to plead Mary's case, but it would serve no point. "Right then; the next time I see you or Mary is at The Harey Rabbit, when this has all been sorted."

He gave the lad an encouraging pat on the shoulder and then began unlocking his front door. However, John lingered, undoubtedly conflicted by his duty to Mary.

"Best be on your way, John. My mind is made up." Sid opened the door and entered. John remained standing there, watching him. "Remember, I'm doing this for Mary."

Sid shut the door on John's downcast expression and went straight to his dining table, bent over, and retrieved the silver button from the floor. Then he went up to his bedroom. If there was to be a meeting with Manky, he wanted to be properly prepared, and *that* meant being armed with more than just information.

He knelt by the side of his bed and slid it a couple of feet towards the window. Then, choosing the 1/16 inch lock-pick from the wallet inside his belt, he leant over the newly exposed floor and used the lock-pick to lever up a small, almost invisible, brass latch. Pulling on the latch lifted a square foot of floorboards, revealing a woollen fleece. The fleece concealed and protected the contents of a cavity constructed between two rafters. It was a fool proof version of the hiding space Liv had stumbled across — *nobody* would stumble across *this*. In any case, it wasn't bursting with coins; it contained something more precious to him.

Sid removed the sheepskin. Underneath it was a locked metal box containing the deed to his house, a letter from his mother and some coins. Next to the box was the object of Sid's desire: a pair of knee-length black boots.

These were no ordinary boots (even though they looked it). They were another gift from Paul Peabody (this time for the occasion of his eighteenth birthday) and had been made by the same craftsman who had created the lock-pick belt. Like the belt, embroidery had been used to conceal what lay within. But instead of lock-picks and other tools of thievery, the spine of each boot contained a dagger. Decorative black leather tassels at the top of each boot were actually attached to the pommels. This allowed for quick and effective access to the sharp blades.

Sid hadn't worn the boots for almost six years; not since he'd given up Adventuring. But now donning them seemed not only necessary but appropriate. He sat on his bed and slipped them on. The supple leather slid over his feet like a lover's caress. He stood and walked around the room; it felt like he'd never stopped wearing them. He smiled to himself. Then he knelt back down, re-packed the sheepskin, replaced the lid and moved his bed back. His hiding space was, once again, virtually undetectable.

Standing up straight, he stretched his arms high before bringing them down slowly in a wide arc. He was rewarded with a satisfying cracking sound as his vertebrae adjusted themselves back into place.

Sid turned around and looked out his window. It was a perfect day: cloudless, with just a hint of a cool breeze. The sun was beaming down as it reached for its zenith; midday was approaching. "The time is nigh," Sid said to himself. Now all he could do was wait and hope Doctor Manky was a man of his word.

Chapter 27

A requetht

SID WAS DOWNSTAIRS, pacing around in his Adventuring boots. It couldn't have been much more than ten minutes since he'd put them on, but anticipation made time drag. He didn't want to arrive at The Duck before Manky, but, at the same time, he'd been waiting all week for this moment.

A sharp rap on his front door wrenched Sid from his musings. What the frig? He opened the door on Manky's servant or coachman, or whatever he was: the small, wiry figure who spoke with a lisp and looked like a vulture (or, now that he was closer, perhaps a turkey was a better comparison). He was bald except for a wispy ring of grey hair that hugged his ears and fell away towards the base of his skull. He had drooping eyes that didn't seem to blink and a large beak nose that sat in the middle of a pinched, oval face. His nose totally over-shadowed a small, thin-lipped mouth and a virtually non-existent chin that melded quickly into a long neck. In the middle of his neck, fighting for prominence with his nose, was a huge Adam's apple. To top it all off, he was dressed in a dazzling ice-blue robe. In fact, it was so dazzling it made Sid squint.

"I have a requetht from Doctor Manky," lisped the turkey man.

"A requetht?" Sid mimicked, not attempting to hide his contempt.

If Sid's tone bothered him, it didn't show.

"He would like you to accompany me to hith plathe of rethidence."

"Would he now?" Sid spat rhetorically, immediately suspicious of the change in venue. The man eyed Sid without emotion, unaware or oblivious that Sid was waiting for a response.

"I was under the impression we were meeting at The Dead Duck," Sid prompted.

"I don't believe that wath the arrangement."

It wasn't the response he was expecting, particularly from a servant. "And, of course, *you* were privy to our conversation."

Once again there was no response; the dazzling figure just stood there regarding Sid from behind his hooked beak. Who the frig did he think he was? Perhaps a sharp slap across the face might register with him. Then the name 'Bertrand' popped into Sid's head — that's what Manky had called him. Well, if the change in venue was Manky's idea of trying to gain the upper hand, he'd have to do better than Bertrand. However, Sid *was* curious to find out where Manky lived. "So, Bertrand… where, exactly, *is* your master's current place of residence?"

The diminutive figure showed no reaction to Sid's use of his name. "It'th a five-hour ride north."

"A five-hour *ride*?" Manky must be mad or desperate if he thought Sid had that much trust in him.

"Aprocthimately. Yeth," agreed Bertrand, calmly ignoring the incredulity in Sid's voice.

"And what if I refuse Manky's request?" Sid snarled.

"That ith your prerogative. I have been told not to uthe forth."

Sid laughed out loud. He was genuinely amused by the thought of Bertrand trying to overpower him.

Bertrand eyed him blandly, seemingly impervious to any human emotion. "What ith your anthwer?"

Sid was about to tell Bertrand to flutter off when he heard his name being cried out. He cursed as he looked to his right. "Bloody hell!"

Mary was fifty paces away, walking hurriedly towards him.

Sid quickly scanned his street, looking for a way to avoid Mary meeting Bertrand; he really didn't want her getting involved with such a creep, and, no doubt, she'd insist on seeing Manky.

To his left, parked on an open piece of land a few houses down from his, was a black carriage. A horse, whose colour matched the coach perfectly, was calmly waiting in its trappings. Beyond the carriage, the street continued for another block of houses and some outbuildings before the cobblestones petered out into a well-trodden dirt road. It arced around Lower Icing, eventually intersecting the northern end of Market Street, just before it became the North Road.

Sid glanced back in Mary's direction. She looked like she was on a mission; obviously his message hadn't been received well (or, more likely, hadn't been delivered well). She waved an arm and called out to him again. Sid was torn; Mary deserved a proper explanation, but this might be the only chance he'd have to find out what Manky was up to. And it was something he was determined to do on his own.

Almost before he realised it, Sid had shut his front door and was addressing the seemingly unflappable figure next to him. "Right, Bertrand. Let's go."

With that, they started running towards the carriage. Over the sound of his boots pounding on the cobblestones, he could hear Mary's voice crying out for him to stop.

As he reached the carriage and opened the cab door, he looked back to see Mary standing in the street outside his house. Her arms were by her side. She looked wretched. Sid felt like running to her, and tell her that all would be all well, that he loved her. However, the moment was broken by a voice that had probably never felt love.

"If you'll pleathe thtep into the cab, we can be on our way."

Sid didn't hesitate. He clambered into the dark interior of the cab and shut the door. Seconds later, the carriage was moving, surprisingly smoothly, over the cobblestone street.

CHAPTER 28

Enough to send his mind spinning

SID'S WORLD HAD suddenly turned black. He'd jumped out of the bright, midday sun into the plush midnight of crushed velvet that lined the interior of Doctor Manky's cab. He felt like he'd jumped into a coffin. It was quite apt, really; this madness was likely to end in his funeral.

The carriage moved swiftly along the dirt road, known colloquially as the Coin Curve after Lower Icing's most affluent resident, Fraser Coin — essentially, the road had been created to provide access to the construction of his ostentatiously large estate house, complete with a row of terraced housing for his servants and workers. It had taken almost twelve years to complete, and rivalled the Upper Bailey in opulence. Even though the estate was little more than a quarter mile from his humble abode, Sid hadn't used the Coin Curve since the estate opened some two years ago.

The Coin Curve curved from north to east, passing through an area of woodland before re-entering the northern part of town. Back on cobblestones, Bertrand steered the horse left onto Market Street. The cobblestones didn't last for long, as Market Street soon became the North Road. Not that Sid felt any difference in the ride; just the sound of hooves changing from clopping to thudding.

Sid spent the first ten or so minutes peering out the cab's windows. He'd never travelled north before and was intrigued to see what lay beyond the smattering of barns and farmhouses that dotted this side of Lower Icing.

For the most part, the scenery consisted of green and brown-tinged fields set amongst lush woodland. The odd undulation in the land wasn't severe enough for the road to deviate from its northern route, and, consequently, Sid soon lost interest in the world outside.

Sitting back in the comfortable seat, he closed his eyes. The battered side of his face was throbbing now. He could imagine Doctor Whysman tut-tutting about rest and recuperation, and Mary, arms folded, looking at him as if he was an incorrigible child.

A week ago he hadn't had a care in the world, and no-one cared what he looked like or how he behaved. But since meeting Manky, Sid had been beaten up, the Duke had been poisoned (for which someone had attempted to incriminate him with the silver button), and his most lucrative business venture had been sabotaged by his sister… his sister: the person who didn't associate with anyone she deemed inferior, yet he'd seen her in some clandestine rendezvous at The Bloody Bell, *and*, more damningly, she was in possession of Manky's book of potions and poisons. Well, she would get her comeuppance one way or another.

He'd also come under the unwanted scrutiny of Sir Richard Upson, who just happened to be the half-brother of the one good thing that *had* actually happened since the doctor's fateful appearance. Still, there was no use wishing he'd never met the bloodless creep; the damage had definitely been done. He'd get answers from Manky, and then he'd confront his treacherous sister.

Hopefully, Mary would understand…

In any case, Manky had said he'd pay Sid another five gold pieces for his information. Five gold pieces? Bugger that! He would demand the original ten be repaid as *well* as the agreed five! Manky could look upon it as just compensation for Sid's troubles. The only thing, of course, was that what was *agreed* and what was *happening* were two different things. He was no longer meeting the pink-eyed practitioner at The Duck; he was hurtling north to an unknown destination in a black carriage driven by a bird-man with a lisp.

He reached into the right pocket of his trousers and felt the reassuring shape of the silver button. Manky would no doubt want some sort of verification of his story, and the button was the only thing he could offer; it might even have some meaning to him. After all, he *must* have suspected *something* was about to happen to the Duke. Why else would he have approached Sid?

And why hadn't he gone directly to the Duke?

And what connection did he have to Sid's stuck-up sister?

And how did Gerald fit into all of this?

Why-What-How-When-Who-Where. It was enough to send his mind spinning… spinning like the wheels of the gently rocking carriage that carried him smoothly to wherever Manky was holed up.

CHAPTER 29

Seems like your kind of place

SID WOKE WITH a start. His first thought was that the carriage was under attack. He stuck his head out the window in time to see the back of another coach heading in the opposite direction. Dust plumed in its wake, and Sid retreated back into the cab. He was now fully alert, heart still beating quickly from the shock awakening. He wondered how long he'd been asleep, how far they'd travelled, and what was waiting for him at the end of this ride.

Sid moved to the other side of the cab and surveyed the scene. The countryside looked much the same as it had before. He leaned out of the window — the air now clear of dust — and looked in the direction Manky's coach was headed. Just past the rhythmic bobbing of the horse's black head, he could see a set of hills in the distance. Sitting atop the highest hill, highlighted by the late afternoon sun, was a small collection of buildings. From the centre of the collection, something golden bronze was catching the sunlight.

Sid's gaze fell to the ground, and for a while he was mesmerised by the verge of wild grasses along the dusty North Road. He could always jump out of the cab — they weren't travelling that fast. Even if Bertrand noticed his escape, he could easily outrun the feeble-looking man. Then it occurred to him that Bertrand had leapt onto the carriage before Sid had even *reached* it. How the frig had he managed *that*? And then there was his laughable remark about not using force against Sid. However, right now, nothing seemed laughable.

Sid slumped back into the black interior of the cab and shut the window. He was tired of thinking. He was tired of other people's games. He was tired of being on edge. He was just… tired. As if on cue, his left eye began to water. He rubbed it; it was still tender. Perhaps Doctor Manky would help him out with one of his poetic potions.

The carriage slowed as the horse worked against a noticeable incline — they had reached the base of the range of hills Sid had seen some twenty minutes ago.

As they meandered up the slope, the land became more cultivated, and villagers could be seen toiling in fields. The first thing Sid noticed was their garb — they all wore varying shades of blue, although nothing darker than sky blue. The presence of the carriage didn't seem to distract them from their tasks, so he assumed the road was well used. Still, it was odd that no-one even gazed in the carriage's direction; it was almost as if they were consciously making an effort *not* to look at it. Sid thought about calling out to an elderly woman working quite close to the road, but decided against it; he'd already reaped more than his share of trouble this week.

After what seemed like dozens of twists in the road, the ground levelled out, and the welcoming sound of hooves on cobblestones clopped through the air.

Sid's first impressions of the village were not good; except for the noise of the carriage, everything was eerily quiet. There were people going about their business, but no-one seemed to be talking, and all the windows and doors were open, yet the place felt strangely unwelcoming.

The carriage slowed to a walking pace and the road opened into the village square. To his left, Sid observed a handful of people quietly preparing what appeared to be the setting for a banquet. Dozens of tables were arranged in a large circle, with seats placed on the outside, facing inwards. The townsfolk were cleaning the tables and distributing plates and mugs. They, too, were wearing shades of blue. There was little emotion on their faces, and even when a scattering of children appeared from inside a stone building, they were purposeful and orderly. And still, none of them seemed intrigued by the appearance of the carriage.

Before Sid had a chance to fully survey the scene, the carriage came to a halt and the door to his right was flung open by Bertrand. He stood motionless and emotionless as he waited for Sid to alight. Sid clambered out of the cab, stretching to the accompaniment of grateful vertebrae.

"Doctor Manky awaitth you inthide the Sun Temple."

Sun Temple? The carriage had pulled up in front of an impressive-looking building that overlooked the town square. Slate steps led up to a massive arched doorway painted a bright pale yellow. The temple's walls, painted a pale blue, were perfectly smooth. The slate roof appeared to taper, but Sid was too close to get an overall picture of its design. Sid had never been inside a temple before, let alone a *Sun* Temple. It suddenly occurred to him that Bertrand hadn't lisped the S in Sun.

"What is this place?"

"Thith ith the village of Bleth-ed Whipping," replied Bertrand.

"Blessed Whipping…" Sid mused — he'd never heard of it. "Sounds about as much fun as it looks."

Bertrand's response was to walk up the dozen or so steps that led to the yellow arched entrance of the temple. Sid followed close behind.

"I take it this is where you hail from, Bertrand?"

"Yeth."

"Yes… seems like your kind of place."

"Motht perthpicathiouth of you," Bertrand responded, seemingly unaware Sid wasn't paying him a compliment.

"Careful, Bertrand, you could cause a nasty injury using a word like that."

There was no response from the small, wiry man dressed in a whiter shade of the local pale blue… perhaps he was some sort of acolyte.

He pushed open the massive yellow doors that filled the arch. They revealed, in Sid's mind, an astonishing sight.

The interior of the Sun Temple was bright and shining, revealing a world of light-blue walls and rows of gleaming wooden pews. A long rug ran down the length of the central aisle; it was an iridescent blue, with gold stars, planets and other celestial bodies woven into it. The rug continued up some steps to an altar stone. On the alter was a gold disc, about three feet in diameter, held in place by a semi-circular bracket sitting atop a four-foot high stone pedestal. Engraved into the plate was the outline of a fiery sun, and other more intricate things that Sid couldn't quite discern, the detail lost in the gleaming afternoon sunlight which streamed down from above, where a glass roof spired upward. It gave the impression the sun was actually shining *inside* the temple. It was brilliant — no wonder it was called the Sun Temple. After a few moments, Sid had to avert his gaze; the light was making his injured eye water.

As Sid followed Bertrand down the aisle, his attention was drawn to the walls either side of him. Painted in shades of blue were four panoramic scenes, two each side. To his right, one scene showed a woman using a bucket to collect water from a river. The other depicted a woman hanging her washing out to dry. To his left, a man was tilling soil and a blacksmith worked at a forge.

Sid had never been to a place like this. Lower Icing only had two temples, and they were more ceremonial venues than places of worship. One was inside the castle, reserved for special people and special occasions; the other was near The Pits, reserved for special people who had something special to hide. (People like Paul Peabody.)

Like the great majority of Lower Icingers, Sid had never felt the need for spiritual guidance or having faith in some celestial entity (*and* he no longer had use for a clandestine meeting place). No, Lower Icing was far more grounded in the corporeal world, and Sid was of the opinion that, in his walk of life, if you watched your step, you stood a good chance of avoiding the horseshit. However, no matter how carefully you trod, you were bound to be shat on by the occasional bird. For the most part, Sid had managed to avoid the horseshit, but this past week felt like a thousand birds had flown over and aimed directly at him.

It was with this thought that Sid followed Bertrand past the golden disc to a door on his left that obviously led deeper into the Sun Temple. The bird-man knocked softly and then silently opened the door. Sid had no view into the room, but he could tell it was quite a bit gloomier; the back of Bertrand's bald head glowed like a misshapen full moon against the dim interior.

"Thir… Mathter Evily hath accompanied me here to thee you."

CHAPTER 30

A bottle of Hyacinthia

SID ENTERED THE room. Doctor Manky was sitting at the end of a large table. Two candles on the table and a blue stained-glass window provided a weird concoction of light that was, at the same time, warm and cold, glowing and glaring. Strewn across the table were various documents, including a large map of what looked like the streets of Lower Icing.

Doctor Manky stood up as Sid approached the table. Like everything else white in the room, he glowed pale blue.

"Dear me, Sid! What happened to you?" There seemed to be genuine concern in his voice.

The only thing that concerned Sid, however, was getting some answers. "I had the misfortune of meeting *you*, Manky," he said almost whimsically, ignoring the doctor's outstretched hand, and sat down across the table from him.

Doctor Manky's pink eyes followed Sid, but his face remained rigid, fixed in its usual smug expression. However, for the first time, Sid sensed an underlying tension beneath the surface, hairline cracks in a porcelain statue.

Doctor Manky's gaze flicked to the door. "That will be all, thank you, Bertrand."

Sid twisted around in his chair. "Yes, Bertrand, that will be all, unless you can bring me some ale or wine. This jolly jaunt's made me quite thirsty."

"Alcohol ith not permitted in the Sun Temple," replied Bertrand — again, there was no lisp in Sun — as he backed out of the room and shut the door.

"I'll take that as a no," Sid responded.

Doctor Manky sat back down and regarded him with what might have been empathy. "If you'd care for some water…"

Sid shook his head; he didn't need water, he needed a drink.

"Alas, it is the only drink permitted in the Sun Temple. It's one of their customs, I'm afraid."

Sid sniffed derisively. "Like the colour blue and scintillating conversation; must be a fun place to live." Then he realised Manky had said *their* customs; he wasn't dressed in blue and, although his conversation was annoying, at least he could express himself... so the doctor wasn't a Blessed Whippinger. What the frig was he doing here?

"You'd be surprised, Sid," replied Doctor Manky. "In some ways, I find their rigidness and predictability very... comforting. The alternative, judging by your appearance, can be quite *un*comfortable."

Condescending creep!

"Piss off, Manky! I wouldn't have thought *you* were in a position to judge *anyone's* appearance."

Doctor Manky nodded, somewhat abashed. "Touché."

Feeling he had the initiative, Sid pressed his point. "Look, Manky, I haven't travelled half the length of the Duchy in your coffin-on-wheels for an evening of cultural commentary. Since you floated into The Dead Duck, I've been beaten, robbed, set up, betrayed and scrutinised — most of it to the accompaniment of a massive friggin' headache. You owe me an explanation and you owe me money. The people of Blessed Whipping can wear blue and drink water until the sun shines out of their arses for all I care!"

His head was throbbing again, and he could feel his left eye starting to weep.

Doctor Manky lowered his eyes. When he returned his gaze, his expression was one of blue-tinged weariness.

He sighed. "Very well, Sid. I approached you because of your relationship to Gerald Hiepants. From all accounts, he is a bumbling fool; the perfect town crier you might say... the ideal person to let slip certain information."

His relationship to *Gerald?* What about his relationship to *Liv?* Did Manky really think Sid was *that* stupid, that he wouldn't find out about his sister's role in his scheming? Still, he wanted to hear it from the doctor's own mouth, to see if he would admit to knowing Liv.

"You sang *that* song at The Dead Duck, Manky. *How* did you know about my relationship to Gerald, and what kind of information were you hoping he'd let slip?" (He almost added, 'That you couldn't get from my sister'.)

The doctor gazed at him; his bacon eyes looked mauve in this light. "Let's just say I did my research, or, to be more accurate, I asked Bertrand to research on my behalf."

Sid grimaced, but not at what he was hearing. The pain behind his eye was increasing and he was beginning to feel light-headed.

"As for the *kind* of information, I am hoping you will be able to confirm the appearance of a certain individual at the castle. I need not reveal any more, because if you *have* heard anything, *you* will be able to tell *me*."

The smarmy git was playing games again. "Is that the best you can do? Is this what I've been brought to the village of the living dead for? You're going to have to do a shitload better than that, Manky!"

Manky looked shocked, then flinched when Sid sprang out of his chair and leaned across the table.

"Stop playing games! You know exactly what has hap—"

"Do you require athiththanthe, thir?" Bertrand's voice didn't sound any louder than normal, yet it cut through Sid's raised voice like a Gerald Hiepant's 'Oyez'.

Sid swung around from Manky. The small man stood calmly in the doorway, shrouded in the blue light of the room. Where the frig had he come from? There'd been no sound of the door opening.

"All is well. Thank you, Bertrand," Doctor Manky replied calmly.

"All is not bloody well, Manky!" responded Sid, keeping his eyes on the diminutive bird-man. It was all beginning to feel like some sort of bizarre dream.

Bertrand ignored Sid and kept his gaze fixed on the doctor. "Are you thure you wouldn't like me to rethtrain your vithitor?"

"I'd like to see you try, Bertrand."

His heavy-lidded gaze flicked in Sid's direction. Sid's fingers were tingling; if bird-man even twitched in his direction, he'd have two daggers to contend with.

From behind him, Manky said, "That won't be necessary, Bertrand. I feel confident Master Evily is a man of reason."

Sid felt like he was dreaming; the blue room definitely had a dreamlike feel to it, and these two characters couldn't *possibly* exist in the real world… they were just too bizarre… in the blueness. Still, Sid steeled himself, ready to spring into action.

"Please, Sid. Sit down," said Doctor Manky soothingly. "I will do my best to answer all your questions."

This *was* a dream. Instead of springing, his coil unwound. He vision began to swim as he looked at Doctor Manky's surreal mauve eyes. Sid closed his own… hopefully the dream would change. Instead, he felt a gentle hand on his arm. Doctor Manky was helping him back to his seat.

"Bertrand. Some water, please. And bring me a bottle of Hyacinthia."

Sid felt the support of the chair beneath him as Doctor Manky released his arm.

"Just rest for a moment. I have some medicine that will make you feel better."

Sid tried to focus on the white figure hovering next to him. "Who are you, Manky?

Sid now felt much more relaxed in the blue room, and he wondered if he'd misjudged the man sitting across the table from him. Bertrand had been sent away for some food, because Sid suddenly felt very hungry.

The few drops of purplish-blue Hyacinthia in a tankard of water had worked wonders. Sid felt even better than he'd done this morning, after Mary's ministrations the night before. He felt a pang of guilt as he remembered her pleading cries.

The potion had also refocused Sid's mind. Ironically enough, if he'd been thinking this clearly before, he'd never have touched the Hyacinthia or anything else concocted by Doctor H. Manky.

The doctor was smiling at him, no doubt pleased by the positive effect of the Hyacinthia. It was annoying. And Sid was already cross with himself for showing fallibility in front of the smarmy ghoul. "So, was that one of your poetic potions, Manky?"

Sid was rewarded with a new expression: surprise. It was gratifying to see.

"How intriguing, Sid."

"Is it now," he replied evenly.

"Yes…" The doctor's milky features curdled momentarily. "Very much so. To my knowledge, there is only one person who has a copy of that particular book, and I'd be very much interested to know if you've met him."

Him? Sid smiled; it was time to give Manky some of his own medicine. "All in good time, Doctor. Right now, I'd like *you* to answer *my* questions."

Doctor Manky returned Sid's smile, but his pink eyes appeared much more intense, and all traces of his recent fragility seemed to have vanished; his porcelain face was as smooth and composed as ever. Perhaps he *had* taken some of his own medicine. "Very well, Sid. Ask away, but I may not know the answers to all your questions. For instance, I have no idea who attacked you or for what reason."

Oddly enough, Sid believed him. "Then let's start with who you are."

"I am as you see me."

Sid had to control an almost overwhelming desire to punch the obfuscation out of his superior demeanour, but, after a short intake of breath, Manky continued.

"I am a doctor of medicine, and, though I hesitate to say, for fear of sounding egotistical, I'm rather excellent at it. In fact, Sid, my medical research has led to discoveries that could revolutionise the way we treat sickness and injury."

He's mad, Sid thought.

"As you would have appreciated from my book of potions, I have discovered ways to ease discomfort, remedy various maladies, and operate without the patient feeling pain."

Definitely mad... the blueness seemed to emanate from him rather than cover him. "Yes, Manky, I'm sure the Duke is *extremely* grateful that you've penned your book of wonder cures," Sid said sarcastically.

Manky's mauve eyes narrowed. "Would you care to explain that remark?"

No, he wouldn't care to at all. In fact, he was very interested to see how the doctor was going to react. If he *wasn't* involved in the attack, he must have at least suspected *something* was about to occur. "Let's just say a certain individual told me that the Duke was attacked by an unknown assailant."

"Marmaduke has been attacked?" Doctor Manky looked genuinely shocked, "Are you sure?"

"Not having seen the Duke myself, I can't say for sure, but I believe it to be true. *And*, what's more, Manky, the attacker used one of your potions, or should I say... *poisons*."

"I have not created any poisons," he said defensively.

"Not even when Paloma Coma has too much orange-spotted mushroom?"

"The book warns against doing such a thing!" Manky was beginning to look flustered.

"Yes, but it also gives people ideas," Sid countered.

"This is outrageous! My potions have been created to *benefit* people, not to harm them! I am not responsible for anyone who chooses to deliberately misuse the book. And, in any case, no-one except me and my..." The doctor halted, as if suddenly realising he'd lost his composure.

Accomplice? Sid wanted to finish, or perhaps Manky was about to say *bitter and twisted associate who also happens to be your sister*.

Manky shook his head, as if genuinely shocked by Sid's information. However, Sid wasn't about to let Manky off the hook. "The poison was on a blade," he said, pointedly. "The wound a minor cut to the arm, and yet, apparently, the Duke remains in some sort of feverish delirium."

"How do you know this?" he said sharply, mauve eyes boring into Sid's brain.

"The Duke's physician revealed his condition to..." Sid stumbled, almost revealing Mary's involvement, and that was the *last* thing he wanted to do. "To an acquaintance of mine."

Manky stared at him, possibly weighing up the truth of his words.

"Then I stumbled across your book of potions. Paloma Coma was marked; in particular, the warning about orange-spotted mushrooms."

The doctor began to shake his head slowly, as if he really couldn't believe what he was hearing. His snow-white hair, tinged blue in the light, hung limply. His mauve-eyed gaze turned inward, seemingly lost in thought. None of it, however, impressed Sid.

"I'm sure it's obvious to a *genius* such as you, Manky, what has occurred."

He sighed, seemingly resigned. "Very well, Sid. Assuming you've been told the truth, it seems likely your conclusion has merit."

"So kind of you to condescend, Manky. However, I'm not seeking your—"

"This alters things," said the doctor, seemingly unaware that Sid was speaking.

"For you, perhaps, but not for me."

"How did you *stumble* across my book?" Manky persisted.

"Who *had* your book?" Sid countered.

The corners of Doctor Manky's mouth were beginning to twitch. "How long ago was the Duke attacked?"

"How long has your book been missing?"

Manky leaned across the table towards him. "Sid, a man's *life* is in danger — the Duke of Lower Icing no less — it may not be too late to save him."

"I care *nothing* for the Duke of Lower Icing," Sid retorted. "He's just another friggin' nob wanting his arse licked!"

"I think you'd discover—"

"What I *want* to discover, Manky, is what the frig this has been about!"

Doctor Manky stared at Sid, frustration evident in his expression. Then his face relaxed. "Very well, Sid," he said quietly. "You leave me no choice." His gaze shifted towards the door. "Bertrand!"

CHAPTER 31
Such drastic measures

THE FIRST THING Sid noticed was a glowing light. For some reason he thought it should be blue. Instead, it was a warm yellow. He could hardly believe it was real… it should be blue…

He reached out to touch it, but he couldn't move. That wasn't right either. He should be able to move. Panic began rising within him. He struggled, and the light dissolved into a room.

Sid was in a seated position. There was a large candle burning in an engraved silver candlestick set on top of a wooden table. Plush-looking chairs surrounded the table and there was an ornately carved cabinet a little to his right, but Sid couldn't see much more than what was directly in front of him. He couldn't move his eyes, so he tried to move his head, but nothing happened. It didn't feel restrained; it just wouldn't move. It was the same with his arms and legs. In fact, his whole body was immobilised. No, it was more than that; he couldn't *feel* his body. He couldn't even feel what he was sitting on. Only his mind seemed to be working, and right now Sid thought he was losing that.

He tried to make a noise, but his mouth wouldn't move either; there was no sound… or maybe there was and he could no longer hear.

But he *could* hear… The room must have a window; its occasional rattling broke the silence. He noticed the flame of the candle flicker shortly after he heard the rattling. It was almost hypnotic. Then another sound could be heard, faintly at first, but quickly becoming louder. Footsteps… footsteps walking on stairs.

A door opened to his right and then shut quietly. Sid waited for the owner of the footsteps to appear, but there was no sound… except for the breeze and his breathing: shallow and steady, barely perceptible. His mind, however, was anything but steady.

Sid tried to move his eyes, tried to move his head, and tried to call out, but it was no use. The tension was almost unbearable; the feeling of impending doom was like nothing Sid had ever experienced. Even the few close calls he'd had during his days of Adventuring we're nothing compared to the heart-pounding panic he was feeling right now. He imagined this was how it felt to be executed… waiting for the axe to fall or the scaffold to open up. He realised that, with the sound of approaching footsteps, he was about to die.

The angel of death was white and wore a benign expression. Sid felt totally removed from the situation; in fact, he felt totally outside himself. He was floating just above his motionless body: a spectator to his own demise. He looked on impassively as Doctor Manky leant against the table in front of him.

"I am sorry to have put you through this ordeal, Sid. I know how strange Rigour Morphis feels, having experienced its effects a few times myself. But I assure you, you will make a full recovery. The effects eventually wear off, but, since time is of the essence, I will have to facilitate a more rapid recovery."

Doctor Manky reached into the right pocket of his white coat and pulled out a small vial. He displayed it to Sid, holding it between his thumb and forefinger. The liquid inside was a translucent orange. "This is Vigour Morphis, an antidote of sorts. I'm afraid it's rather unpleasant. However, before I administer it, I will explain why I deemed it necessary to take such drastic measures."

Sid looked at himself staring emotionlessly at the vial. It was bizarre — not his half-bruised face, but the fact that he was watching himself at the same time he was looking at a white face and pink eyes.

Doctor Manky placed the vial back in his pocket. He then moved off the table, pulled out one of the plush chairs, and sat down directly opposite him. Sid watched from his detached viewpoint, some six feet above the scene. Doctor Manky leaned towards him, his white hair in stark contrast to Sid's black, and his bloodless face bland compared to Sid's blood-filled hues of bruising.

"Firstly, I know your sister, Liv, has my book of potions. And I know you believe she is involved in the attack on Marmaduke."

Sid felt no surprise at the revelation; he didn't even feel curious. It was just information.

"In fact, Sid, you have told me many things about what has transpired over the last week: your annoyance at Elsie's refusal to sleep with you, Gerald's proclamation, drinking at The Harey Rabbit and your subsequent beating, the silver button, the days recuperating, your feelings towards Mary, Reg Puffy's threatening letter, the discovery of your sister's treachery, your altercation with Sir Richard, your sister's assignation at The Bloody Bell, the castle dinner, your discovery of my book of potions, the obnoxious lawyers, and your flight from Mary. You've been most informative and yet… most *un*informative."

Again, Sid felt no particular emotion as he watched the Doctor reach into another pocket and produce a vial containing a light-blue liquid.

"This is Voracious Loquacious, what you might call a truth potion. It is amazingly effective, Sid, even if I do say so myself, particularly when combined with Rigour Morphis."

He flicked the vial back into his pocket, leant closer to the living statue that was Sid, and patted him on the arm, as if testing for a reaction. Neither Sid felt anything.

"Again, I apologise for using such… underhand methods, but your revelation concerning Marmaduke… the formalities, I'm afraid, had to be circumvented. I had to know in what context you'd seen my book. You see, Sid, the only person who has a copy went missing thirteen days ago."

Doctor Manky relaxed back into the chair. He looked weary, Sid thought.

"After twenty years together, I would have thought he'd be able to confide in me, but no doubt he blames me for…"

Then he leant forward again, as if it was important Sid understood the significance of what he was about to say.

"Xavier is the reason I made contact with you. He's been under my… shall I say care… since he was an infant. I've raised him. I've educated him, taught him about medicine. He has shared in my discoveries, witnessed my failures and successes, and been less like the burden he was supposed to be and more like the son I could never have."

Sid wondered, in a vaguely curious sort of way, why Doctor Manky was telling him this. He seemed quite grave, like he was digging into a past he preferred to keep buried. To Sid, everything was just sounds; he understood what was being said, but he did so without emotion or any real connection. The words seemed to float away as soon as he heard them… He felt like he could be floating away with them.

"I've always entertained the thought he had similar feelings towards me, even though he's always known I'm not his father. However, after my carelessness, I fear he may have…"

The Doctor shook his head and dropped his gaze, lost in thought for a moment. Then he looked directly at Sid's lifeless face.

"It was at Marmaduke's command that I've withheld the truth from Xavier about who he is and why he's been left in my care."

Manky wasn't making any sense at all, but that didn't stop him from talking. The sound of his voice continued to stream through Sid's consciousness…

was he conscious, he wondered.

"But times have changed, and when Marmaduke brought us to Blessed Whipping I thought he'd decided to…" Manky shook his head. "I'm sorry, Sid, please forgive my ramblings; it's been a rather unsettling two weeks, and, truth to tell, it feels good to vent my spleen. Bertrand is hardly the listening type."

Bertrand… that's right… scrawny little shit with a lisp… how the frig had Bertrand overpowered him? It was embarrassing, except… Sid didn't feel embarrassed… and Manky was still talking.

"Not that I would have told Bertrand any of what I have shared with you."

Shared with him? What had Manky *shared* with him… words flying past his memory, making no sense as they flew by.

"And, Sid, it's only because of the Rigour Morphis that I'm being less restrained with you. I doubt you will retain much of what I say."

Less restrained… Just like his drifting mind.

"This has all come about because Xavier was born out of wedlock. Not such an unusual occurrence, I realise, and for the first two years of his life, it made no difference to his parents or anyone else for that matter. They were, for all intents and purposes, ordinary, albeit well-off, people."

Doctor Manky glanced to his right.

"Yet, there was *one* thing that *did* make a difference — a *significant* difference. The blood flowing through his father's veins was the same blood that sank beneath the waves on *The Happy Mermaid*."

The Happy Mermaid… Sid was barely five years of age when it sank with the entire royal family on board. His memory of the catastrophe consisted entirely of stories Liv had told him as part of his History education. Bloody hell. It was hard to believe the caring sister of his childhood had become such a bitter, stuck-up snob.

"After such a calamitous loss, the Duchy was in disarray. Power struggles and infighting ensued, and it seemed as if civil war was brewing. So, when Marmaduke was found by Sir Walter Upson, he was immediately proclaimed as the rightful heir to the Dukedom of Lower Icing. I must say, it came as quite a shock to those of us who lived in the humble hamlet of Prickly Thicket."

Prickly Thicket… It sounded like a good place to hide.

"We had no inkling a person of the royal bloodline was living in our midst. Marmaduke later told me it was not something he'd ever embraced, that he and Lucinda had bought a land holding in Prickly Thicket to escape the world of nobility."

Prickly Thicket… Coming, Duke, ready or not!

"It was not who they were, he told me… He was only a distant cousin to the Duke, and he doubted Olivier de la Wrence would've cared about, or even been aware of he and Lucinda."

The words were starting to echo slightly, as if the room was becoming larger. Or maybe *he* was becoming smaller… No, he still looked the same size, sitting there in a trance on the chair. The doctor's head turned back to Sid.

"Therefore, the situation in which Marmaduke and Lucinda found themselves was totally unexpected, and the ramifications abhorrent. They were told they had to leave Xavier behind because he was not 'of the marriage bed'."

Sid wondered what a Prickly Thicket marriage bed felt like.

"In the blink of an eye, their beloved son had become a royal embarrassment. They were assured that the separation would only last a few months, that they would be reunited after the investiture ceremony, once they had established themselves as the new Duke and Duchess. However, Marmaduke and Lucinda were wary of such an assurance; they feared they'd never see Xavier again, that he might even be put to death."

Death… Death… Death. The word echoed. If this was what it felt like to die, it was surprisingly relaxing, in a bizarre sort of way.

"Their first instinct was to run away and start a new life somewhere else. They asked for my help. I was their doctor, I had delivered Xavier, but, more than that, I was their friend. I was also the beneficiary of their generous spirit, which allowed me to delve into my medical research. I had recently created a potion which caused temporary amnesia. Ironically, the main ingredient is the stamen from Forget-Me-Nots."

Nots… Nots… Nots…

"They thought I might be able to use it to help them make their escape, but, unfortunately, back then, the potion only lasted a few minutes. It wasn't nearly enough time, and, as it turned out, too many important people now knew of their existence. Even the more effective version of Forget-Me-Do that I have today would not have made any difference — their lives were now irrevocably set on another course."

It seemed to Sid that Doctor Manky was sounding dreamier; his reminiscing was taking on a far-away tone. Sid felt like drifting far away himself… and he was trying to remember the name of that village… the place where he could play hide-and-seek.

"As you might imagine, they were beside themselves. In truth, I also believed

Xavier's life was in peril. However, all was not lost…"

Lost… Lost… Lost…

"You see, Sid, I had developed Rigour Morphis quite early on in my experiments into natural medicine. We decided to give it to Xavier, to make him appear dead; enough, at least, to convince the powers-that-be. The dose was the tricky thing: too little and he would only appear asleep, too much would kill him. But Marmaduke and Lucinda agreed it was worth the risk. If Xavier was thought to be dead, he would be safe."

Sid regarded himself sitting on the chair. *He* could be dead, even *with* his eyes open. There was no outward sign of life: no twitch, blink or breathing; no movement whatsoever. It was strange. Perhaps he *was* actually dead. Perhaps he'd been given too much…? What was it called again?

"I invented a story about Xavier catching a chill and succumbing to a congestion of the lungs… sadly, not an unusual malady. Needless to say, the ruse worked."

Again, the Doctor cast his gaze right. What was so compelling? Sid wondered. Hovering above himself, floating-Sid looked to his right. Nothing of *him* turned exactly; it was more like the *room* had rotated. It was quite disorientating for a moment.

The room was a large, ornately decorated office, or possibly some sort of consulting room. There was an imposing mahogany desk facing a bay window with clear, diamond-shaped leadlight; one section was open, the other rattling to be opened. Doctor Manky would no doubt have sweeping views of whatever lay beyond — at the moment, all the window revealed was darkness.

Like everything in the room, the desk was beautifully crafted and presented. On top of the desk lay a neat pile of parchments; the top one had something written on it. Next to the parchments was a shining silver ink well with two occupied quill holders. On the corner was a silver-framed portrait which stood about twelve inches high. Sid realised two things: firstly, this was what Doctor Manky was staring at, and, secondly, the portrait was of the young man Liv had met in The Bloody Bell. The man was smiling, but it looked reluctant. Somewhere in the back of his mind, Sid's thoughts were racing. But the part that was currently doing the thinking was calmly floating on air.

Doctor Manky's voice broke through Sid's musings and the room spun back to himself and the white man sitting opposite.

"Marmaduke and Lucinda pleaded with me to look after Xavier, to take him far away from the village of Prickly Thicket and keep him safe until they could send for him. I agreed without hesitation. Even at the age of two, Xavier was a bright child with a calm disposition. So I took the boy north, to the coastal village of Missing Anchor. There, I found comfortable lodgings above a tavern called the Windy Sailor. Shortly afterwards I sent a letter to Marmaduke and Lucinda, informing them of our circumstances. It took a month to receive a reply from Marmaduke. He asked me to continue caring for Xavier and to make sure I kept his identity secret... even from Xavier himself. Marmaduke insisted he was not to know where or who his parents were until the time was right."

The time... What time *was* it? Did it matter?

"For the next eighteen and a half years, Xavier and I lived and worked together above the Windy Sailor. Each month I received financial support from Marmaduke, and, to my delight, the boy was bright and had a natural aptitude for finding medicinal qualities in the natural world. He went from being my assistant to my protégé, then to my equal, and by the time he was sixteen, he had surpassed me in ability."

Suddenly, Sid began to feel weighed down, pulled towards his body. His carefree weightlessness was replaced by a repressive, heavy sensation. Doctor Manky sounded less ethereal, more... connected.

"Then, eighteen months ago, I thought the moment had finally come. Marmaduke sent me a letter, asking me to bring Xavier to Blessed Whipping, where he would meet us and escort us to Lower Icing to be reunited with Lucinda. Xavier was now twenty years old, with no knowledge of who his parents were... a secret I'd continued to keep from him at Marmaduke's request.

"Tragically, Lucinda died before we reached Blessed Whipping. However, I assumed Marmaduke still wished to be reunited with Xavier. In fact, I thought his desire would be even greater. Instead, he distanced himself, virtually ceasing communication between us — just a missive to the Elders of Blessed Whipping to take us in and look after us. Bertrand was assigned to us as a personal servant and protector."

Bertrand? Protector? For some reason that amused Sid. He wanted to laugh, but he couldn't. The air was becoming thick, pressing him down towards himself.

"Since then, the only acknowledgement of our existence has been in the form of a purse of gold coin delivered by coach each month. And so it has continued for the last eighteen months. My letters have gone unanswered, my arguments for a reunion seemingly ignored."

Doctor Manky sighed and relaxed back into the chair. Sid wasn't relaxed;

his head was aching and he was beginning to feel restrained…rigid.

"Perhaps I should have stopped, accepted the inevitable, but I persisted… even as recently as three weeks ago I sent a letter, espousing the benefits of a reunion."

The man in white shook his head. Sid felt like shaking his, but it wouldn't move.

"Fate, I regret to say, finally intervened. Xavier discovered the letter's contents: things that a twenty-two-year-old man should not find out by chance."

Sid was struggling to remain separated from his body. The Sid on the chair, however, betrayed no sign of any inner turmoil.

"It was the day after Forging Day — the summer solstice celebration two weeks ago — that I awoke to find him gone. My first thought was that he'd been kidnapped, but there was no ransom, and he'd taken his clothes, some equipment, and his copy of my book of potions. Then, three days later, the Sunwatcher presented me with a letter that finally shed light on his disappearance."

Sunwatcher?

"Twenty years of secrecy undone."

Sid was suddenly and violently sucked back into his body. Doctor Manky peered at him, looking straight into his eyes.

"The Rigour Morphis is beginning to wear off. Just relax, Sid. Try not to fight it." Then he pulled out the vial of Vigour Morphis. "This will remove your paralysis, but, as I said, the sensation is rather unpleasant. Still, needs must I'm afraid."

As the acrid liquid flowed down his throat, Sid's head began to burn, his vision seared and his eyes started twitching. He felt as if he were surrounded by a thick fog, cloying and suffocating. He inhaled as hard as he could, and suddenly he was gasping, then he was breathing; he could *feel* his tongue — it was dry and awfully bitter. The rest of his face tingled into feeling, like it was being pricked by a thousand small needles. His eye's fluttered open. Doctor Manky's pink eyes bored into his head; his bloodless gaze looked grave.

PART 2

XAVIER

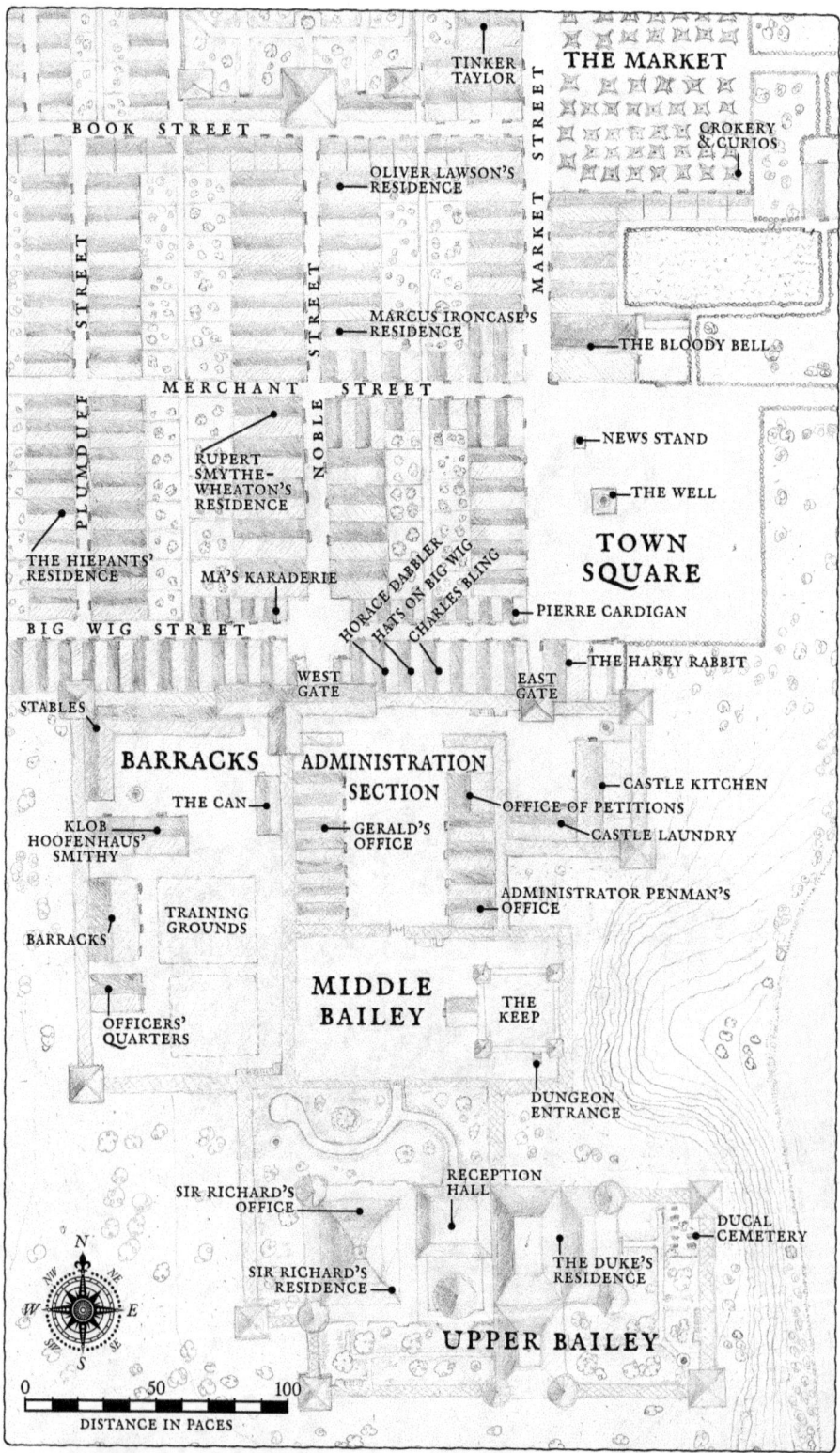

THE MARKET

TINKER
TAYLOR

BOOK STREET

CROKERY
& CURIOS

OLIVER LAWSON'S
RESIDENCE

MARKET STREET

PLUMDUEF STREET

NOBLE STREET

MARCUS IRONCASE'S
RESIDENCE

MERCHANT STREET

THE BLOODY BELL

NEWS STAND

THE WELL

RUPERT
SMYTHE-
WHEATON'S
RESIDENCE

TOWN
SQUARE

THE HIEPANTS'
RESIDENCE

MA'S KARADERIE

HORACE DABBLER
HATS ON BIG WIG
CHARLES BLING

PIERRE CARDIGAN

BIG WIG STREET

THE HAREY RABBIT

WEST
GATE

EAST
GATE

STABLES

BARRACKS

ADMINISTRATION
SECTION

CASTLE KITCHEN

THE CAN

OFFICE OF PETITIONS

KLOB
HOOFENHAUS'
SMITHY

GERALD'S
OFFICE

CASTLE LAUNDRY

BARRACKS

TRAINING
GROUNDS

ADMINISTRATOR PENMAN'S
OFFICE

OFFICERS'
QUARTERS

MIDDLE
BAILEY

THE
KEEP

DUNGEON
ENTRANCE

SIR RICHARD'S
OFFICE

RECEPTION
HALL

DUCAL
CEMETERY

N
NW NE
W E
SW SE
S

SIR RICHARD'S
RESIDENCE

THE DUKE'S
RESIDENCE

UPPER BAILEY

0   50   100

DISTANCE IN PACES

INTRODUCTION

A serious young man

BLESSED WHIPPING WASN'T Xavier's kind of place, but Xavier wasn't the kind of person to complain; he was an adaptor, and for almost seventeen months now he'd been adapting to the odd formality of life in this strange village. He couldn't quite fathom why Horatio had moved here. He and his mentor had been quite content in the port town of Missing Anchor. It was the only home Xavier had known, and, while he hadn't formed any strong personal bonds with anyone there, he did feel somewhat displaced in this landlocked village on top of a hill. And he missed the ocean: the smell of salt in the air and the sound of the waves swashing against the pebbly beach.

Still, from a scientific point of view, Blessed Whipping had quite a lot going for it. There were many species of plants that Xavier had never seen before, and the townsfolk were very enthusiastic about his and Horatio's research.

At just twenty-two, Xavier was a serious young man, devoted entirely to the discovery of new medicines. Being raised by Horatio, it was all he had ever known. In fact, it was at Blessed Whipping that he discovered the amazing properties of what the locals called a Sunflower. The aptly named, bright yellow flower produced an oil that had become the basis of many experiments, one of which had led to the creation of what could possibly be called a rejuvenation potion.

Horatio was very excited about the possibilities, but Xavier was more pragmatic. The experiments were only in their early stages, and the results, so far, had been unstable to say the least. And compared to the discovery Xavier had made on Horatio's laboratory desk, they seemed particularly insignificant…

CHAPTER 1

Pig Dust

Sunday, June 15: Twelve days before Doctor Manky approaches Sid at The Dead Duck. (19 days ago.)

XAVIER WAS ANNOYED with himself. He'd been in such a rush to find the pickled pomegranate seeds before the bubbling mixture turned green that he'd bumped heavily against Horatio's desk. The collision had been quite painful, and as he clutched his bruising kneecap he watched his potion change colour.

"Blast," he muttered to himself as an hour's work went up in green steam. Adding to his frustration was the mess the impact had caused on Horatio's desk. Unlike the one in his study — where everything was immaculate — Horatio's working desk was the epitome of disorder. It was littered with parchments on which were scribed dozens of formulae for his latest experiments. Surrounding the parchments like an eager crowd at a public flogging were glass vials and earthenware jars containing oils and powders derived from an array of flora and fauna. Some of these containers had been knocked over, but, fortunately, none seemed to be broken. However, a lid from one of the jars had been dislodged, and dried pink truffle powder now covered some of the parchments.

As it turned out, it wasn't that difficult to funnel most of the powder back into the jar. The remnants, Xavier blew away into the air with a light puff. He was pleased with the result: most of the Pig Dust was now returned to its jar.

Xavier smiled and was about to blow away the remaining pink granules from the last parchment when he noticed they'd formed into Horatio's immaculate handwriting. The parchment had obviously been underneath a note, one that Horatio had written earlier that day, and his deliberate penmanship had left a perfect impression.

Xavier read the note as a matter of course. He had a clinically inquisitive nature; one born from a lifetime of experimentation. The note would contain information that was useful or not, as the case may be — something either to be acted upon or filed away in his photographic memory to be recalled at some later date. There was, however, nothing in Xavier's nature to prepare him for the contents of this particular note. He felt as though he was being disassembled with every word.

Duke DuMarma of Lower Icing Castle
June 14

Marmaduke,

I trust this correspondence finds you in good health. Blessed Whipping continues to be a most fruitful location, and X continues to make outstanding progress. As I have relayed to you many times, he is a thoughtful, diligent and very intelligent young man who will achieve great things — you would be very proud.

Marmaduke, I realise I have prescribed the following course of action on numerous occasions since arriving at Blessed Whipping, but surely the time has come for you to be reunited with your son. I have no doubt he will help fill the void left by Lucinda's sad passing.

As a friend, I ask you to consider what a boon this could be to both of you. I'm sure you would not regret it. X is your son, and it's been twenty years.

Yours Faithfully,
Horatio

Xavier's head swam in the unfathomable depths of abandonment and deceit. He felt utterly disoriented. He let the note slip from his hands and leant on the edge of the work desk. He'd lived his life nurtured by one man: a man towards whom he felt respect and a keen loyalty. Horatio had been a kind, devoted mentor, and that had more than compensated for the fact that he wasn't his father.

Xavier struggled for reason. All logical thought had dissipated, replaced by something that wasn't a part of his structured existence — certainly since moving to Blessed Whipping — something most people outside this village would recognise as emotion.

The realisation that his whole life had been a lie — the person he was, was not the person he should have been. He should have been the son of Duke Du Marma of Lower Icing (a man he'd only heard of) and his wife Lucinda (the mother he would never know). It was shocking and disorienting. Xavier covered his face with his hands, taking comfort in their warm darkness, keeping the cold reality at bay.

Xavier was upstairs in his well-appointed private quarters some thirty minutes after the momentous discovery. He'd placed the parchment carefully on his desk — the Pig Dust glowed pinkly in the sunlit room, highlighting the message. Rational thought had been quick to reassert itself and he was already formulating a way of meeting his father. It meant saying nothing of his discovery to Horatio; he wasn't sure he could trust him anymore.

His problem, at this point, was how to escape Blessed Whipping undetected. He could not simply sneak out of town. For a start, his only knowledge of Lower Icing was that it lay to the south, was probably a lot bigger than Blessed Whipping, and that it was too far (and perhaps too dangerous) for a journey on foot. This knowledge was based entirely on snippets of conversation he'd overheard from coach drivers who occasionally stopped at the town square to freshen their horses. If he tried to buy passage on a passing coach, he would be noticed. And while his departure wouldn't necessarily be relayed to Horatio immediately, he would only have, at best, a few hours' head start. By Xavier's reckoning, he needed a few days.

He was mulling over this problem when there was a knock at the door. He quickly placed the incriminating parchment in the leather folder he used to keep notes of his latest experiments. Some of the Pig Dust dislodged from its surface, but Xavier wasn't worried about that; a light application of charcoal would easily, and more permanently, bring back Horatio's words.

"Come in," he said.

The door opened and Horatio stood there, dressed, as always, in white. He believed wearing anything dark accentuated his complexion. Xavier didn't have an opinion on the matter; there had been no experiments to compare results.

"Sunhigh is approaching, my boy." Horatio smiled. "I do believe it's hare and carrot pie today."

"I shall see you in the square directly, Horatio. Thank you."

Horatio's brow momentarily furrowed, before returning to its normal, relaxed position. "Very well, Xavier."

The door closed quietly and the sound of Horatio's footsteps diminished as he walked downstairs. Xavier reopened the leather folder, placed the 'invisible' letter underneath all his notes, then closed the folder, making sure he pressed its silver clasp until it clicked into a locked position. Security was something Horatio had entrenched in Xavier from a young age. Information was power, and in the wrong hands could prove disastrous. The key was disguised as a silver pendant. It was secured to a leather cord he wore around his neck at all times.

As he blew away remnants of Pig Dust from the top of his desk, the smell of freshly baked pastry wafted through the window. Xavier realised, with some surprise, that he was famished.

Chapter 2

The Sunwatcher

AS XAVIER WALKED down the stairs, sunlight filtered through the open front door, tingeing the blue-tiled floor of the foyer with a golden, shining glaze. Everything in Blessed Whipping revolved around the sun, both figuratively and literally.

There were three key moments in each day: Sunrise, Sunhigh and Sunfall. These moments coincided with meal times. Not a morsel of the first meal was eaten until the first rays of light appeared over the horizon (which was very easy to see in all directions from Blessed Whipping's hilltop vantage point), the second meal began just as the sun reached its zenith, and the third meal an hour before the top edge of the revered golden orb disappeared below the horizon.

The duty of declaring Sunrise, Sunhigh and Sunfall was given to the Sunwatcher. The Sunwatcher was a person between eighteen and twenty-one years of age who was born on, or close to, the summer solstice (or, as it was known in Blessed Whipping, Forging Day). Needless to say, being the Sunwatcher was a great honour. In fact, it was such an honour that coupling in Blessed Whipping was particularly active around the last two weeks of September. September 21, the autumn equinox, was the most frenetic day of all. (Little wonder it was called Fertility Day.) The result of this mating regime was that most of Blessed Whipping's population celebrated their birthday within two weeks of Forging Day. Sometimes only minutes separated a Sunwatcher from his or her fellow aspirants. The responsibility lasted for twelve months: from June 22 to June 21 the following year. That way, the honour of being Sunwatcher was shared among more Blessed Whippingers. Forging Day was just six days away.

Xavier stepped through the door, out into another bright summer's day. It was quite hot, but not unbearably so — there was a hint of coolness in the light breeze. Days like this had been few and far between at Missing Anchor. It seemed to Xavier that Blessed Whipping was a place of eternal sunshine;

during his sixteen months here, he'd never felt cold. Even the winter had been mild, and although the rain had been regular, the sun always made an appearance between downpours, as if to reassure the town it was still in favour.

Just about everyone in Blessed Whipping wore a shade of blue somewhere about their person. Some wore nothing but blue. Blue was the colour of the sky, the colour that surrounded the sun. Xavier had adopted this custom as a matter of respect, and, in any case, it didn't concern him one way or the other — fashion was not part of his consciousness. Today, Xavier wore a light blue shirt.

People smiled and chatted politely and quietly with one another as they took their places at the various tables that were meticulously arranged around the centre of the town square. Each table displayed a generous amount of food (fruit, vegetables, bread, and what Xavier assumed to be hare and carrot pies).

As Xavier approached the orderly gathering, he was welcomed by the only Blessed Whippinger not wearing a thread of blue. Her name was Beatrice and she was around the same age as Xavier. She had a serene demeanour, but her pale blue eyes belied her playful nature and her straw-colour hair was untamed and free. She wore her simple, loose-fitting robe of pale yellow with unconscious pride. To Xavier, Beatrice was the most alive person he'd ever met. She was quiet and unassuming, yet bright and full of vitality. She was like a butterfly. He'd told her that shortly after he'd met her. It was now a nickname used by some of the younger villagers, and, because it began with the letter B (like the colour of the sky) it was accepted — but not used — by the village Elders.

"It'th good to thee you Thavier," smiled Beatrice, using the indoctrinated lispy speech of Blessed Whipping. S was a sacred letter, reserved entirely for use in the word 'Sun'.

Xavier and Horatio were not expected to spare their S's, but Xavier sometimes found himself unconsciously slipping into the lispy lingo.

"Thank you, Butterfly," replied Xavier.

"You have not partaken of Sunhigh for a few dayth now. It itth not good to thpend tho much time inthide, away from the Sun."

"Horatio and I have been busy, I'm afraid," Xavier replied. "But you are right, we do sometimes become too involved in our work. And it does me good to feel the sun on my face."

"There ith thpace at the Sunwatcher's table if you'd care to thit with me, Thavier."

Being asked to sit next to the Sunwatcher was an honour, particularly to an 'outsider' like Xavier. He'd only been asked once before, and that was on his birthday, just over eight months ago. It had been an unusually cold and mainly overcast autumn day. Xavier had been concerned the Blessed Whippinger's might take it as a sign of the Sun's displeasure, but Beatrice had laughed at the suggestion. Today, the sun looked delighted at her choice.

"Thank you, Butterfly. I would like that." There was gratitude as well as pleasure in Xavier's response. He needed a diversion; he wasn't ready to exchange pleasantries with Horatio.

Beatrice smiled. "It ith almotht Sunhigh. I mutht prepare mythelf for the pronounthement." With that, she drifted off towards the centre of the village square.

Xavier waded through smiles and polite greetings on his way to the Sunwatcher's table. As he sat down, he made eye contact with the only other person not wearing blue: Horatio. The man in white nodded his approval; it was as if he knew something Xavier didn't. But, then again, Horatio often wore that all-knowing expression.

To his left sat Bertrand, who, to the untrained eye, was also dressed in white. According to Bertrand, it was actually the palest shade of blue and could only be worn by the town Elders (of which he was one of six). Up against the pure whiteness of Horatio, Xavier could discern the slight, ice-blue tinge of Bertrand's garb. It did nothing to improve his rather severe appearance, which was why, perhaps, none of the other Elders chose to wear such an extreme shade. But, in an odd way, it suited Bertrand perfectly — he was an extreme sort of individual.

By now, all the villagers had taken their seats. The tables, although separated, formed a circle around the centre of the town square. All the seats faced the spot where Beatrice was standing, where, in six days' time, she would stand for the last time as Sunwatcher.

The villagers were silent as Beatrice, eyes closed, inclined her head towards the midday sun. She raised her arms above her head and extended her arms sunward, her fingers forming an apex. Clasped in the tip of her fingers was a small golden ball: the Sun Orb. For about ten seconds, nothing happened; Beatrice and everyone else were silent and still. Suddenly, the Sun Orb flashed brightly as it captured the moment the sun passed directly overhead.

"Sunhigh," Beatrice announced serenely, then straightened her head, lowered her arms and opened her eyes. Her expression became more animated and natural as she made her pronouncement: "Pleathe partake in the fruit of the Sun."

With that, people began serving themselves and a gentle hum of politely murmured conversation ensued. Beatrice sat down next to Xavier. She looked radiant… as if she really were the sun's chosen one.

She placed the golden ball into a small, leather-bound box. The inside of the box was lined with sky-blue velvet and was completely featureless except for half-sphere impressions in the base and lid. The Sun Orb fitted perfectly.

"May I serve you some food, Butterfly?" Xavier asked politely. The Sunwatcher was only supposed to eat if he or she was offered food by one of the townsfolk. It was part of the honour of being invited to sit with the Sunwatcher.

"Yeth. Thank you, Thavier. Motht grathiouth of you."

Xavier felt warmed by Beatrice; it wasn't what she said so much as the sentiment she conveyed. She had empathy.

Xavier placed one of the freshly baked pies on a ceramic plate and accompanied it with boiled potatoes and green beans. Then he ripped off a piece of bread from a large crusty loaf and handed the ensemble to Beatrice.

Again, her smiled warmed him.

He served himself the same and they began to eat in silence. Xavier gazed at the scene in front him. There were two hundred and seventy-six Blessed Whippingers enjoying Sunhigh on a perfect summer's day. The occasional 'midday meal' he used to have with Horatio at the Windy Sailor, their local tavern at Missing Anchor, seemed very dreary in comparison.

Xavier was now part of a completely communal lifestyle, where people shared just about everything. Every day, before Sunrise, the tables were put in place for the three meals, and every evening, after Sunfall, they were stored away. Xavier used to think it was a waste of time and energy, but like many aspects of life at Blessed Whipping, he'd come to realise it had a certain rhythm, like a beating heart, that kept the community healthy and vital. He also realised that leaving here was going to be harder than he thought.

Beatrice's soft voice broke his reverie. "You look troubled, Thavier."

I am troubled, Butterfly, he thought to himself, still watching the villagers around him. He realised a moment later that he'd actually spoken the words.

Xavier felt the blood of embarrassment rush to his head. He covered his face with his hands and rested his elbows on the table. He took a deep breath and let it out slowly. Then he uncovered his face and looked at Beatrice.

She was waiting for him to speak, a serene angel.

"I have to leave Blessed Whipping."

CHAPTER 3

A beacon to the village

IT WAS MID-MORNING on Forging Day, and Xavier was still in Blessed Whipping. He was relaxed and looking forward to the celebrations. He felt like celebrating. Tonight, after Sunfall, he was leaving. And it was all because of Beatrice. He could hardly believe she'd devised his plan of escape. It was unexpected to say the least.

He had told Beatrice about Horatio's letter while they shared Sunhigh together. (Six days ago, he mused. It seemed liked six weeks.) Predictably, she'd advised talking to Horatio, but Xavier would not be swayed. His course of action, for good or ill, had been decided upon — he would seek an audience with the Duke of Lower Icing, his supposed father.

Later that day, just before Sunfall, Beatrice had approached him while he was collecting water from the stream that trickled down Blessed Whipping's western slope.

"I have been pondering your predicament, Thavier," she said, matter-of-factly, "and I think I may be able to athitht you."

"Athith… um, assist me? In what way, Butterfly?"

"To leave Blethed Whipping undetected."

Xavier looked up at her, the setting sun beaming on her skin, her hair glowing bronze. She was dazzling.

"Bertrand will take you," she continued, as if she didn't really want to speak the words.

And to Xavier, the words made no sense. "Bertrand? He does Horatio's bidding. He would not deceive him."

"Don't be mithlead by Bertrand'th demeanour, Thavier. If I athk him to do thith for me, he will do tho without quethtion. And if I athk him to tell no-one, he will not breathe a word. Of that I am thure."

It had been that simple. Bertrand was taking him to Lower Icing tonight, leaving just after Sunfall, and would say nothing about it to anyone, including

Horatio. He would just be on an errand. No-one asked questions in Blessed Whipping, they always assumed there was a reason.

There's no doubt Xavier would be missed sooner rather than later, but Beatrice had thought of a way to make the sooner a little later. She had informed Horatio that Xavier had offered to help with preparations to the Sun Temple. (The reasoning was simple: Horatio was less likely to notice Xavier was missing if Xavier wasn't standing next to him all day long mixing herbs and combining powders.)

The Sun Temple was a place of meditation and contemplation. Its soothing blue murals depicted the four elements of life: a woman filling her bucket in a river — Water; a man tilling soil — Earth; a woman hanging washing — Wind; and a blacksmith hammering at the forge — Fire. They also represented the Autumn Equinox — Fertility Day; the Winter Solstice — Forming Day; the Spring Equinox — Fielding Day; and, of course, the Summer Solstice — Forging Day.

Occasionally, however, the Sun Temple was used for formal purposes. The most formal of these was 'The Changing of the Sunwatcher', which occurred the day after Forging Day. Beatrice would officially pass on her title during this ceremony. As it happened, it was to be to another girl — Belinda — who was dark-eyed and solemn and, in Xavier's mind, a disappointing replacement to Beatrice (regardless of her birth time).

Although the Sun Temple appeared to be kept in immaculate condition, it obviously wasn't immaculate enough in the eyes of Blessed Whippingers, and so, for the last two days, Xavier had been given tasks that made his research seem like a frivolous hobby.

The pews had to be treated with a resin made by heating pine gum with an alcohol solution distilled from potato peel. It had taken Xavier and a dozen other helpers an entire morning to apply the resin. Still, he had to admit the result was brilliant: the twelve rows gleamed in the temple's golden light. Then the long rug that ran down the central aisle and divided the pews had to be cleaned. It was a painstaking process in which small brushes, dipped in rose-scented water, were gently massaged, inch by inch, into the fibres. Considering the rug was close to seventy feet long, it wasn't a task for the weak-spirited. Not that there were any weak-spirited people in Blessed Whipping; at least, not that Xavier had noticed. In fact, the last two days had been somewhat of a revelation. As much as Xavier thought he and Horatio were dedicated to their research, he'd observed another level of dedication that united this village in purpose, faith and self-belief, creating a warming harmony. He realised, with some regret, that during his time here he'd missed an opportunity to be a part of something more rewarding, perhaps, than just research and experimentation. If he returned, he would certainly readjust his focus.

The rug, like the pews, had turned out brilliantly. The shades of blue glowed and the celestial bodies sparkled. The centre-point was a large golden sun; radiant and beaming, its flaming corona seemed to glow. Even though he hadn't been involved with the rug's cleaning, Xavier shared in the villagers' pride and sense of accomplishment.

While the rug was being cleaned, Xavier had been helping with another painstaking task: cleaning the Sun Temple's glass spire. Sitting atop a six-foot wide, flat, central platform on the otherwise angled slate roof, the spire tapered some fifteen feet to a golden ball about six inches in diameter. The spire was made up of one thousand one hundred and fifty-six individual diamond-shaped pieces of clear glass, sealed with an opaque resin that dried into a solid yet malleable seal. It was a curious substance, one that Xavier had never before seen. It was an outstanding creation, a beacon to the village — it shimmered and sparkled in the sun, dazzling white, rich gold, burning bronze, or even a simmering crimson depending on the time of day.

Working with two villagers, Beth and Brutus, Xavier had spent all of yesterday and half the day before cleaning every piece, inside and out. The inside had been particularly tricky: a special scaffold was erected, but, as they approached the apex of the steeple, manoeuvring became more difficult. The uppermost two or so feet were too confined for even an outstretched hand to reach, so the treated calf skin they used to clean the pieces of glass had to be tied to a wooden pole and used like a small chimney sweep.

The effect, particularly from inside the Sun Temple, was amazing. Light streamed through the spire to the altar directly below. The altar was the focal point of the Sun Temple, for here the Sundisc radiated the diamond-glass light throughout the congregation area. As depicted in the celestial rug that flowed up to the altar, the Sundisc was a brilliant, gold-plated disc with a flaming sun engraved on its surface. Within the sun were numerals aligned to a series of ellipses. These were orbits of the Earth at different times of the year, the numbers signifying the hours of daylight. It was fitted to a metal U-shaped bracket on top of a four-foot high, white marble pedestal. The whole ensemble sat upon a small podium that was draped in blue satin. The Sun Temple was now immaculate in the eyes of every Blessed Whippinger, and ready for tomorrow's 'Changing of the Sunwatcher' ceremony.

Today, however, was Forging Day, and the Sun Temple played no part in the celebrations. Xavier knew Forging Day was the most important day on the Blessed Whipping calendar (having already attended one), but, until now, he hadn't truly appreciated its significance in the hearts and minds of the townsfolk. Working with Beth, Brutus and the other helpers, Xavier had started to see the Blessed Whippingers in a new light. He realised, to his shame, how much he'd chosen to keep himself in the dark, not even considering striking the flint of friendship.

Forging Day... Yes, it was the longest day: a day to be outside, rejoicing under the life-giving sun. And, yes, it was a day of feasting and celebration set around the formality of the Swivelling Sundisc. But, more than that, it was a day of rejoicing in the sun's elemental force and all that it brought to the townsfolk of Blessed Whipping. Not only was the sun the gift of warmth and light, it was also what gave people their inner strength, courage and determination. They were like pieces of iron in a white-hot fire that burned supreme on Forging Day.

The Sunrise meal had finished three or so hours ago, and the normally sedate village square was abuzz with activity as the area was cleared and then prepared for the Sunhigh banquet. Amidst all the activity of cleaning, setting tables, preparing food, and adorning the square with decorations (bunting, pennons and tablecloths of predominantly blue and yellow) stood the calm and concentrating figure of Beatrice. She sat next to the Sundisc, watching it as it captured the mid-morning sun.

Forging Day was the only day the Sundisc was removed from its pride of place in the Sun Temple. The Sundisc, with its purpose-built pedestal, was repositioned in the centre of the square, where Beatrice made her thrice-daily pronouncements. The loosening of two screws in the U-shaped bracket allowed the Sundisc to be rotated and revolved, so that it exactly followed the path of the Forging Day sun, from Sunrise to Sunfall. The Swivelling Sundisc was Beatrice's responsibility. When in the correct position, the Sundisc gleamed. It was a demanding task; the hot Forging Day sun lasted just over sixteen hours, and the Sundisc had to be realigned every few minutes. Beatrice's vigil was made somewhat easier by the constant attention she received from the villagers. Her every need was seen to. However, all she seemed to require was a simple wooden stool and a bucket of fresh water that she occasionally dipped a wooden mug into and drank from.

While Beatrice was focused on the Sundisc, Xavier concentrated his energy on equipping himself for the journey ahead. The trick was to have everything ready without looking like he was packing up to leave. Horatio was very mindful of Xavier's privacy and wouldn't enter his room without permission, but, as that letter proved, major consequences could come from minor oversights. Still, as he regarded his room, Xavier felt he'd achieved his objective: his leather folder (containing his notes and Horatio's letter) was placed neatly on top of his desk (as it usually was); his copy of *Poetry in Potion* lay open next to the folder (as it quite possibly could be); his sixteen jars of essential concentrates, essences and powders, along with twenty-four mainly empty vials, were housed in their purpose-built wooden case, which was now sitting on the floor next to the desk (as it often was), and his clothes were in a trunk at the base of his bed (where they always were). Everything was within easy reach and could be packed into his travelling case (in its usual place under the bed) in moments. The only thing Xavier considered an anomaly was the money he'd taken from Horatio's safe box.

Xavier believed he wouldn't be returning to Blessed Whipping, not for a while at least — either he'd be welcomed by his estranged father or he'd make his own way in the world. It would be a new start either way. The only thing that really mattered to Xavier, the part that he would take with him wherever he went, was his work.

"Sunhigh," Beatrice announced, lowering the golden ball. A sheen of perspiration covered her face and she looked unusually strained and fatigued. Not surprising, Xavier thought; the sun was at its brilliant best today. However, as she opened her eyes and smiled, her expression transformed into one of pure delight. "Pleathe partake in the fruit of the Sun."

The cheering caught Xavier by surprise, even though he was witnessing his second Forging Day. Horatio clapped him on the shoulder. "It is a fine day, Xavier. I feel good things lie ahead."

The bright white of Horatio's clothing was hard to look at in the midday sun and Xavier had to squint at him. Still, it helped disguise his smile when he said, "I couldn't agree with you more, Horatio."

The rest of the day continued with much merriment and without much inhibition (relatively speaking). Xavier mingled, and spoke to Blessed Whippingers he'd hardly noticed before. The Sun Temple experience had provided him with more than just a smokescreen for his planned escaped, it had broken down barriers between him and the villagers; barriers, he realised, that had been created by his own, obsessive behaviour. He was amazed at what his role in the Sun Temple preparations had wrought. People were more open and warmer towards him, and for the first time in his sixteen-month stay, Xavier felt a sense of belonging. It truly was Forging Day. However, his immediate future lay south at Lower Icing: a future of strangers and uncertainty. The irony was not lost on him.

CHAPTER 4

Clopped noisily onto stone

IT WAS AN hour after Sunfall. The black coach was ready and parked outside the Sun Temple. Bertrand waited in the driver's seat, his ice-blue clothing almost glowing in the darkness, radiating resentment. Beatrice stood at the foot of the stairs next to the Sun Temple's entrance, holding the letter he'd asked her to give to Horatio.

"Farewell, Thavier," she said calmly. "I will give your letter to Horathio in three dayth time. He will not know of your whereaboutth before then, you have my promithe."

"Thank you, Butterfly." He didn't know what else to say. It was an awkward moment; a moment where hope briefly flickered in Beatrice's eyes.

"You betht go, Thavier." She sighed, extinguishing the flicker. "I withh you well and hope you find what you theek." Then she kissed him lightly on the cheek.

Embarrassment propelled Xavier towards the coach and he clumsily banged his case into the side of the cab as he fumbled with the door. The sound echoed noisily across the square. Fortunately, Horatio was most definitely asleep, thanks to his exuberant Forging Day celebrations.

"Do you require thome athithtanthe?" There was disdain in Bertrand's voice.

"No. I'm fine, thank you," Xavier replied. He'd always been somewhat intimidated by Bertrand, even with Horatio present. He now felt totally exposed and wasn't at all confident the ice-man would do Beatrice's bidding. Still, he was set on his path, and Bertrand's demeanour would not be a stone on which he'd stumble.

He clambered into the cab. Beatrice stood in the same position as before, quietly accepting. Looking up at the surly coachman, she said, "Thank you for doing thith for me, Bertrand. Thavier ith in good handth, of that I'm thure."

It sounded more like an order than a compliment.

Her gaze falling back to Xavier, she smiled reassuringly. Almost soundlessly, and in an impossibly smooth motion, the coach began moving.

It wasn't the feel of cobblestone streets that alerted Xavier to the coach's arrival in Lower Icing, it was the sound. Xavier had been awake for the entire journey, nervous anticipation driving him on. It was the same sort of feeling he and Horatio shared after a breakthrough in one of their experiments, adrenalin compelling them to keep going.

The journey had been dark and monotonous. The movement of the coach had been more of a curiosity to Xavier: how it was that the ride was so forgiving. Xavier had never been on a road that didn't have ruts, bumps and holes, and he doubted the road to Lower Icing was any different, yet the wheels seemed to absorb every inconsistency.

But such idle musings were discarded the moment the horses' hooves clopped noisily onto stone. Xavier looked out of the cab window. He could just make out the shapes of buildings against the inky gloom.

The coach slowed, the hooves echoing out a walking pace. Xavier leant out of the cab to see what lay ahead. The first signs of life — a light from an upstairs window — flickered wearily onto the street. But that seemed to be the extent of it.

It was warm — much too warm for Xavier's liking. He could feel the heat radiating from the buildings and wondered how hot it was during the day. He leant further out of the window and craned his neck, but all he could make out were more shadowy shapes. Then a raised voice shot through the darkness. It was a woman's. "What time you call this, then? Wakin' us up in the small 'ours with y'bleedin' 'orse. Ain't you got no respect?"

Xavier said nothing, nor did Bertrand. He slumped back into the cab. The horses' clopping suddenly sounded a lot louder, echoing throughout the town, disturbing the peace. The stern tone of the complainant's voice was a harsh reminder to Xavier that he was in a completely foreign place; it had been over a year since he'd heard a raised voice, let alone one raised in anger — not since his time in Missing Anchor. He sighed. The serenity of Blessed Whipping, and the contentment of its people, was another thing he'd taken for granted.

Bertrand steered the coach up a wide thoroughfare that sloped slightly upwards. As they clattered on, buildings of all shapes and sizes loomed ominously, and Xavier saw his first Lower Icingers — shadows walking in the opposite direction to the coach. He leant out of the window, but they merged into the inkiness.

About one hundred paces ahead, he could see the flames of four ensconced torches, two above and one either side of a closed portcullis.

Before Xavier could make out any further details, Bertrand steered the coach left. It was all very disorientating. Moments later, they came to a gloomy halt. Bertrand flashed into view from the driver's seat and opened the cab door. "Thith ith your dethtinathion."

Although Bertrand seemed his usual composed self, Xavier detected an underlying restlessness, a slight edginess in his demeanour, and he wasted no time collecting his travelling case and alighting from the cab. Immediately, the door was snapped shut and Bertrand sprang back up to the driver's seat.

Xavier regarded the ghost-like figure. Was this it? Was he going to be abandoned in a dark street of an unknown town to fend for himself?

In answer to his silent question, Bertrand extended his left arm and pointed to a building. Xavier turned. Some ten paces away, he could see the dimly illuminated sign of an inn. He couldn't make out much detail, but it looked to have a red bell painted on it.

"Mention my name," said Bertrand. Then he was off, sitting atop the smooth-running black coach. He looked as if he were floating: a terrifying spectre, patrolling the streets of Lower Icing in the early hours of the morning. No wonder people had slunk past the coach.

As Bertrand disappeared into the darkness, Xavier realised there weren't any buildings opposite the inn, no vague silhouettes of structure, just shapeless night concealing the unknown.

For the first time in his life, Xavier felt totally alone, and his burden seemed heavier than just the contents of his travelling case. As he carried it awkwardly towards the inn, his sense of dread grew.

The inn was a corner building and, as he approached its foreboding façade, he made out the words 'Bloody Bell' on the sign (also painted in red) under the bell. The place seemed deserted. The windows were boarded from the inside and not even a hint of light came from within. The inn was black and dead, except for the eerie glow of the ominous sign. The red bell rang out a warning inside Xavier's head, but the surrounding darkness and deserted streets left him no choice. Heart pounding, he moved slowly towards the entrance. His leather-soled boots seemed louder than the horse's hooves, echoing off walls to unknown ears that could be just a lunge away. As Xavier reached for the door, it burst open, and a large man wielding a club knocked him to the ground.

CHAPTER 5

Bar and Bertie

STANDING JUST INSIDE the threshold of The Bloody Bell, features dimly lit by candlelight, the man looked angry. Then he looked confused. Then he looked apologetic. All the while, Xavier must have looked terrified; he certainly felt like his heart was about to burst from his chest.

Turning his head slightly to the right, the man spoke to someone inside, "It's alright, love. False alarm."

He put down the club and extended his arm towards Xavier. "Sorry 'bout that, squire. Been havin' a bit o' trouble with a couple o' lads who have lost tha' lovin' feelin' at home, if you catch my meanin'."

Xavier *didn't* catch his meaning, but took the man's outstretched hand nonetheless and was effortlessly brought to his feet.

"Rather stay 'ere an' cause trouble," he continued. "Thought I'd put an end to it, once an' for all."

Xavier glanced down at the club leaning against the door frame. The man smiled. "Relax, squire, nothing murderous — jus' give 'em somethin' to think abou', eh?" He let out a short chortle and clapped Xavier firmly on the shoulder.

Xavier's head was spinning. He literally felt giddy with relief. He found it hard to speak; not that the man was giving him an opportunity to do so.

"M' name's Bartholomew Swill, but only the wife gets to call me that. You c'n call me Bar, the same as what other mere mortals call me."

Xavier smiled awkwardly, then nervously mumbled, "My name is Xavier, and I was… dropped here by Bertrand." It sounded more like a question; he had no confidence in mentioning the name.

"Lucky you, Xavier," replied Bar, sarcastically. "Then you'd be on business I best not know about. Particu'ly since y'been dropped here at *this* hour."

Xavier could only register mute surprise at Bar's acknowledgement of Bertrand. And what did he mean by business he'd best not know about? Xavier decided to clear the air immediately, but a voice from close behind Bar didn't give him the chance. "Who you gasbaggin' to, Bartholomew?"

The large frame of Bartholomew stepped aside and a solid woman in her forties pushed herself into view. "Well, well… what do we 'ave 'ere?" she enquired cheerfully.

"This is Xavier: a package from Bertrand." Bar grimaced.

His wife's cheer disappeared. "Oh…"

It was only a momentary lapse, then her hospitality face quickly returned. "Well, best bring yourself inside then, Master Xavier. Looks like y'could use some nourishment," she said warmly. "An' don't you worry 'bout Bartholomew 'ere. 'Is big club is all show an' no clobber."

This last remark was accompanied by a smile and a wink. Xavier had no idea how to react. Was the woman moonstruck? Bar may not have *hit* him with his club, but the *nudge* had been enough to knock him to the ground.

"Enough of tha', Bertie," Bar admonished with good cheer. "You're embarrassing the poor lad." Then to Xavier, "Pay 'er no mind, Master Xavier. She just can't resist a 'andsome face."

Xavier suddenly felt self-conscious, and bent down to retrieve his case.

"Why she married me, o' course."

"Hah!" She slapped her husband playfully on the chest. "I'll go 'eat up some broth. You take Master Xavier up to one of The Square rooms." Then, as an afterthought, she asked, "You *are* stayin' with us, ain't ya, Master Xavier?"

Xavier nodded mutely. Did he have any choice?

The interior of The Bloody Bell looked much the same as The Missing Anchor, except it was twice the size and, in the weak candlelight, seemed a lot gloomier. Bertie had picked up the club and was meandering her way through an array of wooden tables towards the bar. Xavier was following Bar past a row of shadowy booths to an even more shadowy staircase. From the little Xavier could make out, the inn was very clean and orderly, and that made him feel a bit better. Despite first impressions, Bar and Bertie obviously had some sense of pride in themselves.

"You right with that case, Master Xavier?" enquired Bar as they reached the foot of the staircase.

The case wasn't heavy, just a bit awkward, and Xavier wasn't prepared to trust its fragile contents to anyone as heavy-handed as Bar. He was already worried he might have broken some vials as a result of Bar's club-wielding welcome.

"I'm fine, thank you," replied Xavier quietly. He was aware there could be other guests at the inn and, if that was the case, he didn't want to be responsible for waking any of them.

They ascended into darkness, and Bar's heavy footsteps, creaking up the wooden stairs, were the only clue as to what lay ahead. After some twenty steps, Bar halted. Xavier could just make out the outline of the burly innkeeper waiting for him.

As Xavier reached the top of the staircase, Bar moved off to his right. A faint light emanated from a central corridor. Bar turned left down the corridor, momentarily disappearing from view. As Xavier rounded the corner, Bar was already unlocking the first of three doors on the right-hand side. A single candle halfway down the corridor provided light to navigate by.

Opening the door, Bar indicated Xavier should enter. "You 'ave a room with a view, Master Xavier. Well, least ways, you will when it's light."

Xavier moved to the open door and peered in. From the feeble light that flickered into the room, Xavier could just make out a single bed, pushed against the wall to his right, perpendicular to the corridor, next to a window of darkness. On the nearer side of the window was a square object that was probably a desk. Looking back down the corridor, Xavier asked Bar if he could use the corridor candle.

"O' course, Master Xavier," said Bar, moving immediately down the corridor. "Beggin' your pardon, but we don't usually need much light this time o' night."

Xavier flushed with embarrassment, suddenly realising how odd and, no doubt, inconvenient his arrival must be to the innkeeper.

"Yes, of course," Xavier mumbled self-consciously. "I'm very grateful for you taking me in at such an hour."

"It ain't takin' folk in that's a problem, it's gettin' 'em to leave. Come on, lad." The big man smiled, clapping Xavier on the shoulder. "Unburden yourself and let's get some of Bertie's broth into you. Y'look like y'could do with a bit of a pick-me-up, if you don't mind me sayin'."

Xavier moved to the bed and placed his case at its foot, while Bar used the corridor candle to light another small candle on top of what did turn out to be a roughly made desk. Then he moved to the window, which was already open to the night. "That's the Town Square down there, and you also have quite a good view of the castle."

Xavier joined Bar at the window. The area indicated as the Town Square — where Bertrand had melted into — was inky nothingness, but further in the distance, he could just make out a large towered structure, black against a starry black sky. Xavier felt a light, cooling breeze waft against his face; it was a relief, and the most comforting thing he'd experienced since leaving Blessed Whipping.

Bertie's broth was surprisingly good: a kind of beef, potato and herb concoction. However, Xavier wasn't overly hungry; the remnants of the Forging Day feast still held sway over his appetite.

They were sitting, again by the light of one candle, at one of the bar tables. Bar and Bertie had informed him they'd been married for twenty-three years and had a twenty-one-year-old son, who was an officer at the castle, and an eighteen-year-old daughter who worked at The Bell. They lived on the premises, their private quarters accessed by a door underneath the staircase. At the moment he was the only guest — which was a relief — and room and breakfast cost a silver piece per night. It seemed reasonable to Xavier. He wore a money pouch under his shirt which contained almost eight gold pieces (equivalent to eighty silver or eight hundred copper) in a mixture of gold, silver and copper coins. He'd handed over three silvers, even though he wasn't sure whether he'd be staying at The Bell for three nights. He intended to see his father tomorrow... actually, later today, he corrected himself, and the Duke may well insist he stay at the castle, in which case he would have overpaid Bar and Bertie. However, he could afford to be generous, and he felt they deserved something for the inconvenience of his early-morning arrival.

By the time Xavier had finished his broth, he felt a lot more relaxed about his situation and, apart from the unevenness of the bench he was sitting on, there was only one thing that was nagging at him: Bar's off-hand comment about Bertrand when Xavier had mentioned his name.

Bertie looked pleased at Xavier's enjoyment of her broth, and Bar was happy to have received payment in advance, but both expressions changed dramatically at the mention of Bertrand's name. They shared a moment of concern and then looked warily at Xavier.

"I'm sorry," said Xavier self-consciously, "it's just that you seem to know him. Even after sixteen months living in the same closed community, at a place called Blessed Whipping, I know little about his character. It is obvious that you both dislike and distrust him."

Bar and Bertie gazed at him, the dim light making their features seem more severe. It was Bar who spoke. "What business brings you out at this hour, Master Xavier, if you don't mind me askin'?"

"I had to leave Blessed Whipping on a personal matter. And my departure had to remain unnoticed by a certain individual, at least for a few days. Tonight was my best opportunity, and Bertrand begrudgingly agreed to take me at the request of the…" Xavier was going to say Sunwatcher, but that would mean nothing to anyone outside Blessed Whipping. "At the request of the wise woman."

"Must have some power then, this wise woman? To be givin' orders to a man like Bertrand. Never struck me as the type to take orders from a woman, wise or not."

Bertie nudged Bar with her elbow and gave him a stern look. Bar's expression became more relaxed. He squeezed her arm affectionately. "Well, Master Xavier, as I said before, things to do with Bertrand are best left alone." Then, looking directly at Xavier, he added, "I'll not trouble you about your business with him if you'll not trouble us about ours."

Bertie nodded in agreement. "So, if you'll excuse us, Master Xavier, it's high time we got ourselves to bed." She treated Xavier to another embarrassing wink. "Today's a big day at The Bell, being a Sunday an' all."

Chapter 6

A massive wake of people

XAVIER HAD NO idea what time it was, but it was light. It was also hot and noisy, and it took him a moment to realise where he was. He stretched out of bed and looked out the window. Down below, the Town Square was dotted with people going about their business. Pedlars trumpeted their wares, a group of well-dressed gentleman were holding an animated conversation, a couple of men-at-arms patrolled, young men moved with purpose as they pulled their cart-load of goods, a few people just seemed to be ambling, and, at the centre, about a dozen people were holding buckets, waiting for their turn at the well. Compared to life at Blessed Whipping, it was a chaotic scene.

The Square looked to be almost a hundred paces across, bounded on three sides by buildings. To Xavier's left (east, judging by the position of the mid-morning sun), The Square opened out to cultivated land, bounded by a river, and a large, forested area in the distance. A road stretched across the flat terrain, angling north-east, its progress blocked by The Bloody Bell.

Straight ahead of Xavier, south of The Square, was the castle. It was imposing; the elevated Keep and its four watchtowers looked over the village with impassive greyness. The pennons atop each watchtower were hanging limply on their poles, like they were bored with the view. The Keep was surrounded by a great stone wall with solid, square towers at each corner — at least, Xavier assumed it was surrounded by a wall and cornered by towers; he could only see the northern aspect of the castle, and much of the wall was obscured by streets of buildings. Still, from what he could see, it was impressive. He felt nervous and excited by the possibilities it presented.

He moved away from the window and checked that his travelling case was still at the foot of the bed. It was, and so were its contents. It was a sturdy, hard-leather construction, and Xavier had packed it in such a way that his clothes formed a buffer around his wooden case of vials. Consequently, last night's welcome had caused no real damage except for a superficial scuff mark on the travelling case's exterior. He was also relieved to find that his copy of *Poetry in Potion* and locked leather folder were still secreted within the false bottom of the case. Subconsciously, he touched the reassuring shape of his silver pendant, even though he could feel it was there.

Xavier pulled out some lighter clothing — the morning sun was already making its presence felt — and wondered what he should do about washing and shaving. He wasn't a vain person, but he was meticulous about personal hygiene; being raised by Horatio, his whole life had revolved around remedies for maladies and ailments, many of which were caused by people's disregard for cleanliness. As there was no basin in Xavier's room, he decided to have breakfast first and ask one of the Swills.

He quickly dressed and moved to the door. The room key was still securely in its lock. He turned it and opened the door, and was pleasantly surprised to discover a pail of water, some soap and a small towel placed just outside his room.

Fifteen minutes later, Xavier sat in the bar room of The Bloody Bell feeling much cleaner and more refreshed after his wash and shave. It was already quite busy and noisy; patrons were filling the tables and booths. None of them seemed able to have a quiet conversation, and, judging by the disproportionate amount of laughter, there must be plenty of funny goings-on in Lower Icing. It was also exceedingly light, particularly when compared to the one-candlelight gloom of his arrival. The boards had been removed from the eight windows. Bright sunlight streamed in through the four that faced the Town Square to the south, while the four that faced west looked out onto a shaded street.

Xavier was amazed by the amount of activity happening outside the windows. People streamed past on both sides of The Bloody Bell — it was like the corner of the inn was the prow of a ship under full sail, creating a massive wake of people.

"Sunday's the main market day, Master Xavier. Plenty of things to int'rest a young lad like yourself, if you catch my drift." The voice (and the wink) belonged to Bertie Swill. "It's jus' down Market Street," she continued, nodding in the direction of the west windows. "Jus' a stone's throw away."

"Thank you, Bertie," Xavier replied. He didn't really know how else he should respond. He *hadn't* 'caught her drift', but it didn't matter as Bertie's mouth sailed on regardless.

"You must be well hungry; it's almos' ten o'clock. Must've slept like a baby.

'Ope everythin's to your likin', Master Xavier. We like to treat our guests prop'ly, 'specially when Bertrand—" She stopped herself, then continued as if the 'B' word hadn't slipped out. "Well, anyway, Master Xavier, I'm sure you don' want me chatterin' away like a fishwife. I best be 'bout my business; the patrons can't serve themselves now, can they. You'll have a hearty meal on your table in no time smart."

She gave Xavier a nervous smile and then made her way back to the servery via a few tables where she collected prepared meals.

Before Xavier had finished eating, the table had been invaded by four other patrons, all of whom had spent the morning pulling cart-loads of produce from the fields to the market. They were now determined to invest their hard-earned coin at The Bloody Bell. Like most of the clientele, these young men were loud talkers and loud laughers, but they'd saved their loudest laugh for Xavier after he'd asked them whether they thought he would be able to make an appointment to see the Duke today. None of them deigned to explain why it was so funny, so Xavier had said nothing more while he consumed his breakfast. For their part, the young men did a good job of making him feel unwanted, like a plate of scraps that had yet to be removed.

It wasn't only the young men making Xavier feel uncomfortable, so was the heated stuffiness of the room. Tobacco smoke and enthusiastic flatulence added to the close atmosphere (and, in the case of the flatulence, the hilarity). Given the way he felt right now, this morning's wash might as well have been a week ago. So, it was with some relief that he stood up and bade the four men good day.

"Give me regards to the Duke," one of them taunted. Two of them laughed, while the fourth added, with a mock-noble accent, "Yes, tell him we will be ahround for scones an' tea this harfternoon." They all fell about with laughter.

Xavier made his way through the crowd and left The Bloody Bell. The heat hit him immediately, radiating off the cobblestones and stone walls. The sun felt far more intense at Lower Icing, and he wondered how any Sunwatcher would possibly cope with it. At least the air was clear, and filled with the more agreeable sounds of people going about their business.

He took the direct route across The Square, past the well, heading up the gentle gradient towards the castle. As the castle wall loomed closer (and taller), Xavier realised, with some surprise, he hadn't formulated a logical course of action; he was just following his instinct.

When he reached the other side of The Square, he realised people were funnelling down a short street that led towards the castle. Most of them carried baskets of food or hauled their goods on carts. Two men struggled with a recently butchered sheep as it dangled from the wooden pole spanning between them, rubbing heavily on their shoulders. Xavier had already worked up a sweat simply by strolling for a couple of minutes, and he could only imagine how unbearably hot those two must feel.

As he moved into the street, he passed another inn called The Harey Rabbit. (Its sign was rather comical: a smiling rabbit with big ears holding a tankard of ale.) It certainly looked much nicer than The Bloody Bell, and its patrons more refined. It was amazing what difference a hundred or so paces could make; perhaps being close to the castle was more desirable, or maybe it was a safety consideration. Looking ahead, an open gate and raised portcullis allowed for a steady flow of people to and from the castle. A guard stood either side of the gate and, as he approached, Xavier noticed their posture and expression portrayed casual disinterest rather than alertness.

Quickening his pace, Xavier merged into the flow heading towards the arched gateway. Just as he was about to cross the threshold, he was seized by the shoulder and pulled roughly to his left. He stumbled awkwardly, and would have lost his footing had the grip on his shoulder not been so strong.

"An' just where d'ya think you're goin', sunshine?" The voice was authoritative, but the sweating face of stubble it came from was bemused rather than stern.

Xavier wanted to speak, but was struggling to breathe — heat and shock manifested themselves in a series of gasping noises. The guard smiled knowingly at his partner, then addressed Xavier again. "Take your time, lad. You want to make sure your answer rings true, 'cause I got a partic'ly good ear when it comes to rings."

Even if Xavier had been contemplating some sort of escape, it would have been in vain, as the guard's grip on his left shoulder was vice-like.

"I wish to enquire about seeing the Duke," Xavier eventually replied.

"Do you now?"

The guard turned his gaze away from Xavier and smiled at his fellow man-at-arms who was looking on, across the parade of people, with a similarly bemused expression. "Says 'e wants to see the Duke," he shouted. The other man smiled knowingly.

Eyes back on Xavier, the guard continued his pleasant-mannered interrogation at a volume loud enough for his partner to hear. "An' who, if I may be so bold, were you goin' to make this enquiry to? A vegetable peeler? A scullery maid? An oven stoker? Or were you 'opin' Mr Puffy 'imself would stop overseein' the kitchen an' escort you d'rectly to the Duke?"

His expression was sweet… in a rotting fruit kind of way.

"I'm sorry," Xavier panted. "I've obviously made a mistake. This is my first morning in Lower Icing. I was simply following the flow of people to what I thought was the castle entrance. Please…"

The guard eyed him, all sweetness gone, replaced by a boring gaze that Xavier found hard to return. Then the grip on his shoulder slackened and so did the expression on the guard's face.

"Thank you," he exhaled, not worried about hiding his relief.

The guard began to chuckle. So did his partner. It was now obvious to Xavier that he was the butt of some sort of joke. Embarrassment flowed like sweat from every pore, and the physical pain of his shoulder and the energy-sapping heat left him feeling totally miserable. What was he doing here? These people were all strangers, with uncouth manners and undisciplined ways; this is not where he belonged. What madness had brought him here?

A mocking voice answered. "Enquiries 'bout seein' the Duke can be made at the West Gate, 'undred paces that way," said the guard, thumbing vaguely to his left. "Now, be on your way, 'fore I decide to see if Mr Puffy could use another 'and in the kitchen. Reckon you'd be perfec' f'makin' jelly."

If the walk away from the laughing guards hadn't been slightly downhill, Xavier felt sure he wouldn't have had the energy or desire to continue. Turning left at the first street, in a westerly direction (away from The Town Square), he found some comfort in its relative quietness — there were no goods being carted or hauled and no people rushing by. A smattering of well-dressed Lower Icingers were strolling, or looking in the windows of numerous shops that fronted the street. Amongst the well-presented line-up was a tobacconist, a tailor (with some doublets at half price), a milliner, and shops with an array of colourful earthenware, exotic fabrics and local leather products. Also among the shops was Charles Bling, Jeweller by appointment to the Duke, and, most interestingly of all, an apothecary run by a doctor with the curious surname of Dabbler. It didn't fill Xavier with much confidence; not that that was saying much. Both he and Horatio found 'modern medicine' to be almost archaic in its diagnosis and remedy. The steadfast adherence to the four humours — blood, yellow bile, black bile and phlegm — was a fundamental, and quite often fatal, mistake.

Still, Xavier was not in Lower Icing to enlighten the medical profession. His immediate aim lay around the next corner and through the West Gate of the castle.

CHAPTER 7

Administrator Penman

ADMITTANCE INTO THE castle was surprisingly straightforward. The guards directed him, without any fuss, to the Office of Petitions, housed within the Administration Section of the castle's Lower Bailey.

As he walked towards the office, Xavier was amazed by the sheer enormity of the castle, and the amount of work that must have gone into its construction. The outer stone wall, alone, was twelve feet thick and at least forty feet high, reinforced by square towers at each corner and a large gatehouse at the West Gate (which was obviously the main entrance).

On arrival at the Office of Petitions, Xavier was asked his name, place of residence and the nature of his petition by a small, balding man in his fifties who identified himself as *the* petitions clerk. They were all simple questions, but he still found them difficult to answer — the only name he could give was Xavier, he no longer had a place of residence, so he said The Bloody Bell, and, as for his petition, he informed the clerk that it was a delicate matter for the Duke's ears only. The clerk had written everything down without fuss or comment (apart from a raised eyebrow at the mention of the Duke) and asked Xavier to wait in the antechamber to his left.

The room was about twenty-foot square, with a door in the opposite wall and a number of benches set in rows filling up most of the space. Half the bench space was occupied by people — fellow petitioners, Xavier assumed — whose whispered grumblings echoed throughout the room. Heads turned and all conversation ceased when Xavier made his appearance.

Around two dozen pairs of eyes stared at him as if he was the cause of all their troubles. He smiled self-consciously and quickly sat down on the closest bench. They were a motley collection of people, mainly consisting of middle-aged men, although there was one young family of five who seemed almost as out of place as Xavier. Their scrutiny soon waned and they all returned to their conversations. Most of them seemed to be quite well acquainted. Some listened sympathetically to grievances, while others were at odds with each other.

After fifteen minutes of trying to avoid eye-contact with anyone (in particular, the little girl in the family, who kept pulling faces at him), the door opened and a man dressed in dull grey announced in an equally dull voice, "Richard Pickwick and Archibald Mason."

Two middle-aged grumblers stood up and walked towards the door.

"Now we'll see who has the right of it," stated the leading complainant.

"You've got rocks in your head, Mason!"

"Shut up, wick prick!"

As the door closed behind them, their bickering was replaced by amused chuckles and general support for Mason. Xavier had to sit through ten such announcements before his name was called, some three hours later.

The man in grey, who had identified himself as Administrator Penman, was sitting at his desk, fingering through a neat pile of documents. Xavier gazed around the room. The walls looked as if they were constructed of wooden shelves and rolled-up parchments. The only sign of stonework was a patch of wall above the door and six inches either side of a bow-slit (which was casting a strip of early-afternoon sunlight fifteen feet across the centre of the room to the foot of the door). Although relatively cool, the room was stuffy, and a trickle of sweat tickled its way down Xavier's back.

"Ah… here we are… Master Xavier… let me see now…" Administrator Penman's mutterings became quiet lip movements as he read the petition clerk's report. His bespectacled eyes ran right to left a few times before he laid the report down, removed his glasses, rubbed his eyes, replaced his glasses and looked wearily at Xavier.

"Master Xavier," he sighed. "What, may I ask, are you doing here, apart from wasting my time, and yours for that matter? This," he said, tapping the report, "is not a petition. It is a request to see the Duke. I deal in petitions, Master Xavier — or complaints, if you like. Look around you." He indicated vaguely to Xavier's right. "Over ten years' worth of complaints, ranging from chicken ownership to bridge-building rights, all given due diligence by the Office of Petitions, and not *one* of them, Master Xavier, contains a request to see the Duke on a personal matter."

Xavier was used to frustration; most of his life had been frustration, researching the medicinal properties of thousands of plants, experimenting with their virtually limitless combinations, and finding nothing of consequence ninety-nine times out of a hundred. It had hardened Xavier against disappointment and taught him that perseverance had its rewards. Judging by the expression on Administrator Penman's face, it was time to persevere.

"I am sorry to have wasted your time, Administrator Penman. I was unaware of the petition protocol, having only arrived in Lower Icing in the early hours of this morning. However, the reason for my being here remains: there is a matter of high importance I wish to discuss with the Duke."

"Master Xavier, you're obviously a well-educated young man," said Administrator Penman, making a strained effort to look and sound sympathetic. "Surely you must realise you can't just arrange an audience with the Duke, no matter how important you may think it is."

"Of course," Xavier agreed.

The Administrator nodded and smiled. "Well, thank you for being so reasonable. It's not something that happens very often in the Office of Petitions." He began to rise from his chair.

"So," Xavier said calmly, "how *do* I arrange an audience with the Duke?"

Deflating back into his chair, Penman sighed wearily. "Master Xavier, *you* don't arrange anything. If the Duke wants an audience with you, *he* will arrange it."

It was a logically unsound point, and Xavier was a stickler for logic. "How will the Duke know that he wants an audience with me if I don't have an audience with him?"

It was clear the Administrator's patience was wearing thin. "The plain truth is that the Duke will *not* see you. The only way it *may* be possible is if you have a connection to someone important in the castle, someone who has the Duke's ear. Now, if you'll excuse me, there are other—"

"And who has The Duke's ear?" Xavier persisted.

"No-one who will give *you* the time of day," retorted the Administrator. "I'm sorry to be so blunt, but that's just the way it is I'm afraid."

Xavier knew he was not going to get anywhere trying to argue against someone who worked to procedures and protocol. He decided on a more open approach. "Administrator Penman, if I may take up a little more of your valuable time, I will endeavour to explain my situation in a clearer manner."

"Very well," he said, slumping further into his chair.

"For a start, I *do* know someone who has the Duke's ear, but he doesn't live in Lower Icing."

"I see." Administer Penman's left eyebrow arched above his spectacles and his posture straightened slightly. "And who might that be?"

"He is a doctor," said Xavier simply. "He raised me from infancy and taught me all I now know about medicine. I believe he is a close confidante and friend to the Duke, as he was to the late Duchess."

Administrator Penman sat upright, his expression dubious. "What's this doctor's name?"

"Horatio Manky."

For a moment, the Administrator stared blankly at Xavier, absently rubbing his chin with his right hand, searching his memory. Then he leant forward, rested his arms on the desk, and began to drum his fingers on its oak surface.

"The only doctor I'm aware of who has administered to the Duke is Doctor Albert Whysman. I have never heard of Horatio Manky... although, there is an apothecary in Lower Icing — Horace Dabbler. Could you be confusing the name? There is some vague similarity, I suppose."

"There is no confusion. And, to my knowledge, Horatio hasn't seen the Duke for almost twenty years, so it is quite understandable that you have never heard of him. The Duke has had a good reason for keep—"

"This is all very interesting," Administrator Penman interjected in a disinterested manner, "but, as I said at the beginning of this meeting, I fail to see why you are here, and what you think I can do to help you? If, as you say, this doctor is a close friend of the Duke's, surely *he* could arrange an audience for you?"

"As I was about to say, Administrator Penman, the Duke has a good reason for keeping his association with Horatio a secret. And Horatio would never betray the Duke's confidence."

Xavier paused, his photographic memory picturing the invisible words that had been exposed by the Pig Dust. He sighed. "I was ignorant of all this a week ago. Duke Marmaduke DuMarma of Lower Icing Castle was someone I never thought of. I was content in my research with Horatio. It was all I knew. It was my life. But a chance discovery has changed all that."

Xavier leant forward in his chair. "You see, I've found out that my life has been lie, and I am not who I thought I was. That is why I must see the Duke."

Administrator Penman had listened attentively, but he was now clearly at the end of his patience. "I'm afraid, Master Xavier, you are making less and less sense and I can't afford to give you any—"

"I am the Duke's son!" Xavier shouted, the volume of his voice shocking him just as much as Administrator Penman. He looked at the dumfounded man in grey, and said in a voice just above a whisper, "And I have a document that proves it."

CHAPTER 8

Quiet-ones somewhere quieter

THE SUN HAD set an hour ago, yet its heat remained. Even with the shutters open, Xavier's room was stifling. But it was better than being downstairs with the drunken rabble. A cacophony of voices — shouting, singing, and incessant laughing — permeated through the floorboards of his room and drifted through his window.

What manner of place was this? It wasn't as if he'd never been in an inn before, but not even the old sea-dogs who'd frequented the Windy Sailor were as obnoxious as this flatulent herd of ale-louts. The thought of the Windy Sailor brought a pang of yearning for Missing Anchor, the place he'd been raised, where he'd lived and worked and had felt most at home. The cool, salty air whipping in from the sea used to make his eyes water, and the thought of it almost brought more tears.

It was only because Administrator Penman had reacted so positively towards his revelation and suggested they meet again tomorrow afternoon at five that Xavier felt he could endure another night at The Bloody Bell.

And then, of course, there was the other revelation: one that cast his hosts in a rather different light.

It had been mid-afternoon by the time he'd left the castle. He was just approaching The Bloody Bell when he decided to take Bertie Swill's advice and visit the market. His eyes had finally adjusted to the glaring sunlight, but the heat that radiated from the stone buildings and cobblestones made the walk a rather sole-destroying experience.

If the market hadn't been so close to The Bloody Bell, Xavier wouldn't have bothered at all. It was only his innate curiosity that drove him on against the oppressive conditions. As it turned out, he shouldn't have bothered. Most of the stall-holders had packed up or were in the process of packing up. The only vendors still open for business were those whose wares couldn't rot or spoil.

Xavier's expectations weren't high as he meandered his way through the clamour of voices and stall deconstruction. Why was this town so noisy and chaotic? A few vendors tried half-heartedly to gain his attention with some last-minute bargains, but Xavier only needed his eyes to make a decision, and he'd seen nothing he deemed useful or intriguing.

He was about to give up and return to The Bloody Bell when he spotted a stall of writing paraphernalia: quills, parchment, bottles of ink, blotters, red sticks of sealing wax, and even a selection of paints in small earthenware pots. Xavier needed none of those things. What had caught his eye were the charcoal pencils. He bought six for six copper pieces and then returned to the inn.

As he started up the stairs to his room, away from the swamp life the Swills referred to as patrons, Bar called after him. It was with polite reluctance that he descended back into the mire.

"You look like a man what could be doin' with a cleansin' ale, Master Xavier," shouted Bar from across the bar.

Xavier hesitated, but he realised, with some surprise, that he was parched, and the thought of drinking something cool was very desirable. It was just that the bar of The Bloody Bell wasn't.

As if reading his thoughts, Bar had nodded to the door underneath the staircase. "What say me an' you 'ave a few quiet-ones somewhere quieter, ay?"

The Swill's private quarters were surprisingly neat, and, much to Xavier's relief, surprisingly quiet. He was seated in a comfortable, padded chair with a blue floral pattern that matched the table cloth Xavier and Bar rested their mugs of ale on. Horatio would be delighted by this room; everything seemed to be of high-quality workmanship and, in the case of the two paintings, artistic merit. It was completely at odds with what was happening on the other side of the wall and seemed to reflect nothing of Bar or Bertie's personality. Still, Xavier was content to enjoy the surroundings and slake his thirst.

"So, Master Xavier, how was y'day, if you don' mind me askin'," Bar asked, somewhat awkwardly.

"On the whole, I would say it was satisfactory, thank you."

Judging by the agitated way Bar fidgeted with the handle of his mug, Xavier's response was, on the whole, *less* than satisfactory. The innkeeper drained the mug in three loud gulps, then, almost guiltily, replaced it gently on the tablecloth. "I heard mention that you visited the castle," he said, speaking to his mug, then raised his eyes for Xavier's response.

"That is correct."

"Migh' I be so bold as to enquire the nature of your visit?" The words were pushed out — almost, it seemed, against his will.

Xavier was neither surprised nor affronted by the directness of the question, and had no qualms about being direct in return. "I'm afraid I am unable to divulge that information. As I said, it is a personal matter that has brought me to Lower Icing."

"From Blessed Whipping," he mumbled.

"Yes. Is something the matter, Bar?"

Before he could respond, the door burst open and a young, attractive barmaid flustered into the room. Bar was immediately on his feet. "What is it Bethany?"

"It's the Moleson Twins, Pa!"

"Right," he growled, and strode towards the door. "It's time those two got taught wha' it means t'be barred!"

Remembering the welcome he'd received at The Bloody Bell, Xavier wondered whether there was more club-wielding intent behind the word 'barred'.

The burley innkeeper turned to face Xavier. "Beggin' y'pardon, Master Xavier, I got some unfinished business to attend to." Then he addressed his daughter, "Bethany, love, mind usin' the back stairs t'escort Master Xavier to his room?"

Bethany nodded.

Bar moved towards the door and Xavier stood up to see what trouble these Moleson Twins were causing.

"Be careful, Pa!" Bethany pleaded as he walked into the smoke-filled din.

There was something morbidly fascinating about what was occurring, and Xavier felt a curious urge to bear witness to the unfolding drama. However, Bethany closed the door, and the drama was shut out. "It's best if I do like Pa says, an' escort you up t'your room," she said, respectfully. "Them Moleson Twins don't care what they do, or who they do it to, long as they get what they want."

Xavier regarded the girl; he was about to protest that he might be of some use from a medical point of view, but it was clear Bethany was eager to do her father's bidding — her expression was more of her father's making than her mother's.

Xavier followed Bethany through a doorway on the opposite side of the room and down a well-lit hallway. Her light brown hair was tied with a blue ribbon in a tight plait (like her mother's) and it gently swayed side to side as she hurried ahead; their footsteps were muffled by a plain blue runner that ran the entire length of the hallway. At the halfway mark, they passed a pair of doors that faced each other, and it was there that the truth — in the shape of a golden sun woven into the blue runner — suddenly dawned on him: The Swills were from Blessed Whipping.

He kept following the hypnotic plait as it moved down the hallway and into a stairwell. Bethany was moving quickly, but Xavier's mind was racing. It was all very obvious now that he thought about it: their names all began with B, the decor in the private room was predominantly blue, and the two paintings he'd admired depicted people toiling in fields. The only missing trait was the lisp, but, unless it was a congenital condition, he assumed it was something that would eventually be lost in non-lisping Lower Icing.

Bethany hurried up the stairs, taking two at a time, causing her plait with its sky-blue ribbon to dance wildly. At the top of the staircase, Bethany unlocked a door and ushered Xavier into the corridor that led to his room.

"Third door on your left, Master Xavier; 'ope you don' mind seein' y'self to your room."

With that, she stepped back into the stairwell, shut and re-locked the door, and, judging by the sound of her footsteps, ran back down the stairs. Xavier headed down the corridor; the excited cheers and shouts of a bar room brawl becoming louder with each step. Again, a sense of morbid curiosity infringed upon his common sense, but then the moment passed. He already knew what it was like to be on the receiving end of the club-swinging Bar, and he had no desire to watch people hurt themselves.

Instead, he opened the door to his room. Next to the desk, the pail had been refilled with clean water, and, beside it, a fresh cake of soap lay on top of a folded, clean towel. The neatness of it all bemused him: the person may leave Blessed Whipping, but Blessed Whipping may not leave the person. Kneeling over the pail, he splashed a few handfuls of water over his face. Then dried off with the towel, which, of course, was blue.

Then he checked all his belongings. They were as he'd left them, as he felt sure they would be — if the Swills were still adhering to their Blessed Whipping ways (in private, at least) they'd treat any guest with care and respect. He closed his case, locked the door to his room, and lay on the bed.

Suddenly, Xavier felt very tired. It had been a long day, the heat had drained him, and the refreshing ale he'd shared with Bar had added to his weariness. As he drifted off to sleep, he considered the behaviour of his ex-Blessed Whippinger hosts. It made Bertrand's connection to them more understandable, and he wondered if the Elder had some sort of hold over them... the muffled sounds of shouting and cheering was like a soothing lullaby.

Xavier woke at sunset. (Did the Swills still call it Sunfall, he wondered?) It felt like a thick fog had settled in his head and his shirt was damp with sweat. He felt decidedly uncomfortable: sticky and, judging by his own sense of smell, rather redolent of over-ripe cheese. In the twilight gloom, he removed his shirt and groggily made his way to the pail. The water, warmed in the oven-heat of his room was refreshing nonetheless. After he'd taken some eager gulps, he used the remainder to wash.

Feeling somewhat revived, Xavier sat on the edge of his bed, anonymous in the growing darkness, and watched people walk to and fro, accompanied by the sounds of The Bloody Bell on a Sunday night. He wondered what had happened to Bar and the Moleson Twins, and whether he should disclose his discovery of the Swills' Blessed Whipping past.

CHAPTER 9

No words came out

XAVIER WAS LYING in the darkness of his room. He was feeling hungry and wondered whether he could face going downstairs for a meal. As if on cue, there was a knock at the door.

Xavier unlocked the door and was greeted by Bertie Swill holding a tray of food. *The mind is a wonderful thing*, Xavier mused — the power of thought, if only he could harness it.

"Sorry to interrupt your ev'nin', Master Xavier." She smiled in an uncharacteristically self-conscious way. "But I thought you might be in need o' some nourishment."

The wooden tray contained a bowl of what looked like stew, some slices of bread and a mug of ale. Xavier's mouth began to water.

"Thank you, Bertie," he said, taking the tray from her. "It smells delicious, and you're right: I *am* hungry."

Xavier's response seemed to ignite Bertie's natural, outgoing personality. "Look at you here, sitting in the dark all by yourself," she said, advancing into the room and forcing Xavier to take a few steps back. "Tha's no way for a young man to spend 'is time."

She walked over to the desk and lit the candle. "There. Tha's better. My word, it's warm up here. Sorry 'bout all the kerfuffle s'afternoon; them Moleson Twins been nothin' but trouble since their pa died coupla months back, and Bartholomew couldn' stand for it no more... There you go, young master."

It was with some surprise that Xavier discovered he was holding an empty tray and his dinner had been laid neatly on the table. It seemed odd to him that she could be so matter-of-fact about the events of this afternoon.

"I'll send Bethany up later to collect your plates and bring you some fresh water... My, my, it *is* warm in here."

"Thank you, Bertie," Xavier said politely as she relieved him of the tray. "I take it everything went well with Bar and the Moleson Twins?"

"Oh, right as rain." Bertie beamed. "Bartholomew and a few of our reg'lars overpowered 'em. Then he sent for our boy, Brandon — the one what we tol' you was an officer at the castle? Well, 'e came quick as lightning an' arrested them for breachin' the peace. E's a fine lad, our Brandon."

Brandon, Xavier mused. He'd spent a small part of his people-watching evening pondering the name of the Swill's son, and, finally, without much conviction, had settled on Barak.

"Well, if tha's all, Master Xavier, I'll leave you be, so as you can eat your dinner in peace." By this stage she was backing out of the room.

"It's an odd expression," Xavier said to the retreating figure.

The retreating stopped. "Wha' expression might that be, Master Xavier?"

"Right as rain."

"It's quite common roun' 'ere, an' the 'eavens know we could use some."

"I'm sure it is quite the said thing in Lower Icing, but I've never heard a Blessed Whippinger use it before."

Bertie's mouth was open, but, for the first time since his arrival, no words came out.

Except for the presence of Bethany, there was a sense of déjà vu to the scene: Xavier and the Swills were sitting in the bar room sometime after midnight, windows boarded, the tables and floor cleaned, and the whole place dimly lit by a few candles that could well have melted without any flame. However, *this* late night soirée had been at the request of Bar.

Bar had a swollen, cut lip where one of the Moleson Twins had caught him with 'a glancing blow'. Dabbed over the cut, Xavier was pleased to see some of Horatio's bright yellowy/green Infectus Rejectus ointment (made from a bizarre-looking plant with thick, succulent limbs covered with thorns). He looked grim, and it had nothing to do with his lip.

Bertie had recovered quickly from Xavier's announcement, collected herself and the tray, and hurried downstairs. He'd not seen her again until a few minutes ago. She looked worried (and that had nothing to do with Bar's lip either).

Bethany, as promised, had collected his dinner and brought fresh water and a clean towel. At the time, she seemingly knew nothing about what had passed between Xavier and her mother. However, she had been more forthcoming about her father's condition, and Xavier had been happy to supply her with some of the Infectus Rejectus. He was pleased to see Bar had agreed to the treatment, because Bethany had expressed her doubts. Now she looked concerned.

"Well, it's been a good day for throwin' out the rubbish, that's f'sure," Bar mumbled through his lip. Ironically, it had also given his voice a slight lisp. "And now," he smiled sardonically at Xavier, "it's time to clear the air."

Bertie, who was sitting to Bar's right, gently squeezed his arm and gave him a reassuring smile. Bethany sat across the table from her father and looked withdrawn. Xavier felt very uncomfortable; whatever was in the air, apart from the ale-fuelled humidity, was weighing heavily on the Swills.

"I'm a plain speakin' man, Master Xavier, so I will jus' come ou' an' say what 'as t'be said."

Bar glanced at his wife for further reassurance. She nodded nervously. Xavier wondered what dire statement the innkeeper was about to make; knowing about their Blessed Whipping past couldn't be *that* momentous, surely. It hardly compared to finding out your father and mother had left you to be raised by the local doctor.

"You ain't havin' Bethany. She's stayin' with us! I tol' Bertrand and *now* I'm tellin' *you!*"

The forcefulness of his voice shocked Xavier.

Tears welled in Bethany's eyes.

"Please, Master Xavier," pleaded Bertie, reaching over to comfort her daughter. "Bethany's our only daughter, an' it was all such a long time ago. Surely you can't be so cold hearted."

Xavier was dumbfounded. He looked in disbelief at all of them; had the heat addled their brains? Bar had obviously been hit a lot harder than he thought.

"I have no intention of taking your daughter anywhere."

Bar glared at him, defiantly.

"The thought has never occurred to me, I assure you. I have no idea what you're talking about."

"Lies!" Bar slammed his right fist down on the table.

"Bar! Please!" Bertie interjected.

Ignoring her (and the blood now oozing from his cut lip) Bar leant towards Xavier, and, through clenched teeth, spat, "You'll take Bethany over my dead body! You understan'? An' you can tell that snake, Bertrand, to shove his Deed of Promise where the Forgin' Day Sun don' shine."

No-one had ever spoken to Xavier like this before and he was too shocked to react — he was literally lost for words. Silent tears ran down Bethany's cheek as Bertie pulled her towards her in a protective embrace. Bar leant towards his wife and squeezed her shoulder in reassurance, then turned back to Xavier, every bit of his persona suggesting violence was one wrong remark away.

"May I speak?" Somehow the words had come out of Xavier's mouth.

Bar glared at him, his jaw muscles twitching. "If you want, but don' s'pect me t'swallow any more of y'sweet soundin' words."

Bethany's sad visage regarded him impassively. Bertie looked as if her daughter had already been taken from her. Trying to meet Bar's malevolent gaze, Xavier hoped his expression would convey more than his words. "Bethany is not going *anywhere* with me. She is *your* daughter. Why would I wish to take her from you?"

Bar searched his face, trying to find the truth in Xavier's words. "So what *is* your role in this, Master Xavier? Who *is* Bertrand sendin' t'fetch 'er?" He seemed to have regained some of his composure.

"My role is my own," Xavier replied calmly. He felt like he was no longer within himself and the words were not spoken by him. "And it has nothing, whatever, to do with Bertrand. It was only at the request of the Sunwatcher that he begrudgingly brought me to Lower Icing, and my reason for coming here has nothing to do with any of you."

Bar took a deep breath, massaged his face with cupped hands, and then sighed. "The Sunwatcher," he breathed, his hands balled into fists, and he looked ready to lash out again.

"What is it, exactly, that Bertrand wants from you?" Xavier asked.

"To fulfil a promise," Bertie Swill said quietly.

Chapter 10

Full of restless life

XAVIER WAS MENTALLY and physically drained, yet sleep eluded him. The heat of his room wasn't helping: sweat beaded on his naked torso and soaked into the bed coverings.

Now that he saw things from the Swills' point of view, their behaviour had been quite understandable, and appropriate under the circumstances. Xavier's arrival with Bertrand in the early hours after Forging Day, his connection to Blessed Whipping, his aloofness (and apparent air of superiority), and the secretiveness of his visit to the castle all added up, in the Swills' minds, to the impending loss of their daughter. It had been Bertie who'd finally cleared the air and divulged the reason for their suspicions.

Bar and Bertie had left Blessed Whipping because, at the time, they felt like they had no choice. Bertie had fallen pregnant with Brandon before she and Bartholomew had been Sunblessed by the Elders. It was a betrothal ceremony that not only 'brought light' to the pairing, but also to their children. To conceive without being Sunblessed meant the child would not be ready to 'Face the Sun' (and accept the light) after the darkness of the womb. Although accepted into the community, a 'Shade' could never become Sunwatcher or an Elder (regardless of time of birth or how devoted to the community they became).

Xavier was astounded by all this: even the seemingly harmonious community of Blessed Whipping had its discordant notes, and it saddened him to think that a simple ceremony could influence the fate of an unborn child. He'd only witnessed three Sunblessings in his time at Blessed Whipping, and, like Forging Day, the pivotal moment came at Sunhigh, with the pronouncement made by the Sunwatcher. It seemed such a simple ceremony, not much different from the day to day routine, except the bride and groom wore white and the Sunhigh meal was more of a celebration.

There had been no celebration for Bar and Bertie, however. At the age of eighteen, they'd decided to leave Blessed Whipping rather than raise a child 'in the shadow'. It was language Xavier had never heard before. He wondered whether times had changed in Blessed Whipping, or was it just his failure to interact with its people that had made him unaware of their nuances.

Bar and Bertie had told no-one of their intentions, but, somehow, they were found out by Bertrand. From what Bertie had relayed, he was much the same kind of person then as he was now: fanatical and emotionless. The Swills believed his uncompromising attitude stemmed from the fact that he'd been born three weeks premature (at the end of May) — too far from Forging Day ever to be considered for Sunwatcher. The arbitrary unfairness of it all had obviously played on Bertrand's mind — there's little doubt that he would have considered himself the superior Sunwatcher candidate — and, as his twenty-first birthday passed, so did the finality of his situation. He became a stringent adherer to every Blessed Whipping custom. If they were to rule his life, so be it, but he'd make sure they also ruled everyone else's. Therefore, he'd shown little compassion for Bar and Bertie's situation.

Xavier sat up wearily and leant towards the window, hoping for some semblance of a breeze. But the night was deathly still and quiet, and yet... it *wasn't* quiet. The blackness was punctuated by an array of sounds that a breath of wind would normally carry away: a dog (or what Xavier assumed to be a dog) trotted across The Square, its paws clipping on the cobblestones; alley cats cried from near and far; a window opened (or closed); and even the occasional snippet of conversation was lifted by the heat and carried across the stillness. The night was full of restless life.

Twenty-two years ago, Bar and Bertie's life had also been restless, but in a much more frenetic way. Bertrand's discovery meant they could no longer plan their escape: they had to leave immediately. If they'd lingered, the Elders might have convinced them to stay, where they were safe and cared for. However, the uncertainty of life outside Blessed Whipping was something they had been prepared to risk if it meant giving their child an untarnished start. Their escape had been fortuitous, coming in the form of a coach on its way to Lower Icing.

The similarity of the Swills' story to his own was not lost on Xavier; they'd both left Blessed Whipping quickly and secretively (although for vastly different reasons), escaping by coach and arriving at Lower Icing, with Bertrand playing an unwilling or, in the Swills' case, unwitting role in the escape. And as the Swills were venturing into their new life, Xavier had been venturing into his — he'd been born the week of their escape.

They'd barely had time to collect their clothes and gather a few personal items, and most of the little money they'd saved was taken up in the coach fare, but they hadn't hesitated and managed to board the coach without any of the villagers noticing. Bar had become agitated at this point in Bertie's account of events and she'd laid a comforting hand on his. "It's alright, love; there's no blame to be 'ad 'ere."

"'Course there's blame! If I 'adn't been as stupid to think Bertrand wouldn' know what coach was goin' where at what time… Might as well have written 'im a note."

Xavier could almost taste the bitterness in each word. It had taken Bertrand just three days to find them at The Bloody Bell. They had been hired as a 'man and wife' team to take care of cleaning and general running repairs. They'd been given a small room and meals as payment. And it was in the small room that they'd made their promise to Bertrand.

"It seems so stupid now, but we was scared, Master Xavier," Bertie said, looking for understanding. "This place was so strange to us… we 'ad doubts 'bout what we'd done."

Xavier could well understand how they'd felt — he was feeling it now, sitting in the sweltering blackness. Lower Icing was a chaotic collection of unhappy people, unruly mobs, untrustworthy vendors and undisciplined authority. The contrast to Blessed Whipping couldn't be starker, and Xavier had only spent sixteen months there; he could only imagine the shock of Lower Icing after living an entire life in that closed community.

"Bertrand said we'd been tainted," Bertie had explained, "an' if we didn' come back, we'd be corrupted, an' never be welcome back."

Intimidation had obviously been Bertrand's weapon of choice back then as well. But Bar and Bertie had held true — they had a child to think of, not just themselves anymore. But Bertrand was not to be outdone. He'd presented the young couple with his 'Deed of Promise'. It meant that they would continue to be recognised by the community, and welcomed back to Blessed Whipping whenever they chose to return, provided they promised to present any offspring born on Forging Day to the village before their eighteenth birthday.

"We saw no 'arm in it — not at the time, anyways. Brandon was goin' t'be a September baby, an' any other children… well, we could decide when they was born, if you take my meaning, Master Xavier."

Even the dim light of the bar hadn't been enough to hide Xavier's awkwardness. In fact, the whole situation had left Xavier feeling particularly uncomfortable.

Struggling to find some peace in the still heat of the night, he grabbed his shirt and squelched it in the remnants of the dirty, soapy pail-water that he'd used to wash himself earlier.

"An' if it meant that we could return… well, why not? So we signed 'is bloody deed." Bertie had paused at this point and gazed at her husband. The muscles in Bar's clenched jaw were pulsing, and Xavier wouldn't have been surprised to hear the cracking of teeth. Bertie began rubbing Bar's hand. "'Course, as fate would have it, Bethany was born within minutes of Sunhigh on Forging Day… eighteen years ago."

Forging Day, Xavier pondered, as he wiped his wet shirt over his face and neck. Preparing the Sun Temple with the villagers, sharing in the joy of the day and what it represented, the sun bright and benevolent, beaming its approval— it felt like a dream. Images of Butterfly fluttered through his mind, refreshing his senses and keeping the stinking hot night at bay. He felt a sudden need to return. The Swills were not his concern, and neither were their dealings with Bertrand. He went back to bed. Sleep arrived shortly afterwards.

CHAPTER 11

All seemed to be in order

FACING SOUTH, XAVIER'S room was spared the direct intensity of the morning sun, but it wasn't spared its heat. Nor was he protected from the clamour of the Town Square. This place was just heat and noise, and neither was helpful for his pounding head. He was probably dehydrated. Two mugs of ale before bed wasn't his usual practice, and when added to how much he'd sweated and how little water he'd drunk… Xavier groaned at the thought of facing another day in Lower Icing.

Heaving himself from the bed, he reached out of the window and adjusted the shutters, closing one but leaving the other partially open. It didn't do much for the noise, but it certainly helped reduce the amount of light that flared into his room. He now felt he could fully open his eyes without causing permanent damage.

Bare-chested (except for the silver pendant he wore around his neck) and clammy with sweat, he walked over to the door and opened it. As expected, there was a pail of fresh water and a new cake of soap sitting on a clean towel just outside his room. He was so thirsty that he picked up the pail and greedily drank from it, unashamed of his semi-naked appearance or the fact that there was as much water sloshing over him and the hallway floor as there was being swallowed.

Back in his room, Xavier took much delight in washing and shaving, even going to the extent of scrubbing between his toes — it was as if he couldn't get clean enough. He'd already decided to stay in his room today; hot as it was, it was still better than any alternative Xavier could think of, and he could always work on his rejuvenation potion research. Maybe that would quell his queasiness (which he suspected was just nervous excitement) or at least hurry the hours until his meeting with Administrator Penman.

With that thought in mind, he placed the now-damp towel into the pail and moved across the room. A streak of light passed through the narrow gap in the shutters and dissected his travelling case. Crouching next to it, he took out the wooden case that contained his equipment and the locked leather folder that held his notes and Horatio's letter. He also put on a clean set of clothing and neatly folded his 'soapy-water' shirt, stained trousers and sweat-filled undergarments. They smelt awful, but he would wash them later.

Right now, he was eager to reacquaint himself with his latest project; it felt like ages since he'd worked on his rejuvenation potion. Actually, it was more of a balm than a potion, but Horatio favoured the generic term 'potion' for all their experiments. He also realised, thinking about work, that he was quite hungry. More often than not, Horatio and he had begun their days of research by enjoying an invigorating Sunrise meal as they discussed objectives and procedures. It was another aspect of life at Blessed Whipping that he'd taken for granted. Unfortunately, the patrons of The Bloody Bell's idea of stimulating conversation revolved around how many wenches they could bed and how loud they could belch. Xavier wasn't *that* hungry.

After making doubly sure his door was locked, Xavier sat down at the desk with his wooden case and leather folder. Moving the folder to one side, he flicked open the four latches of the case. It was unremarkable from the outside: made of oak, eighteen inches in length, twelve inches wide and six inches deep. Apart from the simple-looking latches, the only embellishment was a small, rectangular metal plate that had 'Xavier' engraved into it. The case had been a gift from Horatio — something to make the move from Missing Anchor to Blessed Whipping more worthwhile, or professional, perhaps? Whatever his intention had been, the case was something Xavier treasured, and its interior was as beautiful as its outside was plain.

Lined in night-black velvet, the case housed two eleven-inch-square, polished walnut trays, one on top of the other, and five polished walnut drawers, four of them two inches in height and the other three inches, and all six inches wide.

The top tray rested on a small ledge sitting just below the rim of the case. In the corners of the tray, a special spiral nail — or screw, as Horatio called it — was rotated into a matching spiral hole in the ledge, securing it in place. Sparkling against the rich wood-grain was a selection of specially crafted glass vials and jars, each sitting in shallow, carved moulding and secured in place by a silver clasp.

Xavier opened the top drawer and removed an immaculately crafted tool from its designated spot. It was five inches in length, with a turned, polished walnut handle tapered for four of those inches before seamlessly encompassing a solid steel cylinder. The cylinder had been flattened at the tip to form a straight narrow ridge, one that fitted perfectly into a groove in each screw's head.

Placing the tool into the groove, Xavier twisted his hand anti-clockwise. Supplying a downward force, the screw rotated upwards, away from the surface of the tray. The process still amazed him, even though he now understood the mechanics behind it. A few more twists of his hand and the screw was dislodged.

Xavier placed the screw in the drawer that housed the 'screw-remover'. After repeating the process with the three other screws, he carefully removed the top tray and placed it next to the box, its velvet underside cushioning the contact with the desk. The eight small jars and twelve vials sat perfectly intact. The second tray, fixed permanently to the case, was identical to the first.

The drawers contained an amazing array of tools and equipment: a miniature scale with weights, tweezers, magnifying lenses, fine-bladed knives, spatulas, candles, flint, and a collection of small metal rods and clasps that could be constructed in any number of ways to facilitate all kinds of experiments. Everything had its place. All seemed to be in order, and that was just the way Xavier liked it.

He rubbed his eyes; sweat was already beginning to bead on his forehead and his clothes were starting to cling to his skin. This wasn't going to work — the conditions were too extreme for any meaningful experiments. The jar of Dandelion Butter had separated into its base components of oil and pollen paste, while the Sugar Tree sap looked like it had become Sugar Tree plaster. In all honesty, he wasn't sure if he had the energy or concentration needed for working, and he'd never felt *that* way before.

Rescue from despair came in the form of a knock at the door.

"S'cuse me, Master Xavier, I've brought your breakfast."

It was Bethany. Thank goodness; he wasn't in the mood for Bertie's aimless bantering.

"One moment," he replied, carefully placing the tray of potions back into the case.

He unlocked the door. Bethany smiled shyly from behind a tray of fried bacon and eggs, bread, and what smelt like Bertie's special broth. She looked as pink and crisp as the bacon, and her ponytail rested limply over her right shoulder, its blue ribbon withering.

"Good morning, Bethany," he said, ushering her into his room.

She nodded, and placed the tray on the desk next to his case.

"Thank you."

"You're welcome, Master Xavier." She smiled weakly. All of yesterday's vitality seemed to have evaporated from her.

Xavier felt partially responsible; his arrival had caused the Swills no small amount of anguish. "I feel confident everything will work out for the best."

She nodded, but it seemed more out of politeness than in any belief in his words. He wanted to tell her he would tear up any Deed of Promise — if it still existed — when he was accepted into his father's household. But he couldn't do that just yet. Instead, he reasserted the promise he'd made to her parents last night.

"This afternoon, I'm meeting with the Administrator of Petitions and other high-ranking officials at the castle. I will endeavour to find out if Bertrand has any legal entitlement over you. If he does, I promise I will do my utmost to have the deed overturned."

Unexpectedly, Bethany hugged him. It was an awkward moment. Xavier had had little time for emotion in his life; it was something that couldn't be quantified. Still, he managed to embrace the situation, and gently, if self-consciously, offered some physical comfort.

Half a minute later, she was still clinging to him like he was floating wreckage from a sunken ship. "Come now, Bethany," he said, gently prising her away. "Things are often not as bad as they seem. The bond of family is not something to be underestimated."

Xavier saw her nod in mute acceptance, but his thoughts were of himself and the Duke. Would there be any bond between *them*?

The twenty-third day of June, a sweltering Monday, two days after Forging Day. Two days? It felt like two months — time had flowed like molten metal.

As planned, he'd spent the day in his room, the monotony of the oppressive conditions punctuated by various welcome visits from Bethany. She had taken his dirty clothing and returned them washed and dried. Every hour, she had bought him a clean pail of water, fresh soap and a clean towel. Around midday she had, at Xavier's request, dined with him. He discovered she had a fine mind and was obviously a diligent worker. Ironically, Xavier mused, she *would* be an excellent choice for Sunwatcher.

As the day slowly melted towards late afternoon, Xavier prepared himself for the meeting with Administrator Penman. He washed for the seventh or eighth time that day and put on his best clothes: a loose-fitting, white silk shirt with lace-edged cuffs and collar, a deep-green velvet doublet, and white trousers that were tucked into his knee-high black leather boots. The clothes made him feel uncomfortable, both in the way they looked *and* felt.

Xavier had one more task to perform before he left for the castle. He went over to his travelling case and pulled out a small, cloth bundle. Then he returned to the desk and reached underneath it for his leather folder. It lay neatly on top of his wooden case. He'd stored both items there to make room for his lunch with Bethany.

Placing the folder next to the bundle, he removed his leather neck-band and used the silver pendant to unlock the folder. He then put it straight back around his neck; he felt vulnerable without it. Opening the folder, he removed Horatio's letter. As expected, the Pig Dust had dispersed, except for three words near the centre of the page:

achieve great things

Xavier didn't believe in omens or portents, he wasn't the least bit superstitious, yet he couldn't help but look upon the remaining words — in Horatio's meticulous handwriting — with some feeling of encouragement.

Horatio must have pressed harder on the quill at this point, leaving a deeper indentation in the page to trap the Pig Dust. Perhaps he'd been subconsciously, or even consciously, stressing their importance. Xavier felt a pang of guilt. Horatio had, after all, always cared for him and treated him with respect. In hindsight, he could have reacted better to the contents of the letter. However, it was too late to turn back now; one didn't abandon a theory until it was proven to be false. And Xavier was working on the theory that the Duke would find it much harder to resist 'flesh and blood' than a name written on parchment.

Xavier turned his gaze from the parchment to the cloth bundle. He untied the knot and unfolded the shabby-looking material. Inside lay yesterday's purchase from the market: six charcoal pencils. Some of them had snapped into smaller pieces, but that didn't bother Xavier. Choosing one of the broken pieces, he began rubbing it gently across the page. Starting at the top, the parchment revealed its message once more. He now had the required evidence for Administrator Penman. He was prepared to meet his father.

CHAPTER 12

Immediately wary of the uniform

BETHANY SWILL'S HUG was awkwardly tender. "Good luck, Xavier," she whispered as she gently squeezed herself against him. He was standing in the Swill's private lounge room. Bar and Bertie stood behind their daughter, faces smiling through their apprehension.

"Come now, lass, let the poor boy breathe," said Bar in mock reproach.

Bethany released her grip, freeing Xavier's arms. He attempted a reassuring pat on her shoulder, but she turned away too quickly (or the pat was too slow) and his outstretched hand made passing contact with her fulsome left breast. He quickly snatched his hand back, but Bethany gave no indication anything inappropriate had occurred.

"Well, thank you again for your hospitality," he blurted, trying to cover his embarrassment. "I will send for my belongings should I not need to return. And I'm sorry for any worry I may have inadvertently caused."

"Think no more of it, Master Xavier," Bertie Swill said, taking his hand. "It was us what were at fault. We was the ones jumpin' to conclusions. We know you're a good man an' will do right by us."

Xavier forced a smile. Bertie's words were warm, but they were laced with the cool undertones of a mother who would not stand for her daughter to be taken away from her.

"Good luck to you, Master Xavier," Bar said, extending his right hand.

"Thank you, Bar," replied Xavier, shaking his hand.

"If you don' return to The Bell, I'll send the extra money y'paid us with Brandon."

"If I don't return, I'll have no need of it."

Xavier hugged the western edge of The Square, where the shade of the buildings provided some relief from the afternoon sun. The stream of traffic that had swept Xavier to his confrontation with the guardsmen yesterday morning was now just a trickle. A smattering of villagers congregated around the well, waiting to fill their pails.

Xavier turned right into what he now knew as Bigwig Street and was met by an unexpected blast of heat and light. The well-to-do thoroughfare was drenched in glaring sunlight; the scorching sun seemed to hover over its western end. He wondered what the Blessed Whippingers would make of it all. Xavier shaded his eyes with his right hand and, even then, was forced to look downwards. Consequently, the voice next to him came as a complete surprise.

"Excuse me, Master Xavier."

It was a young man's voice: a young man dressed smartly in the livery of a castle guard. His purple and gold-striped doublet was eye-catching against a predominantly black background of boots, trousers, shirt sleeves and round-brimmed felt hat. The brim was pinned on the right side and embellished with a purple feather. Just above his left hip, the metal handle of a sword sparkled in time to his easy gait. Closing the few steps to where Xavier now stood, he removed his hat and nodded respectfully, "Your pardon."

After the altercation with the gatehouse guards yesterday, Xavier was immediately wary of the uniform, and the fact that he had been addressed by name. His consternation must have been apparent, for the young guard immediately attempted to put him at ease.

"There is no need for concern. I have been asked to escort you directly to Administrator Penman's office. Allow me to introduce myself— I am Lieutenant Brandon Swill of the Lower Icing Guard, also known as the Purple Peril."

Asked by whom? was Xavier's first thought. His innate trust in people had been tested over the last week, and he was learning quickly not to take anyone at face value.

"Please to meet you, Brandon. Your family speaks very highly of you."

His face broke into a broad smile, and the resemblance to his sister shone through. "Thank you. They are good people."

Xavier was about to query Brandon on his sudden appearance, but his words were cut off by a friendly slap on the shoulder. "Come along, then. Let us proceed quickly and escape this blasted heat."

Xavier found himself almost jogging next to Brandon just to keep up with his marching pace. As they progressed down Bigwig Street, Brandon talked about his family and how close he was to his sister. By the time they turned left up Noble Street, Xavier was in no doubt who had ordered Brandon to escort him to Administrator Penman.

As they marched through the West Gate, the regular guards, whose doublets were actually *blue* and gold, saluted by pounding their right fist over their heart. Brandon saluted back, and then led the way into the Administration Section of the Lower Bailey. The entrance to the Office of Petitions was to their left, but the lieutenant seemed to have a different destination in mind.

Xavier stopped. The heat and the marching pace had taken their toll. He wasn't willing to take one step in the wrong direction, *and* he definitely wasn't prepared to unquestioningly follow someone who referred to themselves as a Purple Peril. "Where are you going, Brandon? The Office of Petitions is just here," he said, indicating a door to his left.

A look of irritation briefly creased Brandon's genial expression as he, too, came to a halt. Rivulets of sweat were meandering down his face, "That's correct, Master Xavier. However, Administrator Penman's office is *this* way. You have a meeting arranged, I believe, so there is no need to go through the petitions process again."

"Of course," Xavier acknowledged.

Brandon's expression softened. "It is but a few more paces. Come, we will be out of the sun in a matter of moments."

True to his word, Brandon quickly led Xavier into a short entranceway that ended in a small, yet well-furnished, antechamber. The change in temperature wasn't as dramatic as Xavier had hoped, but just being out of the sun was a relief, and the gloomy, candle-lit confines were relatively pleasant.

"Please be seated, Master Xavier," Brandon said, indicating the upholstered bench set against the wall to his left. "I shall inform Administrator Penman of your arrival."

Removing his black felt hat and pinning it under his left arm, feather-side up, he took four purposeful strides towards the door ahead, opened it, and then disappeared behind it without the slightest gesture of reassurance.

Xavier was left, sweat-soaked, to ponder his fate. He ambled across to the bench and sat down. His face was still pulsing with heat and he felt as if he'd been thrown, fully dressed, into a warm bath.

He closed his eyes and let his body sink into the bench. The only sound he could hear was the blood pumping through his head. He wondered if it was nerves or exertion. The whole situation now seemed very unreal. Was he actually about to meet his father, the Duke of Lower Icing? Or perhaps he was still in Blessed Whipping, lying in bed, hallucinating, with some life-threatening fever. He opened his eyes to reassure himself of his surroundings, and then reached for the letter to validate his reason for being here.

His heart leapt as he undid the top buckle of his left boot. The letter was still neatly wedged between his trousers and the inside of his boot, but the once-crisp, white parchment was now limp and translucent with sweat. He carefully loosened another two buckles, hoping it was only the top edge of the parchment that had been affected. But, to his dismay, the stain continued — he could see the charcoal smudged through the damp fibres. He gently removed the letter from its 'safe and secure' hiding spot. (He'd been thinking pickpockets and muggers when he put it there.)

Fortunately, it was still in one piece, and the parchment was of good enough quality to have held its form — there were no rips or tears. There was still hope. The letter had been folded over twice. Although damp, the top edge was still firm enough to be peeled away from the first fold. From there, the second fold opened cleanly. His sweat hadn't permeated through to the centre, and, to his relief, the bottom half of the letter was still legible. Horatio's perfect script still conveyed its meaning perfectly.

and very intelligent young man, and will achieve great things — you would be very proud.

Marmaduke, I realise I have prescribed the following course of action on numerous occasions since arriving at Blessed Whipping, but surely the time has come for you to be reunited with your son. I have no doubt he will help fill the void left by Lucinda's sad passing.

As a friend, I ask you to consider what a boon this could be to both of you. I'm sure you would not regret it. X is your son, and it's been twenty years.

Yours Faithfully,
Horatio

Xavier placed the letter on the bench and re-buckled his boot. He was further bolstered by the thought that the parchment would quickly dry out in this heat, leaving the imprint in place for another application of charcoal. All was well.

Brandon returned ten minutes later. Xavier had begun to worry that Administrator Penman had decided not to keep the appointment. Heart pounding, Xavier stood up. "Is something amiss, Brandon?"

"All is as it should be, Master Xavier," he replied confidently. "I am to escort you directly to Administrator Penman's office."

Relieved, he clutched the refolded letter in his left hand and nervously moved towards Brandon. The young officer still held his hat; his short black hair was flat and slightly slick with perspiration. He remained motionless at the door as Xavier approached. "Master Xavier, may I ask that you address me as Lieutenant within the confines of the castle."

"Oh…" Xavier mumbled in surprise. He had been expecting a final plea for his sister. "Of course, Lieutenant."

"Thank you." He smiled briefly before leading Xavier down a gloomy and noticeably cooler passageway. The hot sweat of exertion was now replaced by the cold sweat of anxiety — he had no idea what he was walking into. And he had no more time to think about the consequences since Brandon had stopped after a dozen paces.

He knocked once at a door to their right, opened it, and advanced half a step into the room. From his position in the passageway, Xavier could see very little of what lay inside, but what was revealed was reassuring: a backdrop of petitions filled the space between Brandon's back and the door frame. This was certainly Administrator Penman's office.

Brandon's back stiffened and he snapped the heels of his boots together. Xavier assumed he was saluting. Then he heard him announce, "Master Xavier, sir."

There was no reply, but Brandon turned towards Xavier and nodded at him to enter the office. Xavier suddenly felt queasy. He inhaled deeply and strode purposefully past Brandon, ready to present his case to Administrator Penman.

Everything in the office was just as he remembered: wall to wall scrolls of petitions, dissected by a streak of afternoon sun that beamed through a bow slit on the opposite wall, and a large wooden desk set against the northern wall to his right. It was still covered with neat piles of parchments, representing petitions that had been successful, unsuccessful or yet to be decided upon. The only change to the scene was the man behind the desk — it was not Administrator Penman.

CHAPTER 13

Naive in the extreme

T HE MAN BEHIND the desk oozed authority; his relaxed demeanour and Brandon's subordinate rigidity was testament to that. Standing in front of the Administrator's desk, Xavier felt more like a wanted criminal than an unwanted son.

"Shut the door, Lieutenant," the man said, waving his hand lazily towards the door.

Brandon obeyed, and then stood statue-like in front of it. Xavier, panic rising, looked at him for a sign of reassurance, but the lieutenant's face remained regimentally impassive.

"So, tell me, what makes a man with no family name, of no fixed abode think he is the son of a Duke?"

Xavier's attention snapped back to the man behind the desk. He sat casually in the chair, looking almost bored, except for his dark brown eyes — they were appraising, and searching for any weakness. Xavier felt totally exposed.

"Well?" the man prompted impatiently.

"I found this letter," Xavier replied, meekly, proffering the folded, damp parchment.

The man's mouth curved into a sardonic smile, his eyes mocking. Then he sprung out of his relaxed pose with a fluidness that shocked and alarmed Xavier. He flinched involuntarily as the man leant forward on the desk, holding out his right hand, indicating Xavier should give him the parchment.

His hand trembling, he placed the letter into the totally still palm of the man. It was a palm that looked like it could command a legion of soldiers. All the while, he could feel the man's eyes boring into him. Looking up, the man was indeed staring at him, scrutinising his every feature. Xavier could feel his eyelids twitching.

The man's gaze dropped down to his outstretched palm, where the letter now lay.

"What's this? Pissed your pants? Not a very *noble* trait."

Xavier flushed with embarrassment. "It's the heat. I sweated through—"

"Enough." The man leant back in the chair and resumed his casual pose, "It makes no difference. If this is what you claim it is, it could be covered in dog shit for all I care."

Xavier cast a sideways glance at Brandon. He remained motionless, gaze fixed straight ahead. Looking back at the desk, the man was in the process of unfolding the parchment. Then he began to read, his expression giving nothing away. While his eyes darted across the letter, Xavier had a chance to study his features. He appeared to be around forty years old and had dark, shoulder-length hair that was immaculately groomed. His neat, short-clipped beard was precisely shaped and speckled with grey. His smoothly shaven neck was bordered by a silver-brocaded collar that was part of a tight-fitting, black velvet doublet. His powerful frame sat perfectly inside the silver-stitched, diamond-patterned torso.

Suddenly his gaze was back on Xavier. It was like someone had ripped out his insides; Xavier felt ill. The man released his grip on the letter and it fell, almost gracefully, to the desk. Then he smiled his condescending smile. Xavier could feel his stomach lurch.

"This letter has certainly aroused my curiosity…"

Xavier knew he was trembling, but he couldn't help it.

"I'm curious as to why you believe it constitutes proof of your… relationship to the Duke?"

He sat up again, cat-like. Xavier, mouse-like, flinched again.

"From the little that is still legible, there is no mention of a Xavier. It could literally be referring to *anyone*."

The man paused, seemingly waiting for a response. Xavier's mind was reeling; this wasn't how he'd imagined events unfolding, "When the parchment dries, I shall—"

"Wipe your arse with it. *This*…" He picked up the parchment between his thumb and second finger as if it had already been used for that purpose, "would be no more revealing in its original condition, regardless of whether it refers to you by name."

He un-pinched his finger and thumb and the parchment dropped to the desk once again. "I am surprised Administrator Penman insisted I see you. He convinced me you may have a case. Instead, you present me with a pissing letter, written by someone, who, like you, *Xavier*, appears not to have a family name.

It proves absolutely nothing except that you are either inept at deception or naive in the extreme."

Xavier heard the words, but he couldn't equate them to his situation. The meaning of the letter was clear, the tone was that of a confidante to the Duke, the information was believable — surely he deserved a more considered hearing.

"I am not a deceiver, sir."

"Then you *are* extremely naive. And I have already wasted too much time on you." The man stood up, predictably tall, and nodded at Brandon. Brandon opened the door and neutrally informed Xavier that he would escort him from the palace.

Xavier felt dizzy; there wasn't enough air in the room and the scrolls were beginning to blur into some sort of madman's wallpaper. He knew he had to think quickly or the moment would be lost forever.

"Please, sir. Allow me to explain the context of the letter." Xavier had never felt so… listless.

"I'm not interested in context. Evidence is what's required and you have provided none." Once again he nodded at Brandon.

Xavier, however, kept his gaze on the intimidating figure in black. "If you speak to the Duke, he will confirm the identity of the signatory, Horatio Manky." Xavier felt Brandon's firm hand grip his upper right arm. "I believe he is an old friend of the Duke." Xavier was being pulled firmly, but not roughly, towards the door. He reluctantly surrendered a side-step. The man looked at him with impatient indifference. "Please, sir. The Duke will confirm—"

"Enough!" the man barked. "Lieutenant!" He jerked his head in a 'get him out of here' manner.

On command, the pulling force increased markedly, and Xavier found himself stumbling towards the passageway. Brandon, now out of the room (and out of sight of the man) looked at Xavier, pleadingly, to stop resisting. It was the same look Bethany had given him in his room at The Bloody Bell, moments before she had fallen into his arms. The memory triggered a connection in Xavier's head and, as he let himself be pulled out of the room, he yelled out two words: "Ask Bertrand!"

Chapter 14

The view is spectacular

XAVIER WASN'T PRIVY to the conversation that ensued between Brandon and his superior after the mention of Bertrand. He'd been left waiting in the passageway for at least five minutes while the two held a muted meeting behind the closed door of Administrator Penman's office. Now, a pensive-looking Brandon had emerged.

He informed Xavier that an audience with the Duke wasn't possible today and that if he wished to pursue his claim, he would need to stay in The Keep, where he could be presented at a moment's notice. Xavier agreed because he felt there wasn't a choice.

The Keep was built within the Middle Bailey, set against the eastern wall of the castle. The view of it from his room at The Bloody Bell was impressive, but standing next to the massive square structure gave him a whole new perspective on this feat of engineering. It had to be two hundred feet tall and at least eighty feet wide. Its grey, stone sides were punctuated evenly by numerous levels of deeply set windows and arrow slits.

At the top of The Keep, towers at each corner reached even farther towards sky. Xavier's head tilted back almost horizontally as his gaze climbed the northwest tower, its conical-shaped peak piercing the vibrant blue sky. However, he was brought back to earth by Brandon's request for him to 'keep up'. He wondered if the pun was intended, but responded by quickening his pace and following him through an impressive fore-building adorned with pennons of purple and gold. Directly below the pennons, black and white tiles in a chess-board pattern led smartly into The Keep. Two massive tapestries — one on each wall — carried the length of the fore-building underneath a row of clear, leadlight windows. The tapestries were both colourful and intricate in their design. The one to Xavier's left depicted a bird's eye view of Lower Icing: the castle on its hill to the south, farmland and the river to the east, the village sprawled mainly to the north. The tapestry on the opposite wall showed a feast or celebration of some kind. Again, the view was elevated, but not enough to obscure the faces of the revellers. Most of them were sitting at tables, eating, engaged in mirthful conversation, or toasting their cups. Some, however, were dancing, and a trio of musicians could be seen at the edge of the scene.

Brandon led Xavier the fifteen or so paces along the tiled floor to a large, double-door archway. The doors — made from heavy-looking timber panels and reinforced with carved bands of metal — were open, revealing a smaller, gloomier antechamber. Another, identical archway — with doors closed — stood some five or six paces further on. Fixed above the first archway was an ornamental shield, blazoned with the standard gold and purple. This time the purple background was broken by the golden head of a unicorn sitting above five silver crowns.

Walking through the first archway, Brandon turned to his left and led Xavier towards a small doorway. It turned out to be the entrance to a spiral stairwell that wound its way up the north-west corner of The Keep. The stone stairs were only a few feet across, so single file was the only option. The stairs were also very steep and tapered from eighteen inches deep at the wall to virtually nothing around the central axis. An occasional bow slit provided some feeble (and very necessary) light for the precarious ascent. They also provided some unwelcome heat. Xavier hugged the roughly hewn stone wall, but after only a dozen or so steps, he was panting and sweating. It seemed to take an impossibly long time to reach the first exit, and, to his dismay, Brandon's silhouetted figure continued spiralling upward.

By the time they reached the second exit, Xavier felt lightheaded and disoriented. And still they climbed. The echoing of footsteps finally ceased at the fifth exit. He lagged a few twists of the stairwell behind Brandon, but eventually gasped his way to where the lieutenant waited for him.

The exit opened up into a passage that ran north-south, above the fore-building to another stairwell in the south-west corner. Arrow-slits on the western wall streaked the passage with golden afternoon light. Halfway down, another passageway opened up on the left. Brandon led Xavier down it. Ahead, some sixty feet away, was the eastern wall of The Keep; a single arrow slit was visible, but the light emanating from it was feeble. Set amongst the stone corridor were eight closed doors, four either side. Brandon walked to the fourth door on his left, unlocked it, and gestured for Xavier to enter.

"This room is the most comfortable, Master Xavier," he announced, "and the view is spectacular."

Xavier responded with mute compliance. He already felt dizzy from the exertion of his spiral climb and, even up here, the temperature was simmering. But he was also wary of his situation, even more so when he stepped inside his 'most comfortable' room. A small wooden-framed bed with what appeared to be a straw mattress, a chair and small table (that looked to have been constructed with about as much finesse as a joke from a regular at The Bloody Bell) and a threadbare rug were the only concessions to comfort in what would otherwise be called a stone cell.

His expression must have conveyed everything he felt about his circumstances, because Brandon quickly reassured Xavier that his stay wouldn't be a long one. "In the meantime, I will have some food brought up, and some water in which to cool down. If you require anything more, send word with the servant."

Xavier stood mutely, listening to Brandon's level, measured voice and taking in the grey surrounds of the room. By the time his eyes turned back to the man in uniform, Brandon was standing outside the door, regarding him with some concern. This was not a place for someone about to meet the Duke.

Xavier found his voice. "Why am I here, Lieutenant?"

Brandon wasn't able to hold his gaze. Instead, he silently closed the door and then locked it. Xavier listened to his departing footsteps until he could no longer hear them.

He had been in the room for what seemed like an hour and no food or water had been forthcoming. Xavier had spent the time thinking about his predicament, and the strange individual he'd known as a village Elder and servant to Horatio, but who was obviously someone with a much greater sphere of influence. However, thoughts of Bertrand were set aside when Xavier finally gazed out of the window. The view was stunning. In that, at least, Brandon hadn't misled him.

The window contained no glass; the waist-high sill was just wide enough for him to lean out, providing a one-hundred-and-eighty-degree panorama of the world north of The Keep. And what a bright world it was. Even in the late afternoon, colours glowed.

To his left, the sun sat defiantly above the western horizon, burning brightly, not ready to give up the day. From this height — well above the castle walls — he could see the distant, brown-tinged grassland stretch out to meet the deepening blue sky. Copses of oak, elm and birch cluttered the gently undulating landscape. On the western edge of Lower Icing, a large cemetery sprawled to the meet countryside, a shallow amphitheatre of the dead.

Inside the castle, the west wall stood stone-strong against the golden rays, casting a dusky blue shadow across the western courtyard. Nestled just beneath the height of the wall was a row of stone buildings. Candlelight already flickered from a few windows, and in the northern-most one an orange glow was punctuated by sparks of white light. The sound of a hammer on metal accompanied the sparks. Some horses, stabled to the north of the buildings, seemed oblivious to the clanging noise.

At the West Gate (where, two hours ago, he had entered the castle) a mounted man-at-arms appeared. The half-dozen guards milling about the gate paid him no heed as he slowly guided his horse towards the stable. Dismounting, he strode past the entrance to the blacksmith's and disappeared into the next building.

Xavier cast his eyes to a lower, internal wall that ran north-south from the east edge of the West Gate, separating the smithy and stables (and what he assumed to be guards' quarters) from the Administration buildings. It was in this central area that the Office of Petitions was located.

A lone figure suddenly appeared from its entrance and headed towards the northern wall. Even though he was little more than a grey outline at this distance, the setting afternoon sun was just high enough to spotlight his progress and glint against his spectacles. It was Administrator Penman. Xavier thought about calling out, but what good would it do? Penman was the one who'd deferred Xavier's request to a higher authority, and that higher authority had sent him even higher: to a cell with a view.

Instead of making his way towards the West Gate, Administrator Penman stayed close to the Administration building. Reaching the corner, he turned right and disappeared behind the Office of Petitions. Imagining his progress, Xavier watched as Administrator Penman reappeared on the other side of another internal wall. This one separated the Administration Section from a courtyard in which stood an L-shaped stone building set against the eastern wall of the castle. It looked to have three levels, rising even higher than the castle wall. It's roof was littered with at least a dozen chimneys, and most of them were smoking, albeit rather lazily in the still conditions. There was a hint of baking in the air, and if Xavier's mouth hadn't been so dry, it would have been watering. The building was obviously the kitchen, domain of the so-called Master Puffy. Xavier watched Administrator Penman walk through the East Gate of the castle; the gate where he'd been accosted by the guard. Two men guarded the gate, but whether they were the same ones, Xavier couldn't tell.

The grey figure walked out of view, behind the castle wall, and didn't reappear. He'd probably entered The Harey Rabbit to slake his thirst, and who could fault him for that. Xavier was parched, and, right now, even a mug of warm ale in the bawdy atmosphere of The Bloody Bell seemed an attractive proposition.

From this aspect, The Bloody Bell was quite a prominent structure, set on the north-west corner of the Town Square, with only stables and a few outbuildings separating it from the patchwork of farmland to the east and the shimmering river beyond. Xavier pinpointed the window of his room. Now in shade, it looked cool and inviting (even though he knew it was neither of those things).

Apart from a line of people waiting their turn at the well, the Town Square (and Lower Icing in general for that matter) looked deserted. A smattering of farmers still worked their patches, but the streets were virtually empty. Everyone appeared to be indoors, escaping the sun, having their evening meal or drinking at the inns. The relentless heat had obviously sapped the energy out of the villagers — it was a condition he could well relate to.

The village was also very quiet. The occasional bark of a restless dog, the crack of a stick over some poor overworked beast of burden, and echoes of muffled laughter as people entered or exited The Bloody Bell were about the only sounds that broke through the more immediate noise of Master Puffy's kitchen.

Xavier cast his gaze directly down Market Street, followed it past The Bloody Bell, past the deserted marketplace, past the houses and other unidentifiable buildings until it joined the main road heading north out of the village: the road to Blessed Whipping.

His vision blurred as he stared at the northern horizon, the trees casting long shadows, streaking black the golden-green countryside. They merged into the face of Butterfly, her golden hair wisped against her tanned skin and her blue eyes full of empathy. Tomorrow night, after Sunfall, she would present Horatio with his explanatory note. How would he react, Xavier wondered. Relieved? Angry? Perhaps a mixture of both. And, knowing him as Xavier did, Horatio would blame himself; he always took the blame when experiments turned out unexpectedly.

Xavier's vision returned to the real world. The shadows were longer, the sun lower, and the world outside his window was now full of dark grey rooftops highlighted in bronze. Lower Icing was melting into darkness.

And still no-one came to his room.

INTERLUDE

SID AND HORATIO

THE BLACK CARRIAGE was darker than the night. Its silhouette was set against the half-moonlit Sun Temple across the square. Bertrand opened the door of the cab, allowing Doctor Manky to clamber aboard with his white case of potions. The cab rocked as he climbed the two steps, sat down on the rear seat, and placed the case next to him. He really did look ghoulish in the darkness of night, and so did the avian-featured man who stood impassively by the door.

"Looking chipper this morning, Bertrand," Sid remarked pleasantly as he followed Doctor Manky into the cab. As expected, Bertrand said nothing. The door was quickly closed behind him and he barely had enough time to sit opposite Doctor Manky before the carriage jerked into motion.

Sid had never felt better; in fact, chipper was exactly how *he* felt, even in the small hours of a Saturday morning. His head no longer throbbed, his left eye was no longer swollen or blood-shot, his bruising had reduced markedly (he could touch it without wincing) and the cut above his eye was now without stitches and looked to be healing neatly.

The remarkable acceleration in his wellbeing was due to the ministrations from the worried-looking man sitting opposite him. After reviving Sid from the near-death experience of Rigour Morphis, Doctor Manky had treated his eye with an unguent made from pulverised thistle and boiled cow's urine. Even though it had been scented with lavender, it smelt foul. The effect, however, was nothing short of miraculous: the pain and swelling had begun to recede almost immediately after the 'Bruise Mousse' was applied.

"You'll find it on page three of *Poetry in Potion*," Doctor Manky had informed him.

"Fascinating," Sid had commented sarcastically.

He was then given a brew of camomile tea and honey. It was a clear, deep-blue colour — certainly not a hue associated with either ingredient — and when Sid had pointed this out, he was informed by Doctor Manky that a few drops of Hyacinthia had been mixed in.

"It will help clear your head."

"Really," Sid had commented dubiously, and then sipped some of the warm liquid. It was sickly sweet and definitely not to Sid's taste, but he'd managed to drain the cup.

Doctor Manky seemed pleased. "Very good, Sid."

"Not how I'd describe it."

Doctor Manky had treated the comment with a knowing smile. "You see, your mind is already sharpening."

Curiously enough, since being brought back from the dead, he'd begun to see the doctor in a slightly different light. He still looked like every child's nightmare, particularly with those bacon-coloured eyes, but his demeanour had become, for want of a better phrase, more human. Sitting in the cab, he looked vulnerable and almost helpless. But Sid knew better; Doctor Manky was a brilliant concocter, and what he was doing right now was concocting a way to gain access to the Duke.

In the brief conversation they'd had between Sid's revival and being bundled into the Bertrand Express, it seemed Doctor Manky required Sid's help to slip unobtrusively into the castle. Sid wondered how he planned to pull *that* off — the only place Doctor Manky could slip unobtrusively would be a Dearly Departed Doctors Convention, or possibly a snowman-building competition.

"Tell me, Manky, was that camomile tea a potion of insanity?" Sid had responded. "Because that's what it would take for me to be part of any scheme you're brewing up."

Doctor Manky had then handed him a purse containing fifty gold pieces.

"Recompense for all the trouble I have caused you, Sid. There will be time enough to weigh up your options on the road to Lower Icing."

The purse now rested on his lap; its contents jingled slightly as the coach made its way back down the winding road that led to the plains below Blessed Whipping. He gazed outside the cab, almost expecting to see blue-clad Blessed Whippingers toiling at the fields, but the still night was devoid of human life.

What a bizarre experience this had turned out to be. Even Doctor Manky had gotten more than he'd bargained for. He'd employed Sid to discover the whereabouts of his protégé, but neither he nor Sid were any the wiser on that count. Sid had never heard of this Xavier person until Manky had decided to unload his burden while Sid was under the influence of Rigour Morphis, and the details were now sketchy to say the least… something about him being the son of someone important and living above a tavern (which sounded pretty good to Sid) in a place called Prickly Thicket, where they were… hiding from someone?

About the only thing he could remember with any clarity was the silver-framed portrait of Xavier on Manky's desk — the same young man Liv had handed her cloth parcel to. Still, for the most part, it was like some strange dream, the details of which were already beginning to blur and dissolve from his memory. The Happy Mermaid had been mentioned, hadn't it? It now all seemed so distant and unreal.

Gazing over at the doctor, he felt a pang of sympathy. Even in the darkness of the cab, Manky looked drained (if that was possible in someone who had a naturally bloodless complexion). Perhaps he was trying to get his mind around the fact that the person he'd raised from a young boy and schooled in the art of medicine was somehow involved in attacking and poisoning the Duke of Lower Icing. No doubt he felt more than just partly responsible for what had happened.

Sid took little pleasure in the fact. If Xavier had been involved, it was probably down to Liv. She was the one who'd seemed in control at The Bloody Bell; Xavier had seemed more like an unwilling accomplice. The evidence was far more compelling against *her* — the pen that had been used to mark Manky's book of potions was the one used to write the half-finished letter to Petronella Whysman, and the perfect, flowery script of that letter was identical to the handwriting in the warning note received by Reg Puffy. It all seemed so unbelievable to Sid. She was his sister who had raised and loved him. How had it come to this?

And another thing that was puzzling him was the silver button, or, as it turned out, *two* buttons — the one planted on Sid and the one found in the Duke's bedroom. Mary said they'd been stolen from Sir Richard's doublet to implicate him in the attack. It had obviously worked, because Mary's nob of a half-brother was no longer Seneschal. So, if the idea was to frame Sir Richard, why implicate Sid? It made no sense at all. And, now that he was thinking about it, why would a reward of a hundred gold pieces be offered for *identifying* the button? Surely Sir Richard must have recognised it.

Sid sighed. He was floundering; the more he thought about everything, the less real it all seemed. If it wasn't for the silver button tucked neatly away in the pocket of his trousers, he could easily believe it was just more hazy Rigour Morphis memories. He ran his hand over the outside of the pocket, then jerked upright — there was nothing there! His hand dived frantically into his pocket. Still nothing! What the frig!

"The silver button is in my possession, Sid," said Doctor Manky, matter-of-factly. "I took it while you were… indisposed. I meant to inform you, but more pressing issues have been occupying my mind." The darkness gave his voice an ethereal texture, his ghostly outline emphasising the effect.

"Well, I consider that button pretty damn pressing," replied Sid, anger quickly replacing relief. "Hell's bells, Manky. What do you think you're playing at? That button is the only thing that—"

"Ties you to the attack on the Duke... I would have thought you'd be glad to be rid of it. After all, it has served its purpose as far as you're concerned."

Sid couldn't argue with Doctor Manky's logic, but he'd acted on supposition rather than fact, and that rankled Sid. "People don't always react as predictably as your potions. We wouldn't be in this situation if they did."

"I take your point. But I consider this situation quite predictable given the emotionally explosive nature of its catalyst. What I am now trying to achieve is a successful result, and I believe the button could be a key ingredient."

What the frig did *that* mean? But Sid wasn't going to be deflected. "Why didn't you ask me for it? Did you *predict* that I would refuse?"

For a long moment, the only sound or movement was that of the carriage.

"What would you have me do, Sid? A man's life is at stake. To save it, I need to reach him as soon as possible. The silver button may aid me in that endeavour."

"Really," Sid drawled, unimpressed. "And how is it going to do *that* exactly?"

"Sir Richard wants it back, I believe — you said as much while under the influence of Voracious Loquacious. Mary asked you for it on his behalf, but you told her you'd lost it in the Icing, which, as you admitted, was misleading."

Bloody hell — that Voracious Loquacious was dangerous stuff. He could imagine the strife it would cause if it got into the hands of someone like Paul Peabody.

"So, if Sir Richard wants the button returned, I shall gladly oblige him... on the condition he allows me to see Marmaduke."

Sid slid back into his seat with a sigh. He couldn't be bothered arguing. He didn't care about Sir Richard or the Duke, or this Xavier. And this silver button wasn't anything to do with him. He wasn't even sure if he cared who had bashed him anymore.

PART 3

BRANDON

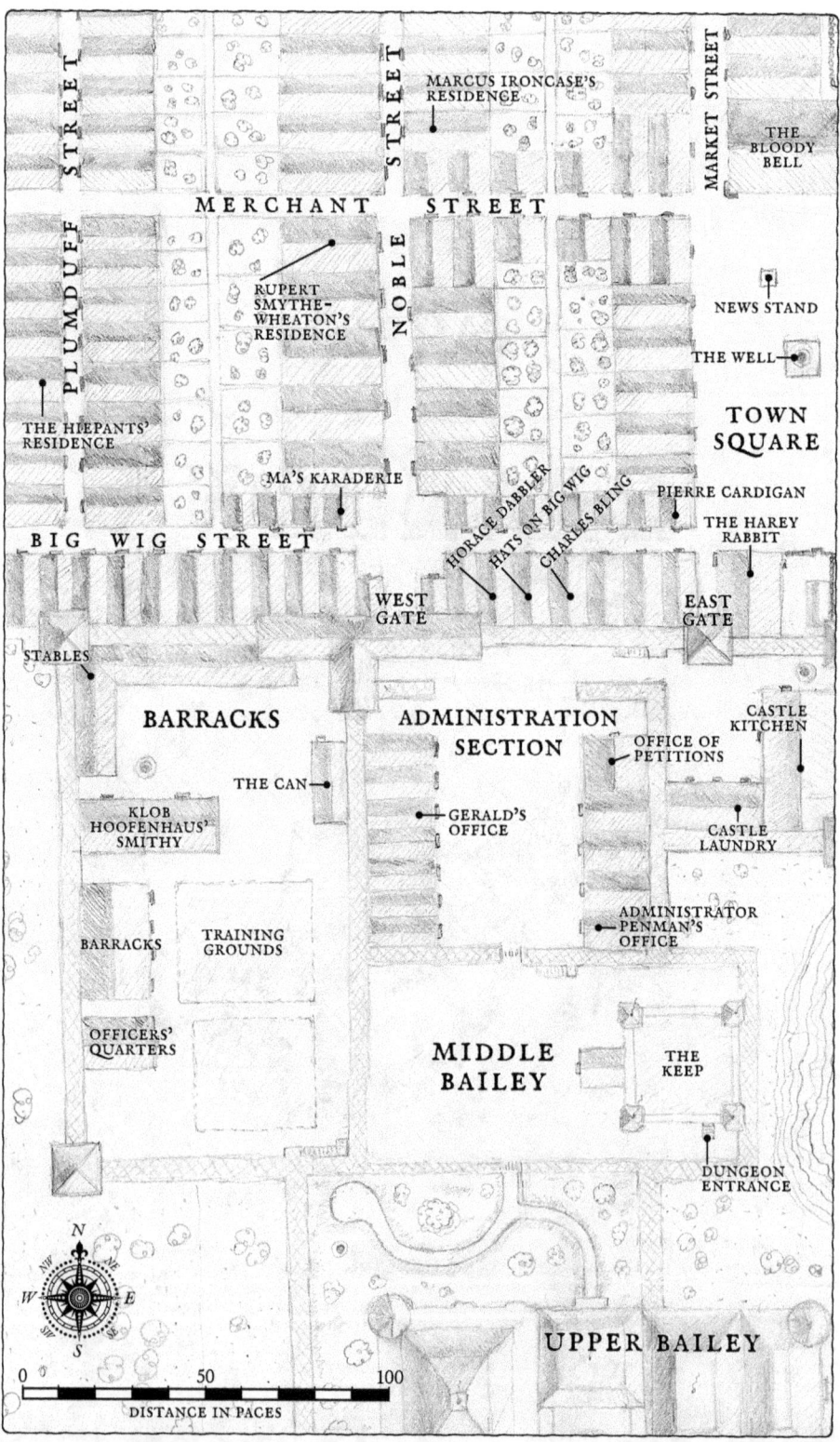

INTRODUCTION
Risen above The Swills

BRANDON SWILL WAS a young man with plenty of ambition. He had been promoted to lieutenant in the Purple Peril and given his own squad of twelve men three months ago. At 21 years and 216 days, he was the youngest ever to achieve this particular feat. (The Purple Peril were also known, by the envious and ignorant, as Cake Eaters. However, the name did have some credence, as Reginald Puffy regularly baked delicious pastries and cakes and often put aside some of them for the Purple Peril.) Brandon was proud of his rapid advancement, proud to wear the purple and gold, and proud to serve Captain Le Sharp, Sir Richard and the Duke.

The two years and three months he'd spent living in the castle barracks had changed him, but it had been a change for the better — he'd gained the approval of his seniors and the respect of his squad. Yes, Brandon was a man in favour, and his focus had been on retaining that favour. He had risen above the Swills, and he intended to keep rising.

That's not to say he didn't love his family. His parents and his sister meant more to him than any people alive — they were the salt of the earth. But that was their problem: they were too earthy. All that sun and colour blue nonsense and names starting with B, it's what had attracted them to The Bloody Bell in the first place. It was embarrassing, and it had no place in Brandon's world of shining boots and polished etiquette (and the occasional cake).

They also spoke like the riff-raff they served and seemed content with their lot, which was fine for his parents — they were pretty much set in their ways — but what of Bethany? *That's* who Brandon was really concerned about. She was smart and attractive and could achieve much more outside the confines of The Bell. And, of course, there was this Sunwatcher business and the Deed of Promise clouding her future. It was all rubbish. No-one in the Office of Legalities had ever heard of a Deed of Promise, and the name Bertrand from Blessed Whipping also drew a blank. However, the sooner he could put his family's minds at rest on *that* score the better. The arrival of Xavier certainly hadn't helped matters.

Chapter 1

Prepared to be disappointed

Monday, June 23: Four days before Doctor Manky approaches Sid at The Dead Duck. (11 days ago.)

BRANDON HAD FELT angry and ill-disposed towards the stranger who had been delivered into his family's life by that worm of a man, Bertrand. He'd arrived like some sort of impatient debt collector in the early hours of the morning after his sister's eighteenth birthday. It had put his parents into a raging panic about this Deed of Promise business. But, thankfully, Xavier had turned out to be something completely different… radically different, in fact.

As he spiralled his way back down The Keep, Brandon found himself feeling sorry for the poor sod. What kind of person would just turn up out of the blue, announce he was the Duke's son without anything to back up the claim except for a sweat-damaged note that anyone could have written, and then actually expect to be welcomed into the castle with open arms? Bloody hell, Sir Richard was right: he was either a terrible opportunist or extremely naive. Brandon favoured the latter.

There were a couple of things, however, that concerned Brandon. One: Sir Richard had changed his mind about having Xavier escorted from the castle after hearing Bertrand's name, and two: Xavier *did* bear a resemblance to the Duke.

He reached the bottom of the stairwell and headed back outside into the Middle Bailey. The deep afternoon shadows stretched across its cobblestoned courtyard as another very hot day sizzled to an end. Also coming to an end was Brandon's shift. All he had to do was report back to Sir Richard and see to it the Duke's 'guest' was fed and refreshed.

Brandon headed through the inner gate into the Administration Section of the Lower Bailey. That was another odd thing: Sir Richard normally conducted any official business in his own quarters in the Upper Bailey. Why he'd chosen to use Administrator Penman's office was puzzling.

He entered the cooler confines of the Office of Petitions and walked down the long, gloomy passage that ran behind three offices and the private antechamber in which Xavier had waited for his audience with Sir Richard. A door at the end of the passage opened up into the petitioners' waiting room, and beyond that lay the reception area where the Petitions Clerk filled in the details of peoples' grievances. It all seemed very tedious to Brandon, but he was proud that Lower Icing had such a system in place. It made his job of keeping the Duke's peace and enforcing Duchy law much more straightforward. It allowed him to think more… politically.

At the moment, however, Brandon's thoughts were of fulfilling his duty. They took him to the end office. After a quick rap on the wooden door, he entered the scroll-filled world of Administrator Penman. Sir Richard was still seated at the desk, reading through some of the petitions. Brandon took a few steps towards the desk before standing to attention and saluting, right fist pounding his heart.

"Sir Richard. Master Xavier is secure in The Keep."

Sir Richard briefly looked up from the petitions. "At ease, Lieutenant," he said distractedly. Then, leafing through the petitions, he continued. "Poor old Penman, having to sift through this excrement every day. He must have the resilience of a barmaid's arse."

"Yes, Sir Richard," responded Brandon, not entirely sure a response was required.

"I mean, just listen to this will you," continued Sir Richard, picking up one of the petitions. "A Paul Pickle is making a claim against an Edgar Roost for, and I quote: *Wilfully and knowingly destroying the composition of his compost heap.* Pickle accuses Roost of taking vegetable off-cuts from his compost to feed his chickens. Roost admits to doing so, but says he repays Pickle by supplying him with chicken droppings to fertilise his vegetable patch."

Sir Richard had a disarming ability of turning a casual observation into a pointed discussion within the space of a few words. His subtle change in intonation was whip-like, cracking through the air of pleasantness. As if to demonstrate, he completed the petition précis with a, "What do you make of that, Lieutenant?"

Brandon could almost feel the lash, but he didn't flinch — he hadn't become the youngest lieutenant in the Purple Peril by flinching. He responded, "It is strange that this petition has been lodged, Sir Richard. It would seem that such an arrangement would benefit both parties."

"Exactly," breathed Sir Richard (rolling up the whip), "and yet these two buffoons are blinded by pettiness and cannot see what is surely obvious to anyone with a modicum of common sense."

Sir Richard replaced the petition and looked up from the desk. Even though Brandon was standing at ease, there was no such thing as 'at ease' in Sir Richard's presence.

"We must be ever vigilant, Lieutenant, that we do not lose sight of what is best for the Duchy of Lower Icing."

"Of course, Sir Richard," Brandon affirmed immediately.

"As loyal servants, we must work *together*, and seize the opportunities that will bring prosperity."

"Yes, Sir Richard."

"And, at the same time, we must be prepared to defend the interests of the Duke, even if it means performing tasks that are dangerous or… unpleasant."

Brandon flushed as he again affirmed Sir Richard's sentiments. For about five excruciating seconds, the second most powerful man in the Duchy of Lower Icing studied him through sharp, appraising eyes. He finally acknowledged Brandon's compliance with a simple "Good" and then casually added, "Then you'll be prepared to deny that fool we have locked away in The Keep any comfort or nourishment."

"Yes, Sir Richard," Brandon answered, obediently, albeit with the slightest of hesitations.

Sir Richard picked up on slight hesitations better than a dog picked up fleas. This manifested itself in the raising of his right eyebrow. "It will just be for tonight, Lieutenant. Give the lad something to think about when you release him tomorrow morning. Is that more to your liking?"

It was a loaded question, but Brandon hadn't risen quickly through the ranks by avoiding confrontation. In fact, he believed that most people in the castle respected what he had to say. "I am simply curious, that's all, Sir Richard."

"I find curiosity usually leads to disappointment." The Seneschal pushed his tall frame out of the chair. "That imposter, now enjoying the Duke's hospitality, is a case in point."

"True, Sir Richard, but, as you said, we must be prepared to defend the interests of the Duke. For such a cause, I am prepared to be disappointed."

Sir Richard released a short bark of laughter. "Well said, Lieutenant." Then he walked around the desk. "Come, it's time to free ourselves from this prison of petitions. My rooms are a preferable place to satisfy your curiosity and slake my thirst. One gets rather parched surrounded by so much…" He waved his right arm, vaguely indicating the office walls, "parchment."

The journey to the Upper Bailey seemed to take a matter of moments. Brandon, following in the Seneschal's wake, had to stop for no-one. Once inside the palatial building set within the royal grounds of the castle, he sailed past an assortment of officials on the wind of unquestionable authority. The streamline, black figure in front of him strode purposely towards his rooms, barely acknowledging the deferential bows. Even though Brandon was only a passenger, the power was exhilarating, and his spirits soared at the possibility of following in Sir Richard's footsteps.

CHAPTER 2
Here on official business

I T WAS WITH a great sense of purpose and determination that Brandon walked through the twilit streets of Lower Icing. He was pleased to be on extended duty, committed to carrying out his orders, and delighted Sir Richard had taken him into his confidence.

His orders had taken him from the castle, down Noble Street and right into Merchant Street. There, some eighty strides ahead, on the corner of the Town Square, was his destination. The red bell painted on its sign always seemed to defy darkness and almost glowed in the quickly fading light.

There was a distinct change in atmosphere as he approached The Bloody Bell. Noble Street had been virtually deserted and calm, but now he was walking down Merchant Street there was no barrier of elegant terraces to protect him from the waves of raised voices and laughter. Underneath the chain-suspended sign, people spilled in and out of The Bell's corner entrance like mad ants.

Brandon had spent the first nineteen years of his life at the inn, but he no longer considered it his home; he regarded The Bell more as the place his family resided (and, of course, the place he grew up). Since becoming a guard, the barracks, and now the officers' quarters, had provided all the comfort he required. But The Bell had also become the place where he, and the twelve men under his command, performed regular patrols and were often called upon to maintain the peace. Only yesterday he'd had to arrest the Moleson Twins for causing a public affray (again). That, however, was the good thing about being raised in The Bloody Bell: he knew just about every patron by name and he knew the troublemakers from the harmless drunks, the informants from the boasters, and the influential from the big-noters; it was another reason why Brandon had moved up the ranks so quickly.

As he reached the inn's entrance, a large man was yelling at someone inside. His blubbery mass took up most of the doorway. Even from the back, it could only be one man: Alistair Bean. In his non-inebriated state, he was a softly spoken, polite gentleman who wrote poetry and popular songs, some of which had been commissioned by the Duke. In his current state, he was loud-mouthed and obnoxious (even by The Bell's standards). The trouble was, he was too educated for the mob and too easily wound up. You only had to call him 'String' or 'Runner' (or, if you really wanted fireworks, 'Jelly') and self-indignation would erupt from his mountainous frame. Unfortunately, eruptions were what the regulars at The Bell came for.

People were squeezing past Alistair to gain entrance, but Brandon was not the squeezing past type, particularly since he was on official Duke's business.

"Please step aside, Master Bean," Brandon announced officially. "You are blocking the doorway."

The only part of the fat, sweat-soaked figure to move was his pudding head. The effort of actually turning around was probably beyond him. Even the mechanics of rotating his neck proved too much and prevented him from actually looking at Brandon.

"What's this?" he shouted dramatically. "Am I to be assailed on all sides by insects and leeches, devouring my spirit and sucking on my soul?"

The big man was obviously the main entertainment for many of the revellers inside The Bell, because a large cheer accompanied this remark.

"Master Bean," replied Brandon calmly — he'd heard all this dozens of times before — "I am not interested in devouring or sucking any part of you. Please move out of the doorway. It's the last time I will ask you."

But Bean's attention had already turned back to the crowd. One of them yelled out something about having a whale of time. This got Alistair Bean moving, and at a surprisingly quick pace. He rocked forward into the muted light of the bar room. Brandon followed in his wake. People were cheering. Some began chanting, "Jel-ly, Jel-ly, Jel-ly," and banging their mugs against the table.

The four main protagonists — laughing and jeering — leapt up on their table to protect themselves from the sudden onrush of flesh and bone. Brandon recognised them — troublemakers the bunch of them — and knew there was no chance of diffusing the situation. It was time to get official.

All guardsmen carried a small bugle. They were mainly used for attracting attention; one long blast usually did the trick, but on the odd occasion, where urgent assistance was required, three quick, high-pitched notes were blown out. Brandon opted for the former; he'd have no trouble with the mob on the table, and he and his father could handle Alistair Bean. In fact, his father was already moving towards the table with his steely, no-nonsense expression that conveyed, even to the very inebriated, his disapproval of their behaviour, and that they were one badly chosen action away from tasting the cobblestones outside The Bloody Bell. (If you were lucky, you'd hit a patch that hadn't been vomited or urinated on.)

The bugle blast eventually broke through the ruckus, and the cheers and the bashing of mugs stuttered to a halt. The same, however, couldn't be said for Alistair. As the huge human frame bounded towards them, the four jesters on top of the table suddenly lost their comic timing, and, just like jesters, they flew through the air as Alistair crashed into the table. Their individual landings, however, were most un-jester like. The crowd resumed its cheering.

Bar retrieved the two closest ones by the backs of their collars, acknowledged Brandon's presence with a nod, and marched them out to the awaiting cobblestones. This was done to the accompaniment of cheers and laughter. The third miscreant decided, with Brandon's blessing, to escort himself quickly from the premises, leaving his hapless comrade sprawled on the floor looking somewhat confused. This was probably due to the fact that he was pinned down at his chest by Alistair's snoring head.

Somewhere out of the mass of merriment, Bethany arrived. She gave him a knowing smile and then knelt next to the sprawled figures beside the still-upright table. Brandon joined her.

The pinned man — Billy Offcut was his name; the youngest of eight Offcut siblings and a member of the renowned family that owned the Duchy's largest butchery — now looked more terrified than confused. Alistair's gelatinous neck, just inches away from Billy's face, was wobbling in time to his snoring. His cavernous mouth was open and a steady stream of drool accompanied his ale and eel pie breath.

"Geddim off me! Geddim off me! Geddim off me!" Billy cried, trying to squirm backwards, but he was already up against the edge of the bar.

"Calm down, Billy," Bethany said matter-of-factly. "This is what y'get for stirrin' the pot."

"It wozzen me. It woz them uvver fellas. I swear." He whimpered, still trying to squirm his way out from underneath the bulk of Alistair's head and shoulders.

Brandon knew Billy all too well: he was an over-indulged layabout who spent most of his time getting drunk and causing trouble. Only his family name, and the free supply of best quality meat to certain individuals, had kept Billy from The Can.

"'Bout time ya got lucky, Billy," yelled someone behind Brandon.

"Yeah, but couldn' ya wait 'til ya got 'im home?" yelled someone else.

Brandon looked up at the crowd of revellers who'd surrounded the scene. "Right, you lot," he said, standing up, "back to your tables, and keep your comments to yourselves."

"Come on, Brandon," objected Daniel Buckwheat, one of Reg Puffy's bread-makers, "it's only a bit o' fun."

Brandon was in no mood for fun. He'd been sent to The Bell on an important assignment; he didn't need this kind of inane bar room banter distracting him.

"I won't ask you again, Daniel," he said forcefully. "Back to your table unless you prefer the comfort and camaraderie of a prison cell."

Daniel looked taken aback, as did his companions. "You'd really chuck us in The Can, Brandon?"

"Do you really want to find out?" Brandon countered.

And upon hearing those words, the onlookers grumbled their way back to their tables.

"Bit harsh, weren't it, lad?" his father said, appearing in the void left by the onlookers.

"Sorry, Pa, but I'm here on official business, not to keep the customers happy."

"Wha' official business migh' tha' be then?"

Before Brandon could answer, Bethany's calm voice somehow rose through the raucous crowd. "I need some 'elp, Brandon."

It required both men to heave the massive Alistair Bean off the diminutive Billy Offcut. In the process, Alistair let out a semi-conscious, eel pie belch that struck Billy right in his flaring nostrils, sending the young man into a coughing fit while he writhed and wriggled (like an eel) to escape. Eventually he was able to slither from under the man mountain. Brandon and Bar let Alistair's head and shoulders go, and he slumped back to the floor with a squelchy thud.

"Go and get some pails of water, Bethany," said their father, wearily. "Get Rosie to 'elp, an' tell y'mother t'heat up some of 'er brew."

"Yes, Pa," replied Bethany.

"As for you," he said, addressing the teary-eyed Billy, who, in some kind of delayed shock, was still sitting on the floor, propped up by the edge of the bar. "I don' want you or y'mates within sniffin' distance of The Bell for two weeks. You got that?"

Billy managed a shaky nod.

"Right! Well get y'snivelling face outta here now!"

Billy jerked to his feet and glared at Brandon and his father.

"Whatcha gonna do 'bout this?" he said, addressing Brandon through quivering lips. "That tub o' lard 'saulted me."

"Don't push your luck, Billy," replied Brandon. "It'll push back one day."

Brandon held Billy's defiant glare, before the youngest Offcut moved sulkily towards the door. After a few paces, he stopped and faced the male Swills. "You ain't 'eard the last of this." Then he made his way out of the inn — flushed with chagrin — to the jeers and ironic cheers of the patrons.

Brandon exchanged a knowing look with his father. There would be consequences for their actions, but nothing they couldn't handle, and Brandon couldn't deny that he felt some satisfaction in chopping that particular Offcut down to size. Their other problem lay sprawled across the floor, face up and snoring.

"We'll 'andle this, Brandon," said his father. "You best be 'bout your official business. Take it 'as somethin' t'do with Master Xavier?"

"It has, but it's nothing for you to worry about. Sir Richard has everything in hand. I've come to collect his belongings. Are they still in his room?"

"Aye, lad."

"I'll send some of the boys around to help with Alistair."

"No need. Y'mother'll sober 'im up. She's got a soft spot for the stupid, fat git. Got a wonderful way of 'spressing himself 'cordin' to her."

Alistair Bean snored on.

Brandon lit the candle on the desk in the corner of the room. He picked it up and held it in front of him. As he turned away from the desk, the candlelight revealed what he'd expected it to: a neatly made single bed next to an open window. On the floor, at the base of the bed on the opposite side of the window, was a reinforced leather case. This also came as no surprise. As Brandon moved towards the rectangular object, he estimated it to be some three feet long, two feet wide and one foot deep. It was lying on its side, with its handle and metal fasteners pointing towards him. Holding the candle over the case, he could see it was in pristine condition except for a scuff mark near one of the corners.

He placed the candle on the floor and knelt beside the case. The two fasteners were easy to unfasten, and the sturdy lid opened smoothly, revealing a very neatly packed arrangement of clothing. It said a lot about the owner: meticulous, regimented and precise. This wasn't the case of an adventurer or risk-taker; this was the case of a person who needed to fit in and have a sense of purpose.

"Interesting," Brandon mumbled. "Let's see what else you have in here, Xavier."

He began to carefully remove the top layer of clothing, which was basically grouped into two piles. Under a white, cotton shirt and a pair of brown, woollen trousers lay a small wooden case. Brandon removed the case and placed it on the bed, next to the candle. It looked to be a very plain oak case about a foot wide and foot and half long: the kind that held tools or trinkets. A small metal plate in the centre of its lid was neatly engraved, identifying the owner: Xavier. Brandon ran his fingers across its dull surface; it was flush against the oak, a perfectly smooth transition from wood to metal. To create such a fit required a great amount of skill. The seemingly simple exterior of the case belied its artistry; a bit like its owner, perhaps, thought Brandon.

Brandon flicked open the latches and lifted the lid. Even by candlelight, the case's contents were mesmerising.

CHAPTER 3

Somewhat more accomplished

BRANDON WALKED DOWN the back stairs, carrying Xavier's travelling case, with all his possessions packed back inside. The oak case, full of its strange and wonderful containers of brightly coloured powders and fluids, and its beautifully crafted drawers of odd tools and devices, was lodged safely in a cocoon of clothing. He couldn't wait to show it to Sir Richard, which was why he was taking the back stairs; he didn't want to get caught in the tide of ale-fuelled aggravation that came in (and went out) every night at The Bell.

His quiet exit was thwarted at the bottom of the stairs.

"That you, Brandon, love?"

He cursed silently, then answered, "Yes, Ma."

She was standing in the hallway that led to the dining room. She began to walk towards him. "Pa said you was 'ere. Is that Master Xavier's case? You takin' it to the castle? What's happened to the lad? Is he in some kinda—"

"Ma," Brandon cut in.

"Yes, love?" She'd closed to within touching distance. She looked worn out.

Brandon immediately felt guilty for speaking to her in such a curt, regimented tone. "Sorry, Ma," he whispered, leaning forward and kissing her on the top of her forehead.

She squeezed his free arm in response. "Tish and pish," she said, dismissing the apology as unnecessary. "I know you got more importan' things t'do than listen t'your ma blabberin' on."

Brandon smiled warmly at her. She really was a selfless person.

"Is everythin' alright, love?"

"Everything is fine, Ma," he said, gently resting his hand on her shoulder. "I've just been sent to retrieve Master Xavier's belongings. He is spending the night in the castle."

"Is he—"

"He is well, but I'm unable to tell you more… and in any case, there isn't much more *to* tell."

This seemed to satisfy his mother. "Okay, love. Be off with you then. Don't want you gettin' in trouble for not carryin' out y'duty… even if it is jus' carryin' a travellin' case."

This was followed by a wink. She often winked — it was part of her personality — but sometimes, like this time, it made Brandon feel uneasy. That wink had meaning.

"Well, be off with you then," she said, playfully pushing Brandon towards the back exit. "Master Bean needs takin' care of."

Brandon gave her a withering look as he reached for the back door handle. "Why do you put up with him, Ma? He's never going to change."

"I know, love," she replied simply. "You take care now." Then she turned and walked back down the blue-carpeted hallway.

Sir Richard closed the wooden case. He'd spent the last fifteen minutes examining it. He'd taken out the contents of the drawers, removed the glass jars and vials from their tray with a tool he'd found in one of the drawers, smelt some of the brighter-coloured powders, liquids and ointments, discovered a second tray underneath the first, with more jars and vials, and then meticulously replaced everything. During the process, he'd barely acknowledged Brandon's presence, but he hadn't dismissed him either, so Brandon simply stood at ease in the opulent surroundings of Sir Richard's private quarters and watched his commanding officer, seated at a large dining table, carry out the inspection.

"Well, Lieutenant," he finally remarked as he secured the second of two latches into place. "It seems our guest is somewhat more accomplished than I gave him credit for."

"Yes, sir," replied Brandon, hoping it was the right response.

Judging by Sir Richard's appraising stare and arch of the eyebrow, he doubted it had been.

"Do you know what this is?" he said, patting the wooden case, but keeping his eye on Brandon.

"I must admit that I have never seen anything of its like, but it looks to be something an apothecary or perhaps an alchemist might use."

"Hmm," Sir Richard mused, before adding in a much more positive tone, "Possibly, and no."

Brandon remained silent. It was the safer option.

"The case is far too ornate for an alchemist, Lieutenant," continued Sir Richard after a momentary pause. "Alchemists are poor; it's rather ironic when you consider it is their mad pursuit of wealth that makes them so. In fact, by definition, alchemists do not exist, unless *you* know of someone who has actually mastered the art of transforming base metals into gold?"

"No, Sir Richard."

"Well, quite," Sir Richard concurred. "As for our guest being an apothecary? It's possible, I suppose, but I doubt it. Those powders and unguents have herbal and floral redolence. I have never smelt their like from any apothecary I've had the misfortune to be associated with."

"True enough, sir," agreed Brandon, remembering the vile-smelling concoction whipped up by one of Horace Dabbler's cronies for a mild fever he'd caught last year.

Sir Richard drummed his fingers against the table, staring into its polished mahogany surface. Then, as if talking to his polished mahogany reflection, he said, "I think we would benefit from another discussion with Master Xavier. Yes, it could be most enlightening." His gaze darted sharply back to Brandon. "Arrange it, will you, Lieutenant?"

"Yes, Sir Richard."

"Leave it until ten o'clock tomorrow morning, by which time, no doubt, he'll be somewhat tired, hungry and thirsty. I, on the other hand, shall be well-rested and nourished by a hearty breakfast." He smiled at Brandon. "Hardly seems fair, does it, Lieutenant?"

Brandon hated these rhetorical questions. "One should always seek to gain the upper hand, sir." It sounded lame, even to Brandon's ears, but it brought a grin from Sir Richard.

"And to make sure we do exactly that, we shall, once again, conduct the meeting in Administrator Penman's office. I don't want him anywhere near this part of the castle, and, in particular, anywhere near the Duke — the fewer people who know about this young man the better. You're not to say a word to anyone. Is that clear?" His voice was unusually intense.

"Of course, Sir Richard," Brandon replied promptly and earnestly.

After a moment's appraisal, he said, "Very well, I shall see you tomorrow at ten with Master Xavier in tow."

Brandon stood to attention and saluted, fist across his heart.

"Good night, Lieutenant." His tone was dismissive, his gaze already returning to the oak case.

"Good night, Sir Richard," replied Brandon, relaxing back into 'at ease'. As he turned around and made his way towards the exit of his commander's private quarters, he heard Sir Richard say in muted tones, "This could be a very unusual case."

Brandon glanced over his shoulder, expecting to see Sir Richard looking at him. Instead, he was deep in thought, stroking the case's metal nameplate. It made Brandon feel slightly uneasy.

The sun had been down for at least an hour, but the air was still warm and the walls and cobblestones still radiated the day's heat. Brandon was looking forward to getting out of his uniform and washing away the sweat and grime of a fifteen-hour shift.

As he walked from the Upper Bailey, across the Middle Bailey forecourt, and past the great stone Keep, he looked up to the window of Xavier's room. It appeared no different to the other windows: just one of many black rectangular smudges smeared onto the gloomy grey edifice. He wondered how the man within the smudge was coping. He couldn't help feeling slightly sorry for him — after all, he'd committed no offense. Unless you counted making false claims against the Duke, but Brandon was no longer sure what he thought about Xavier's claims; even Sir Richard seemed to be reassessing his opinion.

Brandon did an 'about face' and walked back towards the entrance of The Keep. Surely it couldn't hurt to check on Xavier? As he reached the fore-building, he halted. Sir Richard had wanted his 'guest' left alone until the morning; Brandon would be disobeying orders if he continued. He turned around and marched quickly to the barracks.

CHAPTER 4

Your turn to ponce around

BRANDON WOKE the next morning to the familiar sound of bird calls. A family of wrens were nesting in the eaves above his sleeping quarters. Normally he didn't mind a chirpy awakening — he'd always been an early riser — but his sleep had been unusually restless and he wasn't exactly in a chirpy frame of mind. In fact, he felt like he'd spent the previous evening going mug-to-mug with Alistair Bean instead of coming off duty and treating himself to a relaxing soak in the tub.

He wiped the sleep from his eyes and fumbled in the early morning darkness for the flint that lay on his bedside table. Grabbing the small, hard stone, he clambered out of bed and, dressed only in his breeches, stumbled towards the door of his regimented but comfortable room. The three other Purple Peril lieutenants were in identical-size rooms along the passageway and were either asleep or on duty.

Brandon yawned groggily, opened the door, and turned right towards the officers' common room. It was a large, open space containing a sturdy oak table with bench seating for at least twelve. However, the main feature of the room was the large inglenook fireplace set into the southern wall. Brandon clumsily negotiated his way through the feeble pre-dawn light to the massive metal grate housed in the inglenook. It supported the charred remains of last night's firewood. Next to the grate, leaning against the side of the inglenook, was a poker. Placing the flint on the hearth, Brandon grabbed the blackened metal rod and poked away at the burnt-out logs. Bits of charcoal rained through the grate onto a metal tray positioned below. The tray had already collected quite a bit of ash from a night's worth of burning. Brandon thought about emptying it, but he felt too sapped of energy this morning, and, in any case, it was the job of the new recruits to keep the officers' common room clean and provisioned. Putting the poker back in place, Brandon moved a few paces to the right of the inglenook, where a wooden chest was positioned against the wall alongside a stack of neatly chopped wood. The chest contained kindling: small sticks, twigs, and bundles of dried grass. The new recruits had been slack here as well and only a smattering of twigs and a few bundles of grass remained. Brandon sighed as he squatted down next to it; he really felt as if he'd been awake all night. It was a struggle to keep focused. He could feel himself being lulled by the sound of the wrens' whimsical twittering.

Brandon awoke with a jolt, hands flailing for some sort of support as he fell forward into the kindling chest. His left hand came to the rescue, finding purchase against the stack of wood. He was then able to use his right hand to steady himself against the top edge of the chest. The shock had stimulated his faculties. It wasn't long before he had a fire going and water steaming in a blackened metal pot hanging over the flames.

Moving away from the fire, Brandon felt the touch of a cool breeze waft through the open window of the common room. Drawn by the refreshing tendrils, he walked over to the window and breathed in the new day. The window faced east with a view of the barrack's compound and the fortified wall that sectioned the military from the administration. Above the grey stone wall, a thickly clouded sky was in the dawning stage of illumination. The morning was colourless, but the air felt good against his bare skin.

In the waking light Brandon could hear horses spluttering and neighing in the stables, and Klob Hoofenhaus, the blacksmith, preparing his forge. He leaned out the window and looked left towards the northern wall of the castle; in the distance, a couple of stable hands were going about their business and just outside the main barracks, some twenty paces away, three guardsmen stood in quiet conversation. None of them were in his squad, but he knew two of them well; he'd served with 'Giblets' McLean and Edward 'Grippy' Handel before his promotion. The third was a mature-age recruit — George somebody — wearing the plain blue uniform of a cadet man-at-arms.

Brandon gave a short, high-pitched whistle. All three looked in his direction. He beckoned them over. "Morning, lads," he said amiably as they approached.

Giblets and Grippy responded with casual good humour, remarking on his semi-naked presentation. George, however, stood to attention and saluted a crisp, "Morning, sir."

Smiling at his erstwhile comrades, Brandon said, "You two could learn a lot from George here, though I fully understand *your* need to comment on my physique, Giblets."

"Piss off," smiled Giblets, whose physique was comparable to a starving greyhound; you could just about see his insides from the outside – hence the epithet. Grippy smiled, while George continued to stand at attention.

Flicking his gaze to the cadet, Brandon told him to stand at ease. Then, returning his attention to Grippy, he asked, "You lads going on or coming off?"

"Jus' finishin' up, Brando," replied Grippy. Brandon didn't mind familiarity from his former squad members, as long as he wasn't on duty or in uniform. "Took George 'ere on his first night patrol," continued Grippy; "Quieter than a queen's fart."

"No trouble at The Bell then?" asked Brandon.

"Not as we heard," replied Grippy.

"Nuttin' unusual anyways," Giblets chipped in.

Brandon nodded thoughtfully before snapping back into the moment. "Good. In that case, George, before you go off duty, there are a few jobs that need attending to, and you look like a keen sort."

An hour later, Brandon was dressed, fed and ready for the day ahead. George had replenished the tinder box. He'd also run over to the kitchen and brought back two freshly baked loaves of bread, some cheese and ham, and a large pork and parsnip pie. Brandon had been right: he was keen. It turned out that George's surname was Martin. At the age of forty-three, he'd decided to sign up because he needed more structure in his life. (Well, he certainly couldn't be disappointed on *that* count, Brandon thought). George had been fairly vague about his past and, truth be told, Brandon wasn't that curious. About the only personal thing George Martin had shared was his interest in beetles, and he had even offered to show Brandon his beetle collection.

By this time, his fellow Purple Perilians had surfaced and were sitting around the table in various stages of breaking their fast. Brandon was sipping on a brew of honeyed wine mixed with hot water, mulling over the upcoming meeting with Sir Richard and Xavier.

"Come now, old chap, Square Parade is not all that bad, surely?" It was Sebastian Fitzbadly who had spoken, and who was now looking at him with bemused loftiness. Seb was a distant cousin to the Duke and had become a lieutenant simply because of this connection. Fortunately, he was a likeable sort and took his position seriously enough to have earned respect through application (rather than appellation).

He'd caught Brandon off guard. "Sorry, Seb... what about Square Parade?"

"It's your turn to ponce around like a cockerel with a spoon up its arse," Jethro Fowler piped in, delighting in the bad news.

"And keep Gerald the Herald company, of course," added Peter Potts nonchalantly.

It suddenly dawned on him: today was Tuesday and, at two o'clock this afternoon, he and six of his twelve men would be escorting the Town Crier to and from the Town Square. In between, they'd have to listen to him bellowing out inane, and sometimes exaggerated, bits of news about what was happening in Lower Icing. And then there was the ridiculous Posting Ceremony, where new proclamations were officially 'delivered to the people'. However, the only people who stayed around to watch the Posting Ceremony were children, and all *they* wanted delivered was a reaction to their jeering and face-pulling.

Brandon sighed; Square Parade was the last thing he felt like doing.

"Cheer up, Brandon," said Seb amiably, "at least it's a cool, overcast day — should be quite pleasant really."

"Yeah, it may even rain on your parade," smiled Potts.

Jethro stopped eating and struck a thoughtful pose. "So... you'll be pissed on while having the piss taken out of you. Yep, doesn't get much better than that."

They all laughed.

Brandon spent the next couple of hours making sure his uniform (and that of his squad) was Parade worthy. That meant polishing boots, cleaning swords and scabbards, straightening feathers in hats, and generally making sure that everything was presentable. In a way, it was a good distraction from the upcoming meeting with Sir Richard; the plight of Xavier had been playing on his mind, and that, no doubt, was the reason he'd had such a poor night's sleep.

At nine o'clock, Brandon decided to fill in more time by checking in on the Moleson Twins. The cell block — referred to by most people as 'The Can' (although Brandon always thought it should be called 'The Cannot') — was a stone building set on the east side of the compound, across from the smithy.

As he walked past the smithy, he watched Klob Hoofenhaus douse a red-hot horseshoe in a large bucket of water. Klob's massive frame was momentarily obscured by a plume of steam. The towering man was in his early thirties, with long, white-blond hair that was tied back in a ponytail. He also had blond facial hair with a double-plaited beard. Klob was from Longboatia — a country to the north of The Five Duchies where the climate was harsh and cold. Longboatians were great shipbuilders and seafarers, and, according to Klob, hardier and more adventurous than any other people. Still, Klob was a fair man, treated everyone equally, and worked wonders with a hammer and anvil.

"Morning, Klob," said Brandon, regarding the bare-chested muscle giant.

Klob looked up, and, recognising Brandon, replied, "Ar…Yar… Mornink, Lieutenant."

"Keeping busy as usual," Brandon commented for want of anything better to say; casual banter was not something that Klob excelled at.

"Oh yar," he nodded, and waved the three-foot steel tongs around in his left hand as if they were nothing more cumbersome than a pair of nail scissors.

Brandon smiled awkwardly. "At least it's cooler, Klob. It even looks like rain."

"Yar… Cooler is goodt," he said, turning away and walking back into the forge, dousing the conversation like a red-hot horseshoe.

The Can consisted of six small cells measuring some eight feet by ten feet. Each cell contained two wooden sleeping pallets and two buckets — one for drinking water and one for passing water — and nothing more. The Can wasn't designed for long-term incarceration, it was more a place to house drunkards and petty troublemakers for a few days. It gave them the opportunity to sober up and see the error of their ways. (The former was always achieved; the latter, rarely.) The Can was hardly ever empty, although, surprisingly, it was hardly ever full. However, things could get messy on the odd Saturday night when The Can overflowed with ale-louts, supplied mainly by his parents' establishment and, to a lesser extent, The Dead Duck.

At the moment it contained three regulars: a harmless habitual drunk, Willie Trafalgar, and the far from harmless Moleson Twins, Mick and Mal. Brandon had arrested them on Sunday afternoon for, officially, breaching the peace, but, in reality, it was because they were nasty pieces of work that deserved locking up (and for a lot longer than the maximum period of a week that Brandon could enforce). At least he'd taken some pleasure in the fact that they'd been arrested at The Bloody Bell and that his Pa had been man enough to stand up to them. Still, one day they'd go too far, maim or murder someone, and then they'd be subject to the Duke's justice.

Willie was in the first cell. Just as a matter of course, Brandon decided to look in on him. However, judging by the volume of snoring permeating through the reinforced oak door, Willie was still sleeping off another night on the ale. Brandon slid open a small metal panel that was built into the door at eye level. It allowed guards to converse with prisoners without having to risk opening the cell door. It took a moment for his eyes to adjust to the gloomy interior (the only natural light came from an iron-barred opening above the door) and, as expected, Willie lay sprawled messily across one of the wooden pallets. The stench of vomit and urine was overpowering, and Brandon suspected other bodily excretions were also involved in the foul cocktail. He shut the viewing panel; the cell would have to be cleaned out soon. That was another job for the cadets.

Brandon opened the viewing panel of the second cell. Mal Moleson sat on one of the pallets, leaning against the opposite wall. He treated Brandon to a baleful expression, accentuated by a graze on his right cheek where he'd been pinned against the stone wall of The Bell.

"Wot?" he said, challengingly.

"Enjoying yourself, Mal?"

"Piss off, Brandon," he snarled.

"Very well," replied Brandon, calmly. "See you in five days."

Mal leapt up off the bed and was at the door before Brandon had a chance to close the viewing panel. "Woz your game, eh? Reckon y'pretty special inya shiny uniform, dontcha? Well, I know you, Brandon, and you ain't nuffin' more than a dressed-up barrel boy. So y'better watcher self, boyo."

Brandon had heard it all before. "Well, thanks for the advice, Mal. I'll be sure to do that." He smiled, then slammed the viewing panel on the angry, unkempt visage of the elder twin. Mal had always had a mean streak in him, but since his father had died a couple of months ago, the streak had been tinged with madness. So much so, his wife wouldn't have him in the house and he'd had to move in with Mick. And now, the once less aggressive twin had begun to act identically to his identical brother.

Brandon opened the panel of cell number three.

"Wot?" snarled Mick, but there was sulkiness in his tone.

"Just making sure your accommodation is up to standard, Mick."

"Yeah, it's ya standard stinkin' rat 'ole," he said glumly from the opposite corner of the cell, swarthy features obscured by the dim light.

"Perfect for your standard stinking rat then. That's good. We like to make our guests feel at home."

Mick sighed. "Whatcha want, Brandon?"

His demeanour irked Brandon; he was acting like a victim of some miscarriage of justice, like he and his brother's behaviour wasn't totally anti-social and frighteningly aggressive. And the fact that some of that aggression had been directed towards his father made Brandon even less sympathetic to any hardship either of the Moleson Twins might experience in The Can.

"What I want is for you and your arse-wipe of a brother to leave The Bell and my family alone."

Mick made a scoffing sound.

"Because if you two don't start pulling your heads in, you'll lose them. And that's a promise, Mick." Brandon could feel the blood pulsing through his head as he stared at the motionless and expressionless figure slumped casually in the corner.

The heartbeats of silence were broken by Mick's mocking reply, "Is *that* the bes' y'can do?"

Chapter 5

A breach in security

BRANDON HAD WORKED up a bit of a sweat by the time he reached Xavier's room. The cooler day was yet to permeate the sun-heated confines of The Keep, and walking up the spiral stairs, while not taxing, certainly got his blood flowing.

The meeting with Sir Richard was half an hour away, but Brandon saw no harm in making sure Xavier was in a presentable state. He unlocked the door — the keys remained in their locks in this part of The Keep — and entered the room.

The condition of Xavier came as quite a shock to Brandon: he was standing casually next to the window with a cup in his hand, looking relaxed and well groomed. The once-bare table now held a plate and a jug. Lying on the plate was an apple core and the peel of an orange, as well as the pastry-flake remnants of — judging by the familiar smell — one of Reg Puffy's pork and parsnip pies. Also lying on the table was a damp towel, smudged with patches of dirt and grime. Next to the table was a pail of soapy water.

"Good morning, Lieutenant," Xavier said in welcome.

Brandon took a moment to process what had happened and then abruptly enquired, "Who brought you this?"

It was hard to tell whether Xavier looked indignant or embarrassed by Brandon's tone. "A couple of kitchen hands." There was definitely a hint of indignation. "I take it, however, you would like to know who *organised* this for me."

"Listen, Xavier," Brandon said evenly, moving into the room, "this is no time for games, particularly when Sir Richard is dealing the cards."

Xavier smiled sardonically (much like Sir Richard), then took a long drink from his cup. "Excuse me, Lieutenant, I was quite thirsty an hour ago, and, now that you've arrived, I may well be thirsty again. Best make the most of my reprieve."

Brandon felt a flush of guilt; this was not how he would have treated Xavier. However, at the same time, he respected Sir Richard's methods. "I can understand your resentment, Xavier. Certain precautions have been deemed necessary, particularly where the Duke is concerned. Now, as you quite rightly stated, I would like to know who organised this for you."

"And if I refuse?"

"I'd advise against such a stance. After all, it would be a simple enough task to find out the culprit's identity."

"True," the young man acknowledged. He seemed almost at ease and accepting of his fate. But now that Brandon had had a chance to study him more closely, there were signs that his incarceration had been somewhat of an ordeal. His eyes were puffy, and the white lace collar and cuffs that protruded from underneath his green velvet doublet were sweat-stained and smudged with grime. His white trousers were also scuffed with dirt. Once again, Brandon felt a pang of guilt.

"Look, Xavier," Brandon said, dropping the military manner, "it's in your best interests to cooperate. If you are who you claim to be, the truth will out."

Xavier regarded him for a moment, before murmuring, "The Town Crier."

"Pardon?"

"That's who was kind enough to treat me like the guest I thought I was."

"Gerald Hiepants?" Brandon was incredulous.

"Yes. Gerald," confirmed Xavier, placing the mug on the table. "A most amiable man. He was quite outraged over my treatment, particularly after I told him who I was."

"You told Gerald about your... situation?" Brandon could hardly speak; he felt like someone had grabbed him by the throat.

Xavier nodded. "Yes, and he was most interested in my 'situation', as you call it."

Sir Richard was going to explode when he heard about this, and Brandon would be the one standing in the firing line.

Brandon knocked on Administrator Penman's door. He was no longer looking forward to his meeting with Sir Richard and dreaded to think how his commanding officer would react when he was apprised of Xavier's discovery, particularly since it involved, of all people, the Town Crier.

"Enter," came the terse voice of Sir Richard.

Brandon inhaled deeply, and mentally prepared himself for the verbal onslaught that was certainly waiting for him. What he wasn't prepared for, however, was a very flustered-looking Town Crier sitting opposite Sir Richard at Administrator Penman's desk. It could mean only one thing: the news had already been broken. Brandon's stomach dropped; this was a bad situation just made worse, but somehow he managed to salute his commanding officer and stand to attention without faltering.

Sir Richard, dressed immaculately in black (as was his wont), regarded him with disturbing calmness. Underneath the surface, however, Brandon could tell he was seething: his eyes were afire and his jaw muscles clenched and unclenched in a struggle to control his temper.

"Well, Lieutenant. It seems we have a breach in security." Sir Richard's eyes bored into Brandon's, and he dared not look away.

"Yes, Sir Richard," he acknowledged, standing statue still.

"Where is the…" He paused, glanced at Gerald, then back to Brandon, "imposter?"

"In the reception room," Brandon answered, eyes fixed on his superior.

Sir Richard drummed the fingers of his right hand on the surface of the desk, eyes fixed on Brandon. They sounded like the drums of an execution.

"If I may —" Gerald began.

"You may not, Master Hiepants." The sentence was sliced cleanly off at the head. All the while, Sir Richard kept his gaze on Brandon, not missing a beat with his fingers. The same could not be said for Brandon's heart; the tension was terrible.

Eventually, the drumming stopped and Sir Richard took a deep breath. "This is what I propose, Lieutenant."

Brandon concentrated on maintaining eye contact.

"Until the case against this confidence-trickster is proven, he is to be confined in The Keep. However, during that time, he is to be treated with all the comforts befitting a guest; it is something Master Hiepants feels very strongly about."

Sir Richard glanced over at the Town Crier and treated him to an expression one might associate with being confronted by the odour of a particularly ripe cheese. It was only subtle, and momentary, but it spoke volumes of Sir Richard's distaste at having to concede anything to the Gerald Hiepants.

Brandon didn't dare glance in Gerald's direction; he was still at attention.

"I intend to get to the bottom of this," Sir Richard announced, "and I expect your *full* co-operation."

"Well, of course, Sir Richard," replied the Town Crier, as if it was ridiculous to suggest otherwise.

"Yes, sir," Brandon snapped out obediently, just in case the remark was also intended for him.

Sir Richard treated Brandon to a pained look. "Oh, for pity's sake, Lieutenant. Stand at ease."

Brandon flushed with embarrassment. He didn't mind being disciplined, but not in the company of a civilian, particularly one as ineffectual as Gerald Hiepants. And, as the only person standing, he felt even more exposed.

"Master Hiepants," Sir Richard continued, "I don't wish to detain you any longer."

There was an awkward moment of inaction before the Town Crier realised he'd been dismissed. An arched right eyebrow from Sir Richard was all it took for realisation to dawn. "Oh, I see," he mumbled, jumping to his feet. "Plenty to do and all that; must make sure the voice is up to scratch, what."

Sir Richard grimaced. "I'll leave it to you to make the accommodation arrangements. Just be sure it's somewhere in The Keep, and somewhere *secure*."

Gerald nodded compliantly and began moving towards the door. He looked relieved.

"And remember what we discussed, Town Crier. I will be *most* disappointed if you suffer from *any* memory lapse."

Gerald acknowledged Sir Richard's remark with a nervous nod before fumbling the door latch open.

"Oh, and send our esteemed guest in, if you wouldn't mind."

"Yes, Sir Richard," replied Gerald as he disappeared out of the office.

"Sit down, Lieutenant." Sir Richard indicated the seat the Town Crier had just vacated. Brandon complied without a word. "This is an unexpected occurrence, but one that may be turned to our advantage."

Brandon remained silent — even though he was curious to know how Gerald had discovered Xavier — and concentrated on what his commanding officer was about to say.

"Our Town Crier has been completely taken in by our mystery man." His demeanour had changed significantly; he seemed more relaxed and less inclined to have Brandon expelled from the Purple Peril for dereliction of duty. "He is also under the impression that I think him a fool for being taken in, and, while not so far from the truth, it is exactly the impression I *want* him to be under."

Brandon nodded thoughtfully as Sir Richard continued.

"I also want Master Hiepants to feel a sense of injustice at my supposed ill-treatment of this so-called Xavier." Sir Richard paused and regarded Brandon for a moment. "Can you ascertain why I should want this, Lieutenant?"

Brandon wasn't sure at all, so he fell back on the tried and true: "To gain the upper hand, Sir Richard," he answered with as much conviction as he could muster.

Sir Richard smiled his interrogation smile. It had the opposite effect to most smiles — rather than being kind and reassuring, it filled its recipient with fear and uncertainty.

"It's more a case, Lieutenant, of letting Master Hiepants and his… righteous cause think *they* have the upper hand."

On cue, the door was opened by the Town Crier, who nodded encouragingly as he ushered a weary-looking Xavier into Administrator Penman's office. Although his appearance had been improved by his rudimentary wash, he was hardly what Brandon would call healthy-looking: his pallor was a similar hue to the rolled-up parchments stacked across every square inch of wall space. He also looked sun-touched on his nose and forehead, his golden hair was groomed but lifeless and hung limply to his shoulders, and his brown eyes were dull and wary.

"Ah, Master Xavier," said Sir Richard, pleasantly. "Do sit down."

It took a second for Brandon to realise that he was occupying the seat that was being proffered by his superior. Brandon quickly jumped to his feet and moved the chair away from the desk, allowing Xavier to simply sit down.

"Thank you, Lieutenant."

Brandon couldn't help but admire the way the man behind the desk played every role. He was a man of many parts, yet those parts were lost on most people because they weren't aware they were in a play.

"Firstly, allow me to apologise for our treatment of you. It must seem confusing, to say the least."

Brilliant, thought Brandon. It was an apology without any admission of personal wrong doing. He could just as easily be apologising for Gerald's actions. Xavier, however, seemed to accept the apology at face value.

Sir Richard then lifted his gaze to the lingering Town Crier. "Master Hiepants, I believe you have a room to prepare, and you, Lieutenant, will report back to me when all is in order. Meanwhile…" His gaze flicked back to the occupant of the chair, "Master Xavier and I have less mundane matters to discuss."

Brandon followed the Town Crier out of the office, leaving the black cat to toy with his tattered mouse.

CHAPTER 6

Why such precautions are necessary

THE TOWN CRIER looked relieved as he and Brandon exited the eastern Administration building. "Well, what do you make of that, Lieutenant; bit of a change in tune, what? Sir Richard gave me quite a rollicking before you came in, but I stood my ground, of that you can be assured. I can be—"

"Excuse me, Master Hiepants," Brandon interrupted as politely as possible; the Town Crier could talk about himself until the cows came home, "but how, exactly, did you discover Master Xavier's whereabouts?"

The Town Crier gave him a conspiratorial look and tapped his forefinger against the side of his nose. "It's my innate curiosity," he replied, as if he'd just shared something very personal. "I'm not just a bell ringer in a red coat, m'boy. Oh no, I have a nose for news. And my nose led me to Xavier."

It was a curious thing to say. "How, exactly?"

"Glad you asked, m'boy," Gerald said, again forgetting the protocol of referring to Brandon as 'Lieutenant'. "Earlier this morning I was walking, as we are now, towards The Keep. Although, at that time, I was actually walking to the Upper Bailey to ask Sir Richard if he wouldn't mind delaying this afternoon's pre-proclamation meeting by an hour. These meetings are a mere formality, don't y'know; I have the complete trust of the Duke and—"

"Master Hiepants," Brandon cut in a little less subtly this time; the man really was a pompous twit. "I am curious about your talented nose."

"Oh, quite," he said, looking slightly abashed. "I do tend to get swept away with the detail. Part of my job, you see; an eye for detail is a critical part of..." The expression on Brandon's face must have conveyed exactly what he was thinking, because the Town Crier halted himself and refocused. "My nose... Well, as I said, I was walking towards the Upper Bailey, enjoying the freshness in the air. It was then I felt some moisture on my nose. Assuming that it was a spot of rain — which, indeed, it did turn out to be — I looked upwards. As I cast my gaze across the cloud-filled sky, silently rejoicing in its cooling presence, my eyes fell upon something unexpected. High up in The Keep, a face was staring out from one of the old guest rooms."

"I see," said Brandon, somewhat underwhelmed by the power of Gerald's nose — Xavier's discovery had just been lucky (or unlucky) happenstance.

"As you can imagine, I was quite taken aback," Gerald continued, undaunted by Brandon's unenthusiastic response. "Immediately, I surmised that someone had somehow snuck into The Keep and was now squatting there."

"A natural conclusion," Brandon said, more out of courtesy than interest.

"Well quite, m'boy," encouraged by Brandon's response. "But one must keep a level head in a situation like this, what? Didn't want to alert the chap to the fact he'd been discovered, so I continued walking at a leisurely pace towards The Keep."

"Very collected of you, Town Crier."

"All part of the job, m'boy," beamed Gerald, totally missing the hint of sarcasm that had crept into Brandon's voice. "Instinct for a story, that's what makes a good Town Crier, and my instincts told me that this could be a *very* big story. Imagine the outrage amongst the good citizens of Lower Icing?"

Outrage? Bemusement, more like, that someone had managed to put one over the authorities. And good citizens? He should stop frequenting The Harey Rabbit and take a stroll across The Square.

"But not in my wildest imaginings did I ever think I'd stumble across such a remarkable story. To think—"

"Town Crier," Brandon interrupted, indicating their surroundings, suggesting he should quieten his voice (or, better still, silence it). They had just entered the echoing confines of The Keep. While not a particularly busy part of the castle, The Keep was used for a number of purposes relating to the running of the Duchy and was currently undergoing preparations for the Duke of Stymouth's visit.

"Oh yes. Quite right, m'boy," Gerald whispered conspiratorially, as two servants walked past them.

Brandon and Gerald made their way through the brightly decorated fore-building into an antechamber. Beyond the antechamber was a large reception hall. Through the open double-doors, Brandon spied a group of three men concentrating on a set of plans laid out on a banquet table. None of the engrossed figures noticed Brandon's passing as he veered to his left and followed the Town Crier up the spiral staircase.

This time, the twisting ascent stopped at the second floor of The Keep, where important guests of the Duke were quartered. "Sir Richard has given his permission to use one of the guest rooms, Lieutenant," Gerald informed him.

Brandon nodded, and followed the Town Crier as he headed down the central east-west corridor. The layout on this level was similar to the one a few levels above, where Xavier had been holed up, except the rooms were twice the size (and, therefore, there were half as many of them). Unlike the rooms upstairs, these were well-appointed and maintained to a high standard of presentation and comfort.

Gerald entered the eastern-most room. Brandon stepped in after him. The room contained a large bed with a woollen mattress, a dressing table and mirror, a wooden bathing tub, a wardrobe and a dining table. The two, clear leadlight windows had a northern aspect, but, in the overcast conditions, only a dull light filtered through. The room was still warm and somewhat stuffy from the previous day's heat. Gerald walked over to each window, unhooked a central latch, and pushed the two halves outwards.

"That's better," he said, puffing slightly (the Town Crier was not a fit man). "I think this will do quite nicely. Just a few touches here and there and Master Xavier should feel quite at home. Mind you," he said examining the bathing tub that was placed between the windows and the bed, "I imagine he will eventually have lodgings in the Upper Bailey."

This was going too fast for Brandon. Had Sir Richard really given his permission for all this? "Master Hiepants, what, exactly, did Sir Richard instruct you to do, if you don't mind me asking?"

"Not at all, m'boy; delighted to inform," he replied, moving towards the doorway where Brandon stood. "It's quite simple really. I am to make Master Xavier as comfortable as possible pending an appointment with the Duke, though I believe it will be more a case of reuniting a son with his father."

"You do realise that nobody is to know of his existence until then?" Brandon pressed.

"Yes. Sir Richard was most insistent about that," Gerald said, almost dismissively. "Though, for the life of me, I can't see why such precautions are necessary. After all—"

"They are *necessary* because Master Xavier is yet to prove his case," Brandon said firmly. "He could be *anyone*, Master Hiepants. Speaking of which, what of the servants that have already seen him? What have they been told?"

Brandon's forcefulness had cowed the carefree bluster of the Town Crier. "Just that he is a young noble travelling through the Duchy," Gerald replied.

Then, with more enthusiasm, "In fact, I have concocted a rather clever story to explain his—"

"There's no need to concoct anything! The servants don't need explanations, and outlandish stories will only make them more suspicious, which they will be anyway now that he's been moved down here."

"Really, Lieutenant," said Gerald, affronted. "I find this whole situation—"

"Town Crier," Brandon cut in, trying to keep his voice calm, "this situation could have dramatic repercussions for the Duchy. It is not for *you* to decide what is best. Sir Richard is handling this matter, and, like me, you will follow his instructions. If you feel you cannot do that, please tell me right now, and other arrangements will be made."

Gerald's face filled with colour as he battled with being answerable to a 'lowly' lieutenant. "Very well, Lieutenant." He still seemed slightly out of breath. "I assure you that I will be obedient to Sir Richard's wishes. However, let me also assure you, the day is not far away when Master Xavier's claim will be vindicated. *Then* we shall see whose instructions will be followed."

Brandon wasn't sure what to make of that particular statement. If it hadn't been made by Gerald Hiepants, he might have considered it threatening. However, he decided to accept the Town Crier at his word. "So be it, Master Hiepants. I will leave you to see to Master Xavier's wellbeing."

Gerald nodded. "Thank you, Lieutenant. Most kind."

Brandon turned around to leave, but was stopped by a nagging curiosity. He looked back at the Town Crier. "Why are you so certain he's the Duke's son? That letter of his is not proof, and everything else could be lies."

"Ah, true, m'boy," he said, his upbeat nature reasserting itself, "but my eyes don't lie, and what I see is the Duke's son. No doubt you and Sir Richard see it too, what?"

Brandon walked out of The Keep feeling less certain of his feelings than when he'd entered. Who knew what game Sir Richard was playing; he certainly wasn't confiding in Brandon *all* he knew. Perhaps he'd discovered something which connected Xavier to the Duke, something in that wooden box or maybe in his travelling case. Or, maybe, he was simply keeping his options open in case his imposter turned out to be the Duke's son after all.

Brandon knocked at Administrator Penman's door.

"Enter," was the somewhat annoyed reply; it didn't sound like Sir Richard at all.

Taking a deep breath, Brandon entered the office. Administrator Penman was the first person he saw, standing in the centre of the room, arms folded, looking rather put out.

"Oh… excuse me, Administrator," Brandon said, mentally adjusting to the unexpected presence of the Head of Petitions. Sir Richard and Xavier were also in the room, occupying the same seated positions as when Brandon had left the office some fifteen minutes ago.

"Everything in order, Lieutenant?" enquired Sir Richard.

"Yes, sir," Brandon replied. "As per your instructions to Master Hiepants, a room in the guest wing of The Keep is being prepared."

It was Administrator Penman who answered. "Excellent, Lieutenant. Now, Sir Richard, may I have my office back?"

Brandon shifted his gaze back to the Administrator. He had a steely determination about him which was further reinforced by his no-nonsense grey attire. He had to hand it to the Administrator; facing up to Sir Richard was no easy feat.

"Lieutenant."

Brandon immediately flicked his attention back to the man in black, whose dark eyes were suddenly full of intent. "I assume the quarters are of a suitable standard for an important guest like Master Xavier?"

Brandon was in no doubt about what Sir Richard was asking: was the room secure? He'd seen no key in the lock, but he assumed the Town Crier had it in his possession. "The quarters do need some finishing touches, Sir Richard, but I'm sure Master Xavier will find it comfortable enough for a short stay."

Sir Richard's left eyebrow rose slightly.

"Sir Richard," Administrator Penman cut in again, taking Brandon's attention away from his commanding officer, "I understand the need for discretion in this matter. However, I have a number of petitions pending at —"

"Lieutenant!" Sir Richard snapped, slapping his hand down on the pile of petitions.

"Sir!" Brandon snapped to attention, eyes back where they belonged.

Regaining his composure, Sir Richard continued. "In a moment, I want you to go and inform all those good-for-nothing, whingeing petitioners that the office is closed for the day."

Brandon heard Administrator Penman sigh, but he dared not break eye contact with his commanding officer.

"Then you will return here and keep Master Xavier company while I personally see to the adequacy of his quarters. Is that clear?"

"Yes, Sir Richard."

"But, Sir Richard," Administrator Penman protested, "that will just increase the backlog of complainants and create more work—"

"You may go now," he said dismissively, ignoring the Administrator.

Saluting, Brandon moved towards the exit with all haste. Halfway out the door, he was stopped by, "And, Lieutenant?"

"Sir?"

"If any of the complainants complain, throw them in The Can."

"Really, Sir Richard!" gasped Administrator Penman.

Brandon smiled as he closed the door; he would take some pleasure in carrying out *that* order. Then he caught a fleeting glimpse of Xavier staring at him, looking lost and alone, and his smile vanished.

Many of the petitioners did complain, but Brandon allowed all of them to grumble their way home. He couldn't be bothered making an example of any of them. They weren't worth his time and energy, and he felt somewhat haunted by Xavier's forlorn countenance.

Brandon returned to Administrator Penman's office and was surprised to find that Sir Richard had already left, and, even more surprisingly, that he had decided to take Xavier with him. Administrator Penman, now seated back in his rightful position, was particularly disgruntled.

"Sir Richard said that you are to go about your normal duties," he said, not hiding his annoyance, "and that he would send word if he requires your assistance."

"I see," was all the response Brandon could muster. It was perplexing, and he wondered if he had disappointed Sir Richard somehow. As an afterthought, he added, "But what about the petitioners. Why send them away?"

"Why indeed," said the Administrator, shaking his head.

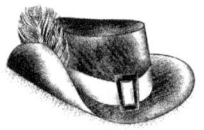

CHAPTER 7

The news is delivered

BRANDON LED THE procession down Merchant Street, past The Bloody Bell to the Town Square. Behind him was the Town Crier — now dressed in his ceremonial, red and gold regalia — followed by six of Brandon's squad members marching smartly and uniformly in pairs. As if the ridiculous formality wasn't enough, Brandon and his men also had to suffer the incessant clanging of the Town Crier's bell. It brought jeers and insults from the afternoon revellers outside the inn. Encouraged by their elders, the dozen or so children, who'd been darting in and around the procession like a swarm of march flies, began to pull faces and make gestures that would normally be accompanied by a good clip around the ears.

Heading towards the well, a smattering of Lower Icingers had already gathered for the regular 'Tuesday at Two' proclamation. Why anyone bothered was beyond Brandon; it was staggering to think that people were actually interested in things like a visiting dignitary or the latest castle fashions. And that was on a *good* news day. If no-one was visiting, then the news could be even more inane, propped up by 'amusing' anecdotes that were submitted to the Town Crier by gossip-loving villagers. That's why they came, of course: to hear who was getting up to no good with whom. The Office of Petitions also supplied a list of settled claims and grievances, but these were usually just pinned up on the news stand next to the well.

The stand was a permanent structure, some fifteen paces to the north-west of the well (or the same distance to the south-east from the entrance to The Bloody Bell, depending on your viewpoint). It resembled a large picture frame, tilted at a forty-five degree angle, sitting atop a waist-high wooden plinth. The frame was double hinged at the top and contained a pane of glass measuring four feet across and two feet high. It acted as a transparent lid, protecting a wooden panel, and was locked in place by the Town Crier's key. It was only ever opened during the Posting Ceremony. The panel itself was pitted with small holes where proclamations and notices had been tacked onto its surface over the last year or so. (It was due to be replaced soon — Brandon would talk to one of the castle carpenters after the Posting Ceremony.) There were about three dozen villagers gathered around the stand, most of whom were women. Some of them had wooden pails that would be filled at the well after the Posting Ceremony.

The crowd parted as Brandon led the clanging procession to the rectangular stone podium on which the stand was built. It marked the beginning of Square Parade. He and his men took up positions each side of the foot-high podium while the Town Crier stepped up onto to it. He placed the bell at his feet and, mercifully, the ringing came to an end.

Reaching into a pocket inside his coat, the Town Crier produced a piece of parchment, tied into a scroll by a purple ribbon. A gentle tug was all that was needed to unravel the ribbon. Brandon braced himself for the next assault on his ears.

"Oyez! Oyez! Oyez!" Gerald bellowed, as he unrolled the official proclamation. And, in case anyone had missed the announcement, the Town Crier repeated the cry with even more drama and volume.

For the next ten minutes, Brandon and his men had to stand to attention while Gerald yelled out a series of 'Castle-approved' announcements, the most interesting of which concerned an increase (from thirty-eight to forty-two) in the number of night-soil collectors. Apt, Brandon thought, because today, more than usual, Gerald and his useless news were really giving him the shits. He then proceeded to bore the crowd with an update on the preparations for the Duke of Stymouth's arrival. He rescued the situation somewhat by announcing that a Henrietta Leksvider was expecting her ninth child. The crowd cheered at the news, and, after rolling up the proclamation, Gerald thanked the 'good citizens of Lower Icing'. This was met with a surprisingly appreciative round of applause, which — judging by his beaming expression — pleased the Town Crier immensely.

Gerald then stepped down from the podium and Brandon took his place; it marked the beginning of the Posting Ceremony. Standing straight, both arms rigid by his sides, Brandon inhaled deeply and barked out the order the collection of scruffy children had been waiting for.

"Squad. Line-for-maaaay-shun!"

The six men-at-arms, stepping in unison, arranged themselves into two lines of three in front of the podium, two yards apart, facing the news stand, creating a guarded walkway. Gerald positioned himself between the pair farthest away from the stand and nodded. This was the signal for Brandon to continue. It was also the signal for the children, who had been held in check by the adults during the proclamation, to do their best to disrupt proceedings. Brandon had made it clear that any man who broke formation during the Posting Ceremony would enjoy a whole month of cleaning out The Can. And, for the three months Brandon had been leading his squad, none had faltered.

"Squad. Faaaace-out!"

Again, his men reacted with precision, the line to his left turned ninety degrees clockwise at the same time the line to his right turned ninety degrees anti-clockwise. Now both lines had their backs to the Town Crier. From both sides, children pulled faces, made rude gestures, or mimicked the movement of the men-at-arms.

"Squad. Preeeesent-blades!"

There was a crisp scrape of metal as swords were removed from scabbards and presented vertically from a horizontally extended forearm. This was Gerald's cue to enter the pantomime. Reaching into another pocket of his cloak, he produced a large key and held it up to show Brandon.

This was the most embarrassing part of the ceremony. Apart from the fact that it was ridiculous in the extreme, it more often than not resulted in unwanted audience participation.

"I have the key!" Gerald yelled dramatically.

Brandon cringed inwardly as a group of older children chorused, "Stick it in ya hole."

Now Brandon had to respond. He did so with a complete absence of drama and enthusiasm. "You have the key. The way is secure. You may proceed."

"To stick it in ya hole," the youths finished off.

Seemingly immune to the heckling and general mischievous behaviour of the children, Gerald proceeded between the two lines of men-at-arms and stepped up onto the podium. Once there, he used the key to unlock the glass lid of the news stand.

"Wrong hole!" shouted the youths, before finally collapsing into fits of laughter.

Gerald opened the lid. Last Saturday's proclamation, along with a list of settled claims from the Office of Petitions, was pinned to the wooden panel. The Town Crier pulled out the tacks, removed the two parchments, and replaced them with the updated current affairs of Lower Icing. He then closed the lid and locked it in place. Turning around, holding the key aloft for anyone who cared to bear witness, Gerald announced, "The news is delivered."

It hardly registered a response. Even the children had lost interest during the parchment exchange, and only a few of the younger ones still persisted with protruding tongues and other face contortions. Gerald slipped the key back into his coat pocket and waited for Brandon's next command.

"Squad. Faaace front!"

Both lines clicked sharply back into position, turning their backs on the news stand. Brandon now stepped off the podium, marched to the front of his squad, and stood to attention some three paces in front of the first pair. This farce was almost over — just a couple more orders.

"Squad. Sheeeeath blades!"

Again the crisp sound of metal upon metal rang through the air. Behind him, Brandon could hear the Town Crier retrieve his bell and take up position between the squad and himself.

"Ready when you are, Lieutenant," Gerald said amiably, and relatively quietly, momentarily slipping out of Town Crier mode.

"Squad. Forwaarrrrd march!"

Rather than return the way they had come, Brandon led the procession down Bigwig Street. As they passed the shop owned by Charles Bling, Jeweller by Appointment to the Duke, it began to rain. Still, Brandon thought, wringing out his uniform was preferable to the Town Crier ringing out his bell.

CHAPTER 8

A grain of scepticism

THE REWARD FOR being on Square Parade was an afternoon of training. After changing out of his patrol uniform into his hardier, combat-training outfit, Brandon joined his complete squad of twelve men in a series of armed and unarmed fighting techniques. As usual, the session was overseen by the Master-at-Arms and Captain of the Guard, Paris (pronounced Parry) Le Sharp. Like Sebastian Fitzbadly, Captain Le Sharp was related to the Duke, but his ties were closer than Seb's: the captain's great aunt had been married to the old Duke's uncle. Not that that meant anything to Brandon — Paris Le Sharp was a high-ranking officer and recognised as the best swordsman in Lower Icing.

Brandon and his men enjoyed training; it was an excellent bonding session, and the skills they learned helped them overcome the many challenging scenarios presented to them by the villains, vigilantes and vagrants of Lower Icing. It also kept them physically fit and strongly toned — so much so that Brandon and his men could tackle just about any confrontation. Most of the confrontations, unfortunately, were with drunken louts who enjoyed stirring up trouble, like the Moleson Twins or Billy Offcut and his mates. Yet, physical altercations were unusual.

They finished at five that afternoon. He and his men were soaked through — a drizzling rain had persisted throughout the entire two-hour drill — but they were now all off-duty until eleven o'clock tomorrow night. Eight of his men were spending the night out of the castle with their wives or families; the remaining four were heading to The Dead Duck for a few drinks. They'd asked Brandon to join them. It was the last thing he felt like doing. He'd placated their good humoured insistence by explaining that he had further duties and assuring them he'd try to join them later. In truth, his mind had already switched from official duty to unofficial duty: he wanted to know what was happening with Xavier, and planned to visit him this evening.

It was nearly seven o'clock by the time Brandon left his quarters. He'd bathed, dressed in casual clothing, then scoffed some beef and broad bean stew with crusty bread. After washing it down with a couple of mugs of ale, he'd felt more like going to sleep than traipsing around the castle. Adding to his weariness was the beating he'd sustained during his sparring match with Captain Le Sharp. But he fought through the pain and fatigue; his hunger may have been sated, but his curiosity certainly hadn't been.

Brandon thought about approaching Sir Richard, but he had no official reason for doing so. He couldn't disturb him simply to enquire about the wellbeing of Xavier — that would be seen as a severe breach of protocol which, at the very least, would incur the displeasure of his commanding officer. However, there was nothing stopping him from going directly to the person in question and making sure he was settling in comfortably. He was also curious to know what nonsense Gerald had been filling the poor sod's head with.

The rain had stopped, but the sky was still overcast, subduing the early evening light. There were no burnished golden highlights to contrast the purple shadows this evening; the castle appeared rather bleak against the dull grey sky.

As Brandon entered the deserted world of Administration, feeble light emanated from the windows, but there was no-one to be seen behind them. Not surprising, he thought; the administrators would have finished their day's work over an hour ago. They were an odd bunch — sticklers for detail, very keen on procedure and punctuality, they worked every minute they were required to, but not a minute more. When six o'clock came, the administrators left. The only exception to that rule was Administrator Penman. There were not enough hours in his day to handle the ceaseless flow of petitions lodged at his office. It never ceased to amaze Brandon how petty some of the townsfolk could be.

Passing through the Middle Bailey gate, he looked up at The Keep to where Xavier was housed. His room was easy to pinpoint because it was the farthest window on the second level and the only one with any light behind it. That was a good sign; it suggested some form of habitation, although it could just as easily be a ruse. With that thought, Brandon quickened his steps across the echoing courtyard.

The Keep's fore-building flickered with the light of two dozen wall-mounted candles, highlighting the gold in the gold-and-purple colour scheme and creating a bright, welcoming haven from the drab stone façade outside. Past the antechamber, the doors to the reception hall remained open and a group of tradesmen were in the process of building some sort of wooden structure.

The Duke was preparing a lavish display for the Duke of Stymouth and his entourage (according to Gerald's proclamation) and, judging by the amount of activity and harried expressions, this display was either ambitious or there was some urgency to complete it on time. However, Brandon's focus was two floors (four twists of the stairwell) above.

It was a hazardous climb in the fading light; you could easily lose your footing on the narrow, tapering stairs. There were no torches in the sconces, because that kind of consideration only occurred when the guest rooms were officially occupied. Again, Brandon felt a twinge of uneasiness about the way Xavier was being treated. He understood and agreed with Sir Richard's position, but there seemed to be inconsistencies in the way it was being handled. If secrecy was of the utmost concern, why put Xavier in a guest room where servants interacted with him? And why allow Gerald Hiepants, of all people, to vouchsafe the compliance and co-operation of a complete stranger. There was definitely something amiss here, and, like his journey up the stairwell, some illumination would be appreciated.

His knock on the door was answered promptly by Xavier, who, it suddenly occurred to Brandon, wasn't actually a prisoner. The door was obviously unlocked, which was fortuitous, because Brandon didn't have the key. Sir Richard must have decided, for whatever reason, forced confinement was unnecessary. Then it occurred to Brandon that Xavier was actually confined by his desire to see the Duke.

"Good evening…" He paused and regarded Brandon with a half-smile, or maybe it was a smirk. "Do I still refer to you as 'Lieutenant' when you're out of uniform?"

Brandon opted for the half-smile and responded with good grace. "I think I can cope with Brandon. May I come in, Xavier?"

Xavier took a couple of steps back into the room, allowing Brandon to enter its cosy confines. The room had been revamped since the morning inspection with Gerald: the bedding had been replaced; the bath had been filled (and used, judging by the opaque soapiness of the water); a brazier had been installed (providing heat for warming water and food); the dressing table, wardrobe and dining table had been dusted (and polished, judging by the fresh smell of sandalwood); and the stuffiness was gone. Xavier was being treated the same way as any noble guest, which was probably just as well from an appearances point of view. Appearances, however, could not last forever.

Xavier shut the door behind Brandon. Turning around, he noticed that a large table had been placed next to the door. Xavier was obviously using it for some kind of research or experimentation. Spread out over the table was a mortar and pestle, a strangely constructed stand suspending an empty glass vial over an unlit candle, an open leather folder displaying loose pages of scratchy notes, a quill nestling in its inkwell, and four small, glass jars containing colourful unguents and powders. Brandon recognised the jars from his inspection of Xavier's finely crafted oak case. The case itself lay closed on the floor next to the table. Sir Richard, it seemed, had returned all of Xavier's possessions, for which Brandon felt surprisingly pleased.

"Making yourself comfortable, I see," Brandon said casually.

Xavier smiled; he was looking a lot less bedraggled. "Master Hiepants has been most accommodating."

He was also displaying an air of self-assuredness that hadn't been present in Brandon's previous encounters with him.

"Has he now," Brandon said as he moved towards the table. Xavier seemed quite at ease as Brandon picked up one of the pages. It was cluttered with drawings and diagrams, as well as a series of letters and numbers joined together with small lines, like some mathematical caterpillar. Near the bottom of the page was a list of ingredients, and directions on how they should be combined. Strange words like 'base compound', 'distillation process' and 'PH factor' appeared amongst the text. Brandon had never seen anything like it.

"It's part of my research," Xavier informed him.

Brandon replaced the page. "And what, exactly, are you researching?"

"Currently I am working on a rejuvenation potion."

Brandon picked up the stone pestle to see what was being pulverised. It was a smooth, orange-coloured paste. Leaning over, he smelled the paste. There was a hint of citrus there, but it was masked by some other floral fragrance.

"Doesn't look like much of a potion," Brandon observed, placing the pestle back in the mortar.

"It's a generic term Horatio has adopted for all our treatments," Xavier informed him. "In any case, this is just a simple part of the preparation: the mixing of cumquat rind, sunflower oil and rose petal to soften the texture and add a pleasant fragrance to the finished product, which will be an unguent applied directly to the skin."

Brandon looked at Xavier, whose smile definitely had a smirking tinge to it. "And what condition will your rejuvenation potion treat?"

"In its perfected form, it will reduce the signs of aging and revitalise the layers of skin, allowing wounds to heal quicker, reducing the chance of contracting an infection."

The most astounding part of that statement was the way he said it, as if he was explaining how to make onion gravy. "Oh, is that all?"

"Of course, it is still in the developmental stages," Xavier supplied, either completely ignoring or totally unaware of Brandon's sarcasm, "but I am making progress."

Brandon wasn't sure how to react. Purple Peril training didn't include dealing with deluded healers. "That's good to know. Looks quite complicated," Brandon offered, half-heartedly indicating the notes.

"Do I detect a grain of scepticism, Brandon?"

Brandon smiled. "More like a wheat field."

Xavier studied Brandon's features for a moment. "You disappoint me. I thought you to be more open-minded."

"And I thought you to be more level-headed," countered Brandon. "This," he continued, vaguely indicating the equipment on the table, "does nothing for your credibility. The son of a Duke is not someone who spends his time in the pursuit of fantastic potions and impossible remedies."

Xavier took the insult in his stride. "Perhaps the Duke would *benefit* from such a son."

"There is nothing to be gained—"

"Do you have any ailments or injuries?"

It was such an unexpected question that Brandon was momentarily lost for words. "What does that have to do with anything?"

"It has to do with my credibility, as you put it."

The young man looked him in eye, and Brandon had the uneasy feeling that he was being examined. In truth, he was quite sore from this afternoon's training. He'd been on the receiving end of a few adept moves by Captain Le Sharp during the sword-play exercises, and even though the swords were blunt and made of wood, he'd felt every slap and jab. A brutal swipe just under his left armpit had been particularly painful and had left a significant bruise.

Brandon decided to concede the point. "Very well, I did sustain a minor injury during training this afternoon."

Xavier's expression remained impassive. "Will you allow me to examine it?"

Brandon felt a flush of embarrassment; he silently berated himself for even mentioning it. "It's just a bruise, it will mend of its own accord," he replied, more tersely than he'd meant to. "But thank you, anyway," he added, trying not to sound ungrateful.

Xavier smiled. "If, as you say, it is just a bruise, I have an unguent that will reduce the swelling and lessen the discomfort."

He made it sound so simple.

"Come, Brandon, there is no shame in the easing of pain."

That was true. He always encouraged his men to seek immediate treatment for any injury or malady. Pride was a man's worst enemy, and for a man-at-arms it could prove fatal.

Brandon complied with a reluctant nod. "Very well."

Xavier returned the nod with one of his own, although his was accompanied by a smirking smile. While Brandon removed his doublet and plain cotton shirt, Xavier retrieved his oak case from the floor. Opening it, he picked up the odd-looking tool Brandon had seen Sir Richard employ, and used it to unclasp a jar from the walnut tray.

Placing the jar on the table, he turned his attention to Brandon's injury. It was an angry-looking welt some six inches below his armpit, the size and shape of his index finger. Surrounding the swollen wound was a corona of purple and yellow bruising. Xavier studied it closely, but said nothing. Then he looked up at Brandon. "As I said, I can treat the bruising, but you've received quite a hefty blow," he said with gentle concern. "Does it hurt when you breathe?"

Brandon felt surprisingly relaxed in Xavier's care. "Not that I've noticed," he answered honestly. "It hurt like hell at the time. That'll teach me to forward thrust with too much weight on my front foot. I won't make that mistake again, that's for certes. Since then, it's just been sore, and if I move my left arm or twist in a certain way, there's a sharpness."

Xavier was regarding Brandon with a serious expression. He then asked him to take a quick, deep breath. Brandon did so, and was rewarded with a stab of pain, causing his body to tense. It was all he could do not to groan as he exhaled.

Xavier nodded to himself, as if silently confirming his own prognosis. "Would you mind turning around?"

Brandon complied. Then he felt Xavier's ear press against the left side of his back. "Is something amiss?" He wasn't used to being examined in this way. Horace Dabbler would have produced a couple of leeches to suck on the swelling, followed by some vile concoction to ease the fever (even if he didn't have a fever).

"Please be quiet, Brandon; I'm trying to listen to your lung."

Of course you are, Brandon thought. He wondered whether 'Lung Listening' was the latest fad in the so-called profession of healing.

"Would you mind taking another deep breath, but slowly this time."

Again Brandon complied. Mentally preparing himself for the sharp pain, he gradually filled his lungs. The pain did come, but it wasn't nearly as shocking.

"Good," said Xavier. "Now exhale slowly."

As he did so, Xavier stopped his lung listening and Brandon turned around to face the strange young man. He no longer looked concerned.

"The rib cage sounds intact," Xavier informed him. "However, you have most likely bruised, or possibly cracked, a rib. This will heal over time, though you will be in some discomfort for the next week. But, as I said, I can ease the pain of the swelling."

Brandon was dubious. "You can tell that from listening to my lung?"

"Yes," he replied, and retrieved the jar he'd taken from the oak case. Removing its lid, he added, "If your rib was broken, your lung would have rattled."

"Rattled?" Brandon wasn't sure he'd heard correctly.

"Yes. Any fluid in the lungs makes a rattling sound. Breaking a rib would have pierced your lung, causing internal bleeding. Mind you, it was just a precaution — you hadn't mentioned the most obvious symptom of such a condition, namely blood in your spittle."

"So, it is as I thought — just a bad bruise," said Brandon, somewhat relieved.

Xavier studied him thoughtfully. Then he dipped his index finger into the jar. The unguent was an opaque, dirty-green colour. It looked like slime, but its appearance was delightful compared to its odour — it smelt like The Can on a Saturday morning. Brandon screwed up his face in disgust and tried not to breathe through his nose. "Hold on, Xavier," he said, recoiling from Xavier's administrations. "I'd rather put up with the pain than that stench."

"It is unpleasant, I agree," — he didn't look as if he found it unpleasant — "but it is absorbed quickly into the skin and there is no lingering odour." Then he held out his finger and showed Brandon the foul, green smear. "You can see how aerated the unguent is; a light application of Bruise Mousse is all that is needed."

"Bruise Mousse?" Brandon had never heard of such a treatment.

"All of our potions are identified by name," Xavier said, sounding slightly defensive; he must have heard something mocking in Brandon's tone.

"I see," Brandon replied.

Xavier leant towards the wound and gently applied the Bruise Mousse.

The bruising welt was tender to the touch, but that was overridden by a cool, fizzing sensation as Brandon's damaged skin readily absorbed the unguent like freshly tapped ale down a parched throat.

"There," said Xavier, finishing the application. "That should make you feel more comfortable."

Brandon could already feel his pain receding. He tentatively rotated his chest; there was still some soreness, but the breath-taking stab of pain had miraculously disappeared. He looked at the serious young man standing in front of him; he was still studying Brandon's wound.

"This is amazing, Xavier," he said, almost in disbelief. "It feels…" Brandon was lost for words as he twisted his upper torso again.

Xavier reacted by placing his hand on Brandon's shoulder, halting his movement. "Be careful, Brandon. Bruise Mousse eases pain and helps the healing process, but it does not heal. You must treat this wound with care and keep movement to a minimum."

Brandon nodded and smiled. Even the foul smell had gone, replaced by a hint of lavender.

"I would also suggest strapping the wound," Xavier continued, "to support the damaged ribs."

Brandon again nodded his agreement; he was literally dumbfounded. If this wasn't some kind of confidence-trickster act, the man was a genius.

While he put his shirt and doublet back on, Xavier secured the jar of Bruise Mousse back in the walnut tray and clamped the oak case shut.

"Thank you, Xavier."

Turning around, Xavier smiled, almost self-consciously. "You're welcome." Then, after a thoughtful pause, he added, "Had I perfected the rejuvenation potion, you would not have any pain *or* injury."

Brandon no longer had a grain scepticism.

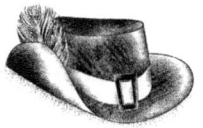

CHAPTER 9
A few more than a few drinks

BRANDON WOKE TO the sounds of chatter and the scraping of metal utensils upon metal plates. The sound that usually roused him from slumber — his chirping family of wrens — also became part of his reluctant awareness of a new day.

The pain of his ribs had been replaced by a pain in his head and memories of last night's drinking session at The Dead Duck. He'd gone there on a whim, after his session with Xavier — actually, more *because* of his session with Xavier…

Xavier had offered him a glass of wine after treating his side. Brandon felt so invigorated — the Bruise Mousse had done more than just ease his pain — that he'd accepted gladly. He was beginning to see why Gerald Hiepants had such a high opinion of the young man. He even found himself asking if there was anything he could do, personally, to make his stay more comfortable.

"I am content, thank you, Brandon," he replied. "Gerald assures me that the Duke will see me tomorrow. In the meantime, I have everything I require."

Brandon wondered how the Town Crier was in a position to make such a statement. Even if Sir Richard had organised a meeting with the Duke, which he strongly doubted, he would not confide that information to a loose-lipped git like Gerald Hiepants. "Oh yes? And what else has Gerald being saying?"

A quizzical expression crossed Xavier's face. "Do I detect a note of disapproval there?"

Brandon inhaled deeply, feeling only a slight tinge of pain, as he considered his response. "I am not in a position to comment, because, in truth, I don't know. I am not, it seems, privy to every decision made on your behalf."

"Nor am I, it seems." His smirking smile spoke volumes, and Brandon suddenly realised just how frustrated and humiliated Xavier must feel. It was a defining moment; Brandon was now convinced that Xavier genuinely believed he was the Duke's son. Whether or not that was the case was yet to be proven.

There was a resemblance — not a strong one, but a resemblance nonetheless — and Brandon couldn't help feeling hopeful for the young man.

He finished his wine and took his leave. On the way out, Xavier asked about Bethany.

"She is well," Brandon responded warily.

"Good," Xavier replied. As Brandon moved to step out of the room, he added, "Please reassure her that I have not forgotten about her plight."

Brandon stopped and regarded Xavier with a growing sense of unease. "What plight might that be?"

Xavier suddenly became a little self-conscious. "As you are aware, there is a document that requires Bethany to present herself at the village of Blessed Whipping by her eighteenth birthday. The man responsible for this document is—"

"A snake called Bertrand," Brandon finished tersely. Xavier might mean well, but Brandon had just about had enough of all this Sunwatcher business. "Look, Xavier, I've been over this a dozen times or more with my family. There is *no* Deed of Promise, Bethany is *not* going anywhere, and if I could find some pretext, I would lock Bertrand in a dark hole and leave him to squirm in his own poisonous company."

Xavier stared thoughtfully at Brandon. "Your parents seemed quite genuine in their concern, Brandon. And, by their own admission, they signed the Deed of Promise."

"They signed something scrawled on a piece of parchment. It was Bertrand who called it a Deed of Promise." Brandon's frustration was building. "There is no such document recognised in the Duchy of Lower Icing. I have already ascertained this from the Duke's lawyers. And, in any case, no such document has been lodged."

"I see," Xavier replied. "Still, I wouldn't underestimate Bertrand's hold over your family. I have lived amongst—"

"Do you know more about this than you're revealing?"

Xavier looked quite shocked. "Not at all, Brandon. I was completely ignorant of this Deed of Promise until your parents mistakenly assumed I was in collusion with Bertrand. I was simply about to say that, having lived amongst the community at Blessed Whipping for over a year, I know how bound they are to each other and their beliefs. Even though your parents left before you were born, Blessed Whipping still influences their lives. You only have to look at their surroundings to know that: the paintings of workers in the field, the sun design on the blue hallway runner, the blue ribbon Bethany wears, and your traditional Blessed Whipping names. You were both born outside the community, yet the custom was still adhered to, even though three *years* had gone by when Bethany was born."

He was right, much as Brandon wished he wasn't. This sun-worshipping nonsense still shaped their attitudes and clouded their judgement. They allowed people to take advantage. His mother indulged every good-for-nothing waste-of-space, while his father was more show than punch.

"What I am saying, Brandon," Xavier continued, more intently, "is that for your parents and your sister, this Deed of Promise is very real, regardless of its legality. And from my limited association with Bertrand, he would see it the same way. He is an adherent to the customs of Blessed Whipping and expects everyone in the community to act the same way."

Brandon felt a bit deflated; he'd come here to test Xavier's integrity, only to have his own put to trial. Ironically, it was *he* who had failed. "Very well, Xavier." He sighed. "Perhaps I have treated this matter too flippantly. I shall endeavour to rectify that."

Xavier looked pleased.

Brandon felt drained and had nothing more to say. "I bid you a good evening."

"Good evening to you, Brandon, and don't forget to bandage that bruise."

In truth, he'd almost forgotten about his injury, but he assured the young man he'd take care of it, thanking him again for his ministrations.

Brandon had planned to go to the infirmary — located in a small room within the main barracks — and then return to his quarters. He achieved the first, but, after being bandaged up by a rather indifferent infirmary attendant, he'd felt in need of camaraderie. So, instead of making the short trip to the regimented coldness of the officers' quarters, he'd opted for the somewhat longer journey to the bawdy warmth of The Dead Duck.

As he made his way down Noble Street, his mind had wandered back to the room in The Keep, where Xavier was biding his time until he met the man he believed to be his father. Would that ever happen? Brandon wasn't sure. It depended on what Sir Richard had in mind. And that was something he wasn't privy to. The whole situation was beginning to trouble Brandon; things weren't as clear cut as Sir Richard would have him believe. Yes, there was definitely something afoot, and to get to the bottom of it, Brandon knew he was going to have to tread carefully.

Brandon had entered The Dead Duck with the thought of having a few drinks with his men, but by the end of the third round it was a clear that a few drinks was just the beginning of quite a few more than a few drinks. Usually, he was able to retain some sort of decorum during his occasional drinking sessions, but the good-humoured atmosphere of The Dead Duck came as a welcome distraction to the intrigue of the castle. And it was nice to be out with some of his squad — they were a good bunch — without having to break up fights or drag drunks to The Can. He'd even joined in a round of singing and had some undergarments tossed at him by one of the barmaids during her rendition of the classic sailors' ditty 'He Always Got Her Knickers in a Knot'. It had been great fun, and he remembered thinking he'd have to do it more often.

Now, lying in his bed, with every scraping utensil feeling like it was scraping against his brain, he was thinking: *I'm never doing that again.*

Brandon's appearance in the officers' common room was met with a predictable reception: Seb, Jethro and Peter all cheered, and then began the traditional, head-splitting bashing of mugs and plates. They kept it up for at least a minute before Sebastian Fitzbadly finally put down his plate and poured Brandon a hot brew of what smelled like beef broth. Brandon joined his fellow lieutenants at the table as the clatter and cheering was replaced by the inevitable ribbing.

"Well, Brandon." Peter Potts smiled. "How was your extended sword-play at The Dead Duck last night? Manage to thrust through some sweet lass's defences?"

They all laughed. Brandon tried to join in, but it hurt his head to laugh (or smile for that matter). Then Jethro Fowler followed up with, "Aye, which lucky wench was on the end of *your* Purple Peril, Brandon?"

More hilarity followed.

Brandon sat through the bawdy banter with as much humour as he could muster. Fortunately, he didn't have to suffer long. They had to ready themselves for duty, so, after some playful parting slaps across the head, he was left in peace.

Peace, Brandon thought, as he forced himself to drink the beef broth. If only his head would stop pounding. At least he had the whole day to recover. The first swallow of broth almost came straight back up. He remembered emptying his stomach of its mainly liquid contents numerous times last night, and the bitter, acidic taint still lingered in his mouth. He tried for a second swallow, but the smell defeated him. Instead, he reached for the remains of a crusty loaf of bread. It was definitely more palatable... if only he had the strength to chew it.

Suddenly the door to the compound burst open. Brandon quickly jumped to his feet, sending a throbbing pang through his skull and a sharp jab of pain to his side. That's right: he had a bruised rib.

It was a surprised-looking George Martin — the beetle-loving cadet.

"Oh!" He hurriedly performed an embarrassed-looking salute. "Excuse me, Lieutenant. The other lieutenants told me breakfast was finished, and instructed me to clean the common room immediately."

Of course they did, Brandon thought. One more prank at his expense. "At ease, cadet," Brandon croaked, barely acknowledging the salute as he slumped back down onto the bench seat.

George remained motionless as Brandon attempted another swig of the broth. "Um…" the mature-aged recruit ventured, "would you like me to get you anything, sir?"

You had to hand it to him, the man was keen. "Not unless you have a miracle cure for…" Brandon suddenly remembered Xavier was supposedly meeting the Duke today. If he was to find out if that was actually happening, he needed to get moving… but that was easier said than done. Fighting through queasy pain, Brandon stood up and addressed the cadet. "Actually, George, you can heat some water and fill the bathing tub."

George saluted and eagerly set about his task.

CHAPTER 10

In good spirits

BRANDON EMERGED FROM the officers' common room an hour later, dressed in his patrol uniform. He wasn't on duty until ten o'clock tonight, but he had a feeling the authority of the purple and gold might be necessary before then. Normally, he wouldn't have afforded himself the luxury of a morning bath, but that had *definitely* been necessary.

While he'd attempted to soak away the throbbing pain in his head, George had brushed down his uniform and cleaned his boots. Lower Icing could do with some more mature-aged recruits like George. The cadet had even re-bandaged his bruise, which was remarkably less gruesome than it had been before his visit to Xavier. So much so, that Brandon had felt somewhat embarrassed by the need for a bandage at all. The words Cake Eater came to mind.

Brandon had no real plan of action as he strode from the barracks to the Administration Section. Yesterday's overcast conditions were now, like his night at The Dead Duck, just a clouded memory. The eight o'clock sun beamed down through a blue sky, illuminating the eastern-facing walls and buildings of the castle. There was already warmth in it, and Brandon found himself gravitating towards the shady side of the Lower Bailey.

A handful of villagers were milling around the Office of Petitions, even though it wasn't open for another hour. They shot him a few aggrieved glances as he passed. He recognised most of them from yesterday: serial complainants and time-wasters the lot of them. Why Administrator Penman entertained anything they had to say was beyond Brandon. He had no time for people who had nothing better to do than complain, and he just didn't understand how they could put so much energy into it. He was in no mood to be cordial this morning, so he returned their sullen glances with one he hoped conveyed his distaste and disapproval.

Entering the Middle Bailey, Brandon was in two minds. Should he go straight to Xavier or try to find the Town Crier? He really wanted to speak to

Sir Richard, but, in his current hazy condition, he couldn't think of a pretext to make such a request of his commanding officer. As it turned out, the decision was made for him — the Town Crier suddenly manifested from the shadowy entrance of The Keep's fore-building. He looked flustered, or maybe it was just that he was wearing a bright pink shirt under his yellow waistcoat. He headed towards the Upper Bailey, seemingly without noticing Brandon.

"Master Hiepants," Brandon called after him, and the colourful figure stumbled on the cobblestoned courtyard. Turning around, he wore an expression of annoyance, but as Brandon moved closer, his features softened.

"Ah, Lieutenant," he said amiably, but it seemed to be more out of recognition than courtesy.

"Is anything amiss, Master Hiepants?"

"Apart from my innate clumsiness, I've never felt better, m'boy."

"I see. It's just that you seemed a bit preoccupied. Have you seen Xavier this morning?"

"Why yes; just had a spot of breakfast with him." His manner was so jovial that Brandon began to think his initial impression of the Town Crier had been inaccurate and probably the result of his foggy brain.

"He must have been in good spirits," Brandon probed.

Gerald nodded enthusiastically, missing the intent of the question. "As a matter of fact he was in rather good form. Such an amazing mind! I take it you know of his research into—"

"Yes, I am aware," Brandon cut in, rubbing his temples. He really wasn't in the mood for the Town Crier's banter this morning.

"Yes, of course. I'm sure you are," said Gerald, slightly put out. Then he smiled as realisation dawned. "Ah… I see. Could it be that you're paying for your own good spirits, Lieutenant?"

Brandon grimaced, but otherwise didn't acknowledge the observation. Instead, he went straight to the point. "Has the Duke agreed to see Xavier today?"

This time, the Town Crier's stumble was a mental one. "Ah… Xavier mentioned that, did he?"

"Well?" pressed Brandon.

"Well," he responded awkwardly, "I may have alluded to the fact that the Duke would see him today."

"And who provided you with that fact?"

His face turned a few shades pinker than his shirt. "I suppose it was more…

Sir Richard led me to believe that a meeting was imminent, and I felt the lad deserved some good news."

Brandon felt a pang of sympathy for the big man; he might be a bumbling fool, but his heart was in the right place. "No doubt you meant well, Master Hiepants, but I don't think Xavier is likely to appreciate your good intentions when he discovers there is no substance behind them."

The Town Crier straightened, his demeanour suddenly stiff and formal. "To be honest, Lieutenant, I find this whole situation *most* unacceptable," he said with a surprising amount of fervour. "The way this young man has been treated is disgraceful, and *I* don't appreciate being put in the position where all I have to offer *is* good intentions."

If Brandon hadn't felt so brain-addled, he would have challenged the Town Crier on that point. After all, his job had nothing to do with deciding who was or wasn't suitable to gain an audience with the Duke; he only had to decide how to present news from the castle, and even that needed approval from Sir Richard. This situation wasn't so different; Sir Richard was just controlling the news going into the castle rather than out of it.

"Master Hiepants," Brandon said with a weary sigh, "I'd be thankful the Duke and Sir Richard are such men who allow you to have good intentions."

The Town Crier gave him a puzzled look. (Brandon didn't blame him; he wasn't sure what he'd just said either.) Finally, he said, "I am indeed thankful for my position in the castle, and I shall be exercising that position when I see Sir Richard in two hours' time. Good day to you, Lieutenant."

Brandon was momentarily rooted to the spot, almost dazed as he watched the Town Crier stride towards the Upper Bailey. His vision began to waver, and he had to force himself to move through the dizziness and the aching. Turning left, he entered The Keep.

CHAPTER 11

Brandon or Lieutenant Swill?

BRANDON FELT SOMEWHAT relieved by the relative darkness of The Keep. The same, however, could not be said for the noise level. Construction in the reception hall was in full flight, and the hammering and sawing of wood pounded into his brain. He still hadn't spoken to a carpenter about changing the proclamation panel in the news stand, but, right at this moment, he felt like his head might explode if he entered the chaos of the hall.

The cacophony receded as he spiralled up the stairwell, and was virtually nullified by the time he reached Xavier's room. The young man seemed pleased to see him, as Brandon was swiftly ushered into the cosy confines of the room.

"How is your rib this morning?" Xavier enquired, offering him a seat at the dining table. The remnants of breakfast were neatly stacked to one side and the redolence of Reginald Puffy's famous pork pies lingered in the air. Normally, Brandon found their aroma highly appetising; today, however, the opposite was true.

"Much better than my head and my ability to hold down food," he said, moving away from the table. Reaching the window, he inhaled deeply and looked out at the new day. About fifteen feet below him was the massive eastern wall, which traversed a rocky outcrop that sloped steeply down to the Icing River. It also intersected the inner defensive wall that separated the Middle Bailey from the Administration Section. Directly ahead, protected by the eastern wall and three defensive towers was Reg Puffy's kitchen and the Castle Laundry. Grey, slate roofs, bathed in golden morning sunlight, predominated the scene — a stark contrast to the shadowy courtyard directly below. Looking down into its empty gloom made Brandon's head spin, and the only thing that kept him from adding some colour to the grey cobblestones was his sense of pride. He would not embarrass himself, nor, more importantly, bring shame upon the Purple Peril uniform.

"Here, Brandon," Xavier said, suddenly standing next to him. "This will make you feel better."

Taking another deep breath, Brandon turned back into the room. Xavier held a mug in his left hand and glass vial in his right.

"And what miracle cure do you have there, Xavier?" said Brandon, sounding more flippant than he'd meant to.

"Not a cure." Xavier smiled his smirking smile, offering Brandon the mug. "An aid to recovery."

Upon accepting the mug, Brandon could see it was half-filled with water, or, at least, what appeared to be water.

"It is as it appears," confirmed Xavier. "However, when I add some of this…"— Xavier held out the vial. It contained a white powder — "it will transform the water into a restorative potion."

Brandon would have scoffed at this point had he not experienced the curative wonders of Bruise Mousse. Instead, he smiled as Xavier removed the vial's stopper. "So, what's this potion called? Fixer Elixir?"

Xavier smiled back, obviously taking Brandon's attempt at humour the way it was intended. "Very good, Brandon," he said. "However, Horatio named this particular potion 'Natron Bomb' after the active ingredient contained in the powder. Natron was one of the salts he discovered in a dry lake bed in the hills just outside Missing Anchor, where we lived before moving to Blessed Whipping."

"I'm not sure the words 'active ingredient' and 'bomb' should be used to describe something I'm about to ingest," remarked Brandon half seriously.

Xavier smiled. "Quite harmless, I assure you. However, when I add the powder to the water, a reaction occurs — call it an explosion of tiny bubbles — so you must drink it quickly and keep drinking until there is nothing left."

Brandon hardly felt reassured by Xavier's explanation. "Is the taste that bad?"

"Not at all. Lemon essence and ginger root are some of the other ingredients. It is really quite refreshing and does wonders for a body recovering from the overindulgence of alcohol."

Brandon stared at Xavier's passive expression as he patiently waited for some sort of response. Whatever this potion tasted like, and whatever effect it had on Brandon's body, it couldn't be any worse than what he was feeling right now.

"Very well, Xavier. Natron Bomb away."

The smirking smile reappeared as Xavier positioned the vial over the top of the mug. "Ready?"

Brandon nodded.

Xavier lightly tapped the open end of the vial with his index finger. A small amount of the powder dislodged from the edge and landed silently in the mug of water. For a second or two nothing happened. Then, suddenly, the water erupted into a fizzing, white foam. Brandon quickly brought the mug to his mouth. Xavier was right, the taste was quite pleasant, but the potion's fizzing made it a challenge to drink. It was a strange, almost burning sensation, and Brandon struggled to keep gulping down the concoction, but he persisted until the mug was drained.

What followed was a moment of extreme discomfort, where he thought his stomach might indeed explode, such was the pressure. Relief came in the form of a belch. Not just any belch, mind you; it was the kind of belch you'd expect from Alistair Bean after he'd eaten half a pig and washed it down with a barrel of ale.

"Well done, Brandon," said Xavier, taking the mug. "That should help with the nausea, and your head should clear within the hour."

Again, Brandon was lost for words; he already felt much better. It was as if his queasiness had been blown up by the Natron Bomb. He could hardly believe what he was feeling. He regarded Xavier with something approaching awe as the young man placed the mug on the table.

"You have a truly remarkable talent, Xavier."

"Thank you, Brandon, but the remarkable talent behind this potion is Horatio's." He then walked over to his work desk and returned the vial of Natron Bomb powder to its place in the wooden box.

"Be that as it may, I'm sure you do this Horatio proud," Brandon said sincerely.

Xavier paused in the process of securing the vial and his expression became momentarily introspective. "Yes, perhaps you are right."

Brandon felt slightly awkward. All he knew of Xavier's mentor or patron (or however the relationship worked) was that he was the alleged author of the letter to Lord Marmaduke and, supposedly, an old friend of the Duke's. "Has Gerald told you anything more of your meeting with the Duke?"

Xavier gently closed the lid of the wooden box. Brandon was about to prompt him, when the young man spoke. "Gerald has a meeting with Sir Richard later this morning," he said, turning around. "The time of the reunion with my father will be decided upon then." He wore a determined look, almost challenging Brandon to contradict the information he'd been given.

Brandon was not about to do that. Unlikely as such a reunion seemed, he really had no idea what Sir Richard was planning for Xavier, and it certainly wasn't his place to make a judgement on the decisions his commanding officer made, no matter what his personal feelings were. "That is good news, Xavier," Brandon responded, trying to sound positive.

A smirking smile appeared on Xavier's face. "So, is this visit simply to confirm what I already know, or do you have some more good news for me?"

Brandon smiled at the perspicacity of the comment. "Actually, I simply came by to make sure your needs were being met."

"Very kind of you, Brandon," he said, without sarcasm. Then, moving back across the room, he invited Brandon to join him for a brew. "It will do you good," he added, noticing Brandon's indecision.

His reluctance, however, had nothing to do with his stomach. In truth, his discomfort lay in playing a regimental role with Xavier, particularly when it was becoming more at odds with his personal feelings. Still, he reminded himself, he wasn't here to interrogate the young man. "Very well," he agreed.

Brandon's second attempt at sitting at the dining table was a lot more successful. The remnants of Xavier's breakfast no longer churned his stomach and he was even disappointed there were no pork pies left — his nausea was rapidly being replaced by hunger, thanks to the wondrous effects of the Natron Bomb.

Xavier reached for the jug resting atop a metal brazier. Judging by the slow tendrils of vapour wafting from the jug, the charcoal embers in the brazier were still hot. Reaching over the table, he filled Brandon's mug and informed him that this particular brew was made from peppermint leaves. "It aids digestion and will help settle your stomach. The villagers at Blessed Whipping introduced Horiatio and I to the benefits of peppermint."

Brandon had only ever seen peppermint used as an aromatic; it was even infused in the buckets of hot water used to wash out the cells of The Can. The thought of drinking a mug of cell-cleaner didn't exactly fill him with excitement, but he wasn't about to share that thought with a man who had miraculously saved him from pain and discomfort twice in the last twelve or so hours.

He picked up his mug and took a tentative sip while Xavier poured one for himself. Again, the taste was surprisingly better than expected. "It's not unpleasant, I suppose," he said, almost to himself.

"True. One might even be tempted to be overly effusive and say that it *is* actually pleasant."

Brandon took another sip of the brew, inhaled the fresh piquancy of mint, and felt the hot liquid flow down his throat to warm his stomach.

"You seem somewhat detached, Brandon. Is something troubling you?"

Xavier was regarding him casually, seemingly relaxed, with his mug of peppermint clasped between both hands.

"What do you hope to gain by meeting the Duke?" The question popped out of nowhere, surprising Brandon as much as it did Xavier.

Placing his mug carefully on the table and sitting up straight, Xavier enquired, "Who is asking — Brandon or Lieutenant Swill?"

Again, his intuitiveness impressed Brandon. "The answer should be the same for both."

"Very well," he said, gazing down at his mug. "I'm not sure what I will gain from meeting my father. There may be nothing *to* gain, but I hope for his acceptance, and an understanding of why he abandoned me. And..." He paused, and then lifted his gaze to meet Brandon's. "I'd like to know what sort of person my mother was."

Brandon nodded. "Understandable... However, I was thinking on a less emotional level." It was clear that Xavier was uncomfortable talking about the Duke.

"What do you mean?"

What *did* he mean? He took a gulp of the peppermint brew to give himself some thinking time. He wasn't sure how to approach the matter. He was making assumptions, and he was speaking out of place. He could almost sense Sir Richard's disapproval: *Remember, Lieutenant, the less you speak, the more you hear.*

Resting his mug on the table, Brandon regarded the serious young man seated across from him, his brown eyes fixed upon Brandon, his forehead slightly furrowed under his golden locks. "I mean," Brandon replied calmly, "if you are officially recognised by the Duke, you will become the son of a Duke, and with that comes responsibilities. This is more than a father accepting you as his son; this is a Duke accepting you as his heir."

Even as he spoke the words, the ramifications of what he was saying hit Brandon like a hot bucket of peppermint-scented water in The Can. If Xavier was recognised... It was all suddenly clear: the unusual treatment and the secrecy. If Xavier was recognised and named heir, Sir Richard would lose his claim to the Duchy.

"Yes, I have considered that, Brandon, and I have no interest in becoming..."

Xavier's words were just sounds outside his thoughts. How could he have been so stupid? Even Gerald had recognised the gravity of the situation: *The day is not far away when Master Xavier's claim will be vindicated. Then we shall see whose instructions will be followed.* It had sounded oddly threatening at the time, now he realised the Town Crier had just been stating the plain, simple truth.

"Is something amiss? Brandon?" Xavier's voice finally broke through his thoughts, and Brandon glanced up to find the young man looking at him with some concern. "You've gone very pale. Perhaps you're having a reaction to the Natron Bomb."

"No. I'm fine," Brandon said in a rather off-hand manner. He felt like he'd just been awakened from a deep sleep. "It's just… never mind."

Xavier was obviously not convinced, but didn't push the matter. "As I was saying, I have no intention of becoming Duke."

The young man was so out of place here. Sir Richard's first impressions had been right: he was naive in the extreme. "You won't have any choice, Xavier," he said more forcefully than he'd meant to. "If you are recognised, you will become the next Duke."

Xavier looked a bit taken aback.

"And that means you'll need to be educated in everything required to fill such a position. No more research into wonder cures; you'll be immersed in a world of politics, diplomacy, economics and military strategy."

"I don't wish to be recognised as an heir, only a son," countered Xavier, "even if it is fleetingly."

Brandon felt a pang of sympathy. "I hope you are given that choice. There are people in the castle who will not see things quite so simply."

Xavier's face flushed. "Are you referring to Sir Richard?"

"Among others," he informed him, "but Sir Richard has the Duke's ear."

"Gerald believes—"

"I wouldn't put much credence in what the Town Crier has to say. Although he means well, and makes himself out to be someone of importance, he has no influence whatsoever in the decisions made in or out of the castle."

"I see… So, the meeting with my father today?"

"I honestly don't know, Xavier. But I wouldn't count on it."

Xavier looked lost. He seemed to be gazing over Brandon's right shoulder, out the window to his other life.

"I think you should forget about seeing the Duke. Return to your life at Blessed Whipping, invest your time in research, use your talents to finish your rejuvenation potion and create other wonderful remedies. It would be a much happier outcome for you, and, I imagine, Horatio would welcome such a decision."

With a flick of his eyes, Xavier's attention was back on Brandon. "Thank you for your advice, Brandon, but I have come to Lower Icing to see my father, and I intend to do exactly that, regardless of the outcome."

There was a defiance in his tone and bearing, and Brandon realised there was no chance of convincing him to abandon his course of action. He couldn't blame him though; he would do the same if he was in Xavier's position.

"Very well," said Brandon. "I will help you all I can. Just don't believe everything the Town Crier tells you."

This brought a smile to Xavier's face. "That's exactly what he said of you."

I'm sure he did, thought Brandon, but he returned Xavier's smile nonetheless. "Then he, also, was giving you good advice."

Brandon downed his brew and excused himself. On the way out, something on Xavier's work desk caught his eye. Amongst the sheets of notes and other experimental equipment was a small book. The gold-leaf title shimmered in the candlelight. Moving closer, Brandon read the words:

POETRY IN POTION
Doctor Horatio Manky

It suddenly occurred to him that this book (and, now that he thought about it, the folder of notes) hadn't been in Xavier's room at The Bloody Bell, nor had they been in his travelling case. He silently cursed himself for his lack of observation; he really needed to lift his game if he wanted to remain in Sir Richard's favour.

"Where did this come from, Xavier?" His tone was curious, not accusatory.

"Blessed Whipping."

Brandon shot him a glance. Was he trying to be smart? It didn't appear so. He looked relaxed, if not pleased, by Brandon's enquiry.

"It is a book of marvellous discoveries and medical breakthroughs, Brandon, including Bruise Mousse and Natron Bomb. Would you care to—"

"What I meant was," he said as the young man moved towards the desk, "when I retrieved your possessions from The Bloody Bell, this book and the folder of notes were not among them. And don't tell me they were in your travelling case, because it was searched."

Xavier moved past Brandon. Instead of picking up the book, he gathered the pages of notes and placed them inside the folder. He then put the book on top of the folder before finally facing Brandon.

"These items are precious to me." His voice was little more than a whisper. "Consequently, I treat them as such. I am sure you can appreciate that."

"Did Bethany hide them for you?" This time the question did sound like an accusation.

It produced Xavier's smirking smile. "Believe that if you want, Brandon. It makes no difference to me."

CHAPTER 12

Not your concern

BY THE TIME he reached the bottom of the stairwell, Brandon's mood had twisted towards the bad. He was angry and frustrated at himself for not realising the full ramifications of Xavier's claim, and annoyed and upset at himself for the way he'd reacted to Xavier's book and folder. It was not worthy of the uniform, and unacceptable in a person who regarded himself as fair and just.

As he stepped out of the stairwell, a couple of tradesmen were carrying lengths of wood into the reception hall, where things sounded even more frenetic. The hammering of mallets and the barking of instructions no longer hurt his head (again he marvelled at the talent of the young man above) and he decided it was time to turn his thoughts to more mundane matters, like finding a carpenter.

Most of the action was centred at the southern end of the hall, where at least a dozen workers were busily constructing some sort of stage. Straight ahead, on the eastern side of the hall, two men stood at a table, talking over what Brandon assumed to be the plans. He recognised them both — Stephen Scaffold, a robust man in his fifties, was an engineer and builder, and the thin, tall man next to him was his assistant, Jerome Sawyer.

The two men were deep in conversation and didn't notice Brandon until he came to a halt on the opposite side of the table. As Brandon had surmised, the men were discussing the plans laid out before them and, in particular, what looked like an intricate pulley system.

"Excuse me, gentlemen," Brandon said in a raised voice, so he could be heard over the din of construction. Both men looked up wearing similar aggravated expressions.

"What is it, Lieutenant?" enquired the engineer, clearly put out.

Brandon was not deterred by his attitude; right now, he had one of his own. "The panel in the news stand needs replacing and I would like one of your carpenters to attend to it as soon as possible."

Stephen Scaffold's eyes narrowed; he seemed unsure how to react, as if he was wondering whether Brandon was playing some kind of practical joke. Jerome Sawyer's expression, however, was very easy to read: jaw dropping disbelief and outrage. He looked to his master for a response.

"Out of the question," Scaffold said dismissively, immediately turning his attention back to the plans. Sawyer treated Brandon to a brief, contemptuous grin, before re-engaging with the engineer.

Brandon waited for a few moments, but when it was clear they were going to ignore his presence, he slapped his right hand down on the table, just missing Sawyer's index finger as he indicated a series of counterweights on the plans.

While the table remained intact, the impact was such that everyone stopped working and the hall was suddenly filled with silence. Again, Scaffold's reaction was minimalistic; only his head snapped up in surprise. And, again, Sawyer's was exaggerated; his whole body jerking backwards as if he'd just been shot by a crossbow bolt. Brandon, conversely, felt quite calm and in control — the slap had had the desired effect.

Fixing his gaze on the simmering engineer, he coolly whispered, "Master Scaffold, I can see that you are busy. All I am doing is informing you of a task that needs attending to. *You* can decide when that task is completed. However, I wouldn't take too much time in allocating responsibility, because the next person who makes this request won't be as courteous or forgiving as *me*."

The engineer slowly straightened, as if he was ironing out the kinks in his back, while his assistant looked like he was about to jump over the table and hit Brandon. Neither response bothered him. Asserting his authority over things he could control was as much of a tonic as one of Xavier's potions. Already, he felt much better in himself.

Not waiting for a response — there was no need; the message had been received — Brandon turned around and marched out of the hall. He'd taken two or three steps when Stephen Scaffold's husky voice barked out, "Tompkins! Over here! The rest of you, back to work!"

Brandon allowed himself a self-satisfied smile as he exited the hall. The renewed efforts of the workers faded as he left the fore-building and headed towards the Upper Bailey.

It was his sense of duty that propelled Brandon to Sir Richard's office. Ironic, he thought, considering it was the same sense of duty that had *prevented* him from approaching Sir Richard before. But circumstances had changed. Brandon was no longer convinced his commanding officer was acting in the best interests of the Duchy, particularly when so much was at stake for him personally. His oath of fealty, he reminded himself as he waited to be admitted into Sir Richard's office, was to the Duchy of Lower Icing, not to any one person, no matter *how* powerful they were.

Brandon had to wait less than a minute for Prestwich, Sir Richard's personal secretary, to reappear in his office, confirming Sir Richard would indeed see him. He indicated Brandon should enter the Seneschal's office, then sat down at his desk and continued scribing at an amazingly fast rate. The man was like a flash of grey: his clothes, hair and even skin were of a similar hue.

Brandon entered the demesne of his commanding officer, located directly below his private chambers in the western wing of the Royal Residence, with a mixture of conviction and trepidation. Like everything else Brandon had seen within this part of the castle, opulence and finery were the norm, designed to intimidate.

He'd been admitted into Sir Richard's office on a number of occasions, and each time he found something new to admire — the expansive room was tastefully adorned with works of art, sculpture and military memorabilia. Sir Richard's gleaming suit of plate armour was on permanent display in the corner of the room, next to a window that overlooked the manicured gardens. However, the most eye-catching item filled a large part of the wall behind Sir Richard's massive mahogany desk. It was a full-length portrait of the man himself, dressed in his customary black. He was standing in the colourful, flowering garden outside, but black Sir Richard dominated the scene. His left hand rested on the pommel of his sheathed sword, his right arm hung casually at his side. And although it was meant to capture a relaxed moment, it was the underlying menace in Sir Richard's stance that shone through.

The real Sir Richard was sitting at his desk, looking like he'd just jumped out of the portrait. Brandon saluted. Sir Richard gave him a cursory glance and indicated he should sit down, before returning his attention to a parchment in front of him. Complying wordlessly, Brandon waited for him to finish reading. It was all part of the power play, Brandon knew that, but he was content to act his part.

Eventually, Sir Richard looked up. "So, Lieutenant, I assume you are here to report that all is well with our guest."

"All is well, sir," Brandon replied. "However…" — As Brandon paused, Sir Richard's left eyebrow arched — "our guest has made an assumption of his own."

"I see," he murmured, either annoyed or uncaring, Brandon wasn't sure.

"Yes, sir," Brandon soldiered on. "He's assuming he will be seeing the Duke sometime after your meeting with the Town Crier."

"Really?" said Sir Richard, sounding bored. "And what led him to that assumption?"

"The Town Crier informed—"

"Hah!" Sir Richard was suddenly more animated. "That buffoon would struggle to inform anyone what day it was!"

True enough, Brandon thought, but he also knew that his commanding officer excelled at insinuation. There was no doubt in Brandon's mind that, at the very least, he'd misled Gerald. An inner voice urged him to speak up for Xavier and ask Sir Richard what he intended to do about the situation, but it was muffled by the thick wall of military protocol.

"Something wrong, Lieutenant?"

"No, sir," he replied, automatically.

"Well, then, if you have nothing more interesting to—"

"Sir, why won't you allow Xavier to see the Duke?"

Sir Richard's dark eyes had looked like dull embers a moment ago, but now they shone like anthracite. His mouth formed into a mocking smile. "Do your loyalties still lie with the Duke, Lieutenant?" His voice was calm, but his eyes pierced Brandon's mind like a forward thrust from Captain Le Sharp's rapier.

"Of course, Sir Richard," he said defensively, "but—"

"I am relieved to hear it," he interjected smoothly. "I would hate to think that the youngest-ever lieutenant in the Purple Peril put the feelings of a charlatan before that of his liege lord."

"That's my point, Sir Richard," Brandon countered, hardly believing the words were coming from his mouth. "Why not settle the matter quickly? Let Xavier have his moment. If he is a charlatan, the Duke will disavow all knowledge of him, and that will be an end to the matter."

The fingers of Sir Richard's right hand started drumming against the desk top. His left hand rested in his lap. For five agonisingly slow beats — enough time for a trickle of sweat to run down Brandon's spine — Sir Richard said nothing.

"Lieutenant," he said, reinforcing Brandon's subordinate position, "I will excuse your... *reasoning* on the grounds you are inexperienced in matters of court."

Brandon tried to maintain eye contact, but the steady beat of Sir Richard's fingers was a nerve-wracking distraction.

"I am an advisor and confidante to his lordship, and he expects me to act in his best interests at all times. By presenting this pretender to the Duke, it suggests I find some credibility to his claim, which, at this point in time, I do not. Therefore, it would be regarded as highly remiss of me, even derelict in my duty, to arrange such a presentation. Has that clarified the matter for you?"

Brandon remained silent under Sir Richard's appraising gaze. The Seneschal's fingers stopped tapping as Brandon fought for the words 'yes, sir' but they wouldn't come. Instead, he counterthrusted with, "Then why give him false hope?"

Sir Richard's hand clenched into a fist, his expression turned bemused, and, when he spoke, his voice was dangerously calm. "Are you questioning my judgment?"

"Just seeking understanding, sir."

"Well, understand *this*, Lieutenant Swill," he hissed, suddenly thrusting forward so his face was only a few feet from Brandon's. "Whatever decisions are made by your betters, you can rest assured they are for the *betterment* of the Duchy, and, let me emphasise this point, *not your concern*."

As Sir Richard reclined back in his chair, Brandon filled with anger. His commanding officer's threatening aura might be enough to make the likes of the Town Crier cower, but Brandon was made of sterner stuff. He'd been raised to stand up for what he believed in. As much as he criticised his parents, they had never shied away from their beliefs, and neither of them had ever taken a backward step when it came to defending their family and home. Following orders was one thing — he believed in the chain of command — but unquestioning loyalty was another. Sir Richard himself had, on numerous occasions, stressed the importance of keeping an open mind. So, instead of meekly surrendering to a more powerful opponent, Brandon decided to throw out a challenge.

"What is Bertrand's involvement in this matter, Sir Richard?" His tone left no doubt that he was making a stand.

Sir Richard regarded him for a moment, as if considering whether he'd like to toy with his opponent before dispatching him. Then he did something that caught Brandon completely off guard: he started laughing.

He slapped his hand down on the desk, like he'd just been told an hilarious anecdote. It landed on top of the parchment he'd been reading when Brandon entered. Picking it up, Sir Richard waved it vaguely in his direction. "Your timing is impeccable, Lieutenant." He smiled.

Brandon's flush of embarrassment was quickly replaced by a prickly sense of indignation. It had been the cry of Bertrand's name by Xavier that had influenced the current course of events; Sir Richard had completely dismissed Xavier's claim until that moment. However, now was not the time to vent that indignation. Brandon remained silent and allowed his commanding officer to continue.

"See for yourself," he said. His amusement had turned grim as he placed the parchment down, rotated it one hundred and eighty degrees, and slid it across the table for Brandon to read. The first things Brandon noticed about the precise handwriting were that the scribe had used only capital letters and that every 'S' had a line drawn through it. It was dated June 24 — yesterday's date.

$IR RICHARD,

I MU$T, AGAIN, BRING TO YOUR ATTENTION THE MATTER OF BETHANY $WILL AND HER PARENT$' OBLIGATION TO PRE$ENT HER TO THE COMMUNITY OF BLE$$ED WHIPPING BEFORE THE COMMENCEMENT OF HER NINETEENTH YEAR, A$ LAID OUT IN THE DEED OF PROMI$E I LODGED AT THE OFFICE OF LEGALITIE$ NINETY-THREE DAY$ AGO (FOR WHICH I HAVE A DETAILED RECEIPT). UNFORTUNATELY, BARTHOLOMEW AND BERTIE $WILL (PROPRIETOR$ OF THE BLOODY BELL INN) HAVE CHO$EN NOT TO FULFIL THAT OBLIGATION. I MU$T IN$I$T, THEREFORE, THAT YOU RATIFY THE DEED OF PROMI$E AND ACT $WIFTLY TO EN$URE COMPLIANCE OF THE $AID PROTAGONI$T$ IN FACILITATING THE IMMEDIATE RETURN OF THEIR DAUGHTER, BETHANY, TO HER RIGHTFUL PLACE IN THE COMMUNITY OF BLE$$ED WHIPPING. FURTHER DELAY$ WILL NECE$$ITATE A MORE DRA$TIC COUR$E OF ACTION ON MY PART.

BERTRAND
BLE$$ED WHIPPING ELDER

Brandon could hardly credit what he'd just read. The man had to be insane if he thought he could get away with this contrived 'Deed of Promise'. He'd been assured by Humphrey Tumbridge-Wills (Lower Icing's resident Historian and Duchy Law expert) that any such Deed was not legally binding.

Brandon looked up from the parchment to Sir Richard's bemused gaze.

"It seems everyone has an axe to grind, does it not, Lieutenant?"

"What do you intend to do about this?" Brandon asked directly. The letter had shocked him out of his subordinate protocol.

Sir Richard acknowledged his tone with a twitching grin. "Well, Lieutenant, that very much depends on which side of the wall your wavering loyalty falls. You seem to be sympathising with a deluded individual, perhaps *I* should do the same."

Brandon felt his stomach lurch and his face flush, his anger only tempered by fear of provoking the man in black. "I assure you, Sir Richard," he said evenly, "my loyalties to the Duke have never wavered. My sympathy towards Xavier is based on his predicament, not his claim."

Another trickle of sweat ran down his back as he held Sir Richard's appraising gaze.

"Very well, Lieutenant," Sir Richard conceded, "but just remember, his predicament is of his own making *and*, I repeat, not your concern."

Sir Richard was manipulating the argument to suit his own ends. Xavier's predicament was, for the most part, a direct result of Sir Richard's decisions, but Brandon now realised that confrontation was not the tactic to employ with a man of such unquestionable authority; it would get him and, more importantly, his family nowhere. Nowhere, that is, except the sun-worshipping community of Blessed Whipping. If Bertrand had some sort of relationship with Sir Richard, so be it. As long as it didn't impact upon his family, he was content to remain ignorant. And if Sir Richard wanted to inherit the Dukedom enough to deny its rightful heir, then so be it to that as well. Xavier was better off continuing his life away from the intrigue and machinations of the court; his research was a far nobler course for him to follow.

So it was with compliance, rather than defiance, that Brandon acknowledged his superior officer's remark. "I understand, Sir Richard."

A self-satisfied smile broke across Sir Richard's face, an exact replica of the one in the portrait above. "Very good, Lieutenant." After a brief pause, he added, "Now, if you'll excuse me, I believe the Town Crier is waiting to vent his frustrations and, as you know, he is a man who knows how to vent."

Brandon stood up slowly and saluted, but remained standing by the desk. He couldn't leave without knowing what Sir Richard planned to do about Bertrand's ultimatum. The man in black regarded him with a quizzical expression.

Brandon gaze flicked to the parchment. "Sir, if you'll indulge me a moment more, I—"

"Ah… of course…" Sir Richard smiled in mock absent-mindedness before picking up the parchment and proffering it to him. Brandon tried to control his eagerness as he accepted the letter, but, judging by the bemused expression on his commanding officer's face, he doubted he'd succeeded. "Would you mind giving that to Prestwich on your way out?"

Once again, Brandon felt his stomach lurch. Prestwich was renowned for record-keeping; he had information on almost every Lower Icinger. He also worked closely with the Office of Petitions and probably knew more about the daily goings-on in the town than Sir Richard himself. It was ironic, really, since the man seemed to spend every minute of the day chained to his desk, scribing, filing, or rummaging through parchments. Once Bertrand's letter had been handed to Prestwich, it would never be lost or forgotten.

Brandon's dismay must have been just as obvious as his initial eagerness, because Sir Richard lost his mocking expression. "It is evidence of a threat made against your family and myself, Lieutenant," he explained matter-of-factly. "For the records, you understand."

"Yes, sir," he replied, trying not to sound alarmed. "And what of the Deed itself, Sir Richard?"

"Ah, yes…" Sir Richard rested his elbows on the desk, his chin touching the tips of his fingers in an introspective pose, "Further evidence of this zealot's coercion against law-abiding citizens of Lower Icing." Then he relaxed back into his chair and looked directly at Brandon. "It is fortunate for your family that I am now in possession of this farcical Deed."

Brandon regarded his commanding officer. He looked and sounded sincere, and his reasoning was, as usual, hard to argue against. "Of course," said Brandon, relieved. "Thank you, Sir Richard."

"Not at all, Lieutenant," he replied pleasantly. "It's simply a matter of doing one's duty, as I'm sure *you* are fully aware."

His smile was warm, but Brandon felt a chill. The implication behind his words was obvious: be found wanting and the Deed of Promise could be found legal. Sir Richard had just made certain of Brandon's loyalty.

Brandon shut the door to Sir Richard's office, leaving behind its stately grandeur, and re-entered the chaotic realm of his secretary. Prestwich's desk was covered in files and record books, seemingly placed at random. It was a far cry from the neat piles and ordered filing system on display in Administrator Penman's office. At least all the archived records were hidden from view in the huge cellar below.

Prestwich looked up from his desk. His eye-glasses glinted in the well-lit room and his neatly-kept, shoulder-length hair shone silver against his drab, grey attire. Grabbing a quill and a large, leather-bound book, he jumped up from his chair and darted the ten or so feet towards Brandon. For a man in his sixties, he was surprisingly spritely, and displayed the energy of a man thirty years his junior. Opening the book and flicking to the correct page, he began scribing as he said aloud, "One letter from… Bertrand of Blessed Whipping, dated… Tuesday, June twenty-four. Received Wednesday, June twenty-five."

After he'd recorded the details, he darted back to his desk, dropped the open book on top of a scattering of parchments, speared the quill back into its inkwell, then darted back to retrieve Bertrand's letter. Brandon had barely taken two steps since entering the secretary's demesne; the manic little man zipped around so quickly there hadn't been time to.

"Thank you, Lieutenant," said Prestwich, snatching the parchment from Brandon's grasp with the swiftness of a toad's tongue. He then scurried back to his desk and began rummaging through a pile of files, seemingly oblivious to Brandon's progress towards the opposite door.

"Tell Master Hiepants to come through please, Lieutenant," said Prestwich as Brandon reached the door.

Brandon turned to look at the man; he was placing Bertrand's letter into a file. He flicked a quick glance in Brandon's direction. "Thank you, Lieutenant. Save me a trip."

Save him a trip? Was he joking, Brandon wondered as he opened the door and left the chaotic realm of the Prestidigitator of Parchment.

The Town Crier, as predicted, was waiting in the reception area, relaxing on a luxurious red velvet divan like a large yellow-and-pink cushion. He looked slightly taken aback by Brandon's sudden appearance and stood as Brandon approached him. "Oh… Lieutenant," he said, grappling for his customary upbeat demeanour. "I trust Sir Richard is in good form this morning?"

Brandon returned Gerald's hopeful smile. "Yes, Town Crier," he replied pleasantly. "Sir Richard is in *excellent* form this morning."

The Town Crier's smile quivered.

CHAPTER 13
No official duty nonsense

BRANDON SALUTED THE guards at the East Gate on his way out of the castle and strode through the usual trail of people to-ing and fro-ing from Reginald Puffy's kitchen. He often wondered how the town would survive if the kitchen wasn't there to provide a regular source of income to the many villagers who worked the land or tended livestock. It was another reason Brandon was proud to serve the Duchy of Lower Icing — everyone, from the man with a small potato patch to the mill owner who supplied bag after bag of flour, was paid for their goods.

Leaving behind the enticing aroma of baking pies, Brandon walked down the short laneway that led to the Town Square. It was now late morning, but the laneway was still partially shaded by the two-storey building to his right. The sign above its door hung motionless in the shade. Painted on the sign was a white, fluffy creature with large ears holding a frothing tankard of ale. It stared down at him with a mocking grin, as if his rank was not worthy of admittance. As he passed The Harey Rabbit, he glanced through a window at the assortment of fashionably attired clientele within. Perhaps the rabbit was right.

However, it was the two-storey building with the red bell sign that Brandon was heading for. The laneway opened up into the bright sunshine of the Town Square. The weather was turning hot again and, as usual, there was a collection of villagers waiting their turn at the well. Most of them were women passing time in conversation while their children scurried around them, playing chasey. As Brandon drew closer, he was spotted by a lad who looked to be around eight years of age. The boy stopped running, stood to attention and saluted. Brandon smiled and acknowledged the salute with one of his own. The boy reacted with delight, gleefully calling out to his mother that the soldier had saluted him. This attracted the attention of the other children, who called out for him to salute them as well. Brandon thought about walking on, but it could do no harm, and showing goodwill to the children would foster trust in the uniform — *that* was worth a salute. So he stopped, faced the dozen or so children, and gave them all, including the adults who were now watching, a formal salute. The resulting cheers buoyed him somewhat as he made his way to The Bloody Bell, where he planned to talk to his family about the Deed of Promise.

It hadn't taken as much cajoling as Brandon thought it would to get his parents and his sister away from the bar room. Just the mention of the Deed of Promise had been enough to get their attention. His mother had literally dropped what she was doing — filling an ale tankard — when Brandon had countered her 'What's this all about, love? We got folk needin' to be served' with those three magical words.

They were all sitting around the table in their living room, immersed in serene blue surrounds. (The bar room had been left in the capable hands of Rosie, who'd been working at The Bell for eleven years, two younger barmaids, Janice and Rhiannon, and 'Handy' Andy, who basically did any job asked of him.)

"Well, lad, what news then?" said his father in his usual no-nonsense manner.

They all regarded him with pensive expressions. His mother held Bethany's hand and squeezed it as if waiting for an inevitable death sentence to be pronounced.

"It's not bad news," he assured them, trying to sound positive. "However—"

"It ain't *good* news," finished Bar. Then he went on the offensive. "Not that it matters, lad. I don' care if the Duke kisses Bertrand's Blessed Whipping arse and gives him three wishes; he ain't havin' our Bethany."

His mother gave his father a supportive nod, whereas Bethany remained calm and introspective.

"I feel the same way, Pa," Brandon said meaningfully, "but it won't come to that. I don't think the Duke is even aware of the Deed's existence. What I was going to say is that Sir Richard has it in his keeping. Bertrand lodged it three months ago."

His mother looked worried, his sister even more resigned, but his father remained steely-eyed. "An' what's *he* gonna do with it?" Bar's jaw muscles were clenching.

"He's keeping it, along with a letter he received this morning, as evidence of Bertrand's unlawful coercion and threatening behaviour."

His father's expression didn't change, but his mother's looked hopeful. "Does that mean Bethany's safe?"

"Yes it does, Ma," he said as convincingly as possible. Then he reached across the table and took Bethany's other hand. "Bethany, nothing will happen to you. I promise."

"Thank you, Brandon."

Bertie put a reassuring arm around her and squeezed her close. "You see, love, we're stayin' together 'ere at The Bell, and there ain't nothin' Bertrand can do about it."

Bethany smiled weakly in her mother's embrace. Bar gazed reassuringly in her direction, before announcing, "Well, best get back to work. Give us a hand with a couple o' barrels will you, lad?"

"Of course, Pa." Brandon stood up with his father, leaving Bertie and Bethany at the table.

They opened the door to the bar room — the sudden noise and chaos was a complete contrast to the calmness of the living room. It was like tapping a badly shaken barrel of ale: there was no hint of its fizzing contents until the seal was broken. Casting a quick eye across the room, Brandon saw that the patrons consisted mainly of night or early morning workers enjoying a bit of sustenance and relaxation after their hours of toil — people like manure collectors and street sweepers who helped maintain the overall cleanliness of Lower Icing, night-soil collectors who contributed vastly to the town's aromatic standard of living, and a smattering of people from more savoury occupations, like bakers and dairy farmers.

As Brandon and his father emerged from the private quarters, there was a subtle, yet noticeable, change in noise level. The late-morning crowd were well aware of how to behave in Bar's presence. He followed his pa under the staircase and into the storeroom. Bar shut the door behind him. Brandon turned around in surprise. His father never shut the door when changing barrels.

"So, lad," he said calmly, "'ow 'bout you tell me the whole truth, an' don' be givin' me no official duty nonsense."

Brandon felt a flush of embarrassment. He hated keeping things from his family, but he often had no choice. On this occasion, he hadn't been given any official orders, just an insinuation of what would happen to Bethany if his loyalty was found wanting. He had no intention of being disloyal, but he'd wanted to spare his family that caveat to his sister's safety.

"There's nothing official about it, Pa," he replied. "That's what worries me."

He then relayed the conversation he'd had with Sir Richard to his father. The noise from the bar room wasn't as nearly as muffled in the storeroom, and he occasionally had to raise his voice over bursts of laughter and chants like "Icing-Icing-Icing-Oi-Oi-Oi... Icing-Icing-Icing-Oi-Oi-Oi... Icing-Oi... Icing-Oi... Icing-Icing-Icing-Oi-Oi-Oi!"

In contrast, Bar had remained silent throughout Brandon's recounting. Even his expression remained fairly constant, with only his furrowing eyebrows revealing his deepening concern. "Hmm," he murmured thoughtfully after Brandon had finished divulging the contents of Bertrand's letter. "Seems Bertrand's got his grubby little hands on Sir Richard's balls."

"Yes, Pa." Brandon nodded. He wouldn't have put it that way, but his father was right. Sir Richard would normally have had someone like Bertrand arrested.

"Well, lad, we're gonna 'ave t'make some plans, an' make' 'em quick, like. I'm puttin' no stock in Sir Richard's assurances, partic'ly if Bertrand can squeeze 'im where it hurts."

Brandon had been afraid of this. The last thing he needed was his father acting irrationally and making the situation worse. "Pa, I think the best thing we can do is—"

"Brandon," Bar interrupted, "ain't nothin' more important t' me than this family. Not The Bell, nothin'. An' I'll do anythin' I can to protect it."

"Of course, Pa," Brandon said defensively, "but if you start kicking up a fuss then it—"

"Who said anythin' 'bout kickin' up a fuss?" He reacted angrily. "Don' worry, I ain't gonna do nothin' t' embarrass you and your Purple Peril mates. You an' Sir Richard talk of loyalty... Well, my loyalty is *here*, to your ma, to your sister, an' to *you*, Brandon. You use y'fancy words in y'fancy voice, an' tell us ev'rythin' is alright, an' that y'sure nothin' will 'appen to Bethany, but you *ain't* sure, an' so all those fancy words mean nothin'!"

Brandon felt completely ashamed. Bar's outburst was a reminder of how deeply his father's feelings went, and he suddenly realised how distanced he'd become from them. A hollow feeling formed in the pit of his stomach and he cast his eyes downwards, no longer able to meet his father's intense gaze. Then he felt Bar's strong grip on his shoulder.

"Sorry, lad. Jus' fear an' anger talkin'. You know I couldn' be prouder of ya."

Brandon looked up; his father was smiling at him. "I know, Pa. What do you want me to do?"

Bar straightened and, with grim determination, said, "Leave this t'me. You jus' go 'bout y'duties, an' don't give Sir Richard no reason t'be questionin' your loyalty."

Brandon was about to protest, but his father headed him off. "You jus' keep your ears to the ground, lad, an' keep me in the know."

"Of course, Pa, but—"

"I'll take care of everythin' 'ere, an' we'll be ready if the worst 'appens."

Brandon didn't like this one bit, but as he stared into his father's face, he knew there was nothing he could do to dissuade him.

"Very well, Pa," Brandon conceded, and then, trying to regain some perspective, added, "But remember, whatever precautions you take are very likely to be unnecessary. Ratifying that Deed would be an unlawful act, and I don't think Sir Richard would stoop to such underhanded methods, regardless of what pressure Bertrand tries to impose. It would be dishonourable, and I believe Sir Richard would rather lose the Dukedom than his honour."

Bar regarded Brandon seriously. "I 'ope you're right, son."

Much to his family's pleasure, Brandon decided to stay on and lend a hand at The Bell. It was approaching midday and the crowd had begun to bustle in for their repast. He changed out of his uniform into some plain attire; the animated environment of the bar room was not conducive to keeping clothing clean. And, in any case, he wasn't officially on duty for another eleven hours, so there was no need for the uniform.

Brandon used to help out regularly at The Bell when he became a cadet, but his availability (and desire) to do so had been eroded away by his new, regimented lifestyle. In fact, he realised, much to his shame, this was the first time since being promoted to the Purple Peril that he'd devoted any of his free time to help out at The Bell. Thinking on it even more, as he walked from his room (that Bertie still kept ready for him), it had to be almost six months since he'd offered his services. He'd been a lieutenant for almost four months, and he wouldn't have worked the bar room for at least two months before that. Actually, it had been the first day of the new year, almost seven months ago! Brandon could hardly believe it. The castle walls were more than just fortifications against enemies; they were a barrier between those within and those without.

Brandon stepped out into the noise and frenetic activity. (Lieutenant Swill had been left neatly folded on his bed.) Much to his surprise, he enjoyed getting in amongst the fray. He'd forgotten how much fun serving ale and bantering with regulars could be. And it was amazing how much people opened up to him when he wasn't in uniform.

By the time he finished, some three hours later (although, it felt a lot less), he'd resolved to work at The Bell at least once every month. This Bertrand business had been a timely reminder about what was important to Brandon, both personally and professionally. The Bell was the connection to his family, but it was also a connection to the townsfolk of Lower Icing. It was a taste of everyday life.

It was with a renewed sense of wellbeing that Brandon strode across The Square. He felt rejuvenated in mind and heart; the time working alongside his family in The Bloody Bell had been as much of a tonic as Xavier's Natron Bomb.

Xavier… He'd almost forgotten the young man in the miasma of smoking, belching and farting. Xavier's arrival had been met with fear and suspicion, but, to Brandon, he'd proven himself unworthy of either. In fact, Xavier had been the catalyst of today's rediscovery of family and place. *What I am saying, Brandon, is that for your parents and your sister, this Deed of Promise is very real, regardless of its legality.* Those words had been ringing through his head when he'd entered Sir Richard's office, and the resulting confrontation had led him to The Bell.

He wondered if Xavier still held hopes of meeting the Duke today. It was a regrettable situation. Xavier deserved more consideration, but Brandon was powerless to alter his circumstances, and he couldn't risk another confrontation with Sir Richard. It was best if he stayed away from the young man, for today at least. In any case, their relationship was probably becoming too personal, blurring the line between duty and courtesy.

His purple-and-gold doublet shimmered in the hot, mid-afternoon sun, and his polished black boots clicked confidently across The Square. His wide-brimmed hat provided adequate protection from the glare as he observed the myriad of colour that was part of a working summer's day in Lower Icing. Most of the clothing was fairly drab and practical, but that just highlighted the baskets of bright red apples, the bales of golden hay, the bunches of vibrant orange carrots, and the brilliance of the deep blue and gold in the uniforms of the guardsmen.

Turning down Big Wig Street, the colours were even more vivid and varied. Shops displayed the latest fashions: clothing, millinery, shoes, cloth and drapery. Charles Bling's jewellery sparkled silver and gold, and even Horace Dabbler's apothecary displayed a colourful range of bottles and vials. And then, of course, there were the people who frequented these places — the well-to-do in their finery, strutting out their taste for all to see.

Upon entering his quarters, Brandon found its dim greyness rather deflating, but its quiet coolness was welcome and relaxing. He planned to have another soak in the tub — the smell of The Bell was in his hair — then get a few hours' sleep, to be refreshed and ready for tonight's duty. He sat down on the edge of his bed and pulled off his boots.

Brandon was woken by Jethro Fowler's less than gentle prodding. His room was lit by candlelight, not sunlight, he was still in his uniform, and his hair still smelt of ale and tobacco smoke.

CHAPTER 14

Behind its jovial windows

BRANDON LED HIS squad of twelve men (in four rows of three) out the West Gate and down Noble Street. He had recovered from the initial shock of falling asleep after Jethro had informed him he still had an hour before patrol — time enough to douse his head in a basin of water and give his hair a good scrub, sate his hunger with a pork and leek pie (and a raspberry tart), and wash it down with a mug of cleansing ale.

Now he felt refreshed and eager for what the night might bring. It was still pleasantly warm and there was an unusual number of people out strolling, enjoying the perfect conditions. When they reached the corner of Noble and Merchant, Brandon brought the squad to a halt.

"Right, lads," he said, addressing the four rows. "It looks like we may be in for a busy night. As you can see, there are plenty of people about. That means there'll be plenty of opportunities for cut-purses, so keep your eyes peeled, and don't just concentrate on the usual venues. Check the quieter places too, and I want a strong presence around The Harey Rabbit. There's going to be a lot of pickled nobs meandering down Big Wig Street, along here, and down to Blancmange and Meringue Streets, all stumbling under the weight of their money pouches."

"T'be sure, t'wouldn't be under the weight of their cod-pieces," chimed in Paddy O'Limerick, the squad jester, obtaining the desired response from the rest of the men.

"Yes, thank you for that, Paddy," responded Brandon, acknowledging the joke with good humour. "Must be why *you're* so light on your feet."

More laughs ensued.

"And remember," Brandon continued, seriously, "stay in your threes. We're outnumbered as it is, even with Lieutenant Potts' squad concentrating on the area around the College and The Pits. And don't be afraid to use this." Brandon patted the small bugle slung over his right hip. "No need for heroics; we're here to help each other. Understand?"

"Yes, sir!" the squad responded in unison.

"Good," Brandon acknowledged with a nod. "Tiller, Mitchell and Fletcher — a visible presence around the Town Square, if you please."

The front three men-at-arms saluted and then headed down Merchant Street towards The Bell.

"Mason, Greyson and Ap Bleddyn — the Noble to Meringue sector."

The three men-at-arms saluted and continued down Noble Street (which ended in a T-junction at the main entrance of Lower Icing College some hundred paces ahead). No doubt they would cross paths with some of Peter Potts' men, but that wasn't a bad thing — the more, the safer.

The next three — Pullman, Oldman and Bean (Alistair's nephew) — were sent to the south-west sector, the streets west of Meringue, a fairly safe area, full of families. It was more a 'seen to be serving the community' patrol.

The remaining three — Wellington, MacHaggis and O'Limerick — waited silently for their assignment, the latter with a playful grin on his face.

"You lucky three have the pleasure of accompanying me through the streets and alleyways around The Dead Duck."

O'Limerick and Wellington (along with Oldman and Greyson) had been part of last night's revelries at The Duck, and both of them smiled and nodded. MacHaggis also seemed pleased. "I'm glad that meets with your approval, lads," Brandon remarked with a hint of sarcasm.

"T'wouldn't be a chance o' patrollin' *inside* The Duck, now would there, Lieutenant?" O'Limerick's remark had been as predictable as trouble following the Moleson Twins.

"Yes, Lieutenant," piped in Wellington. "Perhaps you could give the crowd another rendition of 'She Loved The Prick O' My Sword'."

This was followed by MacHaggis saying that he'd heard about the remarkable amount of undergarments that had been thrown in Brandon's direction during the sing-along.

Brandon took it all in good humour (although the mention of his singing conjured some hitherto forgotten and embarrassing images). "Alas, lads, our role tonight will be one of peace-keeping, not stirring the womenfolk into fits of unbridled passion."

They all smiled knowingly, until Brandon added, "That's why I chose *you* three to accompany me. The sight of your gormless expressions should be enough to douse any spark of desire."

An hour later, the worst thing they'd had to deal with was Jock MacHaggis' flatulence. He came from the highlands of Sporrendale, a cold, mountainous place far to the north, where eating boiled offal was a local pastime (along with throwing large pieces of wood) and where the word 'decorum' translated as 'disembowel' in their dialect. Tonight, MacHaggis' decorum had been exceptional.

"Seriously, Jock," complained Stephen Wellington as they rounded a corner from one dark street into another. "I've smelt better tanneries than you."

"Och, man," replied the Highlander, "'tis only a wee thing to be concerned aboot. 'Better out than in' my mammy used to say."

"Poor woman obviously had no sense of smell," countered Wellington.

"And I wouldn'a t'ought it was a wee thing," added O'Limerick, "t'be sure, 'tis more o' a shi—"

"That'll do, Paddy," cut in Brandon. He'd had just about enough of the privy humour. For all their sakes, he headed for The Dead Duck, where Jock MacHaggis could relieve himself thoroughly.

They heard sounds of singing and laughter well before the inn came into view. And when it eventually did, it was a beacon of light and life, as if the heart and soul of this part of Lower Icing was concentrated behind its jovial windows.

As they approached the entranceway to The Dead Duck, marked by its eponymous sign, O'Limerick couldn't help himself. "T'be sure, Jock, this be the place for you. You could hang that sign over your arse."

Jock joined in the laughter from the other men as they moved to go inside. Brandon stopped them at the door. "Hold up, lads. Before you go swaggering inside, let me remind you we're on duty. That means no drinking, fraternising or carousing. Got that, Paddy?"

O'Limerick had been looking in through one of the windows with an expression that conveyed thoughts of doing all three. He gave Brandon a knowing smile. "I'll be a tower of restraint, Lieutenant."

And with that ringing endorsement, Brandon led his men inside.

The noise outside the inn was a lullaby compared to the noise within. But it was a joyful sound. Some people were singing along with one of the barmaids, others were engaged in animated conversations, and there seemed to be smiles and laughter everywhere. A few of those smiles became looks of concern when their owners spied Brandon and his men, but Brandon did his best to give reassuring signals to any who glanced their way. He even went so far as removing his hat as a gesture of their goodwill.

While they waited for MacHaggis to relieve himself, Brandon took the opportunity to observe the villagers who frequented The Dead Duck. He'd rarely stepped foot in the place while on duty, and never as a lieutenant in the Purple Peril. He'd been here last night as a customer, but that was with his men, and the ale-fuelled evening was all a bit of a haze. As he glanced around the room, he noticed quite a few of the patrons, particularly the women, were now smiling at him. In some cases, their smiles appeared to be filled with more than just good cheer. Brandon felt a flush of embarrassment as imagery of stockings, garters and other undergarments flashed back into his memory. What was MacHaggis doing? On second thoughts, he didn't want to think about that either.

It struck Brandon that, ale and food apart, The Dead Duck was a completely different establishment from The Bloody Bell. This place was full of happiness, whereas The Bell was full of aggression. Here, at least half the crowd were women, whereas the only women desperate or mad enough to be seen at The Bell (his mother and sister excluded) either worked behind the bar or worked the streets. And there was no singing at The Bell, just the occasional chant or drinking game. Yet here, most people were in full voice, joining in on the chorus of a popular ditty, one that was scarily familiar to Brandon:

Your head is swollen and flush,
And you speak in a saucy rush,
In your eye there's a certain twinkle,
But keep your pants on, Mister Winkle.

Brandon wondered how much longer it would be before MacHaggis got *his* pants on. Wellington and O'Limerick were starting to enjoy the atmosphere, particularly since a couple of women had begun flirting with them. At least Wellington was maintaining some semblance of decorum, whereas O'Limerick's 'tower of restraint' looked to be crumbling.

Brandon was about to intervene when he felt a forceful hand on his shoulder. He jolted around, left arm protecting his face, right hand ready to draw his sword; a defensive action that had been trained into him over the last three years. He relaxed, however, when he saw who handled him. The swarthy features of Will Plucker, the innkeeper of The Dead Duck, regarded him from a height advantage of at least six inches (and Brandon was considered tall at six foot).

Will, through necessity, had mastered the art of non-verbal communication, and, with the flick of his head, it was clear he wanted Brandon to follow him. From what he knew of Will Plucker, he wasn't a man to court the involvement of authority, but judging by the set of his dark, bushy eyebrows, there was something that required Brandon's immediate attention. Brandon nodded his understanding and held up a finger to indicate that he needed a moment. Turning back to his men, he beckoned O'Limerick to follow him, while indicating to Wellington to stay put. The 'tower of restraint' reluctantly extricated himself from the young woman who had successfully laid siege to his defences, and joined Brandon.

Following in Will's wake, they barely caused a ripple as they waded through the singing crowd to the opposite side of the bar room. Just like The Bell, The Dead Duck had accommodation upstairs, but it wasn't the kind of accommodation that needed to accommodate someone all night. In fact, in some cases, a few minutes was all that was required. And, unlike The Bell, patrons were allowed to spill up the stairs and onto the first-floor landing.

Will led them under the stairs to a door. Producing a key, he unlocked it, and they entered a large storeroom. It contained rows of three-tiered shelving that housed piles of pots and pans, stacks of plates and bowls, trays of mugs, and other assorted kitchen supplies.

Will shut the door. It blocked out some of the noise, but the rattling plates and mugs were testament to the rollicking enthusiasm of the crowd.

"Your timin' couldn' be better, Lieutenant," he said matter-of-factly as he led them down the central aisle. Brandon followed — he could feel O'Limerick pushing at his back in his eagerness to see what lay ahead.

"T'be sure, I t'ink the man's killed someone," he whispered.

Brandon ignored him.

Will turned right and then came to a halt after a few more paces. Hands on his hips, he looked downwards, his massive frame hiding whatever it was from view, but only momentarily.

As Brandon drew next to him, he could see in the corner, amongst a collection of buckets and mops, a man propped against the wall. He hugged his knees under his chin, not because it was a desired position, but because it was the way the ropes bound him. The man had also been gagged. He began to wriggle and squirm at Brandon's appearance, yelling out an angry, muffled demand. In his attempt to move, he knocked against one of buckets, causing a mop to overbalance and clock him on the skull. The man shook his head in pain and frustration, and his muffled cries become even more animated.

Brandon smiled at the angry bundle before him, unable to hide his amusement. "What have you been up to this time, Billy Offcut?"

CHAPTER 15

It wozzen me, it wozzen me, it wozzen me

THERE WERE NOW seven of them in an alleyway to the side of The Dead Duck: Brandon and his three men (MacHaggis had finally rid himself of his burden), a subdued Billy Offcut, Will Plucker and the person responsible for Billy's imaginative bundling, Tom Skinner.

They'd congregated in the alleyway to avoid making a spectacle of Billy. Brandon wanted a proper explanation of events, not an audience of drunken revellers throwing in their two coppers' worth.

As the Gamekeeper of Lower Icing, Tom was known to Brandon, but more through reputation than anything else. He was rarely seen at the castle, preferring a more natural existence in the Duke's Forest. So, to find Tom here at The Dead Duck under such circumstances bordered on the bizarre.

Like Will, Tom was very tall, but with curly, fair hair and a healthy, tanned complexion. He was also at least ten years younger than the innkeeper. He had an open face and an easy-going manner, despite his intimidating size. Perhaps he'd picked up on the fact that Brandon and his men had little sympathy for the skinny, dishevelled figure slumped against the wall like a broken mop. Billy was still gagged, because none of them wanted to hear his whining protestations of innocence.

Brandon had removed the gag in the storeroom, only to be on the receiving end of a barrage of "It wozzen me, it wozzen me, it wozzen me."

Will untied him, while O'Limerick held him at sword point, taunting him with questions about butchery. "Now, Billy, if I'd want to be havin' a nice piece o' steak where would I slice?"

Billy's squeaks of innocence finally reached re-gagging point when Paddy got around to asking about sausages.

They'd then re-tied his hands and led him through the back door of the storeroom, around the outside of the inn, to where they now stood. Will had filled them in on what Billy had done, as much as he knew, but then told him that the person who knew exactly what had happened was still inside The Duck. While the innkeeper went to fetch the witness, Brandon sent O'Limerick to retrieve Wellington and (hopefully) MacHaggis.

For two or three minutes, Brandon had been alone with Billy. Even in the darkness of the alleyway, there was enough light from the waning full moon to see Billy's features. His eyes darted from side to side.

"Don't even think about it, Billy," said Brandon, conversationally. "You're in enough trouble as it is."

This had brought on more muffled anguish and anger.

"Save it, Billy." Brandon was fed up with the youngest Offcut — not just for tonight, but for all the other times he'd gotten away with things on the back of his name. But now, if Will had the gist of the story right, Billy had finally over-stepped the line of family protection. "If it wasn't you, I'm sure this witness, and, indeed, the *victim* will corroborate your version of events."

Suddenly, Billy bolted, but Brandon was too close and too quick. He stuck out his leg. The wiry figure tumbled face first into the compacted dirt and stone and let out a muffled cry of pain. With his hands tied behind his back, all he could do was roll over. He was now sporting a graze on the side of his chin (to go with the lump on his head from the mop).

Brandon squatted next to him, heart racing from Billy's attempted escape. Levering the boy up by his shirt collar, he looked into his wide eyes. "You really do have offal for brains, don't you, Billy," he breathed, and then propped him against the side wall of The Dead Duck. "Or do you *want* me to add 'resisting arrest' to your *alleged* assault."

Billy looked helpless slumped against the wall, and a lot younger than his seventeen years, but it was time the runt of the Offcut litter learned a lesson, no matter what influence his family held at the Upper Bailey. As Sir Richard had recently pointed out, it was *simply a matter of doing one's duty*.

Will and the witness had been the first to return to the alleyway, chattering away like friends. It wasn't until Will had introduced his compatriot that Brandon realised who he was. He had only ever seen the Gamekeeper a few times, and then only fleetingly. If he hadn't been introduced, Brandon doubted he would have recognised Tom Skinner, particularly in a dark alleyway.

Tom extended his arm in greeting. Brandon responded in kind, and they locked forearms with their hands.

"Well met, Lieutenant," Tom said.

"I'm not sure *he'd* agree with you," Brandon said with good humour, indicating the sorry-looking sack of skin and bone sitting against the wall.

"Ah, yes," he acknowledged with a glance in Billy's direction. Tom's teeth shone in the moonlight, but whether he was smiling or grimacing, Brandon couldn't tell. "He was acting like a wild pig, so I trussed him up like one."

This brought a sulky, muffled response from Billy.

"Squealed like one too," added Will.

At that point, Billy had obliged by throwing in a few muffled, high-pitched protests before Brandon turned the conversation towards the events leading up to Tom's involvement. Addressing Tom, he stated, "Will said you caught him with one of the barmaids."

"Jenny," supplied Will.

"Your pardon, Will — Jenny." Readdressing Tom, he asked, "What was he doing exactly?"

"Put it this way, Lieutenant," he said seriously. "What he *wasn't* doing was treating her with respect."

"Fair enough, Tom," Brandon replied, "but if I arrested everyone who disrespected a barmaid, the inns would be empty."

"We ain't talkin' 'bout a few saucy words an' a slap on the arse 'ere, Lieutenant," interjected Will.

"No, I'd gathered that."

"Look, Lieutenant," said Tom. "This rogue staggered in just before ten o'clock, three-quarters full, and started making a nuisance of himself. Then began making unwanted advances towards Jenny."

"Jenny's my niece," supplied Will. "She 'elps in the kitchen, like. She certainly ain't one t'take patrons upstairs, if you catch my meanin'."

Brandon nodded, and Tom continued. "She's a sweet lass and was scared enough to ask for my help. So I told her I'd watch out for her."

"Why did she ask *you*, Tom," asked Brandon, "and not Will?"

Will answered this. "You know what it's like in there," he said meaningfully. "I can't be lookin' after one lass when there's two hundred people carryin' on an' demandin' all sorts. Speakin' of which, I'd best be gettin' back."

"I won't hold you up much longer, Will, or you, Tom," Brandon assured them. "I just need to make sure of the facts, because there's going to be one hell of stink about this."

It was then that O'Limerick had reappeared with Wellington and MacHaggis.

"Speak of the devil," remarked Brandon, more to himself than the two men next to him.

"Och, Paddy." MacHaggis was in lively voice. "I've seen smaller logs tossed in a—"

"That's enough, MacHaggis." Brandon was becoming increasingly aware of the seriousness of the situation and was no longer in the mood to put up with any juvenile banter. The three men-at-arms joined the gathering in silence and stood around the forlorn shape of Billy Offcut.

Now that all his men were present, Brandon wanted to get Billy to The Can as soon as possible. An alleyway was not the place to conduct an enquiry, particularly at this time of night. Four men-at-arms and two hulking civilians surrounding a bound and gagged whippet of a lad could appear to any passers-by as somewhat excessive. And there would be plenty of passers-by when the music stopped at The Dead Duck. It was approaching midnight and the first revellers would be leaving soon.

As if reading his mind, Tom suggested he accompany Brandon and his men back to the castle, and he would relay the details of the incident along the way.

"That's very good of you, Tom."

"Not at all, Lieutenant," he replied, happily. "It's on my way."

This surprised Brandon — he'd assumed Tom was staying at The Dead Duck. He and Will obviously knew each other quite well, and Tom was trusted enough by the staff that they would approach him for help.

"His lordship's stayin' at the castle," Will interjected. "Too good for the likes o' The Duck these days. Ain't that right, Tom?"

Tom smiled. "Richard has prepared one of the guest quarters; it would be the height of bad manners to refuse his hospitality."

This was even more surprising, and Brandon's thoughts turned immediately to Xavier. However, he wasn't about to heat up *that* kettle of fish. The last thing he wanted was to give Sir Richard any reason to question his loyalty. He had a prisoner to escort to The Can and another six hours of night patrol; *that* was his duty, and he intended to carry it out to the best of his ability.

Will returned to his innkeeper duties while Brandon ordered his men to patrol around the inn and make sure there was no trouble at closing time. There was no point in all of them traipsing back to the castle. Brandon and Will could handle Billy Offcut.

"And *around* the inn doesn't mean *in* it," he emphasised to all of them, but focused his gaze on O'Limerick.

"Yes, sir," they replied as one. Billy Offcut's arrest and the presence of the 'legendary' Gamekeeper of Lower Icing had smartened up their attitude considerably.

"I should be back shortly after closing, but if I'm not, return to The Square and help out at The Bell if needed. And remember—"

"Stay in our threes," piped in O'Limerick.

"Exactly, Paddy," he said seriously. "Now, off you go. Two block radius, thanks, lads."

They saluted and moved off into the night.

Tom grabbed Billy and pulled him to his feet. Brandon regarded the slight shape of the youngest Offcut: a wispy shadow of misery next to the towering figure of Tom Skinner. Although he didn't deserve any, Brandon couldn't help but feel some sympathy for the bedraggled boy. If he'd had some discipline in his life, he might not have turned out so… undisciplined.

"You right with him, Tom?" he asked out of courtesy. It was clear Billy wouldn't be going anywhere except where the Gamekeeper led him.

"Good to see you have a sense of humour, Lieutenant," he remarked conversationally, and then, shaking the limp boy by the shoulder, he added, "There's no fight left in this scrawny leveret."

Brandon nodded and moved across to address Billy, "I'll remove the gag on the condition you keep your mouth shut. Agreed?"

Billy nodded, eyes downcast. He looked rather pathetic.

Will turned Billy around, and Brandon began to prise open the knot at the back of his head. His head moved and jerked in response. Tom was right: the fight had gone out of him. A few moments later, the gag, which was actually an ale (and whatever else) sodden bar cloth, was removed. Billy took a few deep breaths, and they set off towards The Can.

True to his word, Billy remained silent and compliant during the ten-minute walk, even when Tom relayed the full extent of Billy's crime. Fortunately for Jenny (and Billy), Tom had prevented a far more serious crime from occurring, but it didn't diminish the fact that Billy had committed assault. And this time he would pay for it.

Brandon was in little doubt Billy had done this before. Tonight, however, he'd pushed his luck too far. Billy had picked the wrong place, the wrong time, the wrong girl and, worst of all, the wrong man to bear witness against him. Tom Skinner was respected and trusted throughout the Duchy of Lower Icing. Billy's word would never be taken against that of the Duke's Gamekeeper. And, because he had been alone, none of his idiotic associates could provide him with a fanciful alibi or corroborate his version of events. In one fell swoop, all the privileges he had accrued over his young life suddenly amounted to nothing — Billy Offcut was on his own.

The Can was usually quiet on a Wednesday night, and tonight was no exception — Billy had the luxury of a cell to himself (for the time being, at least). Brandon had toyed with the idea of throwing him in with one of the Moleson Twins, but decided that Billy had already experienced a big enough shock to his system. And, in any case, Billy might benefit from some solitude. It would give him time to think about what he'd done.

Tom and Brandon had parted ways after they'd passed through the West Gate. Brandon had thanked him for his assistance in apprehending Billy and for the information he'd supplied pertaining to the incident. Tom had shrugged off Brandon's appreciation with a jovial, "I've had more trouble swatting flies."

Brandon found it hard to be as light-hearted about the matter. Billy was heading for a stretch in the dungeon. Not literally, of course — Lord Marmaduke had put a stop to the horrors of the rack and other forms of torture — but any time spent in the dungeon was still referred to as a 'stretch'. Even so, the dungeon was a particularly unpleasant place to be locked up. The darkness, the dampness and the sparseness of the cells were confronting enough, but what really made Brandon's skin crawl was the oppressiveness of all that stone above your head, being situated, as it was, under The Keep.

Billy was looking at a month. Still, he'd made his own bed and now he'd have to lie in it; except Master Key would more than likely put him in a cold cell *without* a bed, with only rat-infested rushes for comfort.

Brandon untied Billy's hands. He was in the end cell. Next door, a couple of 'drunk and disorderlies' were singing out an inebriated tune. The young man had completely withdrawn into himself, and Brandon removed the binding without resistance or complaint. He had never seen Billy this way before and it was oddly disturbing. He led Billy to one of the two corner pallets and gently guided him into a sitting position.

"See if you can get some rest, Billy," he said, trying not to raise his voice against the background of mournful, drunken harmonising.

Billy nodded silently and lay back on the pallet. Brandon stood up to leave.

"Lieutenant?" Billy's voice was slightly croaky and he sounded lost. "I'm sorry for wha' I done."

Brandon didn't know what to say; he'd only ever met the loud-mouthed, trouble-maker Billy Offcut who *never* admitted to doing *anything* wrong. "Get some rest," he suggested again, and walked out of the cell in silence.

Brandon locked Billy's door and went to the cell next door. Sliding the viewing panel open, he yelled into the darkness, "If you two don't shut up, I'm throwing one of you in with Mal and the other with Mick. Got it?"

Brandon was rewarded with immediate silence. It was an added benefit of having the Moleson Twins in The Can — everyone knew who they were and everyone was scared of them. They were the perfect deterrent. "Right. Keep it that way," he added quietly.

Normally, he wouldn't have worried about such behaviour. In fact, anything to annoy the Moleson Twins was to be encouraged. But tonight it wasn't the Moleson Twin's discomfort he was thinking about — it was Billy's.

CHAPTER 16

Enough spoon for the job

THE REST OF patrol duty was relatively incident free. Once closing time had passed and the last revellers had staggered home, the dark streets became eerily peaceful. Still, the night had been pleasantly warm, with enough moonlight to meander through the familiar streets and buildings without having to use the lanterns. There had been no reason to explore darkened alleys, no unusual sounds had needed investigating, no 'night-wanderers', nothing out of the ordinary to report.

The first glimmer of a new day occurred around half five: fading stars in the eastern sky and a halo of purple-red-orange over the gloomy green canopy of Duke's Forest. The air was still and quiet; it was going to be another hot day.

Brandon's squad was relieved by Sebastian Fitzbadly's at six o'clock, and the streets of Lower Icing were already alive with people going about their business. The contrast to an hour or so ago was remarkable — the silent world of shadows had been transformed into a frenetic world of bright sunlight, full of noise and colour. In fact, everyone seemed to be in a hurry this morning. Perhaps they were trying to out-race the heat. Brandon could already feel sweat on his head as he led his squad back to the barracks. It had been an unusually hot June, but he wasn't about to wish it away, not with all the freezing, rain-soaked nights and icy mornings winter would bring. Still, he was looking forward to breaking his fast and then having a soak. He and his squad were on patrol again tonight; he would bunk down for four or five hours later this afternoon.

Brandon marched his men back into the castle in formation, leading the four lines of three. Once they reached the barracks' compound, he formally dismissed his men and left them to disperse in whatever direction they chose, while he walked towards The Can. He wanted to check on Billy.

He entered the lock-up; the air was humid and scented with peppermint, like a mug of Xavier's digestive brew. The first cell was being cleaned out by a couple of cadets. One of them was George Martin.

"Morning, cadets," Brandon said.

Both reacted the same way. They dropped their mops and saluted with the eagerness of the newly recruited.

"At ease," Brandon said, trying to hide his amusement. "Willie Trafalgar been released, then?"

"Yes, Lieutenant," George informed him, "about half an hour ago. Lieutenant Fitzbadly said the smell of him was putting him off his breakfast."

Brandon nodded — it certainly sounded like Seb. "Carry on, then," he said, and moved to the second cell. Sliding open the viewing panel, he was greeted by a scowling Mal Moleson, reclined on his pallet, back propped up against the wall. Brandon had no intention of speaking to either twin; he just wanted to make sure they were being made to feel as uncomfortable as possible. Judging by Mal's glowering expression, all was well in that department.

He shut the panel and moved on to the other Moleson cell. The expression on Mick's face was a simmering replica of his brother's. However, Brandon was startled by the fact that Mick was standing just the other side of the panel. Before Brandon could react, Mick let fly with a gobbet of spit. It splattered against his left cheek. Brandon recoiled from the panel and quickly wiped the foul-smelling gob on his sleeve.

Brandon's immediate impulse was to lash out, but when he looked back at the smirking visage behind the panel, he knew that was what Mick wanted him to do. Reigning in his anger, he calmly slid the panel shut.

Mick began to laugh out loud. "Got 'im, Mal! Righ' in the face!"

This brought cheers and whoops of congratulations from Mal's cell, and also brought the two cadets out into the walkway to see what was going on.

A concerned-looking George led his fellow cadet towards Brandon. "Everything alright, Lieutenant?" he asked, closing the distance quickly.

"I'm fine," Brandon said sharply, still mustering his self-control. Then, noticing the flush of embarrassment on the new recruit's face, he added more appreciatively, "Thank you, George."

George nodded, but they both looked confused and distracted by the hilarity coming from the Moleson cells. "Don't worry about them," he assured the cadets. "Just concentrate on cleaning out that cell."

They both saluted and turned back down the walkway. Brandon wiped his sleeve on Mick's door, and then strode past the next two cells (which were empty — the two drunkards must have also been released) to the one at the end.

The viewing panel was open. Billy was huddled in the corner, on top of his pallet. He was hugging his knees to his chin, as if he was still tied up in Will Plucker's storeroom.

Brandon turned the key to the door. Billy looked up expectantly, but frowned when he saw it was Brandon. He opened the door and entered the cell. Billy remained in his huddled position. "How're you feeling, Billy?"

Billy shrugged, his eyes cast downwards.

"I'll send someone over to your house," Brandon continued, "to let your family know you're here."

Billy's gaze momentarily flicked towards Brandon, but he remained silent. Brandon wasn't sure what to make of the lad's demeanour. Judging by the acrid smell coming from the piss-bucket, Billy had chucked up the contents of his drinking session. Brandon wondered why he was wasting time on Frank Offcut's good-for-nothing son. He'd certainly get no thanks from the man himself for concerning himself with Billy's wellbeing.

"Right, Billy." Brandon sighed. "I'll leave you to your thoughts. The Witness Statement will be written up this afternoon, and—"

"Torn up this afternoon!" Billy sprung from the corner and was suddenly standing in front of Brandon, grazed chin jutting out in defiance. "You ain't got nuffin' on me!"

Brandon barely restrained himself from flattening the skinny whelp; the vulnerable boy he'd left last night had turned back into the obnoxious brat everyone knew so well.

"Sit down, Billy," Brandon said through clenched teeth.

"You jus' wait 'til—"

Brandon pushed the boy with enough force to cause him to fall back onto the pallet. "I said sit down," he said quietly.

The boy shuffled back into the corner, looking defiantly sulky.

"I thought you might have learned a lesson last night," Brandon said, feeling strangely betrayed by Billy's attitude, "but the morning has obviously reawakened the coward in you."

Billy grimaced, then responded sullenly, "*You're* the one wha' should be scared."

Brandon had had enough. The Can was unpleasant at the best of times, and he had better things to do than spend his time in a hot cell with a bucket of vomit and an ungrateful little turd.

He turned to exit cell. "Enjoy The Can while you can, Billy."

"What d'ya mean by that?"

Brandon ignored him and walked out of the cell.

"What d'ya mean by that?" he repeated, more aggressively.

Brandon turned in time to see Billy get up from his pallet. He eyed Brandon, waiting contemptuously for a response. Brandon almost burst out laughing — everything about Billy was pretence. And in his current, scruffy state, his posturing was about as intimidating as that of a newly-born alley kitten.

Brandon responded by shutting the door and turning the key. Billy rushed towards the door and put his face to the viewing panel. Brandon wasn't going to tempt fate — once spit on, twice shy — and he slid the viewing panel shut on Billy's angry visage.

"You jus' wait 'til me pa get's 'ere," he yelled.

This was followed up with a kick to the door and the typical, inane expletives that were the weaponry of the uneducated and, in Billy's case, the overindulged.

George and the other cadet — something Withers, wasn't it? — were still in the process of cleaning out cell number one. The smell of peppermint was refreshingly welcome, particularly after being in Billy's company. Who would have thought it could have the same effect *inside* the body.

Cadet Withers — Nick… *that* was his name — noticed Brandon first and stood to attention immediately. George followed suit a second later.

"At ease," he said, eyeing the cell and the two buckets of foul-looking mop water. They had done a good job of mopping up the evidence of Willie Trafalgar's stay. "Well done, lads."

This place wasn't doing anything for his appetite; it was time to leave.

Brandon couldn't remember feeling more relieved to be back in his quarters. His breakfast had been hearty, both in sustenance and conversation — Peter Potts and Jethro Fowler were intrigued to hear about Billy Offcut and Tom Skinner.

"Blimey," said Potts, after Brandon had told his fellow lieutenants about Tom's willingness to bear witness against Billy, "the lad's in for it *this* time."

"Aye," Jethro agreed, gleefully. "What I wouldn't give to see the look on old man Offcut's face when he's told that his arse-wipe of a son has been formally charged with attempted rape."

Brandon smiled, breaking a piece of bread from a freshly baked loaf. "Well, consider your wish granted."

Jethro's gleeful expression vanished. "What're you on about, Brando?"

"You're on duty soon. Why not pay the Offcuts a visit and tell them the good news," answered Brandon.

Jethro stared at him, trying to work out if Brandon was in jest.

"It's a nice day for a walk, Jeth," Brandon added with a smile.

"Go on, Jeth," encouraged Peter. "You like stirring the pot, and you don't get a much bigger pot than Frank Offcut."

"That's right, Potts," agreed Brandon, "but the question is, does Jeth have enough spoon for the job?"

Jethro wasn't usually on the receiving end of common-room banter — Seb and Peter were normally the targets — and he didn't seem to be handling the situation well. In fact, he looked very uncomfortable.

Peter, on the other hand, was enjoying the turning of the tables. "No worries there, Brando; Jeth's always going on about how big his utensil is."

It was too much for Jethro. "Right, right... I'll do it!"

"Good on you, Jeth." Brandon was surprised he'd succumbed so meekly. Peter expressed the same sentiment in a delighted smile. All that was missing was one of Seb's "That's the spirit!"

"In any case," added Jethro, a smile returning to his face, "I get to clap eyes on the luscious Ophelia. That's worth the price of admission."

They nodded in agreement. Ophelia was the anomaly of the Offcut litter — strikingly beautiful and beautifully proportioned. And she was wantonly promiscuous to go with it. However, her flirtatious nature was tempered by the knowledge that her father was a foul-tempered madman who often carried a large cleaver.

"I'd say 'clap' was the pertinent word there, Jeth," chimed in Peter. They all laughed, and Brandon finally put the piece of bread he'd broken from the loaf into his mouth.

The tub had already been used this morning by Jethro and Seb, so Brandon had to empty and refill it himself. He didn't mind; he found the preparation made the soak more enjoyable.

Sitting in the warm, soapy water, he was at peace with his thoughts. The sounds of castle life dissolved into the background; the marching of feet and clomping of hooves across the compound, the rhythmic clank of hammer on anvil from Klob's smithy, the barking of orders and the snippets of passing conversations were relegated to Brandon's subconscious.

The vanguard of Brandon's mind was filled with thoughts of his family, and how removed from them he'd become. To think, it had taken Xavier to open his eyes to that particular truth. Ironically, it was his sense of duty (and a bruised rib) that had brought him closer to the young man… a sense of duty that was seen as disloyal by his commanding officer… a commanding officer with a hidden agenda and a document that could potentially break up his family… And for his family, Brandon was willing to do anything, even treat Xavier like a… That was the problem: he didn't know *how* to treat Xavier. Was he a guest or a prisoner? Either way, it didn't change the fact that Brandon believed he was the Duke's son, and he suspected that Sir Richard believed it as well, despite his assertions to the contrary. And then, of course, there was Bertrand — there was more to *that* vulture than met the eye. Perhaps he also knew about Xavier's claim. Xavier had told Brandon that the letter he'd presented as evidence was a chance discovery, an oversight by his mentor, Horatio. Perhaps Bertrand had made a chance discovery of his own, or even been confided in by this Horatio… If that was so, Bertrand might have more compelling evidence than Xavier. Maybe that's what he'd meant by *further delays will necessitate a more drastic course of action* in the letter to Sir Richard.

Brandon heaved himself out of the tub with enough urgency to send a stab of pain through his all-but-forgotten bruised ribs.

INTERLUDE

SID AND HORATIO

THEY HAD BEEN on the road for at least a couple of hours, but the smooth ride and the featureless darkness made it hard for Sid to judge their progress. The first rays of sunlight couldn't be far off, and he wondered what the day would bring. He certainly hadn't been enlightened by the man opposite — the living corpse, sitting emotionlessly in his moving coffin.

If Doctor Manky had formulated a plan to gain access to the Duke, he wasn't sharing it with Sid. And Sid wasn't asking, because he didn't want to be an ingredient in his formulation. Sid grimaced to himself; his thoughts were beginning to sound like Manky's words.

"Something wrong, Sid?" purred the man opposite.

Sid wasn't sure what shocked him more, the sound of Doctor Manky's voice or the fact that he'd been observing Sid closely enough to pick up on his thoughts. For the last half an hour, the ghost doctor had appeared to be in some sort of trance.

"No, no, Manky," Sid replied, sarcastically. "Spending this time with you has been delightful. I'm just sorry it will be ending the moment this contraption reaches Lower Icing."

Even though it was dark, Sid could sense the knowing smile on Doctor Manky's face; his trademark smugness had reasserted itself. However, Sid wasn't about to give him the satisfaction of reacting. He'd become accustomed to that self-satisfied expression and knew it was part of the mind game Manky liked to play. Sid turned his head away from the irksome apparition and looked out the window. It must have conveyed the right message, because Doctor Manky remained silent, leaving Sid to his thoughts once again.

The rhythmic motion of the cab and the hypnotic sound of the horse's steady gait merged with the passing parade of shadowy trees and the pleasantly cool night air. It made his situation seem more unreal. He felt for the purse containing the fifty gold pieces Doctor Manky had given him. *That* was real enough, as was his pouch containing the meagre amount of coin he had brought with him. He'd also checked his boots before he'd got into the cab — all was well there, the daggers still snuggly in place. He wondered if Doctor Manky or Bertrand had noticed them or if he'd mentioned them while under the influence of Voracious Loquacious — neither scenario seemed likely. Knowing the daggers hadn't been discovered was reassuring. If there were any surprises ahead, Sid would be ready with a couple of his own. He wouldn't hesitate in giving Doctor Manky, Bertrand, or whoever else popped up on this surreal sojourn, a sharp lesson in self-defence.

The night landscape continued to pass by, and as Sid stared into its gloomy depths, dark images of his sister insinuated themselves into his mind as if the Rigour Morphis was still affecting him: Liv at The Bloody Bell handing the cloth bundle to Manky's protégé melded with the last words she'd directed at him on her way to the Duke's dinner, *Why don't you crawl back to your world of dirty whores and pathetic drunks.* Then her sunlit face floated disjointedly amongst the dark trees, radiating disgust. *Sid looks for trouble as much as he looks for the ale jug.* She'd addressed that pearl of wisdom to Gerald after Sid, battered and bruised, had bumped into them on his way home from The Harey Rabbit. Then visions of her letter to Reg Puffy swirled across his mind like her flowery script. *It is my opinion that Sid Evily has used his greed and guile to lead you astray.* Then, bizarrely, an image of her dressing-room mannequin, modelling its finely laced, black bustier formed in his head. Her face suddenly appeared on the smooth, plastered head, her malevolent gaze directed at someone next to Sid. *Then you should see that Sid is rotten to the core.* It was Mary she was speaking to. The mannequin shattered, replaced by images of Mary — her beautiful face was joyful, sad, happy, concerned, playful, serious, and countless other expressions she'd shared with Sid in the week they'd been together. Sid suddenly felt a deep longing for the woman who had captured his heart. He would put things right with her as soon as he reached Lower Icing. Manky and his bag of wondrous potions would have to save the Duke without him. Then he would confront his sister. He might even take a leaf out of Violet Le Fleur's book and show her exactly how to Do Well-To-Do Well.

Sid woke abruptly and reached automatically for his daggers. He stopped short of producing them when he realised the scene in front of him had not changed: it was still dark and Doctor Manky was still sitting in the seat opposite. Bloody hell, what was in that Rigour Morphis?

The moment of disorientation passed and Sid rotated his head in an effort to stretch out a kink in his neck.

"I have an ointment for muscular discomfort, if your neck is troubling you, Sid," remarked Doctor Manky.

Sid knew he should be more appreciative of the Doctor's good intentions, but his superior air really got up Sid's goat. He wanted to tell Manky where he could shove his ointment, but that, more than likely, would evoke some clever response — something along the lines of how that particular part of the body required a different ridiculously-named ointment, followed by some long-winded explanation of how it was made and the page it could be found on in *Poetry in Potion*.

"I'm fine, thank you, Manky," replied Sid with controlled politeness. "I've managed to survive *this* long without your ointments."

Doctor Manky smiled. "So you have, Sid."

"Just like the *Duke* has survived without any assistance from me," Sid added, hoping it would wipe the smarmy expression from Manky's face.

It had virtually no effect, except, perhaps, to intensify his pink-eyed gaze. His face really did appear to glow in the dark.

"Very true," Doctor Manky agreed.

"And he will continue to do so," Sid informed him.

"Also true," he acknowledged pleasantly. Sid felt like he was being led through a mental maze again. "However," continued Doctor Manky, "the Duke will not survive without *my* assistance."

"That may well be the case," Sid agreed.

"And for *that* to happen, *I* may need *your* assistance."

Manky was so sure of himself. Did he really think Sid would just follow along unquestioningly?

"Why?" Sid asked.

Of all the times he'd conversed with the man in white, this was the first time he'd been rewarded with a puzzled expression. Sid smiled. Maybe this mental maze wasn't as predictable as Doctor Manky thought.

"Would you mind clarifying that question, Sid?"

"I'm not sure I can make it any clearer, Manky," Sid retorted.

"Who are you questioning," he responded, "me or yourself?"

That made no sense whatsoever. "What?"

"If you are asking *me* why I need your assistance, the reason is patently obvious. As I explained, I may require a diversion to enter the Upper Bailey. If, however, you're asking *yourself* why you should assist me, then I cannot provide the answer for you. Suffice to say that a man's life is at stake."

Sid had never met anyone who could make logic sound so insulting. However, Manky had missed the point of his question. "Dear, dear, Doctor," Sid tutted in mock disappointment. "Only *two* possible interpretations to my question? Clearly there is a third."

If Doctor Manky took offence at Sid's tone, he didn't show it. In fact, he looked more intrigued than offended. "Do please enlighten me, Sid."

"The 'why' was not directed at you *or* me," Sid explained, embracing the role reversal. "It was directed at Sir Richard — the man you seem to hold in such high regard, even though you have never met him."

"And yet you asked *me*."

"Yes."

Doctor Manky regarded him with a bemused expression, obviously waiting for Sid to continue. Let him wait; it was Sid's turn to lead through the maze. A moment later, he was rewarded with a slightly impatient, "Would you care to elucidate; your reasoning is unclear to me."

"Come now, Doctor." Sid was beginning to enjoy this. "I thought it would be *patently* obvious to someone of your intellect."

Doctor Manky's eyes narrowed and his expression became more considered. "Sid, this is not the time for one-upmanship. I am simply asking for your help."

One-upmanship! If *that* wasn't a case of the pot calling the kettle black! Sid suddenly felt like lashing out, but he managed to control his tongue enough to spit out, "Very well, Manky, I am simply asking *why* you need a diversion. Why wouldn't Sir Richard, or any of the other Upper Bailey nobs, welcome you with open arms, particularly if the Duke's *life* is at stake?" Then, as an immediate after-thought, he added, "Hell's bells, Manky, even *Gerald* could get you into the castle if you can save the Duke."

Doctor Manky's expression remained impassive, but his eyes no longer looked appraising, more introspective. "I see your point," he said quietly, "and it is a valid one. However, the answer to that question is staring you in the face."

Why couldn't the man just speak plainly? Did everything have to be a conundrum? Doctor Manky must have seen the frustration on his face because his tone became more personal. "Look at me, Sid. Remember how you felt and what you thought the first time we met?"

How could he forget? Manky's ghoulish appearance had sent a shiver through everyone at The Dead Duck and totally ruined his chances with Elsie that night. The implication of Doctor Manky's remark was clear.

"There's no doubt the first impression you create is…" Sid searched hurriedly for something diplomatic to say and stumbled lamely upon, "memorable."

Doctor Manky smiled knowingly. "Very kind of you, Sid. However, I believe the word 'shocking' is more appropriate."

Sid remained silent, in tacit agreement.

"As you witnessed," Doctor Manky continued, "I can stun an inn full of people in a matter of seconds."

Sid was beginning to feel slightly uncomfortable at the way the conversation was turning. "White is a very… unexpected colour… sartorially speaking, of course."

Again, the Doctor seemed to take Sid's attempts at diplomacy with good grace. "White is my best colour, Sid. It complements my complexion, every other shade accentuates it."

Sid needed to turn the conversation back to the matter at hand. "So you need to sneak into the castle because of your appearance. Is that what you're saying?"

Doctor Manky nodded. "Succinctly put, Sid."

"Surely—"

"I would not be believed, Sid," Doctor Manky pre-empted. "At best, I arouse suspicion, but, more often than not, I am seen as a freak, a bad omen, a harbinger of death, everything…" He faltered, but recovered with conviction, "… everything I am not."

It was the first time Doctor Manky had revealed anything of himself, and Sid wasn't sure how to react. He was becoming used to Doctor Manky's ghoulish appearance, and, oddly enough, it seemed… normal. But he was only able to make that judgement because he knew something about the person. Doctor Manky was right; he would cause an adverse reaction in the best-intentioned people. Those at the castle — with their fashionable finery and polished prejudices — were an inbred bunch of nobs whose associations were based on bloodlines, not a person's character. And as far as bloodlines were concerned, Doctor Manky was sadly lacking.

"Look, Manky," Sid said, trying to sound reasonable, "I understand your predicament, but you're going to have to find your own way into the castle. I'm not prepared to risk a stretch in the dungeon on the off-chance you can save the Duke."

Doctor Manky looked accepting of his response. He'd probably never expected Sid to go along with his insane idea. Not that he *had* any idea; he made creating a diversion sound as simple as applying one of his ointments.

And another thing that didn't make any sense: why was Manky so hell-bent on saving the Duke? Sid had originally put it down to guilt — guilt over the possible involvement of Xavier and guilt that his book of potions had played a part in the attack — but now it seemed more personal.

The Master of Diversions sat passively in his seat, his white frame rocking gently with the smooth motion of the carriage.

"Why is this so important to you, Manky?" Sid asked.

He didn't reply, and Sid wondered if Manky had heard him. He was about repeat himself when the Doctor spoke. "No matter what you think of Marmaduke," he said dreamily, as if he were addressing another ghost, "his life *is* worth saving."

What was he on about now? Maybe he *was* insane. "You make it sound like you know the Duke personally."

Doctor Manky sighed. "I do, Sid. We have known each other for quite some time," he replied, as if revealing something he'd rather have kept to himself.

Sid didn't know how to react. If Doctor Manky was *that* close to the Duke, what was all this subterfuge about?

"Are you *trying* to do my head in, Manky? Or is this some sort of sick jest courtesy of my sister?"

Doctor Manky looked taken aback by Sid's reaction. "I assure you, Sid, my need is genuine."

"Don't bother assuring me of anything. This has gone far enough! As soon as I hear the cobblestones of Lower Icing, this ride is over!"

"That is your choice."

His stoic acceptance just fuelled Sid's frustration. "So, tell me — just out of curiosity — why this diversion nonsense? A long-time friend of the Duke, regardless of appearance, would have no trouble entering the castle, which, no doubt, you have done on many occasions."

The Doctor shook his head. "Alas, Sid, I have never set foot in Lower Icing Castle. Until last Friday, I had never set foot in *Lower Icing*. The only person who could verify my identity is in a cataleptic state, fighting for his life."

Cata what? Was the Duke meowing his way to death? Sid's confusion must have been obvious to the man opposite.

"It means he's unconscious. And even if he wasn't, my presence would not necessarily be seen as a boon."

Sid shook his head in disgust. He was fed up with Doctor Manky's meanderings; every half-answer was multiplied with more questions, every turn in the conversation lead to another turn or a dead-end. Well, Manky could play the mental maze game if he wanted, but Sid had had enough.

A minute or two passed, bringing dawn and Lower Icing a minute or two nearer. Meanwhile, the night continued to roll by. Sid stared at the passing shadows outside the cab, hoping for some signs of light.

"Sid, do you recall anything of what I said while you were under the influence of Rigour Morphis?"

Sid continued to stare out the window. He really didn't want to be confronted by the bloodless visage of Doctor Manky anymore. He thought about ignoring him entirely, but the man had such a compelling manner, damn him; he made everything sound so intriguing. In truth, he now recalled virtually nothing of what Manky had shared. Only Xavier's portrait stuck in his mind for some reason. The rest... "Something about the effects being unpleasant, but I'd make a full recovery," he finally replied. Then, gazing back at Doctor Manky, he added, "Which, by the way, I'm hoping I haven't yet done."

"What I meant is, do you recall anything of what I revealed about Xavier and the reason why his parents left him in my care?"

What was he on about now? Sid had no interest in Manky's missing protégé, or what had been revealed about his parents. And, in any case, how was *that* related to the Duke? It was just more...

Suddenly, out of his fuzzy Rigour Morphis memory, the copper-piece dropped.

PART 4

TOM

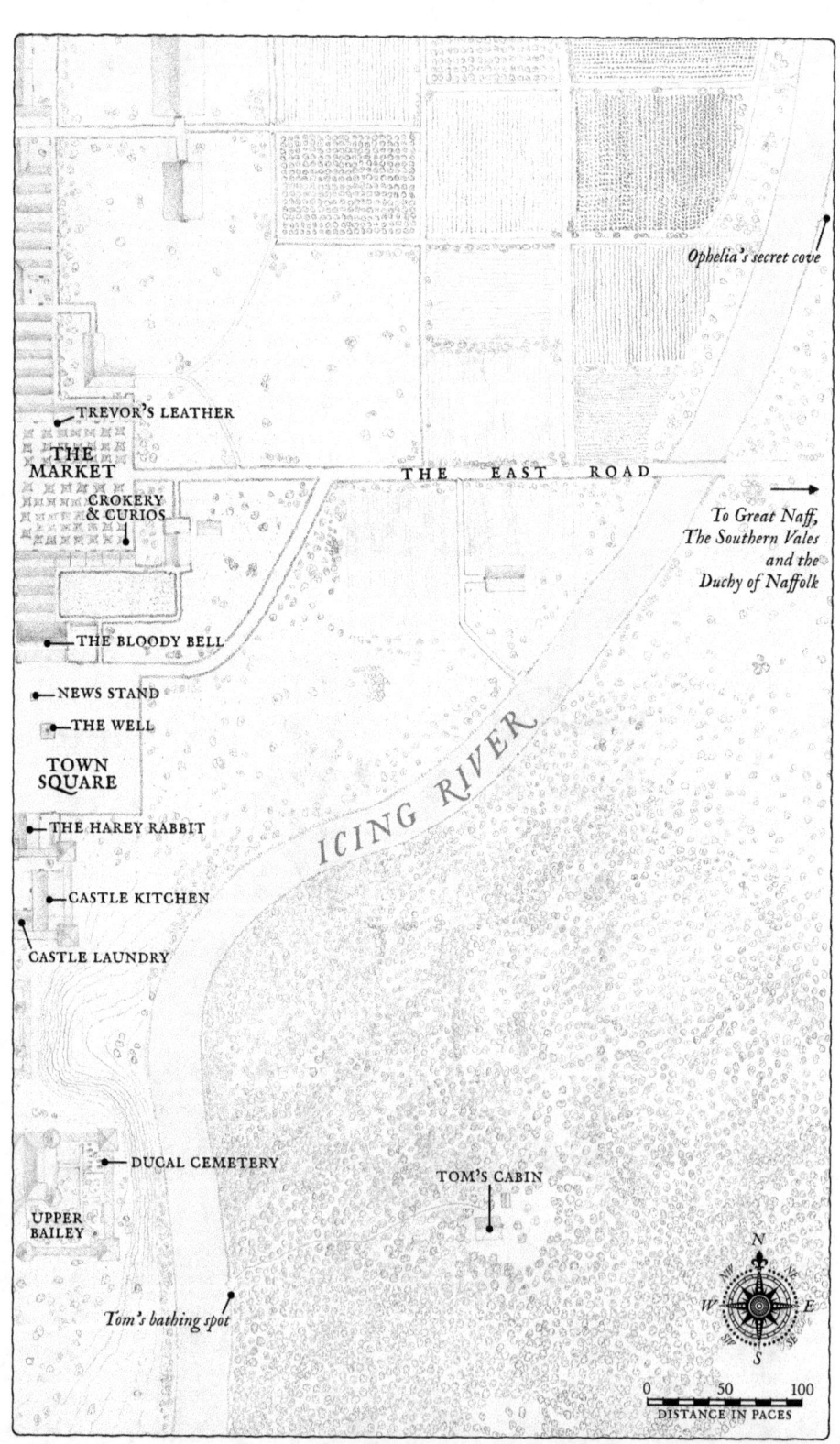

Ophelia's secret cove

TREVOR'S LEATHER

THE
MARKET

THE   EAST   ROAD

To Great Naff,
The Southern Vales
and the
Duchy of Naffolk

CROKERY
& CURIOS

THE BLOODY BELL

NEWS STAND

THE WELL

TOWN
SQUARE

ICING RIVER

THE HAREY RABBIT

CASTLE KITCHEN

CASTLE LAUNDRY

DUCAL CEMETERY

TOM'S CABIN

UPPER
BAILEY

Tom's bathing spot

N
NW NE
W   E
SW SE
S

0   50   100
DISTANCE IN PACES

INTRODUCTION
Follow his love for nature

TOM SKINNER WAS possibly the most contented man in the Duchy of Lower Icing, or, at least, he certainly felt that way. Living the outdoor life and being his own man were things he valued highly. He had a down-to-earth disposition, and being the Duke's Gamekeeper suited him down to the earth. It was as if he'd been born to it, even though he hadn't.

He was born thirty-four years ago, the second son of a wealthy landowner, Harold Skinner. Tom, along with his older brother, Nick, had been raised and tutored in all aspects of running and managing Wet Crossing, the family estate. However, since he was the younger son, it was his brother who would inherit the title of 'Baron of Wet Crossing'. Not that that worried Tom; his aspirations had never flown towards the lofty heights of nobility.

From an early age, Tom had been happy to follow his love for nature. For him, Wet Crossing — so named because the West Road forded a tributary of the river Sty at the southern edge of the estate, en route to the border town of Pashing Madly — had been a place to grow up and enjoy: exploring the woods, observing how animals interacted with their surroundings, learning the art of tracking and hunting, and, most importantly, mastering survival in the wild.

Tom had never acquitted himself to the economic or political wrangling that went with ownership of land; it bored and frustrated him. Instead he favoured the menial, day-to-day tasks of toiling the land. In the process, he'd endeared himself to the fourteen families who lived and worked on the estate. In turn, he felt more comfortable breaking bread with these simple people than he did feasting on pheasant with his family.

At the age of sixteen, his father sent him to Lower Icing, a two-day journey by horse, to be educated in the ways of the landed gentry. Tom hadn't wanted any part of it, but his mother, Juliet, the person he was closest to, had persuaded him it was for the best. Still, it was with a heavy heart that Tom left the green fields, dark woods, and rushing streams of Wet Crossing. After saying his goodbyes to his family, and being farewelled by the workers, he'd begun his journey to Lower Icing, but vowed to return within the year.

On arrival, he was given lodgings at the castle and put under the guidance of a young noble, Richard Upson. Richard was three years older than Tom, but the gap in age was small compared to the vast chasm of worldliness that existed between them. Richard was being groomed by the Duke (and Richard's father, Sir Walter Upson) to be the next Seneschal of Lower Icing. Consequently, his knowledge of politics was extensive and his skill at arms impressive. Unlikely as it seemed when they first met, Tom and Richard became fast friends.

Tom marvelled at Richard's confidence and enjoyed his quit wit. For his part, Richard found Tom's openness and lack of pretension refreshing. And they shared a common passion for hunting and the outdoors. Many a day they spent on the trail of wild boar, stalking king bucks, or just spending time riding their mounts through the great woodland of the Duke's Forest.

As the months passed, Tom found himself teaching Richard more about the skills of survival and hunting than learning how to be a successful landlord. It was an arrangement that suited both young men.

Tom had gradually become accustomed to castle life and the bustling streets of Lower Icing, but he still planned to return to his family and responsibilities at Wet Crossing. Then, a terrible incident changed everything. Ten months into Tom's 'education', the Duke's Gamekeeper was gorged to death by a wild boar. Tom was asked to be his replacement, even though he'd only just turned seventeen.

It was Richard's doing — he had a lot of influence at the castle and was a favourite of the young Duke's wife, Lucinda. Richard had even convinced the Duke to compensate Tom's family by apportioning a fertile stretch of land just north of the estate to Wet Crossing. Tom had been amazed by the offer, and gladly accepted on the proviso that his father agreed. Richard had then penned a letter, endorsed with the Ducal seal, which was sent, forthwith, to Wet Crossing. The reply was favourable, on the condition that should any ill befall his brother, Tom was to return to Wet Crossing and fulfil his responsibilities.

The next few years had been an exciting time — Richard and the Duke, and many other people of importance, often went hunting. Tom's tracking skills, his ingenuity, and his happy demeanour brought him praise and invitations to dinners and gatherings from many influential people. He also helped farmers protect their lambs and chickens from foxes, as well as making sure the forest was safe from poachers.

He'd moved into the Gamekeeper's Cottage, situated near the wooded edge of the Icing River, opposite the castle. It was a simple wooden structure, well-hidden amongst a copse of elm trees. It had a stone floor and hearth, and a ladder leading to a loft bedroom. The ground level contained rudimentary furniture, pots for cooking and heating water, and a tub for bathing (which he rarely used, preferring, instead, to immerse himself in the cool, clear water of the Icing). It was a basic, invigorating existence, and Tom loved it.

Around the turn of each year, he braved the grey skies and biting winds and journeyed back home to see his family. But, as the years passed, Wet Crossing seemed less familiar to him, and his family, apart from his mother, more removed. It was to be expected he supposed; after all, he was living a life far away from the day-to-day routine of the estate.

As time moved on, Tom became even more at one with his natural surroundings and spent less time at the castle or in the town. Richard, too, became more involved in his duties, as the Duke relied increasingly on his judgement and leadership. The Duke was a fine man, generous and kind-hearted, who worked diligently for the betterment of his people, but he was a reluctant leader. He and Lucinda had been plucked from obscurity after the tragic demise of the previous royal household. (The entire De La Wrence family had perished when the *Happy Mermaid* sank in a freak storm while sailing back from Longboatia. They'd been guests at the royal wedding of Crown Prince Stig Maelstrom and Anke Iceberg, the Duchess of Jawland. At the time, the general thought was that marriage was a disaster waiting to happen, but no-one could have envisaged the actual disaster that was about to befall the contingent from Lower Icing.)

Marmaduke and Lucinda had been two years into their rule when Tom arrived in Lower Icing, and the tragedy was *still* fresh in people's minds. And while they were generally content with their new Duke and Duchess, the Duchy craved an heir and the re-establishment of the noble family. However, as each childless year passed, such an outcome seemed less and less likely.

Being somewhat removed from life at court, Tom noticed the subtleties and nuances that others missed, and he had an intuitive ability for recognising people's true emotions, no matter how well they were masked. When he had first met the Duke and Duchess, he'd sensed a deep sadness behind their welcoming smiles. Lucinda, in particular, looked lost and haunted. It was almost as if she'd taken on board the departed souls of those who went down in the *Happy Mermaid*. As the years went by, she became more and more withdrawn, and Richard expressed his concern for the Duchess to Tom on a number of occasions.

Tom remembered well the day she passed away. And passing away was exactly how he thought of it. She hadn't died. Death suggested an ending to life, but Lucinda had been slowly drifting away from life for the seventeen years Tom had known her.

It was the third day of February last year; he'd been riding back from a four-week stay at Wet Crossing. Ironically, it was one of the happiest times he'd spent with his family in many a year — Nick and his wife, Elisabeth, had just had their third child (and third boy) Henry, and the estate was more profitable than ever, thriving from the Duke's largesse, with twenty-four families now living and working upon it.

Mounted on his horse, Tom had crested Look Over Hill, the place where Lower Icing first came into view along the West Road. Two miles away, the castle was the prominent feature, built on the higher ground south of the village. It was a dismal day, and everything looked grey in the mid-afternoon gloom — the castle walls and village rooftops dissolved into the slate-coloured sky. The wind had picked up, and, gazing at The Keep, he could see the four purple and gold pennons fluttering wildly... at half-mast.

Lucinda had died in her sleep at the age of thirty-nine. There had been no sign of illness or malady, just a silent surrender of life. The Duke seemed quietly accepting, almost as if he'd expected her death. Richard, on the other hand, was distraught and seemed angered by her departing.

Her funeral had been held three days later; the ceremonial casket — draped in purple satin, with five silver crowns and a gold unicorn — was paraded through the streets of Lower Icing. The casket was purely for show; Lucinda had been cremated and her ashes scattered in the Ducal Gardens of the Upper Baily.

A month later, Richard was named successor to Marmaduke, the assumption being that the Duke would not remarry, and, therefore, not produce an heir. Richard was thirty-six — only five years younger than the Duke — but his naming was seen by all as a good decision. He exuded confidence and was a man of action. The Duchy would be safe and prosper in his care. The announcement also had a positive effect on Richard himself: he was wrenched out of his mourning by his new responsibilities. At the time, Tom had joked with him about finally having to find a wife. Richard's response had been both memorable and revealing: "At least love is no longer a consideration."

The seventeen months since Lucinda's death had been happily uneventful for Tom. He spent most of his time at his cottage, occasionally venturing into town for a night out at The Dead Duck — he liked Will Plucker (the innkeeper) and people who worked and drank within its cheery walls; they reminded him of the farming families at Wet Crossing. He'd also got to know some of the regulars, including a rogue by the name of Sid Evily. He'd taken Sid on the occasional hunting foray and allowed him to keep the odd bit of game. Not strictly legal, but a few pheasants and rabbits were hardly going to deprive the Duchy of much revenue. In any case, he liked Sid — he was good company and had a ready wit. In fact, he reminded Tom of Richard before Lucinda died, when laughter came a lot easier to him. Not that Tom had spent much time in Richard's company recently. The Duchy had become Richard's life, and his every waking hour seemed to be devoted to keeping it in order. So, the invitation to stay at the castle had come as somewhat of a surprise.

CHAPTER 1

Pig of a man

Thursday, June 26: The day before Doctor Manky approaches Sid at The Dead Duck. (8 days ago.)

THE EARLY BREAKFAST in Richard's private chamber had been going well. Richard was more like his old self, their banter relaxed and uninhibited. However, his mood had changed when Tom relayed the events of the previous night. As he told his friend of the encounter with Billy Offcut, Richard's face gradually became tauter, his expression more serious. There was a time when he would have cheered and laughed along with an exploit such as this, and even jokingly berate Tom for leaving him out the fun. Now, it seemed, there was no room for such frivolity.

"The boy deserved all he got, Richard," Tom assured him, watching his friend massage his temples.

Richard ceased his massaging and looked wearily across the table at Tom. "I don't doubt that for one second, but why did that fool of a lieutenant have to arrest him? I have enough on my plate without adding a serving of angry Offcuts."

"Not so long ago you would have applauded the lieutenant's actions. And since when did a family of butchers hold sway over—"

There was a knock at the door. Richard bade the knocker enter. A rather harried-looking Prestwich flashed into view. "Excuse me, Sir Richard, but Master Frank Offcut is downstairs in the reception hall, insisting on seeing you."

Tom was treated to a withering glance as Richard addressed his edgy secretary. "Tell him I will see him in my office in fifteen minutes," he said dismissively. Prestwich was already on the move before Richard had finished his sentence.

Richard picked up his silver goblet and gulped down the hitherto-untouched spiced wine. Tom shook his head.

"Don't start, Tom," said Richard, seeing his expression.

"Why are you burdening yourself with this matter," said Tom, ignoring his friend's tone. "It is I who restrained the lad, and it is *I* who will bear witness to his actions. From what I understand, it's high time he was taught a lesson. Just tell Frank Offcut to stuff his sausages up his arse."

This brought a wry grin from Richard. "I wish it were that simple, Tom."

"Surely it is that simple. You are, for all intents and purposes, running the Duchy."

"Exactly!" he said with fervour, slapping his hands against the table, the morning sun catching the silver brocading of his immaculately tailored black outfit. "I take it you saw the preparations underway in the reception hall... Well, it's all for Duke of Stymouth's benefit, who *kindly* informed us two weeks ago that his entourage of fifteen, plus an escort of twenty men-at-arms, would be passing through Lower Icing on their way to Great Naff and would we mind putting them up for few nights, suggesting we use it as an opportunity to build closer ties between the two Duchies. Marmaduke agreed readily enough, even though it's been twenty years since the last *goodwill* visit. Stymouth will be here in two weeks."

Tom had never understood why those in power looked upon extravagance as a sign of goodwill and respect. What was wrong with a handshake and a welcoming smile; it had always worked for him.

"What has that to do with Frank Offcut?" he asked, almost amused by Richard's frustration.

Richard sighed and shook his head. "Political diplomacy has never been your strong point, Tom." Then he leant back in his chair and folded his arms. It was a posture familiar to Tom — he'd seen it many times over the years, when Richard needed to play the disappointed tutor. He hoped Richard's discerning eye hadn't noticed his stifled smile. "The Duke's visit, while inconveniently close, *is* actually a rare opportunity to establish a better relationship with the Duchy of Stymouth. Marmaduke believes a lavish dinner will help cement that relationship." Richard paused, suddenly looking tired, then leaned forward and rested his arms on the table. "I'm not entirely convinced, myself. Stymouth is a pig of a man and I doubt the effort behind this occasion will match the expectations of his overinflated ego. Still, I haven't seen Marmaduke this energised since Lucinda's passing, and that, in itself, is a good outcome." Straightening in his chair, he reached over and picked up the decanter containing the spiced wine. Refilling his goblet, he continued. "Anyway, returning to the Offcut matter..."

"I was beginning to wonder whether you'd forgotten about that," Tom cut in, and was surprised by Richard's humourless response.

"Frank Offcut is also a pig of a man. The problem is that when *he* oinks, all the farmers within a ten-mile radius sit up and pay attention. If Frank Offcut had a mind to, he could severely disrupt the supply of food to the castle, and, right now, that's something I can do without. I've already had Reginald Puffy steam into my office, complaining about the lack of preparation time for this farce of a dinner."

Tom could hardly believe what he was hearing — how could a *butcher* have so much influence. "Don't tell me you're going to allow yourself to be dictated to by a—"

The door crashed open and the pig of a man burst through, shortly followed by a flustered Prestwich. Tom had only met Frank Offcut in passing, and never really paid him much attention. His face was a lot ruddier than Tom remembered, but, then again, the foaming mouth and sweating, bald palette weren't exactly part of his recollection either. He did recall, however, his stocky frame and aggressive posturing and, as he closed in on their table, the odour of raw meat also rang a few olfactory bells.

Tom was stunned by the man's effrontery and quickly jumped to his feet. The movement didn't even register with Frank Offcut, whose gaze and gait were fixed on Richard. Richard, for his part, remained seated and unmoved as the butcher strode towards him. In the background, Prestwich was darting about, apologising profusely.

"If y'think I'm goin' t'sit down there and wait for you t'stuff y'face while our Billy's sittin' in the pissin' Can, y'better think again, Sir Richard," he blustered.

One swift punch to the guts, thought Tom; that would knock the wind out of him. He was about to tackle the raving madman when he caught the subtle shake of Richard's head.

"Stay out of this, Gamekeeper," said the butcher, coming to a standstill a few feet away, directing his baleful gaze Tom's way. Then he added with menace, "That's if y'know what's good for ya."

Forget the guts; an uppercut to the jaw would do a much better job of shutting him up, and perhaps improve his unpleasant looks. He seemed ready to burst, panting heavily through exertion or outrage, or both. Behind him, Prestwich twitched from one foot to another.

Richard rose calmly from his chair; he was nearly a foot taller than Frank Offcut, but the butcher's aggressive disposition made up for that particular shortcoming. Richard smiled down at him coolly. His self-control was amazing, and one of the many attributes Tom admired about the Seneschal of Lower Icing.

Defiant uncertainty best described Frank Offcut's reaction to Richard's composed demeanour; he was obviously struggling to keep his uncivil tongue inside his fat mouth.

Richard, his dark eyes gleaming, took control of the situation. "You're quite right, Master Offcut, I should not have left you waiting in my reception," he purred. "It was most thoughtless of me."

Frank Offcut looked wary. Tom smiled.

"Prestwich!" snapped Richard.

The secretary jerked into action, taking two quick steps forward. "Yes, Sir Richard," he said, eager to please.

"Fetch two guards to escort Master Offcut to his son," he said to the nodding Prestwich.

"I don't need no—"

"At once, Prestwich!" he barked over the indignant butcher.

Richard's secretary disappeared in a swirl of grey robes.

"Sir Richard," continued Frank Offcut, still panting. "An escort ain't necessary, all I—"

"I insist, Master Offcut. As you so cordially reminded me, I was remiss in leaving you in my reception, when, in fact, you should have been with your son."

Frank Offcut, clearly frustrated by Richard's unflappable demeanour, took a deep breath in an effort to calm himself down. Then he flicked his gaze in Tom's direction and his outrage found new air.

"Well 'e shouldn't been put there in the first place. It ain't no crime t' touch up a friggin' bar wench—"

"Jenny isn't a bar wench, Master Offcut," Tom cut in.

"Hah!" he spat. "She *your* floosy, Gamekeeper?"

Tom tensed; the urge to teach the bald-headed butcher a lesson in pummelling meat was overwhelming, but the urge was broken by Richard.

"Enough!" he snapped.

But it wasn't enough for Frank Offcut. "An' y'send tha' prick, Fowler, t'tell me and mine *after* our Billy's already spent the night in The Can. This ain't 'ow y' treat nobody, least of all an Offcut. We shouldda been informed!"

At that moment, two guards rushed into the room, clambered to attention, and saluted.

"Sir, Master Prestwich—" one of them began.

"I want you to escort Master Offcut to his son, Billy. He is currently residing in one of the cells in The Can. After that, lock the cell door behind both of them. Master Offcut is also under arrest."

"What? No!" Frank gasped, shock replacing outrage. As the guards approached, his demeanour became more desperate. "Sir Richard, I didn' mean t'cause no offense. Jus' that our Billy is…"

The guards were quickly on him. Frank grabbed Richard by the forearm. The guards tried to extricate him, but the butcher clung onto Richard's arm as if it were a lifeline. Tom would have stepped in, but Richard appeared quite unflustered.

"Sir Richard," Frank Offcut pleaded.

Richard gave him a contemptuous smile, then, in one swift motion, flung his arm downwards, dislodging Frank Offcut's hand. "Take him away."

Frank Offcut immediately reverted to the offensive. "Y'can't do this!" he yelled as the guards forcefully escorted him towards the door. "I ain't done nuffin' wrong."

Richard ignored the protestation and, instead, concentrated on smoothing his crumpled sleeve. Then, almost to himself, he said, "Nothing wrong? The cheek of the man. At the very least, he's nearly ripped a silver button from my sleeve."

CHAPTER 2

A matter of great importance

TOM CLAPPED HIS friend on the shoulder. "Well done, Richard." The door had just been shut behind the fuming Frank Offcut. They could still hear him cursing as the two guards marched him along the landing and down the stairs.

Richard, however, didn't seem very pleased at all. In fact, he seemed unusually on edge, and acknowledged Tom's congratulations with a dubious grin.

"Sit down, Tom," he said softly, moving to do the same. "I invited you here on a matter of great importance."

The sudden change in tone concerned Tom; the heated altercation had obviously shaken his friend. "If you're planning to offer me the esteemed position of Duke's Butcher, I'm afraid I must decline," he said, trying to lighten the mood.

Again, Richard could manage little more than a twitch of a smile. "A pity; it would save me being the meat in the sandwich, so to speak," he said, refilling his goblet. Then he leant over and filled Tom's. Tom acknowledged the gesture with a nod and raised the silver goblet towards the man in black.

"Your health, Richard," he said, before sipping the subtly spiced red wine.

Richard responded with a nod, downed a generous quaff from his goblet, then relaxed back into his chair, seemingly lost in thought.

Tom broke the silence with a question. "Sorry to interrupt your musings, but I'm curious to know what you intend to do about the Offcuts?" Then, after a momentary pause, he added, "And if you'd care to share this matter of great importance, I am all ears."

This brought a reluctant smile to Richard's face, accentuated by his perfectly maintained beard. "It is good to have you here, my friend. It has been too long."

Tom nodded in agreement, responding with levity, "Don't tell me the Seneschal of Lower Icing is suffering from a dreaded fit of nostalgia."

"My apologies," he said, openly smiling, "most absent-minded of me.

Truth be told, I have been rather distracted over the past few months and, clearly, certain individuals have taken advantage."

"Taken the piss, more like. However, as you say, Richard, diplomacy was never my strong point."

"True," he acknowledged.

"So what *do* you intend to do? And please don't say something diplomatic, I might have to slap you."

"Ha! There's no danger of that, my friend — not after what has just occurred. Frank Offcut has taken a great liberty with me. Now it's my turn to repay the favour. Let's see how well he and his whelp of a son cope with a month or two in the dungeon. I dare say that Master Key, being the consummate gaoler, will delight in playing host to the Offcuts; he'll find Frank particularly rewarding. I take it you are prepared to stand by your account of the incident at The Dead Duck?"

"Of course," replied Tom. "And will stand witness to all that occurred here."

"Yes," Richard nodded. "I am confident that between you, Prestwich and I, we'll be able to provide enough convincing evidence."

Picking up on Richard's dry humour, Tom added, "Thank goodness for Prestwich. I'm not sure our word would have held sway over the most revered butcher in Lower Icing."

Richard acknowledged the remark with a grin and took another sip of his wine.

"And what of the Duke of Stymouth's banquet?" asked Tom.

"It will go ahead as planned," Richard replied. "And he'll have no cause to complain." Absently fingering the rim of his goblet, he added, "You're right, Tom; it wasn't that long ago I would have applauded Lieutenant Swill's actions. It's high time Frank Offcut was chopped down to size."

Tom smiled and raised his goblet. "I'll gladly drink to that, Richard." Upon downing its contents, a flush of warmth permeated his body, accentuating the heat of the early morning sun that now streaked through the south-facing windows. It was a good feeling.

Richard also looked re-energised, and it was with a sense of purpose that he finally revealed his matter of great importance. "You understand, Tom, that what I'm about to tell you remains within these walls."

Tom nodded. They both knew it went without saying, but Richard was ever the one for protocol; it was the politician in him. He poured the last of the mulled wine into his and Tom's goblets, and then sat upright in his high-backed chair. His posture conveyed power and self-confidence. Adding to his commanding presence was his impeccable appearance: perfectly groomed, shoulder-length hair and neatly sculptured beard were complemented by finely tailored clothes. The inky-black doublet, meshed with silver stitching and embroidered collar, set the perfect tone — Richard often shone in the darkest of moments. He certainly cut an imposing figure, and it was easy to see why he commanded such respect. It made the Offcut situation even more bewildering.

"As you are aware, the main responsibility I have as Seneschal of Lower Icing is the protection of the Duke and all who live under his governance, as well as safeguarding the Duchy from marauders and opportunists. Fortunately, we are living in peaceful times and the Five Duchies are relatively stable. However, it is during such times that we are susceptible to an even more insidious enemy."

Richard regarded Tom, as if expecting him to supply the answer.

"Mulled wine?" Tom obliged, looking at the goblet resting on the arm of Richard's chair.

Richard smiled and picked up the goblet. "Complacency," he said. Then he leant forward and tipped the purple liquid back into the decanter. It was almost as if he'd orchestrated the moment, to make his point even more meaningful.

"The temptation to rest on one's laurels is always there, Tom. To sit back and enjoy the wine, you might say."

Placing the goblet on the table, he relaxed back into his chair. "To prevent such a dangerous state of mind, I have instigated various measures, one of which has been the recruitment of certain individuals to act as conduits of information within and without the Duchy."

Tom was bemused by Richard's formality. "Or, as most people would call it, a spy network."

"It's not quite that invasive," he replied. "More of an *observation* network."

Tom wasn't sure of the difference, but Richard was a man of subtleties, and the distinction was obviously apparent to him.

"Suffice to say, I have observers across the country. The closest of whom resides at Blessed Whipping."

Blessed Whipping — Tom had never been, but he had heard reports about their strange customs and sun-worshipping ways. It sounded very ordered and confining, but, then again, there were worse things to worship than the sun.

"In late February last year, my observer there sent word that two outsiders had moved into the community."

"Outsiders?" Tom queried; it was an unusual term.

"Blessed Whipping is a closed community, Tom," explained Richard. "Their beliefs and traditions are instilled from birth and it's virtually impossible for anyone born outside the community to assimilate. They are very protective of their way of life. The acceptance of these two individuals was an anomaly, to say the least."

"What made them so special?"

"The community had been sent something that made it very hard for the Elders of Blessed Whipping to turn them away."

This was becoming more interesting.

"A letter, in fact; the seal was Marmaduke's."

Tom raised his eyebrows. "Really... and you were unaware?"

He nodded. "I knew nothing about it."

Tom found that surprising, because Richard was someone the Duke relied on and confided in, particularly since the Duchess' death, and this would have been only a few weeks after her passing.

"It requested that the outsiders be accepted into the community, vouchsafed their character, recommended them as men of great learning, and, most intriguingly, described them as very dear to the Ducal heart."

Richard was being very matter-of-fact, but there was an underlying uneasiness in his delivery, and he'd become very rigid; his hands clasped (rather than rested against) the arms of his chair.

"Not only that, the Duke described them as *noble* and asked they be treated accordingly."

"The plot thickens," remarked, Tom. He was genuinely intrigued by what was being revealed. However, judging by Richard's expression, he had taken Tom's remark the wrong way. Tom reacted defensively. "And so should your skin, my friend. Surely you know me well enough to understand my intent."

"I understand it, Tom," he replied, "but would ask the same of you. This is not some ale-swilling adventure story; it is real and has serious ramifications for the Duchy. I am confiding in you because matters are coming to a head, and I trust your judgement. I would appreciate your thoughts once I have finished my account and you fully understand the predicament in which I now find myself."

Tom felt his face flush. It wasn't his friend who was confiding in him; it was the Seneschal of Lower Icing. "My apologies, Richard."

Richard nodded, then continued. "My observer took it upon himself to personally see to the needs of the new arrivals, and, at the same time, keep me informed. The two outsiders were men, one in his fifties, the other around twenty, and both doctors of some sort."

Doctors? Tom hadn't been expecting that.

"They kept very much to themselves, and, from all accounts, were respectful of the community. In fact, it wasn't long before the community began to regard their presence as a boon. The older doctor, in particular, had made a significant impression. This was due to his striking appearance. Apparently he has milk-white skin and hair and complements this by wearing white clothing. White has spiritual significance to the community, being the colour of sunlight in its purest form. Therefore, to a Blessed Whippinger, wearing white is a declaration of absolute purity. No-one in the community, not even the Elders, regards themselves in such rarefied esteem, and, consequently, white is never worn. Although some, like my observer, have a near-white opinion of themselves."

This was fascinating. To think that a community like Blessed Whipping — What was it? Four or five hours ride north of Lower Icing? — could cocoon itself in such foreign beliefs. Imagine Richard riding into Blessed Whipping, resplendent in black; he'd be about as welcome as an eclipse.

"It was his natural 'whiteness', more than the request from the Duke, which the community embraced. This worked in my observer's favour, for he was able to interact freely with the doctors."

"Excuse me, Richard, but do any of these people have names?"

"Their names are irrelevant at this point in time. Bear with me. All will be revealed."

Tom accepted his friend's words with a nod. "Fair enough."

"One of the responsibilities entrusted to my observer was the safe delivery of sealed correspondence between the older doctor and Marmaduke. This occurred on a regular basis, roughly once a week to start with, then less frequently."

"And your observer had no idea what information they contained?"

"No. As I said, Tom, my observers aren't spies, and we are talking about a Blessed Whipping Elder here. Such activity would be seen as an anathema. I thought about broaching the subject with Marmaduke, but decided, instead, to allow events to unfold. Everyone is entitled to privacy and, as far as the Duchy is concerned, no-one is more committed to its wellbeing than the Duke."

Tom wasn't quite sure he'd have been as accepting of the Duke's behaviour; it seemed totally out of character. Suddenly, an explanation dawned on him. "Is the Duke being blackmailed?"

Richard barked out a derisive laugh. "If only you knew the irony of that remark. Have patience, my friend; you'll soon know everything."

"It's just that you often opt for the long path when a shorter route is available."

"Perhaps. However, it's the twists and turns that make the journey more interesting, and, ultimately, the destination more rewarding."

Tom smiled, acknowledging the truth of the statement.

"To answer your question: No, the Duke is not being blackmailed. However, the same thought did occur to me at the time, and I raised the possibility with my observer. He thought it highly unlikely, simply from the respectful way the outsiders conducted themselves. I took a more pragmatic approach to reach the same conclusion. Every blackmailer sets an agenda, and the situation becomes increasingly tense until, one way or another, the situation is resolved. During this time, Marmaduke was quite himself and presented no signs of duress, or any other unusual behaviour one might associate with blackmail. So the correspondence continued and held its secret for almost a year. Or, to be more precise, until the second day of February this year."

"The day before the first anniversary of Lucinda's death," Tom remarked without thinking. The pain of her passing still burned deeply in Richard, and he mentally kicked himself for his thoughtless words.

"Quite," acknowledged Richard evenly. "By happenstance, my observer stumbled upon one of the letters. It was lying open, ready to be sealed, on the older doctor's desk. Why the doctor had suddenly been so careless who knows, but it represented an opportunity, possibly the *only* opportunity, to discover the nature of their relationship. Fortunately, my observer's curiosity overcame his sense of morality and he took advantage of the opportunity. I received his missive the following day in which he'd copied the contents of the letter. The words are still etched in my mind."

There was a moment of silence. Tom's anticipation must have been obvious, because a wry smile formed on Richard's face. "Fret not, my friend, the destination is upon us... For the most part, the letter was an expression of support for Marmaduke. However, what immediately caught my attention was the tone; it was intimate, like that of a brother. The doctor had obviously shared a past with Marmaduke, yet, in the twenty years I've known him, he has never made mention of this doctor. Does the name Horatio Manky mean anything to you?"

Horatio Manky? Tom shook his head; he had no recollection of ever hearing the name, and it wasn't one he'd likely forget. Manky? Perhaps it was foreign. In any case, he hoped there was something more to Richard's story than the discovery of a mysterious old friend. "Who is he?" Tom asked, expectantly.

"He is the guardian of the younger doctor, who, in the letter, he refers to as X."

"X?"

"It stands for Xavier, and it seems he is the son of Marmaduke and Lucinda."

CHAPTER 3

Choose your next words carefully

TOM STARED DOWN at the parchment on the table in front of him; sunlight through the crystal decanter cast a diamond pattern across its smooth surface. It was the observer's letter. Its capital-letter script with crossed-through S's seemed as bizarre as its contents. It was signed BIRDMAN — the code name Richard had given the Blessed Whipping Elder, a man called Bertrand.

Richard had produced the letter after Tom had argued the implausibility of the Duke and Duchess having a son. He couldn't imagine Marmaduke or Lucinda — *particularly* Lucinda — abandoning a child.

He'd read the letter twice now and still found the information hard to fathom. The question that had come immediately to mind was one of validity. It could have easily been fabricated by this Doctor Horatio Manky, or Bertrand for that matter.

"Possibly," Richard acknowledged, "but I doubt it. It serves no purpose to invent such a story. The author makes no demands, and it explains many things."

"Really?" It seemed to Tom that it posed many questions.

"Yes. It explains Marmaduke's circumspect nature, Lucinda's demise, even the lack of an heir. They played the part of the Duke and Duchess, but, in reality, they were a mother and father mourning their separation from their child."

How did Richard reach *that* conclusion? Tom must be missing something. Focusing in on the pertinent paragraph, he re-read the words for a third time.

...EVEN AT A TIME $UCH A$ THI$, MARMADUKE, THERE I$ A WAY TO HEAL YOUR TORMENT. IT HA$ BEEN NEARLY A YEAR $INCE YOU RELOCATED U$, AND I HOPE THERE I$ NOW ROOM IN YOUR HEART FOR X. HE I$ YOUR $ON, AND, I BELIEVE, YOUR $ALVATION.

If Richard believed the words to be true, why hadn't he acted upon them? And why was he revealing all this now, and to the Duke's Gamekeeper? Surely it was his duty to approach the Duke.

"This was written almost five months ago, Richard. Shouldn't you have spoken to the Duke by now?"

Richard was quick to pick up on the accusatory undertone.

"Strangely enough, Tom, the thought did occur to me." The reply resonated with sarcasm. "However, I deemed it wasn't my place to interfere. If Marmaduke wanted to keep this to himself, it wasn't for me to gainsay him."

Tom couldn't believe Richard had taken this attitude. "Of course it was, Richard. You are his most trusted subject, the heir to the—" It suddenly occurred to Tom exactly what Xavier's recognition would mean to the Duchy, and, more significantly, to Richard.

Richard had been hovering around the table as Tom read the letter. Now he stood still, piercing dark eyes probing for intent. "I suggest you choose your next words carefully, Tom."

Tom felt a flash of anger and stood up to meet him eye to eye. He refused to be intimidated by anyone, and that included the Seneschal of Lower Icing. Before a word could be spoken, there was a knock at the door.

"Yes!" Richard snapped, wrenching his gaze away from Tom.

Prestwich opened the door in a flash.

"What is it?"

"Excuse me, Sir Richard," said the edgy secretary. "The Town Crier is downstairs. He says there is an urgent matter that must be brought to your attention."

Richard groaned and hissed a profanity.

"He wouldn't reveal the nature of this matter," added Prestwich, trying to deflect Richard's displeasure towards the Town Crier, "and insisted you needed to be informed."

Richard sighed. "Very well. Send him up."

Prestwich zipped away. His footsteps tapping across the tiled floor of the antechamber like an Icarumban dancer.

Richard turned his attention back to Tom. "You're about to find out exactly what has transpired and why I wanted to speak to you. Matters are beginning to unravel. Unfortunately, I've had to involve the Town Crier."

"What do you mean, Richard?" Tom felt like he had been sucked into a political whirlpool, with the Duke of Stymouth, Frank Offcut, and now the

Town Crier all swirling around.

"In the early hours of last Sunday, Bertrand delivered Xavier to The Bloody Bell. On Monday, Xavier saw Administrator Penman, claiming that a recent discovery of a letter proved he was the Duke's son. Since then, he has been staying in the guest quarters, just above where you stayed last night. The Town Crier discovered his existence on Tuesday and has, under strict instructions of secrecy, been keeping watch over him while I considered the options."

"Options?" Tom was trying to remain calm, but even he could hear the disbelief in his voice. "Have you informed the Duke?"

Richard clenched his jaw, fighting hard to stay calm. "Not as yet." He managed to grind out.

"Richard. Have you taken leave of your—"

Tom's tongue was curbed by the sound of footsteps and heavy breathing. These were shortly followed by a profusely sweating Town Crier.

He strode into the room, exertion mixed with urgency, then, upon seeing Tom, uncertainty crept into the mix. He greeted both men with a polite nod.

"Apologies, Sir Richard," he breathed, looking rather unsteady on his feet, "but I have some urgent news, um… regarding the, er…"

The Town Crier looked unsure about sharing his urgent news (not a trait Tom associated with Gerald the Herald). Richard, however, was in no mood for any prevarication.

"You make speak freely, Town Crier. Master Skinner has been made aware of the situation."

Only just, thought Tom. He really hadn't had time to take it all in, and he still had many questions.

Gerald still looked uncomfortable, despite Richard's terse assurance. "Jolly good. The more the merrier, what?"

"Town Crier," Richard said, clearly impatient. "Has something happened to the claimant?"

Claimant. That was an interesting description. Richard obviously hadn't revealed all to the Town Crier — a wise move, for certes.

The Town Crier flinched at his tone. "I'm not sure, Sir Richard. That is to say, he's no longer in his room."

The silence was deafening; well, it would have been had Gerald not been breathing so heavily. Richard's gaze flared in the morning sunlight. Gerald produced a handkerchief and dabbed his sweating face. Tom remained silent, waiting for the drama to unfold.

"When did you discover this?" His words were ice, steaming in the warmth of the room. Gerald dabbed at a trickle of sweat near his left ear. Richard closed in upon the big man. "Well?" he snapped.

The Town Crier jerked in response. "A matter of minutes ago, Sir Richard," he replied. "As you can see, I have acted in all haste to inform you." And, just to emphasise the point, he continued wiping the beads of sweat from his face.

"When did you see him last?" Richard pressed.

"Yesterday evening," he breathed. "I was on my way to—"

"I'm not interested where you were on your way to, Master Hiepants. You were supposed to be keeping an eye on our guest. In fact, you assured me you were doing *exactly* that."

"I assured you nothing of the sort," Gerald blustered, straightening with indignation.

So the man did have a backbone, thought Tom. However, the shock of actually using it was immediately apparent on his face. He continued in a more submissive manner. "I'm sorry, Sir Richard. However, I must protest. This situation—"

"Is one that should have been prevented." It was hard to tell whether Richard was addressing the Town Crier or berating himself.

A prolonged silence followed. Richard seemed lost in thought. This made the Town Crier even more uncomfortable, and, in between mopping his face, his gaze turned towards Tom.

"Perhaps Master Hiepants should take me to the room in question," said Tom, casually breaking the silence. "It may reveal a few things about the lad's movements."

Richard flicked his gaze towards Tom and treated him to a sardonic smile. "I think I may have an inkling of the lad's movements, Tom. However, we may as well cover all possibilities."

Tom ignored the jibe; it was how Richard acted under duress.

Then, almost as an afterthought, Richard added, "It's time I saw to the Duke."

The three of them moved down the stairs to the reception hall, Richard leading at a smart pace. A couple of servants flitted below them, one carrying a tray of plates haphazardly decorated with the remains of a hearty breakfast, the other a couple of large ewers. They walked on, oblivious to the descending trio. Everything seemed strangely normal. After what had just been revealed by the Town Crier, Tom had almost expected the place to be in disarray, with the noble folk of Lower Icing milling around, waiting to see if the incredible news of a man claiming to be the Duke's son was actually true. However, the ornate reception hall was luxuriously calm.

Richard stopped at the bottom of the stairs and faced Tom. "After you've been to the room, advise Lieutenant Swill of the situation. He knows about the claimant," he said with a perfunctory calmness that matched the ambience perfectly. "Then tell him to report to me in the Duke's quarters."

Lieutenant Swill? Who *else* knew about the Duke's heir? "Richard—"

"I must see to the Duke, Tom," he interjected. Then, addressing the Town Crier, "I sincerely hope, Master Hiepants, that I am his *only* unexpected visitor this morning."

Gerald flushed as Richard hurried away and disappeared down the passageway that led to the Duke's private chambers.

CHAPTER 4

Taking tidiness into new realms

IT WAS JUST after eight o'clock when Tom and Gerald emerged from the reception hall. The manicured gardens of the Upper Bailey were, for the most part, bathed in sunshine and full of luminous summer colours. The day was already bordering on hot, and the sound of trickling water from numerous water-features provided a pleasant counterpoint. A troupe of gardeners were working away, daintily clipping the symmetrical box hedges, picking up errant leaves that dared to defy the season, turning the soil, cutting and edging the lawns, and diligently tending to the exotic array of flowers, shrubs and trees — manicuring the colourful harmony.

Tom and Gerald strode towards the opening in the twenty-foot-high stone wall that separated the Upper and Middle Bailey. As they approached, two bored-looking guards lazily touched the tips of their hats in a half-hearted attempt at being respectful. Sweeping past the guards, with barely an acknowledgment, they entered a world of grey walls and cobblestone.

The Middle Bailey was essentially a large, open compound, dominated by the massive Keep that shot skywards from the eastern wall; its morning shadow stretched across the compound and climbed over the western wall. Stepping into the markedly cooler shade, Tom and his unlikely companion headed for the entrance to The Keep. From within, sounds of construction could be heard; preparations for the Duke of Stymouth continued in earnest. The temperature dropped further as they marched through the fore-building and entered The Keep proper.

The Town Crier had been surprisingly silent since Richard's departure. The likely cause, in Tom's mind, was a lack of physical conditioning; he was breathing heavily again and looked as if speaking was beyond him. Still, his heavy robe and thick woollen trousers were, no doubt, heavy contributors to his discomfort. As they reached the spiral staircase that led to Xavier's room, Gerald came to a gasping halt. "Please, Master Skinner, a moment to catch my breath."

The man looked like he was about to pass out; either that or chuck up the contents of his breakfast. In this dim light, his pallor verged on the ghostly. "Why not leave this to me, Town Crier," suggested Tom. "You've already been of good service this morning and I'm sure you have many pressing matters to attend to. And, truth be told, I may be able to glean more from the search if I am alone. No offense intended."

"None taken, my boy." He looked relieved more than anything else. "Jolly good idea, in fact."

Tom shared his relief; the journey upstairs might well have been the end of Gerald the Herald.

"Well, I'll bid you good luck," Gerald said, recovering his breath somewhat. "Let me know if you discover anything." Turning unsteadily, he made to leave.

"One moment, Town Crier. Are you expecting me to sniff out the lad's quarters?"

"Oh yes, of course, most absent-minded of me," he puffed. "The north-eastern room on the second level."

"Cheers." Then Tom bolted up the stairs.

As it turned out, Tom probably *could* have sniffed out the young doctor's quarters; the smell of cooked bacon still hung greasily in the air. He had obviously broken fast here. Entering the room, the remains of the morning's repast — crockery stacked neatly on the table — was the only immediate evidence of occupation. It was apparent that this Xavier was someone who liked order. The bed covers lay smoothly across the bed and a large towel was draped neatly over the bathing tub. It was as if he'd prepared the room for someone's arrival rather than made an escape. In fact, he may well have just stepped out for some fresh air and intended to return; there were no locks or guards barring him from leaving, and Tom could well understand the need to escape the confines of four stone walls.

He checked inside the wardrobe and the drawer to the dressing table — they were empty. So, unless the young doctor had arrived without possessions (which he doubted), it seemed that he had, indeed, left. Again, Tom couldn't blame him. From what Richard had told him, he'd been kept in The Keep for two days with only the Town Crier for company. That would cause enough duress for all kinds of unusual behaviour, including taking your leave in the neatest way possible.

What had Richard been thinking? Even the Town Crier had grumbled his disapproval of how Xavier had been treated, and Tom found himself wondering about the motives of his friend. There must be more to this than Richard was prepared, or *allowed*, to reveal.

Tom turned his attention to the bathing tub; it contained a small amount of soapy water. It wasn't enough to bathe in, but certainly enough to wash oneself. Tom dipped his right hand into the water. As expected, it was cold; the brazier hadn't been used. He wiped his hand on the towel. It was damp (again, as expected) and, on closer inspection, the coarse, grey fibre was smudged with soapy grime. So, he had washed; he was either naturally very clean or had been preparing for an encounter with the Duke.

Finally, Tom moved to the table and inspected the crockery. The first of two earthenware pots contained butter, the second — he dipped his finger into its dark, sticky contents and tasted — plum jam. Next to the jars was an empty jug. Tom sniffed it and guessed, by the lack of aroma, that it had contained water. So, he surmised, the orderly doctor wasn't a drinker either, or, at least, not a regular one. Three stacked plates completed the simple arrangement. Placed on top of the stack were a clean spoon, knife and fork, and the unfinished portion of a small loaf of bread. Next to this was a neatly folded, grease-stained napkin. This was taking tidiness into new realms.

Tom picked up the loaf and prodded his fingers into its cleanly sliced surface. Inside the crust, the brown bread was soft and spongy, suggesting it hadn't been exposed to the drying air for long. He replaced the loaf and moved to the window; he was already finding the plush confines stuffy.

Looking straight out at the sunlit rooftops, Tom inhaled the warm morning air. It was a scene of gold and grey — light and shadow — punctuated by the sounds of people at work. Leaning into the two-foot-thick sill, he afforded himself a better view of the world beyond the castle walls. Looking right, he squinted into the morning sun as it broke above the Duke's Forest. Just beyond the east wall of the castle, the Icing River glittered as it flowed its way southwards. A further three-hundred paces on from the opposite bank was Tom's cottage. It wasn't visible from the window. However, if this had been one of the eastern rooms, he reckoned he'd have been able to pinpoint its exact location, even under the canopy of trees, and shoot an arrow down its chimney.

He was looking forward to returning to its peaceful embrace; although, he suspected his stay at the castle may prove to be an extended one. As Richard had said, matters were beginning to unravel, and it remained to be seen what they would reveal. In the meantime, he would inform Lieutenant Swill of the 'situation' and the 'claimant's' disappearance. All he could add was that Xavier had left this room no more than half an hour ago. Where the young doctor had gone was pure speculation, but, like Richard, Tom suspected an audience with the Duke was most likely. The room certainly conveyed a sense of finality.

CHAPTER 5

The price he has to pay

BY THE TIME Tom had walked back down the spiral staircase of The Keep, across the cobblestone courtyard of the Middle Bailey, between the grey-stone buildings of the Administration Section, past the massive West Gate to the barracks, he was feeling a bit stone-crazy. He could never live in this world of grey solidness — it was far too unyielding, and he felt constrained.

There was already quite a lot of activity in this part of the Lower Bailey as men-at-arms either started or finished their shifts. The sounds of banter and laughter were punctuated by the barking of orders and the clanging of hammer-on-steel. Tom diverted slightly from his path. Delivering Richard's message to Lieutenant Swill could wait a few minutes; he hadn't seen the blacksmith in quite some time.

Klob Hoofenhaus acknowledged Tom's salutation with a distracted, "Ya… goot mornink, Tom." It was followed by a hissing plume of steam as the Longboatian doused a red-hot pike blade in a barrel of water.

Tom knew Klob as well as any man — that is to say, not very well at all. However, he was one of the few people to have shared a social drink with the blond-haired giant. Klob had appeared unexpectedly at Tom's cottage one afternoon with Wildflower — Tom's horse — in tow. He'd just re-shoed her and, for some reason, decided to deliver the mare in person. Pleasantly surprised by the appearance of the smithy, Tom had invited him to stay for an evening repast. Klob had accepted, somewhat shyly. However, as afternoon turned into evening and the jugs of cider began to empty, Klob had become more animated, more jovial, and more talkative.

He'd shared stories of his past: how his father's clan had been displaced by a rival clan and they'd had to resettle farther north, where the harsh Longboatian winters — with only a few hours of daylight — made life miserable. However, the hardship had bonded the clan and, working together, they'd managed to make the best of their new home. It had only been after the death of his parents that he'd, literally, gone searching for greener pastures. "So much night and winter-koldt is not goot," he'd said. "Eventually it kills. Why I am smithy, Tom — it is light and heat."

That had been the first and only time Klob had visited. In the nine months since, Tom had suggested on a few occasions in passing that they share a few cups at The Dead Duck — all to no avail.

Moving past Klob's workshop, Tom headed for the barracks. However, his journey was cut short by the appearance of Brandon shooting out from the entrance to the officers' quarters. He was obviously in a hurry — perhaps the Town Crier had already broken the good news. Tom didn't envy him his position. It was going to be a long day for Lieutenant Swill, on top of a rather eventful night (with little, if any, sleep). He was so focused that he would have marched past had Tom not called out.

"Oh… morning, Tom," Brandon said, taking a moment to register the Gamekeeper's identity. He was dressed in uniform, and, while it was in a presentable state, (purple and gold doublet shining brilliantly against black trousers and shirt), a closer inspection revealed the tell-tale remnants of last night's duty: scuff marks on his right sleeve and knee caps (probably from when he'd tackled Billy Offcut) and the odd splash of ale from the more expressive patrons at The Dead Duck. Added to that, the sickly, stale remnants of pipe smoke battled for supremacy with the scented soapiness of his morning bath. Underneath the purple plume of his hat, his short brown hair looked slick with moisture. Clearly, he'd only just finished bathing and the finer points of presentation had been overlooked (including shaving, as evidenced by an even peppering of stubble). Yes, it seemed as if the Purple Perillian had been caught unprepared for an early start.

"Morning Brandon," Tom replied, jovially. "No rest for the Perilous. I see you've already—"

"Your pardon, Tom," Brandon cut in, "but I have urgent business with Sir Richard. I take it you wish to see me about the Witness Statement. I will send word when it's prepared. Then, if you wouldn't mind meeting at Administrator Penman's office, we can—" His words were flowing like jugs of ale on a Friday night.

"Hold on, Brandon," Tom said calmly, trying to control the messy outpouring. "I have not come to see you about the Witness Statement. I am merely acting as one of Sir Richard's messengers. He asked me to inform you of the young doctor's disappearance and tell you to report to him, but, obviously, the Town Crier has already done so. Quite surprising, really; when last I saw him, walking and talking were proving somewhat of a challenge."

The look on Brandon's face was a mixture of confusion and impatience. "Sorry… I'm not sure what you are talking about. I haven't seen the Town Crier, and I don't know anything about the disappearance of a young doctor. Are you sure Sir Richard said—" Realisation suddenly dawned on the youngest-ever member of the Purple Peril, draining his face of its rosy hue. "When you say a 'young doctor'…"

"I mean Xavier, the self-purported son of the Duke."

"Xavier is missing?" he hissed, apparently shocked by the news. "How long, do you know?"

"An hour at most," Tom responded, caught in the urgency of Brandon's tone.

Brandon swore.

"Richard and I found out from the Town Crier about half an hour ago. Richard's gone to see the Duke and wants you to report to him there."

Brandon nodded. He looked distracted.

"Is something amiss?" Tom enquired. "I must say that I am at a loss to know what has actually occurred here. Richard only informed me of the situation this morning and there are many things that—"

"Don't make any sense?" said Brandon, pointedly.

Tom regarded the lieutenant; he was very close to the mark. "You *could* put it that way," he acknowledged. "Perhaps, however, it's more a case of a lack of understanding. For instance, if you knew nothing about Xavier's disappearance, what urgent business did you have with Sir Richard?"

"Very well, Tom," he conceded. "If you'll follow me to the Upper Bailey, I'll explain as we walk."

For a while, Brandon said nothing; they were immersed in the sounds and activity of military life at Lower Icing. Walking back across the barracks, their pace an exact double-beat to Klob's rhythmic hammering, Brandon acknowledged salutes from a number of men-at-arms. Tom cast his eyes over to the stables. The wooden, L-shaped structure, with its angled roof, seemed as if it were propping up the north-west corner of the castle wall. A dozen or so horses stood in their stalls, looking out into the courtyard with studied ambivalence. One of them was Wildflower, her blaze a brilliant streak down the centre of her chestnut head. Tom had to overcome a sudden impulse to go to her and ride away from all this intrigue, back to the simplicity of his Gamekeeper's life. The flight of fancy was grounded by the sound of Brandon's voice.

"Sir Richard's future as heir to the Dukedom is being held to ransom by a man called Bertrand," Brandon said matter-of-factly. Then, through a clenched jaw, he added. "My sister is the price he has to pay."

For Tom, the assertion was like a blow to the stomach; he felt bad enough that *he* was questioning his friend's motives, but Brandon's words were delivered with *unquestionable* certainty. Tom had broached the subject of blackmail with Richard, pertaining to the Duke. His response echoed in Tom's mind: *If only you knew the irony of that remark.*

Could Richard have changed so much in the past year? The man he knew would never succumb to a blackmailer, particularly one who dared meddle in the future of the Duchy.

Brandon's statement raised yet more questions. It was frustrating, and one of the many reasons why Tom had shied away from politics. Every solution seemed to cause more problems. Like the fabled hydra: chop off one head and two more grew in its place.

They were now entering the Administration Section. "What does your sister have to do with the Blessed Whipping observer?"

Brandon looked perplexed. "I've never heard him called *that* before — snake, serpent, anything that slithers, silently waiting for the right moment to strike."

So, Brandon wasn't privy to Richard's informants; he would leave it be then. "And the right moment is now?" he asked, wanting to retain focus.

"The right moment has passed, but since Xavier has declared himself, I believe Bertrand has upped the ante."

Tom's confusion must have been obvious, because Brandon drew to a halt. He quickly scanned the Administration courtyard and buildings, scowling briefly at the collection of disgruntled villagers waiting outside the Office of Petitions, before looking directly at Tom.

"My parents once lived in Blessed Whipping." His voice was little more than a whisper. "They left twenty-two years ago because I was conceived out of wedlock. Now my sister has to pay the price, because of a document Bertrand made my parents sign back then, when they were scared and vulnerable — a document he is pressuring Sir Richard to ratify. For some bizarre, sun-worshipping reason, Bertrand wants Bethany back at Blessed Whipping."

His voice had become more intense and they were beginning to attract some curious looks from the hoi polloi waiting to have their petitions heard. Tom may as well have been one of them for all he'd understood of Brandon's revelation. However, the lieutenant's intentions were clear.

"And you're planning to confront Richard on this matter?"

He stiffened, aware of Tom's relationship with his commanding officer. "Yes, I am, Tom," he said simply. "No-one, not even the Duke himself, has the right to force anyone away from their family."

Tom nodded. He liked the lieutenant; he had a forthright, honourable nature. "True, but do you seriously believe the Seneschal of Lower Icing would place himself above the good of the Duchy?"

"More to the point, Tom, would he place my *sister* above the good of the Duchy?"

Tom didn't have an answer.

CHAPTER 6

Access to Richard's half-sister

ONE OF TWO things had happened in the three hours since Tom last saw Richard: Xavier had been found, or he was still at large. Either outcome had, no doubt, caused Richard severe consternation, but obviously not enough to send word to Tom. In many ways, he was relieved to be excluded from the tension at the castle, but, at the same time, he couldn't help feeling let down by his old friend. Trust seemed to have been lost somewhere in his world of bullying butchers, treacherous observers and dark secrets… or maybe Richard felt betrayed by the woman he couldn't have. To think that Lucinda might have lived such a lie seemed incredible.

Tom reflected on the drama of the morning as he walked from the relative calm of the Administration Section into the bustle of the courtyard outside the kitchen — Reg Puffy's demesne always seemed to be hive of activity. (It was understandable considering the high expectations of those who resided in or frequented the Upper Bailey, as well as having to provision the men-at-arms and sustain everyone else employed at the castle.)

A part of Tom wanted to leave this heated, grey stone world behind: a world of political machinations, half-truths and hidden agendas, where nothing was black and white — it all merged into grey. However, a bigger part of him remained steadfast to his friend, no matter how questionable Richard's actions. After all, he wasn't in possession of all the facts. He was in no position to make judgement. He'd left that to Lieutenant Swill.

In the meantime, Tom had taken it upon himself to find out exactly when the Witness Statement would be ready; he was not one for waiting around at the beck and call of others. Administrator Penman had been most accommodating and marked a time of two o'clock. He'd also assured Tom that Lieutenant Swill would be informed, and present at the appointed time. Tom had almost broached the subject of Xavier with him, but decided against it, not knowing exactly how much information the Administrator was party to. Instead, Tom had thanked the agreeable clerk and, more on a whim than anything else, informed him, should the need arise, that he could be reached at The Harey Rabbit — he had three hours to kill before the signing of the Witness Statement.

The Harey Rabbit was an unusual inn — more like an extension of the Upper Bailey than a public drinking house. Entering its relatively cool confines, the refined, late-morning crowd regarded him with a mixture of curiosity and bemused acceptance. Dressed in his trademark leather trousers and open-neck shirt (with his wayward, sandy-coloured hair and bright blue eyes beaming through his tanned complexion), Tom was immediately recognisable, even to those who didn't know him personally. It was as if an exotic weed had suddenly appeared in a manicured garden of roses.

The inn was comfortably busy, even at this time of day. At least half the patrons were women, attired in the kind of finery Tom associated with grand banquets. Most of them frequented The Harey Rabbit because it was the place to be seen (and overhear castle gossip), but some of the younger ladies were also there to snare themselves a husband of fortune.

As much as Tom might like to think The Harey Rabbit had just hopped into his head because of its proximity to the castle, the truth of the matter was that it was a more considered choice. The venue offered something that no other inn or tavern could provide: access to Richard's half-sister, Mary.

Mary was somewhat of a revelation. Tom had always regarded her as the smart young woman who ran The Harey Rabbit: a natural beauty with a talent for making people feel welcome, regardless of their social standing. It hadn't been until the death of Sir Walter Upson, almost two years ago, that Tom discovered Richard *and* Mary had just lost their father. Tom had been flabbergasted, but Richard shrugged away his disbelief and said, "Mary is content being Mary."

And that she was. She was smiling at him now as he approached the bar. "Well, look what the cat's dragged in."

Tom returned the smile. "Hello, Mary. You're looking well."

"So, Tom, to what do we owe the pleasure of your company. Don't tell me the trees have run out of conversation?" Her bright blue eyes shone within her playful expression.

"They still whisper sweet nothings when there's a breeze," he quipped. "However, I do have a few hours to kill, courtesy of your brother."

"Don't tell me Richard's putting his own interests first?" she said with a wry smile.

Tom laughed. He was already glad he'd decided to look in on Mary; she was a balm for the soul. The three months that had passed since he'd last set foot in The Harey Rabbit evaporated in her warm easy-goingness. "It's good to see you, Mary."

He and Mary were sitting at a corner booth while Dave and a trio of barmaids tended to the needs of the genteel clientele. It had been Mary who suggested they share a drink and catch up on each other's news.

"What about the 'beautiful people'?" he whispered.

"They'll survive." She smiled. "This dainty bunch aren't exactly heavy drinkers. We've got about half an hour before the lawyers and merchants roll in."

It hadn't taken either of them long to realise that nothing had really changed in the last three months — Mary had been running the inn and Tom had been running the forest.

"You're an odd one, Tom," she said after he'd commented on the unusual abundance of wildlife, putting it down to an unusually early spring. "Ever thought of snaring something that can satisfy more than just your hunger?"

"Is that an offer, Mary?"

She flicked his arm playfully. "In your dreams."

Tom laughed. He and Mary often had this sort of banter — not recently, but in times past. They were two individual souls, one happy in his own company, the other seemingly happy in the company of her many patrons. "Well, thank you for your concern. However, when the need arises, I find The Duck a fertile-enough hunting ground. The quarry is not as elusive as The Rabbit's, and it tastes just as sweet."

"Enough!" She laughed. "This is a refined establishment, Tom Skinner, not some rutting den."

He smiled. "In your dreams, Mary."

They both laughed heartily, drawing attention from the demur gathering, which only made the situation funnier. Tears began to well in Tom's eyes. He tried to douse the hilarity, but the looks of bemusement, outrage and disgust from the prissy patrons only fuelled it. Mary wasn't much better; her eyes were crying with silent mirth, her right hand clamped over her mouth.

Gradually they recovered their composure. Wiping eyes and relaxing jaw muscles, they dared not look around the room that was now filled with the sound of tittering conversation.

However, the chance of more laughter igniting was well and truly extinguished by Mary's casual enquiry, "So, have you seen my dear brother, or is he too busy ruling the Duchy on behalf of the Duke?"

Tom's face must have betrayed his misgivings because Mary was immediately focused, her eyes, moistened with tears, shining even brighter. "What's happened?" She seemed more curious than concerned.

Tom knew he wouldn't get away with revealing nothing, and he saw no harm in sharing the fact that Richard had thrown Frank Offcut into The Can.

"Are you serious, Tom?" Mary was not often taken aback, but she certainly looked surprised now.

"He was part of the post-breakfast entertainment," Tom quipped. It all seemed a lot more amusing now that it was over. "Burst into Richard's quarters, looking like an over-boiled pork sausage, foaming at the mouth and ranting about the treatment of his son."

"You're jesting with me, Tom." Mary obviously thought it was too outrageous to be true.

"I assure you, Mary, that man is moon-affected," he said, reacting jovially to Mary's disbelief, "demanding that his son be released from The Can immediately, addressing Richard like he was some commoner-gaoler."

Mary looked intrigued now. "I assume you're talking about Billy?"

Tom nodded. "The lad seems to have acquired a bit of a reputation in my absence."

"Yes, I've heard a few things said about Frank's youngest recently." Then she leaned across the table, closer to Tom, and, in quieter tones, added, "A few of my patrons see him as a potential client and have wagers on when their services will be required."

"I would suggest sometime after two o'clock this afternoon," Tom answered. "That's when I sign the Witness Statement."

Mary gave him another shocked look. "You sign it?"

Tom chuckled. "I haven't forgotten how to write my name, Mary."

She slapped him across the arm. "You know what I mean. You've had Billy charged. What did he do?"

"Well, it wasn't me who actually charged him — that was Lieutenant Swill — but I was responsible for trussing him up like a rabid boar, and Will Plucker was more than accommodating with the use of his storeroom. In particular, the corner next to the slops buckets."

Mary smiled at that. "No wonder Frank Offcut was fuming — humiliating his youngest son like that. So, what had Billy done to deserve a first-hand demonstration of your knot-tying skills?"

"Upset one of the lasses with his not-so-skilful caresses."

Mary nodded her understanding, mirth evaporating from her face. "Then what you did was the least he deserved."

"Don't worry, Mary. Will and I weren't exactly gentle with the squirming little toe-rag."

"Lucky it was Brandon Swill on duty," she added, thoughtfully. "He's about the only officer who'd have the balls to charge Billy and risk the wrath of Frank Offcut."

"Hells bells, Mary!" Tom was outraged. "The way everyone happily chews Frank Offcut's gristle, you'd think he held the fate of the Duchy, not a meat cleaver, in his bloody hands."

Mary stared at him for a moment. "You're right. Frank has become more cocksure of late."

"Even Richard was put-out when I told him Billy had been charged."

"Yes, well, I've always found it easier not to look too deeply into the murky motives of my brother."

Tom regarded the woman sitting across the table from him. Her olive complexion and blue eyes were an exotic mix, and her easy-going nature only enhanced her beauty; she was so far above any of the 'ladies' she served. Maybe he should confide in her and share the concerns he was beginning to have about Richard. The moment, however, was snatched away by the sound of a pompous voice behind him.

"Top-hole, old man," it said, bellowing through the dainty chirping like a blunderbuss at a poetry reading. "Teach the blighter a lesson, what!"

However, there was no need for Tom to turn around; he knew who had just entered The Harey Rabbit.

"Oh good, it's lawyer time," Mary said, smiling through her sarcasm. "Boorish oafs, but they spend like there's no tomorrow."

"Charge like it, too, no doubt."

"Better go and see to their egos. Don't want to be sued for dereliction of duty."

As Mary stood up to welcome them, Tom gently held her arm. "Do you have a room spare? Don't think I could spend another night in that glorified prison cell Richard calls a guest room."

"I'm sure we can accommodate a man of your discerning tastes, Tom." With a playful wink, she waltzed off to greet the lawyers.

Tom smiled, although he wasn't entirely sure what she meant by the remark.

CHAPTER 7

You know where I can be reached

ADMINISTRATOR PENMAN'S OFFICE was hot and stuffy. Tom felt slightly claustrophobic surrounded by the walls of rolled-up parchment. In fact, the castle itself was beginning to have an oppressive effect on Tom. He could almost feel the massive weight of stone bearing down, closing in on him from all directions. Everywhere he turned he was confronted by stone.

Administrator Penman was sitting behind his desk, scratching away at another petition. He was filling in time while they waited for Brandon to arrive. It was almost a quarter past two. Tom was beginning to wonder if something had happened at the castle. The lieutenant didn't strike him as someone who would be late for an appointment, particularly something fundamental to the case against Billy Offcut.

He still had no idea what had transpired since he'd left Richard's company. Apart from retrieving Wildflower from the castle stables and walking her to those behind The Harey Rabbit, Tom had spent all his time in the bar room, waiting for some news from the castle. Instead, all he'd heard was the inane chatter and pompous bluster of Lower Icing's frilly elite. Still, it hadn't been a bad way to spend his time. Dave had a few good stories about some of the patrons, and Mary made sure his mug was kept full.

Stepping out into the afternoon sun had been somewhat of a shock to his slightly inebriated system, and it took a few steps for his senses to adjust to the glaring conditions. Now, in the gloomily lit interior of Administrator Penman's office, the heat was beginning to make Tom feel drowsy.

Again, he was tempted to bring up the subject of Xavier, but decided discretion was, in fact, the better part of valour.

"I'm sorry about this, Master Skinner," said Administrator Penman suddenly, replacing his quill into its stand. "I can't think what could be keeping Lieutenant Swill; he's usually very punctual."

"Perhaps Sir Richard has found a more important matter for him to attend to," he said, pointedly.

A quizzical expression passed across the Administrator's face. "Perhaps," he conceded. "However, if that was indeed the case, I would have expected a messenger by now."

The man was a born clerk, thought Tom — all protocol and procedure, without a curious bone in his body. Well, Tom wasn't prepared to linger in this world of pen and parchment much longer.

"Is the lieutenant's presence necessary for me to sign the statement? Can't you witness our signatures separately?"

"Ah…" He sighed, shaking his head. "Would that it was that simple, Master Skinner."

"Surely it *is* that simple, Administrator."

"Unfortunately, for legal reasons, the arresting officer and the witness must sign the Witness Statement in each other's presence. In essence, they must witness each other signing the Witness Statement. I am merely a witness to the two parties witnessing each other's signature on the Witness Statement."

The Administrator looked pleased with his explanation. Tom had had enough. He stood up. "In that case, Administrator," he said pleasantly, "you can witness me taking my leave. I'd rather not spend the afternoon imposing myself in your work space."

The grey-robed figure sprang up from behind his desk, concern replacing his courteous formality. "I am terribly sorry—"

Tom waved a dismissive hand at him as he walked towards the door. "No need for apologies, Administrator. It is not *you* who is at fault."

Opening the door, Tom turned to face the petitions clerk. "You know where I can be reached."

Instead of walking north towards the town, Tom emerged from the gloomy greyness of the Administration building and headed south, towards the Upper Bailey. The thought of spending the afternoon inside The Harey Rabbit (or any other inn for that matter) certainly didn't appeal to Tom's outdoor nature, nor would it satisfy his growing concern that something had gone terribly wrong at the ruling end of the castle.

As Tom approached the guard-post to the Upper Bailey entrance, all seemed to be normal. The guards seemed just as bored as they had earlier that morning, and, once again, his transitory presence was acknowledged with little more than a half-hearted nod. Still, it was pleasant enough walking through the parapet wall, leaving behind the simmering heat of the Middle Bailey courtyard for the lush surrounds of the noble quarters.

The gardens, now free of workers, were bursting with splendid vitality. It was a moat of vibrant fertility, keeping the dead grey stone at bay. Looking straight ahead, Tom noticed two men-at-arms standing under the grand, marble portico entrance to the reception hall. It wasn't the first time Tom had seen guards posted there, but those times had been when visiting dignitaries were in residence. Tom assumed it meant Xavier had not been found. Either that or the Duke of Stymouth had snuck in unexpectedly early.

As Tom drew closer, the blue and gold uniformed figures resolved themselves into men he recognised. They were members of Lieutenant Swill's night patrol: the Sporrendale Highlander with an overactive bowel and the joker from the Clover Isle. Both were looking rather tired. And both looked, now that he was closer, rather sheepish.

"Afternoon, lads. Didn't think you'd be on duty this early," Tom said good naturedly.

The shorter, swarthier Highlander, with red hair and fulsome beard, spoke up first. "Och, laddie! I'm no' one for lazyin' aboot on me arse. A wee kip's all I be needin'." Like most Sporrendalians Tom had met, his accent was quite thick.

Then the musical voice of the Clover Isle piped up. "T'be sure, what he's tryin' to say, Tommy boy, is that his lazy-arse was booted out of bed by the lieutenant."

"Och, Paddy, after last night, my arse needed a rest."

"Too true, Jock. An' speakin' of which, have you changed your—"

"Lads," Tom interrupted before the bantering went too far into the mirky realms of privy humour. "So, what's happening inside?"

They both shrugged. "T'be sure, we're not sure," said Paddy.

"Then why are you here? What are your orders?"

"If we tol' you that, laddie, we'd be cleaning out The Can for a month."

"That's right, Tommy boy," added Paddy. "We've been ordered not to reveal our orders." Then, after a brief pause, he added, "Course, *you're* free to go inside. We haven't been ordered to keep *you* out."

Tom smiled and walked past them, through the entrance to the reception hall. As he moved into the plush confines of the castle proper, he heard Jock say, "Och man, yoo ra blitherin' idiot."

CHAPTER 8

A feel wouldn't do any harm

THE RECEPTION HALL at half past two in the afternoon was much busier than it had been at eight o'clock in the morning. The marble-tiled floor was alive with echoing sounds of polished boots walking in a number of directions. They belonged to servants for the most part, but there was also a smattering of gentrified soles in the clicking mix. Clearly, Tom wasn't the only person Jock and Paddy hadn't been ordered to keep out.

Tom turned to his right, where, in the corner of the hall, an arrangement of lounges and low tables served as a casual gathering area, and a place to await an audience with Richard. The furniture was positioned around a large bay window that washed the space in light and afforded the occupants a delightful view of the garden.

At the moment, the occupants consisted of three well-dressed men in deep discussion (all smoking pipes) — merchants, come to lobby the Duke about taxes and levies. He was vaguely acquainted with one of them: Fraser Coin. Sitting away from them was a young man and woman. Both of them looked uncomfortable and ill-suited to the fine surrounds. Their clothing, while presentable, marked them as working class. However, as Tom drew nearer, the woman's beauty shone through the plainness of her attire. Catching his eye, she gave him a sultry smile, her full lips gently parting to reveal perfect white teeth — very unusual in the working classes. Tom suddenly felt self-conscious under her appraising gaze and focused his eyes on his destination: the door next to the reception lounge that led to Prestwich's office.

He knocked once. Seconds later the door opened inwards.

"Master Skinner." It was a perfunctory greeting from Prestwich.

"Prestwich," Tom responded. "I'd like a word with Sir Richard."

"Beggin' your pardon, but we was 'ere first."

The voice had come from the reception lounge. Turning around, Tom saw the plain-dressed man was now out of his seat, eyeing him with a mixture of defiance and apprehension. He looked ready to say something more, but his determination gave way under the bemused gazes of the three merchants. Shuffling nervously on his feet, he added, "I's jus' that we bin waitin' 'ere for more'n two hours t'see Sir Richard."

The woman was more at ease with the situation and continued to give Tom lascivious looks, even going so far as positioning her body so Tom could take full advantage of her more than ample cleavage.

"Don't be lured by *that* one, Gamekeeper," piped in Fraser Coin through a plume of tobacco smoke, "unless you fancy the idea of a visit to the pox doctor. I hear a leech on the balls is the favoured treatment for a dose of Ophelia Offcut."

"Yeah, well you ain't got nuffin to worry 'bout 'ave ya, ya nadless prick," Ophelia snapped, immediately losing her allure.

"Pheel!" pleaded the young man, presumably also one of the Offcut clan.

This drew the attention of several servants, who looked ready to pounce on any breach in decorum.

"Feel?" mused another of the merchants. "Well, I suppose a *feel* wouldn't do any harm."

Ophelia leapt out of her seat. "Yeah! Well feel *this,* ya smarmy git!"

She made for the merchant, who still looked bemused, her brother restraining her just as she was about to let fly with her right boot.

"Pheel!" he yelled, as she squirmed madly in his grip.

Servants closed in as the merchant began to rise from his chair. "Oh well," he smiled, "if you insist."

A tap on the arm drew Tom's attention away from the fiery scene that had erupted suddenly from the cool confines of the reception hall. Prestwich beckoned Tom inside his office with a twitch of his head. "If you please, Master Skinner."

Tom hesitated for a moment. A part of him wanted to watch the unfolding drama, but his sense of priority quickly asserted itself.

Prestwich shut and locked the door the second Tom stepped over its threshold. Tom was surprised at how much it blocked out the noise — the screeching curses of Ophelia Offcut were little more than muffled cries.

"My apologies, Master Skinner," said Prestwich, zipping towards his desk. "Those Offcuts are a breed unto themselves."

Tom remained near the door. He felt a certain amount of sympathy for their plight. After all, their brother and father had just been arrested. "Can't say I'd be best pleased if *I'd* been waiting two hours to see someone."

Prestwich was at his desk, shuffling through a mass of documents. Tom closed in on the clerk. "So why *have* they been waiting two hours? Where's Richard?"

Tom's direct tone had an immediate effect. Prestwich's head shot up from his parchment sorting. "I do not know his exact whereabouts, Master Skinner. I have not seen Sir Richard since he had Frank Offcut arrested. I informed Seth and Ophelia Offcut of that very fact when they arrived. It has been their choice to wait."

But what choice did they have, thought Tom. They obviously hadn't had any joy at The Can. "I see," murmured Tom.

Seemingly satisfied he'd answered Tom's query, Richard's secretary went back to his document rummaging. Tom, however, wasn't finished with Prestwich just yet. Knowing how literal the clerk was, Tom asked, "Have you *heard* from Sir Richard since Frank Offcut's arrest?"

This time he didn't bother looking up. "No."

"Then you don't know about the extra guards in the Upper Bailey?"

"Lieutenant Swill informed me about that," he said, scribing away at parchment.

"Did he say why?"

Placing his quill back in its holder, Prestwich straightened and regarded Tom with impatient indulgence. "I'm sorry, Master Skinner, but, as you can see, I have rather a lot on my plate. I'm sure you've as much of an idea for the necessity of extra guards as I do. We are both aware, are we not, of the facts surrounding the Duke?"

"Are we?" Tom challenged.

The man in grey remained silent. Semantics, Tom thought; it hadn't been a direct question. Very well, there would be nothing indirect about what he would say next. Closing in on the wiry, limp-haired figure, Tom said, "What facts, exactly, would you be referring to, Prestwich?"

Prestwich held Tom's gaze without flinching. Years of working with Richard had obviously instilled a certain resolve against aggressive posturing. "Once again, I must apologise. I am not at liberty to divulge any information regarding the Duke or Sir Richard, or, indeed, *any* citizen of Lower Icing without the consent of the aforementioned individuals."

Tom was dumbstruck.

"I was under the impression that Sir Richard had taken you into his confidence," Prestwich continued. "If that is the case, you probably know at least as much as I. If not, it is not my place to inform you. Now, if you will excuse me, Master Skinner, I must attend to some rather pressing matters."

CHAPTER 9

Lusciously defiant figure

TOM EMERGED FROM Prestwich's office disappointed and slightly bewildered. The secretary's officious behaviour was to be expected, even admired in this particular case, but what game was Richard playing? Why had he chosen to involve him in his 'matter of importance' in the first place? Clearly, he no longer valued his advice or respected his opinion. So, what had the breakfast meeting been about? Was it just an unburdening of guilt? Or perhaps he'd hoped Tom would ease his conscience and support how he'd handled the revelation of Xavier's existence. In truth, Tom found it hard to understand Richard's course of action (or inaction). And because their breakfast had been interrupted, he still had questions that were yet to be asked. That was the most frustrating part — not knowing how, exactly, everything had transpired. That, and the role Richard intended to play in its resolution. Sadly, he couldn't shake the thought that his friend was acting in his own interests.

As he shut the office door behind him, his gaze turned towards the staircase to his right. The one he, Richard and the Town Crier had raced down earlier this morning. It seemed ages ago. For a moment, Tom was tempted to race back up them, to see if Richard had returned to his quarters, but, then again, even if he had, it was doubtful whether Tom's presence would be welcomed.

No, he decided; no more running around after Richard or Brandon or anyone else. The rest of the day would be spent on *his* terms. And, right at this moment, some cooling ales and fine fare at The Harey Rabbit seemed like the best option… just in case his presence was required after all. Although, he was already fighting the pull of the forest.

"Just missed the finale to the Ophelia Offcut show, Gamekeeper," said a voice to his left — it was Fraser Coin. "Shame really. Very amusing, and such a colourful script."

"Physically taxing as well, I would have thought," added one of his associates, without removing the pipe from his mouth.

Tom had little sympathy for the Offcuts, but he had even less regard for people who actually enjoyed feeding on the misfortune of others.

Fraser chuckled. "For *her* or the three servants who had to restrain her?"

Barely acknowledging the men within the tobacco cloud, Tom made for the exit. Paddy and Jock were still at their post, but they appeared more alert and jovial than when he'd entered.

Jock was particularly animated. "Och, Tom, y'shoulda seen the Offcut lassie, jus' noo. Cussin' 'n' cursin' 'n' wailin' 'n' flailin' like a banshee in a hoose of horrors."

Paddy was also upbeat. "T'be sure, the wench has a devil of a spirit in her. Took tree of 'em to drag her out. Put most men t'shame, she would."

"Give *you* a roon for your money, Paddy, *that's* t'be sure!"

"An' t'would be money well spent, boyo: T'wouldn't mind runnin' into *those* ripe melons."

Predictably, the Ophelia Offcut Appreciation Society found its level of humour snuggled quite nicely into the ample cleavage area. On any other day, Tom would have snuggled with them, but today his sense of humour couldn't find a way to get comfortable. Richard's prickly mood and irritating absence had made sure of that.

"I would have thought your natural charm would have been enough to win her over, Paddy," Tom commented.

Jock laughed at the dig.

Paddy took it in good humour. "T'be sure, but it's y'nat'ral bulge in y'codpiece that does the talkin' with Mistress Offcut. An' the bigger it is, the more she'll pay attention."

Both guardsmen chuckled. Tom even managed an amused smile.

"Aye, she's a good bootcher's daughter — knows 'er meat," added Jock.

"So, what's happened to the good butcher's daughter?" asked Tom. "I assume her brother was still with her."

"Aye," confirmed Jock. "He was yellin' at 'er to stop screamin', but that jus' made 'er scream looder."

"Reckon *I* could make 'er scream louder," piped in Paddy.

Jock was about to thrust forth with the obvious bawdy riposte until he caught Tom's impatient expression. "Don' know wha' 'appened after they got kicked out, laddie... 'sides from Ophelia not screamin' anymore. Guards at the gate sure t'know more."

Tom nodded. Not too much could have happened in the minutes he was locked away with Prestwich. "Well, lads… think I'll leave you to it. Hope the rest of your afternoon is just as entertaining."

The guards at the Upper Bailey gate were their usual friendly, effusive selves.

"They went that way," one of them mumbled, vaguely indicating the direction of the Lower Bailey.

"Do you know where they were being taken?"

"Didn' ask."

"Of course you didn't."

After striding across the cobblestone heat of the Middle Bailey courtyard, Tom entered the Lower Bailey. This was where the castle came to life, although most of that life tended to converge on the kitchen and the barracks. Here in the Administration Section, only a smattering of people were going about their business. Most were clerks, judging by their attire, but there were also a group of villagers milling about in the vicinity of the Office of Petitions.

Into the mix walked three men dressed in the purple livery of Upper Bailey servants. Judging by their slightly dishevelled appearance, they were the ones who had wrestled with Ophelia. Tom wasn't sure why he was interested in her wellbeing. Frank and Billy were obnoxious individuals, and she'd displayed similar traits, but, somehow, Tom felt there was something more to her. Maybe it *was* just her sultry beauty affecting his judgment, but she (and her brother) still deserved better than the treatment they'd received at the castle.

"Excuse me one moment," Tom said to the leading servant. "Have you just escorted the Offcut siblings from the Upper Bailey?"

The young servant had a friendly face and a disposition to match. "I wouldn' say escorted exactly, sir. She's a fiery one, no mistaking."

The servant to his left displayed a ripped shirt cuff, which he then pulled up to reveal a raking scratch mark that extended from his wrist to his elbow. "Fights like an alley cat, she does."

"An' I got a bruise in a place that only Molly knows," added the third.

Tom didn't know who Molly was, but he could hazard a guess at the location of the bruise. "So, where did you take her?"

"The brother managed to calm 'er down by the time we got to the gate," explained 'friendly face', "so we jus' let 'em go."

"'Course, we told the guards not to let 'em back in," emphasised the scratched servant, straightening out his sleeve.

"Which gate?" asked Tom.

"The West Gate," answered friendly face.

Emerging from the portcullis archway of the West Gate, Tom spied Ophelia leaning against a shop on the corner of Big Wig and Noble streets. He headed straight for the lusciously defiant figure.

She scowled at him from the shade of Ma's Karaderie, a business that sold masks and other paraphernalia for costume parties. Funnily enough, Ophelia was standing next to a sign that read *Wear a happy face*.

"Whatcha want?" she said, folding her arms under her breasts, accentuating a cleavage that didn't need accentuating.

"Where's your brother, Ophelia?" Tom parried, trying to focus on the matter at hand.

She shrugged. "What's it to ya?"

"I just wanted to make sure you were both alright."

She certainly appeared alright, no worse for wear from her exertions. In fact, if anything, she looked more radiant. Tom's attempt at concern, however, produced another scowl.

"What d'*you* reckon, Mister Come 'n' Go As You Like Arse-Licker."

Direct questions were obviously not going to get Tom anywhere; he might as well try talking to the wall she was leaning against. A different tack was definitely needed. The one he took was unexpected to say the least; it was as if he'd put on one of Ma's masks and suddenly become somebody else. "If you'll allow me to buy you a drink, I will tell you something of Billy and your father's fate."

Her full lips turned upwards, the sun breaking through the clouds.

CHAPTER 10

While Ophelia glowed

GRADUALLY THE EVENTS of yesterday afternoon and evening trickled through Tom's quagmire of mind-thumping pain and gut-churning seediness — the alcohol-fuelled ride he'd spent with Olivia Offcut had been both wondrous and regretful. It was as if all his neglected passion of the last three months had been compressed into however many crazed hours he'd spent with her.

He remembered walking to The Harey Rabbit; he'd been in an oddly anarchic frame of mind and taking Ophelia to the den of dainty decorum appealed. Maybe Richard was to blame for his rebellious mood, but, then again, maybe it was the mischievous sparkle in Ophelia's eyes at the suggestion of The Harey Rabbit. Whatever the cause, Tom had been ready and willing to upset the toffy apple cart, without thinking about the bruises it might leave, particularly to Mary.

Ophelia's presence had caused quite a stir — the mix of outrage and leering delight was, like Ophelia's womanly assets, thinly veiled. Mary had taken it all in good grace, for Tom's benefit no doubt. He winced at the memory.

Ophelia, on the other hand, had revelled in the attention, smiling sweetly at the sour, disapproving dainties and blowing kisses to the stiff-upper-lips. Tom had loved every shocked response.

Once settled in a corner table, however, Ophelia the Alley Cat returned, demanding to know what had happened to Billy and her father. Tom had already begun telling her about her brother before they'd reached the inn — she'd seemed more concerned for him than her father.

She'd been angry at the beginning, particularly at Tom's pivotal part in Billy's arrest, and her colourful invective drew unpleasant looks from nearby patrons. Somehow, though, he'd managed to calm her down, and through the course of what seemed like a myriad of marvellous moments, they drank and laughed away the afternoon.

Sometime around dusk, they'd left The Harey Rabbit to get some fresh air. Moving back through the sea of faces had been a surreal experience — everyone seemed a lot happier, smiling and laughing as they spun around him. Even Mary's quizzical face had rotated in and out of his vision. The only anchor to reality had been the woman in his arms, the one who'd looked at him with the promise of unearthly delights in her eyes.

Somewhere deep in his mind, Tom had known he was beyond drunk, but somehow he hadn't attributed it all to the wine and cider — he'd been intoxicated by Ophelia Offcut. And the spinning faces had given their approval. As they'd stumbled out into the warm twilight, stars twinkling awake, all had seemed right with universe.

They'd meandered across The Square. At first Tom had thought they were heading for The Bloody Bell, but Ophelia pulled him in the direction of the river. They were alone on the East Road and could have been alone in the *world* if it hadn't been for the sounds of hilarity and drunken voices behind them. And the world ahead was Tom's world: a dark wall of trees below an evening sky that seemed to stretch on forever.

Then the sounds of the Icing River had percolated through the sounds of Lower Icing. It was too dark to see, but Ophelia, strangely silent, like a whimsical spirit in her white dress — the banshee exorcised — had led the way. She'd held his hand and drawn him north along the riverbank. Tom had been happy to follow. He went with her flow, against the flow of the Icing. The river was full, even this time of year and, in the early night's gloom, it flowed black and strong... while Ophelia glowed.

Then they'd sat down — it felt like sand, still warm from a day's baking. Tom remembered her words, swirling like an eddy sucked from the depths of the river. "This is my favourite place."

Then she'd pushed him onto his back. Tom had stared in wonder at the revolving universe as she undressed him. Then she was on top of him. If there was a celestial paradise waiting for the soul, it had to be close to this.

He'd woken with the sun. His mouth felt dry and gritty. One side of his face was cool and damp, the other warm and dry. Eventually curiosity had won over his desire for sleep — he opened his eyes.

At first, the vista made no sense. All he could see was an impossibly thick forest, where even the trunks were green. Then he was aware of another sensation: something cool was licking at his toes. He'd recoiled immediately and sat up in shock. Everything was suddenly bright, like a bolt of lightning illuminating the darkness. The pain in his head was immediate.

He shut his eyes, but not before capturing a glimpse of his surroundings — riverbank-reeds flared white to red inside his closed eye-lids. It was the river lapping against his toes, the reeds the impossibly thick forest.

Then the sounds of the river had become part of his awareness — not the river itself; *that* was almost silent — the brushing of the reeds, a soothing susurrus to the annoying buzzing of flies that hovered around his face. He waved them away and opened his eyes. Gradually, the new day came into focus.

Apart from his boots, lying within arm's reach, he was relieved to find that he was fully clothed — his shirt was on and so were his trousers (although they were undone at the waist). Gently brushing away the sand that had collected on the right side of his face — coagulated more around his mouth where it had mixed with his drool — he stood. The world reeled for a moment, then found its balance. His head throbbed as his brain finally registered his whereabouts.

Tom stood alone, surrounded by chest-high reeds, in a sandy little beach that stretched no more than six paces along the river. Looking around, the height of the bank obscured Lower Icing, but he was able to pinpoint his location by the position of the East Road Bridge, spanning the Icing some two hundred paces to the south. He was quite surprised at how far away it appeared — last night, the walk along the bank had seemed to take only moments.

There was no sign of Ophelia. She had dissolved into the night. Tom had no memory of her leaving; perhaps he had dreamed her… no, his imagination wasn't *that* good.

Tom's reverie was broken by the sounds of splashing and flapping. A group of ducks had just landed on the river and were already being carried downstream towards the bridge. He watched them disappear behind the reeds.

The river looked inviting. The morning was already warm, flies continued their frenzied circling around his face, and all over his body the scratching sensation of sand irritated his skin.

He removed his clothes, gave them a good shake, and then laid them out on top of the reed bed. In one, smooth lunge, he broke through the clear slate surface of the Icing. The shock of cold water was bracing, a reinvigoration of body and mind. Resurfacing near the bank, he found his feet on the smooth granular surface of the riverbed. Even in waist-deep water, it required some effort to fight the pull of the current.

Facing the forest, he watched the nascent sun filter through the distant trees… where he belonged. If there was no message from the castle when he returned to The Harey Rabbit, he and Wildflower would be breezing through its shady boughs by mid-morning.

Now, as Tom walked back along the bank towards the bridge, the consequences of his actions were beginning to materialise, much like the people who were arriving to tend their crops in the fields between the river and the town. What sort of greeting would he receive from Mary? Had he burned any bridges there? He cursed himself for a fool.

And what of Ophelia? As much as he cringed at the thought of what might have occurred at The Harey Rabbit, the thought of what *had* happened afterwards filled him with excitement. He wondered how *she* was feeling this morning.

CHAPTER 11

Exacted a price for her company

"I'VE SEEN ANIMALS with woollen fleeces that look less sheepish than you, Tom Skinner."

Tom was relieved that Mary's opening remark was accompanied by a bemused smile. "From what I can remember, I think I may have good reason to be." He was surprised by the hoarseness of his voice.

"Don't worry, Tom." Mary smiled. "After you've cleaned yourself up and made yourself presentable for breakfast, I'll take great delight in refreshing your memory."

Tom didn't like the sound of that at all, but Mary had every right to enjoy his discomfort. Even after his river cleanse, he must look like a homeless beggar. He needed a change of clothing, and then he had to be prepared to wear the consequences of his drunken dalliance.

Tom sat opposite Mary in the same booth which he and Ophelia had occupied last night (according to Mary that is; Tom had no recollection of where he'd sat). At least he was feeling better now. He'd washed his face and body, using the soap and perfumed oils provided with a small basin in the room he'd paid for but not slept in. He'd changed into a new shirt, but still wore the same brown leather trousers and short-cut boots. (He had no alternative; the possibility of spending a night on the riverbank hadn't occurred to him when he was packing for a stay at the castle.)

"So, Tom," Mary said with a mischievous smile, "Ophelia Offcut?"

Tom didn't feel as abashed as he thought he would. "The lass has spirit."

"Yes, I know; she had quite a few here last night," she quipped. "And *you* weren't exactly holding back either. I thought you were a skilled hunter, Tom, one who liked a challenge. Anyone could snare Ophelia Offcut; all that's required is a half-unbuckled belt."

Tom was about to respond, but a young lad entered his vision, walking towards the table with a tray, looking self-conscious and uncertain. Following Tom's gaze, Mary twisted around in her chair.

"Ah, John," she said, obviously anticipating his appearance. Then tapping the table in front of Tom, she added, "Here's the patient."

John carefully placed the tray on the table and presented Tom with a complete breakfast selection: bacon, eggs, tomato, sausage, fresh bread, cheese, strawberry conserve, as well as a steaming brew of some herbal concoction. An hour or so ago he would have retched at the sight and smell of this much food, but now it all looked and smelled delicious.

"Anythin' else, Mistress?" asked the awkward serving boy.

"No, that'll be all, John," Mary replied pleasantly. "That should fix Master Skinner's overindulgence." Then she added with a wicked grin, "For the drink, at least."

Tom gave Mary a withering look. She raised her eyebrows playfully.

John twitched out a smile and headed back to the kitchen.

"Well, tuck in, Tom," she encouraged. "We only serve the best Offcut meat at The Harey Rabbit."

It was a while before Tom could take his first mouthful; he found it hard to stop laughing.

The conversation had become quite stilted as Tom scoffed down his breakfast. (The brew turned out to be camomile.) He'd asked Mary whether Lieutenant Swill had come to see him, but Mary informed him there'd been no messages from the castle. He explained that Brandon had missed their appointment with Administrator Penman and, consequently, the Witness Statement remained unsigned. She was perplexed about that and seemed surprised at Tom's complacent attitude. "I thought you wanted to see justice done?"

He shrugged. "I do. However, since no-one else seems interested in pursuing that particular course of action, what *can* I do? I won't be losing any sleep over it, that's for certes."

Mary gave him an appraising look. "So… nothing to do with spending the night with Ophelia?"

Tom felt a flush of resentment. How could Mary suggest such a thing. Was she jealous? Swallowing a mouthful of egg and sausage, Tom regarded his friend and host. Her olive skin coloured under his scrutiny and her eyelids fluttered over her clear blue eyes. "Sorry, Tom," she said, "that was uncalled for."

Tom nodded, his resentment ebbing. "Oh, I don't know, Mary. Who *knows* what I said to the girl."

It was an attempt to reclaim their easy banter, but his smile faded as he wondered whether Ophelia Offcut had, indeed, exacted a price for her company. What lustful boasts had he made to her?

CHAPTER 12
Two different worlds

TOM LEFT THE Harey Rabbit shortly after breakfast. There was no reason to stay. The disappearance of Xavier obviously took precedence over the Offcuts, and since he could not be of service to Richard in that matter, he may as well return to his forest home. In any case, there were tasks that needed attending to. Reg Puffy would be requiring venison and pheasant for the Duke of Stymouth's banquet, parts of the forest used by poachers hadn't been patrolled for some time, and there were always plenty of jobs to be done in and around his cottage.

He rode Wildflower at walking pace along the East Road, pausing occasionally to chat to farmers he recognised. By the time he reached the bridge, his saddlebags were stuffed with four bunches of carrots, a bag of potatoes, some onions and a handful of parsnips: the perfect ingredients for a rabbit stew (and Wildflower liked carrots).

Upon reaching the bridge, Tom looked north and tried to pinpoint the spot where he and Ophelia had lain together, but the thick reeds, glowing green in the mid-morning sun, obscured any sign of the exposed section of riverbank. He was relieved about that.

Across the bridge, he gave Wildflower her head and the mare took full advantage of her newfound freedom. Galloping south and slightly away from the river, she flew through the still air, as eager to return to the forest as Tom.

It didn't take long for Tom to settle back into his routine. After seeing to Wildflower, he walked to the river to collect some water, then prepared the tinder, kindling and wood for a fire. The hearth in his cottage was big enough to roast a good-sized boar, but tonight it would only have to cope with a rabbit or maybe, if the mood took him, some fresh river trout. He then spent some time laying traps along rabbit runs, using a thin twine to make nooses that would tighten against the base of a shrub when the rabbit (or whatever else) ran through it. It was unlikely he would catch anything before dusk, so he decided that he *would* go fishing after all.

It was mid-afternoon by the time Tom made it to his favourite fishing spot, just south of the Upper Bailey. Here, a small pool had been created on the leeside of two massive rocks that extended some ten or so feet into the river. They acted as a breakwater which the strong current swirled around. Over time, silt and pebbles had been deposited, creating the clear, shallow pool of calmness that existed today.

Tom used the pool to bathe. It was hidden from sight from most of the castle's vantage points — only a few of the higher windows in the east and south-facing walls of The Keep were positioned correctly to see Tom's pool. However, as far as he knew, the upper rooms of The Keep were virtually deserted these days, so the chances of anyone glancing down on him were extremely small. Yes, Tom felt quite relaxed in his own private piece of paradise.

Standing on the end of the breakwater, Tom cast out his net. It was conical in shape, trailing eight feet from a circular metal ring which was two feet in diameter. At the tapered end of the net, Tom had tied small pieces of polished metal to attract fish into the cone. Attached to the ring were two lengths of rope (some twenty feet long) which Tom secured to a jagged anchor point on the rock. Throwing the net towards the middle of the river, it hit with a dull splash and disappeared under the Icing's liquid skin. The ropes tensed and began angling parallel to the bank as the net was pulled downstream.

The sun beamed down on him, hot and bright. Tom cast his gaze towards the shadowed eastern side of the castle; it seemed as if the river divided two different worlds. The massive grey structure loomed ominously above the water. The Keep and Upper Bailey, built atop a steep rocky face, looked particularly foreboding. Somewhere in that world, Richard was going about his business… whatever *that* might be.

A bead of perspiration trickled down his face. Tom had sweated out last night's indulgence hours ago (last night… it seemed like a dream), but he still felt lethargic, and a soak in the pool was just the tonic he needed. He could also wash his shirt and undergarments.

He undressed and waded into the cool water. The small, smooth pebbles soothed the soles of his feet, cleansing and massaging them. After a few steps, the water reached his waist. He submerged himself up to his neck. Sticky sweat dissolved in the clear coolness. Then he let his head sink under the surface. Opening his eyes, the world was a silent murky blur, but Tom could just make out the shiny lures dancing in the net. Releasing the air in his lungs, he bubbled down to the bottom of the pool, totally at peace, immersed in a world where nothing mattered. He could easily stay here… he didn't really feel the need to breathe.

Practicalities brought Tom back to the surface. His clothes needed scrubbing and so did he. His methods were simple and effective: to clean his clothes, he washed and wrung them in the pool, then whacked them against a nearby rock before spreading them out to dry; to clean himself, he scrubbed his body with the coarse river sand found at the edge of the pool.

While his clothes dried, Tom made a thorough job of cleaning himself — Ophelia Offcut's reputation certainly played a part in his greater-than-usual attentiveness. After washing, Tom lay on the large rock closest to the bank and basked in the afternoon sun. On the other large rock, the ropes remained taught. For a moment, he felt dizzy — his head swirled with cool currents — but his senses soon adjusted to his horizontal position. He stared at the ropes as they twanged against the rock's jagged surface, strummed by the submerged net as it played in the current.

He closed his eyes, and suddenly he was aware of sounds: birds chirped and cried, insects buzzed and whined, even the silent river seemed to breathe. In the background, Tom heard snatches of castle life: raised voices yelling out orders, laughter, hammering, hooves on cobblestone, crashing kitchen implements, and a convergence of other sounds that couldn't be identified — the giant grey beast was alive. Again, Tom couldn't help but wonder at the contrasting worlds separated by the width of a river.

The brace of trout were just about done. He'd placed them, along with some diced potato, on a metal plate over a small hearth fire. Tom had also caught a rabbit in one of his snares; he'd have that tomorrow. The fire threw out enough light to fill the hearth, but the rest of Tom's cottage was shrouded in twilight shadow. It had been a long day, but he felt good. It was a relief to be back on this side of the river. Tomorrow he would ride out with Wildflower, patrol and explore deep into the forest, out of sight of the grey beast.

He leaned forward and carefully scraped the fish and potatoes onto a wooden plate. It smelt delicious. It tasted better. He washed it down with a couple of tankards of ale.

Fifteen minutes later he was climbing the ladder to his loft. He lay down on the straw mattress, completely sated, and was asleep within a couple of breaths. His dreams were of Ophelia: butcher's daughter to river nymph, foul mouth to sweet lips.

(Sometime during that hot summer night, as he dreamed, the Duke was attacked and Sid Evily walked home alone, cursing Doctor Manky for ruining his chances with Elsie.)

CHAPTER 13

The thrill of expectation

TOM AWOKE TO a chorus of birds, as he did every morning. The loft was stuffy; no breeze wafted through the open window and the trees were dark and still. It was going to be another hot day, but he was looking forward to it.

He sprang from his bed, eager to be about his business. As usual, his first task was to check on Wildflower. As he approached the mare he was rewarded with an excited whinny, and when he rubbed the side of her head, he received an affectionate nudge in return. Tom was sure Wildflower could read his mind; she was certainly able to sense when he planned to go riding.

He then went to the river to have a quick wash. By the time he returned to his cottage, the first rays of sunlight were twinkling through the deep hues of the early morning forest.

An hour later, he and Wildflower were away, cantering through woodland, walking across streams, climbing up hills, and galloping across meadows. This activity was punctuated by rests where Tom would go on foot to check for animal tracks or look for signs of poachers. Around midday, he reined in Wildflower by a small stream under the shade of an elm.

After both slaking their thirst in the stream, Tom replenished his water-skin and then tethered Wildflower to the elm. He removed her saddle and fed her some pieces of stale bread dripped with honey. Tom munched on a mixture of almonds, dried apricots and sultanas, and then had the remaining honey with a wedge of cheese.

He had chosen this spot because it was at the base of a hill whose summit provided one of the best vantage points in the Duke's Forest. He could safely leave Wildflower here; she could drink from the stream and there was plenty of fresh grass for her graze on.

It took thirty minutes to reach the summit. The trees began to thin out over the final stages as the acclivity increased and rocky outcrops began cropping up.

Still, the climb wasn't a taxing one and it was only the heat that made Tom sweat.

The eastern landscape was an undulating forest of summer green. Below and to his left, a strip of felled trees indicated the route of the East Road as it meandered its way towards the Duchy of Naffolk and eventually to the sea port of Great Naff. North of the road, the forest thinned as the land flattened out. Farther north, the land rose again into a series of ridges (the largest of which was known as Dragon's Back) and, farther still, towards the horizon, a range of mountain peaks, the tallest of which was Mount Icing (from which the Icing River flowed, on which Lower Icing was settled).

Turning around, he cast his gaze west. Lower Icing was about eight miles away as the crow flies. Set upon its sloping site, the castle looked like it was sinking into the forest. Tom wondered if it was an omen.

Scanning the immediate surrounds, Tom could see nothing untoward — no obvious signs of poachers. The valley to his east was patched with grasslands and was a favourite grazing place for deer. None were there today, not in the open at least. Like most creatures, staying in the shade was the preferred option.

Tom sat and listened for a while. If it wasn't for the birds and insects, this world would have no sound. He decided not to explore the valley today; instead, he chose to head back to his cottage and try his luck at hunting some pheasant on the way. Tomorrow, he'd start fresh and provisioned, ready for camping overnight at the valley.

Satisfied with his plan, Tom made his way back down the hill to where Wildflower grazed contentedly. He checked her feet; her shoes were intact and her hooves clean. Slapping her affectionately on her chestnut rump, he mounted the good-natured mare. Nudging her into a canter, Tom retraced his route south along the stream, before crossing at a very shallow ford — more a collection of wet rocks and pebbles — and heading west towards Lower Icing and his cottage. Now he could dedicate the rest of the afternoon to finding some of the 'Duke's Poultry' to add to his paltry rabbit.

Pheasants opted for thick grassland or woodland foliage in which to build their nests. They were hiders; they had to be, since they tended not to fly (if they could help it). However, their ability to secrete themselves was no match for Tom's ability to find them. In fact, they were fairly easy prey for most predators. Still, stealth was required, because they certainly knew how to run.

An hour or so later, Tom brought Wildflower to a halt near a small clearing. Dismounting, he hooked the reins over a broken branch and stood silently, watching and listening. On the other side of the clearing, some fifty paces away, was a copse of elder trees, their black berries glistening in the sun. He'd been here before. He always remembered the location of elder trees; their berries had wonderful curative effects and doubled as a refreshing drink when crushed and mixed with water. Elderberry wine had been a popular drink with the families at Wet Crossing, but Tom had neither the patience nor the expertise for such an undertaking. However, he would pick as many of the summer-ripe berries as he could load into his saddlebags, regardless of whether or not he bagged himself a pheasant.

It seemed like he hadn't used his bow in ages, and the thought of pitting his skill against the guiles of the animal kingdom filled him with excited anticipation. He gripped the ash and yew bow in his left hand and pulled the string with his right — the tension felt good, the supple texture of the wood grains were extremely flexible. Tom often wondered how anyone could work with yew. Just about every part of the tree, from its leaves to its bark, was highly poisonous.

Slinging a quiver of twenty arrows across his left shoulder, Tom made his way quietly across the clearing. He stopped at the trunk of the first elder tree and listened. Sure enough, amidst the calls of larks and the whining buzz of the occasional fly, Tom heard the raspy, double squawk of the pheasant — like a rooster's cock-a-doodle-doo without the doodle-doo. Other pheasants answered. Reaching into his quiver, he retrieved an arrow and nocked it, ready to pull and release. His eyes had now adjusted to the blue shade of the copse and he advanced as quietly as possible into the thick undergrowth, bow extended in front of him.

As Tom moved further into the copse, he brushed against bushes and low-hanging branches, and more insects were beginning to land on his neck and face. After about thirty stealthy paces, he stopped again, shook his head free of the clinging flies and, again, listened — he could now discern a nervous fluttering sound. Tom squatted down to give himself a pheasants-eye view, but the foliage was so thick, anything farther than a few paces away was obscured by a tangle of greenery. He knew he was close. He had to be ready to fire; he would only get one chance. Three steps later, the undergrowth exploded with the sounds of flapping and squawking. The copse was suddenly alive. Tom quickly drew back his arrow. He caught flashes of speckled brown, but they were gone in an instant. He ran forward, and more pheasants erupted from their nests. The foliage suddenly became less dense, and the red head of a large male ran across his vision. Tom released his arrow, and the pheasant fluttered to a squawking halt. He let out a victorious cry.

Tom was still feeling jubilant when he and Wildflower emerged from the forest proper into the familiar elm-surroundings of his cottage. The pheasant dangled by its feet, tied to the straps of one of the saddlebags. The bags themselves were bulging with elderberries. Tom had even managed to salvage the arrow that pierced the heart of the unfortunate bird. Yes, it had been a good day.

After unburdening Wildflower of her saddle and bags, he brushed her down, fed her some carrots, and secured her in the stable where she would rest comfortably after a good day's exercise. Tom then set about creating his own creature comforts. Firstly, he skinned the rabbit he'd caught yesterday and cut its flesh into bite-sized pieces, along with the parsnip, potatoes and onions he'd bought from the farmers; he would have rabbit stew tonight. Then he plucked and hung the pheasant, which he would roast tonight and take with him on his explorations tomorrow.

It wasn't until after dinner, as he slowly drained the ale from his tankard, that he thought about Richard, the Offcuts and the missing heir to the Duchy. Was he still missing? Were Frank and Billy still in The Can or had they been released? Funny… he didn't really care; he was tired all of a sudden. The only part of his recent visit to Lower Icing he wouldn't mind revisiting was Ophelia Offcut. That thought in mind, he wearily doused the remnants of the fire, wrapped the roasted pheasant in a heavy muslin cloth, climbed the ladder to his loft, and promptly fell asleep as the sun finally clocked-off its fifteen-hour shift.

Chapter 14

That particular saddle

TOM WOKE BEFORE dawn and began provisioning for the two full days and the one night he'd be away from the cottage: food, water, flint, a small pot for boiling water and vegetables, spare clothing and his deerskin sleeping mat (he wouldn't need to worry about shelter; it was going to be another hot, dry day), his bow (and sword for self-defence; an unlikely scenario, but better to be safe than sorry), and some treats for Wildflower. After double-checking he had everything he needed, it was time to bathe.

The sun was yet to make an appearance as he made his way to his pool, but dawn couldn't be far off now. The croaking of frogs heralded the proximity of the river, but Tom didn't require any assistance to find his way; he knew each of the two-hundred paces from his cottage to the pool.

Naked, Tom slid into the dark water — the cool pebbles rubbing soothingly against his skin. It was, as always, invigorating; although, in this heat, it was also refreshing. He ducked his head under the surface — it felt wonderful to shed himself of sweat and grime. Gliding to the edge of the pool, he grabbed a handful of sand and began scrubbing his hair and face. Then he worked his way down his neck, torso, legs and feet, rinsing at regular intervals. During the process, the violet rays of a new dawn appeared on the eastern walls of the castle; it was an eerie sight. As if on cue, the first sounds from Reg Puffy's kitchen carried through the stillness, momentarily silencing the frogs.

By the time Tom had washed, dried and clothed himself, the violet walls shimmered bronze and the grey beast had stirred into wakefulness. In contrast, his side of the river was still shrouded in gloom. However, Tom felt anything but gloomy as he strode back into the forest.

Approaching his cottage, Tom stopped in his tracks. Through the trees, he saw a black horse tethered next to Wildflower. Tom felt uneasy rather than fearful; whoever was dropping in at this hour would only be bringing bad news (or *was* bad news). He closed in on the stable. Wildflower seemed content to mind her own business as Tom approached the other horse.

Like Wildflower, she was a mare, but a few years her junior — judging by her teeth and her height, she was around three years old. She was quite at ease with Tom's inspection and was obviously well trained. She was also in immaculate condition; her black coat glistened in the early morning light, but this was partly due to the fact that it was slick with sweat. He could feel the heat radiating from her. The ride here must have been made with some urgency.

Then, looking at the saddle, the identity of the rider was revealed. He could hardly credit it; he never thought he'd see the day where *that* particular saddle was strapped to a mare. Tom had only ever seen it astride a fiery black stallion called Black Beasty.

It was with a sense of foreboding that Tom walked across the threshold of his cottage into the shadowy interior. The rider was standing over Tom's table, picking at his roast pheasant, barely discernible in his black attire.

"Morning Tom," said the figure, casually placing a chunk of breast into his mouth. "Hope you don't mind the intrusion. I *did* knock."

"Not at all," replied Tom with equal nonchalance; their casual banter was so ingrained that it overrode normal reactions. "So, what brings the Seneschal of Lower Icing to these humble surrounds at such an hour, and on a *mare!* Your need must be great indeed, Richard."

He smiled. "Beasty is being re-shod, and since it was dark I thought I would risk the public ridicule." Then his smile faded. "And my need, as you put it, is, unfortunately, great."

A chill ran through Tom's spine. "Has the Duke found out about his son?"

"Sit down, Tom." Richard gestured towards a seat at the table as if it were his own.

Tom's heart was suddenly beating faster as they both sat. "You haven't been banished, have you?" he quipped, only half-jesting.

"Do you have anything to drink, Tom?"

Even in the dull light, Tom could see the strained expression on his friend's face. He wasn't a man who accepted fallibility, particularly in himself; it was disturbing to see.

"Richard?" Tom pressed, worried now.

His dark eyes darted towards Tom. "I haven't been banished. Not yet, at least. The Duke is gravely ill: he's been poisoned."

Poisoned? Tom could hardly believe what he'd just heard. Before he could gather his thoughts, Richard added, "And it seems there is an air of suspicion floating around *me*."

CHAPTER 15

Ever the storyteller

THEY'D JUST ABOUT emptied a jug of cider by the time Richard had recounted the events of the last three days. They'd also eaten most of Tom's camping rations. Not that it mattered; he would not be riding to the valley after such a revelation. Richard had scoffed down the food as if he'd been fasting for the last three days. He also looked like he hadn't slept for three days, and had admitted as much, saying, "My mind will not let me be, Tom. No matter how weary I am, it keeps me awake, taunting me with what I might have done differently. This morning, I could not bear it a moment longer, lying in wait for another day, so I came seeking the ear of a trusted friend in the hope that it would ease my restlessness."

At first, Tom had bombarded Richard with questions. What happened? When did it happen? Is the Duke likely to recover? Why are you suspected? Has Xavier been found? What about this Bertrand character? It all seemed so incredible!

Richard had calmly informed Tom that the Duke had been attacked on Friday night by an unknown assailant, cut on the arm with a poisoned blade, and he'd been in a semi-conscious state, unable to speak, ever since. Doctor Whysman was tending to his needs as best he could. However, the symptoms were unfamiliar to him. The treatment, thus far, had been based on trial and error, and, while not successful, the Duke didn't appear to be any worse.

This had caused another broadside of questions from Tom, to which Richard had responded by holding up his hands in mock capitulation. "Allow me to start at the beginning," he'd said wearily. "I will explain all that has transpired since the rather abrupt conclusion of our breakfast on Thursday morning."

He began by saying how relieved he'd been to find the Duke alone in his quarters. However, as a precaution, he'd ordered Lieutenant Swill to post extra guards at the Upper Bailey estate. (Tom had silently wondered if Jock McHaggis and Paddy O'Limerick were who Richard had had in mind.) He'd also put extra patrols on the street, and set the task of finding the young doctor to the Purple Perillian.

"You see, Tom, I had made the decision to *present* Xavier to Marmaduke. 'His most trusted subject' I believe you called me. And you were right; for good or ill, it was time this matter was brought into the open. However, Marmaduke needed to be prepared; I couldn't allow Xavier to just walk in unannounced."

Worryingly, Brandon had no luck in finding Xavier; the young doctor hadn't returned to The Bloody Bell or been seen anywhere else in Lower Icing. Even the mounted patrol that had been organised to scour the North Road had returned without their quarry. It explained why Brandon hadn't been available to sign the arrest document that afternoon. However, it seemed odd for a man of his regimen not to send word to Tom, or Administrator Penman for that matter.

This put Richard into a quandary. Did he still broach the subject of Xavier to the Duke. "I must admit, I was tempted to let sleeping dogs lie, but that just put me in mind of Bertrand and his bloody Deed of Promise."

Richard then explained to Tom about the Swills, their ties to Blessed Whipping, and how their daughter had been 'promised' to the community by the time of her eighteenth birthday. And because the Swills had refused to comply, Bertrand had begun pressuring Richard to ratify this deed, implying he would divulge the existence of Xavier to the *populace* if Richard refused.

Tom kept the fact that he already knew about Bethany Swill's predicament to himself. There was nothing to be gained by divulging the conversation he and Brandon had shared. Knowledge aside, Tom couldn't help thinking the situation with Bertrand was largely of Richard's own making. If he'd been open with the Duke from the start, when Bertrand had first presented him with a copy of the doctor's letter, none of this would have come to pass. And, in any case, Tom believed Richard had a moral obligation to protect the Swills from the likes of Bertrand. However, it seemed moral obligation and politics made strange bedfellows.

Richard continued by describing how he'd finally revealed the existence of Xavier to the Duke; it had been later that night, while he and Marmaduke were relaxing in the Duke's chambers, partaking of a rather fine after-dinner wine (a Chateau de la Chat from the renowned Rouge-Blanc region of Escargotia — a neighbouring country separated from the Five Duchies by a channel of water known as The Funnel).

"He was in good spirits," Richard explained. "Preparations for the Duke of Stymouth's visit were ahead of schedule and he was optimistic about the outcome, buoyed by the fact that the Stymouth's two eldest sons were part of the retinue. Marmaduke saw it as an opportunity to build a longer-lasting relationship, one that would significantly benefit both Duchies. The mention of Stymouth's sons presented an opening I could not ignore: a celestial nudge, if you will. So I responded: 'What of *your* son, Marmaduke? Would not *his* presence *also* be a boon to the gathering?'"

Richard reached for his tankard and took a large gulp of cider, orchestrated, no doubt, to build suspense. Richard was ever the storyteller. "Marmaduke said nothing to begin with. He just looked at me — brown eyes unmoving, eyelids unflinching — frozen in the act of sipping his wine. Then his face drained of all colour, the wine in his glass looking like blood. It was a disturbing sight, Tom, and what made it even *more* disturbing was that, for the first time, I realised there *was* a resemblance between him and Xavier. Not so much in looks, perhaps, but in the expression of naïve realisation, the introspective gaze."

Tom had never met Xavier, but, taking Richard at his word, it made Richard's treatment of the young doctor even more perplexing. It was also the first time he'd heard Richard personally recognise the relationship.

"Marmaduke slowly placed his glass down on the table. It hardly made a sound. In fact, everything was eerily quiet. Then, in a ghostly whisper, he replied, 'Our son died twenty years ago.' I could only imagine the pain behind those words, but his haunted expression spoke volumes. I reached out to him and told him that Xavier was in Lower Icing and wanted to meet him. He recoiled from my outstretched hand as if it was a viper. The look he gave me, Tom…"

Richard paused, shaking his head at the memory. Tom had never seen his friend like this. He always projected self-assuredness, no matter what the predicament, but at that moment he seemed utterly lost.

He went on to say that the Duke had refused to discuss the matter, even after Richard had pressed him with knowledge of the letters to Doctor Manky: the 'men of great learning' at Blessed Whipping who were 'very dear to the Ducal heart', and the fact that he had been shown a different letter by Xavier himself as proof of his relationship to the Duke. His words had fallen upon defiantly deaf ears; he'd been ordered from the Duke's presence with the clear instruction that this matter was never to be raised again or spoken of to anyone.

Tom found the Duke's reaction incredible, to say the least. His son had discovered the truth about their relationship *and* come looking for him. Regardless of what had happened in the past, to dismiss the existence of one's own son seemed incomprehensible to Tom.

Richard recounted how he'd returned to his chambers, feeling sick to the stomach, wondering if he'd caused irreconcilable damage to his relationship with the Duke. The night passed slowly for him — agonisingly so.

When Friday morning finally arrived, it only brought an increasing amount of frustration and concern as each hour went by without Xavier being found. Despite maintaining the extra patrols, the young doctor's whereabouts remained a mystery. Adding to Richard's worries was the fact that the Duke refused to see him.

It wasn't until later in the day that Richard, along with Paris Le Sharp, Fraser Coin (head of the Merchant's Guild) and Gerald Hiepants, was permitted entry into the Ducal chambers for the usual Friday 'Five at Five' meeting. (Each Friday at five o'clock, the five of them gathered to discuss newsworthy topics for the Saturday afternoon Proclamation; it was Fraser Coin who had coined the phrase.)

Fraser Coin, Tom mused. He was the pipe-smoking buffoon who had antagonised Ophelia in the lounge area outside Prestwich's office. He thought he'd recognised those ruddy, jowly features, but it was hard to tell through all the smoke and, truth to be told, his gaze had been somewhat fixated on Ophelia's curvaceous form.

His moment of reflection was broken by Richard's weary, "Not boring you, am I, Tom?"

Tom reddened, but Richard continued without further comment. "As I was saying, we were assembled in the Duke's chambers. I don't know what I had been expecting, but certainly *not* what transpired. It left me wondering whether Marmaduke had fallen into madness… or, more likely, I had pushed him there."

Tom's first thought, judging by Richard's downcast features and air of bewilderment, was that his friend had been stripped of his title and renounced as heir. Neither of those things, however, occurred. According to Richard, the Duke, who usually played the role of quiet observer during these Five at Five meetings, dominated proceedings with an extreme fervour hitherto unseen in the circumspect ruler.

"It was a performance one would expect from a travelling troubadour desperate for a substantial patronage. Marmaduke was madly animated and verbosely optimistic about Stymouth's visit, calling it a defining moment in Lower Icing's history. It was a bizarre display. It's not often Fraser Coin is lost for words, but he, too, was struck dumb by the Duke's behaviour. At one point, Le Sharp thrust himself into the fray by mentioning that the Moleson Twins had been released from The Can that morning and suggesting the Proclamation include an announcement pertaining to the assignment of extra patrolmen, reasoning, quite rightly, that such action would be welcomed by most villagers."

Tom also thought it fitted in very nicely with the fact that the extra men were also looking for a young, blond-haired man, last seen wearing a white silk shirt, deep green velvet doublet, and white trousers tucked into knee-high black leather boots.

"However, Le Sharp's attempt was foiled by Marmaduke's total disregard for any subject other than the banquet. My own attempts at rationality were also blatantly ignored. I even found myself hoping the Town Crier would say something typically inane to distract the Duke from his ranting. Unfortunately, the fool was too busy scribing, trying to record the details for his proclamation: the seating arrangements, the number of courses, the order of the speeches, the choice of entertainment, the diplomatic objectives, the equal representation of Stymouth's colours. It was beyond belief, Tom, the amount of information Marmaduke was spewing forth."

Tom shared Richard's disbelief, and also wondered whether madness *had* claimed the Duke.

"It was only after a brief debrief with a shaken Le Sharp and Coin that the Town Crier finally opened his mouth. He followed me back to my office, spouting some useless drivel about how he'd have to work most of the night to create a proclamation worthy of the Duke's high spirits." Richard scoffed at the memory. "High spirits; *that* was an understatement. I asked him if he was at all alarmed by the Duke's behaviour. You can't imagine the idiot's response, Tom."

Richard shook his head in despair. "He thought it was a *nice change* to see the Duke so happy. *Happy?* Can a man be *that* dim-witted? I couldn't help myself; I had to ask him why he thought the Duke was happy. 'Come now, Sir Richard,' he said in that pompous voice of his, 'no need to be coy. I think it's marvellous you've told the Duke about Xavier.' Then, as if we had a secret pact or some such nonsense, he tapped the side of his nose and said, 'I have a feeling my next proclamation may contain something a touch more momentous than the Duke of Stymouth's banquet, what.'"

Tom smiled at Richard's rather accurate impersonation of the Town Crier, but Richard appeared not to notice.

"As he walked off," he continued, "I actually found myself wondering if the man was all there. I mean, how could have he come to the conclusion that Marmaduke's ramblings were a result of some sort of euphoria over Xavier?

If that were the case, wouldn't you expect the Duke to actually *convey* the euphoric news and not harp on about music selections or wax lyrical about candles? Yet *somehow*…"

Richard shook his head in bewilderment, and Tom added, "He'd made the right connection."

The sun had begun to streak through the trees, illuminating Richard's face in a muted gold which accentuated his dark, chiselled features and highlighted the fact that he hadn't shaved that morning. Apart from their hunting trips, Tom couldn't remember a time when he'd seen Richard anything other than perfectly manicured.

His friend reached for his tankard. "As it turned out, the Town Crier's feeling about the proclamation was more prophetic than either of us could have possibly imagined." He took another deep mouthful of sweet cider, but it failed to remove the bitterness from his face. Still, he pressed on with his recounting.

Richard had been alerted early Saturday morning about the attack on the Duke. He'd been in the process of trimming his beard when Prestwich brought him the news. The edgy secretary had suddenly appeared at Richard's side, apparently out of thin air. "I sometimes wonder if the man was raised by sprites," Richard remarked.

Prestwich informed him that Doctor Whysman had been sent for, and, as he scampered in the wake of Richard's bounding gait, also managed to convey other information: that the Duke's condition had only been discovered in the last fifteen minutes and that the person who'd made the discovery was the Duke's personal attendant — a young squire from Spitting Dipthong named Bradley Lamb.

"Hardly illuminating." Richard sniffed. "Except, perhaps, to highlight the inadequacies of the Upper Baily security. Remember what I said about complacency, Tom? Truly, it is an affliction one needs to constantly guard against. I've let my guard down, and the consequences could not be more dire."

Richard paused for a swig of cider, and Tom took the opportunity to remind his friend that it was virtually impossible to guard against such evil intent.

"I have been a fool!" he shouted, slamming down his mug. Recovering his composure, he added quietly, almost to himself, "No doubt keeping Xavier well amused."

At first, the realisation that Richard suspected Xavier seemed strange to Tom. However, the more he thought about it, the more it made perfect sense. Xavier could well be the Duke's son, but what if he'd come to Lower Icing with vengeful intent? The 'two doctors' story could be an elaborate hoax, the letter a work of fiction. Tom had suggested as much when Richard had shown him the report from Bertrand, his so-called observer. In fact, Xavier and Bertrand could be in collusion, and had devised the whole plan to their mutual benefit. Tom voiced his outrage as Richard helped himself to a wedge of cheese and some bread. "How can *you* possibly be suspected?"

Richard smiled bitterly. "Indulge me a while longer, Tom. There are many things that make no sense, including the way Marmaduke was attacked."

He proceeded to describe the scene in the Duke's bedchamber: the room empty and undisturbed except for Bradly Lamb kneeling at the Duke's bedside, holding a makeshift bandage against the Duke's left arm between the elbow and the shoulder. The Duke lay motionless, as if in a deep sleep. It was oddly serene and tender, not what Richard had expected from an act of violent trespass.

"It wasn't until I drew closer to the bed that I noticed the blood-stained sheets," Richard commented. "I could tell by the amount of blood on the bed, and its brownish hue, that the wound wasn't life threatening and had stopped bleeding some hours before. Marmaduke looked pale, but quite peaceful. Squire Lamb, however, looked deathly ill and was quite distressed. He even had the effrontery to tell me to get a doctor, that the Duke was bleeding to death. He was obviously in a state of shock, but before I could address the situation, Whysman was rushed into the room, accompanied by a couple of guards."

Richard ordered the guards to shut the door and admit no-one, leaving Bradley Lamb, Doctor Whysman, Prestwich and himself alone in the bedchamber of the stricken Duke. The presence of the doctor did not quell the squire's distress — shock had deluded him into thinking the Duke was bleeding profusely and that if he didn't keep pressure on the bandage, the Duke would die. In the end, Richard sent Prestwich to fetch the guards. Their attempt to physically remove the squire proved to be unexpectedly tough. Bradley Lamb, built like an ox, was further strengthened by his deluded belief, and even with one hand pressed against the Duke's wound, he was more than a match for the two guards. Richard put an end to the struggle by rapping the squire on the back of the head with the pommel of his dagger.

"It was a farcical situation," Richard remarked without humour. "Whysman also got himself tangled in the fray somehow and was accidently knocked to the ground by one of the guards. Fortunately, no damage was done. The same, however, could not be said for the squire. He was unconscious, but it was a case of needs must, and, as it turned out, when I questioned him later, the blow had knocked some sense into him."

Tom shook his head in disbelief. His perception of the castle and how it operated was being smashed away by Richard's words. Were the massive stone walls that had stood for over one hundred years just an *illusion* of strength and unity? Were they, in truth, being undermined by incompetence and disharmony? It certainly seemed that way, and it made Tom think how lucky he was to have his forest world, covered by changing skies, nurtured and cleansed by the seasons, fed by streams and rivers, and sustained by an abundance of wildlife. There was nothing pretentious about *his* castle.

"While the guards dragged the squire to a divan in the corner of the chamber, Whysman finally set about the task of examining Marmaduke, during which time Prestwich began pacing around the chamber, offering frequent updates on the squire's condition. It became so irritating I was tempted to use the calming influence of my dagger for a second time. Instead, I ordered him to fetch Lieutenant Swill. I needed someone with a modicum of common sense and enough initiative to undertake a proper search of the Upper Bailey."

The last time Tom had seen Brandon, the Purple Perillian had been on his way to confront Richard with his suspicions of Bertrand's underhanded dealings — well-founded suspicions, as it turned out. However, according to Richard, the lieutenant had been diligently searching for Xavier. His sense of duty had obviously overridden any personal conflict he had with Richard. Then again, thought Tom, with Xavier's disappearance, the hold Bertrand had over Richard would have loosened considerably, and, by extension, so would the pressure to ratify the Elder's deed. Perhaps Brandon had taken matters into his own hands. Perhaps the Purple Perillian knew exactly where *not* to look for Xavier. It provided food for thought while Richard scoffed down more bread, cheese and cider, before relaying Doctor Whysman's diagnosis.

"He began by stating the obvious: the wound was superficial, no more than a deep gash that could be easily stitched. However, he had no definite explanation for Marmaduke's condition; his breathing was soft, his pulse weak but steady. His skin felt cold to the touch, yet a faint sheen of sweat covered his forehead. That's when Whysman told me he suspected a poisoned blade — it explained the small wound at least. He sniffed the congealing gash for a clue as to the nature of the poison, but he could discern nothing useful like the tincture of henbane or deadly nightshade."

Richard stood up, catching Tom by surprise, and walked to the front window of the cottage. Tom watched his friend gaze out at the forest green morning, breathing in the warm elm-leaf air.

"Are you alright, Richard?" Tom asked, thinking that the cider, pheasant and cheese might have been too much for Richard's neglected stomach.

Richard sat on the window sill and smiled sardonically. "As I said before, the nature of Marmaduke's attack makes no sense. Most poisons are administered with the intent to kill. So, it begs the question, what was the intent of the poisoner? Apart from occasional incoherent ramblings, Marmaduke's condition does not seem to have altered. Is he to remain this way? I have been expecting some sort of demand in return for the antidote, but that now seems unlikely."

It made no sense to Tom either. A darker thought then entered his mind: "Might the wound have been self-inflicted?"

"That crossed my mind also," Richard replied, "particularly in light of Marmaduke's recent behaviour, but why administer a poison in such a bizarre way? And where did he put the knife? Nothing was found at his bedside, inside his quarters, or anywhere else in the Upper Bailey. And, again, why choose a poison with such an indefinite outcome?"

Richard's reasoning was sound, particularly since no weapon had been found.

"This was an attack, Tom," Richard continued, his black frame dappled with morning sunlight. "The disappearance of Xavier is no coincidence, and he has in his possession a case of vials and jars that contain all kinds of unusual powders, liquids and unguents. It seems obvious to me that he is, in some way at least, responsible for Marmaduke's condition." Richard seemed reticent to accuse Xavier of the actual attack.

"But not capable of the act?" Tom queried.

"Whatever else he may be," Richard responded, "Xavier doesn't strike me as the knife-wielding type, which leads me to think he has an accomplice. My so-called observer at Blessed Whipping immediately springs to mind."

So, Richard had also drawn a connection between Xavier and Bertrand. Tom considered mentioning the other scenario involving Brandon, but it suddenly seemed less plausible; he doubted the Purple Perillian would stoop to abduction or false imprisonment to protect his sister. And Tom didn't think it was in his nature to disobey orders. If he'd found Xavier, he would have informed Richard; Brandon struck Tom as an honourable man. Something, it seemed, this Bertrand could not claim to be.

Then another thought occurred to Tom. "What if Xavier is being held against his will, and was forced, somehow, to create the poison?"

Richard remained silent for quite some time, as if considering Tom's remark.

Nodding his head slightly, he'd eventually responded, "Possibly. That could explain why the poison has not proven fatal."

Richard pushed himself away from the window sill. "I have to get back to the castle, Tom," he announced. "Time to rattle a few cages. Then we'll see..." He left the sentence hanging and moved back towards the table.

"I need someone I can trust," he said leaning against the table. "Will you help me?"

"Of course, Richard, but—"

"But what?"

Tom wanted to know what Richard had in mind, and he *still* had no idea why Richard was suspected of poisoning of the Duke, and said as much to his agitated friend.

Richard acknowledged the oversight with a grimace. "Come, I will explain while you saddle Wildflower." Then, as an afterthought, he added, "You *do* believe I had nothing to do with Marmaduke's attack, don't you, Tom?"

Tom looked at his friend's stern, stubbled visage, dark eyes piercing into his. He met his gaze. "Of course, Richard."

CHAPTER 16

Some sort of piss-take?

DAPPLED BY THE canopy of elms, the sun seemed unusually bright this morning. Tom and Richard had been talking for over an hour, and the gloomy confines of his cottage had masked the progression of the day. It must be almost eight o'clock, thought Tom, as he stepped outside, saddle in hand.

Richard was already at the stable, securing Wildflower's bridle. The chestnut mare, indulgently calm under his urgent handling, looked relieved to see Tom. Richard's black mare remained nonchalantly aloof.

"I hope you don't treat Black Beasty so carelessly," Tom remarked as he approached.

"Isn't it time you acquired a real horse," Richard retorted, then added, "That's not a side-saddle is it?"

Ignoring the jibe, Tom heaved the saddle over Wildflower's back as Richard finished adjusting the choke strap. "Very well, Richard. I'm all ears. Why are you suspected of the Duke's attack and what do you intend to do about it?"

"A silver button was found in Marmaduke's bed chamber."

He'd said it so perfunctorily that Tom thought he'd misheard. "A silver button?"

"One of *my* silver buttons, to be precise."

Richard stepped around Wildflower's head while Tom pulled the girth strap around the mare's belly. Moving next to Tom, he pointed to the sleeve of his doublet. Three silver buttons glistened against the black material. They were roughly three-quarters of an inch in diameter, engraved with Richard's quill and broken sword insignia. Then he noticed the frayed material next to the button closest to the cuff — clearly, one had come off. Just in case Tom hadn't spotted the missing accoutrement, Richard thrust out his right arm for comparison and, sure enough, it had four buttons.

"I don't understand, Richard," said Tom, as his friend lowered his arms. "Surely the appearance of your button is easily explained."

"Easily *explained*; yes. Not so easily believed, however."

Tom tightened and secured the buckle of the girth strap, then turned to face his friend. "I saw how loose it was after Frank Offcut grabbed your arm."

"*You* saw how loose it was," said Richard, clearly frustrated. "In any case, it could have easily been ripped off during the scuffle with Bradley Lamb."

"Exactly," Tom concurred. "So why is there any doubt?"

Richard shook his head and sighed. "Because of *where* it was found."

He seemed reluctant to continue. "Well?" Tom prompted.

"According to Lieutenant Swill, it was discovered clasped in Marmaduke's hand," Richard said in a voice little more than a whisper.

Tom was momentarily lost for words. No wonder Richard had put off telling him this part of the story. Then his incredulousness found voice: "Someone must have put it there."

"Well, of course someone put it there!"

"Who discovered it?" asked Tom, ignoring his friend's tone.

"Whysman. But the point is, I had no—"

As if sensing the tension, Wildflower suddenly shook her head and skittered a couple of steps forward. Richard casually grabbed her rein and handed it to Tom, before continuing.

"I had no idea I'd *lost* the button, let alone that it'd been found in Marmaduke's hand. It wasn't until yesterday afternoon, *after* the proclamation, that I discovered *that* particular fact. After our fool of a Town Crier had taken matters into his own hands."

"Really? In what way?" Gerald's hands appeared to be at full capacity ringing the bell and rolling out the proclamations.

"Sometime during the morning, he ran into Whysman, who was on his way back to his house to get a tonic or potion, or some such witchery — doctors clutching at straws as usual. In any case, not only did he tell the Town Crier about the attack, he told him about the button *and*, if you can credit it, gave it to him to for safe keeping."

"Safe keeping? Gerald Hiepants?" Tom repeated in disbelief. "What possessed the man to do *that*, and why didn't he come straight to you?" The doctor's actions defied reason.

"I was questioning Bradley Lamb, and I'd told the guards that I was not to be disturbed under any circumstances, save a change in Marmaduke's condition. Supposedly, Whysman tried to inform me of the button, but couldn't gain admittance." He shook his head in disgust and moved towards his black mare.

"Fine time for the guards to begin acting like guards."

Tom watched his friend untether the reins. "So, you're telling me Gerald Hiepants knew about the button before you?"

"Not only that, he proclaimed the facts, as he *mis*understood them, to the townsfolk."

"Without your consent?" Tom was amazed the attack on the Duke had caused so much confusion and revealed so much ineptness.

"*That* small detail seems to have conveniently eluded the Town Crier," Richard said, pulling the black mare alongside Wildflower. "Now the townsfolk are under the misconception that an *unharmed* Duke grappled with an intruder and, as said intruder made his escape, a silver button tore from his clothing."

Tom scoffed, disbelievingly. "Surely this is some sort of piss-take?"

"I wish it was, my friend." A sheen of sweat was beginning to show on Richard's face; his propensity to wear black was not conducive to the summer sun, even in the relatively cool and shady surrounds of Tom's cottage. "He even had the button *displayed* during the proclamation and offered a reward of a hundred gold pieces for bringing the owner of the button to justice."

This was incredible. What had possessed Gerald to invent such a fantastic version of events? Tom shook his head. "Where were Le Sharp and the men-at-arms while all this was unfolding? How could this happen, Richard?"

Judging by his friend's reaction, Tom's disbelief must have sounded more like an accusation.

"Because I am surrounded by incompetence and idiocy! Shall I tell you what Master Hiepant's said when I asked him why he'd changed the content of his proclamation without informing me?" Again the horses became restless; Richard's jaw clenched as he reined in his mare *and* his temper. "He said *Klob Hoofenhaus* inspired him to write it! *That's* the kind of buffoonery I have to deal with!"

Richard then hurled himself onto his saddle, the mare snorting at his angry mount. "Come, Tom. I am eager to return to the castle."

It only took a few minutes to reach the Town Square. Richard had set a fast past through the forest, and, as they galloped along the East Road, across the Icing Bridge, past the cultivated fields, towards the town, he seemed to have little regard for the Lower Icingers or their cart-loads of produce.

Today was a market day; there was a steady stream of people funnelling down Market Street and, as usual, The Bloody Bell was a hive of activity. The Square was also quite busy with a gathering of people waiting to collect their water before the day became too hot.

Richard had slowed the pace of his horse to a walk, much to Tom's relief; it would be foolhardy in the extreme to gallop on these cobblestones. Tom and Richard, riding abreast, were treated to a variety of gazes as they neared the well, ranging from happy and excited (mainly from children) to deferential and suspicious. Richard seemed oblivious to them all. Instead, he drew closer to Tom and indicated the news stand just to their right. "See for yourself the mad ramblings posted by our Town Crier."

Tom steered Wildflower towards the wooden stand. Even astride his saddle, Tom had a clear view of the proclamation pinned safely behind the glass covering. It was all as Richard described, but Tom was surprised by the sketch of the 'missing' button and the offer of such a substantial reward. He turned back to face his friend. "Why is this rubbish still here?"

Richard smiled. "It suits me to leave it there." He seemed to be re-energised from the ride and back to his commanding best. "In fact, the Town Crier may have inadvertently done the Duchy and I a good service. Let the townsfolk partake of this imaginary treasure hunt — who knows what they may uncover — and in the meantime, *we* can concentrate on discovering the whereabouts of Xavier and get to the bottom of all this."

"You're convinced he's still in Lower Icing?"

"Not convinced. However, thanks to your insightfulness, Tom, I believe he may be."

CHAPTER 17

Confusing deference with defiance

TOM AND RICHARD left their mounts in the charge of a couple of eager stable-hands who seemed to work *and* live in the barracks' stable.

Ignoring the salutes of a number of guardsmen, Richard strode quickly towards The Can. Tom matched his pace, but not his sense of urgency — the Seneschal of Lower Icing was on a mission. In the little time they'd had to discuss the matter, it seemed Richard intended to start 'getting to the bottom of all this' by making Frank Offcut an offer he couldn't refuse.

The stink of The Can reached Tom well before they entered the linear stone structure built against an inner castle wall. On the other side of the wall was the Lower Bailey's Administration Section (which had to deal with its own unsavoury characters — less pungent perhaps, but just as nauseating).

Two bored-looking guardsmen jumped to attention as Richard entered the small reception area. If the smell outside The Can had been bad, the olfactory assault inside its stone confines was almost overpowering: the atmosphere of vomit and excrement mixed with the clogged heat of summer; the ambience of drunkards snoring, farting and belching from their ale-abused bodies. One night in here, Tom thought, and he doubted he'd ever drink again.

"Which piss-hole are the Offcuts in?" Richard asked with the back of his right hand pressed against his nose.

"That'd be the piss-hole at the end of the passage, Sir Richard," said one of the guards, conversationally. He was quite probably the thinnest man Tom had ever seen in uniform, but, oddly, he had a healthy, full face.

Richard rolled his eyes. "Typical."

"Big Pa Offcut ain't a 'appy chappy, Sir Richard," said skin-and-bone man.

"I would be disappointed if he *was*, guardsman…?"

"McLean," supplied the guard.

Lean, thought Tom. *That* was an understatement.

Then, in a tone far too familiar for a minor subordinate, he added, "Giblets to me friends."

Richard shared a despairing gaze with Tom; his point about the general ineptitude of the guards was on display right here.

"An' this is guardsman Handel," continued Giblets, seemingly unaware of his inappropriate discourse, "or Grippy, as I call 'im — bein' I'm 'is friend an' all."

Grippy smiled and nodded. "Giblet's got the right o' things with Frank Offcut. He's well pissed, Sir Richard."

Controlling his temper admirably, Richard answered forthrightly. "As I said, guardsman, I wouldn't wish it any other way. Now, if you would be so kind as to hand me the key?"

"Key?" queried Grippy, looking perplexed.

"To the cell!" Richard yelled.

Both guards jumped, literally caught off guard. Giblets was the first to recover. "Err…" he said, wincing and obviously not looking forward to his next few words. "They'll be with the young Miss Offcut."

"She 'rived 'bout ten minutes ago," added Grippy, unnecessarily, then stood bravely by his friend and delivered a further selection of ill-chosen words. "'Ard to refuse *that* one," he said with a wink.

Tom and Richard's reactions were quite different: Richard simmered with disgust, while Tom flushed with chagrin. He could only hope Ophelia would be sensible enough not to make anything of their dalliance, particularly in front of Richard. She should be alright, Tom surmised, as long as Richard didn't provoke her… All of a sudden, he felt ill.

As Tom followed the steaming Seneschal down the steaming passageway, steaming images of Ophelia ran through his head, one's that had nothing to do with official duty. Fortunately, by the time they'd reached Frank and Billy's cell, any inappropriate thoughts had well and truly evaporated in the festering atmosphere of The Can.

The heavy wooden cell door — key protruding from its lock — was partially open. Richard pushed against it with enough force to make it recoil on its hinges. The reaction of the occupants was blocked from Tom's view by Richard's black frame, but he heard Ophelia gasp in shock. Standing in the doorway, Richard looked to his right. "You! Out!"

A pouting Ophelia suddenly emerged from the dim greyness. Richard moved into the room, allowing her space to exit, and watched her with barely concealed contempt as she flounced out of the cell. Ophelia's pout become a lascivious smile when she saw Tom hovering in the passage. To his relief, she said nothing — well, no words at least. Her expression, however, could not be misinterpreted, and the way she ran her tongue across her lips sent Tom's head spinning. As she walked past him, her hand brushed against his and, for a lingering moment, Tom was transported back to a secluded bank on the Icing River.

Fortunately, Richard could not see Ophelia's expression, but when Tom finally extricated his gaze from Ophelia's seductive features, his friend was looking at him with a quizzical expression.

Tom felt the blood rush to his face, but Richard's attention quickly turned back to the remaining Offcuts. Tom risked a glance to his left. Ophelia was gliding down the passageway, hips swaying fluidly. Then, as if sensing his gaze, she turned her head and blew him a kiss. That was enough to propel Tom into the cell.

Billy looked much the same as he had done the Wednesday night he was arrested: sulkily defiant, just dirtier and smellier. Frank, on the other hand, looked wretched, as if he'd been in there for three months, not three days.

"Enjoying the family reunion, Frank?" asked Richard.

Frank gazed contemptuously at both of them. Billy stared at his father, huddled behind his knees. (Almost the same position Tom had tied him in at The Dead Duck.)

"Still, at least the stench should be making you feel at home," he added.

Again, Frank let his expression do the talking. Tom was beginning to see where Billy's surliness came from.

"Even so, no doubt you are missing the sights and sounds of slaughtering animals." Richard paused as Frank straightened himself against the edge of the pallet. "That's why I am prepared to be most magnanimous on your behalf."

Suddenly Frank Offcut leapt up from his sitting position, taking both Richard and Tom by surprise. He sniggered at their response, even though neither of them had taken a backward step.

"Come t'ya senses 'ave ya?" He sneered, yellow teeth on show behind his pink face. He really was a disgusting man.

"How odd," Richard replied, smoothly. "I was about to ask *you* the very same question."

A look of confusion passed across the butcher's face.

"However, it is clear that your senses remain somewhat muddled. For example, you *still* seem to be confusing deference with defiance. What a pity, Frank."

Richard turned away from Frank and his foetal son and nodded at Tom to follow him out of the cell. He hadn't walked two steps before Frank called out. "Alrigh', Sir Richard, wha's the deal then?"

Richard shared a knowing smile with Tom, and then turned back to the stocky butcher, whose bald head was slick with sweat, his expression wary. Billy remained slunk in the corner of the pallet, silently watching his father.

"*Deal*, Frank?" Richard purred. "Such a *distrustful* word. I'd much prefer that we could come to an *agreement*."

Frank flicked his gaze between Richard and Tom as if he was weighing up his chances of escape. Who did he think he was?

"Don't even *think* about it, butcher," said Tom, echoing the words Frank had used on *him* when he'd burst into Richard's chambers three mornings ago. For the first time since entering the cell, Frank Offcut concentrated his gaze on Tom. It was an appraising one, and it suddenly occurred to Tom that Ophelia might have told him of their encounter. Tom tensed, ready to teach the butcher a painful lesson in humility. However, the pig of a man said nothing. Instead, his porcine eyes flicked back to Richard.

"Wha' sort of agreement?"

Richard's smile broadened.

When Tom and Richard left The Can ten minutes later, Frank Offcut was with them — the agreement reached or, in Frank's case, acquiesced to.

He had been released on the condition that he use his influence and resources, as Richard had put it, to find Xavier. Richard had not revealed the details of Xavier's relationship to the Duke, simply describing him as a uniquely talented doctor, but he *had* stressed that time was of the essence, even going so far as to say that it was a matter of life and death. Again, Richard did not name the Duke; he referred to him, instead, as a person of importance. However, to Tom, and, no doubt, to a man like Frank Offcut, the message hidden within the words was clear. Frank had even tried to turn the situation to his advantage, but Richard had laughed in his face.

"Frank, have your wits rotted away in this festering cell? I am offering you a *choice*. Your whelp of a son *will* be leaving The Can. It's up to you whether he goes home to you and yours or is sent to Master Key in the dungeon." Richard had glanced at Billy, who'd remained pathetically huddled in the corner during the whole discourse, saying nothing, as if he felt he no longer existed. "Personally, I think he'd be better off with Master Key." *That* had been enough for Frank to make his choice.

Squinting in the morning sun, Frank looked like he'd had a bucket of night-soil emptied on him. His white shirt was now the colour of grime, sweat, and who knew what else. Oddly enough, it matched his soiled grey trousers and black boots. His face almost glowed pink in the bright light, sweat pouring out of him.

"Dear, dear, Frank," said Richard with mock-concern, "you don't look well. I wouldn't have thought a few nights in The Can could have such an effect."

Frank sneered at the jab. Then Richard went for the full-thrust. "Imagine what a few months in the dungeon could do."

"Point made, Sir Richard. Ain't no need t'keep prickin' away. If this Xavier's still in Lower Icin', I'll find him."

"I appreciate your confidence, Frank," said Richard, eyeing the somewhat subdued butcher. "However, as they say, the proof of the pudding, or, in your case, Frank, the *black* pudding, is in the eating."

Frank Offcut met the Seneschal's gaze. "Am I free t'go?"

"Of course, Frank," said Richard, stepping aside with exaggerated politeness. "After all, every minute counts."

Frank could barely hide his contempt, flicking his gaze between Tom and Richard, before sauntering towards the West Gate of the Lower Bailey.

After a few steps, Tom asked his friend if he really thought Frank Offcut could be trusted, adding, "He's not the type to accept defeat, and he's not stupid."

"No…" Richard's gaze became distant. Then, looking directly at Tom, he added, "That's why I'm counting on him to find Xavier."

INTERLUDE

SID AND HORATIO

Saturday, July 4ᵗʰ

THE COPPER PIECE had dropped, and now Sid's head was spinning. *Marmaduke and Lucinda pleaded with me to look after Xavier, to take him far away from the village of Prickly Thicket and keep him safe until they could send for him.*

The words were Doctor Manky's — ones he'd spoken while Sid had been floating in his Rigour Morphis nightmare. It was like remembering whimsical drunken words the morning after a night on the ale. Except, these were not drunken words and they were far from whimsical.

"Are you telling me your protégé is the Duke's son?" Sid was incredulous.

"I am," said Doctor Manky. "In fact, I have already done so." A look of puzzlement crossed his face; it was amazing how bright Manky appeared in the darkness of the cabin. "Rigour Morphis does tend to affect the memory, but I thought you might have retained the pertinent facts."

More Rigour Morphis words seeped through the haze. *It was at Marmaduke's command that I've withheld the truth from Xavier about who he is and why he's been left in my care.*

It was unbelievable — too unbelievable for Sid to believe. And suddenly he felt violated, like Doctor Manky had planted some thought process into his mind.

Then, eighteen months ago, I thought the moment had finally come. Marmaduke sent me a letter, asking me to bring Xavier to Blessed Whipping.

"Sid," said a more tangible voice.

Sid was surprised to see Manky leaning forward, observing him closely. Bloody hell, what was *in* that blasted potion!

"Are you alright?"

Sid ignored the question; he wasn't interested in Manky's concern. "So, you think your protégé, after discovering he was the Duke's son, raced off to Lower Icing and attacked his father using one of *your* potions!"

He really needed to get out of this cab; the darkness was beginning to feel claustrophobic.

"Xavier is incapable of harming anyone," Manky said, reclining against his side of the coffin on wheels, "let alone his father."

Sid's response was doused in sarcasm. "Well, of course, Xavier is the epitome of goodness, Sir Richard is beyond reproach, and we are two knights in shining armour come to save the day."

The doctor remained annoyingly impassive, matching the motionless confines of the dark cabin. He then reached inside his white jacket and produced a neatly folded parchment. Leaning forward, he proffered the document. Like Doctor Manky, its whiteness seemed to glow. "Perhaps this will help you understand."

Sid regarded it for a moment, wondering what it could possibly contain that would corroborate the Doctor's story.

The Sunwatcher presented me with a letter that finally shed light on his disappearance.

Mistaking Sid's hesitation for uncertainty, Doctor Manky explained the reason for the parchment's glow. "It has been treated with concentrate derived from cows' urine. I accidently discovered it while trying to perfect Bruise Mousse; it stores light, which it then emanates in darkness. The Blessed Whippingers were *most* impressed."

Of course they were, thought Sid. No doubt the Doctor also *bathed* in it. Sid took the parchment. The bizarre was becoming commonplace and any information that helped clarify the reason behind this murky ride was worth accepting.

The parchment was folded into a third of its size, with two precise creases. Typical, thought Sid, as he unfolded it. However, what lay within was anything but precise: a barely intelligible note written in some sort of half-coded scrawl.

H,
btt u rd this, I will b3D gone.
Disc truth re father.
Dnt blame Butterfly.
X

Was this some kind of joke? Sid reread the scrawl to see if he'd missed something obvious. Blaming a butterfly? B3D gone? *Completely* gone, more like. Or maybe this was one of the effects of too much *Poetry in Potion*.

Sid looked up at Doctor Manky. There was a hint of expectation in his ghostly visage. He *must* be mad. "In what way, exactly, is this piece of 'bt turd' supposed to help me understand?"

He tossed the parchment at Doctor Manky, who, unbelievably, looked perplexed by Sid's reaction. The parchment happened to land on the Doctor's lap. Retrieving it, he examined it for himself. Realisation replaced confusion.

"Your pardon, Sid. Over the years, Xavier and I have developed a short-hand. We record everything, you see and—"

"Listen, I couldn't care less if you've developed a short prick. What does that pissing note say?"

Manky's face, as usual, betrayed little of what lay within, but Sid thought he detected just a trace of indignation. "Very well, Sid." Then, without a glance at the letter, he recited: "Horatio, by the time you read this I will be three days gone. I've discovered the truth regarding my father. Don't blame Butterfly. Xavier."

Sid was momentarily speechless. How could he put into words exactly what he was feeling right at this moment? Manky was looking at him as if he'd just shared something profound. But what he'd shared meant nothing, proved nothing. This was *nothing* more than a ride into madness and, more than likely, the dungeon.

"Stop the coach!" Sid yelled.

Sid was rewarded with a rare, surprised expression from the doctor. "Has something happened?" he said, looking around the cabin.

"Yes. I've come to my senses!"

"I'm not sure I understand."

"Of course you don't. Now, stop this contraption. I've had enough of this nightmare."

"I realise there is much to take in, but—"

"*Take in* is right, Manky." Sid was off his seat, leaning forward, his face inches from the pink-eyed man. "I've been taken in from the moment you floated into The Duck. I don't know what your game is, but I'm not going to be one of your pieces. Not anymore. I have no interest in your protégé or the Duke or *you*. Not even your coin interests me any longer. Now, I suggest you stop this coach before the atmosphere in here becomes even more unpleasant."

Doctor Manky nodded. "Very well, Sid."

Sid went back to his sitting position as the white figure rapped twice at the roof of the cab. The coach slowed immediately; the trotting rhythm quickly became a walk, and then there was silence. All the while, Doctor Manky regarded him with a mixture of curiosity and disappointment. What did he expect: that a few madly written words were somehow going to inspire him to risk his freedom (and possibly his life) for people he didn't know or care about?

Sid reached over and opened the door to the cab. Then he glanced across at the silent figure, who seemed more like an apparition than ever, almost transparent, less substantial. Sid experienced an annoying twinge of guilt, but not annoying enough to make him change his mind. "Good luck, Doctor Manky," he said.

"Thank you, Sid." Then, as Sid began to make his way out of the cab, he added, "I am sorry for the inconvenience and injury you have suffered. I never conceived such an outcome as this. Not for Xavier, the Duke *or* you."

Sid stepped out onto the road, then turned to face the doctor, intending to say goodbye. Instead he asked, "How will you get into the castle?"

"I will have to rely on Bertrand's ingenuity," he said, as if the thought of it was unappealing.

Sid nodded and shut the door of the moving coffin. Stepping back, he looked up at the undertaker. His ice-blue clothing gave him an ethereal appearance; he seemed to be hovering in the darkness like a… birdman. Sid decided to have one final dig.

"Cheerio, Bertrand," he said, cheerfully. "Good luck finding a way for Doctor Manky to see the Duke. Shouldn't be a problem for an amiable chap like you. No doubt your charm will win the day."

There was no reaction.

Then, from inside the coach, one quick knock rapped out into the night, and, with the flick of his wrists, Bertrand set the horse into motion. The coach disappeared into the darkness long before the Elder's eerily spectral form floated out of sight. Sid had no idea how close he was to Lower Icing, but he didn't care. He could barely make out the North Road, but he didn't care. There were odd rustling noises in the bushy blackness to his left, but he didn't care. The early morning air was pleasantly cool and fresh; it felt good to be standing up and breathing it in. He felt relieved too. The Manky business was over; he could now return to sorting out his own mess. He needed to put things right with Mary and he needed to find out the truth from Liv.

It was with a sense of renewed purpose that Sid strode south down the North Road. Lower Icing couldn't be *that* far away, nor could sunrise.

PART 5

FRANK

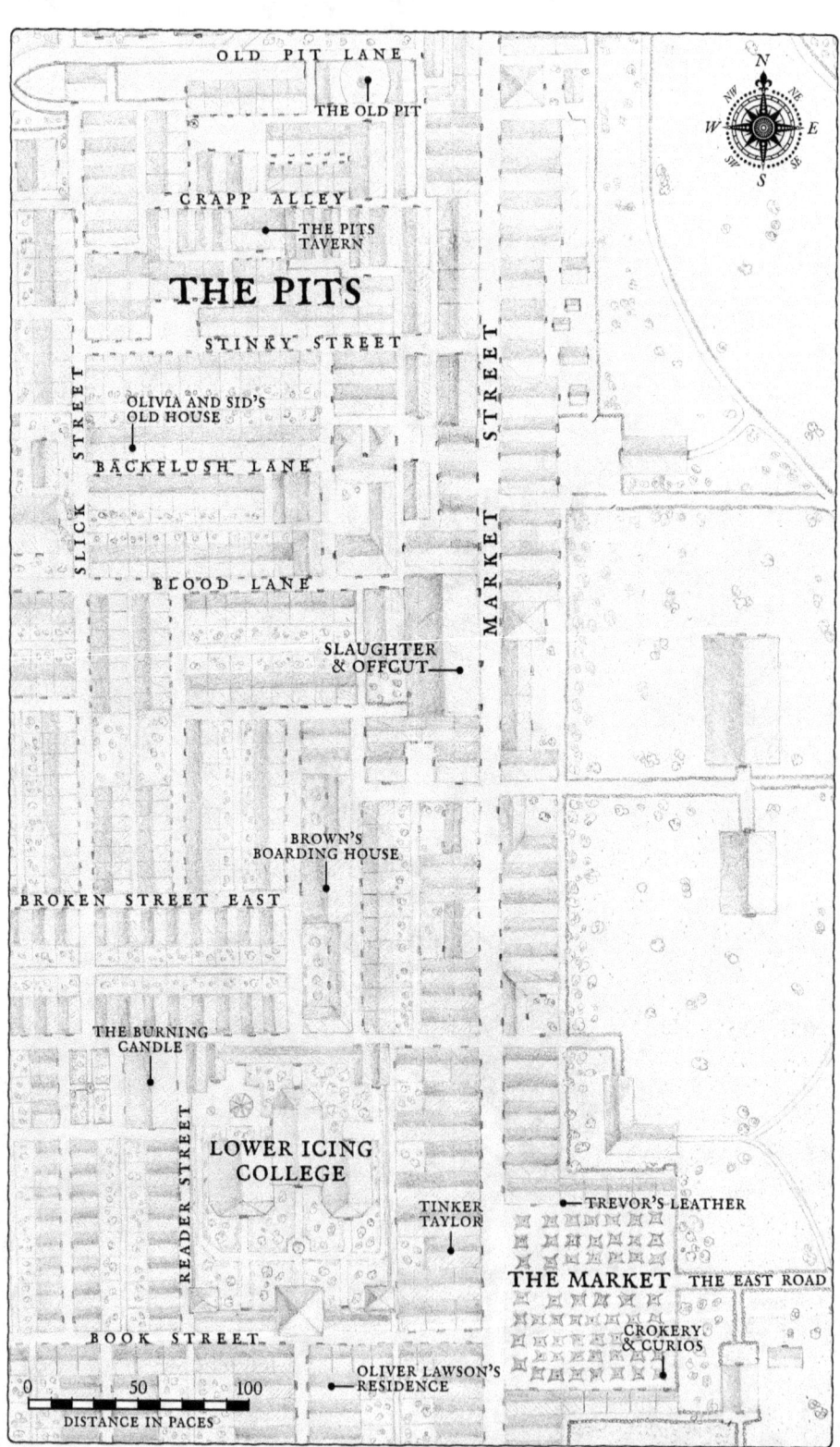

Introduction

A shy woodcutter's son

FRANK OFFCUT WAS an only child, but he was the father of eight children: seven sons and a daughter. He was the son of a woodcutter and a seamstress, Len and Jane Offcut, both dead these past ten years.

Growing up surrounded by piles of wood and rolls of fabric, everything in his world reeked of freshly cut timber. By the time he was sixteen, Frank had chopped enough wood to fill The Keep and was constantly picking out splinters from his hands and woodchips from his boots. His mother's profession was no less annoying. Frank had lost count of how many times he'd been pricked by discarded pins and stabbed with errant needles. Even so, Frank never envisaged himself becoming a butcher, let alone owning Lower Icing's largest butchery and employing almost a hundred workers — well over, in fact, if he counted Great Naff. He still couldn't believe how lucky he'd been, how quirky the nature of chance. It was all because of Maizie. She'd taken pity on a shy woodcutter's son: a young man who never seemed to smile.

Maizie had approached him one Saturday afternoon while he was carrying a load of firewood to The Dead Duck. She'd asked him to Sunday lunch, but Frank had been too embarrassed to accept. She asked again the following Saturday, with the same result. After the second rebuff she'd said to him, "I shall ask you next week, Frank Offcut, and if you decline a third time, I shall ask you no more."

The next week (after some sleepless nights and endless thoughts of Maizie's golden-red hair falling down her open face, past her bright green eyes and warm smile, cascading at her fulsome breasts) Frank had managed to bumble out an acceptance.

Maizie had been eighteen then — the youngest of three 'Slaughter daughters'. Her father, Brian Slaughter, was one of five butchers in Lower Icing. Right from that first Sunday lunch, Brian and his wife, Janice, treated Frank like one of the family. They were jovial people: happy, welcoming and generous.

He had been treated to a roasted shoulder of lamb — Frank couldn't remember the last time he'd had roast lamb — and the smell of it… Even to this day Frank could recall the rich, meaty aroma, so thick it overpowered the redolence of cut timber that seemed to follow him everywhere.

Frank had been invited back the following Sunday, then the next Sunday, and so on until it became a regular occasion. Gradually, he began to regard the Slaughters as his second family and Maizie as his future wife. She was attentive and made him laugh, and to Frank, who was stocky and, at best, could be described as ruddily endearing, she was beautiful.

At first, his mother and father had seemed pleased for him, but as the months passed, Frank spent less time chopping and carrying wood and more time chopping and carrying carcasses. All the years spent using an axe had stood him in good stead; he took to the cleaver like a duck to water. And Frank found he really enjoyed butchery. There was so much more to it than just chopping. It required finesse and an intimate knowledge of anatomy; the specific cuts of meat and the separation of sinew, muscle, fat and bone was an art form. Even sorting through the offal was interesting in a sloppy, sticky, foul-smelling sort of way.

Six months after his first Sunday lunch at the Slaughters, Frank and Maizie were engaged, by which time Frank had also become Brian's apprentice butcher and moved into the Slaughters' home. Neither of Maizie's older sisters — Frannie and Lizzie — had any interest in the business, the former having married a cabinet-maker and the latter now living in Pashing Madly, married to the son of a wealthy wool merchant. Frank, by default, had become the heir-apparent of Slaughter Prime Meats and Smallgoods.

A year later, Len Offcut had been born to the now-married Frank and Maizie Offcut. The next year, Bert Offcut was born, and so on with Tad, Stevie and Fred. There was a three-year gap between Fred and number-six child, and that had been put down to Maizie's grief over the death of her mother. Maizie had desperately wanted number six to be a girl and tried all manner of strange rituals (like hanging out the washing so it faced west, drinking warm milk mixed with ewe's blood, and wearing pink ribbons on her left ankle), but all they had conjured up was Seth. Her much-wanted daughter, Ophelia, arrived two years later.

It had been the happiest time of Frank's life. At twenty-nine, he had much more than he could possibly have ever imagined: a loving, devoted wife; six healthy boys and a beautiful new daughter; and a partnership in Lower Icing's largest butchery.

Just before Ophelia's birth, Frank had convinced Brian that they should make an offer on Bruce Braveheart's butchery, since he was looking to sell. Frank saw it as a great opportunity to expand the business, and although Brian was content to keep Slaughter's as it was, Frank was thinking of the future. Bruce specialised in chicken — it was a niche market that would give the business an extra string to its bow. With Brian's eventual blessing, Frank negotiated and acquired 'Braveheart's Chicken' and, shortly afterwards, 'Slaughter & Offcut' was formed. By this time, Len was ten and had begun working in the business (when he wasn't being taught how to read and write by Maizie). Bert, Tad, Stevie and Fred helped out too. Frank's family were a great source of pride to him.

Two years later, Brian died. He'd caught a chill, which became a fever, which turned out to be pneumonia. Leeching hadn't worked, bizarre concoctions hadn't worked, filling his bedroom with lavender hadn't worked, and so, after a couple of weeks of failed remedies, Brian Slaughter's heart hadn't worked.

It had been a very sad time for Frank, Maizie and the children. Brian had been more than just a father and grandfather; he'd been a friend and mentor, kind-hearted, supportive and generous. Very generous as it turned out. He'd bequeathed the business *and* the home they'd all shared for the last thirteen years to Frank. "Promise me you'll always do right by Maizie and the littl'uns, Frank," he'd said shortly before slipping into a sleep from which he'd never wake. Frank had promised, and, to the best of his abilities, he had kept that promise.

During the next three years, Slaughter & Offcut had continued to expand. Frank bought two of the remaining three butcheries in Lower Icing and, with it, a monopoly on all the meat supplied in the town. He'd also been able to negotiate an exclusivity agreement with Reg Puffy, the newly appointed Head Cook at the castle.

All this expansion, however, had had no effect on the one remaining butchery. John Carver dealt directly with a local merchant, who traded with wholesalers in the mighty eastern seaport of Great Naff, and no matter how generous the offer, John would not sell his business to Frank. Eventually, after a failed third attempt, Frank had approached the merchant directly. He'd offered to undercut John's price by one-quarter, but, much to Frank's disappointment and frustration, the merchant, one Simon Shanks, had refused.

Shortly afterwards, John Carver had confronted Frank. "Wha's your game, Offcut? Think you can 'ave ev'rythin you want, don' ya. Well, me an' Simon goes back a long ways; we got an understandin', see, so's you can forget about undercuttin' me. Got it!" he'd said between clenched teeth, prodding his finger into Frank's chest.

Frank had been shocked; he was only conducting business. John had refused his generous offers, so why shouldn't he try his luck with Simon? The altercation had occurred just outside Frank's new butchery — he'd sold all his assets and ploughed most of the revenue into buying and refitting a large building on Market Street, just down from the market — and had been overheard by a man who'd, shortly afterwards, introduced himself as The Fixer.

The Fixer had told Frank he could persuade John to see sense, for a fee, of course. Assured that John would come to no harm or be threatened in any way, Frank had agreed terms with The Fixer. A few months went by, Maizie fell pregnant for an unexpected eighth time, Len turned sixteen, and Bert turned fifteen — his five eldest boys were growing up and were all involved in the day-to-day running of Slaughter & Offcut. Frank had almost forgotten about the agreement until Tad, then almost fourteen, told him that a 'Mista Fixa' was waiting in his office.

Without preamble, The Fixer had produced a parchment. It was the deed to John Carver's business, signed over to Frank, sealed at the bottom with John's 'crossed cleaver' trademark. All Frank had to do was pay The Fixer the agreed amount. Frank had been amazed and wanted to know how he'd managed such a feat. The Fixer refused to go into detail — just repeated his demand for payment. But Frank wasn't that trusting. He didn't know The Fixer — the non-descript man was not from Lower Icing; he was just a stranger who had suddenly appeared in Frank's life. He'd wanted to be sure that John Carver hadn't been harmed. The Fixer assured him that he was well. Frank agreed to pay The Fixer his commission, but only *after* he'd seen John Carver and paid *him* his dues. The Fixer informed Frank that John had left for Great Naff, and then produced a second parchment — again with John's signature and seal — which stated that The Fixer was to collect the payment on his behalf.

"We had an agreement Master Offcut. I expect you to fulfil your side of it, as I have fulfilled mine," he'd said in his quiet, refined voice. Then he'd added, "In fact, I would be so bold as to predict the future success of Slaughter and Offcut *depends* upon it." There had been no mistaking the menace behind the statement. It was implicit enough for Frank to honour the agreement, even though it was highly probable that it had been gained through coercion and, possibly, something more sinister.

A few months later, Billy had been born prematurely, and Frank barely had time to acknowledge his arrival. He was too immersed in his new partnership with Simon Shanks to be a doting father. Billy was his seventh son, but, unlike his brothers, he looked fragile and pale. Frank doubted whether he would see his first birthday. Still, Maizie and Ophelia (who, at five, was already beautiful and adored by all) were very excited by the latest edition to the Offcut clan and more than compensated for Frank's lack of attention.

The months rolled into years. Both Frank and Simon had put the still-unknown fate of John Carver behind them and concentrated their energies and resources on servicing their meat market. And this they did very successfully: within the next three years, Slaughter & Offcut were not only *the* butcher of Lower Icing, but also the favoured butcher in Great Naff and much of Naffolk.

By the time Frank reached forty years of age, Slaughter & Offcut had established a butchery in Great Naff and he was well on his way to becoming one of the wealthiest men in the Duchy of Lower Icing. Len, now twenty-three, along with Bert and Tad, moved to Great Naff with their families to run the 'Naff Office'.

Frank had also become a man of influence and consorted with influential people. Those people knew people who knew people, who in turn came to know Frank, and favours were done, incentives were paid, and his business prospered. He had also become a man to be courted, because he knew so many people, and some people were willing to do anything for Frank (or, at least, for Frank's money).

Somewhere in all of this, Stevie and Fred had wedded and started families. Seth, the quiet, diligent son, had become a brilliant bookkeeper (and saved Frank hundreds of gold pieces in taxes). Ophelia had turned into a stunningly beautiful woman, with a fiery, independent personality — she was nobody's fool and no man would be her master. The same, however, could not be said of Billy. He'd survived a sickly childhood to become a skinny, awkward boy approaching manhood. At sixteen, Frank's other sons had had key roles at Slaughter & Offcut, but Billy was too clumsy to be trusted in an environment of slick blood and sharp instruments; it would be nigh on a death sentence for the lad. Still, Billy would eventually find his niche — probably in something that didn't involve chopping and cutting. After all, at the age of sixteen, Frank hadn't felt cut out to be a woodcutter.

Now at forty-nine, he was still at the top of his game. Everything at Slaughter & Offcut was going bloody well… *very* bloody well, in fact. That is, until Lieutenant Fowler of the Purple Peril brought him news that Billy had been arrested.

Frank had been outraged. Firstly, Jethro Fowler had delivered the news with barely concealed delight, all the while ogling Ophelia. (Not surprising though, since the Fowlers were a chicken-livered bunch of arse lickers.) Secondly, Billy, at worst, was an immature prankster. Bar Swill had banned him from The Bell again. Well, so be it — that was all part of his rite of passage into manhood — but to be *arrested* for fooling around with some boozed-up floosy? *That* was another thing entirely. But what had really stuck in his guts like a two-pound T-bone was that Billy had been arrested on the say-so of Lower Icing's Gamekeeper. Tom Skinner was a man who lived on his own, surrounded by trees and the smell of timber, spending his days wandering around the forest, like a hermit with a permit — hardly the occupation of a well-adjusted person.

Lieutenant Fowler's gleeful second-hand retelling of events had also included the name of the arresting officer — Frank could have guessed it was Brandon Swill. However, he'd been surprised to learn that Will Plucker had also been party to proceedings. As far as Frank was concerned, that was well and truly overstepping the boundaries of innkeeper.

Frank had decided to go directly to Richard Upson. He wasn't about to waste time dealing with intermediaries; this required a decision-maker (or, in this case, a decision un-maker). He had been certain Sir Richard would see the error of his Gamekeeper's ways and have Billy released immediately. Unfortunately, the error had been Frank's.

CHAPTER 1

Drunken night-soil collector

Sunday, June 29 — the morning after Sid's bashing in the stables of The Harey Rabbit. Sid is currently lying unconscious in Mary's bed.

FRANK SHOULD HAVE felt victorious and vindicated as he passed the indolent cluster of guards at the West Gate. Instead, he felt disgusted. Disgusted by the way he and Billy had been treated, disgusted by Sir Richard's manipulation of the situation, disgusted by that timber-dick Gamekeeper, but, more than anything else, he was disgusted at himself — he'd been humbled and humiliated.

Three days ago, almost to the hour, he'd been manhandled into that stinking cell. Instead of having Billy released, he'd been arrested and thrown in The Can with him. Three days confined with his youngest son — more time than he'd probably spent with him in the last three *years* — and Frank was shocked by how vulnerable he was. Billy, he realised, was a stranger to him; the neglected runt had curled up in the corner of the cell, barely saying a word. Things were going to change once Billy was released — he'd promised the lad *and* himself that.

Sauntering down Noble Street in the glaring morning sun, smelling like the sewer he'd just been released from, Frank was aware of the glances he was receiving. Some smiled knowingly, some glared disdainfully, and some of the daintier individuals gasped audibly. He recognised most of them. Stuff them all, he thought; there wasn't enough substance in this lot to fill a small sausage. Still, it was going to be a long walk back to the shop (and his home) in Market Street; humiliation and shame would follow him the whole way. At least there were a few backstreets he could take.

Frank continued north down Noble Street, across Merchant Street, around Lower Icing College and into a series of nameless backstreets and lanes where Market Street businesses backed onto the homes of common folk. Frank was happy to count himself among them — although he had dined with the Dukes of Lower Icing and Naffolk, he was a butcher a heart.

The storeroom of Slaughter & Offcut backed onto a lane. The entrance was via a solid oak door, reinforced with heavy bands of iron. Frank expected it to be locked and, sure enough, it was. However, it opened like magic after Frank had given it a quick pounding and followed up with, "Get this bloody door open now!"

Donald Rump stood on the other side and quickly moved out of the way as Frank barged into the relatively cool confines of the meat room. Donald was in his twenties, a bright lad and a hard worker. He reminded Frank of himself at that age, but, unlike Frank, Donald refused to concede to the inevitability of baldness — his thinning hair was swept over his crown like flattened summer grass.

"Mornin', sir," said Donald, respectfully.

Frank nodded and looked around the room. Everything appeared as it should: rows of carcasses hung from hooks; all had been skinned and gutted; some had been chopped in half, others into quarters, and some had been covered with a thin gauze (doused in a mixture of salt and Icing River water) to help preserve the meat and keep the room cool. In winter, meat could be kept in here for weeks without risk. In this weather, however, anything longer than a day would be a bit dicey, and Frank didn't do dicey when it came to the reputation of Slaughter & Offcut.

"You alrigh', sir?"

Frank swung around and faced the young butcher. He looked concerned.

"'Course I'm alrigh'. What do…" Frank stopped himself, suddenly aware of how he must look. "I'm fine, thank you, Donald."

Offering no explanation, Frank walked out of the meat room and into the main building. He turned right down a passageway that ended in a door. Behind the door was staircase that led up to the place Frank and Maizie and, for the time being at least, Seth, Ophelia and Billy called home. The entire building had been converted from an old barn: Slaughter & Offcut at ground level, Offcut & Offcut above, including a second floor of loft bedrooms (for the children and grandchildren when they visited). The home was spacious and lavishly decorated, although it looked neither from street level. The front of the building faced east onto Market Street, some three hundred paces north of Lower Icing's marketplace. There were three street level entrances: a black door opened up to the shop, where people bought meat over the counter, a blue door provided entrance to the office, where Seth kept track of all the orders and payments, and a red door (closest to the marketplace) marked the front entrance to the Offcut residence. Behind this door, a small reception area (with space to leave coats and boots) ended in a staircase. Halfway up there was a small landing, where it joined the staircase Frank had just climbed and turned ninety degrees to reach the first floor. The staircase was the only concession to family life on the ground level of Slaughter & Offcut.

Maizie rushed into Frank's arms as soon as he appeared at the top of the stairs. He must have smelt worse than a sheep's large intestine, but she still squeezed him tightly. After thirty-odd years of marriage to a butcher, she'd grown accustomed to a certain amount of foulness. However, it filled his heart to think that Maizie still loved him the way she'd loved that shy son of a woodcutter, the one who'd smelt like freshly cut timber.

"Oh, Frank," she whispered, and then slowly released him.

"'S alrigh', love," he said, holding her gently by the arms. "Everythin' will be fine. I'm gettin' our Billy outta there, don' you worry 'bout that."

"How is he, Frank? What's happened? Ophelia said—"

He gently touched her cheek and gazed into her green eyes — still as bright as they were the day she'd asked him to Sunday lunch. "I promise ya, Maizie, our Billy will soon be 'ome safe."

Tears began to well in her eyes as she nodded her acceptance. As the tears trickled, she smiled self-consciously, and suddenly her playful side reasserted itself. "Best get you in the tub, Frank Offcut. Anyone would think I was married to a drunken night-soil collector."

CHAPTER 2

Now there's a body I recognise

THE WATER WAS hot and clear when Frank edged his way into the tub. Now it was a tepid grey broth. Maizie had infused it with lavender and scented the air with jasmine.

Frank had told her of Sir Richard's deal. Her immediate reaction had been one of concern, but Frank assured her he would find out what had happened to this doctor. In the ten minutes he'd been left to soak in private, his course of action, unlike the tub water, had become clearer.

When Frank emerged from the disturbingly murky liquid, he felt much better and, thanks to Maizie's gentle scrubbing, totally cleansed.

Maizie appeared with a towel and a fresh set of clothes as if she'd been waiting for the sound of sloshing water. She smiled and said, "Now *there's* a body I recognise."

"Thanks, love." Frank smiled back, taking the towel. While he dried himself, Maizie set out his clothes on a nearby chair.

"Do you really think the *Duke* is dying?"

"Ain't sure," replied Frank, running the towel across his back. "Sir Richard wants me t'believe it. Could be a ploy s'pose — make sure of my commi'ment — but I doubt it."

"But why the Duke? You said Sir Richard called him a high-ranking official."

"Come on, Maizie," Frank said, as if Maizie should know better. "The only person Sir Richard thinks is 'igh rankin' is the Duke, an' even then, I reckon 'e thinks 'e only *jus'* qualifies. Anyway, I caught the expression on that soppy Gamekeeper's face; 'e was spewin' tha' Sir Richard was even talkin' to me. I don' reckon 'e'd've accepted me bein' released if it wasn' the Duke whose life was at stake."

"It's not right, Frank," Maizie said, taking the towel and handing her husband a pair of undergarments. "I mean, I hope the Duke recovers, but to use our Billy this way… If *they* can't find this doctor, how do they expect *you* to?"

"The guards are a bunch of incompetent arse-wipes," answered Frank, tying up his undergarments. "An' the officers jus' like poncing around in their purple uniforms, thinkin' their shit don' stink, an' everyone else 'as shit for brains."

"But Billy, he's been charged with manhandling that girl. How do we know they'll—"

"Listen to me, Maizie," he said, squeezing his wife's shoulders in reassurance. "I'll find this bloody doctor, don' you worry 'bout that. Ain't nothin' goin' to 'appen to our Billy. Trust me, love."

Maizie looked him in the eyes and nodded.

"Tha's my girl," he said, kissing her tenderly on the cheek.

The moment was short-lived. The sound of shoes on floorboards forewarned the couple of an imminent interruption. Moments later, Ophelia appeared.

"Pa?" she whispered, disbelief on her face; an hour ago they'd been talking to each other in a cell. She ran into his arms, almost knocking him back into the tub. "Oh, Pa!" she said, holding him tightly.

"Steady on, lass." Frank smoothed her wild, straw-blonde locks; she'd also obviously bathed since leaving The Can. Gazing over at his smiling wife, he added, "Give your ol' man a chance to get 'is clobber on."

She let Frank go, her eyes bright with joy. "Where's Billy?"

"'E's still in The Can," Frank replied without hesitation. Ophelia was a straight-shooter and he'd always been straight with her — no need for fluffery with Ophelia.

"But not for much longer, Pheel," Maizie piped in. "Your pa has an agreement with Sir Richard."

"Maizie!" snapped Frank, snatching his trousers from the chair. The two most important women in his life stared at him: Maizie in confusion, Ophelia in concern. "Sorry, but I don' wan' Ophelia gettin' involved."

"Involved in wha'?" Her hands were suddenly on her hips, her gaze flicking from one parent to the other.

Frank sighed, and Maizie gave him an apologetic look.

"Involved in *wha*?" Ophelia demanded.

Looking at his daughter's determined countenance, he shook his head. It was no use trying to fool her with some fanciful story; she'd see through it straightaway. "Alrigh', I'll tell you." A wave of annoyance suddenly broke over him. "But do y' mind if I get dressed first?"

Sitting around their ornately carved dining table, surrounded by the plushness of Slaughter & Offcut's success, Frank (now fully dressed) had told Ophelia about the discussion he'd had with Sir Richard. Well, the gist of it anyway. he didn't go into detail about the consequences of failure, nor did he make mention of the Duke. In fact, as far as Ophelia was concerned, Frank was aiding Sir Richard in a delicate diplomatic matter: the missing doctor was an eminent physician from Stymouth who'd arrived in advance of the Duke of Stymouth. Frank had further embellished the truth by suggesting that Sir Richard had personally asked for his help because he felt Frank was the only Lower Icinger clever, tactful and well-connected enough to find the doctor.

Ophelia seemed satisfied with his explanation, but that didn't stop her from raising a pertinent point. "'E's been missin' since Thursday mornin'. Tha's three days ago, Pa. 'E could be *any*-bloody-where; driftin' face down in the Icin' would be my guess."

Frank nodded. "Said pretty much the same thing to Sir Richard, but 'e and nature-boy are convinced 'e's alive."

For some reason, Ophelia became slightly flushed. "Wha' else did the Gamekeeper say?"

The question threw Frank somewhat. "Not much. Mainly jus' stood there lookin' like 'e 'ad a pine cone shoved up 'is arse."

Maizie gave him a withering look, but Ophelia quickly chimed in with, "So wha' abou' Billy, then? One favour in return for another is it?"

Frank couldn't help but admire his daughter's intuitiveness. "Aye… pretty much, lass."

Frank finished the discussion by telling his wife and daughter they were to tell no-one, not even Seth, about what had been revealed at the table. "Remember, this affects Billy," he added to hammer the point home, "so we're keepin' this to ourselves, righ'?"

Both women nodded their understanding, but Ophelia looked energised. Then she let loose with a mixed-grill of ideas about where to start the search and who she could sweet talk, reckoning she could find out what had happened to the doctor within the hour.

Frank was having none of it. "You ain't goin' nowhere, my girl. Ain't you been listenin' to wha' I jus' said? I don' wan' you talkin' to no-one. Got it?"

He rarely spoke to Ophelia this way — it went against the grain to raise his voice to womenfolk — and, therefore, the shock of it had the desired effect. Ophelia looked suitably chastised — not an expression she'd worn very often in her twenty-one years. "Got it, Pa. Sorry."

Slaughter & Offcut was closed Sundays, but it was the main market day, so they ran a stall there. Apart from Donald Rump (and Daisy Filler at the stall), Seth was the only person working at the main business today, and he was spending his time tallying up the week's sales.

Frank reached the bottom of the back staircase and opened the door to the passageway. It accessed the office and shop (to the front) and the storeroom and private garden (to the back). He walked through an open doorway, first on his right, and entered the office where Seth was sitting at his desk, head bent over a large ledger, quill in hand.

Unlike Ophelia, Seth's reaction to seeing Frank was more reserved. "Good t'see you, Pa," he said, hugging Frank warmly. Then, as if feeling guilty that he hadn't followed Ophelia's effusive lead, he added, "Ma said we should stay down 'ere and give you a chance to clean up, like. An' she said you'd arranged for Billy t'be released soon. I 'ope 'e's learned 'is lesson."

Frank smiled at his second youngest son — the boy Maizie had so wanted to be a girl. Ironically, he was the child that most reminded him of his wife: sensitive, caring and quietly spoken; a personality Ophelia might have had. But it made no difference to Frank. He was proud of all his children... even Billy.

"You're a good lad, Seth," he said, clapping his boy on the back, before running his eyes over Slaughter & Offcut's ledger. Seth, as usual, had recorded all purchases and sales in fine detail, including deductions for wages and other expenses like the washing of uniforms (particularly those from the abattoir) and bags of sawdust (which were spread over the shop and storeroom floors to soak up the blood). The sawdust made sweeping the floor much easier and gave the spaces a pleasant, freshly-cut timber scent. It was an innovation from Frank's woodcutter days; the irony still amused him.

Frank stepped out of the office into the blaring heat of Market Street. Pacing quickly across the simmering cobblestones, he reached the shaded eastern side of the street, but the buildings wouldn't block the sun for much longer — it was already late-morning.

Still, Frank was confident it wouldn't take long to find out where this doctor was. He had a description of the young man and a time of disappearance; that's all he needed. His information network would do the rest, and that network began at Bert Muggins' stall of 'Crockery & Curios'.

CHAPTER 3

Brown and beige bicuspids

THE MARKET WASN'T busy. It was too bloody hot. Frank couldn't remember a summer being so blazing. It wasn't good for business — people tended not to roast meat in this weather. As he zigzagged his way through the brightly decorated stalls, he checked in with Daisy. She looked as bedraggled as the sagging red and white canopy that covered a selection of small-goods, cured hams and cuts of meat. Like the meat in the storeroom, most of the display was covered in damp gauze.

Daisy's demeanour changed as soon as she caught sight of Frank.

"Mornin', sir." She smiled, trying to look enthusiastic.

"Mornin', Daisy." Frank smiled back, bemused by her bravado. "Bit on the slow side this mornin'."

Daisy nodded. "Not many folk about t'day, sir," she remarked, as if it wasn't obvious. Then, referring to the other stall holders, she added, "'Alf of 'em 'ave already packed it in an' gone 'ome."

"Reckon we should pack it in too, Daisy?"

Daisy looked relieved. "Oh, tha' would be…" She stopped herself, realising that it might not be the correct response. "a bad idea."

"A bad idea?" said Frank, trying to conceal his bemusement.

"Sorry, sir." Daisy was flustered now. "I didn' mean no disrespec', like. I jus'…"

Frank shook his head. What was he doing? The poor girl didn't deserve to be treated like this. It must be the heat. "It's alrigh', Daisy. I'll tell you what, I'll wait 'ere while you run an' fetch Donald, and 'e can 'elp you take this lot back to the shop. It's too bloody 'ot."

Daisy just stared at him, not sure if she'd heard right.

"Well, off ya go. Chop chop as we say in the meat business."

Daisy scarpered.

Frank smiled as she dodged her way through the half-filled market.

Then frowned as his gaze fell on the half-filled stall. Normally at this time only a few pieces, if anything at all, remained. He felt decidedly odd. What was he doing sending Daisy off like that. No wonder she'd looked at him so oddly; perhaps The Can's pissing heat had steamed his brain.

It seemed like only seconds before Daisy and Donald returned. They'd appeared out of nowhere and were staring at Frank, wearing very worried expressions. For some reason, other people, including Bert Muggins, were also looking at him. He felt something cool on the back of his head. Is that what they were worried about, he wondered.

"You alrigh', sir?" asked Donald.

"Course I'm all bloody—" It was then Frank realised he was lying on the ground. "What the?" he said, levering himself up.

"You passed out, sir," Daisy informed him.

Donald reached down and helped Frank to his feet. Momentarily disoriented, he stumbled against the stall, but fortunately Donald had him in a strong grip. The moment of dizziness passed.

"P'r'aps you should sit down, sir," suggested Donald, edging him towards a nearby stool.

"I'm fine," Frank said, gruffly, freeing himself from Donald's grip. Then he added more kindly, "Thank you, Donald."

There was slight throbbing sensation at the back of his head. Frank ran his hand over his smooth scalp and felt a lump the size of a sheep's eyeball behind his right ear. Meanwhile, Daisy had retrieved the damp gauze from the ground and handed it to Frank. "'Ope you don' mind, sir, but I took it from the stall — for your head, like."

"Thank you, Daisy," replied Frank, taking the gauze and gently pressing it against the lump.

Frank's quick recovery had obviously been a disappointment to the small gathering of people; they began dispersing quietly, some actually looking put out by the lack of drama. Bert Muggins was the exception; he looked concerned, in a bemused sort of way.

"Lucky that cranium of yours is as 'ard as it looks, Frank." He grinned, revealing his odd collection of teeth. They ranged in colour from milky white to mud brown, some were large and some were small, and quite a few were non-existent. Surrounded by a craggy, grey-stubble face and wild grey hair, they were Bert Muggins' very own Crockery & Curios.

"Need t'speak to you, Bert," Frank said without preamble. The dizziness had passed and the world was righting itself. "I'll see you at your stall d'rectly."

A knowing (and strangely fascinating) smile grew on Bert's face — a visit from Frank usually heralded the chance to make some quick coin. Doffing a non-existent cap, he turned and walked off towards his stall some twenty paces away.

Frank still held the damp gauze against his head, not because he thought it would make much difference to his lump, but because it felt cool in the oppressive heat. "Righ' then, you two," he said, addressing his employees, "take this lot back t'the shop, pack away everythin' we c'n sell t'morrow, the rest y'can share between y'selves, then y'can knock off."

Both Donald and Maisy reacted with surprise and gratitude. It was unusual for Frank to be so liberal, but he'd been touched by their genuine concern for his wellbeing. Tossing the gauze back over the meat display, he strode towards Bert Muggins' stall.

Frank still felt slightly light-headed, like he'd had a tankard of ale. It would pass, he told himself; he just needed to get used to sunlight again after being shut away in that damn cell. His thoughts turned to his youngest. Billy wasn't coping with his confinement at all, even with Frank to keep him company — frig knows what effect The Can was having on him now. One thing was for sure: Billy wouldn't last a week in the dungeon. Frank would stop at nothing to keep him out of there.

If Frank was light-headed on sunlight, the market looked like it had a hangover. The normally noisy, bustling lines of stalls were orderly and sedate, and even the most enthusiastic sellers seemed laconic and bored. The generous shade afforded by the stall canopies made no difference to the energy-sapping heat. It concerned Frank from the point of view that he felt more exposed talking to Bert — their discussions were usually swallowed up in the hubbub of the market. Still, needs must.

Crockery & Curios was situated on the end of a line of stalls at the river side of the market. Bert was waiting behind his eclectic collection of what Frank would categorise as junk. Even his crockery (of which there was very little) was old or badly made, except for one piece — a plate with, of all things, a large, hand-painted snail — that took pride of place in the display.

Bert was grinning wildly by the time Frank stood in front of him. However, Frank was distracted by the plate; the spiral pattern of the snail's shell was making him feel giddy.

"You gotta good eye, Frank," said Bert, straight into vendor mode.

"Tha's come all the way from Escargotia."

Unfortunately for Bert, Frank didn't like anything Escargotian — stuck up bunch of tossers who thought anyone not raised on blancmange and champagne was an inferior dullard. The Duke was part Escargotian, which was part of the reason why Frank didn't have much respect for him.

"If I was you, I'd send it all the way back," Frank commented, wrenching his 'good eye' away from the mesmerising snail.

Bert's smile momentarily faded, then returned, revealing a different selection of teeth, as his expression adjusted from market vendor to information provider. "So wha' can I do for you, Frank?"

"I need to find someone."

Bert nodded sagely.

"Some young fool outsider," continued Frank, "'as gone missin', an' certain people wan' 'im found."

"Blond 'air, green doublet, white shirt an' trousers, black boots, disappeared sometime early Thursdee mornin'?" Bert looked pleased with himself.

So, the unofficial channels *had* been at work. "Aye, that'd be 'im. So, wha' d'ya know?"

"Zackly wha' I jus' told ya."

"That ain't no good to me, Bert."

Bert shrugged. "Tha's all I got... 'Less o'course you want me to do some delvin', like?" Bert's grin widened in anticipation of Frank's response.

"Delvin' sounds too slow for my likin'. What *this* requires is some rootin' and rummagin' Wham! Bam! Here's Your Man! That kinda thing, Bert."

Bert's grin became thoughtful: a ruminating selection of brown and beige bicuspids.

"Up for it, then?" Frank prompted.

"Course, Frank," Bert replied, taking mock-offense.

Frank nodded. "Good."

"There's an extra charge for rootin' an' rummagin', mind. Sure you can 'preciate that."

Frank reached into the pocket of his trousers and pulled out a small leather pouch. It contained twenty gold pieces — double the amount he had ever paid Bert before. He tossed the pouch over a collection of crudely made stick-men. The vendor of Crockery & Curios caught it in his left hand and a look of delighted surprise spread across his face as he felt its weight.

"I s'pect some damn good rootin' for that, Bert, an' I want it done quick.

Understan'?"

Bert nodded, still feeling the weight of the pouch.

"Find out where our man is t'day an' I'll double it."

Bert's twenty-gold-piece grin turned curious. "Who is 'e, Frank?"

"You don' need t'know that, Bert. You jus' 'ave to find 'im. And know that it's importan' t'me. Alrigh'?"

Bert nodded solemnly. "Y'can coun' on me, Frank."

"No, no, Bert. It's *you* who can coun' on *me*." Then he walked off, leaving Bert Muggins to ponder what he had meant by that.

CHAPTER 4

Your part in your son's behaviour

FRANK WAS GLAD to be out of the sun. The Offcut living space wasn't exactly cool or refreshing, but at least it was bearable. The damp towel draped over his head was helping too, as was the jug of lemon barley water Maizie had prepared for him. Ophelia had sliced some cold corned beef and served it with bread, cheese and a tomato relish. However, the more comfortable he felt, the more he thought about Billy. It wasn't right. The boy was harmless (as long as he wasn't in the vicinity of anything sharp) and Frank doubted he knew the first thing about approaching women. Perhaps that was the problem. He'd probably fumbled and groped at the lass, thinking it was how men went about it, particularly if he was taking his lead from the genteel menfolk at The Bloody Bell or The Dead Duck.

"How you feeling, love?" asked his wife, suddenly appearing by his side.

"Guilty," Frank replied.

She sat down next to him; even their beautifully crafted honey-pine settee from Longboatia now felt guiltily comfortable.

"You're doing all you can, Frank," Maizie said, squeezing his hand.

"Am I?" he replied, pulling his hand away; he didn't want to be comforted.

"Frank? What is it, love?"

Frustration suddenly reached boiling point. He flung the wet towel from his head and got up off the settee. After a few seconds of shocked silence, he said, "It's my fault our Billy's in The Can."

Maizie sprang to his side. "Now listen here, Frank Offcut. Billy couldn't have a better father." She clasped her hands around his and softened her tone. "No-one here is questioning you, love. We all believe in you, and that includes our Billy."

He embraced his wife, breathing in the wildflower scent of her greying auburn hair. What had he done to deserve Maizie? Frank felt the warmth of another body enfold him from behind. He manoeuvred his arm and drew his daughter into the embrace.

The last vestiges of daylight were about to disappear behind Look Over Hill; not that Frank was looking over Look Over Hill — he was sitting in the candlelit gloom of his dining room, picking at the remains of his pork chops. He was in a picky sort of mood. Maizie and Ophelia had made the wise decision to retreat to the kitchen, leaving Seth to bear the brunt of Frank's frustrations.

What was keeping Muggins? Frank had been cooped up all afternoon waiting for the market vendor to knock at the storeroom door with news of the doctor. It was unlike him to take so long — almost nine hours since Bert's confident display of teeth assured Frank of his success. Time enough for the lump on Frank's head to go down.

Seth sat in silence, not wanting to say the wrong thing. Frank was too edgy to put the lad at ease. He'd had enough. He stood up; his patience had well and truly run out.

"I'm goin' ou'," he announced.

Seth nodded. "You wan' me t'come with you?"

"No."

He ducked into the kitchen and made the same announcement to Maizie and Ophelia.

"What about Bert Muggins?" asked Maizie.

He wasn't sure. "Tell him to find me."

"Find you where, Frank?" She gave him a bemused look; she always did when he behaved like an impatient child.

"This ain't Great Naff, Maizie," he retorted, suggesting there were only so many places in Lower Icing that he'd likely be.

She smiled. "Right you are, love."

"You be careful, Pa," Ophelia added, taking on a mothering role.

Frank left via the storeroom, just in case he ran into Bert Muggins. It was wishful thinking, but better knowing than wondering. He opened the laneway door and stepped into the grey-stone murkiness of twilight. Bert was a back-laneway kind of person, but there was no sign of him. Then again, it was easy not to be seen.

After coming from the relative coolness of the storeroom, the air outside was heavy and cloying. Every surface seemed to have harnessed the mid-summer sun. Still, murkiness and mugginess were better than the madness of waiting for Muggins. Time was not on Frank's side — the fate of Billy rested on finding this doctor before the Duke died. Seth had gone to see Billy earlier in the afternoon and said that his brother was much the same: sitting in the corner, hardly saying a word. Ophelia had wanted to go with him, but Frank had prevented her. Women weren't permitted in The Can, either as prisoner or visitor. On the odd occasion a woman was arrested, they were usually sent to the castle washhouse, next to the kitchen, where they'd spend their days up to their armpits in dirty linen and soapy water. It was commonly known as Hysteria House; it seemed agitation and washing went hand in hand.

Frank hadn't questioned Ophelia's visit, or that she'd been given the key to the cell, because he'd been so glad to see her. But now he wondered how she'd managed it. He increased his pace; he needed to see Billy.

Frank strode past The Can guards without stopping, and they didn't stop him; they just nodded gormlessly, one of the two even said 'good evening'. It had been thirteen hours since Frank had been released, but it seemed like moments ago; he wasn't even repulsed by the stench. It wasn't until he reached Billy's cell at the far end of the passage that he realised he needed the key. So *that's* why the guards had let him walk past; having a bit of a laugh were they?

He marched back down the passage and turned into the reception. Both guards were smiling; one of them, sitting behind a desk, was twirling a large key around his index finger. If it wasn't for Billy, Frank would have given the guard a good slapping.

"I ain't in the mood," he said, barely holding his temper. "Give me the key. I need t'speak to my son."

The other guard, leaning against the wall to the left of his comrade, answered, "Well maybe 'e don' need to speak to you. Seems t'me 'e don' need to speak to no-one."

Frank glared at the guard. This was met with uncertain defiance. The key twirler smirked.

"Last chance, boys." He gritted out the words, then extended an open palm towards the key twirler. "The key."

The key twirling ceased and the guard lost his smirk. He glanced at the other guard, who responded with a single, reluctant nod. The ex-smirker dangled the key over Frank's palm. Frank moved to grab it, but the guard snatched it back into his hand. They both laughed.

Frank snapped like an Achilles tendon, drew his arm back, hand clenched into a fist, ready to smash his knuckles into the face of the key twirler and give him a permanent smirk. But the follow-through never happened; in fact, before Frank could comprehend what was going on, his arm was pinned behind his back and he was swung around with his face pressed against the stone wall.

Frank struggled, but the grip was too strong. He tried kicking back, but his boots were wedged. The assailant twisted his arm, causing Frank to cry out in pain.

"Stop struggling, Master Offcut." The voice was calm, polite even. "Listen to me. I will take you to see Billy and no more will be made of this. But if you cannot control your temper, I will lock you up."

Frank was breathing heavily. The rough stone wall was grazing his left cheek, a hand was pressing against the lump behind his right ear, and his left arm felt like it was at breaking point.

"Do you understand?"

What choice did he have? Frank squeezed out a painful 'yes'. The pressure and pain released. Franks arm sprang back to his side as he whirled around to face his assailant. Both guards were now on their feet, waiting by the side of the desk, ready to pounce should Frank decide valour was the better part of discretion. His assailant, however, seemed warily calm.

"My apologies, Master Offcut," said Brandon Swill, Billy's arresting officer. "However, *you* would have been the sorry one should you have assaulted either of these guards." He flicked his gaze to the smug-looking guards and added, "No matter what the provocation." Their expressions changed immediately.

Frank wiped the grazed side of his face with his untwisted right arm. His anger was ebbing, his strength spent. The Swill boy's diplomacy was having an effect.

"Key," Brandon said to the guard holding the key.

The guard placed it slowly onto the Swill boy's palm: a sullen version of what might have occurred moments ago.

"Glad to see you're a quick learner, Beardsley," he remarked without humour. "Lieutenant Fowler will be most impressed."

So, these were Jethro Fowler's offal-brained men. That made sense.

Brandon Swill led Frank towards Billy's cell. Frank's left arm felt sore as it moved in time with his gait; no doubt some muscles had been pulled. And his head was aching. Frank had had better days.

"So, you wanna 'pologise for arrestin' our Billy?"

They'd walked past three apparently empty cells.

The Swill boy stopped and turned to face him. "Let's not have any misunderstanding, Master Offcut," he said, closing in on Frank, enough for him to have to slightly crane his neck to look the lieutenant in the eyes. "I am simply following orders. You are not to be hindered in your search for the young doctor. That does not mean you are at liberty to do as you will, and that *includes* visiting your son. So, look upon this as an act of goodwill on my part. As for apologising for your Billy's arrest, I would look to *your* part in your son's behaviour and his consequent arrest."

Frank bristled; a man barely flown from the nest lecturing *him* about raising children! What the frig would *he* know about it.

The Swill boy turned about and continued down the passage. Frank followed, biting his tongue. Still, he couldn't help feeling there was some truth to the words, particularly when the door was opened and he saw Billy huddled on his pallet in the corner of the cell.

"You have fifteen minutes, Master Offcut," said Brandon Swill. "Then I'll see you in the officers' quarters."

Frank nodded vaguely. He'd heard the words, but his son was front of mind.

Billy remained motionless as Frank sat beside him… except for his eyes. They followed Frank like a portrait of despair.

"You found the doctor, Pa?"

He sounded like a child. Frank fought back tears. *Had* he brought his son to this?

"Not yet, son," he said, resting a reassuring hand on the knees of Billy's bunched-up legs. "But it won' be long now. Don' you worry 'bout that."

Billy nodded, little more than a gloomy shape in a dark stone cell, the feeble passageway light struggling through the open door.

"I'm gettin' you outta here. Your ma an' me 'ave already decided that—"

"Wha' if y'carn find 'im?"

"Listen to me, Billy. I *will* find 'im, I prom—"

"Don' wanna go t'the dungeon, Pa." Billy was getting agitated.

"You ain't goin'—"

Billy suddenly sprang out of his corner and began pacing randomly. Raising his voice, his said, "Them guards carn find 'im. Sir Richard carn find 'im. They gotta ask you, Pa, an' you carn find 'im neiver. Ain't nobody gonna find 'im."

Frank stood up and reached out to comfort him, but Billy lashed out with his arms, keeping Frank at bay, and retreated back into his corner.

Frank was shocked. "Billy, lad," he said, trying to soothe his son.

Billy began rocking back and forward, arms locked across his shins, and intoned eerily into gloom, "Nobody gonna find 'im, nobody gonna find 'im, nobody gonna find 'im."

CHAPTER 5

I want your commitment

FRANK MARCHED PAST The Can guards without so much as a sideways glance and stepped outside. It was now dark. Apt, he thought — he was in a dark mood. Billy's mental state had deteriorated significantly since this morning. He felt guilty and angry. If the fault for Billy's predicament lay, ultimately, with Frank, then why was Billy being punished?

The night was still, carrying banter and laughter from dimly lit windows in the barracks. There was movement in the shadows, the clicking of boots on cobblestone, and something clanged in Klob Hoofenhaus' smithy, but Frank couldn't see anybody in its deep-purple confines. He paid it no heed, he wasn't at all interested in the goings on of Lower Icing's law enforcement community. It was only because the Swill boy was expecting him that he was immersed in it at all.

The officers' quarters were at the southern end of the barracks. Candlelight emanated from an open window to the left of a closed door. Frank walked past the door and looked in through the window. Brandon Swill was sitting at the mess table, talking to another Purple Perillian. It was that Fitzbadly tosser, greedily munching away on a glazed pastry. It was one of a selection piled on a plate at the centre of the table. Bloody Cake Eaters.

"Lieutenant," Frank called out through the window.

Both Swill and Fitzbadly turned their heads in his direction.

The former acknowledged his presence with a measured, "Master Offcut, come in; the door is open."

Frank really wasn't in the mood for all this formality. He sighed. Best to get it over with.

The mess room was very tidy: the stone floor had been recently swept, even the inglenook was free of errant ash, and the kindling was stacked precisely, ready to light. The bench that ran the length of the opposite wall presented a neat collection of crockery; tankards; utensils; two pairs of polished boots;

brushes and cloths; and, in the corner, tucked neatly underneath, a large bathing tub. The room was dominated, however, by the massive table set in the centre; it was easily big enough to cater for twenty men and a spit roast. Currently it was catering for two purple cream-puffs and a plate of cakes.

Swill and Fitzbadly sat opposite each other at the centre of the table, side on to Frank. Both sets of eyes were turned towards him.

"Well?" he said, addressing the Swill boy.

"Sit down, Master Offcut," suggested Swill.

"Yes, do, old chap," added Fitzbadly. "Join us for one of Master Puffy's fine pastries."

Even Swill looked uncomfortable at the comment. No wonder Sir Richard had resorted to engaging Frank's help. "Sorry, Lieutenan', but I got more importan' things t'do than sit around an' eat cake."

"That's rather bad luck for you, old chap."

Frank wasn't quite sure if he was being sarcastic or not, and he didn't care. He got straight to the point. "Y'wanted t'see me, Lieutenant. I'm 'ere. So wadya want?"

Fitzbadly bristled at his tone. "See here, Master Offcut."

The Swill boy was smirking. "Don't concern yourself, Seb. Master Offcut has difficulty communicating to anyone outside the world of butchery."

"I don' mince words, if tha's what y'mean."

"Very glad to hear it." Swill's smirk vanished. "So, what have you found out, Frank?"

Frank was momentarily taken aback by the directness and familiarity of the question. "My boy shouldn' be in tha' pissin' cell," Frank snapped. "You reckon I'm t'blame for 'is behaviour? Then lemmie take 'is place."

"A tempting offer," replied Swill. "However, this is a case of the ends justifying the means." He was a puppy-dog version of Sir Richard, thought Frank. "Billy's learning a lesson and, at the same time, providing you with an incentive to aid us in our search. So—"

"So wha' if 'e don' wanna be found or 'e's already fox food?"

"I say, Master Offcut!" Fitzbadly interjected.

"I don' give a toss wha' you say, Cake Eater!" Frank yelled at him. This was just some sort of pathetic show of power.

Fitzbadly had been about to take another bite of his glazed pastry; instead, he dropped it like a hotcake and rose, knocking the bench seat over.

Frank stood his ground from a distance of three paces; he wasn't at all worried by this posturing, chinless soldier-boy.

"Seb!" barked Swill.

"Damn it, Brandon!" Fitzbadly complained, as if Swill's voice had rooted him to the spot. "I'll not stand here and be insulted by this boorish oaf."

Frank almost asked him where he *would* stand, but Swill took over.

"Leave it, Seb. I'll deal with this."

"This really is intolerable, Brandon; the man should be clapped in irons."

The Swill boy slowly stood and stepped calmly towards Frank. "Master Offcut, I take it you have no information about the young doctor's whereabouts."

"No less than you," retorted Frank.

Swill nodded, and treated Frank to a condescending smile — the tosser really did think he was Sir Richard. "Let me assure you, this man is worth finding. His life *will* make a difference to all concerned, and that includes you *and* your son. To that end..." Frank was about to interrupt, but Swill raised his voice and overrode him, "I will assist you in any way I can."

That sounded more like it.

Lowering his voice, he added, "As for Billy, I understand your concern; I have no wish to see him in the dungeon."

Frank looked at him warily, unsure whether he was being sincere or just diplomatic. Swill sighed. "Listen, Frank..." He sounded weary. "I'm not meant to tell you this, but Billy's Witness Statement is yet to be signed."

"Brandon!" Fitzbadly was clearly outraged.

"It's alright, Seb."

For his part, Frank wasn't entirely sure what the revelation meant. Any statement that contained the word 'yet' should always be met with suspicion. "Tha' mean you 'ave no right t'keep our Billy in The Can?"

Fitzbadly shook his head in disgust.

"Like anyone else," Swill answered, "Billy can be detained for seven days without an official charge. Any longer requires a signed Witness Statement, one of the signatories being the arresting officer — in this case, me."

"So wha' does that mean, then?"

"It means," Swill said, meaningfully, "that if I don't sign the Witness Statement, Billy will be released on Thursday morning."

Frank regarded the Swill boy, trying to ascertain his intent. "Are y'sayin' tha' you won' sign it?"

Swill's brown eyes remained fixed on Frank, his overall expression impassive. "That depends on *you*, Frank."

So… blackmail or bribery was his game. "Go on."

"I want to be kept informed. Anything you learn, I'm next to find out. You find Xavier, you bring him to me."

There was a moment's silence. "Is tha' it?"

Swill's expression suddenly turned intense. "I want your *commitment* to this, Frank."

"My *commitment* ain't goin' t'bring 'im back from the dead," Frank countered.

"Let's assume he's alive, shall we? It is imper—"

"You're wasting your time, Brandon," chimed in Fitzbadly. Frank had almost forgotten he was standing there. "This fellow won't commit to anything that doesn't serve his own selfish needs."

Pompous twat.

"Well, Seb, this is a chance for Master Offcut to prove you wrong." He paused, waiting, perhaps, for Frank to say something. Frank had nothing to say. Lieutenant Swill was repeating what Sir Richard had already said, just in a less compelling way; Sir Richard had the bite to go with the bark.

CHAPTER 6

Stuff all this doctor nonsense

IT WAS CLEAR to Frank that he was going to have to take matters into his own hands. Seeing the Swill boy had been a complete waste of time — as if he needed any reminding that his son's freedom was at stake. And all that talk of this Xavier being such a wonderful person, a life that was *worth* something… What about *Billy's* worth.

Frank walked out of the castle into the night streets of Lower Icing. He was only vaguely aware of his surrounds as he marched down Noble Street. A man with a refined voice, walking in the opposite direction, bid him good evening, but he didn't respond. The man's face was a silhouette in the gloom and Frank wasn't the least bit interested in discovering his identity or swapping inane pleasantries. There was only one man he wanted to talk to and he was to be found at the scene of Billy's so-called crime. Stuff all this doctor nonsense; Will Plucker was the key to Billy's freedom.

The patrons of The Dead Duck were in full voice; most of them were singing along to a bawdy ditty being performed by a bawdy barmaid. Frank watched for a moment while she sang and played up to the crowd.

An' saucily 'e cries, "Sarah, Sarah, Sarah!
Won' y'show me y'wares?"

(To this, the barmaid pushed up her ample cleavage. The men in the crowd cheered.)

"Ah, me lovely, none is fairer, fairer, fairer:
Can I come up y'stairs?"

(To this, the barmaid lifted her loose-fitting skirt and revealed most of her black-stockinged left leg. Using two fingers, she walked her left hand up from her knee to a place barely concealed by the skirt. This sent the men and, unbelievably, most of the women into lustful rapture.)

Frank had seen and heard enough. So *this* was the kind of innocent flower

Billy was supposed to have offended with his advances.

Will Plucker greeted Frank warily and showed him into his office. It was surprising how much the sound of revelry and merriment was muffled by the closed door. Nevertheless, the conversation Frank was about to instigate would have to be conducted in raised voices.

Frank had a bit of time for Will Plucker. He was honest and a hard worker: traits that Frank admired. And even though he'd played a part in Billy's predicament, he hadn't been the one to involve the Cake Eaters. That was down to the Gamekeeper and his distorted sense of morality.

"I ain't 'ere to cause no trouble, Will," said Frank, "an' I ain't holdin' no grudges 'gainst you."

Dark eyes regarded him impassively from within a heat-reddened face. Will's rich, black hair was slick with sweat; the steaming cauldron of The Dead Duck, with its ale swilling, singing and cavorting in the stinking heat must be enough to make anyone feel like they were slowly being cooked.

"I wanna speak t'you 'bout our Billy," Frank continued. "See if we c'n work somethin' out between us."

Will raised a thick eyebrow, accentuating the furrows in his forehead. "Like wha'?"

"Like some sor' of... compensation for y'troubles."

"I ain't had no troubles, Frank."

"Look, Will, we both know wha's 'appened 'ere," said Frank, feeling his frustration build. "Billy's 'ad 'alf a tankard of ale, seen one of y'floosy's song'n'dance acts, an' taken it 'pon 'imself t'fumble 'is way to 'er centre stage. 'E obviously ballsed it up, but, let's face it, Will, it ain't nothin' more than a young lad doin' wha' comes nat'rally. An' we ain't talking about the Queen of Longbotia 'ere. This lass—"

"Is my niece," supplied Will sharply, cutting off Frank's argument. "'Er name is Jenny an' she ain't no floosy, Frank. She 'elps Joan in the kitchen. Your Billy 'ad been botherin' 'er. She told me that 'erself. 'E was told to leave off, bu' 'e still followed 'er into the storeroom. The only reason 'e didn' get to 'ave 'is way with 'er is down to Tom Skinner. Asked 'im to keep an eye out, like, an' lucky for 'er 'e did."

Bloody do-gooder, thought Frank. "The lad's got 'is problems, I ain't denyin' tha'," Frank conceded, trying to regain some traction. "An' some of them problems is down t'me, but 'e don't deserve a stretch in the dungeon. 'E's only sixteen."

"Jenny's barely *fourteen*."

This wasn't going how Frank had anticipated. As much as it galled him, he was going to have to eat humble pie. "You 'ave the righ' of it, Will; Billy was bang out of order with your niece. Wha' c'n I do t'put things righ'?"

Will's swarthy face looked thoughtful, and for a few seconds the two men eyed each other off. "Damage's already done," Will said quietly, barely loud enough to be heard above the laughter and singing coming from the other side of the door.

Will's attitude confounded Frank. Surely he could see The Dead Duck was a haystack of debauchery, and all Billy had done, in his typically clumsy way, was to find the needle of innocence. If he'd approached any other barmaid or frilled-up floosy, he would have been slapped back into place or, if he'd had coin, taken advantage of.

"'Ow much do y'wan' to retract the Witness Statemen'?" Frank blurted out, tired of all the diplomacy. He genuinely wanted to make amends on behalf of his son, but Will seemed to be in an obstinate frame of mind.

Will shook his head and smiled bitterly. "This ain't 'bout money, and the statement 'as nothin' to do with me. I tol' you — Tom Skinner's the one who found Billy all over Jenny. It's 'is Witness Statemen'. Y'talkin' to the wrong person, unless o'course y'gettin' 'round to apologisin'."

Will's gaze was intense, his eyes burning — he could have roasted a boar with them — and his massive hands were splayed out as if he was fighting the urge to gather them into fists. "Y'see, Frank," he continued, grinding out his words, "it's *me* who decides whether there's any grudges t'be 'eld."

Frank wasn't intimidated by any of it. If Will Plucker couldn't see the context of Billy's actions, then he'd overestimated the man. "Well, I guess we ain't got nothin' further t'discuss."

Will shook his head, braced his hands against the edge of the table, and pushed himself into a standing position. Frank followed him with his eyes. He was huge man, particularly in the confines of his office; his massive frame towered over Frank. Still, Frank wasn't cowered by that either. His short, stocky frame had served him well over the years. He stood, joining Will, who looked ruddily defiant behind a sheen of sweat. Mind you, Frank could feel his own beads of perspiration forming on his skull. Absently, he ran a hand across the back of his head and winced in pain as he touched the all-but-forgotten bruise behind his right ear.

Will smiled, but there was no humour in it. "Conscience hurtin' you, Frank?"

"Not as much as someone who'd let 'is *innocen'* niece work in an 'ouse full of whores," Frank retorted.

Will barked out a laugh. "Tha's rich comin' from someone who's sired Lower Icin's sauciest tart."

Frank felt blood rush to his head. His first impulse was to launch himself across the table, head first into Will's stomach. However, the man-mountain's expression — one of piteous contempt — stayed him. Frank realised it was exactly what Will expected him to do. Taking a deep breath, he carefully tucked his chair under the table.

"Tha's another thing y'can ask Tom Skinner 'bout," added Will, glaring at Frank.

"Wha' you on about?" Frank hissed.

Will remained impassive and moved towards the door. "Like you said, Frank, I think you an' me've said all we got t'say."

Frank stepped in front of the innkeeper. "Wha's the pissin' Gamekeeper got t'do with Ophelia?"

He stopped and sighed wearily. "Don' know. All I 'eard was they was drinkin' together with the inn crowd on Friday night."

"Who the bloody 'ell are the friggin' inn crowd?" Frank was imagining some sort of nature-loving sect, drinking weird potions made from exotic fungi and berries, dancing and cavorting naked around the forest.

"Calm down, Frank," said Will. "It's jus' what we call them nobs *you* kowtow to. The ones what drink at The Rabbit."

"Frank Offcut don' kowtow to no-one, specially them chinless ponces at The Rabbit!"

Will pushed past Frank and opened the door. The noise of The Dead Duck blasted through. He nodded for Frank to leave. Frank was happy to oblige.

It was good to be back outside in the relative freshness of a hot summer evening. The sounds of The Dead Duck gradually faded as Frank criss-crossed his way through the streets and laneways that led to his house. Hopefully Bert Muggins had discovered something useful.

His mind, however, was distracted by what Will Plucker had called Ophelia and what he claimed had happened at The Harey Rabbit. The Gamekeeper was the last person he wanted anywhere near his daughter. If he'd got her drunk and taken advantage, Frank would see to it that he shat Witness Statements for a week.

CHAPTER 7

Not ezackly

FRANK ARRIVED HOME around eleven o'clock. There'd been no news from Bert Muggins and that was worrying. Even Maizie's usually optimistic demeanour had wilted in the evening heat. The frustration of not being able to see Billy had sapped the bravado from her. Frank had been honest with her about Billy's condition and, like any mother, she wanted to comfort her son.

He put his arms around her and she squeezed him tightly. As she clung to him, he gently smoothed the small of her back and realised just how much Billy's absence was paining her. Frank had always thought The Can was no place for a woman, but, as Maizie quietly cried into his shoulder, he questioned the reasoning behind it.

Then another question crossed his mind: How *had* Ophelia managed to gain entry into their cell? Frank hadn't thought much about it at the time; he'd just been glad to see her and assumed she'd used her initiative. Ophelia was sharper than the keenest carving knife at Slaughter & Offcut, but what if she'd used something more… obvious? The words *the biggest tart in Lower Icing* echoed in his mind. Bloody Will Plucker.

Frank gently kissed the side of Maizie's head. "Don' cry, Maize," he whispered. "We'll get our Billy back."

She lifted her head from his shoulder. Her tear-filled eyes searched his face for reassurance.

"I promise, love."

She nodded, twitched a smile and wiped her eyes.

Five minutes later, Frank was standing outside his only daughter's bedroom. For his own peace of mind, he had to get to the bottom of the Gamekeeper rumour. He hadn't mentioned anything to Maizie — he didn't want to add to her worries. Trouble was, he wasn't exactly sure how to approach the matter with Ophelia; she was twenty-one after all, and Frank had always trusted and believed in her. Still, images of her living in a forest shack with the do-gooding Gamekeeper, raising a family of sprites and wood-nymphs, was enough for Frank to knock on his daughter's door. He waited for an answer. There was none.

"Ophelia?" he said to the closed door.

He waited a handful of seconds and then opened her door. Ophelia wasn't there. Frank turned down the corridor to his and Maizie's bedroom — she wasn't there. He went back down the corridor to Billy's room — she wasn't there either. He checked the bathing room — she wasn't there. He knocked on Seth's door and entered. Seth was asleep on his bed, propped into a sitting position by a pillow against the wall, an open ledger lying across his chest. He looked like a boy of twelve. Frank quietly put the ledger on the side table, then snuffed out the candle.

He went to the lounge room, where Maizie was also snuffing out the last of the candles. "Where's Ophelia?" he said, trying to make it sound like a casual enquiry, but he already knew what Maizie's response would be.

She faced him, her face illuminated by the chamberstick she held in her right hand. "Isn't she in…?" Then, realising the situation, she added, "She was here just before you arrived home."

Maizie moved towards him, looking more perplexed than concerned. "You don't think she's—"

"Taking matters into her own hands," Frank finished, wondering if he was angry or proud.

Before either of them could think about what to do next, there was an urgent rap at the front door. Frank grabbed the chamberstick from Maizie and quickly navigated his way across the dark lounge room to one of the two large windows that overlooked Market Street. They were both open to let in whatever breeze might happen to waft its way through. Frank leaned out of the window to his right and looked down to see who was at the front door. Even in the dark, he recognised the mad, silvery silhouette of Bert Muggins' hair.

Frank turned around. Maizie was standing behind him. "It's Bert Muggins," he whispered. Even Frank could hear the excitement in his hushed tones. Turning back to the street, he called down, "I'll be righ' there, Bert."

Without waiting for Bert's reaction, he moved back inside and handed the chamberstick back to Maizie. "Stay 'ere, love. I'll 'andle this."

Frank was halfway down the corridor when a voice shot out of the dark. "Ev'rythin' alrigh', Pa?"

"Bloody 'ell, Seth," gasped Frank, heart jumping.

"Sorry, Pa."

"Ev'rythin's fine, son. It's jus' Bert Muggins — nothin' t'worry 'bout."

Frank headed towards the staircase.

"You wan' me t'come with you, Pa?" Seth whispered after him.

Frank didn't want any of his family involved, not even Maizie. If he was partly responsible for Billy being in The Can, then he would be *entirely* responsible for getting him out of it. He was halfway down the stairs before he realised he hadn't answered Seth. He carried on regardless.

Making sure there was no-one else on the street, Frank ushered Bert into the reception area. However, he left the door open; the moonlight provided the only illumination, and Frank wanted to see Bert's face. He could usually tell if someone was lying by their expression. In Bert's case he could *always* tell.

Unfortunately, the light wasn't strong enough to highlight all of Bert's features. It picked up on his spiky, silvery beard and a few of his whiter teeth, but his eyes and nose were shrouded under a canopy of wayward grey locks.

"So, have you found 'im, Bert?" Frank asked, keeping his voice hushed.

Bert seemed to consider this for a moment. "Not ezackly."

Frank felt his stomach sink. "Listen 'ere, Bert, don' give me none of that 'not ezakcly' crap. I ain't payin' for 'not ezackly'. In fact, 'not ezackly' is ezackly wha' I *don'* wanna 'ear from you." Frank was now prodding his finger into Bert's chest.

"Calm down, Frank," Bert whispered, taking a step backwards towards the staircase. "I know who *does* know where 'e is."

"Who? An' why didn' you ask 'em y'self?"

Bert took another step backwards and almost stumbled on the bottom stair. "Ain't no 'mount of coin worth questionin' the Moleson Twins for."

Frank stared at Bert's quivering mouth. The vendor was genuinely afraid. *The Moleson Twins*, thought Frank, feeling suddenly sick in the pit of his stomach. If this doctor had fallen foul of those two thugs, the chances of him still being alive were minimal to say the least.

"I also 'eard they were plannin' to scarper town tonight," Bert added.

Frank swore.

CHAPTER 8
The Pits

JUST AFTER MIDNIGHT, some twenty minutes after Bert Muggins' knock at the door, Frank found himself walking towards a pocket of Lower Icing that was considered highly dangerous by the townsfolk. Well, at least by those who didn't actually *live* in the pocket. Bert Muggins' report had left him no choice. If what he had said was the truth — and Frank believed it was — he had to act fast.

He was concerned about Ophelia, but not worried. She was headstrong and determined, not foolish. He was also angry at her for disobeying him, but he had to find this naffing doctor. Billy was his first priority, and Bert Muggins had given him the lead he needed.

This lead took Frank north up Market Street for two hundred paces, then west into a narrow street known as Stinky Street. After thirty paces, he turned north into an alleyway; it was just wide enough to swing an alley cat (if your purpose was to bludgeon it against the stone walls).

The alley was black. Frank waited for his eyes to adjust, but the gloom was too deep. Gripping the handle of the number four-size boning knife he had sheathed under his belt, he stepped into the tunnel of darkness. It was one of a few grim entry ways into a grim collection of buildings inhabited by an equally grim collection of people.

It was built on the original Lower Icing cesspits, dug some two hundred years ago, but, as the town had grown, the cesspits had been moved to the other side of the Icing River. Still, the pocket had retained it historical significance, so to speak, and was now known as The Pits. The Pits was centred on one main laneway — colloquially known as Crapp Alley — connected to (or protected from) the outside world by twisting alleyways and foreboding architecture. Frank's skin crawled; the darkness seemed to caress him. No-one in their right mind would enter The Pits alone, not even in broad daylight — even the so-called men-at-arms rarely patrolled here — yet here he was, approaching

Crapp Alley in the middle of the night. The tension was terrible; he felt like his brain was about to explode. Subconsciously, he touched the back of his head behind his right ear — it was still tender and his head was slick with sweat.

He was walking like a blind man; left arm stretched out in front of him, feeling for any obstacles, right arm ready to pull out the Number Four Boning Knife. Each step was a battle with fear; his survival instincts cried out for him to turn around. All he could hear was blood pounding through his head. Then, suddenly, the blackness cleared.

Directly ahead, some twenty paces away, the shadowy façade of a squalid-looking building emerged. Frank felt an immediate sense of relief; he could now see his destination. He quickened his pace, eager to be out of the compressed blackness. By the time he reached the end of the alleyway, sounds of life began to filter through the clogging night.

The place smelt of excrement and it was stinking hot. Peering around the corner, Frank looked west down Crapp Alley. Murky candlelight emanated from a few open windows, vaguely illuminating the overhanging two-storey buildings that overlooked the narrow laneway. Frank could hear raised voices and laughter, and a door slammed somewhere, followed by the screeching of a cat. This was the moment of truth. Once he stepped into Crapp Alley, there would be no turning back; the shadows would know of his arrival — he would be watched. The trick was to look like you were meant to be there. Any signs of fear or stealth would be an open invitation for a mugging (or worse). He knew this because he'd visited The Pits once before.

A year or so ago, he'd agreed to supply a whole side of beef to a man known as The Slasher. His actual name was Paul Peabody, but Paul preferred the gruesome epithet, even though he looked and sounded more like a man of learning. He'd insisted that Frank deliver the beef himself, explaining "The Pits is like a bull-terrier — show it you belong and you'll be fine." Then he'd smiled and added, "Don't worry, Frank. I'll keep it on a short leash for you."

Frank stepped into Crapp Alley with The Slasher's less-than-comforting words echoing through his head. Taking a deep breath, he moved west with what he hoped looked like a purposeful gait. He saw no-one — no shadows in the darkness, no silhouettes in dimly lit windows — there was no sign of life at all. And yet it felt like a hundred sets of eyes were watching his every step. He listened for signs of habitation, but The Pits now seemed eerily devoid of life… apart from the cloying stench and the muted light.

Frank had only a vague idea of where he was heading. The Slasher owned and ran — for want of a better word — a tavern. His only visit to the dingy establishment had left him with the strong impression that ale wasn't the only thing brewed up there.

Frank saw and heard nothing. He just felt a sudden, intense pain across his right shin as his legs were kicked out from under him. He fell forwards, arms outstretched automatically to protect his head from impact. The uneven cobblestones smacked into his forearms, punched into his stomach, and grazed his knees. Then his arms were grabbed and pinned behind his back while somebody heavy kneeled on his back. Frank didn't have time to do anything except try to recover the air that had been knocked out of his lungs. The handle of the Number Four Boning Knife pressed into his hip and its sharp blade cut into his left thigh. Frank gasped. Then there was noise… a lot of noise… people laughing and cheering. He lifted his head, only to have it pushed back into the grotty surface.

"Stay still, y'tub o'lard," said a guttural voice. Then he barked, "Pesty! 'Urry up with that friggin' cord."

Frank lashed out with his body in an attempt to dislodge the person from his back, but all he got for his effort was another smack across the head and the suffocating pressure of a boot pressing down on his neck. Then his wrists were bound with what felt like a leather cord — whatever it was, it bit into his skin.

He was dragged to his feet, his head swimming in the gloom, and there were now lights floating across his vision. He wondered if he'd been knocked unconscious, but the pain was too real. The shadows pushed him forward. He stumbled, but was held from falling over.

Risking further assault, Frank said, "I wanna see The Slasher!"

This was met by more laughter and cheering.

CHAPTER 9

You must see the irony

FRANK WAS SLUMPED in a corner booth of what he recognised as The Slasher's tavern. His wrists were still bound; his hands had gone numb and felt dead, like a piece of meat. Only a painful throbbing in his elbows suggested otherwise. He'd been relieved of the Number Four Boning Knife. His trousers were sticky with blood and clinging warmly to his upper left leg. His scraped knees smarted and his head pounded — he was bleeding from a gash in his forehead; the red flow merged with rivulets of sweat and meandered down his face.

The three men who had attacked him had been joined by a fourth. Unlike the mob of muggers, he was clean-shaven and well presented in the neat, practical attire of an open white shirt and black trousers. His brown hair was thick and cropped short, like a leather cap. He wore a thoughtful expression as he sat down. In this light, The Slasher looked ten years younger than his forty years.

One of the muggers was holding a lantern. He placed it on the table and sat down opposite The Slasher. He nodded to the remaining men, who nodded back and then departed into the night.

Once the door had closed, The Slasher spoke. "Well, Frank, what brings you to The Pits on this fine summer evening?"

Frank was finding it hard to come to grips with his situation. It seemed unreal. He was also finding it hard to breathe. "The Moleson Twins," he croaked.

The Slasher raised an eyebrow, and shared a curious glance with his scruffy companion.

"And what business do you have with *them*?" The Slasher asked mildly.

Frank was sitting in an awkward position, one that constricted his breathing, and, with his hands bound, he couldn't lever himself out of it. He felt like he was about to pass out.

"Untie me an' I'll tell ya."

The Slasher nodded at the man across the table. Then he produced Frank's blood-stained Number Four Boning Knife. "Use this, Letch — looks sharp enough."

"S'okay. I can use me fingas."

Frank recognised the guttural tones he'd heard barking out orders to the other attackers.

"You'll have to excuse my un-learned friend here, Frank. He has no concept of irony."

"Don' need no irony to loosen a knot, Slasha."

Frank couldn't care less about irony either — he just wanted to be able to breathe properly. Letch moved next to Frank and turned him onto his right side. Frank felt no pain, just a tugging sensation as Letch worked away at the strapping.

From his new position, Frank could only see The Slasher from the corner of his eye. However, this did not deter The Slasher from continuing the conversation. "Hope you understand why such precautions are necessary, Frank. We get all sorts in The Pits. If only you'd let me know you were coming to visit us at such an unusual time, I could have arranged a more suitable welcome."

Frank wondered what he meant by that as Letch struggled with the knot.

"Unfortunately, you chose the 'sneak in with a nasty-looking knife' option. That kind of behaviour doesn't go down too well, I'm afraid. We're a suspicious lot here in The Pits."

Letch cursed.

"Are you sure you wouldn't like to use the knife, Letch. Poor Frank looks a tad uncomfortable."

"Almos' got the bastard. Pesty's done one of 'is never-slip knots," complained Letch. "An' it's a double."

"Oh… what a pest," replied The Slasher.

Eventually the tugging ceased and the binding loosened. Frank was grabbed by the left shoulder and pulled back into a sitting position by Letch. The blood began to surge back into his hands and fingers, accompanied by a rather uncomfortable pins and needles sensation. The tight leather cord had left creases criss-crossing on the outside of his arms and wrists. He grimaced in pain as he tried to move his fingers.

"My word, Frank," said The Slasher, pretending to be surprised. "You must have struck the lads in one of their more… *enthusiastic* moods." He shook his head reproachfully. "Again, that's probably down to your rather unfortunate timing. I mean, they do tend to drink a bit, and by midnight… well, their judgement is bound to be somewhat blurred."

Frank ignored the words and the sarcastic tone — he was consumed by pain. Apart from his arms, the cut to his thigh was still bleeding and his grazed forehead, elbows and knees smarted like a smack on the arse.

"Which brings me back to my original question: what morbid fascination do you have in the Moleson Twins that you'd be willing to risk life and limb by visiting them at such an unsociable time?"

Frank regarded The Slasher. His reasonable expression was all a façade, he knew that. You *earned* your name in The Pits, and Frank suspected that Paul Peabody (which described his physical presence very well) ruled The Pits with the guile of a very sharp mind. Frank flicked his gaze at Letch, who'd moved back to his position on the opposite side of the booth. He looked bored.

"I jus wanna talk to 'em 'bout somethin' that concerns our Billy," explained Frank wearily. "I 'ad t'come tonigh', 'cause I 'eard they were planning t'leave."

The Slasher's calm "Did you now?" was quickly followed by Letch's gruff, "Who tol' you that?"

Frank didn't answer Letch's question; he wasn't the answering type. He addressed the diminutive, clean-shaven man. "Our Billy's in The Can for gettin' too friendly with a barmaid. It's a stitch-up, Slasher, an' the nobs are gonna send 'im to the dungeon if I don' 'elp 'em find some toss-pot doctor. I 'eard the Molesons migh' 'ave… seen 'im." (He was going to say seen *to* him, because that's what Bert Muggins' had overheard at The Bloody Bell. However, he decided not to risk inflaming the situation — he wasn't sure his body could take any more inflammation.)

"I see," replied The Slasher

"Who tol' you that?" repeated Letch.

"Look…" Frank winced as he leaned forward on the table. "Bloody 'ell, Letch, I think y'broke a rib."

Letch shrugged.

"Anyway, I couldn't give a pig's ear why the Moleson Twins are scarperin' or where they're scarperin' to — I really ain't int'rested. I jus' wanna know wha' they know 'bout this doctor."

The Slasher seemed to be weighing up Frank's request. His eyes glistened in the muted candlelight. Letch also waited patiently for his fellow Pit-dweller's response.

"Assuming you find out what you wish to know, how do you intend to use the information?"

If he hadn't been sitting in the dingy confines of The Slasher's tavern, battered, bruised and bleeding in the company of a hulking scruff called Letch, it could easily have been Administrator Penman speaking to him. Frank knew there was no point trying to be clever with The Slasher; he was too tired anyway.

"The nobs at the castle jus' wan' this doctor found, alrigh'. Don' ask me why, but they're desp'rate 'nough t'get me to do their dirty work for 'em. Long as I poin' 'em in the right d'rection, they'll be satisfied. Won' be no need to go into details."

Again, The Slasher took his time to mull over Frank's words. Then he nodded to Letch.

Letch looked surprised. "Y'sure, Slasha?"

The Slasher shifted his gaze back to Frank. "I think Master Offcut can be taken at his word." Then he picked up the Number Four Boning Knife lying by the lantern and stabbed its sharp point into the table. The embedded, blood-stained knife was left to wag back and forth as The Slasher softly clasped his hands together. "He is, after all, an artisan of anatomy and a sharpener of blades; one might even say a master of the cut-and-thrust world of butchery. It is something to be… respected."

He smiled at Frank. Frank felt the hairs on the back of his neck stand up. He'd never been afraid of anyone before — not even The Fixer. However, there was something disturbing about The Slasher, and Frank came to the unpleasant realisation that he was mad.

Letch wore a blank expression. "If you say so, Slasha," he grumbled, oblivious (or accustomed) to The Slasher's demeanour.

He stood up, exited through the front door, and disappeared into the shadows of The Pits.

"Speaking of your skills," The Slasher continued, conversationally, as if Frank had just dropped in for a social drink. "I must compliment you, if somewhat belatedly, on the side of beef you provided for my fortieth birthday celebrations. It was very well received by our little community."

Frank wasn't sure how to react. He could use a drink.

The Slasher didn't wait for a response. "However, I feel your *questions* won't be quite as well received. Since their father, Morty, died a couple of months ago, the Moleson Twins have become a trifle more unpredictable, and rather more hot under the collar. Truth be known, Frank, I'll be glad to see the back of Mal and Mick."

There was a moment of silence. Frank felt the gloom of the empty tavern close in. *What sort of place was this?* "Is the tavern open?" he asked. He really was parched.

"Alas, I close early on Sundays, Frank," he replied casually. "It's my time for… contemplation. I find endless bar room banter somewhat… tiresome."

Why run a bloody tavern, then? thought Frank. "Any chance o'makin' an exception in this case?"

The Slasher regarded him for moment, as if considering whether Frank was worthy of such a concession. "Very well," he said amiably, snapping out of his reverie. "Why not? It's a rather warm evening, after all… or should I say early morning?"

Frank slumped against the wall as The Slasher stood and walked through the murkiness to the bar on the other side of the room. He could hardly believe he was in this situation — it seemed unreal. The last four days had been the worst of his life: Billy's arrest on Wednesday night; his own incarceration on Thursday morning; and then Sir Richard-bloody-Upson, that goody-goody Gamekeeper, and those puffed-up Cake Eaters all getting him to do their dirty work, twisting his arm with Billy's freedom. And now, here he was in a disturbingly deserted Crapp Alley tavern, beaten up by The Pits' welcoming committee, about to have a drink with their deranged leader, while waiting to interrogate a couple of notoriously unhinged thugs. It made slitting the throats of fully-grown boars seem positively delightful.

Surprisingly, and rather disappointingly, The Slasher returned with a bottle of rum and two small ceramic tumblers — not exactly what Frank would call thirst-quenching.

"This may relieve your pain somewhat, Frank," said The Slasher, carefully filling the first tumbler with the brown spirit, "and help prepare you for your… meeting."

The Slasher stopped pouring and placed the bottle on the table. Then he began to laugh quietly to himself. Frank watched in disbelief, gob-smacked. After a short period of mirthful jiggling, The Slasher managed to regain his composure.

Wiping tears from his eyes, he breathed for control. "I do apologise, Frank," he said, looking like he was about to laugh again. "It's just that I amuse myself sometimes… It's the word 'meeting'. You see, the Moleson Twins' idea of a meeting is where they turn people into meat… and you being a butcher, Frank… I'm sorry, but you must see the irony."

The only irony Frank could see was the blade of the Number Four Boning Knife stabbed into the table just out of lunging reach. He sighed. "I see it orright."

The Slasher filled the second tumbler and pushed it towards Frank. "Not a bad drop this. Comes from the Reggae Islands."

The significance was lost on Frank; he wasn't a rum drinker. He picked up the tumbler and swallowed its fiery liquid in one gulp. It burned at the back of his throat, but Frank showed no sign it had affected him at all, not even a grimace. The Slasher smiled and nodded. He, too, had managed to swallow the rum without any show of discomfort.

"Nice to see you're a man of culture, Frank," said The Slasher, refilling the tumblers.

Frank didn't reply — there was no need.

"You may be interested to know that in Reggae Islander culture, *hair* is worshipped."

Frank *wasn't* interested to know; he downed the second tumbler as soon as it was filled. The rum might not be quenching his thirst, but it was already beginning to make him feel light-headed.

"The Reggae Islanders with the most impressive hair become community leaders and are known as Affros."

"Lucky I ain't a Reggae Islanda, then," commented Frank, under his breath.

The Slasher burst into laughter. "Very good, Frank; I do enjoy wit, particularly in the face of adversity. Well done. Most impressive."

The tumbler was filled for a third time. Again, Frank downed it in one gulp — he was definitely warming to aromatic spirit and, as The Slasher had pointed out, it was doing a good job of numbing his throbbing head. The cut in his thigh still smarted though.

"The Affros also oversee the making of the rum," remarked The Slasher, returning to his cultural commentary. "They regard it as a kind of love potion — an *Affro*desiac, if you will."

The Slasher's eyes glistened, waiting for Frank to respond (with fits of laughter no doubt). The best Frank could manage was a forced smile. Undeterred, The Slasher poured Frank another drink. Again, Frank wasted no time imbibing the sweet fluid.

"Rum is, in actual fact, a depressant and hardly conducive to heightened sexual performance."

Normally Frank would have found this kind of talk uncomfortable (to say the least), but, in this particular time and space, he really couldn't care less what The Slasher was on about. His head was swimming.

"Therein lies the irony."

Frank began to chuckle, and he wasn't sure why.

He was still chuckling when the Moleson Twins burst into the tavern.

CHAPTER 10

Number Four Boning Knife

THE MUTED ATMOSPHERE of The Slasher's tavern burst into angry life with the entrance of the Moleson Twins (and Letch). The lead twin looked ready to explode. Frank knew them by reputation only, and, judging by their menacing demeanour, it was something to be grateful for. They both had greasy, black, shoulder-length hair and a week's growth over thin, pinched features to go with their prominent noses. It was hard to tell the colour of their eyes in the dim light, but they looked dark, like their clothing. To Frank, they were identical.

"Wha' the frig is this all abou', Slasha?" the first Moleson barked, flicking his gaze at Frank.

Looking closer, Frank noticed a scabby remnant of a graze under his growth and felt a cold chill enter his warm, rummed-up world.

"Somethin' amusin' you, baldy?" the second Moleson Twin followed up.

Frank eyed him, feeling somewhat detached from the situation.

"No need for unpleasant language, Mal," The Slasher said, unperturbed by the Molesons' aggressive posturing. "Sit down and join us for a drink. Letch, will you do the honours, please?"

"Look, Slasha, we ain't got no time for muckin' abou' tonigh'," Mal said. Clearly he was the leader of the two. Mick was still glaring at Frank.

The Slasher smiled. "I don't do 'mucking about', Mal. This won't take long. Now, please mind your manners and sit down."

Reluctantly, the Moleson Twins slid into the booth opposite The Slasher.

"I'm sure you recognise Frank Offcut, Lower Icing's finest butcher — *literally* speaking, of course. He is a man of integrity and... admirable determination." Then he flicked his gaze to the motionless figure at the door and added. "Some time before the sun rises, Letch. The boys look particularly thirsty."

Letch moped over to the bar to retrieve the drinks.

Frank sat at the end of the booth, The Slasher to his right, the Moleson

Twins to his left (with Mal sitting closest). The Twins had been in The Can the Wednesday night of Billy's arrest, and also when Frank had been man-handled into his son's cell the following morning. Frank had paid them no heed. The only time he'd even been aware of their presence was when they'd been released on the Friday morning, some twenty-four hours after Frank had been arrested. And now, here he was, in the very early hours of Monday morning, sitting alongside them in Lower Icing's seediest tavern. Still, at least The Slasher seemed to have them under control, and, despite their menacing demeanour, Frank felt quite relaxed. If they tried anything, they'd be in for a nasty shock — Frank Offcut didn't go down without a fight. Still, he wouldn't mind some more of that rum…

The blood-stained Number Four Boning Knife looked strange stabbed into the table, like an ornament to violence, but neither of the Moleson Twins made any comment. In fact, no-one was saying anything.

"Look—" Frank began, but was cut off crisply by The Slasher.

"I think we should wait for Letch to join us with the drinks before we begin." He smiled at them all. No-one smiled back.

As if on cue, Letch loomed out of the shadows with three massive tankards of ale — they must have held at least two pints each. He placed them gently on the table, slid one to each of the Twins, and then sat down next to The Slasher.

"Thank you, Letch," said The Slasher. Then he picked up the bottle of rum. "Would you care for another tot, Frank?"

Frank nodded. The Slasher smiled, filled Frank's tumbler, and then his own. Frank moved a hand towards the tumbler, but was stopped by The Slasher's frown. Frank flicked a glance at Mal and Mick — both had their arms folded, and both looked distinctly pissed-off.

Placing the bottle back on the table, The Slasher raised his tumbler. Letch was quick to follow suit, and the Twins begrudgingly unfolded their arms and picked up their tankards. It all seemed so ludicrous. What hold did The Slasher have over these meat-heads? Frank picked up his tumbler.

The Slasher nodded his approval. "There we are, gentlemen. To your h—" he began, and then paused. A bemused expression crossed his face. "I was going to say 'health', but that's probably not appropriate in poor Frank's case."

Letch let out a chuckle.

Normally, Frank would have lashed out at a remark like that, but he felt oddly removed from the bizarre gathering. He'd been inebriated many times, but he'd never felt like this.

"Perhaps, Letch, a toast to a bright future is more relevant to my late night guests." He raised his tumbler and smiled. "Gentlemen… to a bright future."

Only Letch echoed the toast before diving into his tankard. Frank and The Slasher quaffed their measures quickly, while the Moleson Twins took a few gulps before sloshing their tankards on the table. They all had to wait while Letch emptied the entire contents of his tankard down his gullet. Well, *some* of the contents — quite a bit was dribbling down his scruffy, bearded neck. It was a morbidly fascinating sight; to scoff *that* much ale without breathing was impressive. Frank waited — along with the others — for the explosive finale. The belch that eventually erupted from Letch's mouth vibrated through the table. So much so, in fact, that the Number Four Boning Knife began to quiver.

"Righ'," said Mal, sneering in disgust at Letch, "wha's this all abou'?"

"This better be good, butcha boy," added Mick, glaring at Frank.

Frank knew he should be worried, but he wasn't.

He was about to answer when The Slasher cut in. "It's quite simple… Frank hopes you'll be able reveal the whereabouts of the missing doctor, since you boys were the last to see him, or should I say… have *contact* with him."

There was a moment of silence, during which Letch released a secondary gas-filled tremor.

Mal let out a derisive bark of laughter. "This some sor'ov jest, Slasha?" Then he cast his baleful eyes over Frank, mirroring his brother's expression.

The Slasher remained calm, and a thoughtful expression crossed his face. "No… I do believe Frank is in earnest. Aren't you, Frank?"

Frank suddenly felt cold. This was all just a game to the mad mind of Paul Peabody. Before *he* even realised what he was doing, Frank sprang forward and grabbed the Number Four Boning Knife. Then he whirled to the left and held the point of the slim, bloodied blade against Mal Moleson's neck. "Anyone makes a move an' bother boy number-one gets bled."

Was this really happening?

The Slasher appeared unmoved by Frank's move. "You *see*, Mal, I was right — Frank *is* in earnest."

Keeping his head still, Mal turned his eyes towards Frank and grinned, "You're dead meat, butcha."

Mick looked worried, in two minds, weighing up the chances of disarming Frank before he could stick the knife into Mal's neck. There was no chance.

Letch was a motionless lump merging into the gloom.

"All I wanna know is wha' y'did to tha' pissin' doctor," said Frank. Somewhere, submerged in the depths of Reggae Island rum, he was feeling sick with fear.

"Piss off," Mal said, not moving his jaw.

Frank pressed the point of the knife into his neck, causing him to tilt his head towards his brother.

"Seems like a reasonable question to me, Mal," said The Slasher.

Mick's eyes were darting from his brother to Frank. He looked extremely agitated. "E's serious, Mal."

"I ain't gonna tell the nobs nothin' 'bout you or y'pissin' brother," said Frank, keeping the point pressed into the side of Mal's neck. A small trickle of blood had started to flow. "They jus' wan' this friggin' doctor."

Frank dug a little deeper with the Number Four Boning Knife. The pink skin of Mal's neck was not much different from a pig's; he had no qualms about using the knife from a butchery point of view. Mal grunted in pain and tried to angle his neck farther away from the blade, but his head had nowhere to go and his body was jammed up next to Mick's.

Letch belched again.

"I can't see any harm in telling Frank what he wants to know, Mal," said The Slasher, sounding reasonable and mad at the same time. "The same, however, cannot be said should you decline to answer. As I pointed out earlier, Frank is Lower Icing's finest butcher. I'd say he's just one twitch away from slaughtering you."

Frank ignored The Slasher; he didn't want to see the glee in his eyes. He kept his gaze focused on the Moleson Twins. They might be identical in looks, but, at this moment, they were very easy to tell apart: defiant and angry Mal pinned next to uncertain and frightened Mick. Unsurprisingly, it was Mick who succumbed to Frank's knife and The Slasher's taunts.

"We saw 'im ou'side The Bell," Mick spluttered.

"Well 'e ain't there now," replied Frank. "What 'appened?"

Mal grunted his defiance.

"Shuddup." Frank moved the knife across his neck, opening up a small wound. The trickle of blood became a flow.

Mick gushed out more information. "'E was jus' there, near the back, by the stables… like 'e was…" He paused, looking sick at the sight of the blood.

"Spit it out, Mick," commented The Slasher, adding his casual insanity to the mix. "Your tied tongue may end up slitting your brother's throat."

Letch chuckled. (Then belched.)

"Origh'," breathed Mick. "We done 'im over. 'E was askin' for it, bein' ou' there by 'imself that time o' night."

Frank snarled. He wouldn't be here if wasn't for these offal-brained louts. "When was this?"

"Dunno. Some time Friday nigh'. We'd been in The Can for a week an' needed some coin for drinkin'. Struck gold with 'im, we did."

"Whatcha do with 'im?"

Mick hesitated, casting a quick glance at The Slasher. "We... er..."

"Mick," Mal hissed.

"We beat 'im up," Mick finished.

"'Ow bad?"

"Dunno. Didn' put up no fight. Jus' smacked 'im one an 'e fell. Weren' dead or nothin'."

"An' that's it?" Frank had a sinking feeling he'd come here for nothing. This had happened two nights ago, but, according to the nobs, the doctor had been missing since early Thursday morning. So where the bloody hell had he been for a day and a half before he ran into the Moleson Twins?

"We left 'im there... minus a pouch of coins an' a—"

"Mick!" Mal snapped.

Frank's mind was wandering; he was finding it harder to remain focused, and his right arm was aching, making it difficult for him to hold the Number Four Boning Knife in place. There was quite a bit of blood dribbling down the side of Mal's neck, but it was nothing serious.

"Oh, don't be such a spoilsport, Mal," interjected The Slasher; his voice sounded ethereal in the lantern's gloom. "Mick was just approaching the twist in his tale."

"Irony!" blurted out Letch.

So, The Slasher knew what had happened to the young doctor; he'd just orchestrated this performance for his own sick amusement. Mick looked uncertain — caught between loyalty to his brother and the mocking insistence of The Slasher.

"Go on," pressed Frank. He wasn't quite sure how much longer he could hold the knife. His palm was slick with sweat (to go along with the ache in his arm).

"'E was wearin' a silver pendan' round 'is neck, so we nicked tha' as well." Mick looked very uncomfortable. "Found out the next day there'd been some intruder at the castle, an' then the Town Crier... Well... 'parently 'e said somethin' 'bout a silver button with a feather an' a broken sword 'graved on it.

Turned ou' there was a feather an' broken sword 'graved on the friggin' pendan'."

"Brilliant," said The Slasher, clearly delighted with the outcome. "Of course, by this time," he added, gleefully, "the doctor was no longer where the boys had left him. So, not only were they unable to claim the reward, they were in possession of incriminating evidence."

The story was spiralling out of control. Frank wasn't interested in silver pendants or feathers. Had he heard that right? He was finding it hard to concentrate — all his energy was focused on holding the knife steady.

"Not for long we wasn'," Mick said.

"No, not for long," agreed The Slasher.

Frank's vision was swimming. His body was wet with sweat.

"Kep' the leather cord though."

"Good thinking."

The voices were just sounds. They had no owners.

"Letch."

Something came flying out of the darkness. It was Letch's tankard. Frank's last thought before it smashed into his face was of... irony.

CHAPTER 11

Drier than a bag of sawdust

THE HEAT WAS the same. The darkness was the same. It was the sound that was different: a buzzing noise.

Now that he was aware of the sound, he could feel a tickling sensation on his face. He tried to scratch it, but his arms wouldn't move. It was very frustrating. Then he opened his eyes.

White, glaring light. He shut them.

He tried again, slowly, eyelids fluttering against the brightness. Colours began to emerge. A glaring blue dominated, but there was also a hazy brown, grey and green, with a spot of yellow moving at the edge of his vision.

Now there was another sensation: pressure against the right side of his face, hard and uneven. He moved his head; pain erupted.

He gasped. Parched lips peeled open.

His mouth was dry. He ran his tongue across his lips. It was like leather against pine bark.

Gradually, the light became less intense and his vision focused: glaring blue into sky, brown and grey into soil and exposed rock. About two feet away was a stunted green shrub with a yellow flower. The buzzing returned as a pair of flies landed on his head. He wanted to shake them off, but he was afraid of the pain.

Frank breathed deeply, trying to collect his thoughts. The last thing he remembered was the tankard smashing into his face. Now he was lying on his right side, out in the open somewhere, his hands bound behind his back. He could wriggle them without pain, but they felt grazed. His position made moving his arms difficult. He gingerly tried his legs; they were obviously bruised and battered, but nothing felt broken. He moved his ankles; once again it seemed the pain was only superficial. However, there was a throbbing coming from his left thigh; he must have cut it on a rock or something. No, the Number Four Boning Knife had dug into him when he was jumped by the Letch mob.

He took a deep breath and tried moving his head. Gently, very gently…

his blood began to pulse, a wave of nausea and pain, but he persevered. The wave passed.

He carefully levered himself into a sitting position. He was aided by his downward-sloping position. Nevertheless, he had to overcome a second wave of nausea and more pain. And the sun… it was bright and burning.

The first thing Frank realised was that he had no idea where he was; he recognised nothing, no landmark… nothing. Ahead of him lay a scrubby surface that sloped gently downwards for thirty or forty paces before levelling out. In the distance, roughly two hundred paces away, trees began to appear, until they became a forest covering just about all he could see.

He scanned the vista: he was at the edge of a valley, two or more miles wide, bordered by a steep ridge. To his left, it narrowed and merged into hills. To his right, it extended into a green forest haze. Frank twisted around to see what lay behind him. Again he gasped in pain; his back felt like it had been trampled on by a raging bull. Was there any part of him that hadn't been battered?

As he recovered his breath, he blew away the persistent flies that found his face and head so irresistible. Looking up, he could see he was sitting at the base of a steep slope that disappeared into blinding sunlight. He squeezed his eyes shut and felt pain above his right eye. He gasped. The air was hot and his mouth drier than a bag of sawdust. He couldn't shade his eyes; his hands were bound. He stopped craning his head, squinted open his eyes, and scanned the immediate area. About three paces to his right lay an exposed seam of quartz. Slowly and carefully, Frank shuffled towards the seam — each sideways movement sent a jab of pain up his back and caused his head to throb. It took at least five minutes to cover the distance and he was sweating profusely by the time he'd positioned himself next to the quartz. The sun, directly overhead, continued to beat down on his beaten-up body. He had to get out of its burning rays, but, to do that, he needed to free his hands. Fortunately, the seam of quartz looked jagged enough to do the job.

Frank used his legs to manoeuvre into position, and then used his fingers to feel the surface of the quartz seam. Finding the sharpest section, he positioned his wrists until the binding rested against the hard rock. Leaning back slightly to apply downward force, he rubbed the leather binding against the seam in a sawing motion. This soon turned into a sore-ing motion. His arms ached, his back ached, and his head felt like it was being steamed. To top it all off, Frank was under constant attack from flies and other sweat-seeking insects. He tried to blow away the ones that landed on his face, but that only provided temporary relief. The ones that covered his head and neck were harder to dislodge. Shaking his head caused him pain, particularly on his forehead above his right eye. The tankard… What damage had *that* done?

Frank had to progress in short, frantic spurts. The leather *felt* like it was fraying, but he had no way of knowing. After what must have been close to half an hour, he was ready to give in. He was exhausted, and the leather binding had rubbed against his skin as much as the quartz. His wrists felt as if they had been cut to the bone.

So this was it. He would perish here in the middle of nowhere, left to the scavengers to pick his bones dry… never to see his family again… feel Maizie's comforting caress. He would end like an animal: a carcass to be dined upon. The Slasher would have appreciated the irony.

The bloody Slasher. He'd done this to him. Manipulating bastard, stirring up the Moleson Twins. He knew *exactly* what had happened to the frigging doctor.

"Bastard!" Frank yelled to no-one, and the word echoed across the valley to no-one. And the damn flies… would they *never* desist?

His anger transported him to a place inside his head and he forgot his hands were bound. Instinctively, he tried to swipe the flies. It was then he felt the bindings snap.

INTERLUDE

SID AND HORATIO

Saturday, July 4th

SID AND DOCTOR Manky had parted company half an hour ago. Sid had spent the time following the North Road south, enjoying the fresh, early-morning air. The signs of a new day were evident; the black sky was now tinged red and purple on the eastern horizon, while the silent night was now punctuated by twittering, chirping and squawking.

As pleasant as it was, Sid was looking forward to getting back to the familiar surrounds of Lower Icing, and he was more than looking forward to patching things up with Mary. He wished he was in her arms right now, explaining why he'd run from her. But *could* he explain it? What *had* it all been about? All he could tell her was Manky's fanciful tale about the Duke and his long-lost son. However, if *he* didn't believe it, then Mary was hardly likely to. For frig sake, he'd have to think of something better than that!

At least he was finally away from all that madness. He was glad that Doctor Manky had taken the silver button. Manky was right: it only incriminated him — let the good doctor deal with Sir Richard Up-his-arse. Sid had had enough of being used. He wondered where Manky was now. Had he gained entry into the castle? Had Bertrand charmed his way past the guards? Had they even *reached* the castle? Bloody hell — it *was* frigging madness.

Sid's scrambled thoughts turned to his estranged sister. She had a *lot* of explaining to do, not only because of the letter to Reg Puffy, but due to the fact that she was involved *somehow* with Manky's protégé. Yes, as soon as he'd patched up things with Mary, he'd confront Liv.

And what about Gerald? He'd certainly been very defensive recently. Was he involved with Xavier too? According to Mary, last Saturday's proclamation had been a variation on the truth. Was Gerald responsible for that, or was it someone else, someone who had it in for Sir Richard?

Forget it, he reminded himself. It wasn't his worry anymore; the burden of the button was gone. He wasn't even concerned about *his* attacker. Best put it down to some random mugging and move on… hopefully with Mary. *Would* she forgive him?

Sid inhaled deeply, taking in the cool dawn air. The dark shapes of night were becoming more distinct, but the road ahead was still a smudge of shadows. And, as yet, there was no sign of Lower Icing castle on the horizon.

Sid tried to focus on the positives. He'd found out why Doctor Manky had approached him — mad though it was. He was fifty gold pieces to the good (a year's worth of supplying Will Plucker with Reg Puffy's pork pies) and his face was much better, which, he had to admit, was also due to the doctor. Who would have thought cow's piss and thistles could have such healing properties? However, it was more than just physical wellbeing; Sid also felt fresher in mind and spirit. The fog from his bashing had finally cleared.

Some half an hour later, through the birdsong of dawn, Sid heard a low thudding sound. He stopped walking and listened. It was coming from behind him. He turned around. The North Road stretched out north before him: a light-grey strip surrounded by dark underbrush, tinged violet by the early morning light. It only took a few seconds for Sid to realise that he was listening to horses — two, maybe three — approaching at a canter.

He moved off the road and took cover behind a nearby clump of bushes. Reaching down with his right hand, he felt the reassuring tassels at the back of his boots; his daggers were in place. He might be able to hitch a ride, but he wasn't taking any chances. He'd judge whether to make an appearance when he had a better idea who was riding towards him. It wouldn't be easy to identify anyone in this light, but he *could* see shapes (and whether the shapes were heavily armed).

It took around twenty seconds for the shapes to emerge from the gloom: two horses being ridden abreast. The rider on Sid's side of the road was much bigger than his companion (and looked somewhat sloppy in the saddle). The other rider also looked unnatural in the saddle, but at least he wasn't swaying as much.

Thirty paces away, Sid could make out the flowing blonde hair of the smaller rider and... a second person on the large rider's horse?

Twenty paces away, there were definitely two people astride the horse on Sid's side of the road. The front person was braced between the arms of the one who was controlling the horse, and his head was lolling as if he were asleep. The rider on the other horse looked like a woman. They appeared harmless enough.

Sid stepped out from behind the cover, waving his arms. "Hold," he yelled.

Both horses were reined in. The woman's horse reared slightly, but she managed to keep it under control. They came to a halt about five paces from where Sid now stood on the side of the road. By this stage, the man in control of the other horse had drawn a sword.

Sid had no idea of the highway protocol, so he had a stab in the dark with "Peace be with you, travellers" and held up his hands to show he held no weapon.

THE STORY CONCLUDES
IN BOOK TWO OF THE SILVER BUTTON SAGA:

WHEN FRANK OFFCUT WENT MISSING

AUTHOR'S NOTE

Firstly, thanks for reading *When Doctor Manky Strolled In*… I hope you enjoyed it (and wish to continue your immersion in the intrigues of Lower Icing by reading *Book Two – When Frank Offcut Went Missing*… No pressure).

The world of *The Five Duchies* and *The Silver Button Saga* certainly didn't turn out like I expected — it was supposed to be a shortish story centred around a man who is wrongly accused of robbery. The working title was *A Villain's Story* (super-imaginative, I know). I had Sid Evily as the 'villain' and Doctor Manky as the catalyst, but that was about it — from there, I pretty much made it up as I went along.

The story is set in 'medieval times' (Middle Ages) because I like the era, particularly the history of Britain during this time. Having said that, Lower Icing and the details of daily life within the story are not necessarily medieval or accurate (the Milk & Stout architecture and Hamlet Macbeth character are clearly Tudor references, well past what is considered medieval) but I didn't want to get bogged down in accurate historical detail – that's why there is no year designated to the dates.

The creation of *The Five Duchies* was something else that evolved as I wrote the story. I didn't start with them being aligned to any real countries, but they kind of morphed into Wales, Scotland, Ireland and England… The fact the 'England' gets two duchies is testament to my lack of intent. But then I played upon the idea by incorporating European counterparts like Escargotia (France) and Icarumba (Spain) into the mix.

The various accents – none of which are meant to be derogatory in any way – are written phonetically so readers can get a better feel for the characters and their standing within a class-system of have and have nots, education and ignorance, privilege and place. But, more than anything else, it allowed me to inject more humour into the story and play upon cultural diversities…

Juanita (who becomes a 'real' character in Book Two) was a joy.

The characters were the drivers of this story, they turned a 40,000-word yarn into a 350,000-word saga. They kept me entertained — I hung out with them for 9 years to spend just a few weeks with them in Lower Icing. I really enjoyed writing the different character perspectives. In many cases, I couldn't decide who had the right of the argument. It was super fun being with Sir Richard, no matter what the other characters threw at him.

The only thing Sir Richard didn't have to contend with was religion, which he certainly would have in the real Middle Ages. Apart from the Blessed Whipping beliefs, I purposely avoided any real religion in the story — there was enough for the characters to handle without priests, monks and whatnot sticking their oars in. (And it probably explains why The Five Duchies are at peace.)

The other extravagant departure from reality is the medical knowledge of Doctor Manky and Xavier. Obviously, Poetry in Potion isn't a real medical doctrine, and the 'potions' and their applications are clearly fictional, so please don't try them at home — they may kill you. The only potion that has any medical context is Natron Bomb (the one Xavier gives to Brandon to cure his hangover). Natron (a natural salt mixture found in some dry lakes) was harvested as far back as Egyptian times. It was used as teeth cleaner and mouthwash. Blended with oil, it was used as soap, so it didn't seem too much of a stretch to make it a stomach settler (when blended with lemon essence and ginger root). The other 'medical' titbit of truth is the reference to Chicken Pox being carried by pigeons – one of many theories surrounding the various poxes over the centuries. The poisonous nature of the Yew tree (which Tom's bow is partly made from) is also true.

The structure of the castle – Lower, Middle and Upper Baileys – is based on large castles of the period. However, a doubt whether any of them had an Administration Section, the Office of Petitions would have been seen as the rantings of a madman, and I'd say the luxuriously lavish Upper Bailey is probably more circa French revolution.

Anyway… it was fun mucking around with history.

THE MAPS

The other thing I'd like to mention are the maps. The map of Lower Icing was my COVID lockdown project in 2020. It started off as just the Castle, then I thought I'd include the surrounding streets, Town Square and the two inns (The Harey Rabbit and The Bloody Bell). Then I thought I'd include The Market, Lower Icing College and Slaughter & Offcut, then… you get the idea. In the end, the Castle (drawn on two A4 sheets of paper) had become the entire town of Lower Icing (on dozens of A4 sheets, measuring roughly 1.8m by 1.5m) and six months had gone by (well past lock down). Still, I was pretty pleased with the end result, everything was hand drawn (no ruler was used – which is fairly obvious, I guess) and it gave me a much clearer idea of the geography of the town. Of course, this caused a few rewrites; adjusting distances and times it would take to walk from one place to another… it's not all beer and skittles being a Creator.

The Five Duchies map was conceived as I was reviewing the edits of the manuscript. I had a rough idea of where everything sat in relation to each other, so it came together fairly quickly (within an afternoon). However, I did spend a couple of weeks thinking up some of the more obscure place names. Still, it was little more than a scratchy mud map before being totally transformed in the design process. Seeing it finished made me feel like the Five Duchies really exists (which it kind of does… in my head).

ACKNOWLEDGEMENTS

Firstly, I'd like to thank the people who helped me write this book, all the guys and gals working in cafés supplying me with flat whites and toast. I reckon at least 90% of the story was written in cafés, mainly in Adelaide, but also Carlton, Bondi, Port Douglas.

Rosey's (sadly no longer Rosey's) was where most of it was written, and the last words typed… which was, literally, a champagne moment. Rosey Hume ran the eponymic Rosey's and pretty much lived every chapter of *When Frank Offcut Went Missing* with me. Even though Mary Brewer was an established character by then, I couldn't help seeing parallels. So, thanks Rosey for being so enthusiastic, entertaining and a good mate during those fab Rosey's days.

The next stage saw the story take printed manuscript form, in eight ring-bound volumes. After sifting through it and finding an amazing number of typos and grammatical errors, I shared it with any willing readers, which, as it turned out, amounted to three people. (That makes this next bit a whole lot simpler.) So, thanks, Dave Horbelt — a great friend of mine who couldn't wait to read it, and he did so with sincere enthusiasm and enjoyment. Dave, you propelled me forward; Peter Nelson — another friend, one who doesn't usually read fiction. Peter, I'm grateful for your support and your forensic ability to find twice as many typos as me; and, finally, to Michelle Dottoré (my hairdresser) who provided me with the funniest feedback: "You know what I *love* about this book?" she said. And I'm thinking *wow*, she sounds super impressed. Then she followed up with, "The ring-binding! It's brilliant – the pages stay flat, so you can just rest it on your lap." Of all the comments, this is the one that will stay with me.

After a few years of faffing around with the manuscript, I decided 2020 was the year to begin the process of turning it into a book. (COVID-19 didn't have much of an upside, but I have it to thank for getting my literary arse into gear.)

First cab off the rank was obtaining a professional overview. This fell to Nicki Markus (who also edited the story). Nicki gave the story a general thumbs up and a list of suggestions to turn it into a high five. I agreed with most of them — creativity is a subjective thing. One of her many excellent suggestions was to create a timeline. This proved to be a very worthwhile (if time-consuming) exercise, and completely changed the structure of *When Frank Offcut Went Missing* for the better. Originally, I had Mary, Ophelia and Olivia rotating in order, but from a *chronology* point of view it was a little confusing. So, I rearranged, sliced and diced all the chapters, until they made more chronological sense. The editing process was also extremely helpful, and I now know the difference between 'further' and 'farther'. So, thanks Nicki for your diligence and availability – you helped me write a better version of the story.

And, finally, Rachel Rolfe, who transformed my word documents into what you've just read. Rachel was a 'random' discovery on my Find a Book Cover Designer journey. She was recommended by another designer, Christine Sharp (who was kind enough to respond to my query) and I'm so glad I took her recommendation. Rachel – who told me she wasn't an illustrator – not only designed the cover, but also constructed the chapter illustrations (except the Belladonna), turned my mud map of The Five Duchies into a real map and added all the information to the Lower Icing map. She did the typography and typesetting, managed to interpret my ramblings, and brought the Middle Ages to the pages. It was so enjoyable and relaxing having Rachel on the other end of the line; she is open and engaging, a pleasure to work with. So, now it's my turn to recommend Rachel and her business, Lead Based Ink, for… Anything. You can contact her at rachel@leadbasedink.com.au

ABOUT THE AUTHOR

Tim Thompson has been writing for over 30 years, mainly as an Advertising Copywriter and Freelance Content Writer (separated by a three-year teaching stint in London). The Silver Button Saga is Tim's first long-format story, but he's had a number of short stories published. His first foray into short story writing was titled *Bradman's Thongs*, and was one of ten stories to win publication in *The Advertiser* Summer Short Story competition. Tim lives in Adelaide, South Australia. He can be contacted at timet@internode.on.net

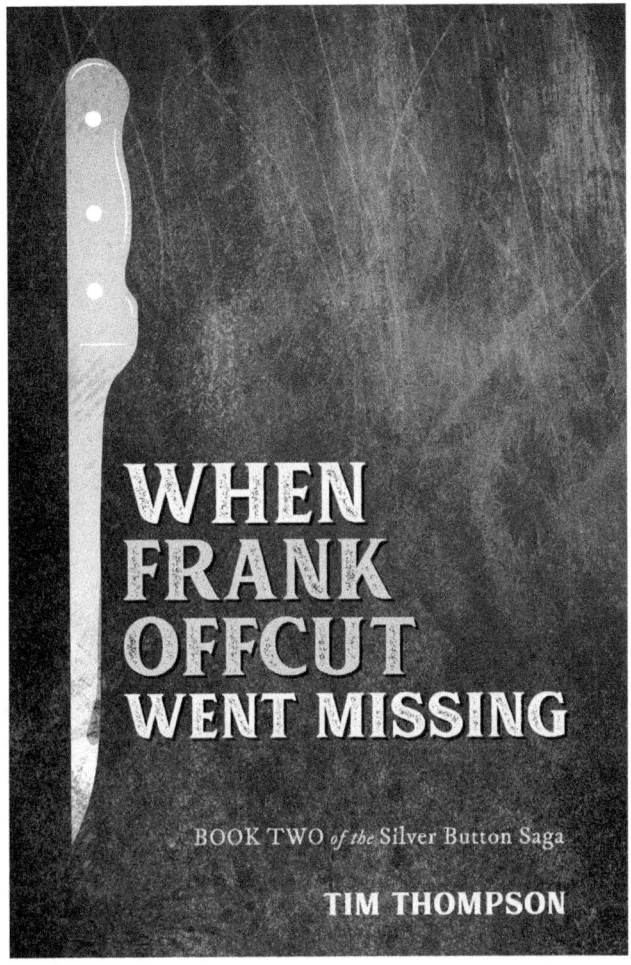

WHEN FRANK OFFCUT WENT MISSING

BOOK TWO *of the* Silver Button Saga

TIM THOMPSON

A fistful of thuggery, an overdose of doctors, a lost memory, a poisonous book of potions, an inspirational blacksmith, a lavish dinner with porky pies, lascivious lawyers, and a dungeon with a view... Emotions spill over like an Icarumban washer girl with a pot of hot water. Is a silver button really the key to the Duchy's future?

Ophelia Offcut, Mary Brewer and Olivia Hiepants are women on a mission... Well, more in damage control. Bad things have happened since the Duke of Lower Icing was attacked, and they look to be getting worse when Frank Offcut goes missing. The Silver Button Saga concludes through the eyes of three different women, each conflicted by duty and desire... if only they didn't have so many 'if onlys' to contend with.

www.ingramcontent.com/pod-product-compliance
Lightning Source LLC
Chambersburg PA
CBHW050841030726
47503CB00007BA/2271